Soldier's Joy

Books by
MADISON SMARTT BELL

The Washington Square Ensemble

Waiting for the End of the World

Straight Cut

Zero db and Other Stories

The Year of Silence

Soldier's Joy

Soldier's Joy

Madison Smartt Bell

TICKNOR & FIELDS

NEW YORK

1989

For information about permission to reproduce selections
from this book, write to Permissions, Ticknor & Fields,
52 Vanderbilt Avenue, New York, New York 10017.

Library of Congress Cataloging-in-Publication Data

Bell, Madison Smartt.
Soldier's joy : a novel / by Madison Smartt Bell.
p.   cm.
ISBN 0-89919-836-8
I. Title
PS3552.E517S65   1989
813'.54 — dc19   88-36822
CIP

Printed in the United States of America

Q 10 9 8 7 6 5 4 3 2 1

The author is grateful for permission to quote from the following songs:
"Freedom" by Charles Mingus. Used by permission of Jazz Workshop, Inc.
"Cripple Creek" by Earl Scruggs. Copyright © 1968 by Peer International Corp.
International copyright secured. All rights reserved. Used by permission.
"Now Is the Cool of the Day." Copyright © 1971 by Jean Ritchie. Geordie Music
Publishing Company.
"Fannin' Street" ("Mister Tom Hughes's Town") by Huddie Ledbetter. Copyright
1936 (renewed © 1964) Folkways Music Publishers, Inc., New York.
"Match Box Blues" by Huddie Ledbetter. Copyright © 1966 Folkways Music
Publishers, Inc., New York.
"Wake Up, Little Maggie" by Doc Watson. Published by Hillgreen Music (BMI).

Every effort has been made to locate the copyright holders of works quoted in this
book. Any errors or omissions are unintentional, and corrections will be made in
future editions if necessary.

ACKNOWLEDGMENTS

My thanks to the usual suspects
who know very well who they are
and to Larry Cooper
for this book and all the others

For Tom Alderson, Tommy Brittingham, and Alan Lequire
For my mother and my father
and
In Memory of Benjamin Taylor

I had tried to be fair. It is the one single thing that no one will forgive you for, neither the communists nor the fascists, the rightists nor the leftists, the white racists nor the black racists. Maybe it is impossible anyway, as many believe. Certainly it is not very diplomatic. One will make more enemies by trying to be fair (marked by impartiality and honesty) than by trying to tell the truth — no one believes it possible to tell the truth anyway, but it is just possible that you might be fair.

— Chester Himes, *The Quality of Hurt*

This mule ain't from Moscow
And this mule ain't from the South
But this mule's had some learning
Mostly mouth to mouth
This mule could be called stubborn . . . and lazy . . .
But in a clever sort of way
This mule could be working
and waiting, and learning, and planning
For a sacred kind of day
A day when burning sticks and crosses
Is not mere child's play
But a madman's most incandescent bloom. . . .

— Charles Mingus, "Freedom"

Contents

I
Cripple Creek
(1970—71)

1

THE SUMMER Laidlaw came back he spent all his time learning to drop-thumb on the banjo. He'd been a better than average Scruggs-style picker before he left, but he didn't put on picks again, not for the first half of that first summer. *Discipline*, was what Laidlaw told himself. *If you want to have any music then you'll just have to play it like this, that's how you learn.* He spent most of his days out on the porch of the clapboard house he lived in. There was a clear view across the yard to the dirt road that came out of the trees and down the hill, and every so often he would see a car creeping carefully down the steep incline, but it was always going somewhere else. Behind the house cleared ground rose and leveled out at a small dug pond with a barn beginning to fall down beside it, and then climbed more steeply to the tree line. The hill pasture was raked with fresh red gullies and the garden on the low side of the house had gone to weeds for two years and most of the rooms of the house itself were full of the plunder of white-trash tenants and God only knew what went on in the woods, but Laidlaw didn't care.

He had back pay and some disability because of his foot and he didn't need to go to work, not right away. Most days he'd play the banjo from morning till night, stopping for a sandwich now and then, or coffee. In the evening he might drink a little whiskey but never very much. The banjo was strikingly heavy because of all the wood in the resonator, and if he was drunk the weight and balance of it could confuse him to the point that he was unsure just what it was he had in his hands.

In the morning he always woke abruptly, found himself bolt upright and unwound from his sheet before he suspected he was coming out of sleep. Usually it was early enough when he awoke that from the pallet he'd made on the floor of the main room of the house he could look up through a sash window and see the morning mist smoking up from the hill pasture into a blank section of sky. It took him a moment or two, most days, to understand just where he was. Then he got up and went back into the kitchen and started coffee in an old stove-top percolator he set on an electric eye. By the time the pot began to chuckle he was already at the banjo.

It was an old Vega, though not one of the very oldest. Laidlaw placed it around the late forties by the cam-type tuners it had, which had become outmoded soon after they'd been invented. There were no frills to the instrument, no fancy fretwork or inlays. Even the Vega logo was simply sketched above the pegs with white paint. Whoever had owned the banjo before him had just really liked to play. The metal fittings were chrome-plated, and a patch on the guard where the right forearm rested was worn through to the brass. The banjo had a plastic head, more reliable than sheepskin for changeable weather, and just by the bridge where a player's ring and little fingers would be posted, the whiting had been rubbed down to transparency, a little peephole Laidlaw could look into if he wanted, to see the steel rod that held it all together and the inside of the resonator.

The resonator was this banjo's secret; deep and heavy, the wood of it a whole inch thick, it produced a fuller, richer tone and more of a sustain than any other he had ever had his hands on. The back of the resonator and the neck had been thickly finished to a false orangy color. On the back of the neck the layers of varnish had been polished back to the pallor of the natural wood by the ball of somebody's thumb traveling up and down it, covering the same route over and over like a man walking back and forth to the well. It must have taken years of playing, hours every day, to accomplish that, which was something Laidlaw liked to remember whenever he picked it up. It was an instrument made to play. No flash, no tinsel, it was all sound.

In the early morning before the coffee had perked his hands moved on the banjo with a soupy clumsiness, though his mind was instantly clear at waking. Knowing it would pass, he didn't let it bother him. With the banjo on the strap, he paced the kitchen from the stove to the enamel sink, peering out of the windows on all three sides of the room. The eaves of the house slanted down over the kitchen and he had to stoop a little to see out. All the while his hands were groping their way through the drop-thumb routine, doing the best they could.

When the coffee had made, he poured himself a big mug of it and went with that and the banjo out to the porch, where he sat down in one of the four ladder-backed chairs that were there. After drinking from the mug he lit his first cigarette of the morning. He was smoking a lot now because of the novelty of being able to smoke whenever he felt like it, but he rarely finished a whole one. Every cigarette he lit would end up stuck under the low-D string next to the peg, where it would burn itself out, raising a thin twirl of bluish smoke and salting the weather-grayed floorboards with its ash. The porch was all unpainted. It ran along two sides of the house, and Laidlaw usually sat near the corner. To the west at the edge of the yard water maples grew on either side of a creek, screening the ragged woven-wire fence around the garden, and beyond the garden there was an unmown pasture. On the south side the yard, scraggly with dandelions and patches of tall grass, dipped and then rose to the fence and the road gate. The locust poles of the road fence were slewed this way and that and the wire dragged to the ground in places. It was all so tumbled over with honeysuckle that in certain areas it seemed that the vines were holding up the wire. The gate, fourteen feet wide and nailed together from one-by-fours, was in fair shape except for a broken board at the top. A rutted track just wide enough to drive on ran back from the gate on the high side of the house and behind it to the barns.

While his hands went up and down the banjo, Laidlaw's eyes wandered from spot to spot, fixing on one thing and then another. There were always birds busy in the yard, and he had fallen into a habit of tossing out breadcrumbs for them. He enjoyed their light movements, something to look at. There was no use looking at his fingers. The left hand already knew what it was doing and the right hand would have to teach itself. In the mornings before the coffee got through to him, Laidlaw could fancy that it was someone else trying to play, awkwardly framing the one-to-one clawhammer beat, the sound of it coming back to him from some distance, while his intelligence drifted elsewhere, above and beyond the body. His thought and senses wound into the landscape while his hands went their own way, chopping steadily at the banjo, lifting the coffee cup, lighting cigarettes. In time, however, he'd come back to himself, the parts of him pulling together. Just short of noon most days there came a kind of melding, so that he knew that it was he who made these exact movements, produced these sounds. Fully awakened, he looked all around himself and saw that he was here, and was amazed all over again at his presence.

In Oakland Laidlaw had had no heart for any kind of celebration. Once off the plane he shook off the company of all the other men on it; though the flight had passed pleasantly enough he didn't care if he never saw any of them again. He hired a motel room to sleep off the trip but woke up after only two hours, tight with nerves though he could remember no dreams. It was still the same morning of his arrival and Laidlaw checked out of the motel and walked down the strip to a cluster of used-car dealers and shopped around until he had found a big blocky Chevrolet pickup, with a lot of cosmetic damage to the body and the bed rusted nearly all the way out, but a strong simple-minded V-8 engine, still in good shape. He paid five hundred for the truck. The dealer was happy to give him the balance of the government check in cash.

Wherever it was not scabbed with rust, the truck was black. Laidlaw drove the California coastline. There were girls on the beaches, whiskey in the bars; you could have whatever you wanted if only you knew what it was. Laidlaw couldn't make up his mind to stop. Maybe, he thought, it just wasn't his kind of country. He tore the map out of the front of a phone book in a gas station booth just south of San Francisco, and set out east with that as his only guide.

The map was on two pages he'd had to rip out separately. Behind the mountains, California was parched. Laidlaw aimed the truck across Nevada. Accident and the phone book map led him to a secondary road winding around Lake Tahoe. He didn't stop to gamble. For the first two nights he tried motels but found he could not sleep enough to justify the price of them. So he took to pulling into roadside rest stops, or sometimes just on the shoulder, whenever he needed an hour or two of a light sit-up sleep. In Utah he was rousted once by a state trooper in a chill predawn, but when the officer had checked his license and his discharge papers he just shook his head and let him be.

Utah was as sere as a bleached bone, baking in its own dry heat. West of Salt Lake City, the landscape became so constant that at times Laidlaw suffered the delusion that the truck wasn't moving at all. That dead alkali white rolled out to impossibly violet mountains, too far away even for parallax; movement suggested itself only by the changing shades of the passing of each day.

The Kansas-Missouri border came at the fold of the map, and when he had crossed it Laidlaw let the first torn page feather down to settle on the floor of the cab on the passenger side. It was around then that he stopped eating, not on purpose at first but from forgetfulness. He drank coffee, Cokes, a pint of milk, but took no solid food across Missouri and Kentucky. The inadvertent fasting affected him little, except that there seemed to be times when he felt unsafe enough on the road to have to pull over, consuming the wasted time with blank staring out the window, since he could still sleep only in one- and two-hour snatches.

Halfway across Virginia he stopped at a crossroads store, one of the old style with dust-covered cans ranked on the shelves, its only brisk trade in saltines and slices of rat cheese slicked onto sheets of wax paper at the counter. Here Laidlaw bought an individual can of Bumble Bee tuna, which he carried out to the hot black vinyl seat of the truck. The can opened with a ring tab at the top, a device which was new to him. Inside were perhaps four ounces of tuna in thick flakes of varying shades of pink. Laidlaw speared pieces of the fish into his mouth with a white plastic fork the storekeeper had supplied. Half the can was enough to sate him altogether. He wedged the pop-top over the remainder to save on the seat of the truck, thinking his appetite would return when it got dark and cooler. But by the time he neared the coast the can had drawn flies and he threw it out when he stopped for gas.

The road was quite familiar now, every bend and curve of it known to him from summer after summer in the back seat of the car, chin propped on the front-seat cushion, peering around his father's boxy head to see the highway signs. Then later, when he was old enough, they'd shared the driving. However, when he reached Virginia Beach it became a little strange, altered, more built up than he'd remembered. There were clumps of condo towers that had mushroomed since he'd been there, and he couldn't seem to find the house they used to stay in. After his second pass along the strip he concluded that it must have been torn down. He parked the truck on the lot of a 7-Eleven and went across the road and between two of the high-rises to reach the beach. Going down a set of concrete steps to the sand, he encountered a squatty woman wearing a frilled bathing cap, and with an unlikely smear of lipstick over her mouth, who immediately began to shout at him that he must stop, that the beach was private here, that he must not walk there. Her accent was foreign and her English unorthodox, and she even followed Laidlaw toward the water, plucking at his sleeve. But it was evening, suppertime, and there was no one else around to back her claim, and finally Laidlaw managed to just walk away.

It was low tide and he walked on the packed sand by the water line, which was easier for him to negotiate, with the limp. By dark he had got away from the high-rises and was passing in front of a row of bungalows, which then fell away entirely behind a rise of sand. Laidlaw sat down and propped his back against a dune. Fronds of sea oats waved and tossed above his head. Just higher than the horizon line, an evening star shone brightly enough to cast a reddish track along the surface of the water, but of course it could not be a star, he realized; it had to be planet: Mars. The light rode toward him across waves that said *hush, hush, hush,* over and over, collapsing over one another on the sand. Laidlaw was quietening within himself and a restlessness that had been in him began to drain away into the expanse of the cloudy water. After a time he rolled over on his side, shoulder and hip digging pockets for themselves in the loose sand, and fell into a black dreamless sleep that carried him all the way until morning.

He woke up hungry, somewhat to his own surprise. When he had found his way back to where he'd parked the truck he went into the 7-Eleven and bought a cup of coffee and a blobby cream-filled donut which he ate all of, sitting in the truck. Though he'd awakened early, the cab was already smoking hot. It cooled a little as he drove out of town, taking the road southwest from nothing more than habit. It was the regular route now, and he no longer needed the map. He got to Abingdon before he'd properly realized that he was going there.

Coincidence, maybe: he was low on gas, and the day was fading into evening. Once he'd filled up Laidlaw didn't go straight back to the interstate, but turned the truck along the main street of the town. It wasn't far, just a bump across the tracks, then two blocks, and he pulled up across the street from the big brick hotel. It had not changed much, he didn't think, though maybe it looked newer, the bricks a rosier shade, as if they had been sandblasted, the columns a fresher white. There were many cars and he could see figures in evening dress passing back and forth across the tall windows inside the portico, engaged in some formal function there.

The main door swung sharply open and out came a woman all in white, a long lacy dress with a train that blanketed the steps behind her as she tripped down them, on the arm of one of the tuxedoed men. It was just a sight, something strange, the sort of thing the mind might feed itself to pass some too quiet night, and Laidlaw did not even register it as a wedding until the car pulled up at the foot of the steps, a gray Mercedes, soaped over with the usual lame jests. Bride and groom scurried into the car and it sped up, swinging around the semicircular drive. The scraping of the cans on the pavement convinced Laidlaw that this event was indeed transpiring. The car turned out of the drive, passing close to him. Briefly face to face with the bride, he saw that she was not beautiful, though enclosed in the icon of dress and setting she had seemed so. The Mercedes went toward the interstate, combing the road with its streamers of cans. Some of the wedding guests who had come out to observe the departure went back inside, while others straggled toward their cars.

Laidlaw turned the truck around and drove it back to the gas station, where he took his duffel bag out of the back and carried it into the men's. The soap on the sink was oil-stained, but it seemed to work well enough. He washed his face and neck and shaved carefully and patted his hair in place with warm tap water. In the duffel bag he had a dress shirt and a jacket and tie, all crumpled but reasonably clean. He'd lost enough weight that his clothes hung on him slackly. In the spotty mirror his look was off, too raw, but he'd done what he could.

A number of ushers from the wedding party were milling through the lobby of the hotel; they all wore red cummerbunds and appeared to be several parts drunk. Laidlaw cut through them to the big oak desk at the rear. He did not feel that they noticed him particularly, though a couple seemed to reel a bit in keeping out of his way. The clerk was young and fuddled easily. While she shuffled cards and papers, Laidlaw turned and set his back to the edge of the counter. The ushers were going in and out of a drawing room at the side, from which he could hear ascending trills of women's laughter. When his registration was finally complete, he paid in cash.

There was a bellboy to the left of the desk, standing on the polished floor as naturally as a tree, so still that Laidlaw scarcely noticed him until he moved forward to pick up the duffel bag. Their hands met on the canvas handles for a moment, until Laidlaw realized what it was all about and let go. The bellboy was black, with a long oval face pitched forward toward the chin. Perhaps he was about the age that Laidlaw's father would have been, though it was hard to tell. He took possession of Laidlaw's key, read the brass tag on it, and began to pilot Laidlaw out of the building, talking steadily in a low voice, not quite a monotone. Carefully he explained where in the annex Laidlaw's room was located, where he could park the truck, where he might seek this or that service, and sirred him so constantly throughout that Laidlaw finally began to sir him back in self-defense. Inside the room he set down the duffel bag and stopped. Laidlaw handed him a dollar bill folded in three.

"Well, thank you, sir," the bellboy said. The bill revolved in his hand and disappeared. Turning as he went out the door, he smiled back at Laidlaw.

"Come from California, do you, sir?"

Laidlaw started, then realized he must have read the license plate.

"I hear it's mighty nice out there. Summer the year round."

"No," Laidlaw said, wondering why it mattered to correct the error. "I'm not from there, I just passed through. I come from Tennessee."

The bellboy looked him in the eye and Laidlaw realized that up to then he'd kept his gaze lowered to his collarbone. The whites of the other's eyes had yellowed into ivory. Both eyes pooled darkly together and Laidlaw experienced an instant of vertigo.

"Well, sir," the bellboy said, voice cool and elastic. "Well then, you're going home."

At noon or thereabouts he ate something, usually beans or a baloney sandwich that went down tastelessly, gulped standing in the kitchen as often as not. As quickly as possible he went back to the porch, to practice now with full deliberation, one of the books of tablature he'd bought propped up on the rail before him. He was essaying only the simplest of tunes. "Sourwood Mountain," and a few other numbers that would have been child's play for him three-finger. Drop-thumbing them was like trying to speak after your tongue had been cut out; the notes stumbled forth disjointedly at quarter speed and with no sense or rhythm.

No more frankly unfeasible way to play the instrument could have been devised on purpose, so Laidlaw sometimes thought, and yet he knew the style had evolved organically, in winterbound shacks up in the mountains, say, where the people were short on amusement, long on time. That kept him going, knowing that it was natural to some and might eventually come naturally to him. But for the moment every movement seemed practically perverse. The right hand was held hooked, fingers crooked stiffly back partway to the palm. The first note was struck with the back of the middle fingernail. The thumb dropped down to pick up the second. And so on. On the fourth beat the thumb came back to the fifth string, ordinarily. It seemed simple enough on the face of it, but the rhythm was very difficult to catch. Beyond that, you were supposed to play exact melodies, note for note, which meant among other things that thumb and finger sometimes had to cross. You couldn't get away with any brush strokes, as in frailing; there wasn't any short cut.

Frailing had its own queer beat, *brush brush* and a *ping* on the high fifth string, one-two one-two. It encouraged Laidlaw to remind himself how long it had taken him to learn it, back in his teens, and how easily it had come to him when it finally came. Even now he'd let himself frail from time to time, to boost his morale a little. You could pick out traces of a melody that way, but your thumb was always stuck droning away on the high G, and the triangular pattern limited what you could really do. Clawhammer would be a lot more versatile, supposing he could ever get the hang of it.

So he spent his sleep-glazed mornings just going after the beat, *chonga chonga chonga,* trying to pry his thumb off the fifth string and get it used to picking up that second note. Afternoons he worked off the tablatures, specific melodies, struggling to hit every note on the button, no matter how painfully slow and awkward it came out, halting like a voice training away from a stutter. When the cool of the evening began to fall, he gave it up for the day. By then he was usually half crazed with frustration anyhow. He took the banjo into the house and tucked it carefully into the red plush lining of the heavy black case and then went outside for a walk.

Generally he preferred the hillside above the house, maybe just because it was harder, chosen with the same stubbornness that kept him hammering at the unlearnable new picking style for most of every day. Climbing was easiest, though the ground was rough and rockier than he'd remembered. He'd cleared the rocks off of that hill as a child, but now it was as if they'd somehow sprouted back. On the way up he could play his limp off against the rise of the ground, cutting across at an angle and keeping the bad left leg on the high side. The limp was no drastic impediment, but it had skewed his balance. His body now tended to revolve around a new axis, a hand span to the left of where the original had been. He wouldn't have thought a few toes would make such a lot of difference, but now it took a good part of his concentration to hold himself back against the sideways spiral.

Retrain. Laidlaw had taught himself to walk with fair confidence up the first grade, to the level ground around the pond, using the slope to cheat a little. *You just have to retrain awhile, that's all.* That had been Sevier's last word on the subject of amputation. Of course if it turned out to be your head then that was another matter. Among other things, Laidlaw was training himself never to think of Sevier even for a half second, of his gestures or his sayings or any other thing about him. Already he'd succeeded to the point that whenever the subject proposed itself there would be a mental jerk, like a skip in a record or a gear slipping over broken teeth, then nothing. Almost nothing. Laidlaw gained the flattened ring of earth around the pond and consciously corrected for the change of terrain. There were three willows weeping into the scummed water, their roots helping to clog the pond, which was mostly silted in. All around the edge there was a plopping of frogs going under at the signs of Laidlaw's approach.

He walked around to the high side of the pond, climbed a careful step or two, and turned back. He'd taught himself to walk without a perceptible hitch on the flat, though it cost him a lot of attention to do it. He rested, looking about himself. On his right hand there was the long sagging dairy barn, relic of some failed tenant enterprise, empty now. A disconnected power fan hung rusting in the short rear wall of it. A stage below, at the side of the track that curved back around the house to the hill, there was another smallish barn: four stalls and a feed room with a hall formed by the overhang of the tin roof. The wood still bore traces of red paint. Around this building what sheep had survived the last tenants' neglect were clustered, waiting to be fed. Below the track was a third barn, bigger than both of the others, all rain-washed gray. That was where the hay was put up when anybody cut it.

Laidlaw turned back up the hill and climbed alongside one of the several gullies, at the edge of which some young scrub cedars grew. The gully obliged him to go up straight, which was a little harder for him. Thistles were growing rib-high all over the upper part of the hill field, headed with their purple blooms. Now and then his foot would slip over the round of a rock and he would have to pause to keep from stumbling.

At the tree line on the cap of the hill he stopped again, turning to rest against one of the red metal posts that supported the three-strand barbed-wire fence. It was far enough. He was not going into the woods, not now. Here he could look out over the barns, the roof of the house, the untilled garden and low pasture, to the line fence where the one dirt road met another, and beyond. At the horizon the hilltops of the ridge that bound this valley blued into the distance, turning shade to paler shade until at last they matched the sky. Into the hills a red sun was falling, hard-edged as a coin.

It seemed possible to look at it, but it wasn't, and after a miscalculated glance Laidlaw started down again, moving at a different angle, toward the barn to feed the sheep. A sunspot partially plugged his vision, black with a yellow aura vibrating. Going down was always harder, each step unpredictable. Then one step seemed to land on nothing, and Laidlaw was falling with such complete abandon that he might as well have been dropped out of a plane. He rolled one whole turn over and fetched up on his back, knocking the wind right out of himself and cracking his right elbow on a rock. A surge of rage and resentment and bitterness shot up in him before he could guard against it. This sort of thing still happened to him quite frequently, whenever his mind wandered away from some rough path. He lay still, fingering the lumps of the necklace he wore privately under his shirt, until he was able to smooth the feeling away and apologize to the world around him for having had it in the first place. He had known of much worse things and believed that they might come to him should he venture to be discontented with his lot. When he was fully calm again he got up and went on, much more slowly and cautiously, toward where the sheep stood, still waiting for him.

When he got back to the house, it was almost completely dark. He picked his way through the dim front room to the kitchen and took a sip from a bottle of bourbon that stood on the table there. As little as he'd eaten, one modest swallow was enough to start a tingle through him. He capped the bottle and went to find the banjo, which he slung to his shoulder and carried to the porch.

Fireflies were hovering all over the darkening yard. Laidlaw stood at the porch rail, watching them while he flexed his fingers, which still buzzed a little from his hitting his funny bone. When they felt right he shrugged half attentively into the clawhammer version of a tune whose tablature he'd memorized by this time, though he'd never managed to play it right.

"Cripple Creek," an old standard, the first tune he'd ever learned to play Scruggs style. Fireflies signaled phosphorescent *green green green* from the dark outside and Laidlaw's hand fell into the beat as simply as he'd had faith it one day would, as if it had emerged from some amnesiac stupor to recall what it had really always known how to do. *Going up to Cripple Creek, going on the run . . .* He played through the verse four times, keeping his eye on the fireflies. He was nervous to glance down at his hand or even shift his feet. On the fifth turnaround he tried the high break up the neck and discovered with a sharp thrill that he could do that too. With his left hand working toward the twelfth fret, he wondered if he'd be able to hit the harmonic, and — just as it occurred to him — he did it, a clean flick across all five strings, every note bright. That was enough, and he dropped both hands away from the strings, letting it ring, boosting the drum over a turn of his hip so that the chime shimmered out of it, rising up and all around him, lifting out of the whole hollow like the air itself.

2

ON THE far side of the big hill the dirt road met a paved road. There wasn't usually much traffic over there, but Laidlaw could hear what there was as a kind of fuzzy shushing sound if he was outside or on the porch. By some trick of acoustics and the lay of the land, a car climbing the hill would seem to fall entirely silent until the moment it came over the peak to become suddenly much louder. From the hilltop the road zigged sharply to the left and then zagged almost straight down, following the turns of Laidlaw's line fence, if you cared to call it a fence. On either side of the tight turns were washboards bad enough to snatch the wheel right out of the hands of any driver not prepared for them. The road was washed down to the pitted limestone and could not be scraped smooth. The county graders restricted themselves to dumping the odd ton of gravel on it now and then, most usually leaving it to be redistributed by the rain.

The red pickup appeared at the top of the hill around its usual time, when Laidlaw had just come out and settled himself with the banjo. The color of the morning was still gray. He knew the driver of the truck had learned the road and tended to take it fast, and today he watched his progress with special interest, because he had seen a county truck drop a load of gravel just past the second downhill turn late on the previous day. The red truck was newish looking, though the side rails around the bed were beaten up. Coming out of the first turn it tracked expertly back and forth to avoid the worst of the washboards, maintaining high speed. Laidlaw stopped playing when it hit the gravel, fishtailing and sliding down diagonally. The driver overcorrected and narrowly missed a fencepost, and the truck went into its second skid angled in the opposite direction. It somehow turned full sideways in the extra space allowed by Laidlaw's gateway, and came to a stop with the corner of the bed just nicking a post, not hard enough to dent it.

The truck had stalled. A sort of fog of gravel dust began to settle on it. Inside the cab, a hand rose from the wheel, hovered for a moment, and fell heavily back on it. Somewhere down the hill a rooster was crowing, the sound coming up clear and bright through the mildly surprising silence the near wreck had left in its wake. Then the truck's engine whirred, missed, and started, and the driver backed and filled until he had it off the road, parallel to Laidlaw's gate. He got out and slammed the door and came around the front of the truck. A tallish man in overalls and an undershirt, wearing a broad-brimmed felt hat. He lifted the loop of rusty chain that secured the gate and replaced it. When he turned to approach the porch Laidlaw saw that it was Mr. Giles. He propped the banjo carefully against the wall beside his chair, took a cigarette from the pack in his shirt pocket, and held it for a moment unlit.

"You like to come through the hard way," he said when Mr. Giles was halfway to him. He kept walking forward without answering, in an even pace that never changed for any break of ground. His left leg was artificial to somewhere above the knee; Laidlaw knew that, but still could scarcely detect any hitch in his movement. Only the prosthetic foot hit the steps and the porch floor with a different tone, as he crossed to a chair opposite Laidlaw and sat. He leaned back and cocked his elbows on the porch rail, grinning. There was something in his posture that gave Laidlaw a brief twinge of *déjà vu*.

"Gate needs fixen anyhow least it looks that way to me." Mr. Giles always spoke in compacted bursts of words, as though he were eager to have done with the act of speech. But that was just the way all the people out around his way had of talking.

"Could be," Laidlaw said. "You want some coffee?"

"Might could use a little drink after that piece of drivin." Mr. Giles gave out a two-syllable laugh, on the beat of *gotcha*, and thumped the rail with the broad heel of his hand.

"I got some if you want it," Laidlaw said.

"Naw," Mr. Giles said. "Come to mention it I give it up."

"What for?" Laidlaw said.

"Doctors."

"Don't want to let the doctors get at you, now."

"No, but though they do." Mr. Giles's mouth shut on a tight line, the creases of his smile hanging slack around it. His face was wide and round, with gray eyes set deep in it. He studied Laidlaw in a grave way that made him mildly uneasy. There was a silence, during which Mr. Giles stroked the folds of his hat, pushing it around his head. Of a sudden bright fingers of light began to spread down the hill with the first rise of sun behind the trees.

"I was right sorry to hear about your daddy."

"Well," Laidlaw said. "So was I."

"Lot of people was," Mr. Giles said. "I looked to come by and see ye but ye'd done gone already."

"Their idea." Laidlaw lit his cigarette, cupping his hand against a light breeze coming up from the direction of the creek. Mr. Giles ooched around in his chair, settling. The smile spread back over his face as with a thick finger he indicated the banjo.

"Been picken on that right much?"

"How I spend most of my time." Laidlaw drew on his cigarette and held it out vertically, admiring the rippling ascent of the twinned columns of smoke.

"Well, hit us a lick on it why don't ye?"

"Nah."

"Go on."

Laidlaw lifted the banjo to his lap and flattened the filter of his cigarette to slip it under the D string. Over the past week he'd learned the clawhammer arrangement of "Turkey in the Straw" and he played it through three times with no slip anywhere while Mr. Giles kept time on the rail with the edge of his thumb. At the end he touched the fifth fret harmonic on high D and sat there happily in the hum of the last note.

"Mind out for that cigarette before it spiles your varnish."

Starting, Laidlaw plucked the butt from under the D string and stubbed it out on the heel of his shoe.

"Always stick'm in there do ye?"

"Trying to get out of the habit of letting them roll around on the floor," Laidlaw said. "I've heard of houses to burn down that way."

Mr. Giles's smile flickered, but it held.

"Seem like ye've learnt that old-time picken style," he said. "Sounds right good."

"Working on it, anyhow," Laidlaw said.

"I'd say ye must be. A body can hear ye all over this holler just about all day long."

"Hope it ain't keeping anybody awake."

"Couldn't tell ye that, I sleep somewheres else." Mr. Giles laughed and slapped the rail.

"You been working out this way?"

"Down the road a piece. Been doen a little for Miz Phipps, worken a garden and such."

"I see the truck go by most mornings. Didn't know it was you, though. That's a new truck, ain't it?"

"Pretty near new. Had it about a year."

"I like that red, it's sharp looking."

"I reckon. Got an automatic transmission to it this time."

"Wouldn't have thought it of you."

"It's a right smart easier in traffic."

"Looks like it handles pretty well on gravel too."

Mr. Giles laughed. "I'd learnt ever bounce on that stretch of road, don't ye know, but I believe they just about had me there."

"Yeah," Laidlaw said. "The county was by late last evening. I knew they'd have somebody before the day was out."

"Well, long as I was here anyway I thought I'd stop in to see ye." Mr. Giles laughed and shifted in his chair. "Time I hit the road now though."

"All right," Laidlaw said. "Stop by again when the spirit moves you."

"Might do." Mr. Giles glanced over the yard in the direction of the creek.

"Not maken ye any garden?"

"Don't look much like it."

"Well," Mr. Giles said. "Can't pick and sing all day. How do ye mean to live then?"

"As birds do," Laidlaw said. "I suppose."

Mr. Giles squinted at him, frowning.

"You don't look like no bird to me."

"But then you never can tell for sure," Laidlaw said.

"You must eat out of cans and such I reckon," Mr. Giles said. "You know Earl, you recall my boy Earl, when he come back he wouldn't hardly eat nothen less it came out of a can. He'd picked it up over there, don't ye know. But now he's getten some better." Mr. Giles laughed again in the *gotcha* way.

"It's late, anyhow," Laidlaw said. "Kind of late to be starting a garden."

"Well, but you could have some late things. Put out some corn and tomatoes. You might make some beans yet."

"I don't know," Laidlaw said. The idea was picking at some part of his conscience, he wasn't quite sure why. He had enough benefits to keep him in baloney through the winter if that was what he wanted to eat. "Not interested in helping out some, are you?"

"Might could. Some."

"You know, I wouldn't have much to pay you," Laidlaw said. "For that much time, I mean. I can pay you something, though."

"Might not need that much time. Tractor run?"

"Hadn't tried it."

"Well why don't ye try it then? Get in there and turn it and disk, if you can get it runnen. Do that and I'll be by one day next week, we'll see where we can get to. What say?"

"Sold," Laidlaw said.

"Well then." Mr. Giles scanned him up and down. "You're looken lively."

"You too," Laidlaw said. "Good to see you."

Mr. Giles stood up. Laidlaw took note how he helped himself, pressing one hand against the rail, but he would never have noticed it if he hadn't been looking. Mr. Giles had been out the leg since well before Laidlaw ever knew him, and only now had he begun to wonder what might have happened to it.

"Hah?" said Mr. Giles.

Laidlaw snapped his head up quickly. Unconsciously he'd been staring at the toes of Mr. Giles's shoes. "Nothing," he said. "Sorry . . ."

"Woolgatheren," Mr. Giles said. "I'll be back by." He pushed his hat up a little from his brow with the tip of his finger. There was a sharp tan line on his forehead and above it the skin was an odd dead white. He resettled his hat and turned and went down the steps into the yard. Laidlaw looked after the blue denim X of his overalls until he got back in the truck.

By midmorning he had resurrected the old tractor, a smallish Massey-Ferguson, once red and now piebald with rust. It ran with a fearsome jackhammer tremble, but never gave out altogether. He spent the afternoon plowing in long elliptical turns through the dense heat, staring out through the shimmer of convection that hovered over the tractor's hood. Next day, with the plowed ground drier, he went back in and disked it fine.

On the morning after that he woke to a thick damp mist that did not break, and went directly to the porch with the banjo and his coffee to wait for Mr. Giles to reappear. Although the instrument held true against the damp, the change of weather altered the sound of it; each note was slightly muffled. The air was greasy and had a metallic taste, and it seemed to raise a sweat on him in answer to the least move he made.

By ten he began to see flashes of sheet lightning to the west. The great silent flare would fill the sky and for an instant suck the color from everything underneath it. Each time Laidlaw responded with a small involuntary flinch, not much more than a tightening around his eyes. A long breath later he would hear the sound of thunder. Because of how the land lay closed round by hills, a thunderstorm would often surround it without striking, and he wasn't sure if it might not be that way this time. Down by the creek he saw that the leaves on the maples had been turned back pale side up by a sudden rush of wind. Then it began to rain everywhere all at once as if the water had been dumped out of an enormous bucket.

The house itself was roofed with tar paper but the porch was covered with tin. The hard rain on the tin roof made an explosive, shattering sound. Windblown water coated the porch rail glossily and began to creep across the boards of the floor. Laidlaw kicked his tablature out of the wet spot and then moved his chair to a drier area. There seemed to be only one slow leak along a joint in the tin to the left of the door, and on the whole he was surprised there were no more. He leaned back in his chair and smoked. The noise of the rain was such that he could barely hear the banjo, and so he left off playing. He could not see farther than a yard past the porch through the rain. Just in front of him the gutter was bent into a sort of pitcher lip which poured a stream of water straight onto the ground below the porch, hard enough to dig itself a good-sized hole.

He was pleased he'd had nothing planted, since it all would surely have been washed out by this time. But such hard rains didn't usually keep up long, and in fifteen, twenty minutes it began to let up. For a moment the sky appeared to lighten in the west and he wondered if it was going to clear up altogether. But instead the rain slacked off to a steadier, gentler pace. Laidlaw picked up the banjo again and began to knock out phrases of "June Apple," a tune he'd been struggling with all week. He had gained some facility with the A line and was beginning to work on the several variations and breaks that were written out in the book he was using. Softer on the roof now, the rain kept up a beat.

It rained all day, a soaking rain, not clearing until evening. When it had definitely stopped Laidlaw put the banjo down and stretched and stood up. The porch rail on the west side had been drenched black and had a stodgy give when he pushed his finger into it. Sunlight made an abrupt return as though a curtain had been drawn from before it. Laidlaw was touched by wedges of light that came off the field through the trees. He walked out over the spongy yard to the edge of the creek, which was swollen and swirling brown with mud brought up from the bottom. All he had on his feet was a pair of old high-top sneakers, and after thinking it over he rolled his pants and stepped into the creek and waded across. The water, just over knee-deep, was cold and the current surprisingly strong. He hauled himself out on the opposite bank and went under the dripping trees to the garden fence. The ground was dark and smooth as a pancake; it looked like somebody had been at it with a huge rolling pin. This work was lost, to be done over. Laidlaw shook his head and went to feed the sheep. The ground dried over the next few days, and he repeated the procedure.

Then one morning he was just getting up from his pallet when he heard something slow down on the road. There was the *chink* of the chain on the gate and the sound of a truck pulling through. He got up and pulled on his pants and shoes and went to the door with his shirt in his hand. Mr. Giles was coming down from where he had parked, just behind Laidlaw's truck up on the track.

"*Ah*-ha," Mr. Giles said, grinning widely. "Been loven up that pillow, han't ye?"

"Been about to give up on you, is what," Laidlaw said sourly. It was true that Mr. Giles got up before the birds but he took an inordinate pleasure in letting you know it. "What would it be, Friday?"

"Too wet to come before, don't ye know. I reckon ye plowed."

"Plowed and disked." Laidlaw sat down on one of the porch chairs and began to lace up his shoes.

"Buy seed?"

Laidlaw's mouth dropped open stupidly. His dislike of going to town had led him to overlook this small point.

"No matter, I brought ye some," Mr. Giles said.

"Must be my lucky day," Laidlaw said. "Obliged to you, that is."

"I'll swap ye the ticket," Mr. Giles said. "What say I go down there and you come on when ye get good and rested?"

Laidlaw let that one pass without reply. Buttoning his shirt, he went back to the kitchen, but decided to pass up coffee so as to get to the garden faster and save whatever was left of his face.

Mr. Giles had driven his truck around to the garden gate and was standing just inside the fence, looking down at the ground as though he and it had just reached a pause in a long conversation. Laidlaw was still irked at being so badly caught out, but his mood softened when he saw that there were two bags of fertilizer in the truck and also several trays of tomato plants.

"Brought it all, didn't you," Laidlaw said. "Nice looking, those tomatoes."

"That's a new cross," Mr. Giles said. "I've had some comen in the last couple weeks. They eat pretty good."

"Glad to hear it," Laidlaw said. He turned over a clod with his shoe and broke it. "Ground look all right to you?"

"Pretty fair. I reckon ye still got hoes and such? Got air posthole diggers?"

"Just let me look," Laidlaw said, giving himself one more mental kick. There was no doubt he was a long way out of practice in these things. He went through the gate and around to where a tool shed stood between the garden fence and the road, a nicely made structure with V-shaped lattices in place of solid walls. The water-swollen wood made the door difficult to wrench open. Inside there did turn out to be hoes, rakes, a couple of pitchforks, and indeed a set of posthole diggers with a dirt dauber's nest caked to one handle. Laidlaw broke it off and shouldered the posthole diggers and picked up two grubbing hoes and went back.

Mr. Giles was walking across the garden toward the shady side. Seeing him in profile, you were more aware of the large belly pouched in the bib of his overalls, though no other part of him was fat. He kept his back very straight when he walked, carrying the stomach like a load strapped to him. At the fencerow he stopped and considered a tumble of old tomato stakes piled among the weeds between posts where the plow had not reached. He picked up one of the lighter scantlings and broke it and handed half to Laidlaw, who had just come to him, along with the free end of a ball of kite string. Laidlaw fastened the string around his stake and, thus hitched to Mr. Giles, walked to the sunny side of the garden. Mr. Giles stooped and pushed his stake into the ground and Laidlaw backed away from him, unrolling string, until he was near the opposite fence, at a place where he bent and fixed his stake.

The string hung suspended a few inches over the dirt, bellying a little in the middle.

They laid off five more rows in like fashion. Laidlaw opened various topics of conversation from time to time but drew little response, and he recalled that Mr. Giles did not much like to talk while he was working. When the rows were marked they each took up a grubbing hoe and began to pull furrows, tightening the hoe handle against the string for a guide. Mr. Giles somehow managed to do this without bending. The brown earth swirled out from the narrow tine of his hoe like the wake of a tiny boat. Laidlaw had to go stooping and was slower to finish.

They did four rows in this way and at the end of the last Laidlaw rested, leaning on the hoe handle, while Mr. Giles went to the truck and broke a bag of 6-12-12 and came back with a coffee can full of it. When he came beside the start of the first row the can tilted in his hand as though it were hinged and a neat stream of the reddish fertilizer began to pour into the furrow.

"Come behind me with that hoe," Mr. Giles said.

Laidlaw set the narrow tine in the furrow and walked behind Mr. Giles, keeping up a light pressure on the hoe handle. The fertilizer mixed and went smoothly under the new turn of dirt. They went up and down the four rows they had hoed out. Mr. Giles's left foot seemed to make a slightly deeper impression in the loam.

"There'll be your corn," Mr. Giles said, indicating the two rows nearest the fence, "and there'll be your beans." He pulled a sack of corn out of an overall pocket and began to walk the outside row, dropping the seed accurately along the middle of the furrow. "Come on behind me."

Laidlaw followed with his hoe turned sideways to cover the seed and smooth over the furrow. In the rare case where Mr. Giles had missed he flicked the seed back into place with the broader blade of the hoe. At the head of the third row, Mr. Giles put up the corn and began with beans. They went on in the same manner until the fourth row was finished out.

"Might could drink some water," Mr. Giles said. He lifted his left foot and rested it in a low square of woven wire and propped his elbow on top of a locust post. Laidlaw walked up to the house and filled a Mason jar with ice and water. Mr. Giles did not appear to have moved a hair when he got back. He took the jar and drank from it and set it down on top of the post.

"Well sir," he said. "Let's see how ye dig postholes."

It was getting steadily hotter. Laidlaw had sweated all through his shirt. The posthole diggers were heavy and somewhat awkward to deal with. With the handles held together he thunked the paired blades into the ground, then pulled them apart to clasp a scoop of dirt, lift it out, and let it fall in the space between the rows. And then again, and again. The handles made a clapping sound when they came together. You could get a good pinch from them if you were careless. Laidlaw was happy that the holes did not have to be deep enough to set posts. When at last he reached the end of the fifth row he set down the diggers and went to take a drink from the jar. Leaning against the locust post, he studied the reddening patches on his hands. Mr. Giles was tapping dirt around a last tomato plant. Then he stood up, gradually, one part of him at a time.

"Blowed are ye?" Mr. Giles said. "Well I'll dig awhile, tired of crawlen."

He took up the posthole diggers and began. Laidlaw looked at the sky. It was near noon and the sun made a hot shapeless hole in the atmosphere. When Mr. Giles had begun his second hole, Laidlaw knelt beside the tray of tomatoes and found the coffee can of fertilizer. He put half a handful in the bottom of each hole and covered it with an inch or so of dirt, detached a tomato plant from its plastic pot and set it in above. The root tendrils coming out of the cubiform greenhouse dirt tickled his palms when he handled the plants. He filled dirt loosely around the stem of each, careful not to choke it, and smoothed the ground back level.

When the last row was done, they passed the water jar; then Laidlaw carried the tools back to the shed. In the shade there he rested for a moment. A dispossessed dirt dauber whined near him; briefly he took it for a wasp. Through the lattices he could see Mr. Giles parking the truck above the house. When Laidlaw got back there, Mr. Giles was sitting on the porch, cutting slices of a green apple and eating them from the blade of his knife.

"Want some dinner?" Laidlaw said. "Piece of meat to go with that?"

"I don't reckon," Mr. Giles said. He pitched the apple core into the yard and pulled a Co-op receipt from his front pocket. Laidlaw read the ticket and went into the house to get money for that and the time.

Mr. Giles put the bills into his pocket without unfolding them. "That should hold ye a while," he said, getting up. "You'll thin that corn. I've left ye the fertilizer. Might put out some squash if ye get the notion."

"Might," Laidlaw said. "I'll manage it, as may be. Obliged to you for the help."

"We'll see ye," Mr. Giles said, shoving his hat back in his usual salute.

When the red truck had bounced down the hill out of sight, Laidlaw went back into the house. Working on an empty stomach had made him a little giddy, but he didn't feel like eating, either. It was hot inside the house. He lay on the pallet, on his back, looking out the window at a patch of sky. The sky was a very rich color of blue and now and then a bird flicked across it too quickly for him to guess what it was. Somewhere outside a mockingbird was trying a single phrase over and over, only changing a trill at the end of it.

Laidlaw closed his eyes, but he felt restless. He began to think about a tune he'd been looking at the tablature to: "Sally in the Garden." He had plenty left to learn about "June Apple," but now he had a real yearning to play "Sally in the Garden" and hear the edges in the minor key. His finger ends rattled on the floor beside his mat, framing a pattern for the tune. Quickly he sat up and for a moment stared abstractedly at the fingertips of his left hand, which were smudged with black lines from the strings across the hardening calluses. His palm was crossed with red blotches which would be blisters soon enough.

He jumped up and snatched the banjo from the case and went outside. Though he could have done with another look at the tablature, he was too jittery to sit still on the porch. He went down into the yard and stopped to drop the D string to low C. C minor was the key. It was breathless out but he felt the need to move, and beginning to play he walked toward the creek. The water had cleared and fallen lower down the banks. He could see through it to the washed gravel on the bottom, the small stones that seemed to rock a little in the current. There was a tune coming out from under his hands but it was not quite "Sally in the Garden." It was something different, but something, and whatever it was he liked it. Keeping time, Laidlaw raised his eyes and looked across the creek to the garden. The least trace of a movement in the air had begun, enough to ruffle the leaves on the tomato plants and start a tremor along the spans of kite string. Laidlaw played whatever he was playing, watching the gentle curve of the kite lines, imagining the seed underground in its first pale uncurling.

3

TRYING TO sleep was like trying not to float: a breathless winding descent that would inevitably reverse itself to spiral back up again. Drawn out from the whorl of unconsciousness, Laidlaw opened startled eyes to the ceiling, which went round and round as the sky will do above a boat. When he sat up the room fell still and, eyes adjusting rapidly to the dark, he could see silhouettes of his furnishings hulking here and there about the room. The air was damp and cool enough to raise gooseflesh on his bare arms and across his back. He put on his pants and limped to the porch with his shoes in his hands.

Outside he could see much more clearly, although no moon had risen. All around the house there was the massive sound of katydids and tree frogs and crickets together, rising and falling like waves on the ocean. Laidlaw tied his shoes and stepped down into the yard, where the dew-weighted weeds and grasses drenched his feet immediately. The choral fabric of the katydids presented a face of complete unity, stitched all through with a great variety of complication. Laidlaw listened carefully to the turns in the sound as he crossed the track and began to climb the hill.

As he drew farther away from the trees into the hill pasture, the sound of the katydids grew more distant. He mounted toward the pond. A month of practice had taught him to walk quite naturally, with his shoes on anyway, and without having to concentrate on the act nearly so much. Surely he was just about effectively *retrained*, he thought, barely attentive to the click and skip his mind automatically performed when it verged upon that particular choice of word. The willows bowed decorously over the pond, a faint silvering of gathered starlight on its surface. Among infrequent splashes, frogs spoke and answered one another from the banks: bass, alto, tenor, bass.

Downhill was a kind of polarization of shade: house, trees, and fencerows thoroughly black, the fields and open spaces startlingly bright beside them. Higher, the line of the ridge was just discernible, black on black against the sky, with the lights of a subdivision cupped on the near side of it. Down in the yard Laidlaw could see a couple of fireflies winking unaccustomably high in the trees. Above, in the hill pasture, those blotches which moved occasionally were sheep. A ewe who had drifted out from the flock raised her head and blatted harshly and scuttled to rejoin the others.

Laidlaw craned his head backward. It was perfectly clear and the stars marked out the curve of the sky with needle-sharp points. He had a sudden and acutely uncomfortable feeling of exposure and he lowered his head and walked quickly down from the pond at an angle toward the fence and tree line. Spooked by his rapid movement, the sheep bunched, turned their heads toward him in unison, and then ran stiff-legged toward the barn. Laidlaw gained the fence and stopped in the shadow of the trees behind it. He was sweating a little and his breath came somewhat raggedly, though there was no reason. But in this position he felt much calmer, and when he'd got his breath again he went on along the fence.

He walked down the hill on the back side of the dairy barn and sheep barn, crossed the track, and passed behind the hay barn. When he reached the creek he sliced his feet into it with toes pointed so as to make no splash and shuffled across without lifting them clear of the water until he came to the other side. This section of the creek was bordered with mock orange trees making squat shadows in the night, and Laidlaw's foot came down on one of the lumpy windfallen fruit, but he was ready and did not stumble. There was a three-strand barbed-wire fence just past the mock oranges and he stooped to go through it and was in the low pasture.

The fescue was tall and gleaming, catching what little light there was. Laidlaw went on along the fence. There was a branch of the creek following the fencerow on the far side of it, and against its steady purling the sound of the katydids was renewed threefold. The tall grass wet him to the waist as he went through it. At the lip of a shallow ditch that cut back across the field he stopped. Ironweed grew along the ditch, darker forms receding into the hay, and where the ditch tapered off to a point a scraggly cedar sapling was growing. Back toward the house, the line of the garden fence was a near shapeless shadow. Laidlaw plucked a long stalk of hay and set it between his teeth, then stepped through the top two strands of the fence and quietly crossed the branch. On the other side he paused again and then went into the trees.

His breathing seemed to stop entirely, as though some glottal trap door had fallen shut across his windpipe. He went forward very slowly, lifting a foot and easing it ahead, careful to register anything that grazed his bare ankle before he set it gently down, committing no weight to the step before he had a clear sense of what was under his sole. There was a considerable amount of unidentifiable scrub over the ground among the trees. For the first few minutes he could see absolutely nothing in the thicker darkness of the woods, but he kept moving, one well-deliberated step at a time. He held the stalk of hay out vertically in front of him, and in this way was able to detect an enormous spider web before he walked into it. Finding out its edges by probing with the stalk, he ducked under it and went on. The sound of the katydids had risen to a roar but what he was most aware of was the violent smashing of his heart.

Then there was another sound and he stopped dead and crouched. The noise did not come again, but he forced his memory back to examine it from every possible angle. It had been light and low to the ground, something small. His hands worked on his knees, wanting to have hold of something, and when he noticed this he stilled them. After a few minutes of squatting, left foot flat and the right on the ball, he began to feel the strain all through his legs. But his heart had slowed and his breath came easier and he was beginning to see, peering from the corners of his eyes, as he'd been taught. Outlines of twigs and leaves began to emerge from the amorphous forms around him. Off to his left there was a minor movement of some longish tapered shape. Laidlaw studied it sidelong, and just as he made out the whole profile, the rabbit hopped farther to the left with the same light fall he'd heard before. Then it was quiet and Laidlaw saw both ears revolving forward, bent upon himself, and then the rabbit thumped noisily away into the bushes, out of sight. Completely calm now, cradled in the rising swell of insect music, Laidlaw smiled.

No matter how hard he worked, how long he practiced, he seemed to need little sleep and in the middle of most nights he'd bob like a cork from the clutch of no dream he ever could remember. It no longer bothered him once he had found a way to pass the time. It had become a habit, to rise quietly and put on pants and shoes (most often he went shirtless) and go out. Now he sought the woods quickly, without hesitation, slipping into them like a knife.

It was possible to go quite far in the shelter of the woods. The cap of trees that sat on the hilltop behind Laidlaw's house had a tail that ran down the west side of it and widened on the flat, alongside the low pasture. It was not far north over the crown of that hill to more cleared ground that fronted on Murray Lane, a narrow paved road that cut between two highways. And going east over the hill you quickly came to a tract-house development that someone had started slapping up and then inexplicably abandoned; there was no one living there. But ordinarily Laidlaw did not care to go in either of those directions.

Widening to the west, the woods took him to better places. They went in the fork of the two creek branches for a good way on the flat and then up the side of another hill. Here someone had once tried to start an orchard, and there were still traces of the terracing, though it had mostly been smoothed down by rains. There were sizable apple trees, bearing small misshapen fruit which never seemed to ripen fully, and not far from them a plum thicket, small bushy trees grown densely together, with little yellow plums in season. The orchard keeper had even tried a vineyard and parts of its trellis work remained, along with numerous knotty vines, though no grapes grew.

The orchard was overgrown with assorted scrub and in certain areas the wild blackberries were so thick as to make it impassable (though the blackberry bushes now produced the sweetest fruit). Above the orchard, where the hill became steeper, a section of rock wall was still standing, at least as old as the last century, Laidlaw knew, made of flat fieldstones laid cunningly without mortar. Climbing up over a tumble-down gap in the wall, he came to a rusty wreck of a wire fence with a half-length gate in it, its wood crumbly with rot. Past this fence to the top of the hill the scrub was thinner, being overshadowed by a wealth of broad-leaved trees: red maples, hickories, black and red oaks, elm, and now and then a sycamore.

The trees were good-sized and gave each other room and it was easy to go among them, down the west side of the hill, until about halfway down, where another string of rock wall fence survived. Not far beyond this spot began a grove of cedars, grown thick and close together. Their tops and branches intertwined so densely that at night virtually no light at all could reach the woods floor underneath them, which in this area was humped with odd mounds of earth and little hollows full of different kinds of moss. Going out of the cedar thicket at the foot of the hill, Laidlaw reached a small round pond, a runoff pond formed naturally at a lowering place in the land. Past it the assorted hardwood trees began again, climbing up a lesser slope, a ripple in the ground, and declining down the other side of it to a vestige of fence along the dirt road where Laidlaw's property ended.

It was weeks of nights of not much sleeping before he had the whole woods registered in a mental map. At first he moved extremely slowly, learning his way by the most delicate touches, educating himself to see. For some time each stand of trees and turn of ground remained alien to him, strange and strange again each time he came upon it, in half light or in no light at all. Then eventually, in a convergence of touch and sight and recollection, every inch of the land was known to him, so that he could walk it quickly and quietly with no misstep and in fact detect any alteration of a given spot since the last time he had passed it.

It was not only a sharpening of the senses by which he learned to welcome himself into the dark under the trees, but a deeper internal shift, so that he navigated not only by what he could see and touch and hear and even smell but by an inner gyroscope which found an increasingly true balance against the rise and fall of the wooded land. Then it was enough for him to step through the fence from the pasture and cross the creek into the trees to utterly, perfectly disappear. A dissolving darkness rose around him, in time to the throb of insect voices; continuous with the woods he passed through like a breeze, he could become invisible, even to himself.

After many nights, when the whole plan of his own place was so stamped into him that he could have found his way all over it not just in the dark but blindfolded probably, he grew more ambitious. The hilltop behind his house was a joint in a backbone of ridge encircling the entire valley, and once up on the top of it he could walk for miles, well above the world that people lived in. In his first explorations he relapsed to extreme caution, falling back on the slow-motion footfall, the probing stalk of hay. But soon he knew the new territory well enough to travel with swift confidence, unsettled only when at times he had to cross a pasture or a road.

No respecter of boundaries, he freely crossed the fences of other farms, though he kept well away from the houses and particularly avoided the couple of subdivisions in the valley. The concentration of the people unnerved him somewhat, though sometimes he would choose a high vantage point, securely inside a screen of trees, and watch the patterns of the house lights for a while. Sometimes too, if he came back that way, he was drawn to inspect the empty subdivision behind his own hill, where the skeletal forms of the undone houses threw queer shadows across the half-plowed roads intended to connect them.

He kept clear of the farmhouses mainly because of dogs, and yet he had the ability to outwit most dogs most nights, blindsiding them, arriving silent and downwind. Probably he could have stolen chickens or robbed gardens if he wanted to, which he did not. The couple of times dogs found him out he was able to calm and befriend them before any of their people were roused, as if they sensed there was no harm in his intentions. But on the whole he stayed away from the lights and people and their creatures, preferring to remain swathed in the deeper darkness, a familiar of whatever else moved in the night.

The moon was bright enough to give Laidlaw a shadow as he crossed the pasture to the trees. It was a hard white color and somewhat asymmetrical, a day or so off the full. Inside the woods the darkness was sudden, and he moved on instinct for the few minutes it took his eyes to adjust. He went quickly up the edge of the orchard, pausing when he came to each trace of terrace to look around and listen. On his left hand it was relatively open among the apple trees and moonlight spangled the clumps of blackberry bramble in among them. Laidlaw climbed under the edge of the plum thicket opposite, meaning to merge his shadow with the short shadows of the trees.

There was a little tick and rustle among the blackberries when he stopped at the third terrace, and when he studied that direction he could make out a black oblong something at the foot of a bush nearby. He bent and quietly put his hand on a rock and flipped it in an arc, not at whatever it was but near it. A groundhog stood up on its hind legs and rotated its bullet head in the direction of the thump. Laidlaw laughed inside his belly, letting no sound escape, and tossed another stone, more accurately. The groundhog dropped to all fours and waddled away into the bushes, wagging a fat behind. Laidlaw went to the edge of the blackberries and stooped to peer where the groundhog had gone into the thick of them. There was a small arch in the briers, which he could not see far into, but he knew that it would be a maze, a warren for groundhogs and rabbits and possums and coons. That touch of musk he could just smell was very likely a fox after them all. He stood up and reached over the curve of the blackberry bush. The birds had gleaned the berries off the top and he had to reach far in to gather a decent handful, with the thorns pricking at his wrists. Continuing up and above the orchard, he put the berries into his mouth one by one and let them dissolve, sharply sweet with a tingling aftertaste on his tongue.

When he gained the top of the hill he did not go down the other side, but held to the left along the crest. He had been along this way enough to beat out a path with his feet, and though habit made him chary of breaking branches, he'd learned where they all were and could duck them without slowing. He could not quite run, but had contrived a kind of lope that carried him rapidly to the dip between peaks of the ridge where the dirt road passed through. There was a tear in his own fence for him to go through; he darted across the patchy gravel and vaulted the fence by a post on the opposite side, landing not quite evenly but without actually tripping. He was off his own land now. Here it was scrubbier and brambly and he picked his way more slowly back to the top of the ridge, where the trees stood farther apart and slashes of moonlight marked out the way in front of him.

He went down from this peak and up the next and then, where the line of hill curved away to the south, he kept on straight, skirting another blackberry patch to go down deeper into a new valley. When he had got past the briers he cut around in front of them and now, through bigger gaps among a stand of walnut trees, he could see a clearing shimmering up ahead of him. Sometimes there could be people there, though usually not so late, and he stopped well inside the trees and listened and waited before he stepped out into the graveyard.

Above, there were clouds floating by the moon, each one a fleecy white. There was the common illusion that the moon was sailing and the clouds were standing still. The graveyard was not fenced. The stones went in uneven ranks down a slope just steep enough to be unplantable. The older stones were higher up and most were topped with carvings, chunky lambs and squat angels, made by the old black stonemason who had served these dead, who were also black. Laidlaw walked softly among the upper rows of stones, looking at the carvings. It was not only that they were weather-worn but some touch of the carver left the impression they had grown out of the stone as much as been cut into it. These older graves were sunken and the stones had settled at odd angles and the names on many were worn away and few of them were tended. Lower in the plot were newer stones and sometimes a brass plate, with wreaths of plastic flowers spotted among them. Without inspecting the new graves, Laidlaw went away among the trees. There was a trail that went out of the foot of the cemetery and led to the white frame church at the edge of the highway, but he kept off that, knowing it was sometimes used by teenagers come to drink or spoon or just to scare themselves.

South along the curve of the hillside, cedars began to mix among the other trees, tall old cedars that cast a richer darkness underneath themselves somehow. Laidlaw was getting near the highway, 431 to Nashville, and though he couldn't see it he could infrequently hear the drone of a car rising to a rush as it passed the nearest point, to drop into a fading whine. He turned and went farther down the slope and stopped at the edge of the clearing where Wat's house overlooked the road.

Two log rooms with the chinks cemented in, and a short patched dog run connecting them. Over the right-hand room a bent tin stovepipe broke the line of the roof. It was not the first house Wat had had since moving out of the one Laidlaw lived in now, but he'd been here a long time. His full name was Henry Redmon, though no one ever called him anything but Wat; the origin of the nickname was so deeply lost that the old man himself claimed not to remember it. Laidlaw had not seen him since he'd been back, or even long before for that matter, though recently he often thought of going. At times, pausing in this spot, he'd heard the old man's voice querulously raised and once had even seen him moving arthritically toward the outhouse in back.

Wat's present wife was a bootlegger of some prominence, known up and down the county by her first name of Martha, though she was sharp-natured and encouraged little familiarity from either her black trade or her white. In this respect she was unlike Wat's first wife, a more temperate personality who was buried in the cemetery Laidlaw had just passed. But Laidlaw understood she now made most of their living. Martha's trade often went late into the night, cars stopping briefly and squalling back out, but not so late as this. The house was dark and still as a coma. At lengthy intervals a wedge of headlights flashed by on the far side of it without slowing. Laidlaw turned away from the clearing and started back.

Going home, he took a slightly different route that brought him to the lower edge of the woods pond. Back in the shadows beyond the bank, he squatted on his heels and looked up into the open round formed by the treetops. The clouds had grouped in layered rings descending from the moon, a dome that sprang direct from the elevation of the trees. A faint breeze from across the pond stroked at Laidlaw's face. A cramp in his arched neck began and passed away, and he remained there without moving, entranced in the architecture of the sky, until the moon began to set.

There was just a taste of blue mixed in the sky when he heard a ripple on the far side of the pond. Over there were four, five slim outlines with heads bent to the water. As Laidlaw noticed them one head raised up: a four-point buck. He did not think the deer had seen him. Then the breeze interrupted itself and swiveled around to his back, and all five deer were running back into the cedars.

There were three does and what he thought was a juvenile buck. He went around the edge of the pond and after the deer in the queer rapid lope he'd learned, but the dark was immediate under the cedars and he had no hope of finding them. Dropping back to a walk, he went up through the cedar thicket and down through the orchard and came at last to the edge of the low pasture.

Though it was dawn already, he was not really tired, just a little chilly and stiff from holding that long crouch. Mist floated up from the pasture as the night began its dissolution into gray. The seed tops of the fescue were bent over with a weight of dew. And over near the garden fence the top of the hay was moving. Laidlaw had just barely noticed that when he saw the lead buck rise vertically from what must have been a flatfooted spring and clear the fence with a foot to spare. Then the others were going over after him with that same breathtaking grace.

Laidlaw fell into a staggering run toward the garden. He wanted to shout but could not bring himself to do it, and instead he began to flap his arms like the wings of a flightless bird. When he was nearly there the deer saw him and came rocketing out of the garden neck and neck like hurdlers. They swept clear of him in a semicircle as he ran up to the corner of the fence. Hanging himself on the post there by the bend of his elbow, he swung back to watch the white flashes of their raised tails bouncing back into the woods. When he glanced back into the garden, he saw that his fragile rows of corn sprouts were still there, which was a marvel; he thought that they'd been in there long enough to eat it all. His surprise turned into a giddy relief, so strong he couldn't stop himself from laughing. Now that it was daylight anyway, it seemed all right to laugh out loud.

4

LAIDLAW WENT down the second row of corn, working around each plant with the broad blade of the grubbing hoe. The corn that had survived was tall now; it came to the top of his rib cage when he was standing straight. He had replanted in the gaps and the newer plants had grown to roughly half that height. It was late afternoon and there was an intermittent breeze from the west that turned and rattled the oddments on the high wire he'd strung around the garden. This wire was looped over tomato stakes he'd tacked to the post tops and on it were festooned the cans he ate from and old cartons and plastic containers and some foil disks he'd fashioned for their glimmering. Some aspect of this arrangement kept away the deer; they'd not been back since he'd rigged it up, though he sometimes still encountered them, if the wind was in his favor, in the woods by night. He'd had a notion that the reflections from the clumps of foil would also keep away the birds, but the barrier seemed less effective in this respect.

The hoe said *chop, chop,* sinking into the dirt, clanking whenever it hit a rock. A big rock set deep, of which there seemed to be some few, could send a stinging vibration up the wood of the handle to jar it halfway loose from Laidlaw's hand. Then, if he had the patience for it, he knelt down and dug around the edges of the stone with his fingers until he had it rooted out, and stood up and flung it over the fence into the creek.

It had been a hot day, but with a dry heat that faded quickly as the sun went down. The breeze came up at regular intervals; Laidlaw could hear it fanning through the garland of trash above the fence before it touched him, and each time he got that signal he stood up to receive it. Letting the round tip of the hoe handle rest against his ribs, he set his hands to his hips and arched his back to ease it, turning one way and another. The wind ruffled the corn all around him and dried the sweat that ran in various tracks down the sides of his body. He opened and closed his eyes to clear and adjust them to the distance where the great copper round of the sun fell behind a line of trees that shivered its light, and then when the breeze began to die he took told of the hoe again and went on.

He'd started late to have the cool of the day, and when he got done it was nearly dark. The rows of plants were melting into a twilight that dropped through dimmer blues toward the final color of night. The breeze blew steadily and much cooler now and fireflies were coming out across the field, hovering just above the hay. Laidlaw looked at the fading garden with a half smile; he *had* a garden now, despite certain defects of both diligence and talent, though certainly it was often less kempt than it should have been. The corn was beginning to tassel and he had good-sized green tomatoes that would be ripening soon and he had already been able to pick a couple of baskets of beans. On his own initiative he'd gone out for the wherewithal to plant a row half in cucumbers, half squash, and had set out a row of bell pepper plants. It was pleasant to stand in the dusk and contemplate the rows in their reasonable order, more pleasant than it was to work them. But now he could hear the sheep bleating nervously around the upper barn because he was late for feeding. Lifting the wad of his shirt from where he'd hung it on the wire, he left the garden and went to tend them.

A little brown wren had nested in a hole in the third locust pole down from Laidlaw's gate. In the very early mornings he saw her come out and begin to hop desultorily just past the weeds in the fencerow. With her tail sticking straight up in the air, she hopped in cautiously widening circles that finally brought her to a spot under a big hackberry tree where Laidlaw usually threw out breadcrumbs. He had hauled a flat rock out of the creek bed and laid it there to make a clear space in the weeds for the crumbs, and on his last trip to the Co-op had even bought a fifty-pound sack of birdseed to supplement the bread. He watched the wren's approach from his chair on the porch while his hand revolved over the drum of the banjo, coaxing melodies out of the modal tunings he was now beginning to explore. A shy bird, the wren preferred to stuff her crop in relative privacy, though she would tolerate the presence of a sparrow, a titmouse, an occasional chickadee. Now and then a few grackles or a pair of blue jays would arrive and frighten all the smaller birds away, but Laidlaw didn't much object to that; he'd as soon watch one bird as another.

Then one morning there was a heavy flap and a hideous squawk and Laidlaw turned his head to see a peacock clasping the top slat of his gate with horny gray feet. It snaked its blue neck around, overlooking the yard as if with outrage, and then fell onto the track with a thump that raised a puff of dust. Laidlaw stared at the peacock, now advancing splayfooted into the yard. He'd heard that squawk a time or two before, coming out of something reminiscent of a bundle of rags which was jammed in the fork of a tree by the unfinished subdivision over the hill, something about the size of a turkey, though it surely didn't sound like one. So this was a peacock, then. It had molted its tail feathers, all but a few that dragged tattered or broken behind it, but the blue of its neck had an impressive sheen, and gold feathers fanned out along its back, bright as new coins edged over each other in rows.

The peacock moved pace by pace toward the stone with the birdseed on it, moving its neck in reciprocal whiplike strokes. When it had come up to the stone it cocked its head one way to bend its right eye on it, reversed the motion to look with the left, and stepped closer to rapidly peck up what seemed a large quantity of seed, grain by hasty grain, preferring, as Laidlaw noticed, the sunflower seeds above the others. The peacock went on eating for ten or fifteen minutes, then sprang up on the rock and erected its leftover snaggle of tail feathers, presenting this display in Laidlaw's direction with a shivering rattle and a hiss. After remaining a minute or more in this position the bird made a reverse turn and showed Laidlaw the cloud of gray down that covered its behind. There was another loud rattle; Laidlaw could now see how this was accomplished by a movement of the fan of brown feathers that supported the tail, when there was any tail to support. The peacock hopped down from the rock and strutted a few steps across the yard. With another squawk, it folded away its feathers, and giving the yard a last comprehensive and contemptuous glance, walked around the back of the house. Laidlaw, who'd been startled out of playing, shrugged and started up again.

That evening, when he went to feed the sheep, he found the peacock loitering around the barn. He fed a mix of corn and pellets bound with molasses in a long trough in the open hall of the barn, and it appeared that the peacock was able to retrieve some of the spillage. At any rate it was busily at work along the ground beside the trough.

The sheep, who'd lain up all day in the barn to hide from the heat, had come out to stand in the area of the feed room door, waiting and watching Laidlaw out of their yellowish eyes. There were six black-faced ewes and a four-year-old, part-Dorset ram with a fine double curl of horn. Only four lambs had survived the spring to see Laidlaw's return, but now they were sturdy and woolly enough: three little rams and a ewe. He climbed into the feed room and the sheep pressed up to the raised doorway, heads turned sideways to lick spilled sweet feed from the floor, then fell over themselves turning to follow him when he came out with the loaded bucket. They packed so closely around his legs that it was hard for him to keep his balance, and as usual he finally had to dump part of the feed on their thick heads, which they kept obstinately in the way of the trough.

The peacock had been startled away a little by this activity, but now was reapproaching the knot of sheep around the trough, step by considered step, neck winding back and forth in inspectorly gestures. Laidlaw withdrew to prop himself on the iron frame of a rotted wagon nearby and waited to see what would happen. When the peacock was in neck's reach of the trough, the ram pulled out of the crush and made a short springy run at it, head lowered, driving it several yards back from the barn. The peacock regrouped and advanced again, and this sequence repeated itself two or three times over, until the ram apparently lost interest in his part of it. Laidlaw watched, shaking his head, as the peacock gained the trough and thrust among the sheep and draped its beak down in among the other feeding mouths.

He stayed for a while on the rusty wagon tongue to see what would next occur. When the trough was empty and the sheep had spread out in the pasture under the first pricks of stars through the twilight sky, the peacock began a zigzag climb up the hill from the barn, then turned and took a running start and sailed itself back to the roof of it. For a minute or two it walked up and down the rooftree, surveying the possibilities, and finally flapped laboredly into a locust tree that overhung the barn. Laidlaw watched the bird make short wingspread leaps from branch to higher branch till it found one that suited it and settled itself there and put its head beneath its wing. Well, it seemed like it knew what it was doing, Laidlaw thought, laughing quietly and privately as he went on back down the hill.

The obligation to the garden cut into Laidlaw's banjo-playing time a little. But on the other hand, a man who didn't need to sleep had time to spare. Then too, he picked up tunes more quickly now that he'd got the knack of clawhammer better. There was a discount stereo in the house that he'd recently ordered through the mail, and he had also found a place to order records from, rare old Dot and Folkways sides. They were pricey and he chose among them carefully, checking the mailbox for the flat cardboard cartons over and over till they came. When the heat of midday drove him inside, he'd sit next to the turntable, with a glass of ice water near at hand, and repeat a cut interminably until it fixed itself in his head and then try to sound it out on the banjo by ear. At times he'd get the tune just so, at others it would take him off on some new tangent of his own. Whichever, he didn't really mind, unless he was slowly starting to prefer the latter.

When a tune had fully captured his fancy, he would sometimes neglect the garden, drop back into the habit of playing all day long till he had it down. Meanwhile Johnson grass would shoot up among his plants, and morning glory vines would climb them, strangling. Beans grew fat and waxy tough and birds pecked apart the ripe tomatoes on the vine. The whole project sank rapidly toward decay, until Laidlaw mastered whatever phrase he'd been studying and remembered to pay attention to it again.

Then there was the house, which never had been much. The front room, where Laidlaw slept and kept his banjo, was the largest. Adjacent was a smaller room, meant for a bedroom probably. At any rate there was a bed, along with two cracked chests of drawers, a steamer trunk with sprung hinges, and a quantity of the ambiguous junk that was spread all over the house when Laidlaw first returned to it. The kitchen, long and narrow, stretched across the rear side of the other two ground-floor rooms. Upstairs, on opposite sides of the steps, were two small rooms whose ceilings slanted with the eaves.

Every room had been left a jumble; you could have started a salvage store by hanging out a sign. Laidlaw had seen such moves in progess, had assisted in a few, and he knew how the abandoned things, no longer held in sympathetic order by the presence of their owners, could cave into the spaces left by whatever was taken away. He had not met his last tenants, had had to handle the whole affair by proxy, from a distance. They had left no old appliances or derelict cars around the yard; really they hadn't been there long enough to turn over much of that kind of thing. But every room was stuffed with the sort of junk you might not recognize as useless until you had to think of moving it somewhere else, trash hung on to in the vain hope that it might one day transform itself into something more worth having.

The stuff seemed to have its own considerable inertia, and Laidlaw coped with it by shifting it from place to place, as though the house were a closed system from which nothing could be absolutely removed. He disposed of the clutter in the rooms he was using by piling it into the ones he wasn't. After all, he needed only so much space to live in, the front room and the kitchen would serve.

With the front room emptied of everything he didn't need, the tattered walls looked wrong somehow, and one day he took hold of a loose tail of wallpaper and pulled it free. A spade-shaped patch opened on the wall, disclosing multiple layers of faded color. He ripped away another gout of paper. The chunk in his hands had a smoky smell, overlaying a musk of human oil. Laidlaw began to claw recklessly at the walls with his fingers, seemingly everywhere at once. The paper was an inch thick most places, regular wallhangings and plenty of newsprint too. The wallboard crumbled in so many spots as he worked that in the end he tore all that down as well.

It took him a whole day to tear the walls back to bare two-by-fours and a good part of the evening to bag up the remnants and find somewhere in the unused rooms to cram it all. He liked it better bare, the crisscross of the posts and joists didn't bother him, but in the winter he knew he'd freeze. In mid-August he finally made himself go out to buy fresh drywall and some insulation. Hanging drywall was within his skill, and he made a fair job of it, cutting the board carefully to the corners and odd spaces, spackling over the nails and seams.

He planned a trip for paint and never made it. A point of accommodation had been reached, where dirt, disorder, and incompletion no longer troubled him because it was all his own. The wall remained unpainted and the junk-filled rooms stayed shut. The house had settled fully into a new state, imperfect as it might have been, and now he had only to live in it.

There was no guilt involved in quitting on the house, as there would have been if he'd given up entirely on the garden. Nothing in the house was growing; nothing relied on him for life. Nevertheless he had at times a vague suspicion that the tenants' abandonings, shut behind their doors, remained in some half-animate state of being. They had an aura about them that disturbed him in the same ill-defined fashion that the patina of humanness caked to the walls of the front room had done. Occasionally, at the moment of his midnight wakings, he might feel that aura coalesced into a presence, but it never got more definite than that, did not become an image or a voice. What shadows marked the room by night were plainly cast by the things he chose to keep there; Laidlaw did not believe in ghosts because he could not afford to.

5

LAIDLAW PLAYED the banjo against the rising and falling pitch of
the tractor, which was winding around and around the field behind the garden. The noise of it built to a peak as the tractor approached the garden fence, and then the sound curved away gradually
toward the far side of the field. Walter Giles was driving the rake;
Laidlaw didn't own one and wouldn't have known how to run it if he
had. It bothered him to be sitting on the porch playing more or less
in Walter's presence, although there was no possible way Walter
could hear him; a person could barely have heard a gunshot from the
middle of that hammering tractor engine. His impulse was to go in the
house, but then he wasn't going to be driven inside just because
Walter Giles was there raking hay. It was hard to put a finger on it;
Walter just made him uncomfortable in a variety of obscure ways and
without really doing much to accomplish it.

Annoyed at himself, he set the banjo aside and got up and went
into the house. In the slightly cooler dim he stood irresolute for a
moment, then went to where the banjo case was propped open
against the bare wallboard. In a plush box fixed inside the neck part
of the case was a set of finger picks. He took them out and went back
to the porch, tossing them lightly in his hand so that they separated
and then gathered back together in his palm. There were three of
them. The thumb pick was made out of black plastic and the two
finger picks of perforated metal, with a patent application number
stamped on the lower side of each.

He slipped on the picks, pinching the sides of the metal ones to fit
them tightly to his first two fingers. The metal came to a soft point
just past the ball of each finger, like some sort of obverse fingernail.
It was a curious feeling to have them on; he'd spent some time, at
other times, remembering how it felt. He picked up the banjo and

played "Cripple Creek," slowly at first, then warming up, putting in all the slides and hammers that three-finger playing encouraged. But what if you tried it the other way? Playing the notes of the clawhammer arrangement, but three-finger, with the picks? He tried it. Well, it was difficult, for one thing. It worked against all the new habits he'd been forming, and the tune came out very slowly on the first couple of runs through it. It also came out bright and sharp and with a clean melodic accuracy. He kept trying it, gaining a little speed and balance. Supposing a person could ever learn to do it fast, why, they might be on to something.

Bent over the banjo, watching his fingers move, he grew so absorbed that he didn't notice when the tractor cut out. He was just becoming aware of an increase in quiet when he looked up inattentively and saw Walter walking along the track toward Mr. Giles's red truck, which it appeared that he had borrowed for the day. Walter walked heavily, his steps swinging out from his body in curves instead of coming straight. He was a big man, built on the same frame as his father, but hog fat all over, stuffing his overalls tight as a sausage sack. Laidlaw got up and lit a cigarette and went after him, catching up as he reached the truck.

"All through?"

"Yep," Walter said, biting off the word. He was not a big talker. Turning his head, he spat to the downhill side.

"When would I look for you all again?"

"Tomorrow'r Wednesday." Walter's lip wrenched up on the right side. It was not a smile, only an adjustment of his tobacco wad. The teeth on that side were browned from it. Walter wore no shirt under his overalls, and his skin was the same boiled red all over, the color even showing through his blondish stubble of hair. A knuckled birthmark ran down the right side of his jaw, shaded the purple of a bruise. He looked at Laidlaw out of slit, piggy eyes. The look might have been taken for surly, but Laidlaw saw that it was simply without expression of any kind. He had a couple more questions, but he decided they could wait.

"Good enough," he said, turning and starting back for the house. He heard the truck crank up behind him, but he didn't look back to see Walter go.

Tuesday came and went with Laidlaw too wrapped up in figuring the new finger-picking notion to care very much about baling hay. But he was surprised when no one appeared on Wednesday morning, and when around noon it began to thunder beyond the ridge, he became positively fretful, finally putting down the banjo to go over and stare gloomily into the field. The hay was lying in a long brown braid against the green, coiled toward the center of the pasture, ready to be rained on and ruined. The leaves on the maples were turning back in a fitful wind, and when Laidlaw started back to the house he saw that the sheep had bunched nervously on the hill; they thought it was going to rain for sure. But finally the storm passed on south of the encircling hills, and it was clear and hot again by midafternoon.

That evening Laidlaw cranked his B string a full step up to C and started working on "Sail Away, Ladies" in this third new way of playing. He was doing the transpositions faster now, and he had it coming pretty well by moonrise, an intricate little tune with a sweet wistful flavor.

> Don't you children weep and cry . . .
> Sail away, ladies, sail away . . .
> You'll be an angel by and by . . .
> Sail away, ladies, sail away . . .

He didn't sing the words out loud, just kept them running in his head as a way of keeping to the beat. The song worked on him like a lullaby, and next morning he overslept, not waking until some metallic clattering entered his sleep and broke it. He got up and peered out the window to find that it was Walter again, with a hay baler clunkily in tow behind the truck. Maybe it had taken him two days to get there at the rate he was going now. Laidlaw decided not to go out; there was no point striking up talk with Walter for purely social reasons, and he already knew where to find the field.

He played the banjo out on the porch until up in the afternoon, defiantly, as it were. *Let old Walter think what he wants to, let him just think I'm nothing but a picking and grinning fool . . . that don't know how to run a hay baler, that don't even know how to get a few of his fingers ripped off in the works of a hay baler yet.* Later he went out to the garden fence and stood there for a long time watching the baler work. A scoop at the front gathered the coil of raked hay, each length of which was somehow mashed into a block in the moil of the machine's interior, then bound with two loops of blond raveling twine and excreted tumbling from the rear. Half the field was spotted with new bales pitched this way and that. For a wonder, the baler didn't break down all day.

Walter would have left again without an interview, and Laidlaw had once more to ambush him at the truck.

"You all be back with the wagon tomorrow?"

A hawk and spit. The tobacco lump rolled under Walter's puffy cheek.

"Sa'rdy."

"Saturday, hell." Laidlaw shot his half-smoked cigarette up the track with an irritable snap of his fingers. "They're calling for rain tomorrow evening, don't you know that?"

There was a pause while Walter looked blankly back at him. If he was moved in any direction it didn't much show.

"Well," he said at length.

"Well?" Laidlaw said.

"Well, might not rain." Walter got in the truck and began to back toward the gate.

Well, it's all on the knees of the Lord now, ain't it? Laidlaw thought, but he held back from saying it. Instead, he went to where the pitched cigarette smoked thinly between the ruts and tromped it completely out.

As it happened, the forecast was dead wrong, which was by no means uncommon, and Friday night passed in clear bright pools of moonlight. Saturday morning Laidlaw was out before dawn, dressed and ready when the truck and flatbed wagon rolled up to his gate, and he walked over to let them in. Mr. Giles looked a bit put out, he thought, not to have been able to catch him asleep. Walter was featureless as ever, but there was a kind of cloudiness under his moon face that made Laidlaw picture him being hauled out of the sack at four in the morning, feet first maybe, bonking his head on the floor. This image rather pleased him. Mr. Giles held authority over his sons, lumpish and inert as they might be, and could have done something like that if he'd been in the mood for it.

"Thought you'd have Earl with you," Laidlaw said. "He coming on behind?"

Mr. Giles frowned. "Earl turned up a little po'ly this mornen," he said.

From the passenger seat, Walter surprised the world with a volunteer remark. "Earl turned up a little bit puken drunk this mornen, is what Earl did."

"Shut that fat mouth now why don't ye Walter?" Mr. Giles said rapidly, the words so compacted together they could hardly be made out. Then to Laidlaw: "We best jump to it."

I'd say so, Laidlaw thought, vaulting into the truck bed without saying anything out loud. He braced back with a foot pressing a wheel well as the truck and wagon jounced down toward the creek. It annoyed him a little that Earl hadn't showed; he'd have sooner had Earl than Walter on any account, and it would make a rougher day with just three people.

No matter the early start they had, the work was active enough to make them all hot even before the sun had really started to work. Laidlaw took the first turn on the ground, walking ahead of the truck, which Mr. Giles drove at a deliberate speed. Reaching a bale, he stood by it and waited until the wagon came near, when he stooped, catching each strand of baling twine in a fist. As the wagon began to pass alongside him he straightened, swinging the bale up across his hip and boosting it into the wagon bed, where Walter might be waiting to catch it, or might not be quite ready. Then he walked forward past the truck and got set to do it again.

The bales handled heavy, as if they might be damp, and Laidlaw worried over that, wondering if they might have taken so much dew they would mold. But only time would tell him that, and at least it hadn't rained. He was grudgingly obliged to admit that Walter had a hand for working the wagon, cross-tying the bales expertly so that each new level rose as tight as masonry.

When the first wagon had been stacked high, Walter gave Laidlaw a sign and he climbed on the tail of the wagon to sit with his back against the bales, as Mr. Giles turned the truck in the direction of the barn. Walter remained standing, propped against the hay, now and then sending a squirt of tobacco juice down behind the wagon. Laidlaw lowered his head and watched the ground change patterns as it spun back between his feet. The warmth of the sun was savory on his neck and shoulders, so long as he didn't have to move.

With the wagon parked on the high side of the barn, a man standing on the wagon bed didn't need to reach much over his head to heave a bale into the loft. On the other hand, that little distance began to tell after a while, and it got longer as Laidlaw worked toward the bottom of the stack. Mr. Giles and Walter were in the loft because they had more skill in stacking a stable tie. They'd set up a relay, with Mr. Giles snatching bales from Laidlaw and barreling them back to Walter, deeper in the shadows of the loft. That meant Laidlaw had to keep corkscrewing back and forth without a pause.

"Walter'll spell ye in the field," Mr. Giles said, coming back out of the loft once they'd cleaned the wagon to the boards. Laidlaw considered. He was tiring a little, but the change would leave him working the wagon, since Mr. Giles would keep driving by prerogative of age and his injury. The thought of stacking didn't much appeal to him because he feared he'd botch it. Foolish pride, you might call it, but then if they spilled a load it would cost them time.

"That's all right," Laidlaw said. "It suits me where I am."

Halfway through his second turn around the field Laidlaw felt himself starting to tire. He had not eaten anything that morning and was beginning to regret it, as his head got progressively lighter. The sun marched toward its meridian, moment by moment more yellow and more hot. Laidlaw moved forward from bale to bale like an automaton, his mind wandering elsewhere. Riding back to the barn on the second load, he hooked his arm around a bale and allowed himself to doze.

"We'll rest a spell," Mr. Giles decided when they'd got the second load into the loft. Laidlaw invited them down to the house, but they declined. He went to the house himself, where he splashed handfuls of water on his face to rouse him. Some way refreshed, he folded bread around a heavy slab of yellow cheese and gobbled it, surprised at the depth and sincerity of his hunger. Then he filled a jar with ice water and went back.

Mr. Giles and Walter both leaned against the bed of the red truck, Mr. Giles feeding himself slices of apple from the blade of his jackknife in his habitual way while Walter pushed the last of a can of Vienna sausages in between his jellied lips. They passed the water jar among them, then Laidlaw took it into the barn and set it inside on a rail. By the time he came back, Mr. Giles had started up the truck.

"Swap out will ye?" Mr. Giles said.

Laidlaw shook his head, walking past the truck into the field. The break had allowed his arms and shoulders to stiffen some, as he discovered when he bent for the first bale, but the soreness passed by the time he raised the fifth. His hands were rubbing raw against the fraying baling twine, so that his first lifting snatch at every bale brought a short sharp pain like a punctuation mark. Combined with the stooping and turning, the sun was starting to make him a little batty. The field yawed around him, and sometimes when he turned back to it, the truck appeared in another quadrant from the one in which his sense of direction had placed it. In the brief pause standing beside each bale, before the wagon reached him, he would shut his eyes and against the hot red of his inner eyelids see disparate images flashing.

When the last load had been brought back the sun was far enough to the west that the barn cast shade on the wagon. In this comparative cool, Laidlaw slung bales toward the square hatch to the loft. Now he was tired enough that his throw was an inch or two short as often as not, so that he had to give the bale an extra shove to keep it from falling back on him. When a third of the load was cleared Mr. Giles joined him on the wagon bed and the pace picked up. Walter had stacked close enough to the door that they no longer needed the relay.

"*Ah*-ha," Mr. Giles said when they'd finally cleaned the wagon. " 'Bout wore ye out I'd say."

"If only I'd been resting myself in the cab of that truck all day," Laidlaw said, "then I might be as bushy-tailed as you."

Mr. Giles laughed again, apparently not displeased. Laidlaw patted his pockets down and found a folded envelope of cash to present.

"All right," said Mr. Giles, putting the packet away. "We'll haul that baler and rake on out of here sometime the next couple of days."

He pushed his hat back and got in the truck, where Walter had already installed himself, ready to depart. Laidlaw went through the double front doors of the barn and took a drink from the jar. The water was still somewhat cool. He wiped his mouth on his forearm and went to stand in the doorway, watching the truck and wagon pass through the gate and down the washboards of the hill. Then he turned back and looked up to where the loft began, a second level just a few paces into the hall.

The loft had no wall at that end, so Laidlaw could see the line of bales lipped up to the edge of its floor. Walter had stacked it about halfway to the roof, leaving a passage at one side by the wooden steps that ran up from the ground. Laidlaw went up and walked back along the wall to the hatch they'd loaded through and looked out to where the sheep grazed high on the hill, near the tree line. As few sheep as he had now, he might make it through the winter without having to buy more hay, that's if this load didn't mold.

He moved away from the window. The hay was piled to about his chin height. He reached over the top of the stack, got hold of a band of twine, and swung himself up, rolling across the tops of the bales and coming out spread-eagled on his back. The tin roof came to its peak directly above him; it was warm underneath it, but not unpleasant. The round rafter poles still had the bark to them, now coated with a twenty-five-year thickness of powdery yellow dust. There were huge amounts of this dust all over the barn, and what Laidlaw had raised by his movement swam lazily all around him. Wherever they crossed the bars of sun that leaked between the boards of the walls, the particles of dust blazed suddenly into light.

When he awoke he was very stiff and sore, every joint creaking as he went down the steps and outside. He'd slept all the way through to the evening chatter of the birds. Barn swallows whirled and darted all around the path of a cable that ran from house to barn, their forked tails lashing against the royal sunset colors of the sky. Half dazed from sleep, Laidlaw saw their movement sketching out bar upon bar of what, it seemed to him, might just as well have been a song.

6

IN THE mornings there began to be a sharpening chill that lingered and lengthened in the air. Laidlaw overhauled the stove, knocking clots of soot down from the pipe, giving it a coat of polish, checking it all over for serious cracks. He began to take note of the position of deadfalls in the woods. But it was not yet quite cold enough for fires. An extra blanket got him well enough through what part of each night he slept. The crisp cool of first light faded by midmorning and the air became warm and hospitable again.

That overnight cold sank into Laidlaw's fingers, making them not exactly numb, just a little stiff and distant. He frailed abstractedly to limber them, looking away into the top of the hackberry tree, whose misshapen leaves had just begun to yellow and shrivel back to the stem. A bunch of small birds fluttered up from the feeding stone at the weighty approach of the peacock. As his hands began to loosen, Laidlaw started to dip his thumb down toward a hint of some melody line.

In the rear of his mind he registered the fade of a car motor climbing the back side of the hill, and when it broke over the crest he automatically glanced over at it: a newish bottle-green Volvo, proceeding at the nervous creep which the drivers who sometimes tried the road as a short cut between subdivisions tended to employ. It wouldn't be anyone he'd know, so he was rather sharply startled when the car stopped at the gate. The man who hauled himself from under the wheel had shortish legs and an almost cubical trunk packed into a screaming madras jacket. As he moved around the front of the car toward the gate, Laidlaw jumped out of his chair and went into the house and put the banjo back into its case.

"Hey, good buddy!" The voice came from halfway up the yard.

Laidlaw walked to the front door and draped himself into it so as to fill it up, a hand braced on either side of the frame.

"Goodbuddy," he said, expressionlessly as an echo. Goodbuddy Clemson was walking up the steps, a smile of canned heartiness daubed across his flattish face, one meaty hand outstretched. Laidlaw realized he'd completely forgotten Goodbuddy's real first name, that tag he applied without prejudice to anyone he met had adhered so firmly to himself. He took the hand without moving out of the door frame, then let it go. Goodbuddy took a turn around the porch, stopping at the west corner to look out across the garden and the field. He thumped the corner post with the flat of his hand and then looked at the palm as though it had done something special to please him. The jacket was so tight across his back that the seams were all pulled crooked. It gave Laidlaw a feeling of disproportion to see Goodbuddy out of green fatigues, though he'd known him, by sight at least, for just about all his life. There was a thinning spot, he noticed, in the back of his sandy hair.

"Sure is a pretty place," Goodbuddy said, turning to drop into a chair. His legs stuck out straight before him like double-jointed milk cans. He wore a pair of penny loafers with an oxblood shine.

"Mmhm," Laidlaw said, thumbing a cigarette into his mouth.

"Course, it is a shame about the big house, now. Reckon you'll build back on the site?"

"Hadn't planned on it," Laidlaw said. The cigarette dipped on the edge of his mouth as he spoke.

Goodbuddy's eyes cocked up.

"Well, I surely don't see why you wouldn't. You could put you up a one-story ranch, for instance, wouldn't set you back too much. Or you could build you a mansion, really, if you wanted. If you cared to sell off a little bit of the back here, you could just about build yourself the Taj Mahal, I expect. You're sitting on a gold mine here, I don't know if you know it."

"Is that a fact," Laidlaw said.

"You know, I could draw you a contract . . ." Goodbuddy fanned at the air with his hands. "I mean just a kind of a dummy contract, you know, to where you could just get an idea of what you might get. Would that interest you at all?"

"It surely would not," Laidlaw said. He pulled a pack of matches out of his pocket and drew back hard on the cigarette in lighting it.

"Only asking, only asking," Goodbuddy said, making parrying motions with his hands.

Laidlaw crumbled the head off the dead match and snapped the paper stem into the yard. "Was that all that brought you?" he said.

"No siree," Goodbuddy said. "It just now happened to flash across my mind. I'd heard you was back and I just thought I'd be neighborly."

Laidlaw considered this notion in silence for a time.

"Well here I am," he finally said. "Big as life and twice as natural. You know, I hate to say it, but I was just now fixing to go into town for some things."

"Now don't let me hold you up," Goodbuddy said, rising. His face squinched with discomfort, as though something had stuck into him, and he ran a hooked finger all around under his collar. Then his expression eased. "As a matter of fact, there was just one thing . . ."

"Mmhm," Laidlaw said.

"My peacock." Goodbuddy glanced down into the yard where the peacock, completely tailless now, pecked morosely through patches of unevenly withering grass.

"Goodness me," Laidlaw said. "I never suspected that was your peacock."

"Well, you know that development me'n Daddy's got over the hill back yonder —"

"Looks like it kind of stalled out?"

"Just a little slow spell, I'd call it. Anyhow, we had this peacock for what, you know, a kind of a classy touch. To show people and so on. Had a girl peacock to keep him home, but I believe something must have got her. Anyhow, the one's not much good without the other, and I've found somebody would buy this'n off of me, make a long story short."

"Well," Laidlaw said. "I'd kind of got into the habit of thinking of him as *my* peacock. He's eaten about fifty pounds of my birdseed, anyhow. You're dead sure this one's the same?"

"Well . . ." Goodbuddy ripped the finger around his collar once again. "You really think . . ."

"Nah," Laidlaw said. "I'm just funning you, Goodbuddy. Go on ahead and take him if you want to."

"What, just like that?"

"Sure, go ahead."

"Well . . ." Goodbuddy stepped down the stairs into the yard and paused. His shoulders jigged up and down under the tight coat. He went slowly toward the peacock, laying each foot down with considerable circumspection. When he was within about five feet the bird began to move ahead of him, maintaining the same distance between them, though with no great sign of alarm. In this manner they made a complete circuit of the hackberry tree. Laidlaw felt a sort of seething in his chest that was not quite a laugh, although he knew it should have been. Goodbuddy stooped to make a tackling run at the peacock and missed it all except for a wing feather. Squawking, the peacock flew to the house roof, turned twice around crying angrily out, and then flapped off in the direction of the barns.

Goodbuddy had not quite fallen down in his attempt, though he'd come close. The boiling under Laidlaw's ribs still would not resolve itself into a laugh. Goodbuddy stood looking up the hill, where the peacock had landed and was now proceeding on foot.

"Maybe you might could feed him in a shed for a while," he said thoughtfully. "You know, throw the seed in a shed or a stall for him and then shut him up one time. That might be a little bit easier, you know what I mean?"

"Probably would," Laidlaw said. "Tell you what, I'll let you know when I get around to it."

"You know I'd appreciate that," Goodbuddy said. There was a light beading of sweat across his forehead. He was still looking off toward the barns. "Good to see you again and all . . . Say, are you using that old dairy barn at all? Because you know that old barn siding goes for a right good price these days. People been using it for paneling, panel their dens and what not. Why, I expect I could get you —"

Laidlaw had taken some quick jerky steps across the yard. *Can't you see I wouldn't sell you a handful of gravel?* was close enough to what he was thinking, but he couldn't say that or anything else because everything inside him had all speeded up, he was breathing much too fast, and he was convinced he was about to ——. With a mental wrench, he brought himself to a stop a couple of yards from Goodbuddy, who was just turning back in his direction.

"Say," Goodbuddy said, taking a rapid few steps back. "You don't look too sharp, Laidlaw. You're looking kind of pale. Think you might have a touch of the flu? Maybe you better lie down or something." With surprising agility, he backpedaled to the gate. "Anyhow, I'm gone."

Even after the dust of the Volvo had settled, Laidlaw remained fixed to the middle of the yard, rigid as if nailed. He was angry at himself more than anything but he still couldn't quite bring himself around. For God's sake, you didn't blow your whole fuse box because Goodbuddy Clemson came sniffing around after some barn siding. But then it was all the little things that slipped up on you. You could be wrong-footed that way at times. *Don't let nothing get at you till you can get at it* was what Sevier always used to — Laidlaw stopped. *Inhale. Exhale.* He breathed carefully, with long deliberate strokes of the diaphragm, until his tension had eased enough for him to walk back to the house.

No sleep. Laidlaw turned over and over in his blanket, tightening it around him as though screwing himself into a threaded sleeve. Under his breath he was talking to himself. Goodbuddy's drop-in had given him a real turn, though he wasn't entirely sure why. It might have been that rapacious greed that always shone so brightly through his chummy manners, or maybe just the way the very sight of him conjured up the whole REMF constellation all over again. Goodbuddy Clemson, the quintessential Rear Echelon Mother —— Oh, what was the use of thinking about all that? But the choice seemed either to be haired up about Goodbuddy in some way or other or else be uneasy without knowing why.

He rolled up from the pallet and padded barefoot to the door. The chill of the outer air raised gooseflesh on his upper body. He went back to the place near the pallet where he'd dropped his shoes and a flannel shirt, and then slipped out into the night. What time was it? The moon had risen fat and bloodshot red, a harvest moon, but climbing to the sky's roof it had shrunk and paled toward ivory. Laidlaw walked around back of the house, not able to stop himself from shivering. Soon there'd be a killing frost. He swung into a lope to warm himself, jogging north around the curve of the hill.

When he made the top of the ridge he dropped back to a walk. He'd been traveling fast enough to warm up some, not quite so fast as to break a sweat. The movement had bled him dry of anxiety, and now he was fully tuned to the minute sounds and movements around where he was walking, along the backbone of the ridge. He walked briskly enough to cover ground fast. Going down a dip in the ridge, he paused while a car sped by on a narrow paved road, then crossed it behind the disappearing taillights. The road was mostly made of patches and it humped up in the middle. Laidlaw got across it quickly, and began climbing the hill on the other side.

Just over the top he came out of the woods and cut across a steep gully-ripped pasture of a tenant family called Hobart. There were cows spread farther down the hill, white-faced Herefords, and halfway across he saw something coming up rapidly through them, a dark splotch passing low over the moonlit grass, the Hobart dog. The dog raced around Laidlaw in an ecstatic circle and then dropped into a deep crouch to fawn at him, its plumed tail curved and waving over its head. The dog had long brindled hair and slanted eyes like a Chinese clown. Laidlaw knelt and ran his fingers into the fur at the base of the dog's ears and rubbed there. The dog licked his face and pawed at him and Laidlaw rolled over into a dead-man's-float position, keeping his arms and legs bunched under him while the dog nuzzled deliciously at the back of his neck. Then he jumped up and went on, crossing a fence back into the trees.

The dog followed him a little way into the woods and then turned back. Laidlaw went ahead, smiling. He liked the dog, who he could now hear winding back toward its own house and barn. It was ever alert, but had never barked at him, not once. Any night he passed near enough the dog would sense his presence and come out to greet him and go with him a part of his way. At times he had thought of stealing it but the dog seemed content to return home each night and he thought things were better left as they were. He went down another fall of land and crossed the same paved road again; he'd traversed a bend of it in going across the Hobart woods and field. Passing through a thin screen of trees, he came within sight of a low open pasture, and before he entered it he stopped.

Like his own, this field had been cut back for hay; now moonlight pooled on the close-cropped expanse of it. On the opposite side, just out from the tree line, he could see the deer. He counted; tonight he made out seven. There was scarcely any wind, but he wet a finger and raised it for a test, then began carefully circling the pasture against what breeze there was. Keeping a pace or two back in the cover of the woods he made it within fifty yards of the deer before one of the younger bucks raised his head and began to study the patch of brush which hid him. Laidlaw stopped moving. The deer did not break. When the buck had begun to graze again, Laidlaw lowered himself softly to one knee. He remained there for some time watching the deer as they nosed their way farther into the field's center, spreading apart minute by minute as each explored its separate patch of grass.

It was about an hour before the cold began to reach him again. He got up a little stiffly, making a small crunch of something that brought up the heads of the three deer nearest him. Not to disturb them anymore, he retreated as carefully as he might the way he'd come.

Going back he made a somewhat wider circle, coming out on the far side of the hill above his house. He was meaning to keep in the woods entirely, but there was a patch of brambles in his way, and to get most easily around it he cut across a knob-shaped clearing at the head of the pasture on that side. His third step away from the trees landed false, on something round and long that turned and rolled in the arch of his foot, unbalancing him enough to bring him down. Landing propped partway up on the elbow he used to break the fall, he found himself eye to empty eye with a long cracked yellow skull. Next he saw the bones strewn all around him, shanks and spines and yet more skulls.

Laidlaw shut his eyes. He felt that he was up to his neck in dark noisome water; he could feel its thick warm surfaces sucking all along the bottom of his jaw. He had a footing of sorts on slick underwater mud, but it was most unsure. The water had a slightly fetid smell to it. Its surface was black as tar and perfectly flat and still and, because of the low angle of his head, it seemed to stretch out before him for an amazingly long way to a something which must have been the dike, though in the near-absolute absence of light he could see it only as a local deepening of the general darkness. When he opened his eyes the skull was still there, but now he could recognize it as belonging to a sheep. He sat all the way up and took the skull onto his knees and looked at it.

After all, it was only a thing, an animal leaving. The satirical expression that had flung him back had just been something he'd imagined. Laidlaw made to roll the skull away, then, thinking better of it, put it gently down beside him, right side up. He remembered well enough now: this was the spot they always towed the sheep to, whenever disease or wild dogs got one. High above the house and barn, the carrion smell rose straight up to the buzzards, drawing them down to where they'd clean each carcass back to the mealy-white core. Laidlaw stood. The bones were scattered all around him; there was no telling which belonged with which. It was just that he'd been taken by surprise. All summer the bones had been drowned there in the long grass, and it was fall, the falling off, that brought them back to the surface.

Below, the hill went down in terraces. Where the land leveled was the rail-fenced riding ring and then just past it the horse barn. Laidlaw could make out the white trim on the stall doors; washed in the moonlight, the paint still looked fresh. Ahead of the barn an asphalt driveway made a flattened loop before the scar on the ground where the house had been and then bisected the big front field on its way to the road.

Laidlaw walked down the hill to the next terrace, where he stopped. He'd never meant to end up here, but now he had, he thought of going down there, going all the way. But then he thought, For what? Even the ashes had been mostly rained away; there was nothing but a charred spot on the ground and a few of the flat fieldstones on which the house had been raised. It had been no mansion, just a big free-handed farmhouse, square, with porches running all four sides of it. What he remembered about it most clearly were the doors, how each one of them, inside and out, had been heavy and tall and a full arm span wide, as if the house had been built to accommodate bears. Well, no one would be walking through those doors another time. Laidlaw would have liked to go away but he couldn't quite bring himself to it, and somehow he remained standing there until the beginning trace of dawn began to dilute the moonlight into blue.

7

HONED TO a brighter, sharper edge, the cold began to hold for a good part of each day. Now Laidlaw's first business upon waking was to rebuild his fire. His insulation job seemed reasonably tight (though there were drafts around the door and windows), so if the damped-down stove had kept a few coals through the night there'd be some faint warmth clinging to the room at morning. He cleared ash from the stove till the coals were bared to their jewel-red glow. Blowing on them brought them back to flame, and he opened the damper and fed them kindling and wood until the stove leapt with a freshened fire. But as often the stove would have burnt itself completely out and he woke to a chill settled low over the whole room. As quickly as he could manage he'd clear the stove back to its dusty iron floor, shoveling the ashes into a bent tin foot-tub, and start a new fire from scratch.

For safety's sake he dumped the ash bucket daily in the creek. Ash puffed up in dusty rings while the small embers that were always hidden in it sizzled and steamed on striking the water. Holding the empty tin bucket warm against his thigh, Laidlaw turned back to the house. It was cold enough that his breath came smokily from him. He walked around the side porch, set the bucket down, and picked up a sledgehammer and wedges from where he'd left them the previous morning.

He'd towed two trees down out of the woods, a hackberry and an ash, and hired a chain saw from Mr. Giles to cut them into rounds. The fat circles of wood were bunched on the ground back of the house, covered against rain by long black sheets of plastic. He'd put out an especially knotty round to use as a chopping block, and now he pulled others from the plastic cover and began to set them up.

He had three iron wedges, one newer than the rest, which still had traces of blue paint up the sides of it. The older ones were browned with rust and frayed across their narrow ends and curled down around the top from year upon year of hammering. Laidlaw raised an ash round to the block and set a wedge in a crack of it with a couple of taps from the choked-up sledge. Then he stood back and struck at the wedge from the shoulder. There was a ring and the wood jumped into two pale halves, the wedge tumbling out from in between them. The ash was dry and easy to split, though on the other hand it didn't last long on the fire and parts of it had the dry rot. Laidlaw split the halves in quarters and then began on a chunk of hackberry.

The hackberry tree had been felled by lightning. Green and complicated with many knots, it made for troublesome splitting, cleaving to itself with cunning recalcitrance. Laidlaw worked with a pair of wedges, using one to free the other, each in turn. If he miscalculated he might sometimes need the third. This wood did not split so much as rend. When he had finally got it torn in quarters, he went back to the ash for a break.

Alternating the two kinds of wood, he kept the hammer swinging into the wedges, the ring of it echoing back at him from the hill behind, a sharp clear repeat in the cold air. He wore a blanket-lined denim jacket, short enough to let his arms move freely. The work was enough to keep him reasonably warm once he had set a pace. He sledged until he became a little lightheaded, the hammer handle jarring in his hand and the wedges bouncing crazily back at him, and then stopped and went to sit on the back porch floor and light his first cigarette of the day.

Coming hard after the exercise and on an empty stomach, the tobacco made him pleasantly giddy. He leaned back against the kitchen wall, stretching his right side in the thin warmth of the first sun. On the wooded hill, the trees were a billow of red and orange, the cones of a few cedars standing out darkly among them. Above, the sky was a dense blue, with the pale ghost of a daylight moon still riding low on the curve of it.

He snubbed his cigarette out on a plank, rubbed at the black mark until it was cool, and got up, taking hold of the splitting ax which was propped against the wall. The ax head was much like a wedge itself, only somewhat sharper, with the same solid weight. A crack in the wood handle just below the head had been bound with silver tape. Laidlaw went back down into the yard and began to set up the quartered rounds, smashing them into smaller pieces one by one. He had a certain knack for this, or at least he was better at it than at hoeing. As if directing itself, the ax swung in an arc up and back of his shoulders and then down to meet the wood with an enjoyable shock of contact. He took off the point of each quarter first, then split the remaining chunk at the opposite angle. The ax handle jumped springily in his hands. He found a beat and ripped through all the quartered wood in less than twenty minutes.

The split wood was scattered in a half circle from the block, shining bright along its fresh-cut edges. Laidlaw rested, breathing a little hard, leaning on the ax he'd propped against the block. Then he gathered the new split wood in armloads and added it to a pile he'd started under the shelter of the side porch roof. When all the wood was stacked he went into the kitchen to make a pot of coffee. Enough heat leaked back from the stove in front to warm this little room. When the coffee burbled black in the glass knob of the pot, he poured a cup and had another smoke. Then he went in the front room and fed the fire and opened up the banjo case.

With the weather now turned more definitely cold, it took his fingers longer to unbind. Playing on the porch was over for the season. Laidlaw sat with his feet on the stove's iron apron, picking out the simplest patterns till his hands came back. Then he moved away from the heat to a chair by the table that held his record player and now a tape recorder too.

These days less of his time was spent on playing standards. He had detuned the banjo, knocking it down about two full steps, so that the notes were low and a little hoarser, and held longer, almost as long as the notes of a guitar. Tuning the strings to one of a variety of minor chords, he tried out different picking patterns, arrangements of plucks and strums he could play off against lines of the melodic picking he'd derived from the clawhammer style. What came of this was something different, something strange, a kind of low drone that hummed from one pitch to another, stitched all over with brighter designs of more particular notes.

Never quite certain what he was doing, Laidlaw didn't bother writing tablature, too slow and tiresome a process for him in any case. Instead he loaded the big open-reeled tape recorder and switched it on before he started playing . . . whatever. You couldn't exactly call it composition, but it was something, he was almost sure. When he sat at the table, he kept the leather strap of the banjo slung loosely on his shoulder, and often he would find himself up and wandering around the room, hardly having noticed getting up. Reeling in the filament of what tune he might be following, he paced from wall to window, stove to door, just half aware of any immediate aspect of the surroundings: layers of warmth and cool in the room, stripes of spackle down the wall, a faint odor of hot stove polish not quite yet burned away, movement of a sheep or a bird he'd register on the bits of hill or sky the little windows showed him.

A pale stripe of sunset-red lay down along the side of the hill. Behind the fencerow it was darkening among the trees. Four sheep drifted laterally across the slope, cloudlike and seemingly with no greater plan or direction, over the thin dry grass. A big black dog trotted quickly around the brow of the hill above the sheep and went under the three-strand fence into the woods. The sheep were unalarmed and did not bunch. Within the thickening shadows of the trees the black dog quartered a patch of leaves, its muzzle close to the ground.

Laidlaw put the banjo aside and found his jacket and went out. It had got colder than he'd looked for, and he shivered inside the denim, hearing the door bang behind him. Soon he'd need some kind of winter coat. His breath clouded the air as he went up the hill and came among the sheep, who scattered a little away from him. "Baaa," Laidlaw said, his mood turned weirdly playful, "maaa," rolling the vowels back in his throat. The sheep lifted their heads to look at him but were not taken in. Laidlaw could see the shadowy movements of the dog retreating through a stand of hickories on the wooded part of the slope. He went along the fence until he found a post set solidly enough to bear his weight and climbed the fence and followed.

It looked to Laidlaw like about the biggest dog he'd ever seen, nearly the height of a small Shetland pony. He thought it must have some Great Dane in it; it had that huge hammer-shaped head, but he doubted that was all. However, he couldn't get near enough to see for certain. The dog was shy of him and was keeping well ahead, though it went on circling with its nose to the ground. There were a number of fallen hickory nuts scattered through the leaves and their hard oblongs made uneasy footing. Laidlaw stopped and tried a whistle.

"Hey. Hey . . . dog . . ." His voice was loud and sounded foolish. The dog stopped and turned to face him, head lifted. Laidlaw went forward slowly, holding out his open hands.

"Hey, now, boy . . ." He had another five or six paces to go when a shudder ran over the dog quickly as an electric shock and it turned and ran a little farther away, stopping on the track that separated two patches of woods on its way over the hill to the horse barn.

"Hey, now, it's all right . . ." Laidlaw kept up as soothing a patter as he could manage, his voice deliberately low and softened. The dog waited until he had come out of the trees and then turned tail and bolted into the woods that ran down behind the low pasture.

"Oh, what the hell," Laidlaw said, sniffing. His nose was starting to run a little. He went toward the house, stopping now and then to give a whistle or a call behind. It was getting too dark to see very far though the woods, but the third time he stopped he distinctly heard dog feet slapping on the dry leaves back of him and he smiled behind his hand. He made a detour to feed the sheep and then went on to the house.

When he went in he let the kitchen door stand open, walking through to the front room. The take-up reel of the recorder was still aimlessly winding, trailing an end of tape. Laidlaw shut it off. Glancing in a square of mirror he'd tacked to one of the walls, he saw that coming into the warm had reddened his face. He went back into the kitchen and got a slice of bread, dipped it in the can of bacon grease, put it on a plate, and took it outside. The dog was standing on the track above the house, looking down at it. Laidlaw set the plate down halfway between the track and the house and started back. As he reached the door there was a snapping sound and he turned to see that the dog was at the plate and the bread was gone. He sopped another slice and carried it slowly out at arm's length toward the dog, who retreated doubtfully, backing up the slope. Laidlaw stopped and tossed the bread in the direction of the plate. The dog jumped and caught it in midair, jaws meeting with a wolf-trap clash. It did this much in the manner of a wild animal, not as if it had been taught a trick.

Back in the kitchen, Laidlaw tore into a package of hamburger and put half of it into an iron skillet to fry. The dark windows threw his own dim reflection back at him now, but though he could not see the dog he was sure the smell of the cooking meat would keep it somewhere nearby. He hashed the meat around with a fork, and when it began to brown he broke an egg into it. Once that had set he turned the food onto a second plate which he set down on the outer door sill. Then he backed up and sat in a chair just inside the front room doorway.

The kitchen door cast a wedge of yellow light in which Laidlaw could see the dog getting nearer the plate through a sequence of hesitations. When at last it had reached the door sill it gave Laidlaw one hard look and then began to vacuum up the food. Laidlaw watched, not moving a hair. The dog was mostly Great Dane, sure enough, but something else too, maybe bear. It definitely was the biggest dog he'd come across, though wretchedly thin, with all its big square-cut bones standing out sharply under sagging skin, ribs like the bars of a cage.

The dog's flanks pumped with its eating. It had a rolled leather collar, but no tag. Laidlaw had a fast involuntary picture unrolling back of his eyes like a film strip. He saw the dog running down some dirt road in the wake of a disappearing car. As the distance between dog and car lengthened the dog ran harder and more frantically, big paw pads splaying in the gravel, legs beginning to slip out to the sides. When it could not run any longer it stopped, tongue lolling, and looked after the plume of dust which was slowly settling along the path the car had taken

The dog had finished eating now and remained half in the doorway with its head partly lifted. Laidlaw got up slowly and took the skillet from the stove and set it down in the middle of the kitchen floor. Then he poured two fingers of bourbon into a jelly jar and went to the front room, picking a seat from which he could still see into the kitchen. The dog came in one piece at a time, rolling its great head toward the corners of the kitchen. In the confines of the small room it looked even bigger than it had before. When the dog became fully involved in the grease on the skillet, Laidlaw got up and made a careful approach. As he crossed the door the dog shied, but somehow without moving its feet, only lowering and cringing in its same position over the skillet. Laidlaw came nearer, slow and steady, until he had a hand on the dog's taut back and could begin to rub and scratch, up and down the neck and between the shoulders. Gradually the dog relaxed and straightened, then abruptly leaned into Laidlaw, dropping all its considerable weight against his side. The size of this dog, Laidlaw thought, slightly incredulous. The dog's shoulders came just above his hip, and he himself was on the tall side. The dog's eyes had fallen shut. Laidlaw kept up his stroking, moving up to the ears while with his free hand he reached over and swung the kitchen door quietly closed.

Sometime past midnight a scratching at the kitchen door blew

Laidlaw up from his pallet like a rocket. He was standing in the middle of the floor before he remembered about the dog, who only wanted to go out, of course. Nice thing it knew to ask . . . He opened the door and the dog slid past him and trotted out of sight through the long fronded shadows thrown over the yard by pale light from a chip of waning moon. Though it was cold, Laidlaw left the door ajar and remained standing near it, smoking and breathing the smoke through the crack and watching it unfold in the outer air. It crossed his mind that the dog might not return. He went back in the front and fed the fire, flicking his cigarette end into the stove door behind a twisty chunk of ash. There was a small creak and he looked over to see the dog shouldering its way back into the kitchen.

Laidlaw swung the back door to and returned to his pallet. He was not so restless as he'd usually be, waking suddenly in the middle of the night, but not especially sleepy either. Lying curled up on his side, he could see the cracks in the stove's body flashing a merry red. The dog was flopped out just beyond the warm iron apron, breathing with a steady hiss. Its back was just within arm's reach. Laidlaw put a hand out cautiously to feel the other warmth, then closed his eyes. Till now, he'd hardly noticed he'd been lonely.

8

WITH THE passage of time it developed that the strangest thing about the dog was her absolute silence. Over weeks in Laidlaw's house she became more natural in most other ways, but remained voiceless. She gained back the weight and the bulk she'd lost during her homeless time, grew even more massive than Laidlaw had suspected when he'd first seen her. She became fully at home in the house and its surrounds, confident of it as her own place. It was plain enough that she was quite well aware of anything that happened within her sight or hearing, but she never barked or growled or whined or made any other of the familiar canine noises.

Hard frosts had come, the ground was freezing solid, each day was locked in an iron cold. In the evening, Laidlaw fed the sheep their grain and then went around back of the barn, dragged out a bale of hay, and broke it open for them on the high ground there. He kicked the hay apart and paused a little away from it to smoke a cigarette while the sheep skirmished over the scattered flakes, and at a farther distance the black dog trotted in intent looping figures over the ground, nose tight to some tracery of scent. Overhead a crow cried out with the sound of a rusty hinge. Both Laidlaw and the dog looked up to see the crow flying low over the hill pasture, harried by a pair of smaller birds that darted at its eyes. Driven by the little birds, the crow went on harshly calling in its dragging flight down into the trees on the low side of the hill. The piece of sky where it had been was darkening. Laidlaw whistled up the dog and headed for the house.

Done eating the dish of meal and drippings Laidlaw set before her, the dog scratched to be let in and settled herself before the stove. In the kitchen, Laidlaw was hacking up a chicken for stew; cold weather had revived his interest in hot food. The knife slipped off a bone and nicked his finger, and all at once in the other room he heard the dog scrambling frantically over the floor. It was usual for her to register passing cars by trotting from window to window to observe their progress, but this was something else. When Laidlaw came to the front room she was trembling at the door. He placed his hand on her back to calm her, bending to peer out the window himself.

Mr. Giles's truck was parked up on the track and he himself was mounting the porch steps. Laidlaw, busy in the kitchen, hadn't heard him coming; he was a little chagrined at that now. He opened the door, and as he did the dog surged forward so quickly he was just able to catch her by the collar, holding her reared back on her hind legs.

"God Amighty," said Mr. Giles, who'd come to a frozen halt. "Where did ye get that thing?"

"Get down," Laidlaw said. "Get down, dammit, you can't act that way." It was difficult to tell for certain whether the dog meant to menace or embrace. A growl would have been revealing, but she remained utterly quiet. Laidlaw rapped her across the nose and she subsided quickly and completely, slumping against his side in that deadfall way she had.

"Go lie down," Laidlaw said sharply. The dog withdrew to the square of floor she'd marked off as her own. "Come on in," he said to Mr. Giles.

"Dog won't mind it?" Mr. Giles stepped into the room and pulled the door shut behind him. "What are ye doen with somethen like that anyhow?"

"What she's doing with me," Laidlaw said. "She's kind of a volunteer dog, you might say. I found her running in the woods, just about starved to death. Somebody dumped her is my best idea."

"They'll do thataway," Mr. Giles said musingly, keeping an eye on the piece of floor over which the dog was now spread at full limp length. "Ain't starven anymore though, not that I can see."

"No," Laidlaw said. "She's a real good eater. The funny thing is she never barks. Never makes a sound at all."

"Ha," Mr. Giles said. "Trained that way could be."

"Maybe so," Laidlaw said. "Hadn't thought of it, really. Take a seat if you want to," he said, taking one for himself.

"Can't stay," Mr. Giles said. "I'm on my way out home, what I wanted to tell ye was we'll kill hogs Saturday if the weather holds up. Us'n the Tomlinsons."

"It's the time of year," Laidlaw said.

"Tomlinsons'll sell a hog," Mr. Giles said. "Come on and kill with us and ye'll have a little somethen to hang in the smokehouse this winter."

Laidlaw considered. "Corn-fed hog?"

"Sure it is."

"The bottom rotted out of my saltbox, I believe."

"We'll salt yours down with ours, bring it on out to you when it takes."

"I don't know," Laidlaw said. Shifting his hand, he knocked the clot from his cut, and seeing it begin to bleed fresh, he licked at it.

"Ha," Mr. Giles said. "Better come on then. So starved for meat ye'd eat your own finger . . ."

Laidlaw laughed. "All right, I'll be there. Tomlinsons take a check?"

"Cash'd be handier I expect," Mr. Giles said. "You can come early as ye want to. And you can leave that dog to home."

He was up early on the Saturday but a tire on the truck had gone flat overnight, and because the lugs had been smashed on with an air hammer it took him longer than it should have to change it. It was as cold out as predicted, cold enough that his hands reddened and stiffened as he changed the tire. When he looked down at the house he could see the dog moving uneasily from window to window; she didn't like it any time he drove away. The sky was a lowering bellying gray and the smoke from the stovepipe was going straight to the ground. Once he got out on the main road a kind of spitting snow had begun, as fine and grainy almost as sand.

By the time he reached the Giles place the snow had stopped, though enough had stuck to spangle the ground. Some cars and trucks were parked alongside of a wall-less barn, a roof raised on poles. Nearby he could see steam still rising from a scalding trough, but he was so late he'd missed that stage. Eight headless hogs hung by their hind-leg tendons from a cross pole just outside the shed, already gutted, their fresh-scraped hides a bluish white. The ninth was split across a wooden table, where Charles Tomlinson was busy blocking it out, chopping the backbone loose from the ribs with short chunking strokes of an ax.

There was only one woman, of indeterminate age and hatchet-faced, who was cleaning chitlins at one end of the shelter. At the other end two teenaged boys, Tomlinsons probably, had started trimming shoulders for sausage. Mr. Giles himself stood over Charlie Tomlinson, as if to study the way he handled his ax. Walter and Earl Giles were loading a wheelbarrow with hams and side meat, ready to trundle it off to the smokehouse. Laidlaw came up beside them and began to help relay the sides of meat.

"Got lost did ye?" Mr. Giles said briefly.

"Flat," Laidlaw said. Earl greeted him with a nod, while Walter seemed scarcely to have marked his arrival. The temperature was still dropping, Laidlaw thought, and the wind that was intermittently blowing had a cutting edge to it. So he was happy enough to help Mr. Giles salt meat once the first wheelbarrow was ready; there was no fire in the smokehouse but it made a windbreak and had an encouraging smell of ash and old lard. There was no window and no light except a little from the open door. He stood behind Mr. Giles and passed him the meat to be laid in the saltbox. When they had done the first two loads Mr. Giles went off to some other task and Earl took his place. Laidlaw kept on with what he'd been doing, passing Earl meat or the salt bag on demand.

When the load was salted down Earl kept kneeling near the box. There was a tumble of old sacks on the floor and he rooted a pint bottle out of them, from which he drank. Whatever it was had a heavy sweetish smell coming out of it like a cloud. Earl stood up, overbalancing slightly, and offered the bottle to Laidlaw, who after a tick of hesitation took it, screwing the slobbery neck through his palm before drinking. Peach brandy, vilely sweet and very strong. The warmth of it began to bloom in him as soon as he had swallowed.

"Lick that cold," Earl said, hiccupping as he took the bottle back. Unlike his father and brother he was on the skinny side. He had faintly reddish hair bleached to a strange chrome yellow, so light he seemed to have no eyebrows, which was a strange effect. His skin was an unusual milky white, blued slightly by veins running shallowly beneath it. When Earl grinned, swaying back after another drink from the bottle, Laidlaw noticed his eyetooth was missing on the left. It was also plain that he was very drunk, which would account for the hiccup he couldn't seem to shake.

"How long —" The hiccup undid him. "Dammit . . . How long you been back, Laidlaw? Been out . . ." His voice trailed off as he reached behind him to steady himself with a hand on the rough board wall.

"Since the summer," Laidlaw said. He reached for the bottle and took a bigger hit; this time the sweetness seemed less cloying and the warm patch inside him expanded.

"Uh-huh," Earl said. "Lessee, I must've come out around three, four months before that then. Where were you at over there?"

"Around," Laidlaw said. He hadn't had one of these conversations since Oakland and he didn't much think he wanted to now.

"Around where?" Earl said. There was something to the tone of his voice that Laidlaw couldn't completely pin down, and he remembered that Earl could be a nasty drunk sometimes, though he was nicer than Walter when sober.

"In Four Corps for three months or so," he said, playing it more or less straight. "Then the Central Highlands. You?"

"Tracks," Earl said. The bottle, three-quarters empty, fell among the pile of sacks with hardly a sound. It was unclear whether Earl had tossed it or dropped it. "Which crowd were you with?"

"Why don't we go get some more of that meat, hey?"

"Hah," Earl said. "Psy Ops, I bet, smart feller like you."

"Lurps," Laidlaw said. So long out of company, he'd lost the knack of lying. Earl shot him a curious look, but said nothing. A moment passed, then he spat on the floor and walked out of the smokehouse. Laidlaw saw his back hunch as the cold hit him. He waited long enough to light a cigarette and followed.

By the time the last hams and shoulders were down in the salt it had started snowing again, and coming out of the smokehouse Laidlaw stopped to watch it whirling down white from the off-white sky. Then he went over to the shed and found a place between Mr. Giles and Charlie Tomlinson at the trimming table. Tomlinson was the best and fastest butcher of the lot, for all his right hand had only two whole fingers on it, so that he had to hold his knife wedged among the nubs somehow. The knife swished quickly and neatly through sections of backstrip and tenderloin, which he passed to the grim-faced woman to be wrapped from a roll of white freezer paper.

There was no conversation; maybe it was too cold. Laidlaw picked up somebody's spare knife and began to carve strips of meat from the near side of the shoulder Mr. Giles was also working on. When he had got a few big pieces he began to chop them into smaller bits, mixing fat to lean at about two to one. The extra fat he added to a common mound in the middle of the table. There were some tin washtubs on the ground by the table for the trimmed-out sausage meat. His hands and the wood of the knife handle soon grew slick with lard, and now and then he had to rub them with a rag so as to be able to keep his grip. The knife seemed to dull very quickly too, and at ten- or fifteen-minute intervals he called for the flat file that was making the rounds of the table and used it to freshen the edge.

"Go on and take ye some bones for that dog of yours," Mr. Giles said finally, his first remark for at least an hour. By then the table was piled with shoulder bones trimmed as closely as was reasonable, with odd-shaped scraps of meat and fat still clinging to the hard-to-reach hollows of them.

"Well, I will," Laidlaw said. He stacked three or four of the grease-coated shanks together. "You'll let me know when to come for the meat."

"Might bring it to ye." Mr. Giles was piling lard into a bucket. He seemed tired and a little remote. Laidlaw hugged the bones against his chest; his jacket was already so thoroughly greased that a little more wouldn't make much difference. Beyond the overhang of the shed's roof the light was failing into a dim white generality. The snow had stopped again, but nearly an inch had stuck.

"Hey."

Laidlaw looked back, across his truck bed.

"Hey, wait a minute." Earl was coming toward him along a parabolic path from the smokehouse, where he'd no doubt just been finishing off that brandy. Laidlaw opened the door of the truck for a windbreak and waited in its shelter.

"You like barbecue?" Earl said, coming up. "Pit barbecue?"

"Well," Laidlaw said. "Sure."

"Come on by the trailer then, we gone have some. Me'n Walter saved out two shoulders from this mornen."

Laidlaw stared at him. He was flushed from the brandy but he didn't look especially crazy. "Well, it sure is nice weather for it," he said. "Who did you plan to have dig the hole, Earl, the ground's been frozen solid for ten days."

"We dug it in the summer, fool," Earl said. "Ain't gone be no trouble about the hole."

"Did I hear you say whole shoulders? Sure, it'll be cooked about this time tomorrow too."

"Hell, don't come then, I ain't draggen you. But Terry Tomlinson's had it on the fire since just about noon today. And it's Saturday night, anyhow, 'less you're scared to chance missen church or somethen."

"Saturday night," Laidlaw said in the contemplative manner of someone learning a new word. "I'll bring along something to drink, I guess."

It was nearly night when he got to Earl and Walter's trailer, back from a short run to the nearest liquor store, and their fire stood out well against the dark. There was a thick smell of hickory smoke coming to him as soon as he got out of the truck. He walked toward the firelight with the half gallon of Early Times he'd bought hanging from one crooked finger of his hand.

"Hey, cooken with gas now," Earl said. "Had oil while ago."

"It's a little cool for beer at that," Laidlaw said, though he noticed people were drinking it anyhow. No problem to keep it cold, at least. There were six men around the good-sized fire: Walter and Earl, the two Tomlinson boys, and two hard-favored long-haired men Laidlaw didn't much think he'd ever seen before. The pork shoulders sputtered on a hardware cloth rack set across a coffin-sized hole in the ground, from which the smell of cooking fat rose in a pleasing blend with smoke. Everyone was sitting in folding lawn chairs and Laidlaw took one that was free, raised the bottle to his lap, and broke the seal. Earl handed him a stack of paper cups and he poured one half full for himself and passed the others with the bottle.

As earlier in the day, there was little talk, and no one bothered with introductions. The two strange men were talking in low tones Laidlaw couldn't distinguish from across the fire. When the bottle reached them they each raised their cups as in a toast, and one of them, catching Laidlaw's eye, reached in a shirt pocket and produced a joint which he held out. Laidlaw nodded. Had he done that? The stranger pulled a burning stick from the fire for a light and threw it back. The joint began to go from hand to hand; among so many, Laidlaw thought, it would not come to him more than twice. He took a gulp of neat bourbon to chase his hit. On the second round, Earl pinched out the tiny roach and swallowed it. Laidlaw was as happy to see it go.

It was reasonably warm in front of the fire, at least it warmed the side you kept to it well enough, and the wind had fallen off, which helped. Laidlaw was on the downhill side of the fire, facing the house trailer which sat farther up the slope. As he took note of it the door came open, a patch of yellow light, and a woman's form passed through. When she came in range of the firelight, Laidlaw saw that she was young, with pale hair combed straight from a center part, a pretty face, and bad skin. She set down a skillet with a brush in it near the pit and started back out of the circle. No one spoke to her, though Earl made a halfhearted grab at her hips as she passed near his chair, which she dodged efficiently, with no sign of interest or surprise. Laidlaw noticed that these sudden movements seemed to linger in an unusual way. There was a strong taste of something like cedar in the back of his throat. He glanced over at the pit and his eye stuck upon the dark area that was expanding away from it in the thin snow. As pearls of fresh water melted out of it, the body of the snow was hollowed into a kind of three-dimensional filigree, as a bone can be worked by long underwater erosion. It seemed to him that he could actually hear a trickling sound from the melting of the snow, but then the thought came to him, in slow jerky sections like different cars of a train, that this was unlikely; instead there must be a stream somewhere nearby that he hadn't noticed when he arrived. A building sense of unease which he'd hardly yet become aware of was quieted when he thought of the stream. His mouth had become almost painfully dry, though, and a drink of whiskey didn't help it any. He wanted to light a cigarette but he didn't want to, really, because of that papery feel in his mouth. These two contradictory notions echoed a number of times over in his head, leaving him arrested with a cigarette stuck in his mouth and the matchbox in his hand. Across the fire one of the strange men addressed a remark to Terry Tomlinson and Laidlaw found that he could not understand either the question or the reply. He listened more closely; though they were both speaking quite audibly he could not make out so much as a single comprehensible word. The conversation seemed to run in a rapid succession of sharply inflected syllables, full of expression but vacant of meaning. Laidlaw passed a hand over his forehead and it came away slick with sweat. The uneasiness he'd just dismissed now returned in the form of panic. The faces of the speakers seemed oddly slanted and strangely colored by the fire, and the way that the two strangers seemed to disappear into their long black wedges of hair unnerved him so that, not to see them any longer, he closed his eyes. At once image after unlooked-for image appeared on the back of his eyelids, flashing so rapidly over each other that he could hardly see any one of them whole. He must be remembering these things, he thought; they didn't come from nowhere, but they were fractured and rejoined into a kaleidoscopic spiral that made them impossible to identify. Then he remembered that he did not want to identify them. With an effort of concentration, he closed, as it were, a third eyelid, an opaque curtain drawn across the floor of his mind, on which the images now broke into splashes of dull color on a field of black.

"Hey, Laidlaw, hell, boy, don't go to sleep on us yet."

He opened his eyes then to see Earl, who'd hitched his chair close enough that Laidlaw could smell the peach sweetness under the bourbon on his breath. The realization that he was understanding language again suffused him with a grateful euphoria.

"Lookee here," Earl was saying. "Got a little somethen to show you." He placed a small but exceedingly heavy object into Laidlaw's palm. Opening his hand to the firelight, Laidlaw discovered a small silvery revolver. It was a snubnose, no longer than his hand, but it felt like it was the weight of a brick. Holding it sideways, he could see the butt ends of cartridges in the crack behind the cylinder. Now he was suddenly rather cold and his mind had stopped that aimless roving; he stared at the gun transfixed, not able to think a thought at all.

"Ruger, three-fifty-seven Mag," Earl said on a note of contentment. "Don't find many, small like that is. Take a body's head off, though."

"It would do it," Laidlaw said. He'd forgotten the cigarette stuck in his mouth and when he spoke it fell. With what seemed to him great craftiness he bent over after the cigarette and as he did so lowered the gun behind his knee, thumbed the cylinder open, and shook the shells into his palm. The gun flipped shut with a little click as he straightened up with the cigarette back in his mouth again. He switched the pistol from hand to hand and passed it back to Earl while with the other hand he slid the cartridges into his pants pocket.

"Mighty fine," he said.

"Ought to be," Earl said. He dropped the pistol into his pocket without looking at it. "The bastard cost two hundred dollars. I think it was hot too."

"You and your damn pistol," Walter said. "I believe he's in love with that thing."

"Well, it's as nice a one as they come," Laidlaw said. Now, now he would go on and smoke, though his mouth was, if possible, even drier than before. However, he discovered that the cigarette was so wet it was falling apart, and then he had to forage on the ground between his feet to find his matchbox. When at last he found a fresh cigarette and got it lit, the tobacco smoke brought back that curious cedar taste and this time Laidlaw recognized it as . . . hash. It was the opium in it, that flavor, of course; that was it. Probably only five or ten minutes had passed since they'd finished the joint, even though it seemed like at least an hour.

That recognition made him considerably calmer, even though he was still high as a kite. If you made an effort you could control it. Anyhow, he'd come down in an hour or so, itself a comforting prospect. Try to enjoy it a little. The thing was — as he'd one time figured out — to pay close enough attention to what was around outside you that you didn't fall into staring at the inside of your mind.

He kept his eyes wide, as though propped with sticks. The talk between the strangers and Terry Tomlinson had fallen back away to silence, and the only sound to be heard was the hissing of the meat over the pit or, every now and then, a chunk of wood falling in the fire. Walter and Earl were tending the pit. They used the brush in the pan as a baster, coating the meat, which was getting done now, with runny red drippings of sauce. There was a long-handled shovel which one or the other used to reheat the pit with scoops of red coals from the core of the fire. Nested on the shovel blade, the coals drew Laidlaw's eye. They were like stones but living, changing their colors on the pattern of animate breath. When he looked at them they pulled him down into their hot changes, but at the same time his mind would begin to turn and wander inwardly if he stared at them for too long. Still, the time was managing to pass a little more quickly.

He was drinking quite a bit of bourbon, since the heaviness of it seemed to help anchor his mind, help keep it from spinning beyond his control. Among the seven of them they'd done a good amount of damage to the bottle. Earl went to sleep by stages, his head propped on a hand slipping farther and farther to one side, until the head and hand went completely limp together. Soon after, Walter began to pull gobbets of meat off the shoulders and hand them around, wrapped in paper towels. The warm meat oiled Laidlaw's hands and he ate with an eager appetite which the pepper in the sauce seemed to prick and urge on. The cold itself sharpened the flavor, so that the idea of winter barbecue began to seem less crazy to him than it had before. All around the fire there was a steady rhythm of chewing.

"Might ought to wake up old Earl for a piece," somebody said.

"He's dead to the world, sure enough," said one of the Tomlinsons. Earl had been snoring, with a rasp, for the past half hour.

"Thought he'd come to of hisself when he smelt the meat go round," one of the strangers said.

"Well, I know what'll rouse him," Walter said.

When he smiled, Laidlaw noticed how very thin his lips were; his mouth was like a cut across the meat of his face. He filled up a shovel with coals and held it at the handle's length up under Earl's seat. There was no immediate reaction. After about a minute Earl shifted position, though he didn't appear to wake.

"Reckon you ought to keep on with that, Walter?" somebody said.

Walter's smile tightened to an even thinner line. "*He* kept ahead on, time he done it to me."

He jacked the hot shovel higher, not more than an inch from the bottom of the seat. In another minute there came the bad smell of burnt plastic, then Earl shot out of the chair with a harsh yell, jumping so far forward that he scattered half the fire with his boots. On the other side the two strangers had melted aside from their chairs with catlike alacrity; they must have seen even before Laidlaw how Earl's pistol had flown as of itself into his hand. He went on dry-snapping the stubby gun, though it was angled too high to hit anything much, and chances were he didn't yet know what he was doing.

"Put that thing on up now, Earl," a voice said out of the dark where the strangers had gone. "It was loaded, you'd like to kill everbody here."

"Loaded?" Earl said.

He shook himself, and appeared to notice the gun for the first time, as if it had that minute fallen out of the sky into his hand. He wasn't quite awake yet, but getting there. Laidlaw got up quietly and walked off in the direction he thought the others had picked out as a latrine. Once well away from the light he doubled back and found his way down to his truck.

9

NIGHT. Halfway submerged in sleep, Laidlaw felt himself turn back as the tide turns. Any effort to go deeper against the current seemed only to make him more buoyant than before. However sleep still tugged at him, he rose lighter and more rapidly until he finally broke the surface, gasping. As if a wave were knocking him up the beach, he rolled over onto his back, one arm unwinding from his body so that the back of his knuckles cracked on the wood floor as his eyes came open. The room rocked deeply, then came to rest. He lay. He had come undone from his blanket, and although the room had grown rather cold he seemed to be sweating quite heavily. Behind him, the last coals in the stove were barely ticking and the dog sighed as she slept.

The moon was full or nearly and it filled the room with a frosty bright light. Long shadows tumbled in over the window sill and sprawled crazily on the floor. A net of tree branch shadows was etched in black on the far wall and now and again it shivered and pulsed. Staring at it, Laidlaw tried to time the movement against the rise and fall of the wind outside, hoping to catch some beat that might send him back to dozing again. But the edges of the room were growing sharper, sharp enough to cut. He sat up cross-legged and lowered his head to his feet. The string necklace he wore dangled forward, then clicked back against his chest when he straightened up. His head felt heavy as a bell. He wagged it from side to side and then stood up with the room blearing all around him.

Since the barbecue he'd had more trouble sleeping; he'd got used to little sleep but now he found it hard to achieve even that small amount he needed. Fatigue dulled his mind progressively and he never knew what might eventually slip around the blunted corners. In the dead of winter, night stalking was not so appealing as it had been in warmer weather. However, he rebuilt the fire, waking the dog with the clanging of the stove door, and dressed: jeans, boots, a sweater, a knit watch cap. He'd bought a second-hand leather jacket that had been in a motorcycle crash or two; the back and sleeves were scraped to a limestone-gray, but it fit him tight enough to seal out almost any wind and the lining of it was good. Pulling the zipper to his chin, he walked into the kitchen and stopped at the back door. It was colder in the kitchen and the four glass panes of the door were opaque with intricate layers of frost, in which a small hole began to open under Laidlaw's breath. He could hear the wind rising to a whistle and then falling off again in a long sloping wavelike pattern. The dog padded across the floor and leaned against him in a companionable manner. Laidlaw pushed the door open and they both went out.

The cold seemed less than he'd been looking for; he hardly felt it as he stepped outside. There was perhaps an inch and a half of snow, brilliant under the light of the moon. He'd worn a furrow through it going back and forth to the woodpile, which hulked low to the ground with snow weighting down its plastic cover. The snow crunched slightly under his boots as he walked up the rise toward the track. The dog had gone in the other direction and lost herself in the shadows of the trees that lined the creek. Midway up the yard, Laidlaw stopped and crouched to study a pattern of tracks that spiraled over each other and then made a straighter line down toward the water. They might have belonged to a cat, but he suspected from the length of the toe points that it was more likely a coon. That idea pleased him; one night he might stay up and try to catch a sight of it, if it became a habitual visitor. As he was considering this prospect the cold suddenly cut through to him and he stood up, shook himself, and loped off in the direction of the woods.

When he crossed the tree line the dog rejoined him briefly, cantering in a loop around him and then plunging off ahead. Laidlaw ran as best he could. His eyes streamed a little from the cold and his breath puffed out ahead of him in compact little clouds. Going farther into the woods he felt himself beginning to emerge from the fogginess that had blanketed him the first little while he'd been awake.

Enough of the scrub had withered back in the cold that it was fairly clear going through the first patch of trees. With the roof of leaves fallen in, the moon poured a clear colorless light all over the ground. Laidlaw jogged up through the orchard, cutting around the blackberry patch, which ran back around the curve of the hill in tight interlocking coils, a glittering coat of ice upon its thorns. On the other side, tree trunks spun back by him as he ran, the gaps between them measuring out intervals of shade: light and dark and light. By the time he reached the rock wall he had warmed himself through and he slowed to a walk, continuing up the hill and into the hardwood groves.

Under the hard moon the woods floor was striped with the long shadows of the trees. When the wind died down the whole landscape fell into such a stillness that each part of it might as well have been carved into place. The highest treetops wove themselves into many-ribbed arches beyond which the moon kept gliding, a cold light shaped in an imperfect circle, worn down on one side like a worry stone. There was a glowing ring around it, betokening, perhaps, more snow. Laidlaw stopped and leaned against a walnut tree to look up at it; the extreme cold seemed to bring it nearer, or else it made the sky more clear.

As he came to a stop he heard dogs finding somewhere, first one and then a couple more, their voices blending. Just as he wondered where his own dog was she appeared below the crown of the hill ahead of him, pausing a moment with ears pricked to listen to the others and then trotting away to the left, about her own affairs. The coon hounds were far away yet, on the other side of the valley, Laidlaw thought, though he wouldn't have sworn. The different baying voices tumbled over each other like currents mixing in a stream, a couple of trebles and below a deep bass note which seemed to touch his memory as he began to climb again.

He'd once known a dog with such a profound voice as that — yes, a redbone hound, one of Wat's dogs, it had been. He couldn't recollect the name but he remembered it quite clearly, a big amiable floppy creature. He wasn't supposed to feed it because — because they were going to hunt, wasn't it? But it had licked his face, the warm drippy tongue sliding over his cheeks like it was really on its way to somewhere else. Right, while he was standing up too, he must have been less than ten. That would have been a dead dog now for around a decade.

The pitch of the dogs' crying changed a little as they climbed, running something up the ridge. Laidlaw came to the hilltop and stopped. He could see all the way out through the winter trees to a flickering orange light on a hill across the valley which would most likely be the coon hunters' fire. Diehards, they must be, out on a night like this when it was almost too cold to sit down even, unless you managed to find a hospitable log somewhere. No doubt there'd be a little whiskey. The wind rose suddenly and the trees around him trembled, bare branches rattling. Laidlaw trembled a little too as the wind chafed at his face.

On the other hill they'd all be listening, waiting for the dogs to tree. Those with the ear for it would know if it was coon or possum or fox being run, could follow every nuance of the trail as clearly as if they themselves were running with the dogs. Laidlaw had never picked up the knack of it, but of a sudden the memory opened and he saw himself going along this same hillside, with Wat holding back branches for him as solicitously as for a woman as he led the way. He'd been no taller than Wat's hip then; he must have been six or seven. They'd bundled him into a bulky corduroy coat, with little clips that held the mittens to it, though it wasn't as cold as it was now, it had been before the snow. He wore a kind of knit helmet that had a damp woolly taste where it passed across his mouth; there was that and also the feel of the quilted jacket Wat wore over his overalls, which he held on to for guidance when they went single file. Wat had been peculiarly silent for someone who was usually an eager explainer of everything, able to concoct some kind of answer to any question, whatever it might be. Now Laidlaw could see that that was because he was so intent on the dogs, though it had puzzled him at the time. It must have been fairly early in the fall; there'd have been leaves on the trees because it was so dark that the other men disappeared only by taking a few steps away. Or else it was the dark of the moon. He had not been frightened, but sensed a mystery, a language composed of the dogs' tolling and the shape and sound of the woods by night which the black men understood when he could not.

On the far hill the small red blade of fire flashed up and down. The hounds seemed to be running the ridgetop now, and Laidlaw admired how elaborately they managed to stitch their several voices together. Then a long shudder ran all over him from the very base of his spine; he'd stayed still for too long and let the cold get through. He stamped his feet and again started running, not back toward the house but in the other direction, toward the highway.

In this rough weather it seemed that no one had had heart to tend the graveyard. The stones and their figures were shrouded in snow, and the changes to their shapes made Laidlaw mildly uneasy, though he'd never been spooked in these woods before. He halted behind the border of the trees to breathe. His lungs felt a little raw from pumping so much cold air, and the cold had also made his mouth go very dry. He crouched and made a pellet of snow to pop into his mouth, and stood, sucking the moisture from it, and went on around the south side of the graveyard, keeping back in the woods. He could hear a radio booming a little before he came in sight of Wat's house, which meant it must be turned up mighty loud. Some long Motown wailer, not what he'd have guessed to be Wat's style of tune. When he got in view of the shimmer of snow in the clearing the song ended and a low, honeyed voice reported the call sign of the Nashville R & B station, then somebody turned the radio down to a murmur. Laidlaw halted. The dog came and snuffled into the palm of his hand and went back away.

The two little rooms of the house were blazing with light and a thick post of smoke stood out of the stovepipe, a gray column on the black of the sky. Laidlaw found himself surprised, but what had he expected? That Wat would be out with the coon hunters, he reckoned. But he was too old for that now, or if you wanted to get really accurate, too drunk. Then again, it was late for such a party here; what would it be, two or three in the morning. Maybe Wat was out with the dogs after all, with the cabin turned over to somebody else.

Laidlaw wanted a smoke but his habits restrained him from striking a light. Instead he took a wooden match from a box in his pocket and set it between his teeth. Now that the radio had been turned lower he could hear a low bubbling of talk from the house, which argued for a considerable crowd, since the doors and windows would be battened down against the cold. There were some unfamiliar cars pulled up on the slope below the house: a couple of cavernous old Chevys, a white Lincoln with a scrape across the front fender. As he was contemplating these he heard the creak of a door spring and turned his head to see someone coming out the back.

The moon was not quite bright enough to show the features; it was just a man-shaped silhouette coming away from the house as the door clapped shut on its spring, chopping short the noise of the people inside. Whoever it was crunched across the snow of the yard and stepped into the woods not ten yards from Laidlaw, merging with the shadow of a tree. He heard a hiss of urination start and stop. The other began to whistle softly as he stepped back into the clearing and Laidlaw broke out all over in gooseflesh because it was the first two bars of "Goodbye, Pork-Pie Hat," and that was Rodney's signature tune.

Where did you come from? The line switched on in his head like a light. That ritual greeting had evolved into a code that even Sevier could not quite penetrate. With a tremor he realized that he must have muttered it aloud, or slipped into some other careless noise, for Rodney had stopped dead, half turned to listen. His head was profiled against a yellow square of window for just long enough for Laidlaw to know it really was Rodney even before he heard his voice.

"Who's that?" Rodney said.

Laidlaw's breath caught. He knew he really should declare himself, but it would have looked too peculiar and the prospect of explaining his presence was not at all attractive. Hesitating, he saw Rodney tuck in his head and sprint for the woods, not quite straight for his own position but reasonably close. Typical enough. Thoughtlessly he peeled out up the hill himself before it occurred to him just how very visible he'd be, in motion under the moon and against the snow. On the other hand Rodney had just come out of a lighted room, so it should take him a minute or so to adjust to the comparative darkness. The interesting question was just how jumpy he might really be, and whether he might have a pet firearm of some kind or other, like Earl did. At least he was not the sort to start busting caps without a target, although possibly that was not so much of a comfort when you began to think about it carefully. Laidlaw ran a few paces into the reassuring darkness of the cedar grove and stopped.

Somewhere behind, Rodney had stopped too, abruptly; he would be hoping to get a fresh bearing on Laidlaw by sound. *Ha*, Laidlaw thought. *I'm ahead of you that far, at least.* When he saw Rodney begin to come forward again he began to move himself, working his way cautiously deeper into the cedar thicket. He felt easier now; he'd have the advantage of terrain, unless Rodney had also spent the last six months prowling these woods by night. The evergreens blocked out the moon and cut the reflection of the snow. After a little longer groping among them, Rodney was going to start to wonder what he'd really seen or heard.

"Whoowee," Rodney said.

Laidlaw stopped moving and looked back. Just outside the cedars he could see the dog framed against the snow for a moment before she moved on into deeper shades.

"*Big* momma dog," Rodney's voice said. Laidlaw had lost him, but he didn't sound very close. "Did you give me a turn or what?" Rodney chuckled, the familiar throaty sound.

When he moved Laidlaw could see him again, coming clear of the cedar grove and retreating toward the house, beginning once again to whistle. After he had gone out of sight Laidlaw could still hear notes of "Goodbye, Pork-Pie Hat" rising, then sharply cut off by the slap of the door.

The matchstick had dropped from his mouth when he ran, and he wondered briefly if Rodney might find the chewed stub if he came back to nose around by daylight. Of course with the snow there'd be an easy trail, but Laidlaw doubted he'd bother; the sight of the dog would have satisfied him. He felt surprisingly good after the short evasion, keyed up to a pleasant tingle. Maybe he was turning out to be an action junkie after all. Well, it was kind of nice to see old Rodney again, especially when he couldn't see you, ha ha. He recognized that kind of mental yappiness that would sometimes come on right after something had just stopped happening, but it was probably harmless enough to indulge it, here and now. Old Rod, still going to and fro in the earth after all. Any reason to think he wouldn't be? He just hadn't expected to find him working this particular patch of it, though that was nothing but a failure of foresight. Why wouldn't he come visit his daddy anyway? Well, of course, there could be reasons. But if he did, it would mean they must be in one of their getting-along spells, which surely could be nothing but a good thing.

When he began to move again he found he was still jittery from the contact. His feet had gone numb to the ankles, and to liven them he broke into a trot, heading back the way he'd come. Still, his head kept buzzing. It had been a shock, all right, whether it should have been or not. Rodney had disappeared, and he had let him. He hadn't been thinking about Rodney at all, and he wasn't sure if it was time to start. But this was as much of an outing as he needed, and to spare. He picked up his pace and ran for home.

10

ON THE hill where the sheep pastured the snow was so pocked by their wandering trails of hoofprints that it began to resemble a moth-eaten garment. Around the barns and especially at the feed room doors they'd churned the snow into the dirt and whipped up peaks of mud that froze again, making tricky footing for Laidlaw to stumble across. The sheep pressed closely around the door as he filled the bucket with grain, long black faces urging upward out of ruffs of grayish wool or turning sideways to lap spillage from the floorboards. Despite the cold, the lanolin smell of the sheep came through to him, clear and acrid. They milled around him, jostling, as he shoved through to the trough and filled it and withdrew.

Propped on the cold tongue of the decaying wagon, he lit a cigarette and studied the sheep, their dung-wattled rears shifting around the trough as they jockeyed for superior position. The peacock, discouraged by the weather, had not come down to share this feeding with them. It hunched miserably in its roost in the hackberry tree, feathers ruffling up from the back, head retracted between the clamped-shut wings. Beyond the treetop, outlined against the drear sag of an unpromising sky, Laidlaw saw the shape of some fair-sized raptor. Hawk or buzzard? Hawk, a redtail, probably. It wound in an aimlessly loosening spiral, shrinking to the size of a punctuation mark on the cloud cover as it rose.

Laidlaw flicked his cigarette end away and watched it burn a hissing hole for itself in one of the cleaner patches of snow. He turned his attention back to the sheep, who'd cleaned the trough and were beginning to spread back out across the hillside, getting on with the business of foraging. Their heavy winter fleeces made them all look enormous, especially the ewes, who were all fat with lambs. He'd better start paying some attention to them; this flock had a

way of lambing early. As that thought crossed his mind the ram
trotted out of the hall of the barn in his direction and came to a halt
about eight feet away.

"What about it?" Laidlaw said. The ram made a number of
hooking motions with his head. With the movement, his whole
knotty body seemed to bounce.

"Sure," Laidlaw said. "Spring's coming."

He hadn't thought of it before, but he had sensed it. The taste of the
air was beginning to change, and it was clear enough the animals felt
something too. The ram dropped his head to butt and charged across
the short distance separating them. Laidlaw switched his leg to the far
side of the wagon tongue, but the ram brought his charge up short. He
turned and rubbed the base of his horns on the spongy-rotten corner
of the wagon bed, then backed off and looked up at Laidlaw.

"You better watch it," Laidlaw said. "Your days could be num-
bered from right now."

The ram bobbed his head, a pure coincidence. Laidlaw thought he
was four or five years old, a dangerous age for rams. That admirable
twirl of horn made two inward turns already, enclosing each of his
soft white ears. The ram peered up at Laidlaw out of a hot yellow
eye, full of a sort of stupid knowingness, thoroughly unaware of its
limits. Really, he was not much more than a hammer on legs,
Laidlaw thought. Powered by the gonads. The ram's head jerked
again to underline the thought.

"Can't have you breaking my leg now, can I?" Laidlaw said. He'd
have the force to do that too, with a solid hit from enough of a
distance. "No, pal, first time you really try to butt me you'll find
yourself hanging in the smokehouse with your insides all turned
out."

The ram's head bobbed.

"Got that?" Laidlaw said.

The ram turned to the side, profiled for a moment with his nose
in the air, and then charged away to scatter the ewes and mingled
back into the flock.

Two weeks after he'd become aware of the first hint of the season's
break, it began to rain. For one whole day it poured, sluicing the
snow down from the hill and out of the pastures, pounding the fields
to a dull slippery green. The drenched, leafless trees acquired a
rubbery look. The creek ran rich boiling brown and finally over-

flowed its bank, flooding Laidlaw's front yard with cloudy water up to the top of the rock on which he fed the birds.

Next there was a plague of grackles. Laidlaw woke one morning to a solid wall of bird noise, a great swell of maniacal twittering. When he went out to the side porch he saw that the whole of the low pasture was coated with the scurvy black birds, who seemed to blow over it like trash blown across a beach. There were no individual birds among them; they were just a horde, moving and cohering like a fluid. At night they roosted so thickly in the bare trees that they seemed to leaf them once again. They were there for four or five days, and then, one morning, gone.

Entangled in some complicated passage on the banjo, Laidlaw forgot the sheep until it was already dark. There had been a measured solo bleating through the afternoon, on a tone that might have signified distress, but he had not really noticed it until it stopped, when the sudden absence of the repeated sound finally got his attention. He swore at himself, getting up to put on his cap and jacket, picked up a flashlight, and went out with the dog following.

It had begun to rain again. The ground was so sodden and soft that his boot heels tore out big chunks of grass as he labored up the slope to the barn. When he played the flashlight into the hall he saw the sheep lumped gloomily there, in a cloud of that ineffable wet-sheep smell. The area around the feed room was a soup of mud that sucked hard at his boots, and he was relieved that the sheep were too listless to crowd him tonight. However, as soon as he'd fed them they revived and rushed around the trough. Laidlaw stepped back and counted tails, once and again to make certain.

Sure enough, a ewe was missing. Laidlaw kicked at a stall door. Doubtless that accounted for the wretched bleating he'd been half hearing through the latter part of the afternoon. It would be nice if he could remember the direction it had come from. That it had stopped was probably not the best of signs. He went out from under the eaves and switched the flashlight off for a moment. At once there was such a darkness that there seemed to be no space ahead, only a flat black surface vaguely streaked with rain. He shook his head and turned the light back on and started hunting.

It took half an hour, or a little longer, to eliminate the gullies and work around all the edges of the hill field. Laidlaw paused at the top of the pasture, where the crown of trees began. The three-strand fence here was a gesture. The sheep went through it easily; the wire was tufted with wool to prove their passage. The dog arrived and leaned heavily into his hip. It was clear that all she wanted was to go back home.

"No, baby," Laidlaw said. "Find the sheep."

He ducked through the fence and went into the woods. Within ten paces he was convinced it was hopeless. Had it been dry he probably could have found her. But he was shut in a box of rain and the flashlight served only to mark out the walls of it. Rain was trickling into his collar, for the wool of his hat had by now been soaked through. He shook his head to clear his eyes and kept on going.

When he reached the top of the ridge he saw that the rain had started to freeze. Now the flashlight's beam was answered by a thousand glittering reflections, as every twig of every tree and bush gathered a layer of ice. Pretty, but his teeth were chattering. He stopped them with an effort of his mind. That did it, really. And, of course, the ewe could have been anywhere, in some completely different part of the woods, not necessarily this patch. The dog turned up and leaned on him again.

"All right," he said. "We'll go in."

He walked a little farther across the hilltop and then started down by a different path, moving carefully because the way was glassy with sleet now. Ahead, the dog's hind end jogged alone in the narrow cone of light. Halfway down, he saw her pause to sniff intently at something on the ground before she lost interest and ran off to one side.

When Laidlaw came to where she'd been he found a lump of afterbirth. It had been rained on for so long that the color was almost completely washed out of it; what remained was a pale fibrous pink. Probably he'd have missed it, if not for the dog. He studied it for a moment, listening to the clicking whisper of ice forming on the trees, and then began to circle.

Fifteen yards away on the downhill slope he found the ewe slued over against an oak tree as if she might have fallen and slid there. She was still flexible, still warm, but her eyes were clouded over and a coat of ice was forming on them. Her way of lying was not that of a living thing. On the far side of the tree trunk a black-faced lamb was stretched. When he lifted it the head and legs hung pendulous. This smaller body was already cold.

He carried the dead lamb back to the carcass of the ewe and stood there looking down on her, his insides twisted in self-reproach. A little attention could have stopped all this. When he stooped to lay the lamb beside the ewe, he remarked another form half hidden under the stiffening hind leg; so there'd been twins. He drew the second lamb gently clear; this one still had a little warmth, which maybe clung from contact with the mother's cooling body. It looked to be a throwback, mostly black, with a few light speckles in the wool that thinly coated the wrinkled skin. As he examined it, it gave a hint of a kick and seemed to try to lift its head. There was a twitch of life still caged within it somewhere. Hastily Laidlaw opened his jacket and zipped the lamb inside, leaving its head clear just at his collarbone. Cradling the bundle with one hand across the belly, he hurried down the hill for home.

Once in the house he made to lay the lamb before the stove, but reconsidered when the dog came hastening to investigate. He dragged his table over to a spot in front of the stove's apron, and set the lamb down on the side nearest the warmth. It lay full length, its overlong legs splayed across each other. Its head stirred slightly but failed to raise. The eyelids were lowered, almost shut, and the slits of the nostrils flared and relaxed with barely perceptible hints of breath.

Laidlaw himself had begun to shiver. He peeled off layers of his wet clothes, looking down on the exhausted body of the lamb. Its skin seemed improbably delicate, barely enough to contain the inner workings; he felt he could almost see through it to the vitals. He pulled off his soggy sweater and tossed it onto a chair so that the room's warmth reached him faster, but still his shivering took some time to stop. There was a twitching pulse on the lamb's hollow flank, irregular as the final few ticks of run-down clockwork. The little movement held him transfixed until the dog came to snuffle curiously at the table's edge. Laidlaw tapped her lightly on the nose as a warning and went out into the kitchen.

The dog followed, nose pressed to the small of his back, her signal that she didn't much care for what was going forward. He got a dishrag and went back, picked up the lamb, and daintily patted it as dry as he could manage. When he had done he lifted it and tried to set it on its feet on the table top. The square-boned legs, twice the length of the body, hung disjointedly as the limbs of a marionette. He noticed that the tiny hooves were still soft and seemed only partially formed as yet. When he took his hands away the lamb's legs spun crazily out from under it and it collapsed softly into a heap. It tried again to lift its head, then stretched out full length, that hint of a pulse still ticking. Staring, Laidlaw noticed that it was a little ram.

He had to feed it or it would surely die. With that in mind he went back to the kitchen. There was a carton of milk, not quite the right kind though it would do, but there was no bottle and no nipple. He'd have to think of something. Wondering what, he poured a cup of milk into a saucepan and while it warmed went back to check the lamb, which still lived, by the hardest. The dog had subsided and lay in a corner to which she'd withdrawn, some hint of resentment in her pose.

Laidlaw stood over the stove, testing the milk with a finger till it reached body temperature, or a little over. When it was warm he took the saucepan out to the front room table and drew a chair up to it. He scooped the lamb into a sort of sitting posture and lifted its head with his left hand. Along the inside of his forearm he could feel the ticking of its life as if there were no skin between them. He dipped his right forefinger in the milk and introduced it to the lamb, parting the small jaws as gently as he might. The lamb shrugged and its head sagged limply away from the finger. Laidlaw tried again, to more or less the same result. It was no good; the effort was only weakening it further, he could see. He was never going to get enough milk into it to matter, not this way. It would have been kinder, maybe, to have left it for the ice to finish. Now he was going to just sit there and watch it die.

Not a sight he especially cared to see. He lowered the lamb back down on its side on the table and went back into the kitchen, where he leaned into the door. A ghostly outline of his face appeared in the black square of the glass pane there, with sleet intermittently rattling against the back of it as the wind's direction turned. His mind ran a plaintive little string of *ifs*. *If only there was* — *If I'd gone out a little sooner* — *If the feed store was still open* — Well, no need to take it so seriously, was there? It was only a lamb, not a baby, after all.

He turned and leaned his back against the door, listening for something, what? With a sense of his own foolishness he realized that he was waiting to *hear* the lamb die, like the crack of a twig breaking, something like that. His eye ran idly over items in the room, canned goods in the open shelves, a red towel slung carelessly over the sink faucet, trailing over a day's unwashed dishes, a yellow pair of rubber gloves pulled through a cabinet handle . . . Laidlaw pounced on the gloves and held one up, the fingers dangling, and grinned at his murky reflection in the window glass.

Full of milk, the glove was bloated like a drowned man's hand, the fingers sticking out at silly angles. Laidlaw closed the wrist with several turns of a rubber band. He took a straight pin and pierced the middle fingertip. A droplet of milk appeared, which under a light pressure on the palm of the glove became a narrow stream.

Again he raised the lamb more or less upright, atop the jumble of its legs. With his own finger as a guide he worked the rubber one into its mouth. The extra fingers of the glove floated blimpily on either side of the small head. He gave the swollen palm a little squeeze and milk ran out the lamb's lower jaw, matting the wool down its wrinkly neck. *No, no, you've got to swallow it.* He squeezed again, more softly, at the same time massaging the throat with two forward fingers of his supporting hand. This time the milk did not spill out. Laidlaw repeated the procedure.

Of a sudden there was a ripple of autonomous movement down the body of the lamb. Its legs scissored; it raised itself a little more upright. Cautiously Laidlaw withdrew his hand and the lamb stayed in a kneeling position, holding itself up with its own strength. And it was really nursing, head ducking and thrusting weakly but deliberately at the glove. Now he only needed to press hard enough to keep the nipple from collapsing. The lamb's eyes drifted voluptuously shut as it pushed its muzzle into the glove. Laidlaw noticed how long the eyelashes were, a kind of feminine touch. And there was even a hint of a wag at the base of its scraggly tail.

He let the lamb suck till it seemed sated, having emptied half the glove, then he took the glove away and set it in the saucepan. Tomorrow, if all went well, he'd get some more advanced equipment. But for the moment this system seemed to be working well enough. The lamb remained sitting up, legs curled beneath it. The feeding had tightened the skin over its small stomach and its breathing was distinctly more vigorous. On an impulse Laidlaw reached around the rib cage and lifted the lamb once again to its feet. This time the hooves seemed to find some purchase on the surface of the table. When he took his hands away the lamb stayed up, knock-kneed and atremble, but standing. Its head moved from side to side, black eyes searching into the space of the room. It lived. Laidlaw leaned back gently, not to disturb it, while inside his own pulse shouted applause.

11

A FREAK spell of warm weather fooled a row of daffodils up from the ground. Laidlaw had not known they were there at all, or had forgotten about them. The bunchy green shoots must have been sprouting for a week, two weeks, he didn't know how long it took. He didn't notice them until one morning they were blooming, warm buttery daubs of color running in a line from the hackberry tree to the rise of ground at the edge of the yard, standing out brightly against a field of winter gray.

Laidlaw took the lamb out to pleasure itself in the false spring. He lowered the little creature to a standing position in the middle of the yard, and then retreated to the porch to observe it, not bringing out the banjo for once, though it was nearly warm enough. The lamb stood shakily, uncertain, till the dog, who'd accepted it by this time, came along and gave it a lick and then passed on. The lick seemed to bring the lamb to life. It began to stagger around in looping circles, balancing awkwardly on stiltlike legs. As it gained confidence it essayed small leaps and prances, pausing after each with an air of surprise at its own spontaneity. Laidlaw let it play till it seemed to have tired itself out, then gathered it up and replaced it in the cardboard box he'd fixed for it to live in, in the house.

After four days the weather reverted, as he'd known it would. There was a freeze that caught the daffodils off-step. Going out one morning to split wood, he found them glazed with frost and instantly withering. In a day they had collapsed back into the sodden ground and were invisible. A few buds were frozen to the trees, and that was all. Laidlaw resumed his winter routines, interrupted now by the lamb's feedings three times daily, then twice when it got bigger. The other lambs, meanwhile, managed to be born without catastrophe. As each arrived he'd shut them with their mothers in a bedded stall and keep them there for a day or so, till they'd found their legs, and turn them out to pasture with the others. By the time the last one had been released, spring had come for real.

The bottle-fed lamb grew quickly, rounding out to a chunky form seeming yet more solid as its wool grew thicker. When he felt it had become sufficiently robust he returned it to the sheep lot. For half of its first day there it stood with its nose poked through the weave of the fence above the track, bleating in piteous quarter tones to be restored to Laidlaw's society. It being a fair day he brought the banjo out to the porch and played vigorously enough to mostly drown the lamb out. He'd gone back to drop-thumbing again, a softer note for the season.

By noon the lamb had given up, or lost interest, or worn out its vocal cords temporarily. It left its post by the fence and went up the hill to mix with the other sheep, where it seemed to find acceptance readily enough. That evening it acted as though fully resigned to remaining a sheep for life, though it still recognized Laidlaw and seemed glad to see him — him or the bottle he'd brought for it.

As the season circled further into spring, the hackberry tree budded and put out dainty slivers of leaf, the palest green and almost the texture of skin. In time it shaded the yard again, blocking sunshine that grew increasingly hot, while Laidlaw sat in the roof's overhang, playing with an almost effortless facility. Inside the house the stove went cold, a thin trail of ash remaining on its apron from the last time he had emptied it. Certain birds were coming back, or else he was just beginning to attend to them again. The wren had built a new nest in the same hollow locust pole. Laidlaw went back to spreading seed on the flat rock, and the wren and other birds began to feed there, learning to ignore the dog, who spent hours of each day stroked out in some sunny spot of the yard, never bothering the birds or even lifting her head to notice them.

It might almost have been the year before, except that he could drop-thumb like nobody's business now. That and a couple of other details . . . Soon it would be dry enough to plow. No doubt Mr. Giles was due to appear, with half-mocking or reproving suggestions for that and other worthy projects. One early morning he'd seen the deer standing by the garden fence, just faintly visible in a heavy mist, as if they were impatient for him to plant. Laidlaw found himself looking forward to the sweat and soreness and even the boredom of the work he knew he'd soon be doing. Even the tedium of it looked somewhat reassuring from his present position, like a proof that he'd survived, and would continue.

He no longer woke in the exact middle of the night, but reliably around four in the morning, as if he'd set his clock for it. Frequently he'd wake with the feeling he'd heard something which had roused him, though he could never make out what it was. With only a short time to wait for dawn he seldom bothered to explore the woods, but usually he was too restless to stay in bed either. He'd rise and dress and walk slowly around the borders of the fields, studying the night's gradual disintegration. Most days he'd climb the hill behind the sheep barn and sit with his back to the sunrise, letting the slow warmth of it reach him, watching it cover the land below with light.

In the hour before sunrise he often saw the deer. Somehow they always managed to appear on the opposite side of the field from wherever he was walking, and yet they did not seem to fear him much, so long as he kept that distance. There were a few spotted fawns among them now, but they were shy and he couldn't manage to count them. It puzzled him what drew the deer so close to the house and barns, since there seemed nothing out of the ordinary to attract them. In any case, they'd all fade away as soon as the light grew full.

It was possible, he thought, they'd been a little spooked by small-game hunters in the woods. In the half hour before sunrise Laidlaw frequently heard a thump or two of distant gunfire, quite far away, the sound blanketed by the range of intervening hills. It made him uncomfortable the first time or two he heard it, but he suppressed that feeling. He knew from the sound it wasn't close. It would only be some other early riser improving the hour with a shot at a little wild meat, rabbit or squirrel or groundhog, he surmised. No harm in that, nor was it any of his business. Still, he supposed it might have been enough to drive the deer from certain sections of the woods.

Chin on his knees, Laidlaw sat on a big pitted rock at the head of the hill pasture, his back to the fence there, watching a line of light approach from the far side of the low field as the sun began to lift clear of the trees behind him. There'd been a heavy dew which hung like fruit on the heightening grass and the buckbushes and the sprouting thistles which he knew he really ought to be uprooting. As the light climbed the hill the numberless globes of dew began to shine as from within. When he felt the sun full on his back he stood and began to go down the hill, passing on the far side of the pond from the barns. The sheep saw him anyway and began to bleat a protest that he did not come to feed them right away.

The dog had slept through his departure, but now she was up, impatiently scraping at the door. Laidlaw let her out the front and went back to the kitchen, where he started coffee for himself and mixed milk formula for the lamb, which he poured into a king-sized Coke bottle and set in a pan of simmering water to warm. His high tops were soaked through from the dew, but the feeling didn't bother him. There was just enough time for him to swallow a small cup of coffee before the bottle was ready. A black rubber nipple lay waiting on the drainboard. He sniffed it and gave it an extra rinse and pulled it over the neck of the bottle, then went back out.

As soon as he had stepped into the sheep lot the lamb hit him like a woolly cannonball. It slammed at his knees, thrusting blindly with its whole body. Laughing under his breath, Laidlaw lowered the bottle. The lamb made two more missed lunges before it found the nipple. When it did achieve the connection, Laidlaw had to hold the nipple on with his fingers so the lamb would not pull it off. His knuckles were quickly covered with froth. The lamb sank almost to its knees to improve its angle, sucking with its eyes squinched shut. It emptied the bottle in a matter of seconds, and when Laidlaw heard the first empty hiss he pulled the nipple away. The lamb gave his knees a couple of halfhearted bumps, hiccupped once or twice, and wandered away.

The other sheep had gathered in the feed room door, from where they all looked down, waiting for Laidlaw to have done with the lamb and get along to themselves. He climbed to the barn and shoved through them, setting the empty bottle down inside the feed room door, to free his hands to fill the bucket. The sheep surrounded the trough, lambs struggling to nurse while the ewes fed. Coming back with the empty bucket, Laidlaw took a cigarette from his top pocket and hung it in his mouth. He put the bucket back in the feed room and, standing in the open door, began to pat his pockets for a match. Then he heard gunfire, not thumps this time but clear sharp cracks. There were two shots close together, then two more separated by longer pauses. Laidlaw walked around the south side of the barn and stood there for a minute, rubbing his chin and looking at the woods, but the sound did not come again. He went back and got the bottle and latched the feed room shut. The bottle twirled in little *esses* from his fingers as he walked down toward the house. The cigarette was stuck in the corner of his mouth, forgotten, still unlit.

Inside he got a cup of coffee, then settled on the porch with the banjo. The birds gathered on the rock; the dog returned from somewhere and flopped onto a warm spot of the lawn to nap. But Laidlaw couldn't seem to concentrate, or couldn't arrive at the form of self-dismissal which allowed him to play well. He suspected himself of a bad conscience on one subject or another. The notes all came off dead sounding, though his strings were new, and he couldn't even get his timing right. After half an hour he replaced the banjo in its case and returned to sit still on the porch, fingers laced, listening to the shushing sound of the wind on the leaves combining with the whistle and chatter of the birds.

He pushed himself up from his chair and walked down to the shed by the garden, where he selected a grubbing hoe which he carried up the hill above the sheep barn. Midmorning, it was getting pretty hot. The young thistle plants were buried in the longer grass, but there were so many he'd have no trouble finding all he wanted. The broad leaves were spread flat on the ground in round clusters like place settings. He hoed one up and then the next. The earth was moderately soft from the rain and it was not terrifically hard digging.

Still, when he had rooted up the fourth he was hot enough to remove his shirt, which he tied around his waist by the sleeves, arching his back to loosen it a little. Beyond the first ridge the blue hills were slightly hazy. Laidlaw moved and clumped his hoe at the next thistle without really aiming. The tine snagged on something which had a peculiar weight when he pulled back against it. He looked and then jerked back with the cold will-less recoil he'd always get whenever the sight of a snake surprised him. Cool black loops of flesh went swirling around the hoe handle. On second glance he saw he had not hurt it and was glad. The snake freed itself from the hoe and wound into a coil from which it snapped its head forward to hiss and gape at Laidlaw. It was a chicken snake, one of the bigger ones he'd seen, four feet long or more and inches thick in the middle. He held still, and after another token strike the snake unknotted and poured off into denser grass, downhill.

Laidlaw's interest in thistles was diluted. He cocked his head to the woods below as if he were expecting to hear those shots again, but there was only an internal echo. Sharp as they'd sounded, he knew they'd certainly been somewhere on his land. He was reasonably sure it was a rifle, not an especially light one either. It wasn't going to be so easy to ignore it, after all. He unwrapped the shirt and put it back on, took a cigarette from the slightly crumpled pack in the top pocket, and started down the hill.

At the sheep barn he paused to prop the hoe against the feed room door and then walked on around it. On the low side the peacock had commenced to strut. Its tail was full again now, the hundred Argus eyes, green, gold, and a miracle blue. It turned tail on Laidlaw with its customary perversity, and he waited, finishing the cigarette, until it swung back. The cock shivered, emitted a kind of strangulated croak, then folded its feathers and stalked away. Laidlaw went farther around the hill's curve and crossed the fence into the woods.

Trees joined over him, forming a green cave of leaves. He could not think when he had last been in the woods by day. Every plant was crawling with new foliage. There was among other things a luxuriant spread of poison ivy low to the woods floor, the wicked-looking slitted triplets of leaf. Laidlaw walked through it; there was no way around and at least his sneaker tops were high. He walked halfway between the two branches of the creek, so that he could hear each burbling on either side of him for a while. Once he had crossed the first stone wall the water fell out of earshot and the poison ivy abated on the higher ground. The dog appeared momentarily beside him, though he had not called her to come along, then rattled off into another part of the woods, out of his sight.

He came to the top of the hill and paused. The whole of the woods was frantic with life. He felt that he was constantly just missing small movements out of the corners of his eyes, whether it was birds or rabbits or squirrels or only the trembling of the trees themselves. There was a wealth of bloom he could hardly identify. The tent of leaves was shot full of water, turgid, and the cool damp which suffused everything seemed charged.

Two blue jays startled him, chasing and nattering at one another through the treetops nearby. He could see them flashing and jerking along, shivering the thin branches where they lit. They goaded each other out of earshot to the north, and as their noise faded Laidlaw heard a mockingbird intoning a low watery tune at some farther distance from him. He shook himself alert again and went on.

The cedars began once he crossed the second line of rock wall, first sparse among the other trees, then more frequent. He went into a rough arch of them and was enclosed. In the cedar thicket it was almost clammy and no direct sun could penetrate. The light was pale, subaqueous, and the cedar smell was dense. Fern and moss grew richly all over the uneven little hummocks of ground. Cedar spines tingled and stung his arms a little when he brushed among them. Under every footfall the moss bled water like a sponge, and he was going along so softly that he was scarcely aware of his own progress.

At the lower end of the thicket two big cedars formed an ogive framing the approach to the woods pond. The runoff area was slick and muddy; Laidlaw saw a little reddish toad beginning to hop across it. Beyond, the pond was full, its smooth surface swollen with light reflected from the sky.

An overhead crash brought his head up. A gray squirrel had made a mistimed jump from a cedar to a maple tree and was hanging by its nails from a dipping branch. Laidlaw watched it recover itself and run springingly across the top of the tree, finally leaping with more grace and a better aim into a neighboring black oak. The squirrel ran to a central fork, made a circuit of it, and then began to descend the main part of the trunk. Halfway down, it paused at some queerly alien contraption, as if puzzled how to negotiate it, and that was how Laidlaw found the deer stand.

Some scraps of one-by-six had been hammered to the trunk on the far side of the pond, with two tenpenny nails apiece to stop them from turning underfoot. Laidlaw thumbed the rough edge of one, and then began to climb. When he'd come eye-level with the stand he stopped. It was quite an ugly thing, to his taste at least: a stubby wooden platform painted a gummy black with rubber loops on top to hold the hunter's feet secure. Three lengths of angle iron held it tight to the tree's bole; big wing nuts brought the metal edges cuttingly into the bark. Laidlaw peered around the trunk. The position commanded the opposite bank of the pond and he could see well into the sparsely set trees on the other side of it. Among them, the crosier blooms of three small dogwoods tossed in a breezy dance of white on green. Laidlaw backed down the makeshift ladder. Raking through the loam on the high side of the tree, he found two shells from a 30.06, enough to convince him there were two more somewhere he didn't really need to find. Tread marks from the cheaper brand of rubber boots the Co-op sold went north around the edge of the pond and Laidlaw followed them.

It was an illusion of some kind, or the general birdsong of the woods had gone abruptly quiet. Laidlaw picked his way through thickish undergrowth at the pond's edge. There was a sort of bubbling coming from a laval center in him, an acutely uncomfortable sensation which he seemed unable to control. It increased when on the far side of the dogwoods he found bloodsign and the marks of something being dragged. He followed this new trail a hundred yards or more, over a low lifting of the land, which dropped more sharply on the other side into a depression where the dead doe lay.

The hide still had a gloss to its color, the muzzle a velvet softness, but the open eye on the upturned side had been thoroughly mucked over by death; it looked like a slug had crawled into the socket. Laidlaw made an effort not to see it. There had been a decent shot, entering just behind the shoulder. Maybe the hunter had gone for two and missed the second. When he turned the doe over by a foreleg, he found an exit wound the size of a railroad tunnel. Another shot had creased the join of the rib cage, as he now could see. The hindquarters had been hacked off with startling clumsiness, and the lower part of the doe's belly was scored over with almost random slashes, as though the butcher had had no notion how to begin. From the place where the carcass was truncated an oily spill of entrails had uncoiled onto the ground. There was no smell he could detect as yet, but three or four green bottle flies had been drawn. Laidlaw looked in another direction. Through the trees downhill he could see a bright green swatch of pasture and a section of the road. That bubbling sensation had stepped up to a hum. He stared back at the hump of viscera as though at any moment it might begin to tell his fortune.

12

DARK FILLED up the windows, slow as an inky liquid dripped into a glass. Laidlaw lay on his back, watching it crawl over the panes. He could not think how he had been passing the rest of the day; whenever he tried there was a click, skip, and a long empty glide over white space. From time to time the dog came and leaned her heavy head over him, dangling loose jowls, but he could not even manage to reach up and give her a reassuring touch.

As it grew dimmer, he heard the sheep begin to bleat, singly as in question-and-answer and once in a while in accidental chorus. Laidlaw remained lying on his pallet in an almost Egyptian pose, the toes of his sneakers pointing straight up, palms flat and stiff against his sides. A smoky darkness swirled into the room, blotting out its furnishings. He heard the harsh cry of the peacock going to roost in the tree above the barn. Some time afterward the sheep left off bleating and an oddly deep quiet fell over the room. During the lengthy pauses between his own conscious thoughts, Laidlaw became irksomely aware of the sound of his own breathing; it was as though the room breathed with him, interrupted at intervals by the nervous *click-clack* of the dog's toenails crossing an area of the floor, or a creak or groan within, as if the house's structure were grinding on itself. It struck him as peculiar that no sound at all reached him from outside, not a car passing on the road nor the wind moving branches on the trees. After a long, weary spell of inertia, he sat up, then stood. The room seemed to make a little spin around him, though he couldn't really see its contours. The lightheadedness clung to him as he began to move around the room, setting each foot down almost in sections in a pointless effort to make no noise. The room became no clearer; it was strange how dark it stayed. The windows gave off a faint sheen that located their panes but seemed to let in no light at all. He worked his hands in front of him as he crept around the room, avoiding bumping into things by touch. When he heard the dog come clicking toward him he stopped, and as she reached him he lowered a hand and rubbed around the base of her ears until she seemed appeased.

The click of her feet went away from him and he heard the sound of her settling. He went on around the edge of the room, fingertips stroking along the wall. He had turned three corners when his knee found a chair seat, and he let himself fold into the chair, spreading his hands flat on the surface of the table in front of it. Now he could hear the slow tap of water dripping from a worn valve of the shower in the next room. He let his hands crawl forward across the table, finding an empty tape reel, stray banjo picks, the base of the lamp. One hand climbed the lamp's gooseneck and turned the switch. Yellowish light pooled on the table's corner and spilled over it to the planks of the floor. Laidlaw noticed the dog sitting in a long shadow thrown by the stove, upright and attentive, a little fretful. He rubbed his eyes and a fragment of a plan came to him, as though it had been worked out beforehand and then in some way concealed.

He sat still for a moment more, looking at the backs of his curled hands in the lamplight, then stood up and dragged the table aside. You could hardly tell anything funny about the quarter-round molding along the edge of the floor, but when he pulled at it a four-foot section easily came loose. Beneath it, against the wall, there was a small hole sawed out of the floor, shaped like a hand grip. Laidlaw knelt and lifted at that, and a yard and a half of the floor folded back on hinges concealed beneath it. He stood and adjusted the lamp so that it lit the hole.

There was a two-foot drop to the dirt under the house, and directly under the trap door was a regular wooden house door, set in a frame of bricks rather clumsily daubed over with mortar. The door had been tarred to waterproof it, and it was shut with a hasp and a steel padlock, which Laidlaw had bought when he'd found the hide-hole quite a while before, in between the comings and goings of various tenants. Though they'd never spoken of it, he was certain enough that Wat must have built it for Martha's whiskey stash. It had the marks of Wat's workmanship: clever carpentry and indifferent bricklaying. If Laidlaw's father had ever discovered it he would have gone crazy, but in other and unpredicted circumstances Laidlaw had found it a useful corner to have.

He went into the kitchen to get the two keys of the Master lock, which hung on a short nail behind the refrigerator. The padlock had rusted slightly and at first refused to give. He had to squirt some oil in it and wait to let it penetrate. Next time he'd better wrap a plastic bag around the lock, or do something to keep it dry. After a five- or six-minute soak of oil the lock turned and he took it off the hasp and pulled back the door. Below it was a four-foot-deep cavity, big enough to hold a fair number of cases of booze, but it was empty now except for a tin trunk pushed against the far wall.

Laidlaw hopped down into the hole. The light from the lamp was a little too dim here, but he didn't want to lower it through the floor. It would shine through the lattices that closed off this space at the front of the house, so that somebody on the road might conceivably see it, though of course it was doubtful that anyone would care.

The trunk was snubbed shut with two spring clasps, but not locked. Laidlaw snapped open the fastenings and lifted the lid. On top there was a layer of books and a few papers, which he removed, setting them aside on the bricks. Underneath he found a long weighty bundle wrapped in several turns of a greased piece of sheet, which he unwrapped, discovering a twelve-gauge pump shotgun. He turned and straightened up, raising the shotgun to the light to examine it. It appeared to be in good order, perfectly clean, still shedding a little gun oil on his palms. The dog had come to stand at the edge of the trap and was hanging her head perplexedly in the hole over him.

"It's okay," Laidlaw said, and crouched again into the interior of the brick safe. He wrapped the sheet back around the shotgun and laid it in the trunk again. Groping along the trunk's dim bottom, his hands moved over small cubes that were boxes of shotgun shells, then came upon something flat, which he took out: a knife with a round rubber grip in a brown leather sheath about five inches long. The sheath had no belt loop, but stopped at the hilt. There was a little stud on one side of it as if for a snap, though there was no snap to match it.

Laidlaw stood up. This squatting and standing seemed to be giving him short strokes of vertigo, and he raised a hand to steady himself on the floor's edge. When his eyes came clear again, he unsheathed the double-edged blade and whisked it once forward and once back across the top of his left forearm. Both edges shaved away a little hair. Laidlaw blew the blade clean, sheathed the knife, and rolled it from one hand to the other as if it were hot. Then he shoved it through the bottom two buttons of his shirt and down into his jeans. Pressed to the inside of the waistband, the little stud held the knife snug.

Sevier's recipe for concealed carriage of a knife in more or less public places: *No need to leave it slap against your leg, now is there?* This once, Laidlaw let himself entertain the voice. *That's your private business, my friend, and you're entitled to keep it to yourself.* The tip of his tongue stroked over dry lips. Consideration of Sevier's aphorisms brought him a voluptuous tingle, like returning to a drug or some other abandoned vice. Like whenever you lit that first cigarette, coming out of the bush, it would give you that deep dizzy thrill.

He knelt and repacked the books into the trunk and shut it. The vertigo hit him hard when he climbed back up through the floor, and he had to lean on the wall for a full minute to recover. If he had eaten at all that day he could not remember it. The dog pranced anxiously in front of him while he contemplated the hot golden dots that hovered and swam across his eyes. *Eat something, stupid.* Laidlaw snapped his head around. *You'll bitch everything all up for sure if you go out in the shape you're in now.* The voice was detaching itself, becoming independent. He squelched it with a mental clench. It was sound advice, wherever it came from. He went into the kitchen, turning the dog out on his way to the refrigerator.

Choice was limited; he'd been putting off a trip to the store for a couple of days. There was a hunk of yellow cheese and he whacked off half of it with a table knife and rolled it in a piece of bread. It had no particular taste when he bit into it, and in fact the lump seemed to get no smaller no matter how long he chewed. Finally he swallowed it whole, it felt like, and went on feeling the shape of it in his throat long after it had gone down. The faint smell of gun oil on his hands began to oppress him, and he got up and washed them very thoroughly with soap. His mouth was terribly dry, not a good sign, and when he drank some water it soaked it up like blotting paper and remained dry still. He contrived to swallow another piece of the sandwich with the help of water, like a pill. Then the dog scratched, and as he let her in he offered her what was left; it disappeared from his fingers with a snap.

So much for that . . . He went back to the refrigerator and took out the two eggs he had left and put them on the table. They rolled, clicking together along an invisible tilt, and stopped at the lip of the enamel. Laidlaw looked down at them balefully for a moment and then picked one up and broke it into the jelly glass he'd been drinking from and knocked it back quickly without looking at it. It went down easily enough. He repeated the drill with the second egg, then nested the four halves of shell into each other and slid his back farther down on the chair. The fabric of his shirt pulled tight over the haft of the knife as he leaned back, and he shifted position to loosen it. For ten or fifteen minutes he rested with his eyes closed, breathing deeply and deliberately, opened them and quickly stood up. This time there was no slap of dizziness; he was all right again.

Time. Laidlaw shut off the kitchen light and stepped out into the yard. When he had gone a few slow steps the dog thumped against the inside of the door and then began to claw it curiously. She'd be whining and barking too, if she were the whining and barking kind of dog. Laidlaw stopped at the edge of the yard and waited till she quit.

The darkness was so complete that he had the illusion he could have touched some kind of bucket lid if he stretched a hand above his head. There must be a heavy cloud cover, and also it was the dark of the moon. But by the time the dog had subsided he could see enough to get by. Though still a bit lightheaded, he no longer felt weak. This was a different lightness, suggesting that his body and bones had been hollowed out to receive a foreign visitor. Laidlaw crossed over the low field and drifted into the woods like a wisp of a bad dream.

Though he hardly expected to encounter anything to be concerned about on this side of the hill, he went with maximum care all the same. It might have taken him as long as an hour to reach the top of the hill; then again, his sense of time was beginning to warp at the edges. The forced slow pace brought tension with it but he did not find the feeling unpleasnt. Noticing that he did not feel at all bad now made him realize how very bad he must have felt a little while before.

Dark as it was, he had to operate ninety percent by ear, for under the trees he could see next to nothing. That alone would have made him go slowly, if nothing else had. There was the usual insect chorus but aside from that the woods were quite still, and most of the gaps between his slow paces were empty of any more particular sound. When he stopped after crossing the second rock wall he heard something moving at a brisk trot a little way farther down, maybe a wild dog, or just possibly a fox. He remained frozen to the stones for a few minutes afterward, eyes straining toward where the sound had been, but there was nothing to see and the noise was not repeated. In its decline he heard a dog take up howling, but that was a long way to the west.

He crept on down the hill in slow motion, taking special care that the underbrush that clung to his legs should not rattle or snap back behind him as he went. The fluting ascent of that howling came again and again, at one-minute intervals where the dog paused for breath. That seemed to be the nearest sound, and it too faded when he came among the cedars, as though the denser stand of trees had baffled it.

The thicket fit over him, tight as a sleeve. Here the dark was palpable, a viscous moil through which he swam. All the same, he moved more at ease within it; there was less scrub and the moss ensured the silence of his steps. At his left was the trickle of a runoff stream fed by wet-weather springs that flowed among the hummocks down the grade, and he piloted through the cedars using that sound as a check, keeping his path parallel to it. Once the ground began to level off he knew he must be near the pond, though he couldn't see it, and he undid a button of his shirt to have a handier reach in to the knife. When the sound of the frogs singing around the pond grew loud he stopped and dropped into a crouch.

For the first few minutes, the space in front of him looked black as a slab of slate. Then the wall began gradually to crumble. That hollowness he felt in his body was coming to life. A wave of tension swelled and rolled over its own crest and began to dissipate. Now he could just barely see a flat dull glisten of the pond's calm surface. The sky above it must have cleared a fraction, allowing the water to gather a little starlight. He heard the frogs splashing but there was not nearly enough light for him to see the ripples. As he kept looking, he saw the pond begin to split on either side of a dark vertical that was the trunk of the black oak.

Hold tight . . . Another phantom instruction, but this time Laidlaw didn't let it make him twitch. Only his right hand glided into the gap of his shirt, closed over the knife's handle, and stayed there. It moved and his hand moved with it, riding the swell of his diaphragm as a thread of air filled the bottom of his lungs. The slight give of the rubber handle was reassuring to him. If he held his breath he could hear the knife just barely beating, from where its tip touched the pulse of his femoral artery.

His intuition was that the stand was now empty, but . . . *A feeling don't know anything. Don't go till you know.* Okay. He waited, ears pricked for anything: cough, throat clearing, the little scrape of someone scratching, anything at all. Time turned elastic, stretching wide or suddenly contracting. The only reliable measure was to count heartbeats or breaths. Every few of what he took to be minutes he raised a little in his crouch without moving his feet, to loosen his legs enough that they would not cramp. For a long time he heard nothing but the frogs. A mosquito's whine came past his ear and he felt the feather touch of it settling on his cheekbone, then the sting and spreading itch as it withdrew.

Don't touch it, fool. Do you think I would? The itch brought his mind sharply to a point. Time. *Says who?* Nobody could keep quiet that long. *But you?* That's right. He let himself slowly rise and began to inch forward at a rate almost below his own threshold of perception, the speed of the minute hand on a clock. He thought it took him twenty minutes to move some fifteen yards to a spot half behind one of the biggest cedars, the next tree to the oak. From that angle he could see a corner of the lowest of the slats nailed to the tree, outlined against the pond's dim glow. He chose a spot on the invisible ground where his left foot would go next time he moved. Then one more step and he could be on it.

Although he couldn't see it yet, he knew the stand was empty. This close he knew he'd smell the hunter, would hear his lightest breathing. All right. That he was coming back was just a feeling. Odds were the deer wouldn't use this pond for a long time. But he had left the stand there. Sometime somebody had to make a mistake, that was a rule of things.

And it could always be you, too . . .

But not this time. Waiting was a rubber band, accordion, a yo-yo. A rising breeze coming off the pond brushed his hair back and for some reason raised gooseflesh on his arms. When the breeze fell he heard behind it a hiss of a car traveling far away on the paved road, some late-night reveler returning. Somewhere beyond the pond a screech owl gave a low hoot and repeated it. After a few minutes another, somewhere behind, began to answer. He rolled his head, following the owls' cloudy voices as they moved from quadrant to quadrant. When the wind rose again it had some hint of morning coming, though it was dark as ever. There was the hiss of another car, but this one stopped short instead of fading.

Somewhat later there was a dim slap that might have been a slamming door. His heartbeat climbed up into his throat. *Get a hold, man!* He made himself breathe slow and deep, his pulse jackhammering twenty to one against it. Regular breathing brought him down to another spell of waiting. Five minutes. Ten. He was easy now. False alarm, anyway, somebody parking in front of a house. When he heard the first footsteps the last of his jitters dissolved suddenly and completely, leaving him cool and empty, body and mind bored out. This was not much of a stalker. He went slowly and showed no light but he made God's plenty of noise. No doubt he'd be counting on an hour or so on the stand before dawn, to let the woods recover from his racket. After the long wait, his movement around the pond's edge seemed loud as an approaching train. Laidlaw took the chance for a last limbering flex, and rolled up on the balls of his feet.

Something shapeless blocked the pond's gleam for a second and was gone. He was close, but not yet to the tree. Laidlaw stared at the corner of that slat till it grew an aura. When it disappeared he shot forward like a spring released. *Right foot push, left foot set —* He was there, swinging the knife under the other's right arm from behind and up, pushing the point just a quarter or half inch into the frog-belly flap of skin under the jaw. His left hand met the right on the knife's haft and he pulled back a little. There was a sulfur flash as the rifle fell against the tree and fired. Laidlaw sent it slithering into the runoff with a lucky kick almost before he heard the round twanging off among the branches overhead.

"You're dead," Laidlaw whispered. The hunter sagged back against him; Laidlaw's mouth was at his ear. The alien body had a clammy feel and Laidlaw smelled the bitter sweat of fear; he'd recognized it on himself at times before. The hunter had fallen into a total stillness, only his breathing groaned like a saw. Besides the sweat he smelt a little of tobacco and some strong sweet liquor too. The litte cut in his gullet was nothing serious as yet, but with a choice of short definite movements Laidlaw could either rip out every part of his throat or push the knife blade clean to the top of his head. What now? He was waiting for an order, but it didn't come. No, here was the place where anything went, where he'd expected never to find himself again. He leaned back against the oak and the other came helplessly along with him, the edge of his ear sliding between Laidlaw's lips, just touching a front tooth. A kiss! Laidlaw had an urge to giggle, but did not. Time took its little bow and disappeared.

The scream, one part pain and the rest raw fear, sounded far away as the horizon when he first became aware of it, then it broke through some kind of membrane and was deafeningly immediate. It occurred to Laidlaw that he might be the one who was screaming, but that was impossible, because his jaws were clamped tight shut, grinding and worrying on something. Unless it was a dream, of course. He'd heard of people having dreams such as this, so perhaps he was finally having one of his own. When he cleared his throat to spit out the obstruction the screaming broke into a kind of sob and then he found that he was running up a hill.

At first there was the sound of someone else running too but that was in another direction and the sound faded rapidly. There was only himself, running all out, careless of branches that slapped and scratched his chest and face, stumbling constantly to the left over his limp. A knife jigged up and down in his right hand and he knew he had to stop and put it up before he fell on it and killed himself but instead he went on endlessly running until he broke into some clearing, he had no idea where, and was stopped by a total loss of breath.

It amazed him that he still had not woken up. A pain like a steel shank in his side made him jackknife, bracing his hands on his knees. The handle of the knife glanced off his shoe with a little bump. His breath began to come again in crying gasps and he straightened and looked up, where now bright stars went twirling through the sky. That taste in his mouth was certainly of blood, and vaguely he heard a familiar voice telling him that once acquired it was extremely hard to cure.

II
Follow Me Down
(1970–71)

13

FUNNY THING, Rodney Redmon was thinking, how so many of the deadbeat bars down South were green. In New York they were mostly brown, the slick clammy brown of tobacco spit. But this place here had two tones of mint-green paint rolled over its walls, with a neat tape line joining them at around eye-level, like in a hospital, as though someone might think the place could pass itself off as a hospital or a school. Fluorescent lights too. Redmon had picked a table by the window, where they couldn't shine on him quite so much. It was a bright sunny morning outside and he could see cars and trucks moaning and groaning up and down Lower Broad, their racket almost completely muffled by the thick plate glass. When a big truck passed on the near side it darkened the window enough for dim reflections of the rows of lights to appear on the glass, and nearer, a cloudy outline of his own head also materialized. Though it wasn't definite enough for him to see his features, he could feel how he was keeping on smiling and grinning as helplessly as a fool.

The truck went by and sunlight poured back in across the oilcloth on the table, slanting through the tall fluted tumbler of beer that made a point of a triangle with Redmon's two hands. He studied the rising strings of bubbles, how they joined the top layer of foam and broke and disappeared from it. This was his first glass of beer in three hundred and sixty-six days, and he intended to get the most out of it he could. When the head was down to an eighth inch he reached for the glass and drank off a quarter of it. The tingle that followed was nothing but excitement from the first taste of beer after so long a time, not the measly amount of alcohol involved. As it flushed through him, a wisp of some song floated into his mind.

Well, I been sitten here wonderen . . .

Now how did the rest of that go? He reached for the glass again
and changed his mind (a quarter of it gone already) and instead
hitched his chair around, facing the inside of the place. From the
layout it must have started out as a cafeteria as much as a bar.
There was a sizable steam table there as you came in the door, with
a tilted glass front on it, but no food was in it. And it was cold. It
ran along the side wall and joined a high Formica counter that went
all the way to the back, behind which the barman was humped on
a stool, a mound of sagging flesh trussed up in a stained white
apron. A line of tables and chairs were set before the big front
window, which had some contradictory decal lettering peeling
from the back of it, words that Redmon didn't trouble to spell out
backward. Deeper into the room there were two lines of booths,
one in the middle and one against the rear wall, all painted a kind
of gummy green, just off the shade of the lower band of color on the
walls. An ancient Seeburg jukebox hulked on the near side of the
door, all its lights off.

Been sitten here wonderen . . .

Wondering what, hey? Get your head hung on something like
that, it would start to feel like an itch on the roof of your mouth.
Quit thinking about it, Rodney, why don't you? It was slow in here
this morning. Bound to be nearly noon, people coming off work were
starting to make the next thing to a crowd on the sidewalks, but this
place wouldn't draw much lunch business, would it, seeing it didn't
seem to stock any food. Nobody in here but him and an old man
humped over a long-neck Bud in one of the center booths. His face
was gray, silvered with a three- or four-day beard, and he had a deep
phlegmy cough. The banked lights overhead might be making him
look sicker than he was, but he did look pretty sick. Broke out of the
Union Mission, most likely. The old man hoisted his bottle.
Redmon saw how he took the whole neck of it into himself,
gumming all the way to the place where it curved out, a queer
picture that made. A man with any teeth couldn't do that, probably,
even if he wanted to . . . Redmon picked up his own glass. That's
half of it gone. It wasn't that you couldn't *get* beer up at Brushy
Mountain. You could get that and just about any other goddamn
thing you wanted to go with it, except *out* of course, so long as you
could somehow pay its price or trade for it. It was that he hadn't

wanted to risk one small minute of his good time. The sweet little
things of life could wait till he was back on the outside again.

This made the third time he'd come out, if you counted the army,
which he didn't quite. But the third time's supposed to be the
charm . . .

Just sitten here wonderen . . .

He shook his head to knock the scrap of song clear of it; he
couldn't even recall the tune, not really. Closing his eyes, he was
surprised to find himself picturing Chandler, parole-board Chandler,
with that deep pink face you get from drinking, though he was such
a fussy little man you didn't figure him to drink. Neat little blue suit
with a light pinstripe, a little something on the comb when he put
that razor-sharp part in his white hair, dab of sweet Eau de Whatever
behind the ear, and that's Chandler, setting his fingertips together in
that prim way he had whenever he was getting ready to speak. The
clicking sound his voice made bore out the rumor that he'd had his
natural harp cut out for cancer or something and replaced with a sort
of talking machine.

Well, you do pretty good time, now don't you, Rodney?

Like he thought it must be some kind of a trick.

Yessir, I always try my best.

Make it *yessir* not *yassuh* for Chandler. He was said to get
suspicious if you pulled the wool too hard. Still, you were better off
to ring out with that *sir* nice and sharp every time, and keep your
eyes no lower and no higher than the point of his chin. But let's quit
thinking about that too, Rod, because with a little patience and a
little luck you might never clap eyes on Chandler again, or the like
of him either. As long as you're out you've won the game no matter
how many points they took from you.

He reached for the beer glass again, but drew his hand back empty.
It fidgeted for a moment on the table's edge and then dipped into his
pocket and pulled out a quarter. For a minute or so he busied himself
trying to stand it on edge. The checked oilcloth was so lumpy it
made it hard to do, and when he got it balanced he eased his hand
back and admired it for a while. Then a sharp flick of his middle
finger sent it spinning in a curve across the green and white checks,
winking back the little flashes of sunlight it caught. When it slowed
and began to topple he dropped his laced hands over it and caught it

between his thumbs. Once more he got it standing, Washington's profile turned his way. With the most delicate care he lifted the glass and drank from it and set it back.

The coin trembled but did not fall. Redmon took out a cigarette and lit it, taking a deep draw and holding it in. Not much came back out when he finally let go. He tipped ash to the floor, there being no ashtray handy, and lowered his head to examine his clothes. A gray sport coat, second hand but a good fit and not too worn. White shirt with a standard collar (he had the tie rolled in his jacket pocket for now). A thin leather belt through the loops of blue work pants from Sears, so new the crease on them was still sharp. Black socks and a pair of high-top white sneakers, also brand new, what they'd call felony shoes in New York, but they'd do him no harm down here. All told, he'd spent around forty dollars. With the tie on he'd be okay for the interview. Mr. Henry Cantwell, Smart Raccoon Warehouse, somewhere north on White's Creek Road, August second, eleven o'clock, *and make sure you're there on time, Redmon, or a little early might be better yet.* For a nothing warehouse job. To hell and gone out White's Creek Road, he'd have to take a bus, supposing there was one that went anywhere near it, or else hitch.

He was going to go, though. If nothing don't happen, if the Lord willing and the creek don't rise . . . Oh he'd be there, bright and early. No choice, really, at least not a good one. Three more days if you counted today. He pulled the torn envelope out of his inside jacket pocket and smoothed it over his knee. Tuesday, Wednesday, show and tell with the parole officer on Thursday, Friday see Cantwell, and start work on Monday, Rodney, if you have any luck. He pressed the ends of the envelope to make it gap open and thumbed past the forms and the letters with the addresses and appointments to the slim green sheaf of money they'd paid him out of his fund, what little three hundred and sixty-six days in the laundry added up to. It was new money, the edges stiff and crisp. He folded the envelope over and put it back in his pocket, on top of the tie, without counting the bills, since he already knew how many there were — or how few, he meant to say. Little enough that he was already walking a high wire to that first paycheck, if it came in two weeks from the Monday, which was probably the best he could hope for. He'd need to start out somewhere he could rent by the week, and move later, whenever he could swing it. Then food, then carfare, then cigarettes, better get a carton . . .

His own cigarette was burned nearly to his fingers and he went to stomp it on the tile floor, since there were enough butts flattened there already that it clearly made no difference. However, thinking better of it, he snubbed the cigarette out on the underside of the table, then slipped it under the cellophane of the pack, right in the red center of the bull's eye. For a rainy day, babe. It was because he liked that picture that he smoked Luckies in the first place, but what he really ought to do was go back and buy some shag and papers, save five or ten bucks a week that way maybe, though he didn't like the idea much because it reminded him of his daddy. There wasn't going to be a whole lot to spare for *beer*, for damn sure, and, annoyed by this thought, he picked up the glass and drained it. When he put it back down the quarter tipped off balance and he snapped his finger at it before it could fall, sending it droning out across the table again. It made a faint whir on the oilcloth, a kind of hollow developing in the center of its motion as it slowed. Heads? Tails? The coin's buzz intensified as it settled, turning up George Washington in his pigtail, letters marching back over his bald crown: LIBERTY. Hell, Redmon thought, I forgot what I bet.

As he stood up the old man in the middle booth fell into a more violent coughing seizure that doubled him over the table's edge, almost as if the table had been kicked into his stomach. Redmon paused to watch him, wondering if he might be going to die then and there. After a couple of minutes of what seemed a single solid cough, the old man hawked up something highly unpleasant looking which he dribbled into an ashtray in the center of the table. Then he sat slowly back, cleared his throat raggedly, and engorged the long-neck bottle to its hilt once again. Redmon shrugged and went up to the counter, twirling his empty glass.

"Nother'n?" The barman's lips rested slightly apart, yet somehow he seemed to speak without moving them.

"No," Redmon said. But he remained standing there, palms placed lightly on the Formica on either side of the glass. Would one more beer do him any damage? He was a little lightheaded, but that wasn't the beer, just excitement, nerves, just that he'd been too jumpy for breakfast and had had nothing to eat on the long bus ride into town. He'd walked up Sixth Avenue from the station to Broad Street, only meaning to scout out a hamburger before he started looking for a place to stay, when he happened to tumble across this place.

Well, I been sitten here wonderen . . .

Yeah, yeah, yeah. He did feel giddy, so light he might float right away. The first day out had its way of putting you a step or two off balance. One of Chandler's little monologues started up in his head, without invitation:

Now Rodney, I wonder if you know how many people are due to come out of the Tennessee correctional system around the same time as you. And do you know how many of them will be right back within the year? Well, I can tell you just this much: it's not a very encouraging statistic, Rodney. Nosiree, not very encouraging at all.

Nosir, Mr. Chandler. Reckon not. Rodney glanced up at the spotty mirror behind the bar. He could see the back of the barman's balding head and the pasty roll of fat turning over the blackened collar of his T-shirt. *Difference is, Mr. Chandler, the ones coming back in might not be a thing more than numbers falling down one of your columns like falling down a hole. Whereas and on the other hand, I'm thinking and planning and figuring out the way I'll never see inside again, not for so much as one minute.*

The mirror showed him he looked pretty sharp, the parts of him he could see, at least. Probably worth it, what he'd spent on the clothes. He watched his face: skin the color of coffee with cream, his daddy's high cheekbones making it slightly cat-shaped, not a whole lot of expression. The smile he felt stretching all over his jaws didn't seem to show, which pleased him, and only a dancing of his light eyes gave away a hint of how high on the edge he felt. Question is, is this a pretty good boy got in a little jam a time or two, or is it a bad mean worthless nigger can't keep out of jail long's two weeks? Let's have us a beer and think on it a spell.

"Let me have . . ."

One more beer couldn't hurt anything, he knew that for a fact. Nor probably one more after that, three wasn't really a lot, though on an empty stomach he might feel it a little, considering he was out of practice. He watched a white moth land on the mirror just above the image of his head, its powdery wings pulsing like breath. In fact, probably he never would know which one exactly it was that hurt him. No, just one after another till you started a little whiskey with it so it didn't go down so cold, until you got worked up to go out looking for some weed, some speed, looking to jump salty with some woman or a man over some woman, or otherwise do something deeply stupid. No, man, can't set foot on that road. The truth of it was, he *still* had to pull good time. The walls might look like they'd come down, but that was an illusion; one wrong step would bring them snapping right back up in his face. And for how much longer? Don't ask that. It's for now.

"Yeah?" Another word leaked through the gap of the barman's mouth.

"An . . . Never mind it. Nothing." Redmon leaned on his palms, looking into the mouth of the empty glass, and of a sudden the whole verse of the song that had been teasing him came back, out in front of the throb of a big twelve-string guitar. John Lee Hooker had cut it, he remembered now, but the version he was thinking of was Leadbelly.

> *Well, I been sitten here wonderen*
> *Would a matchbox hold my clothes?*
> *Don't want to be bothered with no suitcase on my road . . .*

"Don't have to worry too much about that yet, anyhow," Redmon said out loud, and laughed. Without moving his head so much as a hair, the barman twitched his eyes toward him for a second, then away. Redmon pushed himself back from the counter and walked toward the door. The thick new soles of his sneakers put a pleasant bounce in his step. As he pulled the door open he heard the barman speak, to himself it must have been, since the old man had his back to him and was at the far end of the room besides.

"B'lieve that boy must been on dope."

Redmon shook his head and spat on the sidewalk, going on out.

14

"WELL, YOU got this good discharge," Cantwell was saying. He had a big gray pompadour, swept back and sculpted to a ducktail behind; it looked a good deal like Johnny Cash's hair except for the color, and Redmon was thinking how maybe Cash dyed his. Underneath the forward swell of the hair Cantwell's face was long, lined and boned like the face of a country man, and Redmon couldn't quite picture it to himself, a man with that kind of face fixing up such hair, standing before a mirror, putting on hair spray and things. "Even got you a decoration or so to go with it." Cantwell paused; a long double-jointed thumb slipped into the top of a gray folder.

"Yessir, reckon so," Redmon said.

His mind kept lunging in tight little circles, speeding up, slowing down, thinking about the wrong thing all the time. He couldn't figure out which tune was right for Cantwell, so he'd mostly just been patting his foot. The office was a cramped cinderblock hut slapped up against the inside front wall of the warehouse. The walls were lined with metal shelving that held rolls of tape, files, a few books, and some loose papers. At a desk beside the door a white girl in a ribbed blue T-shirt typed slowly, a stroke at a time. From the corner of his eye Redmon could see a pink pouch of bubble gum breathing in and out of her mouth. He was facing Cantwell across the rubber mat on his desk top, with his back to a kind of picture window that looked out on the whole gloomy expanse of the warehouse, and this position made him slightly uncomfortable. Cantwell's deep-set eyes slid away from him now and then to cover some movement back there over his shoulder, and whenever they came back he felt they were cutting into him more deeply than before.

"Got a few college credits too, I see. Reckon you might finish school?"

"Wellsir, I would like to try that. Pick up a night course or something. Soon's I get settled, that is."

"Mmhm. Mary," Cantwell said from the side of his nearly lipless mouth. "You go ahead now and take your break."

The girl stopped typing in midline and stood up, pulling her top down to cover a gap at the hip, and slouched out the door. Cantwell looked back at Redmon.

"Well. You'd seem a right steady feller, Rodney." He coughed and reached for a Styrofoam coffee cup at his right hand. "What I'm tempted to wonder is how you ever come to go to the pen."

"Fraud," Redmon said. "What the court called it." He was surprised to see that Cantwell looked surprised.

"Now what kind of fraud might that be?" Cantwell said. His hand went to his shirt pocket and pulled out a cigarette pack from behind the plastic pen holder there. Eves. Redmon's eyes locked on the pack. This gentleman was truly hard to figure. But come on, Rodney, quit staring at them things.

"Care for one?" Cantwell lit up, expelling a cloud of sweetish smoke.

"No, thank you."

"Well?"

"Yessir?"

"What kind was it?"

"That," Redmon said. Cantwell snapped the folder against the desk mat with the edge of the thumb. Don't he have it spelled out clear enough for him in there? Why, sure he does — just wants to see if I'll lie. "Not to make a long tale of it, it had to do with some people puffing the price up on some buildings out in Williamson County. Some buildings that never did quite get built. I was working in one of the offices had to do with it all. It was a kind of a complicated thing. Truth is, I never quite understood it myself, not all the way."

"Mmhm." The skin around Cantwell's eyes creased. "Innocent feller, were you?"

"I don't see it makes much difference either way." Redmon's eyes fastened now on the filter of Cantwell's cigarette, which carried a picture of a naked woman looking out through some colored leaves, same as on the pack. Mighty fancy for a cigarette butt. He didn't bother pulling his eyes away from it because he had a definite feeling that this interview was already fried. They couldn't do more than send him on another one, but it made a step in the wrong direction just the same.

"Would you do it again?"

"No." Meaning, *No, you ain't got the answer to that one told you ahead of time in the paperwork.*

"Well now, Rodney. I've had a good deal of prisoners, ex-prisoners, to work here at one time or another. Some here now, as a matter of fact, though I won't tell you who." Cantwell ground his cigarette out in an ashtray Redmon noticed was lipping full of butts of the same brand. "By and large they've been no better nor worse than anybody else. I've had all kinds. Murderers, what have you, I don't much mind them. Long's they don't do it on the company time. Only thing I can't abide is thieves."

Cantwell paused here, but Redmon made no answer. Have to suit yourself, he thought, already measuring the walk back to the bus stop in the shimmering midday heat. And I guess I need to dream up a better line about that conviction.

"Reckon I'll start you out in receiving," Cantwell said. "We been needing somebody there." Hot dog, Redmon thought. It wasn't a blowoff, it was a warning. Who'd've thought it? It's *pretty good boy* after all. Thank you, Jesus, that first bit was in another state and name.

"You know how to run a towmotor?"

"A what?"

"Forklift, you might call it?"

"Hadn't done it much," Redmon said, meaning, *Not any.*

"They can learn you anyhow, don't much matter. I'll take you back to the dock here'n a minute, introduce you to Mitch, he'll be your supervisor."

Cantwell swiveled his chair around to the shelves behind him, stuck the gray folder in among other files, and began to hunt for something else. With great surprise Redmon saw his own right hand seize the instant to snap out, whip a cigarette from the pack of Eves, and tuck it away in his own top pocket, just barely fitting this sequence of movements into the pair of seconds it took for Cantwell to turn back around. The hell you do *that* for, Redmon, looking to blow the whole thing? Ain't really *stealing* though, just borrying. Besides which, he did offer you one.

"Any place you got to be the rest of today?" Cantwell said.

"Nowhere particular."

"What I'd suggest to you, then, is you go on out on the dock this afternoon and learn a little something about how it goes. Account of it gets right busy over there Monday mornings, there's a big truck comes in. That be all right? I'll get you a card and clock you in, put the time to your first check."

"Fine by me."

"In the normal course of things," Cantwell said, "you'll be getting your first check two weeks from today. But if you're short I can fix you up an advance, just one time only, you understand."

"Thanks," Redmon said. "Could we take it up later, maybe? I mean, if I get down to it? I'd rather not borrow ahead unless I have to."

"Ask me if you need it. I don't reckon you got any car? You able to get out here all right?"

"Pretty fair. Takes me a couple of buses."

"Where you living at?"

"Just north of Charlotte, up in there. For now, at least."

"Lessee." Cantwell coughed a little, dry and rasping, and sipped again from the coffee cup. Them Eves must be mean, Redmon thought, and then, oddly, felt as sorry for it as if he'd said it out loud. "Mr. Maddox lives out that way, I'll have Mitch point him out to you. He might could ride you, some of the time."

"Obliged. I do appreciate it, Mr. Cantwell."

Cantwell held his hand out across the rubber mat.

"Ay, I'll hope it works out for you."

Redmon took the hand. Cantwell's pressure was dry and hard, soon over. He stood up, tall and almost as hipless as Stringbean on the Opry. The small room seemed to stoop him slightly.

"Come on then, let me show you where you go."

The double-wide door of the receiving area was a flash of bright daylight punched through the vague gray of the warehouse wall. Redmon could see down the drive to White's Creek Road, through the wavy heat patterns coming off the edges of the rear end of a truck marked ROADWAY which was backing in. A shortish, chunky man with carrot hair paced back and forth on the lip of the dock just past the door, crying out "M'on back, m'on back" very loudly but to no visible effect. Back inside the warehouse, a skinny, sharp-boned white boy with the beard and hair of a blond Jesus was positioned at the controls of a green electric forklift. There was a cluttered desk near the dock's opening, near which Mitch the supervisor sat in a spavined rolling chair, his blubbery legs poked out at opposing angles.

Redmon stood in front of him for a minute or more after Cantwell had finished the preliminaries and headed back toward the center of the building. God Amighty, he thought, mind going fidgety on him while he waited for something to happen. This one's even got fat eyes. Mitch was looking up at him with an expression of epic indifference. His head was the shape and consistency of a baby's and his face was glossy with sweat. In fact, he was sweating so hard it appeared that the dye of the purple pullover he wore was bleeding. He breathed with an audible wheeze. It ain't hard around here so far, Redmon thought, but it's kind of boring. He smiled and Mitch came partially to life.

"Gitchee some skids," he said. "Put'm down over there'n get ready hep Timmy lay out that Roadway truck. He'll show ye how it's done."

Okay. Redmon walked toward the back to a stack of wooden pallets and began to put them forward on the floor, side to side along the wall toward the front, taking his time. The boy on the forklift glanced over at him, and when Redmon raised a finger in greeting he responded with a faint neutral nod. The tailgate of the Roadway truck flipped out onto the dock with a clash and the forklift drove up it into the truck's body, then backed out with a skid piled high with boxes on its tines. The boy set the first skid down near Redmon, reversed to disengage from it, and drove back up into the truck. Redmon had nothing better to do but lean on it, not till somebody told him different. Must have been forty boxes, lashed to the skid with metal bands. He nudged one with the heel of his hand but it was strapped too tight for him to guess its weight.

Uneasy from not knowing what to do, he turned back toward the interior of the warehouse. The loaded skid covered him from Mitch's desk, which seemed just as well to him for now, though on the other side, in the rear wall, there was a small square window in which a woman's head appeared at times, Redmon didn't know whose. On the opposite side of the receiving area was another row of skids loaded with more cardboard cases. A heavyset black-haired man came and lifted a skid on a pallet jack and trundled it off toward the shipping area. Redmon waited, tapping his fingers on the dusty wall of cardboard next to him.

The carrot-headed man came suddenly around the corner of the skid, already in midsentence: ". . . you get the packing list off this order? You got the PO yet?"

Redmon noticed that his mouth turned down in hooks at the corners, the approximate curve of a snapping turtle's beak. This would be Timmy, he supposed. He cleared his throat. "Just show me the way, boss."

"Yeah," Timmy said. Unlike most of the others Redmon had yet seen in the warehouse, he wore a uniform shirt, with a name patch reading T. ROWAN. "Where them band cutters at?"

Like that, is it? Redmon thought. He made his voice thick and slow. "Well, you know, I don't believe I seen'm . . ."

Timmy Rowan made a spitting movement with his mouth and turned away, his rubber shoe soles shrieking against the concrete as he pivoted. Redmon took a step away from the skid. This is how I get showed, he said to himself, they'll make me out to be a slow learner. Whether it was a color thing or something else didn't bear thinking of; the idea was to stop his irritation taking hold before it got a good start. The boy with the Jesus hair drove by and dropped another skid, and Redmon stared after him, wondering if it might not be better to get next to him, if and when he got down from the forklift, either to ask questions or just watch and see until he could figure out how the job was supposed to be done. As he was considering this possibility there came a loud snap and a singing sound at his side and he jerked his arm up reflexively, stopping the metal band an inch or two from his face. He whipped the band clear of him with a sideways motion and glanced at his forearm, where it had made a vivid print that stung along one side from a minor cut. Two and a half long steps took him to the other side of the skid, where Timmy Rowan seemed to be waiting for him to appear.

"What, you still back there?" Rowan said. He'd popped his eyes wide in mocking surprise and Redmon noticed that his mouth was hooking the other way at one corner now. "You know them bands can come off pretty quick."

Redmon stopped just out of arm's reach of him and inspected him from neck to knees: Rowan was a head shorter with a correspondingly shorter reach, but probably outweighed him fifteen or twenty pounds all the same. He had short legs, solid arms, and next to no neck. His shirt was untucked, falling loosely off a thick chest, making it hard to be sure if it was fat or meat. A mixture of both, Redmon figured. You wouldn't want to get too close in, not until you had him hurt; you wouldn't want to let him get a hold . . . He let his mind track aimlessly on in this direction: it meant nothing, only a silent bleeding off of steam. Anything but lose that good time, now. He'd played out a hundred such fights in his head the past year, and he could gradually feel himself calming.

"Hey," Timmy Rowan said. "You still with us, son?"

"Yassuh," Redmon said. "I reckon I best be a little more careful, thassall."

Mr. Maddox also wore a uniform, and he drove a brown Ford Fairlane in pretty good shape if you overlooked a small rust-trimmed tear in the rear fender. The inside of the car was neat, with a plastic bag hung on a radio knob for trash, some splits in the upholstery patched with plastic tape. Mr. Maddox had a smooth oval face, with a high forehead and a mustache a little like Martin Luther King's had been. The uniform was clean and he wore it tidily tucked and buttoned, every flap in place. He was a careful driver, on the slow side, although not jerky or overcautious. The car was going through moderately heavy traffic up White's Creek Road toward town.

"How you maken it so far, back there in receiven?" Mr. Maddox's voice was gentle and slow. No one had mentioned him by any other name but Mr. Maddox, including Mitch and Timmy Rowan; Redmon had been struck by that.

"Fair," Redmon said. "It's new to me. They a little long on white folks, that department."

"Not letten Timmy Rowan get to you now?" Mr. Maddox said. "Ain't no point in that."

"That way, is it?" Redmon shifted to pull his package of Bugler out of his hip pocket.

"He like that with just about anybody," Mr. Maddox said, making the left on Lafayette Street. "Bossy, kind of. White or colored, anybody'll let him get away with it."

"Oh," Redmon said. He looked down at the line drawing of the bugle player, white on the green box of tobacco, then recalled the Eve saved in his shirt pocket and put the loose tobacco away. "I thought maybe he was taking some kind of a special dislike to me."

"Ain't a whole lot of that, out there," Mr. Maddox said. "More of them than there is of us but everybody pretty well goes along. Mr. Cantwell an evenhanded gentleman."

"It does seem so."

"They all right in receiven, it ain't a bad spot. You'll be getten busy and stay that way on up through the fall. After Christmas, it slack off. They been short, till you. I will tell you one thing," Mr. Maddox said. "What's eaten on Timmy Rowan is they made Billy

Bird the assistant supervisor there, 'stead of him. So he just looken for somebody else he can boss around. And ain't nobody 'cept Willy, and he too dumb to be much fun to boss." Mr. Maddox laughed very softly, a whisper of a laugh. "And now you."

"Nice for me," Redmon said. He broke out the Eve and ran it under his nose, getting the hint of perfume. The picture of the woman, he noticed, was embossed on the filter in some material that felt like wax.

"Well," Mr. Maddox said. He turned onto Eighth. "You just want to be easy about it. Billy Bird's a right nice boy, quiet but good-natured."

"Which one's he?"

"With that beard and hair. He's the one to try, you got a question, problem, what it might be. Ain't no harm in Willy but not much help either. No particular harm in Mitch but you know, he mainly just supervises now. Him and Timmy's some kin, I believe."

"Well," Redmon said. "It's nice to know where the help's at." He lit the Eve, first ready-made for a day and a half . . . "Because I would have said this Timmy Rowan had him a little mean streak."

"Reckon he does have. But just leave it roll off you, that's all you do. Leave it roll on by." Mr. Maddox came to a graduated stop at a traffic light on Charlotte.

"That how you handle him?" Redmon looked for a second at the scabbed scratch on his arm. A nothing cut but it irked him to see it there.

"Thank the good Lord," Mr. Maddox said, putting the car back in gear. "I don't have to handle him any way at all. I don't answer to Timmy Rowan."

Redmon drew on the Eve. It was weakish and had a flavor of bathroom deodorant, but still it made a change from roll-your-owns. He was wondering a little about Mr. Maddox, who didn't really seem to answer to anyone in particular. It appeared from his movements during the day that he was a kind of department of one, going between all the others, engaged in one task or another.

"I been there twenty-two years now," Mr. Maddox said. "Can still remember my first week there, went to bed ever night and couldn't see a thing but boxes. Boxes on the ceiling, boxes ever which way — I couldn't hardly sleep for it, for a while." He laughed, again half under his breath. "But you get over that."

"I'm proud to hear it," Redmon said.

"Oh yes, it'll pass. Three more years," Mr. Maddox said, "and I pick up my watch and go home for good."

Company man, Redmon decided, stubbing the cigarette out in the armrest ashtray.

"Though I ain't altogether a company man," Mr. Maddox said. "I just float on down with the current, it's easier that way. Where can I take you?"

"Don't really matter. I'm in walking distance now."

"No trouble to me."

"On up Twelfth, then, if you want to."

The car turned. Mr. Maddox began to whistle, a single low note, then stopped.

"I might carry you in on Monday," he said. "If you want me to."

"Wouldn't want to take you out of your way."

"It ain't enough to notice, I suspect. I live right on out Twelfth."

"Well," Redmon said. "That bus is slow."

"Slow and don't go too close either."

"Ain't it the truth," Redmon said. "I could pay you some gas. After I get my check, that is."

"If you want to. We still headed right?"

"Right here'd do me fine."

Mr. Maddox pulled the car to the curb and looked about him blandly, showing no hint of surprise, though the whole block on the left was completely overgrown and vacant except for one house with the roof caved in and scorch marks from an old fire around the empty door and window frames. On the other side of the street a steep embankment climbed to a highway bridge.

"I'll just meet you right here Monday," Redmon said. Not wanting to be dropped at his door had just come over him for no good reason at all, and though he felt a little silly about it, to change his mind now would look sillier yet. "About what time you go?"

"Say seven-fifteen or a little after."

"I'll be right here. And I appreciate it."

"That's all right."

"Monday morning, then." Redmon stepped out of the car and waited till it pulled away, moving sedately to the peak of a little rise in the road and falling out of sight beyond it.

15

THROUGH THE thin wall beside his bed came the only slightly
smothered sound of the next man's record player banging out the
Temptations: "Don't Look Back." A few irregular thumps accompanied it as his neighbor tried to move around his room in time to
the music. When the song ended there was a pause while he moved
the tone arm back and then with a hiss and a scratch it began again.
Yesterday it had been the same. Redmon lay through two repetitions
with his eyes squeezed shut; he had planned to sleep longer, because
it was cheap. When the song began for the third time he reluctantly
let his eyes roll open onto the twirl of flypaper that hung from the
ceiling overhead.

Really ought to move that thing . . . He had put it there in the first
place because it had seemed easiest to reach the ceiling by standing
on the bed, but it had begun to irritate him, especially when he woke
to see it studded with the fat black flies that droned in constantly
around the screen, which fit poorly under the sash of his window. As
there was only one screen he could open only one window at a time,
though on the other hand it made little difference, since the screen
did not keep the flies out anyway. The room was already hot and
bright, so perhaps he had managed to sleep an extra hour after all. A
faint breeze that stirred the flypaper only brought in more heat. He
suspected that as soon as he moved he'd start to sweat.

Peeling the sheet back from him, he sat up. The walls of the room
were a bilious green, with some lighter color bleeding through that
made them look moldy, though they really were not. It contained a
wooden chair, a cardboard wardrobe, and a waist-high unit against
one wall which tried to be a sink, a stove, and a refrigerator all at
once, not succeeding very well in any of these functions. Redmon
walked over to it and coaxed a little water from the tap to splash on

his face. He dressed and went down the hall to the bathroom and then, turning the key on his room door as he passed back by it, went on out.

Warm outside, though not yet choking. Few people were on the street. He walked a block in the direction of the Farmers' Market, meeting no one. On the next block he encountered an enormous fat woman stuffed into a white satin dress as into a sausage sack, wearing a hat shaped like a biscuit. She drew a small shaved-head boy, dressed in shorts and a white shirt and a tie, along with her by his wrist. The boy kept pulling aimlessly to one side in the manner of a leashed dog and whenever he did so the scowl on her face deepened. Late to church, Redmon thought as they passed him, and realized then that the Farmers' Market would be shut, since it was Sunday. The thought depressed him slightly. He had meant to buy a cabbage or some greens for his dinner, and he could have got yard eggs too. He'd been eating mostly greens and eggs cooked in his room in a crazily dented aluminum pan he'd bought for a dime at the first of the week. Eating out was beyond him for now, and he could hardly afford to buy meat, or anything fit to cook it in, for that matter. Boiling was about as much as his present pan was up to. Although he knew that Cantwell's offer of an advance on the first check was genuine, the prospect of staying a week or so behind for the next several months did not appeal to him. The lean spell could not be eliminated, only displaced. Better to get it over with.

Check on Friday, six more days. He turned to the right, walked down a block, and started back toward the I-40 overpass along the railroad track, thinking what he could get with the money. He had paid out a month's rent after all, which was why he was so strapped, so there should be at least a little breathing room when the check came, and also he had several hours of overtime. But there were a good many things he wanted: a fan, some crockery, better cookpots, a coffee pot, a carton of cigarettes, and just some meat, man, because this steady diet of nothing but greens was beginning to make him weak. He wanted a radio or something too, to fight back against the record player on the far side of his wall, but he didn't know if the first check could be stretched that far, not with another two weeks to make it till the next one. Wait and see. Maybe he could put off the fan . . . or he might buy a radio as-is and try to fix it, though he lacked his daddy's talent with such things.

He came through the underpass and stopped for a moment,

looking at the railroad switch on the other side of the street. A string of three rusted boxcars was tipped on a downhill siding. Across the tracks, there was a long low shed that looked disused. Weeds had grown tall along its walls, partially blocking the doors. Redmon turned onto the street and began to walk back toward his own block, up a low hill and alongside a storm fence which closed off a crumbling concrete area that might once have been a playground. He stopped to look into it, being in no hurry. There were a few beer bottles settled in the concrete rubble, along with some discarded syringes. More weeds sprouted through the many cracks, growing thicker and thicker toward the rear until they overtook the area completely. There was no fence at the far side. A couple of water towers made a line into the distance. He went on up the hill.

At the collapsed house where he'd been meeting Mr. Maddox he paused again. The morning sun was full on what remained of the building. There was a For Sale sign pushed into the ground in front, which struck Redmon as laughable. Some billboards for Falls City beer were nailed around the door frame, but it was hard to tell whether they'd been meant as advertisements or had been put there to insulate or reinforce the structure. Enormous weeds grew all around the house, some even rising out of the holes in the roof in the rear. On an impulse he walked up to the door and peered in. The damp smell of rotting wood met him. In the fan of sunlight on the floor he saw another handful of spikes scattered. This time the sight of them gave him a sort of electric shock and he felt a tingling in his arms and legs that faded gradually as he hurried away.

Getting a little squirrelly, he told himself, with all this nothing-to-do. He turned back onto his own block. The apartments were laid out almost like a motel: long one-story buildings set perpendicular to the street. They were painted a peeling green and had huge white numbers at the ends, reaching from floor to roof: 1 2 3 4. Redmon was living in 2. The room offered a poor choice of pastimes now. He had some instant coffee but it was almost too hot to drink it and he expected his milk had probably soured in the weak refrigerator. There was half a canister of grits which tempted him no more. Nothing to read he had not already finished. He might have walked to the library but it was a fair distance and the heat was discouraging. He went on to the end of the block, turned, and walked up to Jefferson Street.

A beauty parlor and a bakery he passed were both closed. Sunday.

Brother Pig had not yet opened its doors but there was movement inside and he could smell the meat cooking. The same was true at Mary's Bar-Bee-Cue a couple of doors farther on. Shoulder's, the third barbecue house on the strip, had burned sometime before. Its rear wall had fallen in and you could see daylight through its scorched and blackened window frames, which looked across the street upon the Church of God Apartments. For the moment Redmon was alone on the strip; others were in church or still asleep. At the end of the block there was a junk stand with bright squares of cloth hung on a line above it, perhaps as flags, for they had no other obvious function. Redmon stopped to poke in the bins. The junkman wore a knit hat and a padded coat despite the weather, and he watched Redmon with a yellow and motionless eye. No whole radio, though there were many electrical parts that might have been almost anything, scrambled among dolls and old photographs and pipe fittings and pans in worse shape than the one he'd bought here earlier, and all manner of everything else. Redmon found a cache of paperback books with the covers torn away and he looked through them carefully, but they were all either romances or stroke books. He put the last one down and turned his back on the stand.

On the diagonal corner the pillbox that had once been Shorty's BBQ had been freshly painted in bright green and white. Above the door lintel a white crescent moon and star appeared in plywood cutouts. Redmon smiled. He'd come upon the place the week before but it seemed to startle him afresh each time he noticed it again. There would be at least one other man out of church at this hour, and probably out of bed. Redmon crossed the street and hesitated before the plate-glass window but it was too dim for him to see inside. The phrase MOSQUE 37 was stenciled on the glass, and in smaller letters in the corner below: HEALTH FOOD RESTAURANT. The door was open, except for a screen. Its spring whined when Redmon pulled it open.

"Raschid?"

There was no answer, but when his eyes adjusted to the dim Redmon saw him seated behind the counter that went down the left wall. A heavy book was spread open before him. He walked down and took a stool.

"No customers this morning?"

"Only you."

Redmon laughed softly. "I'm just a forward observer."

He took out his Bugler, folded a paper, and shook tobacco into the crease. The room smelled vigorously of clean, and once he had rolled his smoke he hesitated to light it. A big fan mounted on a pole near the door to the back room was kicking out a pleasant breeze. Redmon stuck the damp cigarette behind his ear. Raschid was reading as intently as if he were sealed off under an invisible dome. His robe, as usual, was a shattering white. A tuft of gray hair escaped from under his skullcap. He wore fragile-looking glasses rimmed with gold wire.

"What's the health food restaurant got on offer today?" Redmon said. "You reckon I could get me a barbecue sandwich?"

Raschid turned a page. "Perhaps I could interest you in a Shabazz potato pie."

"I doubt it," Redmon said. "I just got a hankering for a big old drippy hunk of hogmeat."

"Something might be wrong with your sense of direction," Raschid said. "You've come in the only place on the block that can't accommodate that request." The tone of his voice was without sarcasm.

For a few minutes Redmon watched him read. The pages of the book before him were tangled and knotty with Arabic. At times he glanced over to another book at his left in which Arabic and English appeared in alternating bands: a grammar or a dictionary of some kind. There was a buzzing and a shadow movement and a huge fly settled onto the back of Raschid's hand. He did not react. Redmon watched the fly take a step to the left, a step to the right, and begin to fidget with its front legs before its big hemispherical eyes. Beside the fly, Raschid seemed still as a mountain; only his eyes moved, tracking print. The longer he let the fly remain on him the more uneasy Redmon felt. He himself could let a fly walk across him if there was some reason to. He had once held himself still as a post while a snake slid over his left foot. But if there was no reason it seemed crazy. He had an itch to swat the fly himself, though he knew it would be unwise. Then Raschid turned a page and the fly lifted, circled loudly, and went quiet somewhere in the shadows of the ceiling. Raschid frowned at the new page of print.

"Sure you got it right side up, now?" Redmon said. Raschid looked at him for a moment, then stood up and drew a stream of something steaming from an urn behind him into a thick-walled cup which he reached to set before Redmon.

"Hey," Redmon said. "How much is that?"

"Free to you," Raschid said. "The duties of brotherhood." He shut his book and folded his hands on top of it.

"Hot tea on a day like this?"

"It will make you feel cooler," Raschid said. "Believe it or not."

Redmon sipped. The taste was of mint, and faintly sweet. Finding it good, he drank more.

"So," Raschid said. "What's in the world? What's out there this morning?"

"Not a whole lot." Redmon considered. "Fresh crop of spikes down Twelfth Avenue."

"That's Saturday night."

"And Sunday morning."

"Did you ever use it?"

"Not much," Redmon said, feeling again that electric pulse. "Not for a long, long time."

Raschid rubbed at his chin. "So," he said. "You're still doing it by the book."

"Sure," Redmon said. "Aren't you?"

"Different book," Raschid said. "I might tell you that the Quran offers more to sustain the spirit than the Inmate Rules and Regulations."

"But you won't," Redmon said. "Besides, there's a different one once you're on parole."

Raschid smiled.

All right, Redmon thought, so it's only a little bit different. "Can you really read all that jive?" he said.

"If I take the time," Raschid said, stroking the book. A character was stamped on the cover in gold. "It's slow. A difficult language. It would help to have a teacher but there's no one around here."

The fly started up again, whining around the room several times and finally lighting on the screen door.

Redmon discovered that he felt mildly ashamed. "Thank you for the tea," he said formally. "It's very good." He took another sip as if to prove it.

Raschid inclined his head, then pulled an ashtray from under the counter and shoved it in Redmon's direction.

"Go on and smoke it if you want to."

"Didn't know it was allowed."

"In the restaurant." Raschid glanced toward the door to the back room, where Redmon now noticed he had begun to cut an onion-shaped form, through the lintel and above it. "Not in the mosque." He smiled. "Blow some my way, if you want to. I miss it a little myself, it's a weakness but I do."

"Hell," Redmon said. "Who's watching?"

Raschid shrugged. "I am."

The fly buzzed on the screen, then found a tear in it and sailed out.

"You got the job?" Raschid said.

"Yeah. Holding my breath for the check."

"It's all right?"

"Fair enough. Plenty overtime. Mostly white folks. There's one mean cracker at my end. Supervisor's a jarhead, assistant's okay. I been getting a ride from a man lives up in here, and he's all squared away."

"Lincoln Maddox," Raschid said.

"You know him? I'd have picked him for a Baptist."

"He is a Baptist," Raschid said. "He likes tea."

"Oh," Redmon said. "Well, he's buttoned down pretty tight, but he's not bad. And the big boss man is all right out there. Decent dude, really."

"But he's still the devil."

"No, he ain't," Redmon said. "He's been straight with me."

"It's a snare," Raschid said. "You'll find the devil has a lot of them."

"You know what," Redmon said. "That really ain't going to go over so good around here. You really ought to go on back to New York. Not doing any business nohow."

"But I'm here."

"Till the KKK or somebody come along and set your shop on fire. And you along with it, most likely."

" 'And for them await gardens,' " Raschid quoted, " 'beneath which rivers flow.' "

"If you say so," Redmon said. "But why not go where there're some others? What for you need to be here?"

"And what are you doing here yourself?"

Redmon shrugged. "It's home."

"There you go."

"Wait a minute," Redmon said. "You lived in New York ten years. You were born in Memphis, didn't come here till you were eight."

"Follow that reasoning and you should be back out in the country right now, holding horses for old man Laidlaw, like you did when you were a kid."

"Never again," Redmon said. "Anyhow, he died. Died and the house burned down. Or the other way around, I forget."

"I didn't know that," Raschid said.

"It was in the paper. Been over a year."

"What happened to your daddy?"

"Ah," Redmon said. "He moved off the place before that. Old man fired him for selling whiskey."

"You been to see him?"

"No."

"You ought to go."

"Ain't in my book," Redmon said. "Might even be associating with known criminals. They still sell whiskey, don't you know."

"Sounds pretty weak to me."

"Hear the wisdom of Rastus 3X," Redmon said. "Adviser to prophets and kings."

Raschid pushed his chair back and placed both hands behind his head. "Now, Cousin Rodney," Raschid said. "I've known you a good little while now. I even knew you when you were calling yourself Jimbo Pepper, waiting trial at Riker's for . . . what was it? Some liquor store anybody but a country cousin would have known was a fort. Now, on the off chance you might've got a little bit smarter since then, I'm going to try and tell you something. What I'm doing here may look foolish to you. At one time it might have seemed so to me too. I've been up and down in the world and I've had things and then lost them. Time's come in my life when I want to have something I can't lose. That nobody can take away from me, or lock me up away from it, or whip it out of me. Now I have that thing. I breathe in *Ah*, I breathe out *lah. Allah.* That's the size of it. Want to tell me what you've got?"

Redmon looked in the direction of the door, admiring the way the sunlight caught on the fresh-torn points of the screen.

"It can be very difficult to find something of that kind," Raschid said softly. "You ought to know it can be."

"I'm sorry," Redmon said, turning back. "I don't know what gets into me."

"You're confused," Raschid said.

"Then why don't you try to sell me the business?"

"Because you ain't buying any right now. You've armed yourself against it. You're a library of smart remarks. You wouldn't be here now if you had any other place to be. Like you were saying a minute back, the world is full of alternatives." Raschid rocked his head slowly back and forth in the cradle of his arms. "Trouble is, they're all terrible. And you got no resources, Rodney. Nothing to call on, at least nothing you're willing to."

Redmon looked at a leaf dried to the edge of his cup. He felt that Raschid's words were hammering him into a box. As he stared at the tea leaf the digits of a phone number entered his mind as if someone had spoken them; it was a moment before he even recognized what number it was. It was a fluke association, nothing to do with what Raschid had been saying at all. But he had been toying with the idea of making the call all week.

"Phone work?"

"Any time you got a dime."

He stood up and went to the booth and fed in the coin. Sunday, he thought as the dial tone clicked out and returned, he won't be in the office anyway. So as not to look foolish before Raschid, he dialed. Clemson's voice burst into his ear almost before it seemed to ring.

"Dammit, Marty, now where have you been? Now listen, we got to get this zoning figured out some way, too much riding on this one to get hung on some kind of . . ." Redmon let the voice roll on, smiling a little, saying nothing. How do you like that? he was thinking. He's putting in a little OT himself. When Clemson finally stopped for an answer Redmon waited, listening to him breathe.

"Hey, what is it, cat got your tongue? Marty? Who is this, anyway?"

"Rodney," Redmon said. He felt a queer unreasonable exhilaration. "Rodney Redmon."

A beat was skipped.

"Hey, good buddy," Goodbuddy shouted. "Didn't know you were . . . ah . . . back in town. You are back now, hey? I looked to hear from you any time these last few months, now didn't I tell you to send if you needed anything?"

Why, you pointy-head bastard, Redmon thought. Why didn't you just put in for a conjugal visit if you missed me all that much?

"Just didn't need nothing, thassall," he said, slurring the words on purpose.

"Mighty good to hear from you now though, Rod. How was . . ."

Goodbuddy trailed off. Redmon said nothing. He propped his back to the wall. At the counter, Raschid had gone back to his book.

"Say," Goodbuddy said. "You're not mad with me, now are you, boy? 'Cause if you are . . . why, we just have to find the way to straighten it out, that's all."

Redmon didn't answer. Perhaps he still wouldn't have if he'd been entirely sure what the answer was. But he didn't know if he was mad or not, not at this moment. Certainly he was feeling something. For a moment he tried to remember whether Goodbuddy usually called everybody *boy* when he wasn't calling them *good buddy*. Probably he did. He had hated Goodbuddy wholeheartedly at different times during the previous year but he couldn't quite get a fix on what he felt now.

"Hey, you still with us, Rod?"

"Sure," Redmon said. "I might come and see you sometime."

"Well, you be sure and do that, Rodney. Come ahead on whenever —"

Redmon hung up and walked back to the counter. He felt almost as jumpy as if he were walking into a fight. Raschid glanced up at him, light from the door flashing from the circular lenses of his glasses.

"Anything out there?"

"I don't know," Redmon said. He did feel cooler now but he wasn't sure whether to credit the tea for it. "Sure, there's something out there. Only I can't quite tell what."

16

HE WAS sweating a little, as much from concentration as from the heat. A tiny globe of solder trembled at the junction of the wire and the fine-tipped soldering iron; carefully he coaxed it down to join what he hoped was the broken circuit. A hit. He leaned back and set the iron and solder aside and watched the lump cooling. The radio rocked on the bed with his movement. It was cooler in the room than it had been for a while; a morning rain had broken the heat and the air coming in through the windows was fresh. He'd bought another screen when he cashed his check and some heavy tape to seal the edges of both. Now and then a fly still penetrated from the hall but there were much fewer of them than before.

When the solder had set he pushed the blob with his fingernail to make sure it was hard and reached down and pushed the plug of the radio into the socket beside the bed. Nothing. He flipped the power switch back on and off and fiddled with the volume knob but still there was no whisper of sound. Just then he noticed the burning smell and snatched the soldering iron away from where it had bored a pinhole through the landlord's bedspread. Stupid, he just wasn't used to this kind of work. He'd been using the bed for a table, since there wasn't a table, but now he thought he'd better shift it all to the floor. The hole was not a serious problem — there were bigger ones left in the spread by the cigarettes of previous tenants — but on the other hand it would be real trouble if he set the place on fire. He unplugged the radio and lowered it down, its parts spilling out of the cracked case, the speaker loosely trailing from a hank of wire. Next he moved the soldering gear he'd borrowed from Raschid and the library book on home electrical repair. The book had a section on radios but it was primitive and none of the situations it described seemed exactly similar to the one he had here. He squatted on the floor for a moment, frowning at the diagrams in the book, then put it down and stuck the plug back in the wall. At once there came a roar of too-loud gospel music which faded out to an announcer's voice:

"The Golden Tabernacle Choir, just warming up the crowd for the controversial Brother Jacob, on the stands here outside Baton Rouge. Reported numbers in excess of —"

The voice was so loud it buzzed, but when Redmon touched the volume he killed it altogether. Damn. He picked up the case and gave it a shake and a different voice appeared, this one measured, rich, and calm:

"Brothers and sisters, I know you've all heard it said time and again that God is Love. God is Love. Now what could that *mean?* Some special kind of a . . . a kind of a Heavenly Love? Could be. Surely it wouldn't be *just* the ordinary kind. Surely, must be something different. Special. Out of this world we live in here and now. But though each and every one of you must have some little bit of love saved up in you somewhere. The upright man and worst sinner alike. They each of them have stored up a little love of *some* kind. Secret, could be. Well hidden, no doubt. Twisted and bent up in some crazy shape till you can't hardly tell what it is anymore at all. But love must *be* love, don't you think so, brothers and sisters? Why, it's the same word, now ain't it? And what that must mean —"

Redmon moved the tuning knob to look for music and the radio died again. He shook it but this time nothing happened and he laid it back flat on the floor. Didn't have the flair for this kind of fiddling, that was clear. Daddy might have fixed it, sober anyway, he could have. Redmon stood up and as he did his temper snapped — for a second all he wanted to do was tromp the radio into the floor. Instead he walked himself to the window where he'd left his cigarettes. The full blast of smoke from the ready-made was a pleasant change from Bugler and by the time he had smoked half he was calm. He might get it working yet, but right now he needed a break.

There was a pay phone at the end of the hall by the bathroom door and Redmon idled toward it, pinching the end of his Lucky to get the last drag. He stopped opposite the phone and began to read the numbers penned or scratched on the greenish wall beside it, mostly the names of bars or of women. When the cigarette scorched his fingers he dropped it and crushed it under his foot, then picked up the phone and dialed. Like the previous Sunday, Goodbuddy's voice filled his ear at once, but this time he was prepared to snap the hook down fast enough that his dime came tumbling back. Working two Sundays straight, he thought. Man might have got himself in another tight spot already . . . He dropped the dime on top of the other change in his pocket and started for the hot hole of light at the doorway out of the hall.

Dumb idea, he was thinking when the bus gave out on him and he had to start to hitch. This'll end up killing a good deal more time than you needed it to. It figured to be around noon, the sun coming straight down on the top of his head and so hot that the asphalt of the highway was tacky under his feet. He had been walking down Hillsboro Road for a half hour, he thought, and it was tiresome walking, the same boxy houses on either side, same neat yards and tidy trees. Each bend of the road was terribly slow to come nearer. When he finally got to Old Hickory the big church on the corner was just letting out, half the cars headed his way, out toward Franklin. He switched backward and hung his thumb in the road, but it must have been the wrong kind of church. Nice cars, mostly new, many big and fancy, kicking off painful spurs of reflected light as they ripped past him up the long grade ahead. They'd be air conditioned too, he imagined. You'd have thought a good Sunday morning service would build up enough Samaritanism in a congregation this size to cover one spade hitch-hiker, but it just didn't look like it had. When the traffic thinned he turned back around and walked faster, facing front.

What would it be, about two more miles, three? He might end up walking the whole distance, though there were a couple of hills on the way he didn't expect to enjoy. As he was considering that, a blue truck stacked high with hay tilted to a halt beside him and over the engine noise he heard a voice call down from the cab.

"How far ye headed, son?"

Redmon stepped up on the running board. "How about you?"

"Out past Franklin a ways."

"More than enough." He pulled on the sticking door till it popped open and swung himself up on the seat and sat back. A prickle on the back of his neck startled him and he turned and saw that the back window was gone from the cab so that the stubble of hay poked through.

"Not goen far, air ye?"

"Just to the store and that Mobil station there, if you know it?"

"Ain't far atall."

"Still rather ride than walk it."

He glanced over at the driver, a man up in age, a blue cloth cap switched backward on his head, overalls over a graying undershirt. Purple veins were popped out across his nose and on his cheeks, where they sank over missing teeth. There was a sibilant sound to his breathing. His hands on the wheel were knotty, moving stiffly as he downshifted on the other side of the hill. The shade and the breeze of the movement were beginning to cool Redmon down. He unrolled the cigarette pack from his shirt sleeve and shook out two, offering one to the driver, who accepted with a nod.

"Light?" Redmon struck a match and extended it.

"Thank ye."

The truck strained up the next hill and crested it. Redmon saw the white frame building of the church spin by on his left and remembered what was coming next just before it appeared. The dog-run cabin Daddy'd moved to, along with that fat old mean old — He glanced over just long enough to make out two junked cars among some other, less distinct trash in the yard, then closed his eyes and rocked his head back against the door post of the truck. Almost as an afterimage he saw his daddy standing over some car parts spread up the grassy slope of an embankment, a hand-rolled cigarette gummed to his lip and a wondering look on his face. But he had fixed that car, that time, hadn't even been able to get all the pieces back inside it, but it had run. A gift . . .

"You haven a dizzy spell there, son?"

Redmon opened his eyes. The road rolled back, blank and gray, hemmed close by woods on either side. He'd have gone walking right by there; how could he have not thought of it?

"I'm all right," he said. "Just thinking."

"That noontime sun can touch a body."

"I'm holding up."

Out the window the woods broke into fields and fences, a rock wall. A small brick church appeared, then a string of houses, then the market and gas stations came into view.

"Anywhere particular 'long in here?"

"Don't matter. By the store if you want to."

The truck coasted to a stop and Redmon knocked the door open and stepped out.

"Thanks," he said, setting foot on the pavement. He lost the answer in the rise of the engine as the truck pulled off, load swaying at the top.

Across the road the realty office was just where it always had been but he wasn't quite ready to go over there yet. So as to be doing something, he walked up to the store and got a Coke from the machine under the eaves. Drinking it, he looked around from the rise the store sat on. There were the two service stations just down from it, and across the road a seed and hardware store. Next to it the realty office looked the same as usual except that the name REDMON on the partnership sign had been replaced by DOBBINS. It was a perfectly square little building, with a raised porch running around all four sides of it and some of the jigsaw trim that went with what they called "colonial style" when they tried to sell the houses. It fit as naturally into the surrounding countryside as if it had recently been dropped from a plane. A big blocky gray motorcycle was parked in front and that was all.

Redmon set the empty bottle in the rack and walked back down to the road. Though there was no traffic he hesitated for a minute before he crossed. On the other side he stopped to inspect the bike: really a nice one, a BMW, solid and conservative as a car. An inexplicable purpose of stealth came over him and he went up the stairs softly so that they would not creak. The door was shut but unlocked when he tried it. He peeped in the window beside it and saw no one at the secretary's desk. In smooth slow motion he drew the door open just enough for his free hand to slide through and silence the little bell that hung on the inside. Cupping the bell, thumb on the clapper, he slipped through the door and pulled it shut and stepped away from it.

It was all much the same. Orange shag carpet, the slick brown paneling, the cheap pictures of the sad, big-eyed children on the walls. The bric-a-brac on the secretary's desk had not changed and he assumed it must be the same one, Joan. He walked around her desk, setting his sneakers down soundlessly on the carpet. The door to Goodbuddy's office was just ajar and he could hear the sound of typing past it, also the drone of a window-box air conditioner, which would help cover his own movements. He pushed open the door of the other office. Nobody. The desk had been moved to the opposite wall and on it was a name plate reading HENRY DOBBINS. Spread on the desk were maps and plats and planning commission reports and some contract forms, the usual kinds of paper. No family pictures.

Dobbins had one paperweight of petrified wood and another of dried flowers trapped in Lucite, neither of which did much to tell whether he might be as big a fool as Redmon had been.

He left the room and went to stand by the crack in the other door. Goodbuddy was seated at a rolling stand beside his desk, straining at the typewriter with as much apparent force as if he might be trying to push it across the room. He was in shirt sleeves and wore no tie. His head was bent over so that Redmon looked down on the thin patch in the hair on top of his head; nothing of his features appeared but the slack red dangle of his lower lip. He pushed the door open hard and took one long step to the edge of the desk. Goodbuddy sat back so suddenly that the spring of his rolling chair almost threw him out the window. Redmon saw with a sense of real accomplishment how it was taking Goodbuddy more than a minute to get the smile plastered firmly over his face again. Now he knew why he'd wanted to arrive without warning.

"God save us, boy," Goodbuddy said. "Did you come out of the floor or what? Give us a knock on the door next time. Why didn't you call up, anyhow? You might just as well've missed me, Sunday and all."

"That'd been a shame," Redmon said. "I couldn't find a dime, is all."

Goodbuddy's hand, square as a side of bacon, came out across the desk.

"What the hell, Rod, it's good to see you any old time." He was getting back in the swing of it now. "*Good* to see you, boy."

"I knew you'd be happy about it," Redmon said. He took the hand briefly, then let it drop.

"Go on and sit down, why don't you?"

Redmon fell into the indicated chair, a leatherette item angled in front of the desk.

Goodbuddy sank into his own seat with a creak. "What's the good word?"

Redmon let the question float, having no answer ready, while he looked around the room. Goodbuddy's office too was much the same as he remembered it. A tooled leather blotting pad on the desk was flanked by framed photographs of a woman and three children in various casual poses. It was Goodbuddy's second cousin and her brood, though Redmon had frequently heard him encourage people in the assumption that the family was his own. "Inspires confidence" was what he'd say of it. His real name, Owsley Clemson, was inlaid in abalone shell on the wooden name plate near the photos.

"Not a whole lot of news to interest you," Redmon said. "I mostly been in the pen, if you recall."

"Sure, now Rodney, I know that." Goodbuddy's hands shifted, covering each other on the blotting pad. "You know my thoughts were with you."

"You actually would say that out loud?" Redmon said. The window behind the desk was bright enough with the afternoon sun that it cast Goodbuddy's face in shadow. Outside in back was a cut field going yellow and at its far edge some tract houses under construction, with a raw new road torn in between them.

"I mean, since you got . . . since you been back, that is. All settled in? They find you a job and everything all right?"

"Oh yes. They found me one. Made me a box lifter, don't you know. And pay as little as the law allows. So I'm settled, like you might say. I'm settling into a kind of a sink hole in there by Jefferson Street. Right there in the heart of town."

"Well . . . you'll get on your feet. I know you, you got talent." Goodbuddy reached across the desk for a stick of Wrigley's and shucked it out of the silver paper. "You know I'd do anything in the world for you, but seeing how we been fixed . . ."

"Oh, I know that as well as you do," Redmon said. "Matter of fact, it might even say something about it in my parole papers. Anyhow, I see where you got all the help you can use. How about this Henry Dobbins, is he any 'count? Smart fella? Understand the business pretty well?"

"Oh, he's pretty fair," Goodbuddy said, turning his hands palm-up. "Not that we don't miss you."

"Must be hard on you, I know."

Goodbuddy snapped his gum. "Listen here," he said. Redmon could tell he was trying for firm, but it was just coming out loud. "I don't know if I'm real sure what you're getting at, Rod."

"Me neither," Redmon said. "Hard to say." He pulled a cigarette from his pack and hung it in his mouth without lighting it.

"Ashtray right behind you," Goodbuddy said.

"Took me two hours to get out here, I must be getting at something," Redmon said. "Hitchhiking too, in this heat. Ain't got no car or anything, you know. And you know what else? Hardly anybody wanted to pick me up."

"Well," Goodbuddy said. "That's real friendship for you."

"I stood up for you," Redmon said. "I stood up for you and all the others. I didn't have to. Nobody made me. Over the last year or so I've sometimes wondered what I did that for."

Goodbuddy cast a glance in the direction of his phone.

"Oh, it's all right," Redmon said. "I don't want anything. I just came out here to let you know I love you." He leaned forward quickly across the desk, placing his elbows next to Goodbuddy's hands, his nose an inch from Goodbuddy's nose. Knowing that Goodbuddy was not really all that smart, Redmon had a good idea what he would be thinking. He would just be wondering if it would make a bad impression if he moved back a little bit, or if it would look better to stay right where he was. "Body language," Goodbuddy called it. He spent a good deal of his time worrying about things like that.

"Uh-*uh*," Redmon said. "Better not move. If you even thought about it I could just sink my teeth right into your face."

"Always a joker," Goodbuddy breathed.

"Yeah." Redmon sat back. For the first time he noticed a key ring with a BMW tag lying at the corner of the blotter. "I'm a laugh and a half."

Goodbuddy released a sigh. "Everybody appreciates it, you know they do," he said. "What you done."

"They ought to," Redmon said. "But that's not what I'm saying. I'm looking for something to *explain* it." He took the unlit cigarette out of his mouth and looked at it. "What I think it is . . . it must be love. Don't you think it has to be?"

"I couldn't hardly say."

Redmon laid the cigarette on the desk and picked up the key ring. "Maybe you couldn't," he said. He tossed the keys and caught them. "God is Love, did you know that? I heard it on the radio today. God is Love."

"Sounds familiar," Goodbuddy said. "Hey, I'm real happy you stopped by . . ."

"It's all right, I can stay awhile," Redmon said. "I'm not pressed for time."

"Well," Goodbuddy said. "That's great."

"Nice little motorcycle there out front," Redmon said. "It yours?"

"Yep. Use it weekends mostly," Goodbuddy said. "You know, it ain't much use for business things."

"I don't suppose you'd be willing to let one of your special friends take it for a little ride."

"Well, sure I would," Goodbuddy said. "Trouble is, I don't know about the insurance and all . . ."

"I understand," Redmon said. "Can't be too careful about insurance and things. It'll trip you up before you know it."

He flipped the keys up and caught them overhand, his fist closing on them with a crack, smashing down so hard on the keys that his knuckles paled and veins leapt out on his forearm, which after a minute or two began to tremble. When he let up and opened his hand the teeth of the keys were vividly imprinted on the skin of his palm.

"Hell, go on and take it out, then," Goodbuddy said. "I don't reckon it'll do any harm. Just make sure you don't hurt yourself, now."

"Oh, I'll be careful as can be," Redmon said. "That's mighty nice of you and all."

"Amongst friends," Goodbuddy said. He waved his hand, a little shakily, Redmon thought.

"Of course," Redmon said. He stood up and collected the loose cigarette. "Just be sure and let me know whenever you need it back."

17

NOW WHEN he woke the first thing he saw was the sleek gray motorcycle, kicked onto its stand in the space between the all-purpose appliance and the outside wall. He had got a table too, some shelving, some better pots and pans, some posters to cover cracks in the walls, but the bike was still the most opulent piece of furniture he possessed. Every day when he came home he humped it over the single step and through the door and wheeled it down the hallway to his room. It cost him an effort but he knew it never would have lasted on the street. There had been no complaints from the other roomers, only a few funny looks, impatient shrugs, or sighs if people had to wait in the hall for him to clear the bike out of the way so they could pass. It was not the sort of place where complaining got you very far, at least not in any direction you'd be apt to want to go.

There were advantages to that, Redmon believed. He lay on his back, eyes slitted, admiring the silvery glow of the motorcycle in the first dim morning light. The sight of it gave him a feeling of satisfaction whether it was really his or not. He had the use of it; Goodbuddy had made no effort to get it back, had made no overture of any kind, for that matter. So it became like the New York time when ownership had hardly been a question; *yours* was whatever you had the power to control, until maybe one day you no longer had it. Bad way to be, over time, and Redmon had meant to put it behind him, had almost completely done so. But like Raschid said, you had to have something. He smiled. Of course a fancy motorcycle was a long way from what Raschid really had in mind, but it was not the thing, only the control of it, that mattered. And it made a hedge, a little pad, between himself and nothing.

The wood floor was cold enough it seemed to clutch at the bottom of his feet when he got out of bed. The room had a fairly effective electric heater running down one of the baseboards, but it cost, and he did not run it at night or if he was going out. An army surplus sleeping bag unrolled across the bed was enough to warm him while he slept. He dressed quickly, jeans and boots, a flannel shirt, the leather bomber jacket that had cost more than he should have paid for anything but that he absolutely needed to ride the bike in cold weather. Seven-thirty by the white plastic clock. With bad traffic he stood a chance of being late. He slapped together two meat sandwiches, rolled them and a Mars bar into the same paper bag he'd saved from yesterday, and dropped the package into one of the storage compartments on the bike. There were four of these, two behind the seat and two in front. One was full of tools but there was enough space in the other three that he could just about have moved house in a single trip. Of course that said something about the house too . . . He put on his gloves and wheeled the bike outside.

There had been a helmet hanging on the bike when he had first taken it, which he hadn't much cared to use in the summertime, but now it was handy, just for warmth. A curved face plate lowered over the whole front of it, making a perfect windbreak. It was tinted to cut the glare and looked flat black from the outside, so that if he wore the helmet in front of a mirror he seemed to have an outsized bowling ball for a head. How he must look to everybody else too . . . There were a lot of things the bike was good for, but a half hour or so of stop-and-start traffic was not really one of them. He was happy to get off when he had finally reached the warehouse.

Ten minutes early, after all. Despite the cold he stayed out in the rear of the parking lot long enough to cut a smoke. Could have had one in the break room but he liked it better in the open. He smoked the cigarette slowly, with the visor pushed up just enough for him to bring it to his mouth, cupping it to stop the wind from taking it. Through the tinted curve of the visor he stared across the lot at the building. On the corrugated roof of the retail wing, a gigantic plaster raccoon was clambering. It managed to annoy Redmon in some fresh way almost every time he caught sight of it. He turned to face the traffic on White's Creek Road. There was a steady current of cars pulling into the lot all around him, and now and then somebody waved. Four trucks were lined at the receiving dock, and the first one was a Yellow, which meant they'd be in for overtime for sure.

At three to eight he went in at the shipping door and fed his card into the clock to get it stamped, then walked back to receiving. They had already cut the seal on the Yellow truck and Willy was stacking the first boxes out of the back of it onto a skid at the edge of the dock. One thing about Yellow was that the orders seldom came on skids. Another was that they were small, numerous, and jumbled up all over the truck, with their packing lists cleverly hidden most of the time. Just to get the boxes off the truck and agree on the count would take everybody most of the morning, and meanwhile there would be other trucks piling up behind. Redmon was looking at another twelve-hour day. The before-Christmas rush was shaping up to be everything Mr. Maddox had promised, and more.

Billy Bird and the Yellow driver stood just inside the warehouse door, studying the shipping bill. Mitch seemed not to be in yet and Timmy Rowan was seated in his chair by his desk, smoking a Kool with grand gesticulations. Smoking was forbidden all over the warehouse, but in the rear, out from under Cantwell's eyes, people frequently ignored the rule. Redmon went to the shelves just past the desk, set down his helmet, and slowly began pulling off his gloves, finger by finger. There was no point in taking off the jacket, since he would certainly spend his first hours working in the wind at the open door.

"Better get a move on," Timmy Rowan said. "You got you a long day ahead." Redmon's head turned a bare degree in the direction of the voice before he stopped the movement with a clench. He went on drawing off his gloves at the same rate as before.

The break room was not exactly a room at all, only an area hemmed in by shelves halfway between the warehouse and the offices in front, though the office workers usually did not use it. Redmon and Billy Bird walked in together at one o'clock. They'd waited late to take their lunch break, since it was shaping into another long day. Few others were there at that time. Mr. Maddox sat at one of the round white tables, along with a man who went by the name of Bullhead. Billy Bird sat down with them. Redmon dropped his lunch sack on the table and went to start a fresh pot of coffee. What was left had cooked to a pasty crust in the bottom of the machine and he made a face when he saw it would not rinse out.

"How you all maken it back there?" Bullhead said.

"About usual," Billy Bird said. "We'll see sundown and then some."

His back to the others, Redmon contemplated the rank of vending machines. After thinking it over he got a can of chili, same as he did almost every day. The machine had a device that heated the can as it came out, and he liked that, though in all other respects it was terrible chili. He poured himself a coffee, dumping in a large amount of powdered creamer in hopes of cutting some of the acid, and sat down at the table with the rest. Billy Bird was eating. Bullhead was smoking, a tin ashtray gathered in the meaty black crook of his arm. Mr. Maddox sat with a cup of coffee in front of him, next to half of a hard-boiled egg which sat on a crinkle of plastic wrap. The conversation, such as it had been, had stopped.

Redmon unwrapped his sandwiches, popped the top of the chili, and began to eat.

"Coffee's ready to get up and hit you," he said when he had finished the first sandwich.

"Always let it burn," Billy Bird said.

"I quit drinken it," Mr. Maddox said.

"What you got in that cup, then?" Redmon said.

"Instant. Bring it from home." Mr. Maddox reached out with great deliberation, picked up the egg half, took a very small bite from it, and set the remainder back on the plastic.

"Stretching that out?" Redmon said.

"No," Mr. Maddox said. "I just ain't got much of a appetite lately, is all."

The talk stopped again. Redmon chased around the inner edges of the chili can with his plastic spoon, then pushed it away and peeled his Mars bar. Bullhead lit another Kool from the butt of his first. Billy Bird hooked his wadded lunch bag toward the wastebasket in the corner, missed, and went to pick it up. He stayed down at the far end of the room, slumped on a couch by the wall, watching the floor through lidded eyes. Mr. Maddox lifted the egg slowly, bit it, and put it back.

"Think you'll quit around quitting time today?" Redmon said.

"More'n likely," Mr. Maddox said.

"Must be nice," Redmon said.

"Ah, what're you fussen about?" Bullhead said. "Doen you a favor, pay you all that good OT for your Christmas gift."

"Yeah," Redmon said. "I'm just so happy about that I don't hardly know what to do."

Bullhead swiveled his neck around. Rose had wandered into the area on her jumpy long legs.

"Come on and give us some *sugar*," Bullhead said. At the coffee pot, Rose switched her blond ponytail behind her like a horse switching a fly, and gave their table all her back.

"Don't be shy now," Bullhead said. "How come you such a timid thing?"

Rose turned and walked past the table, clutching her two coffee cups as for balance, eyes fixed on the middle distance. Her hair was tied back so tight it seemed to stretch the skin over her small cat-shaped face. She had the movements of a nervous cat as well. It was so easy to tease her that Rodney could not really see the point of it. She left the break room as if walking on cockleburs.

"Uh uh *uh* uh uh uh *uh*," Bullhead said.

"You'd just smush her," Billy Bird said speculatively. "Ain't nothing there to hold you up."

"Naw," he said. "You don't know me, do you. I float just like a cloud."

"You float like a bucket of melted-down pavement," Redmon said. "Swap you a Lucky for a Kool."

"You got it." They made the exchange and Redmon got up for more coffee. Back at the table he watched the lumps of creamer stain and sink into the viscous black, not bothering to stir it. Mr. Maddox took another minuscule bite from his egg. Redmon lit the Kool and took in a long gust of menthol. Breath freshener, ha ha. He stirred the coffee and took a sip.

"Poison," he said.

"What do you drink it for?" Bullhead said.

Redmon didn't answer. Willy was just then shuffling into the break room.

"Hell," Billy Bird said. "We must be due back, Rod."

But he made no move to get up. There was a clock on the wall over the drink machine but Redmon didn't look up at it. Willy stood in front of the candy machine, looking back and forth from its window to some coins in his palm. His expressions were always those of a child and now his face was crumpled. After a minute he turned away from the machine and came to sit down at the table. His face was flat and hammy, with black brows almost meeting in a frown.

"Need me to lend you some change, Willy?" Redmon said.

"Ain't that," Willy said. "I just can't see nothen there I want."

Redmon stood at the square window in the back of the receiving area, tapping on the glass. In the bright box of fluorescent light on the other side, two women sat typing at a cluster of desks while a third perused a microfiche reader. Redmon gave up knocking. Let them take how long they pleased. After a minute more Rose stood up from her typewriter, swayed over to the window, and slid back a half section of it. Redmon passed a sheaf of packing slips in to her.

"Hunt me up a PO on that, would you?"

Rose's plucked eyebrow arched but she said no word. She carried the wad of packing slips to a file cabinet in the back and began to sort through it.

"Goddamn, shut that window, why don't you," one of the others said. "You're about to freeze us to death in here."

"Fresh air," Redmon said. "Good for you."

"Sure, Rodney, sure it is. Why don't y'all hustle up out there, anyhow. We just want to go home."

"Why, ladies," Redmon said, pouring syrup into his tone. "Now, you *know* we jess doen the bess we can."

Rose came back to the window and handed Redmon his packing slips, on top of a stack of green-and-white-striped computer forms. Redmon glanced briefly at the mess of paper, then folded it over once and shoved it in his jacket pocket.

"What time you got?" he said.

"Five-thirty," Rose said with a smirk, as though it was his fault. She slapped the window shut. Redmon stuck a cigarette in his mouth and walked back across the concrete floor. By this time receiving was only half choked with unlogged orders, but Timmy Rowan was still ferrying away the last of what they'd processed off the Yellow truck in the morning.

Billy Bird stood up from where he was counting off another set of boxes. "When we goen home?" he called.

"Clear the dock," Mitch said in a monotone. It was a robot reaction at this hour of the day. You could have told him *naked lady* or *house afire* and he still would have come back with *clear the dock*, would still be sitting lumpish and inert there at the desk, sweating heavily from his blood pressure pills no matter how cold it got. Redmon threaded his way through boxes and skids, stepped through the loading door, and struck a match to his cigarette. Ordinarily he didn't smoke back in the warehouse, not because of the rule but because it made a bigger difference between work time and break time, and if he'd smoked all through the day it would have been another pack gone and he'd have a sore throat by quitting time.

He was only having this one in memory of when quitting time ought to have been. He screwed the cigarette into his mouth and put his hands in the warming slash pockets of the jacket, sucking in smoke and staring out over the road to where the sinking sun had stretched a scarlet band along the tree line of the opposite hill. Timmy came racing back from shipping, speeding the towmotor, and as he passed the desk he threw the machine into a spin, the empty tines lashing around like tusks. Redmon glanced over at him and then away.

"Yo, my man Rodney," Timmy called. "You on break?"

Redmon didn't answer.

"Ain't no smoken back here, now don't you know that?"

Redmon took the cigarette from his mouth, looked at it, and took another drag. Cold air sucked all around his head. He turned his back full on Timmy Rowan.

"You hear what I say?" Timmy called.

"Timmy," Mitch said. "Are you the boss?"

No answer.

"I said, are you the boss?"

"No I ain't," Timmy said, throwing his whole troll's body into a sulk.

"Who *is* the boss, then?"

"You the boss, Mitch," Timmy said. "You the big boss man."

"All right," Mitch said. "Rodney, you come on back and do us some work here."

Redmon snapped his butt over the rim of the dock and watched the sparks scatter on the asphalt and wink out. Then he stepped back into the warehouse.

"Shut this door?" he said. There would be no more trucks coming this late.

"Okay, go ahead," Mitch said. Redmon found the pole and hooked the catch of the rolling door and hauled it on down to the floor. With the draft from outside cut off it began to seem warmer almost at once. Redmon took his paperwork from his pocket, shrugged out of his jacket and laid it on a shelf, and went to the table in back to start filling out his cards.

"Sure you don't want us to wax the floor now?" Billy Bird was saying.

"Can if you want to," Mitch grunted. "Ride me about it a little more and you will."

It was a quarter to eight. Another twelve-hour mind twister. There were still skids on the dock but everything had been sorted and written up. Redmon made a point of not thinking about how soon he would be back here again. He stuck the cards on his last order and went to the can in the overflow section and washed his hands and dried them. When he returned the girls were leaving, walking across the floor toward the time clock, their heels sounding cross clicks on the concrete. By Mitch's desk the others were putting on their coats. Timmy Rowan had picked up Redmon's jacket and was holding it spread by the arms.

"Mighty nice," he was saying. "Whoowee, this here's what I'm gone wear next time I go pimpen down Jefferson Street." He checked Redmon for a reaction but none came. This baiting had only bored him for a long time now; it did not touch the buried fist of anger. The others paid no attention either. Billy Bird was making a call, and Willy was telling Mitch a joke involving a man named I. P. Freely. Redmon put on his gloves and his helmet and turned and stretched out his hand.

"Let me have the jacket, Timmy."

Timmy took a step back. "Aw, now," he said. "Don't you want to loan it to your old buddy a while?"

"No," Redmon said. "Sure don't. Come on, it's too late to be fooling around."

He took a step forward with his hand held out. Timmy made another teasing retreat, draping the jacket in front of him. Redmon snapped his face plate down; it seemed less trouble than keeping his expression blank. He took two steps and then doubled his stride and had the jacket before Timmy realized he had reached him.

"Grabby grab," Timmy said. The corners of his mouth hooked down. "You want to go out in the parking lot?" This invitation was meaningless too; he made it to someone almost every day.

"It's where I'm headed," Redmon said. He didn't much care if Timmy could hear him through the helmet or not. The others were straggling toward the front and he went after them. The time clock struck his card its hammer blow, and he went down the outside steps and started for the bike.

18

NOT MINDING the knife edge of the weather, Redmon had taken off his helmet once he reached the dirt road so that he could sink into the sensation of speed more completely. He had no notion how fast he was really going, but it was as fast as the road would take; a few more r.p.m.s would have snapped him right out of the next bend to cartwheel across a field or into a patch of trees. As it was, torque was bending him right down to the ground on the turns, and the howling of the engine seemed to come from a couple of lengths back behind him. His eyes streamed with the wind slicing into them, and the colors of the road ahead ran liquidly together, red wedges of light the low-angled sun spread through the trees at the fencerow bleeding into the gray and white of the gravel and ice. He swept into a turn tilted all out, the breath mostly flattened out of him, then felt his lungs expand again as the bike came back up of itself on a straight stretch, finding the crown of the road. The next bend was already there and something went funny as he entered it: the road shifted under him, sidled out of position, as if all along he'd been riding the back of a sleeping snake that now was just awakening. He'd lost it, the touch was gone, bike stiffly skidding first over ice and then rock, throwing up a spume of gravel. He was gone, had just time to realize that before he pulled out of it, heeled over too far in the opposite direction, then brought himself back through a corkscrew wriggle that took him to the hump of the short bridge over the creek, where he went airborne for a second and then by a miracle came down straight on his wheels on the downhill slope across it. He coasted on a few more yards and stopped, setting down his foot. Across the near fence a horse the color of blue cheese snorted and ran in a short half circle and turned back to stare at him again, twin trunks of steam pushing up from its flared nostrils.

Redmon was breathing fast and hard, as if someone were pumping his body like a bellows. He hadn't been scared like that for a long time and he was enjoying the feeling. As the panic rush tingled away the world came back much sharper and clearer than it had been before. For the few minutes he stayed there propping up the bike, nothing at all intervened between him and the bright transparency of the winter day. Gradually he became aware of a stinging at his knee, where he'd just frayed his pants and a square of skin along with them, but even the pain was a kick now. The cold air rushed tidally in and out of him, crossing back and forth through his smile.

The horse snorted again, disdainfully it seemed, and trotted farther off into the field. Redmon watched it, looking across the withered snarl of honeysuckle vine tumbled all over the fence. Under him the bike bucked and hiccupped. He gave the throttle a twist to clear its throat and cut it back. *Death junkie,* he said to himself, starting to think in words again, and laughed out loud. *Lord, but it's freezing.* His whole face had gone numb. He dug into one of the storage boxes for the helmet and put it on, then shoved the bike upright and idled along the road.

At the intersection over the next rise he turned left and drove along the pale stripe of Murray Lane at a sightseeing pace — he'd had all the speed he needed for one day. Though the sun was behind him, the fields ahead glared. The snow on the road had been burned off by traffic, swept into dirty lumps of slush along the ditches, but it still sheeted the pastures. On the north side livestock had trampled it, but to the south, in the front field of the Laidlaw place, the snow was pristine, white and blank as nowhere at all.

Redmon drove slowly along the board fence, noting that the paint was peeling from it and a plank or two had sprung loose. At the front gate he braked to a stop, drawing the bike up between the fieldstone gateposts, just short of the cattle gap. Nothing had been up the drive since the snow and only a slight depression, a shadow, marked the path of it. His eyes tracked it up to the loop in front of the house, but where the house ought to have been there was just nothing, not even a scar. If the ground was still scorched there, it had been snowed over. A bare plate of snow rose uninterrupted to the trees on the hilltop. Above the trees he could see a faint haze against the paling sky that might have been smoke from some chimney on the other side. Back down, off to the right of the house site, the barn was still standing, though obviously empty. Redmon supposed the horses would have been sold. He smiled, thinking how Mr. Laidlaw, the old man, would have raised Cain if he could see him now, racing a bike hard enough to scare people's horses. But they weren't his horses now; the old man didn't own anything at all anymore, unless it was a shaft somewhere in the frozen ground. Redmon pushed the bike back from the gateway and wheeled off down the road.

At Manley Lane he turned again and went down in the deep dip where the unfinished subdivision started. The half-built houses had hardly changed at all since the last time he'd been prancing around this bottom with his clipboard in his hand. Where they'd been left open to the weather the wooden wall frames had gone gray and some looked rotten; that wood had never been treated for out of doors. Pink tails of torn insulation still dangled from some. On the couple of houses that had been far enough along for windows, the panes had all been broken. A few minutes of fun for kids farther up the road, Redmon reckoned. He had been all for this development at the time, but now he would have wished it back the way it had been before, the narrow lane barely wide enough to admit a car, cutting through the wild land he'd played in and hunted and hidden in when he was a child himself. He passed the last skeletal house, drove on to the crest of the hill, and stopped.

The sun was gone and the light was draining quickly out of the sky. As it darkened, the cold began to seem more cutting, but still Redmon pushed up his visor of his helmet to light a cigarette. On this side nothing had changed much. The graded subdivision road stopped short at the crest of the hill and the old road, no more than a narrow spine of limestone, twisted down into the next hollow. Outside the second barn on the steep slope of the pasture below him he saw a string of sheep feeding among scattered flakes of hay, their backs a dirty white against the bluish tones of the snow. Must be a new tenant, or it wouldn't even have to be that new. There was smoke from the stovepipe and a warm orange light at the windows of the house. Well, he had paused here like this a few thousand times before, probably, waiting a minute or two before he went on down, on in to Momma'n Daddy. With the foolish vividness of a dream he smelled supper cooking, though it was plain enough that no one was cooking anything anywhere near him at the moment. The wind changed direction and he saw the smoke from the house turn with it, lowering to skim the ground. Nope, ain't no Momma'n Daddy down there now. He flicked his cigarette end over the fence and watched it sizzle out in the snow on the other side. When he started down the curves of the hill, it was dark enough that he needed to turn on the headlamp.

What he wanted was out of this neck of the woods, but he made himself go slow. People had a way of slopping the turns on this stretch of road, and if a car or a truck hit him along here it would be no contest. Dark came down fast at this time of year, and when he reached the highway on the other side of the valley, night was complete. Back on the pavement, he opened the bike up a little wider and streaked toward town. Again, the dog-run cabin came up and whipped past him before he quite had time to notice it, and this time it connected with something in his mood that slowed him down. He waited for a break in the line of cars coming south from Nashville, then popped a U-turn and started back.

He went slow again, coasting the shoulder barely fast enough to keep the bike from wobbling, thinking it over. A couple of cars slowed to a creep behind him, then honked a time or two and whizzed on by. Opposite the cabin, Redmon hitched the bike onto the gravel below the pavement and waited, five minutes, ten, trying to make up his mind. An old Chevy and a beat-up Lincoln were pulled up on the hump of ground before the cabin but he had no idea whose they might be. Lights were on in both the rooms and he saw a silhouette pass before one of the windows, then cross back. Might as well, else he'd never know what he'd missed. He drove the bike across the road and parked.

The door was set in the middle of the dog run and Redmon knocked and waited but no one came. After a minute he noticed a loop of string passing through a knothole which when he pulled it jingled a bell inside. A voice called out something indistinct and there was a sound of someone moving. Then Martha snatched the door open and stood square in its frame.

"Whatchoo need, cowboy?"

She was bigger than Redmon had remembered, seeming to fill the door from post to post. Maybe it was just a smaller door. Martha had on a purple print dress with a grimy apron over it, fuzzy black tube socks, and a pair of saddle shoes her fat feet seemed to have sprung. Her face looked not simply fat but swollen, proud flesh rising on her cheeks from some distemper, squeezing her eyes half shut. Redmon supposed she might have looked a little better to him if he had disliked her a little less.

"Let's hear it, boy. Is the cat got your tongue?"

"Ain't buying, Martha," Redmon said softly. "This is a personal visit."

"Unh-uh," Martha said. "Don't get personal with your kind. You can buy sumpn or ease on out of here right now, ain't gone be no free sample."

Redmon set his foot in the door as it began to close. "Hold on," he said. He wasn't as put out as he might have been. In a way it pleased him as much as not to pass unrecognized by Martha. "It's Rodney here, you know, your loving stepson? Daddy home?"

"Hah?" Martha said. She let the door come back open and shifted so that light behind her fell on Redmon's face. "Well now. B'lieve it could be you after all. Crawled out from under that rock again, God hep us. I thought you was in the pen."

"It's always a pleasure," Redmon said. "You must be getting cold standing in this door. Daddy home?"

Martha snorted and stepped a pace back from the doorway, a single step that was enough to bring her up against the rear wall of the dog trot.

"Yeah, 'Daddy home,' " she said, pointing to the room on the left. "Right on back thataway." She stumped back off in the opposite direction, leaving Redmon to his own devices.

As he stepped in and shut the door, the light in the hall went out. It was only three or four steps to the room she'd pointed out but the dog trot was cluttered and in the dark he had to slide his feet carefully along the floor to keep from tripping or smacking his shin. There was a step up, apparently, and then he had to stoop to pass under the low lintel. When he stood straight on the other side his head was almost scraping the sagging ceiling and he found himself staring into the overhead light fixture. Beyond its low-watt aureole he could see his daddy and another man sitting at an angle on the same spavined sofa so as to face each other across a checkerboard raised on two cushions between them. Redmon saw that his daddy's hand was hovering over the board as if it had been quick-frozen there.

"Got somebody visiten here, Wat," the other man said.

Redmon didn't think he knew him. He watched as his daddy switched slowly around to peer up in his direction. The hand swung with him in the same hovering position, with an odd catatonic rigidity. It had been a year or so since Redmon had last seen him and at first he thought he looked very different, but as he kept looking he could find no definite change to fix on. Still the same close-cut graying hair, mustache curving down around the corners of the mouth, coppery skin stretched tight on the high slant of his cheekbones. He looked to be in pretty good shape even, though his shiny black eyes were blurred. Maybe it was that he seemed a little smaller.

"Pepper," he said. The hand dropped onto his knee with a slap. "Is that sho enough you there, boy?"

"Nobody else," Redmon said.

The hand rose driftily up again. "Come on here, son. What you hangen back there for?"

Yeah, what is the matter with you? Redmon thought, for it seemed to him that everything on the other side of the room was something he was watching on TV, like either he or they were only someone's imagining. He took one step and then another and when his father's hands closed over his wrists the illusion faded. Seeing how the old man's eyes glimmered with delight, he shut his own. A wild phantom music materialized in his inner ear and with it a phrase he might once have spoken. *Daddy, won't you play the fiddle now?* He prised his eyes back open. Damn it, when had he got so small? His overalls made a basket of wrinkles that had nothing to do with the shape of the body that had disappeared inside the garment. You could hardly see anything of him but the head floating and the two lean forearms coming up out of union suit sleeves. But the grip on his wrists was powerful, strong as the clasp of a drowning man.

"How's your arthritis?" Rodney said stupidly.

"My arthuritis . . . been treaten me *pretty fair.* Not troublen me . . . much as *usual,* you know . . ."

"Nothing much the matter with your grip yet, anyhow," Rodney said. A grin flashed between them. They both had the grip, it came from milking. It was said once you had it, it would never go away.

"Ain't *nothen* wrong . . . with that." The old man's hands slid away. "Pepper . . . this here's Buster. You recollect Pepper, don't you now, Buster?"

The other man nodded. "Ain't seen you since you 'as a boy, don't reckon. How you maken it?"

"All right," Rodney said. "Getting by."

"Go on now, Pepper," Wat said. "Go on and set down."

Redmon glanced around the room. It was strangled with furniture; there was only a kind of cross pattern on the floor where a person could walk. There were two chests of drawers, a cracked pie safe, and a kind of china closet, it might have been, with most of the glass broken out. It appeared that there were two armchairs as well but both were piled so high with clothing that they seemed to be nothing more than large balls of fabric. Rodney backed up a step and sat on the edge of the bed, which tilted forward sharply as if it meant to buck him off. He was conscious of his scraped knee poking through the tear in his pants, but the others didn't seem to notice it.

"Wet your whistle?"

Rodney saw that Buster was wiping off the neck of a fifth bottle and holding it across the gap between them. He took it to his mouth and swigged. A burn and then an afterburn. He held the bottle away from him to look at it through watering eyes and saw that though the peeling label was for J & B the liquid inside was more or less clear.

"Martha trading in moonshine now, is she?" he said, passing the bottle back to Buster. Wat was frowning at the floor.

"Won't hear . . ." His hand jerked up. "Won't *hear* a word against her, now . . ."

"Forget it, Daddy," Rodney said. "I never meant a thing." However, he was wondering if the whiskey might really have been distilled in old radiators, as Martha's enemies would claim.

"My arthuritis . . ." Wat said, slipping back to a safer subject. "Now, it ain't been *too* bad. But you know . . . Pepper, I have been having a little trouble . . . with my *heart.*"

Whiskey help that for you? Rodney thought, but he held his tongue. The trailing way his daddy spoke was beginning to madden him, as it frequently had. He would hesitate interminably before a word, and when at last he had seized it he might hold it in his mouth indefinitely, like it was a piece of that all-day cannonball candy they used to sell out of jars. It got considerably worse if he was drinking. Rodney put little stock in the heart complaint. The old man could claim a dozen problems of one kind or another and they all wound their way back to whiskey in the end. And this was some mean whiskey and no doubt about it, his head was already starting to swim with just the one belt. He heartily hoped there was no lead in it, or at least not much.

"Jesse! Will! Come on . . . come *on,* down here." Wat's hand floated out dreamily to signal two more men just ducking into the room. "Take you a seat now . . . lookee *here* . . . My boy, Pepper . . . done come to see us. So we gone *have* . . . a *real* good time."

"Hello, there, Will, Jesse," Rodney said.

He knew both slightly from when he was a kid. They were some shriveled and whitened now, but no more than you'd expect. He noticed gratefully that Jesse was trailing a bottle of Cabin Still that looked the right color to be the real thing. Will shifted the clothes out of one of the chairs to the floor, digging himself a seat. Jesse joined Rodney on the bed.

"Watch yourself," Rodney said. "She's a little tippy."

"Ain't gone tip me," Jesse said. "You big enough to take a drink now, Pepper?"

Rodney grinned and reached for the bottle. He cocked it up and held it for a couple of gurgles and when he lowered it the clench of sadness in him began to loosen a little. Someone had switched on a radio and he rocked on the bed in time to the music. Sure now, he thought, we gone have a real good time.

It was some time later, really a good while later, that he decided he'd better get up to make sure he still could. The floor did a roll under him as he stood, but he balanced himself, mastering its motion, before he tried to walk. In the dark dog run he smashed his leg into something sharp and hard, right on the bone, and loudly cursed.

"Drunk old fool." Martha's voice came from the next room. "Oh, it's you," she said as Rodney dragged into the kitchen and steadied himself against the wall. Another equally hard-favored woman was sitting with her at the table. While Redmon collected himself against the door, waiting for the room to stabilize, they resumed their conversation, mouths at work like chewing meat. He couldn't quite make out what they were saying.

"Don't mind me, ladies," he said thickly. Neither replied.

He lurched around the table and went out the back door and paused by the outside wall. He was so hot with whiskey that it took a minute for him to feel the cold tightening on the skin of his face and hands, but when he finally did he felt better, and a good deal less drunk. Beginning to whistle, he walked to the edge of the woods and took a pee. When he came back into the clearing his eyes had adjusted and it looked almost as bright as day. He looked up; there seemed no distance at all between him and the moon. He felt an affection for it that moved him to begin whistling again, the opening bar of "Goodbye, Pork-Pie Hat," slow and stately, each note bending a little as he uttered it.

There was a slight echo and he stopped to listen to it fade, but instead he seemed to hear a voice somewhere in the woods behind. He whipped around toward it and then on reflex took off running in more or less the direction of the sound, hardly knowing what he was thinking just to get into the cover of the trees. His drunk sank completely away from him; now he only felt charged. There might be something, someone ahead of him, moving quickly from one tree to the next, but he could not be quite sure of it, and before he could gain, a wall of shadow that a grove of cedars made had blotted out the details of everything in front of him. He stopped on the dark side of a tree, shadows blending, to get his breath. Not going in there, not without knowing what he was after. As he rested and blew, the most monstrous dog he thought he had ever seen in his life walked into a pool of moonlight some twenty paces up the slope from him. The dog was almost as big as a bear, he would swear it. A small bear, anyway. It stood looking back at him with its ears pricked interestedly up.

"*Big* momma dog," he said aloud. If this didn't explain all he'd seen, he thought it came close enough. "Did you give me a turn or what?"

Slowly the dog wandered off into the shadows, and Rodney began to laugh. Still laughing, he turned and started back down toward the house. His drunkenness remained shriveled inside of him, a closed hand. All he felt was the tingle from the sprint, and the rush that the brush with who-knows-what could bring. It occurred to him that this was the second time he'd had that kind of rush today. He shook his head, stepping into the clearing, and began to whistle again.

The women seemed to be still chewing over the same subject in the kitchen and Rodney passed through quickly, keeping his eyes off of them. Once in the dog run, he hesitated. The sour smoky closeness was smothering to him now he'd come in from the clear cold, and he could feel the whiskey rising back in him, more like a sickness this time. From the next room he heard his daddy's voice meandering among the voices of the others, but he felt all of a sudden that it would be no use to go back in there. To say goodbye? Nope, leave it all to another time. He opened the door and stepped down into the yard, patting his pockets. Yes, he had his cigarettes, his keys. The helmet hung on the handlebars of the bike by its strap. He stooped and scooped up a ball of snow and scrubbed it across his face, the sting of it bringing him as alert as he was likely to get. Still and all, he was kind of drunk for a motorcycle. Third time's the charm, he thought with a twisting smile. It would just be a little like flipping a coin.

19

THE SCREAM blew him out of bed altogether and even its declining echo had enough lift to hold him floating in the center of the dingy space of the room. Though his palpable body lay leaden in the bed, frayed cover pulled to his chin and clutched there with his finger ends as though he might have been an ailing child, another more genuine self went on hovering, held high on the top of the roaring column of the scream. He didn't know if it had happened or if he'd dreamed it, this time more than another, not for sure. It was the kind of house where screaming could and did occur, but it seemed a little unlikely that one would repeat itself so regularly week by week at this same hour of the morning. He mused on this problem, drifting in the wash of the vague dawn light that was stealthily strengthening itself in the room. His mind ticked ahead, in time to the clock's slight buzzing, but with less definite progress. If he had wanted to he could have remembered and rehearsed his dreams, but he was sure enough he didn't want to.

An hour or so passed in this way and then he began to think of getting up, considering this notion for some time before he could carry it out, even sending little ineffectual messages to his arms and legs which resulted in no movement, as if he truly was unable to bring his real willing self back down from its suspension a foot or two below the flaking ceiling. After fifteen false starts a signal penetrated to his limbs, and sweeping the coverlet aside he rolled up to his feet. The set of imaginary bones parallel to his own had all been fractured during the night, and as he crossed the room to the stove top he could feel their splintered ends scraping over one another. He put on coffee and glanced back at the clock. Eight. No matter, it was Saturday. He could have slept in, could have slept all day if he wanted, but though he could have used another hour's sleep he didn't much think it would come to him right now. As the coffee pot struggled to a boil he went across the room to the wardrobe, opened it, stooped, and pulled from an old shoe a pint bottle of Bacardi Gold, three-quarters full. The first pull of it revolted his insides at once but after the uncoiling came a warmth that soothed him. He stood and took another drink. This time the urge to gag was less and he could feel the shattered second skeleton beginning to dissolve. For a moment he shut his eyes and let his body sway forward, then to the sides, just drawing back from a topple in each direction.

Eight-fifteen. The coffee had been bubbling, how long? He could smell it on the edge of scorching. Having removed the pot from the eye, he took a damp mug from the sink and splashed it a quarter full of rum, filled the rest with coffee, and topped it off with the last of a pint of milk that remained in the refrigerator. It seemed to him that the drink had an innocent sweetness to it, like a milk shake or cocoa, but its warmth was more than simple heat. He moved to the motorcycle and lifted himself gingerly onto its seat, sitting sidesaddle, his bare back against the wall and his knees pulled up under him, warmed by the edge of the mug which he held against them. His next swallow brought a pleasant drowsiness from the midst of which he almost felt he could no longer hear the scream at all.

From where he was sitting he could look through the near window onto a scrabbled ribbon of lawn that ran between the building and the parking lot. Dandelions had begun to sprout in the patchy grass, though none of them had yet achieved a bloom. The little area of green was faded by streaks of sun; it would be a bright day, and warm maybe. A big gray squirrel hopped onto the square Redmon's window framed and stopped, sat up, and looked more or less in his direction with its polished button-black eye. The squirrel was fat and seemed overconfident, maybe even a little bit stupid. It hopped in an oblong of quick, abrupt movements, now and then sitting up on its haunches to look about itself. A scroungy white dog appeared on the grass and routed it, barking crazily, then crossed back and was gone.

Redmon sipped again from the mug and turned his glance back inside. The dimness caused a hot red to rise behind his eyes and he was aware of the scream's echo intensifying. There was a triangle of sunlight on the floor that gradually lengthened its point toward the front wheel of the bike. A cockroach came hurrying along the shadowed side of it and then tumbled away into a crack along the baseboard. Redmon considered stepping on it but by the time this idea was complete the bug had gone. His wish for a cigarette was not quite strong enough to bring him down from his perch to look for one. A breeze came rustling over the window sill and he felt that side of him break out in gooseflesh. At first it was a pleasant springy tingle, then it began to chill. He had on nothing but his shorts and it was a little cold for that.

He got down from the bike, drank off the rest of the coffee and rum, and went over to the bed, collecting a pack of cigarettes from the corner of the table on his way. Slithering underneath the cover, he found the warm spot his body had left and settled back into it. There was a pack of matches pushed up under the cellophane of the cigarettes. After he had lit up he dropped the dead match into the empty mug, which he'd set on the chair seat by the bed, on top of the pants he'd been wearing the day before. A groaning of pipes was audible through the wall in back of his head. He lay smoking quietly, finding patterns in the cracks of ceiling up above. When the cigarette was done he dropped it into the mug and as it hissed out he shut his eyes.

Though he'd believed at first he might float back to sleep, the slight noises of the building began to irk him almost as soon as his lids had dropped. Others were rising, beginning to pump the plumbing and bang doors and call out to each other. When he heard his neighbor's record player scratchily commence he knew the project of sleep was hopeless and he sat back up on the edge of the bed. The giddiness in him was no longer so pleasant, and he felt very jumpy down underneath it, which might be the fault of the coffee, he supposed. Everything was going sour. For a stuttering half second he wondered if his daddy's mornings were generally like this, but then he forced that idea from him. He lit another cigarette, though his mouth was dry, and stood up and began to dress.

Outside, the spring air had the soft feel of a washed-out cloth, a kind of gossamer entwining. There was still a coolness to it that helped bring him back alert as he walked off his own block and started up toward Jefferson Street. The rum bottle, shoved in the inside pocket of his jacket, slapped back at his rib cage whenever he took a long step. Though it was turning into a beautiful day, he felt that he was only halfway in it. The other half of him was masked, coated by a thin layer of something indefinable, still a little deafened by the scream.

On Jefferson Street he turned and walked stiff-legged over what already seemed to be a slight wave motion of the crumbling sidewalk. Too soon. The warm place in his belly was turning hollow. He pushed at the glass door of Brother Pig and when it gave he stumbled in. With a special effort at steadiness he approached the counter, which a heavy-lipped girl in a striped uniform shirt was streaking with a mucky cloth.

"I'll have the double meat with extra hot . . . and coffee."

"We close," the girl said, rolling an eye toward Redmon and away. "Open ten o'clock."

"Ah, go on," Redmon said, peering down at the top of her head, which was tightly laced in corn rows. "I know you got the meat, just lemme have the sandwich."

The girl turned to the urns behind the counter and drew a cup of coffee, which she slid across the counter.

"That ain't but half of it," Redmon said.

"Well, take it and set down."

He carried the cup to the bathroom out back and doctored it from the bottle, then returned to the Brother Pig dining room and sat at a table near the door. His elbow had gone a little weak on him; he'd turned the coffee nearly the color of tea. After he'd smoked a cigarette he slipped effortlessly into a half doze, broken after he didn't know how long, when the girl brought the barbecue. He paid her and ate, the vinegary sauce burning a track down him, observing the other people who'd come in while his eyes were shut. When he had done he went out the back again. You went clear outside to get to the stalls, but Redmon didn't bother going into one this time. He stopped by a runner of Virginia creeper that was climbing the cinderblock wall and took a long slug from the bottle neck, chasing it with what remained of the coffee mixture. When he squinted at the bottle it was down to a quarter, but his last drink had set off a euphoric explosion in him which lasted all the way through a cigarette he smoked, admiring the turns of sunlight on the leaves twining up the white wall.

When the good feeling had begun to dwindle he passed through Brother Pig again and bought a roll of breath mints at the front counter. Outside, he went on in the same direction he'd been headed, taking care not to trip over the occasional loose squares of paving or bump into other passersby. Opposite Mosque 37 and Health Food Restaurant he chewed up the first mint and stuck a second one into his mouth. The menthol taste was rising up the back of his nose and he thought it would surely do, but then again he felt abashed to catch himself caring whether or not the liquor smell was covered. Allowing himself no time to hesitate, he crossed the street and went in. A bell jingled; that, he thought, was new. Raschid was seated in the back with a woman named Maggie, who sometimes came to him for instruction. He glanced up when Redmon entered but did not immediately rise. Redmon sat at a front table by the window, hitching his chair a little way from the others, looking back out. The glass changed the tint of the outside and all it contained, and he felt a swirl of excitement when he noticed that, for the image mimicked his whole experience of the day. But the meaning of it slid away before he could quite grasp it, leaving him dulled again. The double-meat barbecue was sinking in his vitals like an anchor with a barb. He was no longer sure what he'd come in here for, and was even beginning to think he'd come into the wrong place altogether.

"Need anything?" Raschid had slipped up behind him.

"I'll have the tea." Redmon nudged a quarter onto the table.

"I'll trust you." Raschid receded, then came back with a hot cup.

Redmon covered it with his hand, listening to the burr of question and response that had resumed at the rear of the room. Arabic — it sounded like throwing up or being strangled to him, no matter which of them was speaking. He had no way of supposing whether Maggie was getting any better at it or not. His chair squeaked on the linoleum as he pulled it around from the window. Maggie was a skinny woman with a cone of gray-streaked hair pulled back to a tight point at the back of her head, dressed as a church-going woman might be for Sunday. Her face was made to seem narrower by wide eyes that spun like the eyes of a shying horse whenever Raschid said anything that startled her. Redmon watched them like a pantomime till the lesson ended and she shrugged into her short jacket and stood up to go. Raschid walked her to the door, exchanging politenesses, in English now. When the door closed on her he scraped a chair back and settled at Redmon's table.

"The first disciple," Redmon said.

"In the beginning," Raschid said, "was the beginning. Among other things." He stroked his forehead below the line of his skullcap. "She's trying."

"What they used to call a God-fearing woman."

"Devil," Raschid said automatically. "We're trying to turn all that around."

"Well," Redmon said. "I believe she's here on a love jones anyhow. Likes the way you feel out that whatchamacallit . . ."

"*Djellaba.*"

"Jelly jar."

"I see where you're in a mood to be nasty this morning," Raschid said, considering. "I don't know if I really am going to need that today or not."

"Looks like it's another slow day."

"We'll have the lunch business."

"Ah," Redmon said. He made a wide gesture of his hand that nicked his cup, which rocked but didn't quite spill. "I take it all back. I'll be just as sweet as you please."

Raschid watched the tea, still shuddering in the cup from the jostle. "What are you on, Cousin Rodney?"

"Just high on life . . ."

Raschid looked up at him.

"Aw, now," Redmon said. "You telling me it shows?"

Raschid smiled. "You look like you been washed and hung to dry."

"Wish I had been," Redmon said. "Well, I had a little drink. It's early for it."

"Just that?"

"Yeah. I'm not cut out for a morning drinker. Like Daddy, that way."

"Hmm," Raschid said. "You seen much of him lately?"

"Every week or so, I'll go."

"How is he?"

"Drunk, most likely." Redmon touched the surface of his tea, trying to just bend it without breaking through. "But I'm not like that, you see."

"What are you doing it for, then?"

"Man," Redmon said. "When did they make you my parole officer?"

"Well, you come in the door in about a half a dozen pieces," Raschid said. "I didn't lay any trap for you, did I? About ten more minutes, I got to go back in the kitchen and you can have yourself back to yourself."

"You know," Redmon said, "I just got up on the wrong side of the bed. Went down the hall and all over the bathroom they got spoons with black on the back . . ." He pushed his open hand away from him. "Friday night, you know how it gets."

"That's all it takes?" Raschid said. "Boy, you better move out from that place. Quick as ever you can."

"No," Redmon said.

That wasn't all it took. His face dropped into his hands with a meaty slap and he opened his eyes to check that the darkness was complete under the cover of his palms. The last reverberation of the scream had left him and along with it he'd lost the place where he might have reentered his dreams if he'd chosen to do it. Now it was all a blank, with a half-drunk swirl boiling before it. When he took his hands away his eyes burned a little from the light.

"Sometimes I think everything's still going on," he said. "Everything I used to be into."

"Well," Raschid said. "Sure it is. I might say the same."

"I mean, I'm still doing it," Redmon said. "Even though I'm not. There's like another me. *Still* doing it. All of it. Just every so often, we meet up."

"Oh," Raschid said. "You're talking about Hell."

"Yes," Redmon said. "I guess so."

"Overseas?" Raschid said. "That kind of thing?"

"Sometimes," Redmon said. "Not necessarily."

"You could go down to the VA."

"Not me," Redmon said. "I'm not one of *them*. Besides, it doesn't happen that often, you know. Once in a few weeks, I can manage that. Just the wrong side of the bed, that's all it is."

Raschid slowly shook his head. "No," he said. "You don't want to be on anybody's plan, do you?"

"No," Redmon said, "I don't. Other than my own."

Raschid's voice dropped. "What you need to do is . . . sleep." He was speaking very slowly. "You can go on in the back and lay down and sleep back there. On the mat. When you wake up, you're going to feel a whole lot better."

"It's all right," Redmon said. He pushed himself up from his chair. "I can make it home, ain't far."

"Sure?"

"Yeah."

"Well then," Raschid said. "*Mashallah.* Don't go racketing around now, and you'll be better off. Let me hear from you before too long."

"I will," Redmon said, making for the door. "Hope you make out on your lunch trade."

In an alley back of Jefferson Street he finished off the bottle. The fall of his arm from the last gulp turned into a wind-up and he flung the bottle sailing high over a vine-wrapped storm fence into a blind brick wall on the other side. The smash, a perfect scintillating circle, allowed him an instant of sheer delight before cross voices took up a protest somewhere in a yard beyond the fence. They couldn't see each other. He went on down the alley, walking slowly enough to prove he didn't care anything about them.

Going between two cars pulled up in the gravel parking space, he came on the same squirrel of the early morning, or one a lot like it, sitting upright in a spangle of sunlight on the sparse grass. His approach did not seem to trouble the squirrel at all and for some reason that annoyed him. Fat and sassy . . . He veered onto the grass and as the animal dropped to all fours he lunged at it. The squirrel disappeared, and Redmon, bent to snatch at it, lost his balance and went over in a complete somersault, landing on his back. A woman in the building shoved her window up to glare out at him for a second, then slammed the sash back down. Redmon laughed at her, though he felt a little queasy. He hadn't really expected to catch the squirrel, but maybe he had taught it a little something; more than likely it would be a slightly more nervous squirrel in the future.

20

TIMMY ROWAN was in a funny mood. He was quiet but not sulky, though these two states ordinarily went together with him. Redmon had expected him to make some crack or other when Mitch had paired the two of them together to pull orders, but for once he'd had no smart remark to offer. He sat at the controls of the towmotor, as serene and abstracted as though he'd been absorbed into a dream.

It could always be laid to the weather, maybe. The molten heat was such that it warped everybody's behavior. At the start of the summer the warehouse had kept reasonably cool, holding pockets of winter chill in various of its recesses. Like the subways, Redmon thought, it trailed behind the season. Now it had caught up and then some, was slowly baking all through. There was no avoiding the heat. Mitch sat at his desk with some paperwork pinned under his elbow, forgotten, its leaves stirred only by a rotating fan that whirred back and forth on the nearest shelf, with precious little other effect. The meager breeze it pushed out was not even enough to dry the sweat that sprang in waves from Mitch's rolls of flesh. A few feet past the desk the breeze stopped dead, as if it had rebounded from the stubborn air.

Billy Bird sat at the rear table next to a microfiche reader, struggling to explain some new procedure to Willy. He'd tied his Jesus hair back at the nape of his neck, tightening it all down to his head, oily and slick-shining as a cue ball. Both of them were wilted toward the weak blue light of the reader's screen. Timmy Rowan's towmotor planed quietly across the empty dock, back and forth between shipping and overflow. At least it was a good slow day. A week or so into August it would get heavy again . . .

Redmon had been there almost a year. Considering this, he rode a skid back into overflow, loaded it, rode back among the boxes.

Halfway across the receiving floor he hopped down and Timmy drove away to shipping. Redmon had time to walk to the door, but the air there was no fresher, only a little more bright. Ninety-eight percent humidity, you could almost see it there, like a floating wall.

Timmy drove back, teased an empty skid down from a stack onto the towmotor blades, and waved to Redmon, who stepped onto it. He set his feet carefully on the slats and braced back against the towmotor frame. The machine glided back into the dim greenish cavern of overflow, traveling a long slow way. The buzz of the warehouse attenuated and finally disappeared.

"Top shelf," Timmy said, braking the machine. "You ready?"

Redmon crouched and set his palms on the boards. "Okay."

The concrete floor began to recede under him. He watched it drop back through the gaps in the skid. The top shelf must be what, nearly two stories up? Looking down over the back of the skid, he could see through the mesh that roofed the driver's seat Timmy's carrot head bent over a clipboard on which he puzzled out the orders and crossed them off as they were filled.

"Lessee," Timmy called up. "We'll have . . . two Sunbeam crock-pots."

Redmon reached for the boxes and stacked them to the back of the skid.

"Rolling," Timmy called.

"Okay." The raised skid floated past two more shelves, swaying a little bit, out at the towmotor's farthest extension. The movement made Redmon a little dizzy, though not in a completely unpleasant way. The skid came to a stop with a slight jerk.

"Three *Crockpot Cookery,*" Timmy said.

Redmon moved forward and the skid tipped a bit with him, then caught on the tines by its bottom slats. "Swing it in a little," Redmon said.

"All right."

"I don't see but one and a half *Crockpot Cookery,*" Redmon said.

"Sure? Well, put it on, then. We're rolling."

The skid passed another shelf and stopped.

"One *Sunbeam Mixmaster.*"

"Got it."

"We're rolling. Six Coronet complete cookware set."

"*Six!*"

"You heard it."

Redmon shifted the boxes, stacking them in a careful tie, adjusting the others around them. "We're loaded," he said. "Take it on down."

At twelve-thirty he took his lunch. The break room was airless, smothering, so he got a cold drink from a machine and carried it back out to the steps that went down from the shipping dock, where Mr. Maddox was already sitting, his emptied lunch bag refolded on his knee.

"Hot, ain't it." This phrase had become a standard greeting.

"Sure enough," Mr. Maddox said.

Redmon opened a sandwich. In the heat it seemed gluey to chew; he had to wash it down with big gulps of Coke.

"Be glad when this weather breaks," Mr. Maddox said.

"If it ever does."

"Oh, it will. Everythen in its time. Hey," Mr. Maddox said. "Almost your anniversary, ain't it?"

"Of what?"

"The job here."

Redmon rolled his bag up around his second sandwich. He didn't feel like eating much, not in this kind of heat.

"So it is," he said. "Reckon they'll bake me a cake?"

Mr. Maddox let out a dry hint of a laugh. "Wouldn't count on it," he said.

"I'm not."

"You ought to be getten a quarter raise, though."

"Well," Redmon said. "Let me think now. What'll I spend it on?"

"Don't get reckless," Mr. Maddox said. He turned his arm over to glance at his watch. "Time I got to head back."

"We'll see you."

Mr. Maddox stood up a little stiffly, using the rail to hoist himself. "Hot, ain't it?"

"Yeah," Redmon said. "Sure is."

He watched Mr. Maddox's square green back fade into the gloom of the warehouse, then turned back to face the parking lot. In the noon glare the chrome trim on all the cars seemed to fizz. A year. The time had passed slowly, though nothing much had happened in it that seemed worth remembering now. It was better than jail, though, he did believe that. But the idea of staying here another twenty-three or -four years gave him a nauseous tremble. He shook his head hard to knock the thought out, reaching for a cigarette. The bottom third of his Coke had gone brackish on the hot concrete step. Redmon wet his mouth in it before he lit up. It was almost too hot to smoke at all, not quite.

Timmy was waiting for him, sitting at the controls of the towmotor with a complete stillness that struck Redmon as odd, since he was usually a fidgety man, always moving himself around a little. When he saw Redmon coming he turned on the juice and spun the towmotor in a little pirouette on the empty floor, coming out facing a skid that lay away from the stack, by itself.

"Will you ride that skid?"

"Sure," Redmon said, walking toward it.

The question was an unusual token of good will, coming from Timmy, but he saw little particular about the skid itself. It was different from most of them, with a solid planked floor instead of the usual gapped slats, and he thought that would be all right; he wouldn't have to look down quite so much that way. It had no slats across the bottom, but he thought nothing of that. He stepped onto the skid as Timmy scooped it up, raised it a foot or so off the floor, and aimed it back into overflow.

"Lessee . . . Barbie Doll regular, two of them."

"There you go," Redmon said, flipping the boxes onto the skid.

"One Barbie Doll Beachwear."

"Got it," Redmon said. They were doing middle shelves, he was only raised about halfway up the rack. The towmotor moved ahead and stopped.

"Assorted Matchbox models," Timmy said. "Three of them."

Redmon peered over onto an empty bay of metal. "Uh-oh," he said. "Don't look like there's any of that here at all."

"Sure?" Timmy said. "Check on either side of it?"

"Okay," Redmon said, leaning. "Nothing there."

"Well," Timmy said. "Scroobie doobie."

Redmon looked over the back of the skid to see him scribbling notes on his pad.

"Somebody made a miscount or something," Timmy said. "You log in that last bunch of them, Rodney?"

"Sure didn't," Redmon said, with no idea if he'd done it or not.

"Well, get set, anyhow, you're going up on top."

Redmon sat back on the skid, in front of the boxes he'd already loaded. Its floor was comfortingly solid, like he'd expected it might be. He twisted around to watch the silvery pistons of the lift apparatus pushing out of the green piping. The skid wavered to the top shelf and halted.

"Let's have regular G.I. Joe," Timmy Rowan said. "Four boxes."

"Coming up," Redmon said, and stepped to the end of the skid. As he moved he felt the whole towmotor buck and lurch backward and the floor was teetering out from under him in a long sick dip that opened up a vision of the drop to the floor and then he jumped and clawed his way onto the opposite shelf, flopping across several boxes of G.I. Joe. When he looked back, the skid was still seesawing on the point of the tines, there being no slat across the bottom to hold it level. One of the boxes he'd stacked at the back fell forward and though it couldn't have weighed more than a pound or so, it was enough to flip the whole thing over. It dropped end over end to the floor. Redmon poked his head out over the edge of the shelf, gripping the posts on either side as hard as he could to help control a hard tremor that had come all over him. The skid had sprung and splintered its wood on the floor and scattered the boxes everywhere. Two of the cases had split open to spread shiny doll packages down the aisle. Redmon made a fist and smacked the post, then when his arm began to shake he took hold of it again. When he looked at the towmotor he saw Timmy Rowan peering up at at him through the mesh roof.

"You all right up there?"

"Yeah," Redmon said. "Thanks for asking."

"Well," Timmy said. "Can you climb down out of there or you want me to get another skid for you?" He pointed. "This one here's busted."

"I see it is," Redmon said. "I'll climb."

He waited a minute more and then began to lower himself from shelf to shelf, taking great pains over every hand- and foothold because he still had a tendency to shake. When he reached the floor he let out his first full breath, standing in the middle of the jumble of dead-eyed dolls and cracked wood, and looked at where he'd been, the forklift tines angled toward each other, over him. He'd have liked to lean back on the shelving, close his eyes, but he didn't want to show it. Timmy Rowan was looking at him expressionlessly through the pistons of the lift.

"Okay," he said. "Guess you better get to cleaning up this mess."

Redmon's chest squinched down too tight for him to make any

reply. He stared back at Timmy for a minute, then walked around the towmotor, heading for the front.

At the end of the aisle he heard Timmy calling after him. "Hey. Hey, where you think you're going?"

Redmon went on without answering. He had no destination. A shimmer of golden motes hung at the edges of his eyes and he felt his twinned self very near him, eager to take on the body of flesh it had been missing, hot to rise up and look out of his eyes and speak from his mouth and make its own use of his arms and legs. He could feel the anticipatory tingling and unstringing of all his limbs. The twin knew that Timmy Rowan was following and wanted to draw him in a little nearer. Redmon walked into receiving. No one seemed to have shifted since lunch. The bare floor was glossy and pooled with the blurred reflections of the light fixtures above.

"Hey, you think — You can't just walk off like that, boy . . ."

Redmon stopped.

"All right." He heard the flat toneless voice of the twin speaking. "Tell me what I can't do."

"Are we down to it?" Timmy said. "I'd hate to have to tighten you up."

Redmon whipped around. His left hand rose and pushed Timmy Rowan in the chest, just a measuring stroke, and dropped back.

"Come on," the voice said. "Come on then, Timmy. I'll go out in the parking lot with you now."

Timmy hesitated. Billy Bird raised his head slowly from the microfiche reader.

"He's not fooling around, Timmy," Billy Bird said in a perfectly neutral tone; he might have been talking about football, or fish. "I'd let him alone if I was you."

Timmy backed up.

"Where you going?" the voice coming out of Redmon said. "Come on, now."

Timmy took some more steps back.

"Come on and let's go," the voice said.

Redmon stepped in. His left hand had become heavy and was rocking back and forth at the loose end of his arm like the pendulum of a clock. Timmy had backed to the edge of the table and his eyes were beginning to slide around, looking for somewhere else to go. On the far side of the table Willy had sat up very straight, and Billy Bird was watching with the distant expression of someone looking

at TV. Then Mitch appeared in between them. Redmon wouldn't
have thought he could have moved so fast, or would have, into
something like this. Mitch's face was tomato-red and he squawled
like an angry baby, his fat arms jigging up and down.

"All *right*, that's *it*, that's *enough* now. You, Timmy, you *get* back
on that towmotor. *Now*, hear me? Willy, you go hep him in back.
Out back *right* now. Rodney, you get *back* there behind that table
now. Billy, you find him sumpn to do, hear?"

Timmy came out from the table, moving behind Mitch's twitching, gesturing hulk, and stalked back off toward overflow. The back
of his neck was turning dark. Willy was coming out from behind the
table to go after him.

"Go on, Rodney," Mitch spluttered, pushing his stubby arms forward like somebody shooing an animal. "Get on back there now."

Redmon felt himself cooling down, returning to possession of
himself. If he'd thought he could get away with it he might have
laughed.

"Yassuh," he said, and went behind the table.

Billy Bird was smiling behind his hand and shaking his head,
looking not at him but at Mitch, who was still windmilling his arms
and swearing, all by himself in the middle of the floor. "Goddamn,
you all drive me crazy, make me run around in this heat — If you
want to *fight*, then hit the *clock*. We come in here to work, you
know that . . ."

Still arguing, he lumbered across the floor to the desk and crashed
back into his chair. His momentum sent the chair gliding on its
wheels a couple of yards till the shelving stopped it. He hauled out
a handkerchief and began to sponge his face.

Redmon turned to Billy Bird. "Okay," he said. "Find me something to do."

The afternoon passed in a storm-center quiet. Redmon stayed
behind the table, learning the microfiche system from Billy Bird. It
wasn't a bad slot, more interesting than humping boxes, but he had
trouble keeping his mind completely on it. The picture of himself
splattered on the floor back in overflow kept popping up between
him and the screen. He was sure enough that Timmy Rowan had
been willing for that to happen, if he hadn't actually nudged it along.
But who would have thought that Timmy could be backed down as
easy as that? If he'd known it, suspected it, he might have saved

himself a whole ration of trouble and pain. It was a puzzle. For the first hour, he glanced up reflexively whenever he heard the towmotor coming, but Timmy never seemed to be looking his way and after a while he stopped paying attention.

They all quit at quitting time, five sharp. Redmon was parched and after he had clocked out he went back to the break room for a Coke, which he carried back out to drink in front of the locked receiving door, swinging his legs off the edge of the dock, watching cars pull out of the lot. By the time he'd thrown his can away and started for the bike, the lot was nearly half empty. He'd cut across a rank of cars and was passing between a red pickup and an old blue station wagon when everything went to pieces.

If not for the shout, that half-choked scream, he'd have been gone before he knew anything was happening. As it was, he just had time to turn partly around and get his left arm up in a half block. There was a mass between him and the light and he felt a bone-throbbing shock to his forearm. He slipped to one side and Timmy Rowan came down past him, holding a tire iron two-handed, smashing a wide dent in the hood of the station wagon. His face was so richly purple that Redmon had the silly thought that if he let him alone he might just have a heart attack. Meanwhile he hit him over the ear with a crosscut to slow him down a little and tried to vault over the station wagon, but his hurt arm wasn't working and the jump turned into a fall. Timmy Rowan was coming around the front of the car faster than he'd have believed possible, the tire iron cocked back, ready to swing again. Pulling himself up, Redmon snapped the aerial off the car and slashed three times at his face with the torn end, opening up a zigzag cut from his forehead down across his cheek, then kicked a leg out from under him as he rushed in. Timmy fell onto extended arms and Redmon stamped him just above the elbow and saw the joint crunch backward.

"Hold up, man, hold up, it's over." Billy Bird snatched him by his shoulder seams and dragged him back a step or two, then jumped away as if he'd touched fire.

Redmon turned. His left arm was still limp. "Where'd you come from?"

"I waited, man," Billy Bird panted. "I saw he was hangen around so I did too but —" He shook his head. "It happened too fast, I couldn't get here." Billy Bird's face was pinched. "I tell you what, this is a mess."

"Yeah," Redmon said. He turned back to look at Timmy, who had hitched himself up against a wheel and was staring down at his smashed arm draped across his lap. The cuts on his face weren't much, Redmon didn't think, though they were bleeding a lot now, but that arm . . . "It's a mess, sure enough." Behind the adrenaline rush of the fight he was beginning to feel very tired.

"Well," Billy Bird said through his grimace. "You better get on out of here."

"Nah," Redmon said. "Probably better if I wait for the cops."

"Ain't gone be no cops," Billy Bird said. "You go on now. I'll get him to a doctor."

"Don't you want help?"

"Rodney," Billy Bird said. "I want you out of here, now git."

"All right," Redmon said. "Fine if that's how you want it."

He bobbed his head and turned. Walking toward the bike, he lifted his left arm with his right to look at it. It bent where it was supposed to, very painfully, but it worked. He could see he'd been hit just in front of the elbow. There'd be one hell of a bruise, but probably nothing was broken. He swung his leg up over the bike. Queer how the most irrelevant movement brought fresh pain to that arm. He'd got the best of it, though, that was clear. Billy Bird was walking Timmy in the opposite direction, toward another car, and Timmy's face had gone dead white; he'd be starting to feel it now. Redmon set his left hand on the handlebar and squeezed the brake lever.

"Hey," he called to Billy Bird. "Sure you don't need any help?"

Billy Bird shook his head, swung an arm to wave him away. Redmon started the bike and flexed his hand on the brake again. The arm would have to work to get him home.

21

AFTER A rain that lasted from midnight till just before dawn, it was a graciously cooler day, with a bounce to it that reminded Redmon more of spring than fall. He was up and out, early, waking from a sleep that had been light but sustaining. In other circumstances it would have been a good-feeling start to the day. His arm had stiffened overnight and sprouted a lump the size of a tangerine. He filled the small basin with water heated hot as he could bear it on the stove, and stood hunched with the crook of his elbow pushed down in it until the warmth unlocked it. It hurt to wheel the bike outdoors, but it wasn't so bad to ride.

He was early at the warehouse; all the bay doors were still shut down. As he crossed the empty parking lot the door to receiving began to rise, the slash of sunlight spread diagonally across it disappearing, replaced by the shadow of the space behind. Billy Bird hooked the pull chain to a stud inside the door frame and stepped forward into the light, cupping his hands around a cigarette. In the early sunshine, the smoke came out sharp blue. It was quiet everywhere; the traffic down on White's Creek Road was no more than a hiss. Redmon vaulted up onto the dock and Billy Bird gave him a crooked smile.

"Good man, Rodney. You just made me ten bucks."

"How's that?"

"Mitch bet me you wouldn't show up, after yesterday."

"Yeah," Redmon said. "Will it make any difference? Other than that, I mean?"

Billy Bird stepped to the edge of the dock and tipped ash over it, frowning. "Maybe not a whole lot. Cantwell's waiting to see you, I guess you got to know. You didn't clock in yet, did you?"

"Nope."

"Well. He said for you not to. If I was to catch you first."

"Uh-huh," Redmon said. "Well, can't say I didn't expect it."

Billy Bird held out his cigarettes.

"No thanks," Redmon said, smiling a little. "They ain't going to shoot me."

"Reckon not," Billy Bird said. "I'm sorry, for what it's worth."

"Not a dime," Redmon said. "But I appreciate it. I had been wondering one thing, though."

"What's that?"

"Is Bird your real family name, or what?"

Billy Bird laughed. "Hell no," he said. "It's Carruthers."

"Carruthers," Redmon said. "Is the man up there?"

"Yeah," Billy Bird said. "He's there."

"Well," Redmon said. "We'll see you. Sometime, maybe, I mean."

It was dark back in the warehouse, with most of the lights still off, making the light at the office window look brighter, whiter, up there by the shipping area. Redmon felt gas-headed, a little drifty, walking up toward it, like maybe he was coming down with the flu. Nerves showing out maybe, but why be nervous? He'd only be losing a little good time, nothing worse than that. He whistled a couple of bars of "Goodbye, Pork-Pie Hat," listening to the boomy echo off the back wall, then stopped as he came near the little box of the office.

"Cigarette?" Cantwell said, scooting the Eves across the desk.

"I thought these things were supposed to be for women," Redmon said.

"Do I look that much like a woman to you?"

"No," Redmon said. "Not really." He struck a match to Cantwell's cigarette, then pulled out a Lucky and lit that.

"Not worried about your luck?" Cantwell said.

"What?"

"Two on a match."

"What luck?" Redmon said. "Anyhow, it's supposed to be three, if you believe in it."

"If you say so. You were the one in the service."

"Where I was at," Redmon said, "one was enough."

"I suppose," Cantwell said. "Coffee?"

"Mr. Cantwell," Redmon said, "we had the interview last year."

"Right," Cantwell said. "Well, Rodney, I'm going to have to tell it to you like it is."

"Shoot, then," Redmon said.

"Now, I wouldn't say this to just anybody." Cantwell set his cigarette down in the overfull ashtray and leaned back, knotting his fingers behind his head. He kept silent long enough for Redmon to begin to wonder whether or not the ashtray might catch on fire.

"Timmy Rowan," Cantwell said at last, still looking up at the ceiling. "He never has been a whole lot more than what I would have to call a worthless son of a bitch, when you get right down to it. Not a whole lot of use, really, for anything other than meanness. Devilment, and such. I think you know what I mean by that."

"Maybe," Redmon said. It was not quite the direction he'd been expecting the conversation to take. Cantwell leaned forward and picked up his cigarette.

"If everything was equal," he said, "I'd a lot sooner get shet of him than you."

Shame it ain't then, Redmon thought. Cantwell frowned at him, almost like he'd heard.

"Well, you see where we're at," Cantwell said. "Fact is, I'd have had done with that boy a good while ago if nothing was holding me back. But the other thing is, there he is laid up in the hospital and here you are walking around in not too bad shape. See what I'm saying to you?"

"I guess so."

"Now, I do know he jumped *you,* Billy Bird told me that." Cantwell reached to stub out a loose butt that had begun to smolder in the ashtray. "But it's what fell out, see, that I got to worry about. How it's apt to look to people around here. I don't know if you take any satisfaction from it, but you messed him up pretty good. He'll be laid up for a while altogether and he's due to get worked on a while after that. Lot of fancy doctors and he'll cost us an arm and a leg on workmen's comp. You see what I'm saying."

"I see where you're going around the barn with it," Redmon said. "I figured you were going to cut me loose when I came in here."

"What it comes down to," Cantwell said. "I called up Branch and Caldwell, don't know if you ever heard of that place?"

"Can't say I did."

"Warehouse over there on Murfreesboro Road. They could use somebody. Could use you, in fact. It's a smaller place than here," Cantwell said. "Real quiet. I believe it pays the same. Sound all right to you?"

"Sounds a lot better than what I was looking for," Redmon said.

"Well," Cantwell said. "You're in, then. I can call the parole people and tell them some kind of thing, if you want me to. Tell them we slowed down here, or you had a better opportunity, some kind of thing like that."

"Yes," Redmon said. "That would help."

Cantwell pulled open a drawer.

"Here's a check," he said. "Severance pay, I believe they call it. Two weeks' worth. They won't look for you at Branch till Monday week. So you can take a little vacation if you feel like it."

"You been to some trouble," Redmon said.

"It's about the best I can do," Cantwell said.

"Mr. Cantwell," Redmon said, "I'd say you're doing pretty good."

The tight line of Cantwell's mouth bent faintly toward a smile. "Well," he said. "I'm proud you think so."

Redmon swung in the door of Mosque 37 and Health Food Restaurant a little before noon. He was hungry, had had no breakfast, and meant to beat the lunch crowd, if there was going to be any such thing. It seemed he'd timed his arrival right, for there was no one in the place except for one man sitting at a corner table, his back to the room. Raschid was busy gluing blue tiles around the onion-topped doorway to the prayer room in back. When he heard the slap of the door he moved back around behind the counter.

"Don't you be getting that mess in my dinner," Redmon said. "I ain't quite ready to die."

"Don't fret about it," Raschid said. "You hauled it all the way over here from White's Creek Road, did you? Should I take that as a compliment to the kitchen?" He turned to the sink and began to scrub his hands with a thick bar of yellow soap.

"Take it anyhow you want to."

Raschid turned around and leaned forward on the counter, his hands wrapped in a dish cloth. "I'm getting the best of you all's trade today, looks like."

"What's that?" Redmon said.

Raschid pointed to the rear corner as the man there moved his chair around to face them. It was Mr. Maddox; Redmon hadn't recognized him from the back.

"Rodney, what you doen, runnen loose?" Mr. Maddox said.

"I guess I might ask you the same."

"Called myself in sick," Mr. Maddox said. "I caught me some kind of bug or other."

"Sorry to hear it," Redmon said. He turned back to Raschid and slid the check across the counter toward him. "Think you could cash that for me?"

Raschid glanced at the check.

"Not a chance," he said. "After lunch, I might could do it. Or you could take it over to the liquor store."

"Don't make much difference," Redmon said. "Well, guess I'll have the stuff on rice. If it's ready, that is."

"Would you mean the vegetable curry?"

"Is that what we're calling it today? I'll have it whatever it is."

"In a minute," Raschid said. "Sit down, I'll bring it to you."

Redmon crossed the room to Mr. Maddox's table. "You mind?" he said.

"Come ahead," Mr. Maddox said.

Redmon sat down. "You really sick?" he said. "You're not maybe just playing hooky, are you?"

"Ah," Mr. Maddox said. "Nothen I hate any worse'n a summer cold."

Raschid came over with a steaming plate, which he set down in front of Redmon. He took a knife and fork rolled in a napkin from his apron pocket and handed it over, then sat down in a third chair, taking a folded newspaper from under his arm. Mr. Maddox blew his nose lengthily into a handkerchief and folded it and tucked it away.

"Believe maybe you *have* got something," Redmon said, spearing a carrot. "Hey, this ain't bad, Raschid. All it needs is a little —"

"You can furnish your own hog jowl," Raschid said, glancing up from the paper. "And somewhere to eat it at too."

"Yessir," Mr. Maddox said. "I caught me a good one. I believe this here tea helps it some, though. Lot of good herbs in it, you know."

"Hey, Raschid," Redmon said. "You been wasting your good herb on this tea?"

Raschid flicked through a few pages of the paper. "I love to see you happy," he said.

"You're taken kind of a long lunch yourself, don't you say?" Mr. Maddox said.

"Permanent," Redmon said. "I'm afraid I went and got myself fired this morning."

"No," Mr. Maddox said.

"Yessiree bobtail billikin," Redmon said. "Cross my heart and hope —"

"For what?" Mr. Maddox said.

"Ah," Redmon said. "I took a piece out of Timmy Rowan last night after we got off. After he tried to stove my head in with a tire iron, that is."

"Who's Timmy Rowan?" Raschid said.

"He's one mean and worthless piece of white trash," Mr. Maddox said, shaking his head.

"That's about the size of it," Redmon said. "He's been riding me ever since I got there, pretty near. I must have said something about him a time or two."

"I guess maybe you did, at that," Raschid said. "Must be I forgot the name."

"I thought that dog was mostly bark," Mr. Maddox said. "He really come after you with a tire iron?"

"From behind," Redmon said.

"I reckon that would be his style," Mr. Maddox said.

"Yeah, well," Redmon said. "He'll be sneaking up on them down at the hospital for the next little while. According to Cantwell."

"What did he have to say about it?" Mr. Maddox said. "Cantwell?"

Redmon shrugged. "Said he was sorry. But he bumped me over to another job somewhere. And he said he'd put it over with the parole board for me."

"No fooling," Raschid said.

"He did," Redmon said. "It was one of the nicest kiss-offs I've ever had."

"You can always count on him, for some things," Mr. Maddox said. "Don't surprise me, really."

Redmon pushed his plate away. "Well, it was good today, Raschid," he said. "Seriously now. You're getting the touch."

"Sure," Raschid said. "And all that for only a dollar, too."

"Well, I'm sorry you're gone," Mr. Maddox said. "We'll miss you out there, you know."

"You know how it is," Redmon said. "You'll live. Probably I was due for a change anyhow."

"Here it is," Raschid said. He folded the paper down into a square. "I'd been meaning to show you this when you next came in." He passed the paper to Redmon, marking an ad with his forefinger. There was a small photograph with print under it reading THOMAS LAIDLAW AND FRIENDS — CLAWHAMMER BAR & GRILL, with dates and times and an address.

"Think it could be the same one?" Raschid said.

"Couldn't really tell you," Redmon said. "There's always some Laidlaws around somewhere or other."

"How about the picture?" Raschid said.

"Can't make it out much, can you?"

There were three people in the smudgy little photograph, but you couldn't really see their faces. The one in the middle was roughly the right size and shape for Laidlaw, though it could just as well have been somebody else.

"These people you know?" Mr. Maddox said, leaning over the newspaper.

"Not sure," Redmon said. "He did use to play a little, I remember. Never was a pro, though, that I ever knew of."

"Just thought you might like to check it out," Raschid said.

"You ever been to this place?" Redmon said.

"I been past it. Never cared to go in."

"Planning to go?"

Raschid snorted. "Ain't none of *my* white folks. You can tell me about it."

"Maybe I'll try it," Redmon said. "Long as I got all this time on my hands."

The Clawhammer was a block or so up a side street off West End. The building had been converted from something or other; its original shape a little disguised by a barnlike extension built off the back. Out of the orange windows of the addition he could hear the tinny flailing of a bluegrass band. He turned off the bike and listened a minute, still in the saddle, then he stepped down.

The front room was hardly big enough to hold a short bar with four stools in front of it and an undersized coin pool table. A waitress carrying a tray of long-neck bottles had to turn sideways to get between the corner of the pool table and the counter and enter a short narrow hall leading to the room in back. There was a man sitting on a stool in the passage who pulled back a door to let the waitress through, and Redmon caught another burst of the music, its timbre lowered now that he was in the building with it. He stepped to the bar and half sat on a stool, keeping his feet on the floor. The bartender did a take when he saw him and covered it as fast as he could. Hell with it, Redmon thought, feeling a bubble in his stomach that might have been either anger or nerves. The bartender coughed.

"What'll you have?"

"A Bud, I guess."

There was a click of pool balls behind him, and he turned to look. Two long-haired, snake-eyed men were playing, both of them looking like they'd just climbed down out of trees. He heard the pop of a cap and turned back as the bartender pushed the tall brown bottle toward him.

"There you go."

"Thanks." Putting his money up on the bar, Redmon bumped his bruise and flinched.

"Whoo, that's a mean lump you got there," the bartender said, picking up the bill. "How'd you get that one?"

"Fell on it," Redmon said. He took a long pull at the beer.

"Yeah?" The bartender winked, shoving a couple of coins back. Odd how talkative he suddenly seemed to have become. "Looks like a what-do-you-call, hema-something or other . . . You ought to get some heat on that, is what you really should do."

"Could be," Redmon said. "I came for the music, matter of fact. Okay if I go on back?"

"It's two dollars," the bartender said. "We don't generally charge no cover but this ain't the regular house band tonight."

Redmon reached to his hip pocket.

"Wait a minute," the bartender said. "This set's about over anyhow, you might do better to wait."

Redmon glanced back at the pool players. The one not busy lining up a shot returned his look with the expression of a wild animal surprised by something it doesn't much like. He switched back to the bar.

"I might take a walk around the block or something."

"Hang on a minute." The bartender walked to the end of the counter. "Steve? You know how much of this set is left?"

"Whyn't we take his money and send him on back?" the man said from the passage. "He could stay over the break. I believe they're on their last number, or just about."

Redmon held up two dollar bills folded over.

"No, you pay that at the door," the bartender said. "Go on and carry your beer, if you want to."

There was a round of applause as he ducked under a low lintel into the back room; the band had just come to the end of a tune. It was dimmer here and Redmon stepped to one side of the door and paused, waiting until he could see better. There was not any stage exactly, just a cleared area behind some mike stands at the far end of the room, lit with a few clip fixtures attached to a pipe in the ceiling. An open path ran back to it through the tables from the door. The "friends" must have been taking a break, because all Redmon saw was one man sitting on a high stool, boot heels hooked on the rungs, bent down over a banjo he was retuning. Redmon looked around for an empty table, then for one that wasn't all white people, but there wasn't one of those either. Might be more room after the set, he was thinking when the banjo let out a kind of low groan.

The player was still hunched over the instrument, staring into the drum, it seemed. The neck stuck up at a sharp angle with his long pale hand climbing around it. Longish black hair hung down the near side of his head, shadowing his face, so Redmon couldn't really tell if it might be Laidlaw or not. The banjo was making a horrible clashing noise, deliberately painful, the rasp of a saw cutting steel. It gathered speed and dissonance together till, at the point where he began to think he couldn't stand it anymore, it began to turn slowly from the sourness toward sweet, breaking out at last into a light easy melody. The effect was of beginning to breathe again, after being strangled for some little time. Unaware of himself, Redmon took a few steps forward down the aisle. The banjo built up to breakdown speed and then took a sidestep into another register, an oddly complex net of notes which stretched out for a time and finally stopped on a full rest. The player shifted position on the stool, still keeping his head tucked. In the dropped beat it was quiet enough to hear the people breathing around the room. Then the banjo walked down a couple of octaves through a slow sliding bass line and fell out the bottom into a gentle tune you might have whistled, a clear, faintly mournful rippling. The last line repeated twice and ended with an upward brush that rang the bright chime of the fifth string as the player stepped off his stool and bowed.

Redmon set his bottle down on the edge of somebody's table and began to clap along with the others. There was a lot of clapping going on. When the banjo player straightened up, his face came into the light and Redmon could see that it definitely was Laidlaw after all, stooping to lay the banjo in a case near the stool, standing up again with a faint smile at the edge of his wide mouth. Two people came out of the shadows on either side to join him, a young woman and a middle-aged man, and the applause picked up as they arrived, but Redmon was paying attention only to Laidlaw. He had hardly changed except for his hair, which was longer and looked shaggy, like he'd probably been cutting it himself. In the black frame of the hair the face was what it had always been, nose slightly flattened from a break, the long jaw and hungry hollows in the cheeks, eyes set back under the bushy, weirdly pointed brows. The applause began to peter out and Redmon looked for his beer, but he'd lost it in a forest of other long-necks, couldn't even remember for sure what table he'd put it on. The house lights came up when he was two-thirds down the aisle toward the stage area and he stopped moving, startled by the glare. He'd been so busy wondering whether or not he wanted to see Laidlaw that he'd hardly considered yet if Laidlaw would want to see him. But then Laidlaw had seen him already and was coming up toward him with his arms stretched wide.

III

In the Cool
of the Day

(1971)

22

LAIDLAW RAN through a changing light across First Avenue at the foot of Broad and rattled over the railroad tracks into a graveled crescent on the far side where people sometimes parked, though there were few enough cars this far down tonight. It was more or less the river bank, though it was built up to where you couldn't actually see the water. The air hanging over the bend of the Cumberland was almost as thick as a fog, and unmoving. It was breathlessly hot, crazy weather for May. He reached over and pushed down the lock on the passenger side and dragged the banjo case toward him over the hump of the gearbox and got out.

A long truck came rattling down from the bridge, headlights passing over Laidlaw as he stood by his pickup, making him squint a little. He locked the driver's door with the key, and as the wedge of light slid off him he started walking back toward Lower Broad. Just by the traffic light he stopped to inspect what seemed to be a long pimpmobile parked on the gravel: lemon-yellow Cadillac with its old paint going brown along a rusted scrape that creased across both doors. Under the rear windshield was mounted a stuffed black cat with little red light bulbs for its eyes, dark now. The driver had gone off too, to seek his fortune somewhere up the block.

The banjo case sagged on its loop of cord as Laidlaw crossed the intersection under a pool of street light and walked up by the locked doors of the feed store on the south side of the street. The pawn shop on the other side was brightly lit but locked behind its gates. A little liquor store beside it still appeared to be open. At the end of the feed store building a pair of feet were hanging out of an alley so narrow you'd have had to turn sideways to get into it, choked with bottles. Laidlaw hesitated, then crossed the opening with a long step. There were too many such crannies in this part of town, so that he always felt there was something unaccounted for at his back. This was no longer his kind of terrain. At the next light he crossed and went hurriedly up Second Avenue North toward a square electric sign that said PICKING PARLOR, the banjo case thumping against his thigh.

"You here for the open mike?" the man on the door was saying. "Left it a little late, my friend. We fixen to finish up at midnight and they's a world of people ahead of you."

Laidlaw passed a sandpaper tongue across his lips; his mouth had gone suddenly dry. "That's all right," he said, making a half turn away. "I'll try it another time."

"Well, I never meant to bar you the door. Come on in and listen. All I'm sayen to you is you might not get no chance to play."

"It's okay," Laidlaw said. "I'll get here earlier. Next week."

"Suit yourself, my friend. We'll still be here."

Laidlaw went out. A wash of relief came over him as soon as he heard the door fall shut. Either it had turned up a little hotter or he'd broken a fresh sweat from nerves. But he had to get over this, he told himself, walking back down to Broad. Too much time spent for it all to come to no account, and his money wouldn't hold out forever either. He turned back on Broad the same way he'd been going, up the hill, dawdling before pawn shops to look at the instruments in their windows.

Past Third Avenue the street was more active. Schools of people drifted among the souvenir shops, mini-cinemas, the bars from whose doors he could hear the pounding of different bands. Fools were abroad in large numbers. Again Laidlaw grew ill at ease, with so many people around him on all sides, most of dubious intent. He stopped to take out a cigarette and for an instant came face to face with Ratman in the light of the Showbud display window. He'd shaved off his beard but still he'd have sworn it was Ratman. He was even dressed about the same: green fatigue pants and a raggedy field jacket. Laidlaw's mouth dropped open so loosely there was a click, but Ratman went on by him with no answering sign of recognition. Laidlaw turned to gawp after him. Whoever it was had Ratman's same scuttling step, but it couldn't really be Ratman, not possible. Ratman was shut up in some hospital for the duration, he wasn't even in the state. One of the Washington hospitals, it was supposed to be; he couldn't quite recall the name just now.

Laidlaw swung back, meeting the eyes of a man and woman who were leaning on a parked car just by him. They both had on tank tops and they were inspecting him in a sidelong fashion as though he might qualify as prey. As the woman seemed about to hail him, Laidlaw lifted the banjo case and went on up to the small lamplit sign of Tootsie's Orchid Lounge.

"Quiet, ain't it?" Laidlaw said.

The front room was empty except for a barmaid, a stout middle-aged woman with a massive bosom propped on the inside rail of the bar. Laidlaw settled the banjo case between the legs of his stool and the bar and set one foot on top of it to make sure he knew where it was.

"Uh-huh," the barmaid said. "Wednesday's a slow night, generally. Most everybody's up there with the band anyhow. You can go on up if you want to, ain't no cover charge."

"I'll wait a while," Laidlaw said. "Could you let me have a bourbon?"

Waiting for the drink, he swung around on his stool. The walls of Tootsie's were papered with thousands of old promo pictures, all the way up to the ceiling on every side, all so faded and greasy you could scarcely make out either the face or the inscription. They looked like they'd had a bad coat of varnish, though Laidlaw supposed it was no more than age and smoke. Through the ceiling there came the muffled sound of an electric bass — *bomp* bomp, *bomp* bomp, *bomp* bomp bomp bomp — and then someone had started singing, something by Johnny Cash, he thought, not quite on the beat. He reached behind him for the glass the barmaid had set down and walked over to the jukebox that was winking purply at him from a corner.

"I wish you wouldn't play that thing." Laidlaw turned and saw the barmaid pointing to the ceiling. "The singer's kind of tetchy about that, you know, if you don't mind."

"All right," Laidlaw said. He carried his glass back to the bar. "I'll just have another one of these. With a little less ice and more whiskey, if you can work that out."

By the time he left Tootsie's they had been asking him to for ten or fifteen minutes, and the band had just started to load out their amps. Laidlaw sprinkled some change on the bar for a tip and hauled the banjo outside. He'd hoped the fresh air might clarify his head, but the air was not fresh. The street had deadened while he'd been in the bar. Some of the movies were still bright but most of the bars had gone quiet and the cars parked along the street were much sparser. A squad car came gliding up from the river, lights languidly revolving, and Laidlaw made a special effort to straighten his steps until it had passed on by.

Nothing but a wasted night; he'd have done a lot better to stay home. At this rate he'd never get the music off the ground, never have anything to show for all the practice . . . No point in drinking so much either. Whenever he got completely drunk it worsened the limp, which now brought the banjo case crashing into his leg with every other step. Foolishness, nothing but foolishness. Still he was not really in the mood to go home, though he was just two or three blocks from the truck and he knew he should. He stopped and set the banjo down to look for a cigarette and from the doorway next to him heard the dim thudding of another bass. Surprised, he stepped back to look at the entry. There was a neon Budweiser sign in the corner of the window, hardly any other sign of life, but when he pushed the door open he saw that was only because the window had been mostly blacked out.

The bar was not exactly lively but it was definitely still open. A railroad bar, just an alley cut back from that front window into the depth of the building. The space was just wide enough for one rank of short tables in the deep gloom opposite the counter. Halfway down the front room they had skipped two tables' worth and stuck the band in there among a nest of cables on the floor: two lean and weary men on electric guitar and bass, and a woman singer who was winding down "Stand by Your Man." No light shone on them. Back of them were pieces of a drum set but no one was at them and they were not arranged to play.

Laidlaw slipped his banjo case between a stool and the bar and sat down with his back against the counter. The band had only a pair of small amps but in the narrow space they were fearfully loud, hammering like a headache. There was just barely room to pass between them and the bar, down an aisle that led through a double doorway in the back. The back room was brightly lit with a fluorescent tube swung over a pool table. Laidlaw stared glazedly toward the hard white light. Two men circled the pool table slowly, and he could see a couple more sitting back there. A tap on his shoulder brought him back around to face the barmaid, a woman of uncertain age with a mannish sidewall haircut, frosted silver along the top.

"Now fella, if you just come in here to rest your feet you better get on down the road. I got to sell you a drink at least, this ain't no auditorium."

"No problem," Laidlaw said. "Bourbon, easy on the ice."

He paid with a ten and sipped; the whiskey was watery but at this point he thought that would do him little harm. After he had drunk most of it he got up and went to the bathroom in the rear, carrying the banjo along for safety's sake. On his way back he tarried to watch the pool game, wondering if he might want to join in, but there were three or four men besides the players who appeared to be waiting for the table, all of them listless under the harsh, crackling light, and a row of quarters was already lined along the dust of the rail. He went back toward the front with his mind about made up to leave, but he somehow let the barmaid slow him down.

" 'Bout ready for another'n?"

"If you say so."

Laidlaw dropped back onto his stool, barely lucid enough even to wonder why. There were just three other customers in the front. A woman with a tall bluish beehive perched on a stool at the corner of the bar, where the barmaid seemed to gravitate in the long intervals between serving a drink. A couple of stools over sat a man Laidlaw couldn't tell much about because his face was buried in his arms on the countertop. At a tiny table by the painted-over window another man was sitting, dressed in a red satin shirt with a western yoke, wearing a ring on every finger. He had hair styled after the fashion of Porter Wagoner and there was a fancy black cowboy hat on the table next to his beer bottle. He kept ducking his head to peep out through the tubes of the beer sign, like he was looking for something out there. The sign threw strange lights back on his face, making him look more anxious than perhaps he was.

Laidlaw picked up his fresh drink and switched around to contemplate the band. A white slice of light falling through from the back caught the guitarist and part of the singer, leaving the bass player wholly in the dark. By the singer's foot there was a gallon jar with a sign taped to it that said, "Band Plays For Tips Only." I bet they do, Laidlaw said to himself. As the guitars lurched to the end of an intro, the singer unclipped her mike from its stand and began to howl out the first verse of "I Never Promised You a Rose Garden." Laidlaw watched her roll from foot to foot, her movement more like the sway of a drunk than like dancing. She was a tall woman with undone straight black hair and an oddly masculine shape, breastless and square at the hips and shoulders, with a small belly pushing at the loose tails of her shirt. He might have taken her for a transvestite except that she seemed a good deal less occupied with her appearance than most transvestites were. She clung to the mike stand as she rocked back and forth, as if it might save her from drowning.

"She's flat," Laidlaw said, turning back to the bar.

"I wouldn't let her hear you say that," the barmaid said. "She cain't hep her looks."

"I mean she's singing flat, that's all," Laidlaw said.

"Yeah, well," the barmaid said. "Lynn Anderson won't available tonight." She moved a few steps over and seized the dozing man by his elbows and flung him forcibly up. It seemed for a second that he would surely flip all the way over onto the floor, but he caught himself and sat upright, shaking just a little.

"Get a hold of yourself," the barmaid said. "You ain't in your hotel here." She smirked and served the man a beer, though he hadn't asked for it, paying herself from a limp stack of bills by his elbow. Then she stepped back to Laidlaw.

"Don't suppose you could do any better."

"I don't sing much," Laidlaw said.

The barmaid smiled. "Thought not. Maybe you could outpick 'em then. Looks like you're pretty attached to that ax, anyhow. Can't take a leak without it."

"Outpick this crowd?" Laidlaw said. "Hell, they sound like they're breaking rock for the county."

The barmaid's eyes widened a little but just then she was distracted by the door flinging open. Laidlaw swung around to see a dark skinny girl in a fringed leather vest bursting in wide-eyed, her mouth open in a questioning round. The barmaid pointed and the girl reversed herself and then skidded into a chair opposite the man with the rings, who immediately leaned forward and gripped her by both arms above the elbows, like he was trying to hold her in focus. The barmaid turned back to Laidlaw.

"Hot dog, huh, how come I don't know you? You Earl Scruggs in a wig?"

Laidlaw's chin slipped off his propping hand and his whole head sagged heavily forward. "Never mind it," he said a little thickly, pushing his empty glass forward.

The barmaid narrowed her eyes on him. "Say bud, I don't know if you really need another one. You look to me like you might have had just about enough."

"You — you —" Indeed, Laidlaw couldn't quite seem to stretch his tongue around the *r*, though he didn't feel all *that* drunk. "You the one pushing'm." He shoved his glass a little farther along.

The barmaid was reaching behind her for the bottle when the front door popped open again and in came two couples, all wearing matching powder-blue T-shirts inscribed "Nashville!" in a bold cursive script. That and their accents marked them as package tourists, most likely, who'd lost their bus or skipped it. Three of them settled at a table, giggling among themselves, while one of the men came up to the bar and asked to have a pitcher. Told there was no tap beer, he ordered four bottles of Miller.

The music had crawled to a full stop and Laidlaw glanced over his shoulder to see the two men propping their guitars against the wall. They headed back in the direction of the pool table while the singer came to the bar and was served a beer. It seemed no one was going to bother to pass the jar.

"Hey, what is this?" said the new man at the bar. "Quitting just when we get here? Come on."

"Break," the barmaid said. In the back room, the guitar and bass player were measuring pool cues; it seemed they were being let into a game in progress.

"They'll start up again after while," the barmaid said.

"Well, hey," the man said, bunching his beer bottles to carry. "But we're almost all the audience you've got."

The barmaid jerked a thumb at Laidlaw. "Hot dog here might pick you one."

The man glanced at Laidlaw, then down at the banjo case. "You really play that? Can you play 'Foggy Mountain Breakdown'?"

"He's Earl Scruggs in disguise," the barmaid said.

The man looked up into Laidlaw's face. "No."

"You calling my mother a liar?" Laidlaw said.

"*Get up there*, you smart son of a bitch," the barmaid snapped. "Put your money where your mouth is."

Laidlaw stood up. A bucketload of bourbon sloshed in him as he moved and for a moment he thought he was going to lose it then and there, but the feeling passed when he took hold of the banjo case, and the weight of it seemed steadying. He hitched the case over to the snarl of cables where the band had been playing and laid it flat and opened it. From the corner of his eye he could see that the little red lights on the amps were still glowing. He found the set screw on the mike stand and dropped the mike to waist height, tapped it to be sure it was live, and stooped to pick up the banjo. When he straightened up, the strap tightening over his back, he saw that the out-of-town bunch had arranged themselves in postures of expectancy, though no one else seemed to be paying him much mind, only the barmaid, whose glare was revealed by the little hooded lamp over the cash register near where she stood.

He scooped the set of picks from the pick box and bent them tight on his fingers. Odd how the besetting nervousness that had plagued him even on the doorstep of the Picking Parlor was gone now, so far that even noticing its absence wasn't quite enough to make it return. Drowned in a lake of whiskey, he supposed, which couldn't be expected to do much for his playing either. He must be drunk enough that even that idea didn't worry him much. Turning away to the wall, off-mike, he brushed the strings to be sure carrying the instrument around hadn't knocked it out of tune, and found the open D-minor chord he'd left there last. The fifth string had gone a little flat and he gave the peg a partial twist, but he wouldn't spend any more time fine-tuning, he had a small mouthful of butterflies now. There was a one-beat pause in which he heard the amps buzzing a little, then he hit the low twelfth-fret chime and pulled the banjo head around to the microphone, snapping into the first phrase of "Nashville Blues."

The first two bars went by automatically, before he noticed how sharply the sound came bouncing back off the wall behind the bar. What that really made was a fractional delay, something to put you off your beat, but he realized in time he couldn't get hung up on it, had better just listen to it inside his head. After that it was all right again, the third string slipping along the crease of his callused finger easily as a silk cord, and then he dropped back to repeat the first part once more. Two times through and then a break, that was the plan. He caught himself looking at his fingers and shut his eyes, then opened them to find the two dots at the seventh fret and hop-scotched over into the melody break that was usually left for fiddle, mandolin, maybe guitar. Now even the echo off the wall sounded right to him, note for note, on the button, leading him back down through the verse again and toward his second surprise move on this tune, a break he'd made up himself that started low and climbed steeply to the high chime at the fifth fret, where it ended. His forward leg, cocked up on the toe to raise the banjo up to the mike, had begun to shake a little bit, and he took a full rest in the fall of the chime to shift his feet, then played through the verse again and stopped.

Only the out-of-town table bothered to clap a little, but in a quick look around the room Laidlaw took in that almost everybody had quit what else they were doing for a minute. Even the man and woman at the table under the window had switched their chairs around in his direction. The two guitar players were standing in the opening to the back room, leaning on their cues, and the singer had moved over beside them. There was just enough light for Laidlaw to see a little of their faces, expressions not of interest quite but the kind of masked attention that bystanders to an accident might have. It was something. He unslung the banjo and put it back in the case and closed it, retying the cord to the handle.

"Hey," somebody said from the out-of-town group. "You're going to quit now too?"

"While I'm ahead," Laidlaw said. His hands were jittering now, sure enough, and he lit a cigarette to cover it, then stepped to the bar to finish his drink.

"You ought not to been able to do that, drunk as you are," the barmaid said in a tone of the faintest curiosity. "You new in town or what?"

"Not exactly," Laidlaw said.

"Sessions man? I know you ain't been playing anywheres downtown at least."

"No." Laidlaw set his glass down empty, palm over it so she'd pour no more.

"Well, if you knew any more like that one you might make something of it."

Laidlaw hoisted the banjo case.

"Bring it on back if you get in the mood," the barmaid said with her sour smile. "Next time you might hit the heavy tippers."

"All right," Laidlaw said.

Three long steps took him out the door. It was not so hot as it had been. His drunk had been hovering a distance away from him the whole time he'd been playing and a little after, but now it dropped over him again, a soggy blanket. He was about to get the whirlies standing, but he made himself walk the imaginary tightrope, remembering how well he'd stand out on the empty sidewalk if another prowl car passed, so late. Nothing became of him before he got to the truck, but when he had hauled himself into the cab he knew he was too far gone to drive.

A damp chill woke him, so he thought, though it might have been a noise or a light. The first thing he was conscious of was that the unseasonable heat had broken, a glad relief. He leaned over to check the banjo and sat back up. A police car was pulled up with its lights locked onto the old yellow Cadillac. Both officers were out and had backed a tall black man against the car. He faced them with a long twitchy smile, fluttering hands, trying to explain something. Laidlaw took a look around; his was the only other car left on the lot and he came to a snap decision he'd be better off moving. He felt sober enough, pulling out, and the police didn't even bother to look after him.

His head hurt him dully all the way home, but at least it made sure he didn't doze off. It was getting daylight, barely, enough so he could begin to see patches of sky above the trees lining the roads. When he had reached the top of the hill behind his house it was bright enough that he could shut off the headlamps. He slammed the truck down over the well-learned washboards, the steering wheel jolting in his hands, then pulled it up short in his gateway. For a moment he didn't get out to let himself in, though he could have used an aspirin, though the truck's noise had waked the dog, who was now scrabbling urgently against the inside of the house door. Elsewhere everything was glassily still, only a way farther down the hill somebody's rooster was crowing on a long interval, every minute and a half. Laidlaw's sheep grazed their way across a pasture still silvery in the early light, their blunt heads all aimed at the barn. He slumped back in his seat, watching them drift along. As trips to town went for him, this one had been pretty good on average, even an ice breaker of a kind, but he was glad to have it over. He sat without moving a while longer, watching the gray hillside gently brightening into green.

23

As the hour pressed toward noon, Laidlaw worked down a row of new corn in the swelling heat. He was crawling along on his hands and knees, thinning the new plants so they wouldn't choke each other out. It was dry, but the powdered clods had mixed in his sweat and gloved him to the elbow with a fine coat of mud. He whisked the soft shoots he chose to uproot into his left palm, and whenever he had a good handful he got up and walked to the fence to toss them over. Just by the garden gate, the dog was flopped full out in the sunshine, legs pushed straight away from her, head stretching up toward the house. Sometimes she seemed to take pleasure in the heat but it always made her very sluggish. She was still as death now, except for a flank pumping slowly as she breathed. Laidlaw dropped a corn stalk on her ribs and she raised her head to look at him gravely and lowered it slowly back to its hollow of grass.

Laidlaw went back to crouch over the corn, crawling and plucking. He left what seemed to him to be the most hardy plants in each bunch, making eight- or ten-inch gaps between them, hoping he was picking the winners. At the end of the row he stood and arched his back against the dull pain in the small of it and then stepped to pitch the leavings over the fence. On a post here he'd left a jar of water and he stopped to take a drink. A strange car was creeping down from the crest of a hill and he watched it half attentively until it had gone by and turned out of sight past the edge of his place, then looked down at the reddish prints his muddy fingers had made on the bright walls of the jar. The heat was beginning to make him sleepy too. He turned back toward the gate and saw the dog shifting herself, raising one leg at a time and bunching them under her to stand. Once up, she walked slowly over to the shade of the maples along the creek and fell out there once again.

Laidlaw stared down the corn rows. They at least were taken care of for now. There was plenty left to do, tomatoes to stake, one thing and another, but it was getting too hot to keep at it much longer. Leave it till the afternoon grew cooler. He dumped the last of the water out of the jar onto the ground beside the corn and went back over to the gate to let himself out of the garden. As he went by the creek the dog raised herself again to follow him. Alongside the path that went up from the creek toward the house, the peacock stood presenting its spread tail and Laidlaw paused to admire the spectacle, turning the empty jar in his hands. The peacock switched its head around to fix its sideways look upon him, letting out a sound which was part croak, part hiss, then turned its back and shook its fan at the road.

Laidlaw walked on. He was surprised that the peacock kept on staying, hopeless of a mate here, and that no cat or fox had got it yet. Even Goodbuddy had lost interest in retrieving it, hadn't come around since that first time last summer, though with the hot weather Laidlaw caught himself half expecting him to appear again. Forgetting the peacock, he walked up the steps, across the porch, and through the house back to the kitchen, and set the mud-streaked jar down in the sink.

Two or three hours in the full sun made the dim of the house seem the deepest black for the first few minutes he was inside. From the kitchen he looked back through the front room, and in the glow of the front doorway he saw the dog rotating to settle across the sill, making herself a sort of canine trip wire. Laidlaw shook his head and peeled off his T-shirt and pulled off his jeans, which were caked with mud at the knees from all the crawling, and stepped up into the tin washtub and turned on the shower taps. There was no curtain and he made his movements conservative, so as not to spread too much water on the floor. The faintest cross breeze ran through the house from the front door to the back and Laidlaw stayed under the shower for a long time, letting the water and the light ripple of air combine to cool him down.

Done, he stepped down from the tub and went into the front room to put on fresh clothes. Back in the kitchen he cut cheese onto a slice of bread, put it on a plate, and added a lumpy dill pickle from a jar. There was beer in the refrigerator which he thought might put him to sleep if he drank it, but he reached for a can anyway. He took a bite of bread and cheese and walked back toward the front of the house, chewing, carrying the plate. In the front room he hesitated and then sat down before the long table that held his tape recorder. Piled around one of the speakers were a lot of cassettes and a stack of padded envelopes. He had been planning to send out another mailing of his banjo tape to places around Nashville that hired live music, and this batch needed to be addressed and needed cover letters as well. He picked up a ball-point pen from the jumble and pulled an unruled pad of paper toward him.

The pen point traced out the words "Dear Music Manager," then slid out across the paper in a shaky spiraling doodle. Laidlaw frowned at the page, let the pen fall and roll across it. Ought to be typed, anyway, but he had no typewriter. People were bound to think he was crazy. The fact was, he had about lost hope in this approach. All it had accomplished so far was to waste a lot of money making the dubs. He had finally paid to have the phone reconnected too, but it didn't seem to be ringing any. There were too many extra banjo players running around Nashville anyhow, with or without him added on, and that was a large part of the problem. And no one seemed to care too much for the idea of a solo banjo act, never mind how he might arrange and rearrange his tape. He had a feeling not many of the people he was sending it to managed to listen to it at all, and he couldn't seem to work himself up to push harder, make calls and go knocking on doors. Not his kind of thing, on the whole, though he'd probably have to screw himself up to it eventually. Or keep on doing pickups, open mikes, play once in a while for a pass of the hat . . . What he could use was some kind of a band, guitar or fiddle or maybe both, and not just backup either but something better than that. A group would go over easier, he knew, but he didn't know where he would find anybody he'd really care to play with.

The whole operation was stalled on the tracks, and this stack of tapes had been gathering dust on the table ever since he'd had them made. Real dust, he could streak his finger through it. A fat fly that had leaked in through the screens came bumbling along toward his plate and he waved it away with the back of his hand, then reached across the heap of cassettes to switch the radio on.

". . . so bear it in mind, we are *all* blood kin. We're all of us cousins through Adam and Eve. Any man, any woman or child, scratch deep enough down in there and you're bound to all the others, down there under the skin. Bound in your blood to the flesh and bone of every other human creature on the face of the whole big earth . . ."

Laidlaw squinted at the flicking needle on the dial of the tuner. He knew he'd heard that voice before; it stuck in his head because it was a different inflection from the average radio or tent preacher. He pulled the tab on his beer can, trying to call back the name.

"Blood calls out to blood, brothers, I know you all know that. That's a proverb, just about, that's what we call the tie that binds. And sometimes, when the time turns on you, blood may call out *for* blood. Because, don't you know it, we're kin through Cain and Abel too . . ."

The trick to the voice was that it always stayed cool and even, not whipping itself up to hoarse peaks and frenzies in the old evangelical style. It was almost as quiet as somebody just barely thinking out loud at times, and yet it had a rhythm that could draw you all the way in and hold you there. Brother . . . Brother Somebody, never mind. Laidlaw got up with his plate and can and went to push at the screen door. A couple of shoves brought the dog sulkily to her feet and she moved out of the way to let him through. As Laidlaw came out the door she sat down again at the far end of the porch, over by the steps. Laidlaw lowered himself into a chair and set his beer on the rail and then glanced over to meet the gloomy gaze she'd fixed on him.

"Well, did I tell you to lay down across the door?" he said. "Then what have you got to sulk about?"

As if those words released her, the dog let her head drop down and rolled over on her side on the shaded planks. Laidlaw bit into his pickle. He could still hear the radio murmuring from the room behind.

"The pride of blood is a deadly pride. Might be the deadliest of all. And pride goeth, brothers and sisters, before destruction, yes it does, and leads the way right up to it."

Laidlaw finished his bread and cheese and set his plate down on the floor. The dog's eyes rolled around to see what crumbs there might be left, none worth her getting up for.

"That's why I'll claim no race nor color. Ask am I black or white and you can't tell it. Ain't no matter anyhow. For I'll claim kin with each and all of you and make no difference. Under the great round eye of our Almighty God . . ."

Laidlaw leaned back and put his feet on the rail, pushing the chair back on its hind legs, cradling the beer can in his lap. Best finish it off before it got too warm. From the corner of his eye he noticed that near the steps a board had sprung and raised two rusty nails like fangs. One more thing . . .

"Have you give any thought to God today, I wonder? Better ask if He's give any thought to you. For if God was to stop thinking of you for as long as one second, then you would no longer *be.* Children of God, I tell you, you owe every breath to His attention. And you know He sees the sparrow fall . . ."

The tab rattled in the empty can, and Laidlaw lowered it to his plate. He slid down till the back of his head caught on the top rail of the chair back, and let his eyes sink shut. What comes of beer drinking on a warm afternoon.

"For thoughts in a single mind to war is nothing but Bedlam madness. Children of God, I tell you, you *must* try to be sane. Be easy with one another, that you may be at ease in your own mind . . ."

The banging of a car door brought Laidlaw back fully awake. He didn't think he'd been asleep entirely, but the circumstantial evidence ran against him. The radio was playing gospel now and he'd developed a slight crick in his neck. Mr. Giles had gated himself into the lot without his noticing and now he was halfway from his truck to the steps of the porch. Laidlaw dropped the front legs of his chair back to the floor and began to search his pockets for his cigarettes.

Mr. Giles clumped up the steps and settled himself in a chair. Spreading his arms on the rail behind him, he looked Laidlaw up and down.

"Put in your own garden this year, did ye?"

"A hint suffices me," Laidlaw said. "Anyhow, you hadn't been by." He pulled his last cigarette from the flattened pack he'd discovered and struck a match to it.

"Dry weather, kindly."

"Ain't it the truth," Laidlaw said. "I've been having to water some already."

"Got ye one of them seeper hoses?"

"Not one that's supposed to be," Laidlaw said.

Mr. Giles laughed. "Might get ye one. They come in right handy at times."

"I wouldn't doubt they do," Laidlaw said, "but you know, money's tight."

"Lord yes." Mr. Giles brought his hands down from the rail and folded them on his knee.

"How you all been?" Laidlaw said.

"Oh," Mr. Giles said, turning his head to look down toward the garden. "Pretty fair I reckon." His eyes switched from the garden into the field. "When ye aim to cut hay this summer?"

"Didn't think it was quite time yet, did you?" Laidlaw said.

"Must have lost track," Mr. Giles said. "Go and get started on it, that's what ye ought to do."

"Lot of things I ought to do," Laidlaw said. "I ought to fix the barns and fill in all those gullies and mend this porch we're sitting on. I could do with about five miles of new fence, if it comes to that. Trouble is, I'm a little light on cash."

"I suspect it'll be high to buy hay though," Mr. Giles said. "If it keeps on dry like it has been."

"Well, you're right about that too," Laidlaw said. "Can't win for losing, I suppose."

"Best get it done then."

"I know," Laidlaw said. "I just don't know how much help I can hire."

Mr. Giles took his hat off and fanned himself with it. Gray tendrils of hair stuck sweatily round the edges of his bald crown.

"Cry poor if ye want to," he said. "Land's bringen a smart price, around here at least."

"I expect I don't want to hear about that," Laidlaw said.

"Know that real estate outfit down on the highway? Clemson and all that crowd?"

"Better than I need to," Laidlaw said. His cigarette had burned out on the filter and he reached down and dropped it through the keyhole of the can.

"Whoowee." Mr. Giles shook his head. "What they been offeren for land . . ."

"They triple it, too," Laidlaw said. "Putting up all those little box houses. Would you sell to them?"

Mr. Giles laughed shortly, shaking his head again. "They ain't made me no offer. We're too far out yet."

"No, but would you if they did?"

Mr. Giles put his hat back on and straightened it. "I doubt it. The boys might want to but I doubt I would."

"There you go," Laidlaw said. "They ain't got anything but money."

"But ye got to have that too, don't you know?"

"All right," Laidlaw said. "I'll get the hay cut, some way or other. You're going to scout me out a mow, I guess? Maybe Earl could come and run it?"

"Maybe Walter," Mr. Giles said. "Or I might could do it myself. Earl's laid up in the jail right now, truth to tell."

"No," Laidlaw said. He made sure his cigarette pack was empty, then folded it double in his hand. "What for?"

"Shot somebody."

"Damn," Laidlaw said. "Kill him?"

"No, we had that much luck." Mr. Giles took his hat back off, hung it on one hand, and began to spin it in a circle with the other. "Didn't even hurt him all that bad. Just winged him, broke his shoulder a little bit."

"What brought it on?"

"Nothen but a barroom fight. Outside the Black Cat there on Highway a Hundred, ye know it?"

"Over anything in particular?"

"Not that I know of. Had'm a big fist fight and it spread out in the parken lot. Earl had that little old pistol he carries, ye know. T'other man had a rifle he got out of his car."

"A *rifle?*" Laidlaw folded the cigarette pack in four. "Sounds like pretty poor odds for Earl, I'd say. He didn't get hit himself?"

"I doubt either one of them could have hit the broad side of a barn," Mr. Giles said. "Not on purpose anyhow. They smoke that marijuana, ye know, and take all kind of pills. And drink on top of that." He stroked the creases of his hat, looking down on it. "I drank a bit myself one time," he said, "but I don't know about all this here."

"Well," Laidlaw said. "He ought to get off, though, if the other man had a damn rifle."

"We're hoping it," Mr. Giles said. "Hired him a lawyer. But they won't come to trial for another while yet."

"What, can't he make the bond?"

"Not without I help him," Mr. Giles said, releasing a pale smile. "I thought he might better stay put awhile, settle himself down some."

"Hell," Laidlaw said. "Get him out and let him raise his lawyer fee."

"I don't know," Mr. Giles said. He looked past Laidlaw to the dog, who was getting up and stretching. "I couldn't tell ye where he's headed. He don't much care to farm no more seems like, and the place can't keep us all nohow. He don't know much anythen else but trouble."

"It's hard times," Laidlaw said. "Anything I can do?"

"Not that I can think of." Mr. Giles put his hat on and stood up. "He wants to hunt him a job in town if he once gets clear of this thing. I'd doubt he'll do much good though."

"Well," Laidlaw said. "Let me think if I know anybody. You tell me how you all do in court."

"I'll tell ye," Mr. Giles said. "I'll stop by the next day or so and let ye know about that hay mow too."

"Oh, and I got the telephone hooked back up," Laidlaw said. "Just a minute while I get you the number."

He went into the house and back to the table, where he scrawled the number on the bottom of the sheet he'd been trying to draft the letter on, and tore the piece off. When he came out again, Mr. Giles had walked down into the yard and was standing near the stone where Laidlaw fed the birds. The dog had followed him partway.

"There you go," Laidlaw said. "Might save you a little driving, now and then."

"Might do," Mr. Giles agreed. He tucked the scrap of paper into the top pocket of his overalls. "Well, I'll be back after while."

"Tell Earl I'll be pulling for him," Laidlaw said.

Mr. Giles nudged up his hat, then turned and walked away. Laidlaw waited in the yard, watching him take the truck out the gate, two-minded about whether he would go stake the tomatoes or try doing something else instead. Dream up some way to get hold of some money . . . The dog walked stiff-legged halfway to the fence and stopped to watch the dust the truck had raised as it settled back all down the hill.

24

OPEN MIKE night at the Clawhammer was more crowded than Laidlaw had ever seen it yet — with pickers; there was no audience to speak of. Maybe it was the warm weather that brought so many of them out, like it did weeds. Outside there was a thick and gluey heat that nightfall had only made more constricting. A pair of window-box air conditioners in the back room of the place turned the air clammy and no less damp. He sat down a few empty tables back from the musicians' circle and put his feet up on his banjo case. Another banjo player in the group signaled him to come up and join in, but he stayed where he was. After a minute he took a cigarette out and lit it.

The music was no better or worse than rain pounding a loose tin roof. Laidlaw couldn't really make out what it was they were trying to play. In the stage area a dozen or more pickers had pulled their chairs into a circle, so that half of them had their backs to him. There were three or four guitar players you could hardly hear. A mandolin and a dobro, both pretty well drowned out. Two worse-than-average fiddlers scraping dismally away. And five, no less than that, five banjos hiding everything else behind a wall of noise.

Here was what people meant, Laidlaw supposed, when they complained that bluegrass music sounded all the same. He tipped his cigarette butt into the neck of somebody else's empty beer bottle and glared in the direction of the outsized band. Five banjos were at least three too many, and in most cases four. Some of them were probably pretty good too. In fact, he knew some of them were, but you wouldn't know it now. You might as well have had the same number of typewriters going, or maybe a couple of jackhammers if they were about a quarter mile away. And that was not all, either. There were ten or twelve more pickers revolving in small groups around the main circle, tuning, warming up, waiting their chance to come in.

He stood and picked up his banjo and ducked through the low door into the small room in front. Two men trying to shoot a pool game had to weave their way among three more banjo players who were trying to tune up over each other's racket in the narrow space between the pool table and the wall. Laidlaw bought a long-neck Miller and sat down at the bar to nuzzle it; the beer tasted a little bit sour but he was inclined to blame that on his mood. From the next room, only slightly muffled, the same tune rattled on and on; like anything else with a thousand legs and no head, it couldn't tell where to stop. He picked listlessly at the seal inside his bottle cap. Any one of these people might have turned out to be the one he was looking for if he could manage to catch them playing alone, but it was plain enough he wouldn't catch them that way here.

He hadn't expected the drive to Smithville to take him any more than an hour or so, but his idea of going the back roads had not served him as well as it might. His map didn't seem to show what was under construction, and one of the roads he picked turned out to be torn back down to the bedrock. Not much more was left of it than a ridge running back down the country, with a lot of mysteriously unattended grading machinery parked alongside it. Laidlaw was the only person who seemed to be trying to use this route, and he had to go at a snail's pace to keep the truck from breaking in half. No matter how slow he took it, the banjo slapped back and forth on the floor of the passenger seat beside him whenever he went over another bump, setting his teeth on edge. It was midafternoon when he finally came to the town, though it didn't matter all that much, since the fiddlers' convention was not due to open till noon the following day.

A big platform had been raised in a fairground area which was not more than spitting distance from the town square. Some way beyond that an array of multicolored tents had also been put up, a craft fair spun off of the fiddlers' convention. Laidlaw took a turn among the booths, wagging the banjo along with him, since he was nervous to leave it in the truck. It was country hippies mostly, selling leatherwork and jewelry and pots. There was a good crowd of customers, mostly from Nashville, Laidlaw guessed, and confirmed it by sampling their license plates on his way back to the square. No doubt they'd all come humming out on I-40 like sensible people, and stood to be home the same way before dark.

The courthouse was new, a squat concrete pillbox, but there was a quorum of old men gathered on the benches out front. The other three sides of the square looked older, the two- and three-story brick fronts aged blood-red. There was a small feed and seed store, a hardware store, what looked like some doctor and lawyer offices, and a small café on the corner, with a sign over its door too faded to read. Laidlaw, who had yet to eat that day, went in.

"Be picken for us some tomorrow?" the counterman said, glancing down at the banjo case. He had big soft eyes and a small chin and mouth. It was slow inside the place, too late for lunch and early for supper, and once he'd taken Laidlaw's order, it seemed like he was ready to talk.

"Hadn't made up my mind yet," Laidlaw said. "Could be I'll just listen."

"Well, you know," the counterman said. "Tell me it's right high to sign on to play."

"Didn't know they charged for it," Laidlaw said.

"Right steep, what they tell me, around fifty dollars or so."

"Damnation," Laidlaw said. "That'll make up my mind right quick."

"Might be I misheard it," the counterman said, and turned to shout back toward the kitchen. "Get a move on with that cheese-burger, will you?"

Laidlaw had a cheeseburger and a slice of blueberry pie, paid, and went back outside. He was leaning on a parking meter, wondering what he would do next, when he thought he heard somebody hailing him.

"Mister, can you tell me —"

Laidlaw turned. A lean sunburned man in a torn straw hat was standing in the open door of a red Ford Fairlane with part of the left front bumper torn away. The man squinted into the sunlight that came slanting down over Laidlaw's shoulder into his face.

"Tell me, would this here be Huntsville?"

"Huntsville?" Laidlaw said. "Huntsville, *Alabama?*"

"That's the one we're looken fer."

In the front seat of the Fairlane sat a massive black woman in a print cotton dress, cradling a very new baby. In the back were a reedy white woman in charge of a little boy with a bowl haircut and a black girl who looked around ten or eleven.

"I don't know where you're coming from," Laidlaw said, "but I'm afraid you're pretty well out of the road."

Doors opened on an old green pickup parked beside the Fairlane and two black men came forward to join the man in the hat. They resembled each other and seemed enough apart in age to have been father and son. Both looked worried, or maybe only tired. Their clothes and faces were filmed with the same gray gravel dust that covered their truck.

"You all look like you came the same way I did," Laidlaw said. The younger man smiled faintly but had nothing to say.

"You say this here ain't the revival, then?" the man in the hat said.

"Not that I know of," Laidlaw said.

"We seen them tents and thought we 'as here," the older black man said.

"It's the fiddlers' convention," Laidlaw said. "You're in Smithville, Tennessee. Maybe one of you has got a map?"

"Nosir," the man in the hat said. "Hadn't got nairn. We had some directions but I reckon we crossed'm up."

"Where was it you were coming from?"

"Straight down from Flynn's Lick."

"I don't know it."

"Round about Carthage, thataway."

"Oh," Laidlaw said. "Well, you might be on the way to Huntsville after all." He pulled his own map out of his hip pocket and took a step forward to spread it on the hood of the red car. "Let's see here, you want to go on out of here on Fifty-six and head for McMinnville, I guess. Once you get there you'll get on Fifty-five and go toward Tullahoma."

"I ain't studied them numbers," the man in the hat said.

"You can just go by the towns, then," Laidlaw said. He took a notepad and pencil from his pocket and began to jot down the names.

"Believe I must've left my glasses to home," the man in the hat said. "Sissy, just you step over here and have a look what the man's writen."

The little black girl appeared at Laidlaw's elbow. Looking down at the top of her head, he noticed how tightly her hair was pulled out to the pigtails over her ears. As he watched her frowning over the notepad it dawned on him that she must be the only one of the party who could read. He straightened up and rested his hands on his hips.

"Who's preaching this revival you're looking for?"

"Brother Jacob, that's the one," the man in the hat said. "Do you know of him?"

"I believe I might have heard him on the radio a time or two."

" 'At's what we did," the older black man said.

"He speaks pretty fair," the man in the hat said.

"He must do if he can bring you all the way from Carthage to Huntsville," Laidlaw said.

"Well, he just don't seem to get up in our part of the world," the man in the hat said.

The little girl nudged Laidlaw in the hip and held the pad up toward him.

"Mister, you got a mighty rough handwriten."

"Hush that," the older black man said. "This gentleman tryen to hep us out."

"It's nothing but the truth," Laidlaw said. "Can you make it out all right?"

"Yessir," the little girl said, dropping her eyes to the sheet. "McMinnville, Tullahoma, Fayetteville . . . and *Hunts*ville." When she hit Huntsville she gave a big smile.

"That'll get you there," Laidlaw said, and turned to the man in the hat. "Here, go on and take this map."

"Oh, now, we wouldn't want to do that."

"I don't need it."

"We'll git there. I wouldn't take it from you."

"All right," Laidlaw said, and turned to point out the bottom of the square. "Go straight out there," he said, "and McMinnville will be the next good-sized town you hit. You can ask the way to Tullahoma from there, I guess."

"We sure thank you."

Laidlaw tore the top sheet from the pad and handed it to the girl. "Sure you won't take the map, now? I don't have anywhere to go but back home."

"Oh, no," the man in the hat said. "We sure thank you though."

"Luck to you, then," Laidlaw said.

He picked up his banjo and walked off to the corner, where he paused for a moment to look back. The man in the hat and the older black man were standing with hands on each other's shoulders, looking out down the road. Laidlaw kept watching them till they moved apart and settled behind their separate wheels. That Brother Jacob, he was thinking as the cars pulled out and fell in line, he must be some draw.

Toward sunset the western sky fanned into red mares' tails as more and more musicians began pulling into town. They set up in tents or camper trucks, unpacked food and drink and instruments, some built fires. Laidlaw wandered through the encampments, falling into conversation here and there. A time or two he was asked to play but he wasn't quite in the mood for it. A good many others seemed to show the same reserve, saving their best licks for tomorrow.

By eleven or twelve the camp was quiet, and Laidlaw lay in the bed of his truck on a pile of burlap feed sacks, staring up into the blank dark of the sky, which had clouded over shortly before nightfall. It was too warm for him to need any cover, but just as he was about to drift off a raindrop struck his face. Just one — he might have imagined it, even. He turned onto his side and another hit his eyelid. Laidlaw sat up and waited, but there was no more rain. A moment after he'd lain back down, another drop tagged him on the nose. He got up and crawled into the cab of the truck, padded the door handle with a feed sack, and tried to stretch out, but the seat was too short for him to straighten his legs. After fifteen more minutes or so he got out and kicked his cramps loose, took the banjo case and wandered off toward the square.

The café was still open, though it had drawn no trade. The counterman declared that he'd stay open on the off-chance, though he looked for a lot more business the next night. Laidlaw had another piece of pie and then a beer, but he was still wide awake when he went back outside. The rain kept dripping along at the same irregular pace as before, no more than an occasional tick. The banjo had begun to drag on his arm, but he was still afraid to leave it untended. Somewhere off the square he heard the faint sound of somebody playing a guitar and he wandered off in that direction.

The music drew him down a street and around a corner, quickening his step. Whoever it was was flat-picking "Black Mountain Rag," clear and true as Laidlaw had ever heard it played. By the time he came in sight of the player the ill temper of his sleeplessness had dropped away from him.

The man sat under a street lamp at the far end of the block. He was short, stubby-armed, and barrel-shaped, and his guitar looked child-sized, though its tone was plenty rich. Laidlaw walked around in front of him to watch the flat pick dip and stitch. If the other was aware of him he gave no sign of it. In the thin bluish light of the street lamp Laidlaw saw something fat and glistening on his upper lip; it looked for all the world like a big black slug. He squatted over his banjo case and went on staring. It was some concentration to be so deep in the music you'd let a slug crawl across your face before you'd interrupt it.

The man brought the song to its end with a downstroke and shifted to acknowledge Laidlaw. Whatever had been on his lip was gone; maybe it was just some trick of the dim light. His face was circular and calm as the moon.

"Evening," he said. "Name Martin Brown. Not keeping you up, am I?"

"Not a bit," Laidlaw said. "I'm Thomas Laidlaw. You play pretty good, don't you."

Martin Brown changed position in his chair. A webbed lawn chair, he must have brought it with him.

"What kind of guitar you got there?" Laidlaw said after a minute had passed.

"Gibson. It's special made."

"You have it done?"

"Bought it at a flea market. It suits me a good deal better than most. My arm's too short to go over the regular size. Won't go easy anyhow."

"It's got a real good sound. Especially for one that small."

"Does at that. What you carrying in that case?"

"Well," Laidlaw said. "Let's have a look." He stood up and slung the banjo to his shoulder. "What will we try?"

"Do you know 'Salt Creek'?"

"Go ahead and start it up," Laidlaw said.

Martin Brown struck a note and darted into the tune. Laidlaw came in vamping softly on the second measure. The guitar sounded out the same steely blue as the light that fell over both of them from the street lamp. When he had been two times through the verse Martin Brown gave Laidlaw the nod and Laidlaw took the break. His fingers succeeded each other smoothly over the fretboard, locked in their known pattern, keeping steadily on, for all his head kept growing lighter, buoyant with some sense of fresh discovery. When he finished his break he took a step back and bobbed his head, sending it back to Martin Brown.

The guitar player's round hand was choked up the neck, fingers busy and fluttering. Laidlaw watched him, marking time himself, vamping the chords out lightly, once in a while following some melodic notion but never more than a little way. The air was damp and caught the light, seeming to enclose Martin Brown in some bright cloud or orb. Laidlaw saw the same glisten appear again at the edge of the guitar player's top lip and was startled enough to almost drop the beat, not quite. This time the other's face was more turned toward the light, though he'd lowered his head a little, not to watch his fingers but to stare at a patch of crumbling concrete a few feet out in front of his chair. Laidlaw watched the shining thing spread out over his lip and up to his nose and all at once he understood it was nothing but his tongue, pressed out of him inch by fractional inch as he tightened further down into the music.

Just as he recognized the tongue for what it was, it sucked away back out of sight as Martin Brown lifted his head and winked to turn the melody over to the banjo. Laidlaw started where he'd been chording, high up the neck, trying an experiment or two, and practically heard his breath catch when he realized the guitar was following him in unison. At the end of his bridge he dropped to the lower octave, playing it straight for the last time around. The guitar was locked tight to the melody, missing no trick. Laidlaw ducked his head as a signal and the guitar's last chord came on the button as he chimed out to end the tune.

"Let it ring," Martin Brown said. His hands had fallen to his sides; the guitar stood balanced of itself, upright on his knee.

"I hadn't touched it," Laidlaw said. He lifted the banjo a little by the edges of the resonator, turning it upward, letting the last echo of sound shimmer out of it like steam rising from a bowl, not moving again till it was all gone.

"Well," Martin Brown said with a short chuckle. "But could we do it again by daylight?"

Laidlaw let the banjo drop back to the length of its strap. "You'll win that flat-pick competition," he said. "I'll bet any amount of money."

Martin Brown shook his head. "Won't be in it."

"You're fooling with me," Laidlaw said.

"Can't play in front of that crowd of people."

"Did you ever try it?"

"Never cared to chance it. If I just even think about anything like that it makes my hand start to shake already."

"I've had that problem once in a while. It goes away, though, once you get up there."

Martin Brown shook his head some more. "I wouldn't know about that."

Laidlaw took a step forward and another one back, then stopped to kick some scales of concrete out of the loose patch on the sidewalk.

"Hiding your light under a bushel," he said. "Where are you from, anyhow?"

"Nashville," Martin Brown said. "I got me a little metalworking shop out the Charlotte road."

"A metalworking shop," Laidlaw said.

"I make trophies and such, to order. It leaves me time to play."

"It must do," Laidlaw said. "Don't you know you could be playing all over the country? And bringing home hatfuls of money too."

"Not hardly," Martin Brown said. "Like I say, I get nervous up in front of folks. I don't care for them lights they shine on you neither, can't see good that way."

"I might could solve that problem for you."

"How's that?"

"Turn them out," Laidlaw said. He crouched down, cupping the drum of the banjo, to look straight into the guitar player's face. "Now listen here, I got some new tunes, some I think you might like pretty well. Would you play again with me at least?"

"Be proud to," Martin Brown said. "Wait till I write you down my address, you could come by the shop most any time."

"All right," Laidlaw said. "We'll just start with that."

Those fitful rain clouds had blown over by the time he got back to where he had parked, and he lay in the truck bed washed in the light of a pale half-moon. Still and all, he was too pleased and excited to feel very drowsy, and what sleep he did manage to get was thin. At the first crack of dawn he woke for good and got down out of the truck, stiff and a little woozy from the mostly wakeful night. His shirt and trousers were damp with the dew that also wet his feet through his sneakers as he crossed the grass back toward the town.

The café on the square still had its lights on, burning into the gray of the morning through the plate glass in front. Laidlaw went in and found the same attendant slouched on a stool behind the counter.

"Been up all night?" he said.

"Oh, I closed up from one to six," the counterman said. "You're keepen me in business, aren't you? Up kind of early yourself."

"Out to get that worm," Laidlaw said. "Could you fix me up a fried egg sandwich and a large coffee to go?"

"Not leaven us, are you?" the counterman said. "Why, the show don't even start till noon."

"No call to stay," Laidlaw said with a crocodile smile that split his face from ear to ear. "I already found what I came for."

25

MARTIN BROWN'S shop smelled mostly of glue, several different kinds of glue with their strong odors all overlapping, while fresh-cut wood and metal shavings ran neck and neck for second-place smell. Glue vapor had almost done Laidlaw in at first. It made him a little dizzy when he first came in, and after he'd been there an hour or so he'd feel the tickle and scrape of a slight sore throat, but it always went away as soon as he was back outside, and after a week of practicing in the shop he seemed to have stopped noticing it at all.

Martin had all the free time he'd claimed and was perfectly willing to use it to play. Laidlaw turned up most days around midafternoon, pulling his truck up in front of the small cinderblock cube of the shop, which was recessed well back from the road and wedged in between two big tire warehouses. When he went in he'd just be able to tell from shifts in the machines and the packing boxes that Martin had been working at his trade. The greater part of the single room was used for the business and was full of heavy-duty equipment whose uses Laidlaw did not fully understand. There were strips of fluorescent lighting hanging from the ceiling, but they were always turned out by the time he got there, leaving all the machinery wrapped in a thick coat of shadow. The windows running in a band at the top of the front wall were so grimy they did not actually admit any light but only displayed it, pressed and flattened under the glass like something in a sample case. From the chair he sat in while he played, Laidlaw could glance up and guess the time from the color of the windows, like looking at a clock.

At the far end of the shop, the opposite end from the door, Martin had cleared a little space for his personal use, marked out by a semicircle he kept swept clean of the wood and metal dust that covered the rest of the floor. Inside this fairy ring was a card table set against the wall, and on it a coffee pot and an ashtray and a six-pack-sized cooler in which Martin packed his lunch and sometimes a couple of cold drinks extra. Facing the card table there was a swaybacked stuffed chair with its arms sagging out to the sides, which was where Laidlaw sat down when he arrived, to unpack the banjo and raise it to his knee. Most days Martin would have already started playing by the time he got there, sitting in a metal folding chair beside the card table, intent on the music, his head ducked down and his tongue pushed out against the base of his nose like maybe a big slice of Spam. He had a strong lamp on an arm and clamp but he had put it in a place where a machine split the beam, throwing a deep shadow over the place where he sat.

For the most part, Laidlaw had become the leader, because Martin was the better at following. Martin had the more accurate ear and could get the notes out to his fingertips a little faster. Also they'd mostly been working on the fiddle tunes Laidlaw had learned to drop-thumb and then rearranged in his new three-finger style: "Sail Away, Ladies," "Jay Bird," "Needle Case," "Forked Deer," "Fisher's Hornpipe," "Soldier's Joy" . . . They had a good number of them down solid now, enough, as Laidlaw kept on saying, to take on some stage or on the road. Martin had decided to handle that as a joke, and any time Laidlaw raised the subject he would just smile down at his shoes, wait a half beat, and strike up some other tune. Laidlaw could do nothing but count out a measure, tapping a toe on the concrete, before Martin joined in. They'd take up the tail of the music's thread and keep on reeling it in till all the windows had turned black above them.

Martin played in his work clothes, a half uniform of khaki pants and a khaki shirt, the shirt cuffs chewed with pale stains that sometimes crossed the seams and ate their way toward the elbow. He wore a pair of heavy black-rimmed glasses, a little outsized on his moon face, which Laidlaw thought might be safety glasses, though he wasn't altogether sure. What he liked to watch more were Martin's hands, which when at rest were plump, a little doughy, entirely inexpressive. They had no sign of personality but for the close-bitten nails. Lifted to the guitar, they danced into a different life, bobbing and weaving, whirling and spinning, racing each other to a peak of the heart's desire. "Blackberry Blossom": Laidlaw vamped to keep time and watched, half hypnotized, Martin's pick hand tracking an intricate pattern over the black sound hole of the guitar, drawing the stream of music up and up like he was pumping it out of a well, till it filled itself completely, till it would run over — then it stopped.

"We're ready," Laidlaw said, crossing his hands on the banjo drum. "Ready any time."

Martin switched positions in his chair and reached across the table for his coffee cup. Back behind a batch of machinery, the small air conditioner groaned and went off. Laidlaw unhooked the strap from the banjo and lowered it into the case at his feet.

"You're not going to quit already, are you?" Martin said, running a short trill on the guitar. "It's early for that yet."

"Well, I'll tell you what." Laidlaw stood up and pulled a half-crushed cigarette pack from his hip pocket. "I decided we need us a fiddle player or something like that, you know, before we turn pro with this thing."

"Is that what you decided?" Martin said. "Where did you plan on getting you one?"

"Ad," Laidlaw said. "Can I use the phone?"

"You know where to find it," Martin said, and propped the guitar up against the wall.

The phone was fixed to the wall beside the frame of the outside door. Laidlaw lit his cigarette and cracked the door for light, then spread the little square of newsprint against the cinderblock.

> A. Wells, Fiddler
> Bluegrass, C&W
> Play for Fun
> Or Profit?

He'd been reading such entries for a couple of weeks now, but this was the first one he had clipped so far, for no real reason but that you had to start somewhere. No more than a feeling . . . An address was listed, the Commodore Apartments, somewhere off West End, and a phone number, which Laidlaw now dialed. There was a rash of clicks and a busy signal. Laidlaw hung up and tapped the phone with a fingernail, folded the ad and slipped it back under the clear wrapper of his cigarettes. There was a hiss and a sigh as the air conditioner switched back on. He pushed the door shut and went back toward the card table.

"You get him?" Martin said.

"Line's busy."

Martin reached over and clasped the neck of the guitar. "Let's pick us another one, then," he said, "and you can try again after while."

"I don't know," Laidlaw said. "It's been busy all day."

"Must be he likes to talk on the phone."

"Could be," Laidlaw said. He squatted down and flipped the case lid over the banjo and began to snap the catches closed.

"Hey, what're you doing?" Martin said.

"Think I'll just go on over there."

"You think you really ought to do it just like that?"

"Why not?" Laidlaw said, retying the rope from the case to the handle. "It's a pretty safe bet he's home."

Laidlaw drove west through stop-and-start traffic, squinting into the slanting sunset-colored light. The apartment building turned out to be not quite so easy to unravel from the snarl of short streets back of Vanderbilt as he might have expected. He made a complete circle around the outskirts of the campus on false trials and tentatives, gradually becoming a little annoyed. The sidewalks were crowded with long-haired children — he automatically seemed to think of them all as children now, though a good half of them were probably older than he. And his own hair was getting fairly long too, come to think ... The apartment building was in sight of the stadium when he discovered it at last, but for a wonder there was room to park.

Inside the building, he walked up four flights of a broad staircase and turned into a hall. Number 7, lucky for some ... He knocked and after a minute or so had passed he tried again, a little harder. The door drew backward on a chain, wide enough to disclose a green eye under a thick shock of light hair.

"What is it?"

A woman's voice. What if the guy works? Laidlaw thought. That hadn't occurred to him.

"I'm looking for A. Wells," he said.

"He's sleeping," the voice said. "Is it that important?"

"I don't know if he'd call it that or not," Laidlaw said. He unfolded the ad from the cigarette pack and held it where the eye could see it. "It's about this. I've been trying to call —"

"Oh," the voice said. "You play?"

"Banjo."

The eye tracked down and took in the instrument case, then returned to Laidlaw's face. He watched the door push to and then open back up all the way. There stood a girl in a man's white shirt and jeans, bare feet with long toes splayed on a wood floor. Her eyes were a little puffed with sleep.

"Come on in," she said, and stood aside.

Laidlaw stepped into the room and set his case down on a worn Persian carpet in the middle of it. His eye drifted around the area, stopping at a half-open door in the rear, through which he could see the corner of a bed.

"No, it's me," the girl said, turning back from shutting the door.

"What is?" Laidlaw said.

"The A is for Adrienne."

"Oh," Laidlaw said. "Interesting name. I kind of thought —"

"You're supposed to," Adrienne Wells said. Laidlaw couldn't place her accent, but she had a pleasant clear voice, somewhere in the middle range. "I didn't want any weirdos coming around."

"Well, now," Laidlaw said. "I guess I got in easy."

"Oh, you look all right," she said. "You've got a banjo. My phone's been out of whack ever since I ran that ad and I didn't want it to go to waste . . ."

"Well, it's T. Laidlaw," Laidlaw said. "The T is for Thomas." He'd forgotten he'd ever known how to flirt.

"Sit down then, Thomas," Adrienne said. "You caught me asleep, this heat knocks me flat."

"It's hot," Laidlaw said. "It should let up a little after dark."

"Maybe," Adrienne said. "I'm going to try washing my face and see if that does any good. Just a minute and I'll be back." She walked through the bedroom and went into another door behind it.

Laidlaw remained standing in the middle of the room. From back behind the bedroom he could hear the sound of running water. A breeze stirred a yellowed blind on a window facing the stadium and passed across the room to another open window in the kitchenette on the other side. The living room was square and sparsely furnished: three chairs, a plush couch, and a long low table, college-looking stuff, or perhaps one cut above. Some posters of Impressionist paintings were tacked to the cream-colored walls. Near the windows opposite the kitchen there was a music stand and a violin case with a separate fabric slipcover of the kind classical violinists tended to favor. Laidlaw's spirits sank a little when he saw these; he mistrusted classical musicians crossing over. More often than not they had too much precision, too much technique, and not enough natural feel for the music. But give it a try anyway, he thought, now he was here.

The door bumped the wall and Adrienne came back into the room, drying her face with a small green hand towel. He took in again how thin she was, half lost in the billow of the outsized white shirt. Her hair was very thick and cut around her face in a sort of helmet shape. Her face was smooth, reserved, with some childlike quality that appealed to Laidlaw, but he was more drawn to her hands, which were quite strikingly larger than the rest of her. They were squarish, ropy with blue veins, and had long slender blunt-ended fingers. The sight of them cheered him up considerably, for whatever reason. His eye tracked them as they jigged the towel up and down and then slung it over the back of a chair.

"So," Adrienne said, glancing over at him. "You want some coffee or a beer or something?"

"No thanks," Laidlaw said. "Let's just play."

"Old Joe Clark" was almost a toddler's tune, though it could also be used as a fiddler's showpiece, and Laidlaw struck it up without telling her what it was. He was still feeling a little mean, enough to think she ought to know it. She let him go once through the whole verse, watching him solemnly across the fiddle, and then came in tight to it as you please. When she started her break Laidlaw experienced a kind of relaxation that began as simple relief and then became a blush of pleasure that spread out from the center of him all the way to his finger ends. This was none of your bland, book-mastered perfection; she could saw herself all the way out on the razor's edge. Laidlaw didn't even *like* "Old Joe Clark" all that much, or hadn't before now. They had started up standing and now began to circle each other, a slow waltz powered by the music, each passing through and again through the sinking yellow bar of light that ran in through the window. The breeze seemed to have turned a little cooler already, lifting and light. Laidlaw kept on walking through his break, observing how steadily she looked at him across the fiddle and bow, as if she'd just become intently drawn into some conversation. The look was a sort of challenge too, and he made sure he didn't let it drop. Every time she passed through the light her eyes shot a brighter glowing green, then sank to a deeper shade, swimming back out of the beam. They played through the last round of the tune together, stopped on a dime, and stood stock still and staring at each other.

"So," Adrienne said, lowering the fiddle. "Will I do?"

"No question," Laidlaw said. "What about me?"

"You'll do."

"You're a fiddler, no doubt about it," Laidlaw said. "I was afraid you were going to turn out to be a violinist."

"I'm both," Adrienne said.

"Ah," Laidlaw said. He tucked his thumb under the banjo strap, raising the weight a little from his shoulder. "Why don't we sit down a minute and you tell me about that."

"Interview?" Adrienne said, moving to a chair.

"Oh, just curious," Laidlaw said. She'd spoken so demurely he wasn't sure whether or not to be embarrassed. He propped the banjo against the couch cushions and sat down next to it. "You're not from around here, I wouldn't guess," he said. "At least, you don't much sound like it."

"I'm from just about everywhere," Adrienne said, shrugging. "I was born in Norfolk. Lived in Florida and then in California for a while."

"Military?" Laidlaw said.

"Navy." Adrienne drew a cigarette from the pocket of her shirt and Laidlaw struck a match and watched her lean toward it.

"Then I lived in New York for a few years," she said. "While I was in music school."

"Would that be Juilliard?"

"That's the place."

"What do you want to mess around with this kind of thing for, then?"

Adrienne blew out a long blast of smoke and watched it swirling, flattened in the shaft of sunlight still fading in through the window.

"Since you ask," she said. "What's available for a second-rate classical violinist these days isn't really all that interesting to me."

"Oh now, you couldn't be second-rate," Laidlaw said.

Adrienne gave him a look sharp enough to have made him acutely uncomfortable if she'd held it very long. "I could even be third-rate," she said. "It's kind of touch-and-go."

"Sorry," Laidlaw muttered.

"I'm not," Adrienne said with another long smoky exhalation. "I'm good at what I do now, and I like it."

"You make a living at it?" Laidlaw said. "I mean, if you don't mind telling."

"More or less," Adrienne said. "I teach a little here and there, but I'd quit that if I could. And I play sessions too."

"Sounds all right," Laidlaw said, sliding his hand slowly down the smoothed back of the banjo neck. "I've been trying to find a way myself . . . You know, to add a little profit into all this fun."

Adrienne fixed her eye on the banjo head. "Have you ever done sessions?"

"No," Laidlaw said. "I never really thought about trying to, tell you the truth."

"Can you read music?"

"I read tablature," Laidlaw said. "I don't think I could sight-read a regular score but I could probably dope my way through anything they'd use a banjo for."

"Half of it's head sessions around here anyway," Adrienne said. "Maybe I could put you in touch with some people. The money's good if you can break in."

"If I wouldn't get in your way," Laidlaw said.

"As long as you don't take up the violin." Adrienne smiled and he smiled back.

"While we're at it," he said, "what about playing on stage with me some time? If we could get some dates. Maybe travel a little too?"

"Especially if I could get paid for it," Adrienne said.

"I know the feeling," Laidlaw said.

"I make a terrible waitress," Adrienne said. "I drop things and I also lose my temper."

"Right," Laidlaw said. "Well, I'm at the place where I have to do this if I'm going to."

"With just fiddle and banjo, you think? Sounds a little thin, doesn't it?"

"I have a guitar player," Laidlaw said. "One of the best. Only trouble is, he's shy of the public."

"Will he rehearse?" Adrienne said.

"Like a demon," Laidlaw said. "I'll get him out there somehow. I've been thinking up a couple of ways."

"Just three pieces, then? No bass?"

"Who needs that?" Laidlaw said. "I can keep time. Just three people and a three-way split. We might not get rich but it could be something."

"Do you sing?" Adrienne said.

"Not where anybody can hear me, as a rule," Laidlaw said. "I could drone along in the background without doing too much damage."

"It might work," Adrienne said, lowering her chin into her palm and giving Laidlaw a considering look. "I can sing. I could double up on mandolin."

"Really?" Laidlaw said. "I don't suppose you're shy of performing, are you?"

"Not since I was seven or so."

"In that case," Laidlaw said, "you must be the answer to my prayers."

26

"YOU MIGHT just want to take your guitar along with us," Laidlaw said.

He was standing with his boot toes just in the circle of lamp light that shone around the card table. Adrienne was wandering around somewhere in the front of the shop among the machines, now and then pausing to run a finger over some surface of one of them. It was a habit she seemed to have picked up over the last few weeks, during lulls in the practice times. Laidlaw couldn't think what it was about them that attracted her attention so. It was a little spooky, anyway, especially now, well after dark, when the shop was so dim he could hardly make out where she was. He had noticed that Adrienne moved around in a feline silence, a quality of his own that unnerved him slightly in others. He kept listening for any move she might make behind his back while he watched Martin fussing around the card table.

"What would I need it for?" Martin said. He took the black-rimmed glasses off and blinked at Laidlaw, rubbing the side of his nose. "Are you all going to take yours?"

"Sure we are," Laidlaw said. "See, this crowd might like to pick with us some, maybe, after the show. In the back, or something. You know, they like to play."

"I doubt they'd be wanting any other guitar."

Laidlaw tapped his right toe on the floor, not hard enough to make a sound. Behind him came a sulfur-blue flash and he half turned to see the bright point of a cigarette lowering in an arc from Adrienne's mouth.

"I wouldn't doubt they could fit a guitar in easier than almost anything else," he said. "You best bring it along, just to be on the safe side. Anyhow, we need to get on the road before we're late, it'll be a half hour to Franklin."

"All right, then," Martin said. He stooped and uprighted the chunky black case of the Gibson and lifted it by the handle. "I'll just follow you on out there, I reckon."

Coming through the light at Old Hickory, Laidlaw's gear stuck going into second and he coasted across the intersection, pounding the stick and stomping the clutch till it gave in. The truck went into third easily enough after that and, picking up speed, he checked the rearview mirror to make sure that the headlights of Martin's humpy old Chevrolet were still back there.

"Ah," Laidlaw said. "Time for a new clutch, looks like. That or a new transmission . . ." Adrienne, on the seat across from him, lit another cigarette without speaking.

"Fire me up one of those, would you?" Laidlaw said. Adrienne passed the one she'd just lit over to him, and Laidlaw reached over the banjo case, upright on the seat between them, groping for the spark. Their fingers brushed and he had the cigarette, took a drag, and tipped ash out the window. There was the flash of a second match, and he looked over to see her face, cheeks drawn, in the small yellow orb of light.

"*You're* not getting nervous, are you?" he said. "Not going to choke on us now?"

Adrienne wrung out the match and sighed a cloud of smoke. One hand rose to rub at the back of her neck. "Not on my own account," she said. "I don't know about Martin, though. It's kind of a dirty trick."

"All depends on your point of view," Laidlaw said. "You might just as well say I'm saving him a lot of trouble not giving him any time to worry about it."

"He wouldn't need any time to worry about it," Adrienne said. "He just wouldn't do it. You know, this thing could just backfire right in our face."

"Maybe you should have been telling me that last week," Laidlaw said. "Where are we going to find another one like him, anyway? The others are all already making money."

"True," Adrienne said. "So far, you have a point."

"Look," Laidlaw said. "They throw kids in the water all the time and mostly they don't drown, now do they? And there's no way possible at all for somebody to drown standing up in the back of the Millwheel Tavern."

"I don't know," Adrienne said, tapping a finger on the windshield glass. "I just hope it works out."

"Well, so do I," Laidlaw said. "Why don't you reach down in that bag by your feet and get us out a cold beer?"

He listened to the rustle of the bag and the faint pop of the cap giving, then reached for the bottle, took a swallow, and set it down between his legs. Out ahead, the Franklin road was bare and a little whitish in the headlights, spinning back under the truck. There was no traffic except for Martin coming along behind.

"This'll cool us out, I guess," he said, sipping again on the beer.

"I'm cool enough already," Adrienne said, "personally. What you need to do maybe is toss one back to Martin."

"Funny," Laidlaw said. "I never have seen him out of the shop, hardly. I don't even know if he drinks."

A little way out the road past the town square, the Millwheel Tavern sat raised up on a hump of asphalt, marked by a small electric sign with the mill from which the name was drawn. Laidlaw pulled in beside Mr. Giles's truck. On the other side of it he spotted Goodbuddy's green Volvo. There were maybe three or four cars he didn't know. Under all the circumstances, he thought it just as well if the crowd was thin, and anyway it was a small place. He leaned over to slip his empty bottle back into the bag and then got out of the truck. Martin had just pulled up on the near side.

"Okay, this is the place," Laidlaw said.

Martin got out and banged his car door to.

"Better grab your guitar now," Laidlaw said. He was aware of Adrienne rolling her eyes at him from the other side of the truck. "Might not be too safe to leave it in the car."

Instruments in hand, they filed into the Millwheel. Inside there was a short counter with wooden stools in front and six or seven square tables covered in worn red oilcloth. The walls were just bare plank, a little smoke-stained, spotted here and there with calendars, election posters, and the like. There was not any stage, but a space at the far end of the room had been cleared for the musicians. The place was far too small to need any kind of sound system and the stage area was unfurnished except for a gallon jar with a note taped to it that read, "For The Band."

"Well, *hey* there, good buddy . . ."

Laidlaw moved to Goodbuddy's table first and introduced Adrienne and Martin, warmly as he could manage. In return, Goodbuddy presented to them the woman he'd brought along, masked in makeup, with a tall slate-colored beehive and long red nails. There was a little back slapping. Laidlaw's smile felt tight as if it were held in place by clothespins, though having to be cordial to Goodbuddy was packaged into the evening, he'd known that all along. He had wanted to ensure that there'd be at least somebody there, and there hadn't been all that many he could think of to ask. Mr. Giles hailed him from the next table over and Laidlaw moved on with a sense of relief.

Mr. Giles was dressed to the nines: a yellow satin shirt with a cowboy yoke, tight white breeches, a needle-sharp pair of tooled boots. Beside his glass of orange juice on the table was a new-looking Stetson hat. He had with him a woman he introduced as "Auntie." Laidlaw didn't much think she was anybody's aunt, though she looked a little older than Mr. Giles and was much more plainly dressed, so that together they looked like peacock and hen. Earl was with them too, drinking a mug of beer, but Walter was nowhere in sight.

The greetings done, Laidlaw drew back chairs for Adrienne and Martin and then sat down himself. Past Mr. Giles's table he could see that a couple more tables were occupied, by people who looked like they'd come to eat, families with a couple of children. The Millwheel served hamburgers, sometimes fried catfish. Well, maybe if they liked the music well enough they would stay on. It occurred to Laidlaw, as he watched the bartender approach with a pitcher and glasses, that he might have bargained for a dinner all around, as well as the free beer. He poured a glass from the pitcher and raised it.

"Thank you, James."

"I know you all'll be good for it," the bartender said, starting back toward the counter. Laidlaw poured out a glass for Adrienne and one for Martin, and shoved the pitcher toward Earl, who refilled his mug.

"Thanks," Earl said. "How you maken it?" He flashed his gap-toothed smile.

Laidlaw took note that he looked reasonably sober tonight, though his eyes were red and a little stary. Maybe Mr. Giles was right and the spell in jail had pulled him straight.

"All right," Laidlaw said. "Proud to see you out and about." That was about as much as he could say on the subject without the risk of giving offense.

Earl ducked his head in acknowledgment and then took a drink of beer. "Shame they ain't got nothen stronger here," he said. "Settle your nerves down some before you all have to play."

"I don't have any nerves," Laidlaw said, cutting a quick glance over to Martin to see if he was paying any attention, which he didn't seem to be. Adrienne was talking across him, saying something to Mr. Giles, and Martin had just tasted his beer and was looking down into the glass as if it might have done something to surprise him. So he does drink sometimes, Laidlaw thought, and as he turned back he noticed too that the eyeglasses were gone, so probably they were just safety glasses . . . Earl seemed to be about to say something more and he moved to cut him off.

"What was it I had to tell you, now?" he said. "Oh, right. You still looking for work in town?"

"Might be," Earl said. He took out a pouch of Drum and began to roll himself a cigarette. "Do you know of any?"

"You know that Esso station at Old Hickory and Franklin Road?"

"I expect I could find it if I had to," Earl said, licking the cigarette paper shut.

"They're about to start looking for somebody to pump gas and train for a mechanic," Laidlaw said. "Man told me so just yesterday when I bought my gas. Name's William Hull, he's not a bad fellow. Fixed my truck a time or two. I don't believe they ran any ad yet, so you might get in ahead of the crowd if you stop by the next day or so."

"Well, I might do that," Earl said, and patted his shirt pocket. "Hey, you got a light?"

Laidlaw flipped him a match book and stood up. Time to get the show on the road. Somebody was bound to say something soon that would absolutely force Martin to cotton on to what was happening. He crossed the floor to the counter.

"Hey, James," he said. "Could I fool around with the lights a little?"

"Suit yourself," the bartender said. "Switches're all back here."

Laidlaw ducked through the gap in the bar and stood up on the inside. There was a flat metal plate with ten or twelve switches fixed to the underside of the countertop.

"What's what?" he said.

"Try and see," the bartender said. "You better just leave them back there some light to eat by, though."

Laidlaw began to flick the switches, and the lights, bulbs in cone-shaped fixtures hung from the low ceiling, began to go out in alternating pairs. He found he could more or less dim them over the tables without darkening the room altogether, and leave the stage area comparatively bright. Not a Grand Old Opry set-up, but it was good enough. He scooted out under the counter and went back to the table.

"Well, lookee here," Mr. Giles said merrily. "Looks like the show must be fixen to start."

Martin swiveled on his seat to look at the bare bright end of the room. "You don't mean it," he said. "Where's that crowd that's supposed to play?"

"Right here," Laidlaw said, coming across with another clothespin smile. "It's nobody but us."

The next few minutes were some of the queasiest that Laidlaw had lived through in quite a long time. He could tell at once that Martin was going to go through with it, or try to; the trap had been timed tidily enough for that. So much the better, but Martin didn't look good. He picked up his guitar case and followed the others down to the end of the room to unpack it, but he was so rigid and tight with nerves that the latches were slipping through his fingers. He would not meet Laidlaw's eye. The clumsiness was communicable and Laidlaw found himself dropping his picks, stumbling over the open banjo case in pursuit of them, dropping them again. Only Adrienne was unaffected, standing a little apart, fiddle tucked under her chin and bow poised over it, looking at Laidlaw now and again with the distant curiosity that a man climbing into a grave he'd dug for himself would inspire. Martin got his guitar strapped to him and straightened up. Laidlaw saw how odd he looked that way, given that he almost always played sitting down.

"Want a chair?" he said, half turning.

"Don't matter," Martin said, staring straight ahead, his lips barely moving at all.

The lowered lights made what audience there was seem a little misty and somewhat farther away. Laidlaw noticed that three more men had come in while they'd been fumbling around, and were now clustered at the bar. From the Giles table came a few whistles and stomps; they were doing an impression of a fair-sized crowd. Laidlaw took a step forward, dropped his D string to C, and plucked it once: *bong*.

"Don't suppose we need an introduction," he said. He glanced at Adrienne, then at Martin, and said in a lower tone, "Why don't we try 'Soldier's Joy'?"

He went into the tune just a little stiff, but he was playing pretty well on track. Though there were some words to this one, they had always done it as an instrumental, featuring banjo the first time through the verse, the fiddle coming in stronger on the bridge, and then over to guitar. After that, they all could fool around according to what notions struck them. If there *was* any after-that, this time. Laidlaw was afraid even to look at Martin now, but he was listening for him, wondering if he was only imagining something mushy and a little sluggish in the guitar, which was only playing rhythm so far anyway, *boom-chunk boom-chunk*, with the alternating bass.

Adrienne finished her first conservative fiddle break and made a scything motion with her bow as she lowered the instrument, her style of flourish. A couple of isolated claps came from the shadowed area of the tables as Laidlaw took a step back, out of the way, and nodded at Martin to take up the melody. Now he knew why he hadn't wanted to watch Martin, who looked like he'd eaten some bad shellfish, or just survived a car wreck, or been forced to witness something indescribably terrible from which he was still in shock. He also totally dropped the cue, just went on thumping the same C chord, eyes fixed hopelessly on something or other well beyond the box of light they all were standing in. Laidlaw, marking time up the neck, had a horrible hollow feeling of free fall.

Then Martin turned around toward Laidlaw and, with one absolutely despairing look at him, attempted to go into his break. It was only a second or so before Laidlaw knew for certain it wasn't going to come off. He couldn't stand to look at Martin's face, just stared at his pick hand as it stuttered over the line of strings in futile little bounces. That kind of flat-picking, once you had missed one note you stood a good chance to miss all the rest, and Martin wasn't just wobbly, he was completely lost. Laidlaw heard him come floundering out of the melody in entirely the wrong place and fasten himself to a G chord with the clutch of somebody drowning.

Clenching his own eyes shut for a second, Laidlaw contemplated the spectral possibility of starting all over again to hunt for a new guitar player. Then he shucked the picks from his finger ends and moved forward, drop-thumbing the tune on a slightly softer note, as a diversion. Martin had pulled himself together just enough to find the right chord again and was back to playing the rhythm line, grimly hammering on. Laidlaw stepped partly in front of him, between him and the audience, as you might move to shield somebody from the wind. When he had played through the verse he winked at Adrienne, who picked up the bridge, playing with a slight jazzy slither this time around. She looked and sounded perfectly unrattled, and that raised Laidlaw's spirits just a little. He reached overhead and loosened a light bulb from the fixture just in front of Martin. It went dark and he unscrewed the next, then reached across Martin's shoulder and got the one behind him. Now they were facing each other, both shut in a triangle of shadow. Laidlaw pushed his picks back on, fingers smarting a little from handling the hot bulbs, and began to vamp along behind Adrienne, who'd come back down to the verse.

"Okay," he said, leaning over to Martin, who inclined his head a little toward his whisper. "You're back home in the shop, that's all. Just once through it, now." He counted Adrienne down through the bottom of her break: "One, two, three, four —"

Laidlaw swung back around into the brighter light, facing front again. Right away he could hear that Martin was doing it this time, the melody sparking out in its tightest pattern, and every note shining like new money. Laidlaw stole a look. Though Martin was in shadow, you could see him well enough this close. His eyes were lightly shut, like someone dozing, and his tongue was beginning to peep up out of his mouth as he played on. He didn't look exactly happy, but he was surviving, and everything he played was coming out just fine. As he came over toward the last piece of his break he opened his eyes and glanced at Laidlaw, giving him the cue. Laidlaw retrieved the lead for the last run through, hardly noticing what he was doing until of a sudden the tune had ended, to a sparse patter of applause.

"Well, thank you all for coming out," Laidlaw said, noticing that his breath was coming rather short. "On fiddle, Adrienne Wells." Adrienne bobbed her head, smiling very briefly. Laidlaw peered at Martin. His face was shellacked with sweat, but on the whole he looked like recovering, like maybe he had just broken a fever. "On guitar, Martin Brown." Another small spatter of applause. Laidlaw sighed, his chest unfisting. "You mostly know me, and you know the tune: that was 'Soldier's Joy.' "

27

ADRIENNE SAT at a small tippy table in the back corner of what they'd come to call the No Name Bar, wrinkling her nose a little against the criss-cross smells of stale beer and the bathrooms, which were right through the thin wall behind her. Laidlaw was still playing and playing, sitting on a bar stool under the little circle of bluish light, sitting down now probably just because he was too tired to stand up any longer. Martin had gone home at least an hour before, at the end of the third and last official set, but she'd hung in there for a while longer, as she usually did when Laidlaw didn't want to quit. She'd finally had enough for one night, though, and would have been happy to leave any time.

Laidlaw was hunched down over the banjo like a big old daddy long legs, knees practically in his mouth, head tucked too low for her to see his face. He'd told her how once in this very bar he'd had to drink himself all the way out the bottom of the bottle to get up the nerve to play before strangers, but now he wasn't self-conscious anymore, and barely aware of the audience either, a good deal of the time. Oh, he knew they were there, in a glazed kind of way. He would talk to them. But she had learned that he preferred to wear through that good-time, half-social part of the evening, collapsing into this kind of total privacy from which the music rose like a trail of smoke from a secret fire — the kind that could gnaw your house down before you had really caught on that anything was burning. It was not the most engaging performance manner imaginable, but it seemed to draw a lot of people in. There were only a few people left in the No Name but all of them looked like they were well hooked. Adrienne took a look at the tip jar shoved up against a leg of Laidlaw's stool. It was a little better than half full, with a comforting amount of paper money, though the bills would be singles and they tended to wad up and look like a lot more than they really were. It wouldn't be getting any fatter either, not this late at night.

She lit her thousandth cigarette of the evening and took a sip of beer to chase it. The amount of free beer she'd been drinking lately, she was starting to get the bloat. But she had heard people say you could live on it. And it used to be prescribed for nursing mothers . . . Laidlaw was playing one of his minor-key melodramas, a long chanting train of melodies building up into a dirge. They were quite good, those things of his, she knew they were, though from the most specialized points of view they could have been called naïve. And a bit on the interminable side too, sometimes. He was not the best musician she'd ever been around, or even close, but he certainly was different. He could play his original numbers like he was pulling a long filament up from the hollow of his bones. And technically he was getting better all the time. He worked out quite well as a sessions man, as far as sheer ability went, though he was a bit moody for the job in other ways.

Laidlaw dropped a foot to a lower rung of the stool and the neck of the banjo cocked up higher, like a counterweight. Adrienne sat up straighter when he began to play harmonics, not just the usual chimed chords but a lucid harmonic melody, the sort of difficult fingering stunt she'd only heard jazz guitarists pull off before. He must have been practicing that line in secret, only she wondered where he found the time. Laidlaw hit his final note, let it whir until it died, and then stood down from the stool. There was a sprinkle of clapping, but the few people remaining were too drunk, or just too stunned with exhaustion, to be up to very much. Laidlaw smiled thinly, glancing foggily around the room. Adrienne watched with distinct relief as he stooped and laid the banjo in its case and began to shake the tip jar into the canvas sack they always carried.

People were emptying their cans and glasses, getting organized to leave. Laidlaw moved molasses-slow, rolling the sack, tucking it in the case under the banjo neck, fastening the lid down. Well, she felt draggy enough herself. But when he got over to her, Laidlaw was smiling and looked a good deal brighter than she'd thought.

"How'd you like that last one?" Laidlaw said.

"It's a good one," Adrienne said. "I'd heard it before."

"Not all of it," Laidlaw said, and grinned. You really couldn't rattle him, not when he knew he'd done one right.

"Okay," she said, smiling a little herself. "You're right, the new bit's nice. Must have taken you a while to whip that up . . ."

"Why, thank you," Laidlaw said, offering a hand to help her up. "What say we go shoot a game of pool?"

"Are you out of your mind?" Adrienne said. "Do you have any idea what time it is?"

"It's Friday night, I know that," Laidlaw said, leaving the hand hanging in front of her. "Just one game. Maybe they won't even be open."

"All right, one game," Adrienne heard herself say, and wondered why in the world she had, as her hand closed on Laidlaw's and she hauled herself upright.

Two doors down was another railroad bar, practically indistinguishable from the No Name except that it had a slightly better pool table and much brighter lights, which set forth all the grime of the place, along with the sorry condition of the customers. This late, they were mostly winos who'd come there to sleep, strewn across the furniture like empty sacks, too far gone even to take note of the door opening or case new arrivals as panhandling prospects.

"Want a beer?" Laidlaw said.

"I'll drown," Adrienne said. "Let me have the banjo if you're stopping at the bar."

She took the case from him and moved to a table in the rear corner, checked that the floor was reasonably dry, and pushed the case under. Then she put the violin case on the chair, turned around, and bent to put a quarter into the pool table's slot. The balls dropped with a rumble and she stood up and began to rack. Laidlaw was coming toward her, carrying two cans of beer.

"No stopping you tonight, is there," she said.

"Tomorrow's a holiday," Laidlaw said, bouncing a cue on its rubber butt end. "Want to lag?"

"Go ahead and break," Adrienne said, and lifted the rack off the balls. Laidlaw stroked his stick and the wedge flew apart, the five ball coming off a cushion and then making a long slow trickle into the far corner pocket.

"Luck," Adrienne said, and yawned on the word.

Laidlaw stuck a cigarette in his mouth and began to walk around the table, surveying it. He was limping a little on his left leg, as she'd noticed he sometimes did when he was tired. He made an easy shot on the two ball but gave himself an impossible leave, which he straightened up to study, his cigarette still hanging unlit. Under the harsh overhead lights his face was pale, eyes two holes of shadow. Adrienne sat down on a metal chair, crossed her legs, and unconsciously took a drink of the beer he'd bought her.

Laidlaw leaned over the table, ready to try something. The door to the street popped open and someone walked in, cast about briefly, and called out his name.

"Laidlaw, there you are."

Laidlaw straightened up.

"Wilbur. What are you doing down here this late?"

Adrienne rubbed her eyes and squinted at the newcomer. It was Wilbur Small, Clawhammer's manager, buttoned up to the neck in his denim jacket.

"Looking for you all," he said, nodding to Adrienne. His wire-rimmed glasses flashed in the light. "Thought I'd missed you clean, but they told me down the block you might have come in here."

"What's up?" Laidlaw said, turning to peer down into the pool table again.

"Mostly trouble," Wilbur said, and rubbed at the thinning patch in the front of his pale frizzy hair. "Uncle Jerry and the band were coming back from Knoxville and the van blew right over on them."

Laidlaw turned to stare at him.

"*Blew* over, you say?" he said. "How bad?"

"Nobody killed," Wilbur said. "Nobody crippled, not for good, but Lord, they got a good supply of broken arms and legs. And fingers."

"I see," Laidlaw said, and struck a match to his cigarette. "Well, I hope they get better before too long."

"Me too," Wilbur said. "Meantime, you can start tomorrow night. After that, Wednesday through Saturday, I could give you a month or six weeks for sure. Maybe longer, I don't know. Sound okay?"

"In theory," Laidlaw said. "We'd have to talk to Martin. What would you be paying?"

"Hundred a night," Wilbur said. "All you can drink and still keep in tune."

Laidlaw leaned across the table, tried a weird bank shot, and missed it. He walked the cue over to Adrienne, who stood up to take it from him.

"What do you think?" he said to her while his back was turned on Wilbur.

Adrienne walked to the edge of the table and popped the fifteen ball into the corner without really breaking her stride. "You pay Uncle Jerry more than that," she said.

"Do I," Wilbur said. "Well, there's not but the three of you, after all."

Adrienne took the twelve with a bank shot to the side pocket, and got a bad leave. She looked the table over, then glanced at Wilbur again.

"A hundred's kind of hard to divide by three," she said. "If you're not all that good at arithmetic."

"Don't forget you get it every night," Wilbur said.

Adrienne pushed the cue ball to kiss the fourteen, sending it idling down the rail to plop into the corner pocket.

"Hundred and fifty," she said.

"The lady is hot," Wilbur said, staring at the whitening felt of the pool table. "Okay, then. Deal? Deal." He turned back to Laidlaw. "First set starts at eight o'clock. It would ease my mind considerably if you got there some time around seven."

"I expect we can make it," Laidlaw said. "I'll buy you a beer on it, if you got time."

"I'm beat," Wilbur said, shaking his head. "I'll buy you one tomorrow."

"See you," Laidlaw said.

Wilbur went out. Adrienne had a straight shot on the ten but she hit it too hard and it bounced back out. She passed the stick back to Laidlaw, who stood chalking it and looking at her across the tip.

"The lady is hot," Laidlaw said. "Nice going."

"Probably we should have asked for two hundred," Adrienne said. "He came across awful easy."

"I wouldn't worry about that," Laidlaw said. "It's folding money, any way you look at it. Now, aren't you glad you came?" He bent over the table, sank the four, and toppled the eight ball into the corner on the rebound.

"Ain't that pitiful?" he said, leaning the cue against the wall, digging a quarter up from his front pocket.

"One game, you said," Adrienne told him. "I'm going to hold you to it."

"You couldn't call that a game," Laidlaw said. "That was an accident."

"Come on, now," Adrienne said, stepping over to him. "I want you to take me home."

Laidlaw shrugged. "I'll walk you to your car," he said.

Adrienne slipped her hand into the loose collar of his shirt, balling fabric into her palm. Her knuckles came coolly against his collar bone. The contact felt completely familiar, one more of the dozens of little accidental touches. She tightened her hand until she felt a little tingle, looking Laidlaw in the eye.

"We'll get the car later," she said. "I mean, home with you."

"Oh," Laidlaw said, eyes barely widening. "All right."

It was still in the cab of the truck, driving out. They sat at their usual distance from each other, the instruments laid between them. Going out of town, she could see Laidlaw's face profiled in flashes against various lights that they went by along the way. Whenever they had to stop for a signal, he would glance over at her and smile a little, then face front again. They said nothing out of the ordinary. After a while the road got narrower, and darker, and they stopped talking at all. Adrienne could hardly see Laidlaw anymore in the dark. She supposed he must be nervous, a little bit at least. Lines of possible conversation floated up in her head — *you do live a long way out . . . seems a little cooler in the country* — but she chose to speak none of them out loud. Though she too was a little nervous it was no more than a pleasant edge, and she was quite sure she was in control, though of what exactly she couldn't have said.

The truck hauled itself up a good-sized hill and jounced partway down the other side of it, then Laidlaw pulled into a gateway between two humps of vine. He got out and opened the gate, pulled the truck through, and shut off the lights and the engine. In the fall of the motor noise, Adrienne began to hear the fleeting voices of birds. She heard a scrape and a clink as Laidlaw shut the gate, and then he was back, on her side of the cab, leaning in the open window, brushing at her cheek with something damp and leafy, something with a dense sweet smell.

"What's that?" she said, drawing back a little.

"Honeysuckle," Laidlaw said. It was too dark for her to make out his expression, but he seemed different, easier than he'd been in town. "Wait, I'll show you something." He snapped off a blossom and slipped the torn end of it into her mouth.

"Taste it," he said. Adrienne pulled at the stem of the little bugle and drew in a fine thread of sweetness. The surprise of it connected to something else that started an electric flutter in her, and she took hold of the top of the door as if she needed it for balance. Laidlaw pulled the door open, bringing her along with it.

"Come on," he said. "This is it." Adrienne went with him along a rough track, lumpy feeling under her feet, holding on to his elbow as a guide. Halfway down, her eyes began to adjust to the night and she stopped to take a look around. Below, where they were headed, she could make out shades of a grove and a blacker square which resolved into an unlit house. Somewhere beyond it there was the sound of water running. On the other side a silvery hill rose smoothly to a crest which was darkly crowned in trees. The sharp lights of a mesh of stars hung from horizon to horizon.

"Fantastic," she said. "You live here?"

"Yes."

"Where's the moon?"

"It went down," Laidlaw said. "It's nearly morning, hear the birds?"

Going through the grass of the yard, her shoes got damp and she kicked them off when they got up onto the porch. Something seemed to be moving behind the door while Laidlaw fumbled at the latch.

"I've got a dog," he said. "Big but harmless . . ." An enormous animal came skidding out as Laidlaw pulled the door open, and she saw him catch it by the collar.

"New friend," Laidlaw said.

The dog snuffled all around her waist and then relaxed. Laidlaw released it and it walked down the steps and trotted across the yard.

"She'll stay out a while," Laidlaw said.

"Absolutely fine."

"She's been shut up all night . . ." Laidlaw entered the house.

Adrienne stepped over the door sill and stopped in the pitch-black interior.

"Here we go," Laidlaw said. A small lamp came on at the far end of the room, making a puddle of yellow light on a cluttered table there, throwing long shadows over the rest of the area. Adrienne came farther in, taking in the bareness of the room; it looked like someone was in the process of moving either in or out. She followed lines of spackle around the bare wallboard, stopping at the telephone mount, where the wall was scribbled over with numbers and notes. Then she walked to the stove and drew her finger along its flat top. Laidlaw had gone into the kitchen. She dusted her hands together and looked down at the blanket folded across the pallet's foot. Laidlaw came back in carrying two glasses and a bottle.

"Nothing fancy, like you see," he said. She saw that he was looking just a little jumpy. "Want a drink?"

She crossed the floor to him in a long step or two, pulled him down into a kiss, and held it. The bottle met the glasses behind her back with a little click. It startled her slightly to find their faces meeting almost level; she hadn't realized she was almost as tall as he. After a minute she stepped back, pulled her shirt off over her head, and took a whirling step in the direction of the pallet. The movement left her a little giddy, with a cool gooseflesh patch rising along her bare shoulders.

"You put all that down and come over here," she said, and sat down on the blanket.

Laidlaw put the bottle and the glasses down on the table behind him, unbuttoned his shirt, and shrugged out of it. With it off he looked even thinner, so thin there was a sag in the waistband of his jeans. Adrienne noticed with some surprise that there was a clutch of what looked like little bones hanging from a long loop of fish line on his chest. Never had seemed like the beads type to her . . . Laidlaw was staring dumbly down at his feet.

"Now you take your shoes off . . ." she said, prompting.

"I know that," Laidlaw said, and reached around behind him to turn out the light.

After a while a deep blue light began to spread across the window above the pallet and the singing of the birds grew louder. Adrienne got a little cold and she reached down and pulled the blanket up over both of them, the coarse fabric prickling a little at her skin. Laidlaw's breathing was light and even.

"Sleeping?" Adrienne whispered.

"No."

She shifted a hand and flattened it on his stomach. Laidlaw reached down for it, and brought it up to his mouth.

"I like your hands," he said.

"Really?" Adrienne said. "I always used to think they were kind of ugly, they're so huge."

"No, they're great," Laidlaw said. "They look like they really can do . . . all they can do."

Adrienne laughed. "I'm double-jointed too," she said. "See?" She bent her thumb straight down to her wrist and held the contortion up over him.

"Too dark," Laidlaw said. "Who says I want to, anyhow?"

Adrienne dropped her hand back onto his chest and let it rest there a moment. She had passed through fatigue into a kind of ambiguously sparkling state that buoyed her up like a small bright cloud. After a little time she spread her fingers and found herself touching the lumps of Laidlaw's queer necklace.

"What is this, anyway?" she said.

Laidlaw sat up and there was the pop of a match, then he lay back down, smoking. After a couple of drags he held the cigarette to her mouth so she could draw on it. It was still too dark to see the smoke come out.

"I guess I might as well tell you," Laidlaw said, lifting the cigarette away. "Don't be startled, now. You've noticed how I sometimes limp a little?"

"When it's late."

"Well, it's my toes."

"Your toes?" Adrienne laughed, then quickly stuffed her knuckles in her mouth. "I'm sorry," she said. "Sorry, that was stupid of me . . ."

Laidlaw laughed softly, a swallowed sound.

"No, but it really is funny, though," he said. "Why, I even laughed when it happened, too."

"When what happened?" Adrienne said.

"Well, I was helping some guys unload this truck," Laidlaw said. "Real heavy cases, big enough to be pretty awkward to handle. It was so hot I didn't have boots on, just these little cotton slippers. And they were these wooden cases with metal strips down the edges, you know. So one of those strips came loose on the bottom and it was kind of sticking out like a knife blade, and" — Laidlaw laughed — "that just had to be the one that got dropped on my foot. It was just like a guillotine, really. Sheered right through my whole shoe, toes and everything else. So I just sat down there and I picked up my toes and I decided right then I was going to keep them. For luck, if you know what I mean. It didn't hurt any yet at all and I just sat on the ground and kind of tossed my toes around in my hand and bled all over everywhere and I just laughed and laughed and laughed . . ."

"Did they think you were crazy?" Adrienne said. "The others, I mean."

"I doubt it," Laidlaw said. "Things like that used to happen all the time. It really was funny, anyone would have thought so, to get hurt in a fool way like that after all the time I spent —" He cut himself off with a long drag on the cigarette, exhaled slowly, and took another drag without speaking again.

"You were in Vietnam," Adrienne said.

"Yeah," Laidlaw said, his voice rather tight. The lower part of his face lit up again in the glow of the cigarette and then it disappeared.

"Hey, I'm a navy brat, remember?" Adrienne said. "My brother was in the air force, too. You can talk about it."

Laidlaw snubbed the cigarette out somewhere and turned on his side, toward her. He brushed her hair back from her forehead and kissed her lightly over the eyebrow.

"I believe you," he said, more easily. "But now we just ought to go to sleep."

"And what if I'm not sleepy?" Adrienne said, listening to the birdsong rising out of doors. It was slowly beginning to turn pale in the room, though there was not yet enough light to see.

"We'll sleep," Laidlaw said, and drew his hand down over her eyes like a curtain drawn over everything.

28

IT WAS Saturday night and the front row of tables had been taken up
by a crowd of stompers, a thick-necked, red-faced bunch of what
might have been fraternity boys, maybe, though some of them
looked a little older than that. They clapped and whistled and beat
their feet and called for the most familiar standards. Banjo was what
they mostly came to hear, but anything at all out of the ordinary
soon left them restless, and Laidlaw thought them a boring audience,
no matter their enthusiasm for the tunes they liked. Coming down
to the end of the second set, he stood between Adrienne and Martin,
a little ahead of them, knocking out the banjo break to "Little
Maggie" just as fast as ever he could. He'd played the tune such
hundreds of times he could hardly hear it anymore, and he was
barely listening to himself now. When he looked down and saw his
fingers whirling over the banjo's white drum they didn't even really
seem to be his own. Just a few feet out ahead of him the stompers
were working up a good flush and sweat, pounding out the beat on
the floor and table tops.

Laidlaw played mechanically on, looking out past the first row
into the darker area at the rear of the room. It looked like they'd
pulled a pretty good crowd, full almost all the way to the back. The
small cover charge Wilbur had tacked on didn't seem to be keeping
anybody away. Behind the last table, the door to the bar was open,
with one of Wilbur's helpers taking money from somebody just
coming in. Laidlaw's left hand drove up the neck in a long slide, his
right spun in a dervish movement, but his eye locked as the new
arrival straightened up into the light and hesitated, looking around
for a free seat or maybe for whomever she might have come to meet.
She was a tall woman in a long flowered skirt, with heavy chestnut
hair parted in the middle and combed back in glassy wings to a long

straight fall down her shoulders in back, and she was a dead ringer for Kate Sevier.

There was the wrong kind of twang and Laidlaw jerked his head back as the end of the broken fifth string whined past his face. He didn't know if he'd clutched and broken it with some especially clumsy motion, or if it was a simple coincidence, or if Kate Sevier's appearance had signaled some sort of gremlin attack. The fifth string was supposed to be wound to a tension peg, which now popped loose from its socket as if the devil had plucked it free, and rolled in a drunken spiral away from him on the floor. Laidlaw shot Martin a *save me* look and stooped, pressing the banjo back against his chest, to chase the peg under one of the tables where it had tumbled.

Martin had caught the melody clean where Laidlaw had broken off and was carrying it tidily forward. Laidlaw smiled, listening to him; he was steady enough on his performance legs these days, though he still claimed he disliked getting up there. Laidlaw guessed he might still be a little fearful of the crowd, but maybe it was the thrill of that small scare itself that hooked him. Laidlaw had been jostled way off balance himself, so much that his hand actually seemed to be shaking some as he fumbled the peg back into its place. Fifth strings were ever prone to break, and so he always had a spare, and he straightened up and felt for his back pocket where it was supposed to be, turning his back on the audience. Martin was playing fast and hard, with his chin tucked tight to his collarbone and his eyes squinched shut. It was a little funny looking, maybe, but it seemed to work to settle his nerves. Trying not to rush himself, Laidlaw uncoiled the spare string and slipped its loop over the hook and fit it into its notch on the bridge. Adrienne winked at him, put down her fiddle, and picked up the mandolin. Laidlaw threaded the string to the peg and tightened it up, listening to Adrienne, who'd stolen up behind Martin on the mandolin and was beginning to drop her own odd trills and echoes into his break. He thumbed the new string and twisted the peg till the note came true, then turned around and joined the others in time to bring the tune to a strong finish. There was a solid round of applause, and he let it go on for a minute or more while he searched the tables in the back, but he couldn't see Kate — if it ever *had* been Kate — anywhere among them. Adrienne stepped up behind him and gave him a poke in the ribs.

"Thank you," Laidlaw called out to the crowd. "Thank you so much, and we'll be back in just about half an hour."

The stompers were still stomping and calling for more, but he turned his back on them and went to lean the banjo into the wall.

In the front room he went and collected a beer from the bar, deciding against a whiskey to go with it; there was still one more set left to play, after all. He drifted over to the pool table, sipping from the long brown bottle. The crowd of stompers had begun to jumble out the door, and he was just as happy to see them go. There was no further sign of the woman who had looked like Kate Sevier.

"Saved you a game, Laidlaw," Earl Giles said, and handed him a stick.

"Oh," Laidlaw said, just slightly startled. "Sure, thanks."

Earl moved around the front of the table, broke, and followed up his shot. He might look a little bleary-eyed tonight, but his aim appeared to be quite good. Laidlaw guessed he must have come straight in from Hull's gas station; he had on an oily pair of jeans and a striped shirt with a name patch that read HARRY.

"Who's this Harry it says you are?" Laidlaw said.

Earl glanced down at the tag and shrugged. "Beats me," he said, and passed Laidlaw the cue. "Nothen but a free shirt so far as I'm concerned."

"Job okay?"

"Ah, you know," Earl said. "They'll keep a body hoppen. I'm bound to get bad knees walken that concrete all day."

Laidlaw lined up his shot and missed as a tall woman with a long skirt came through from the back, but it wasn't the same one. Or at least it wasn't Kate, though he wasn't absolutely sure she couldn't have been mistaken for Kate, maybe at a longer distance. Whoever it was bought herself a beer and went back into the other room.

"What're you moonen about?" Earl said, blowing beer breath past him as he took the cue away. "Dreamen up some new tunes to play?" He turned to a third man, who was leaning into the corner as if someone else had propped him there. "Hey, this here's Fowler, by the way. Fowler, you want to meet the music star?" Earl stooped and made to shoot, then paused to peer at Laidlaw. "Thought you and Fowler might have met up some time or other, matter of fact. Seems like you were in some of the same places, you know, overseas."

"Evening," Laidlaw muttered.

For a minute he couldn't manage to raise his eyes as high as Fowler's face, but when he finally did he was fairly sure he'd never seen the other man before. Never more than once in passing at the outside chance, and more probably not at all. Fowler's face was equally blank of recognition; in fact, it was blank of anything else too. He was of middle height, thick through the chest, with a peeling red face and close-cut curly hair that had been bleached yellow-white by time in the sun. His eyes were colorless, Laidlaw saw. Two holes punched through him all the way to nothing. He wondered for just a second what he might look like to Fowler. Fowler's shovel-shaped hand rose palm-up in a greeting, then fell back to bump against his thigh like it had been shot dead. He's not any more in the mood for this than I am, Laidlaw thought. Fine. He turned his attention back to the table, where Earl was making balls right and left; he looked fair to run the table clean. After a minute, Fowler pushed himself off the wall and brushed by Laidlaw, going toward the bar. When their shoulders grazed, Laidlaw felt the sort of chill he might have had from touching a snake, but he thought he must be imagining that, or it was just the idea of running into Kate again that had left him feeling spooky.

No, Fowler was just another guy, a little burned out, maybe, but no worse. Anyway, he might never see him again, with a little luck. Chances were there was no harm in him; chances were he felt the same.

"Don't mind him bein quiet like that," Earl said. "It's just his way."

"What? Oh," Laidlaw said. "Nothing to me, is it?"

"Reckon not." Earl picked up the short cue to make a shot on the eight ball from a place hard by the wall. He gestured, stroked the cue, and Laidlaw watched the ball bank and roll back into the side pocket.

"You lucky dog," Laidlaw said.

Earl leaned with his palms on the table rail, grinning up. "A quarter'll buy you the chance to prove it."

"Well, I would," Laidlaw said, tossing off the last of his beer. "But I guess I better go start getting us tuned back up."

"You've got a mood on," Adrienne said. "You've been acting funny ever since you broke that string."

Laidlaw did not reply, just kept on driving, staring out over the hood at the long straight stretch of road his headlights cut loose from the dark. She let a mile go by in silence and then reached across the instrument cases to give him a jostle.

"Hey. You."

"How can you tell?" Laidlaw said.

"You're not talking."

Laidlaw's laugh was as dry as a rasp. "Lots of times I don't talk."

"Not like this time . . ."

Laidlaw pulled up to a stop sign, the last fork but one before his place. There was nothing coming, but he sat there for a little while, making no move to go on.

"So keep it to yourself if you like it that way," Adrienne said. "I just kind of doubted you would be that undone over nothing but a string, that's all."

"Ah, yes," Laidlaw said. He shifted gears and let out the clutch, turning right instead of left the way they usually went.

"Where are we going?" Adrienne said.

"Oh," Laidlaw said. "Just . . . the long way."

The road ran ahead for half a mile, three quarters, curving steadily to the left. Laidlaw was building up his speed, maybe going a little too fast. Then with no warning he pushed out the lights, and shifting into neutral, cut the motor too. Adrienne caught her breath as he twisted the wheel hard left. The truck freewheeled through the sudden dark and silence, jolting off the road and across a cattle gap between two fat gateposts, and drifted partway up a drive before it coasted to a stop. Adrienne sighed her breath out as Laidlaw set the parking brake. On either side of them was spread a wide low pasture, bright with the moon. Dead ahead the driveway flattened out into an oval turned upon itself, as it would have done before a house, though no house was there. Farther back and to the right a rougher track led up to a big barn and twisted around to the rear of it.

"I haven't done that, oh, for a long time," Laidlaw said. The truck seemed to settle underneath them, the engine popping and creaking as it cooled. "Not since I was about sixteen."

"Where are we, anyway?" Adrienne said. "Teenage fool."

"Come on," Laidlaw said, and got down from the cab. "Let's go see."

Adrienne got out and fell in step alongside him as he walked up the rising path to the barn. Above, the moon was a bright creamy oblong, covering everything with a cool lucid light. The white *X*'s of trim stood out sharply against the darker paint of the barn doors, and the tin roof seemed almost to glow. In front of the barn was a flat apron of bare dirt, packed hard and coated with a fluffy layer of fine dust. When Laidlaw stopped, Adrienne stopped with him. He was looking back down the slight slope they'd come up, over to where the truck was parked in the drive. The moon was so bright they cast shadows that way.

"So who owns all this?" Adrienne said. "Do we stand to get shot for trespassing here?"

Laidlaw turned his head to face her. There was enough light for her to see the crooked smile. "It's mine now," he said, and pointed up the pasture to the tree line on the hill above it. "My house is on the other side of that hill there, see? That same track goes around the side of it and comes down between the barns . . ."

"Oh," Adrienne said. "I never knew you owned this far over."

Laidlaw walked to the wall of the barn and touched it with his hand. After a moment he began to walk to the left, dragging his fingers along the wood. At the corner he detached himself from the building and walked a few yards across an open space to a circular board-fenced riding ring. Adrienne caught up with him and they turned together to lean back against the top rail of the fence. Now they were facing the front of the truck, could sight over the top of the cab straight down the drive between the gateposts. From this angle, Adrienne was able to see a great scorched rectangle on the near side of the oval drive. Laidlaw lit a cigarette and passed it to her, then lit another for himself.

"There's been a fire here," Adrienne said. "Right?"

"Right." Laidlaw blew out a cloud of smoke, pale and ghostly in the moonlight.

"Big house."

"That was my father's house," Laidlaw said. "He bought it falling down and spent about ten years fixing it. Built the barn and all that too . . ." He swept his arm out, the spark of his cigarette cutting a red loop, then let it fall back to his side.

"What happened?"

"Well, nobody knows for sure," Laidlaw said. "He was always careful about fire. Old wooden house, you have to be. He had a Coleman lantern, though, he used to use outside at night, you know, he liked it better than a flashlight, for some reason." Laidlaw hesitated, stroking the palm of his left hand with the forefinger of his right. "He had some pretty bad heart trouble, which I never did know about till afterward. What they figure is, he had a big heart attack one night just when he came in with the lantern. Doctor guessed it must have killed him right away, else he probably would have got out. Anyhow, you drop one of those lanterns the wrong way and it's about as good as a fire bomb."

"Where were you?" Adrienne said.

"Army." Laidlaw shrugged. "I got compassionate leave for the funeral. Then I went back and extended, I couldn't have stood to come back yet a while, I don't think. I had the horses auctioned and the tack and all, and threw it in with the insurance money. It makes about enough to keep the land tax paid."

"And you never thought about building the house again?"

"Not me. Not with dead man's money . . ." Laidlaw said. "Couldn't do it, anyhow. It wasn't any kind of mansion, just a big farmhouse, but it was old. So old it was mostly pegged, and all that kind of thing. Can't build that back, nobody knows how to, and if they did you couldn't pay them." Laidlaw scraped his cigarette out on the top board of the fence and tossed it onto the weedy track inside the ring. "I don't much care to even come over here anymore, to tell the truth," he said. "It just gives me a funny feeling."

"What was he?" Adrienne said. "Your father."

"I never really knew a whole lot about him," Laidlaw said. "He fell out with his family and came down here from Virginia. I met a few of them at the funeral, only time I ever did. They were more uptown than I would have expected. Hunt country kind of people." He vaulted up to sit on the top plank of the fence behind him. "My father was a horse trainer, horse trader too. And a blacksmith." He pointed off to the left. "He had a little forge down there by that oak tree, it got broken up and sold in the auction. He used to work the horse-show circuit as a blacksmith. He'd go down to Texas once a year for a while and bring horses up here to sell. He boarded a few horses here, and sometimes he'd hire somebody to give riding lessons." Laidlaw lit another cigarette. "He used to have a lot of things going, and always working like a crazy man, that finally killed him, I suppose. He was a stubborn old bastard, right to the end."

"What about your mother?" Adrienne said.

"I didn't have one."

Adrienne poked him in the leg. "Come on, now, everybody has to have a mother. It's a rule."

"Well, I never even knew her name," Laidlaw said. "Either she was taking riding here or teaching it or boarding a horse or maybe they just bumped into each other on the show circuit, I don't know. Anyhow, they bumped into each other and she came away pregnant." He laughed a dry laugh. "You didn't get abortions so easy back then. Daddy did offer to marry her, I'm told."

"He told you that?"

"No. He never told me a thing about any of it himself. I might have just dropped down out of the sky for all I ever heard from him. Wat was the one that told me."

"Wait a minute," Adrienne said. "Now I'm really going to be confused."

"Wat was a tenant we had when I was a kid. Lived in the house where I do now. We used to split a garden with him and he would help with the horses. He and his family took care of me when my father was on his trips, and Wat used to tell me all kinds of things." Laidlaw laughed. "Some of which might even be true . . . He used to like to add on to stories, Wat, but I think this one is pretty close."

"Why didn't they marry, then?" Adrienne said. Laidlaw's hand drifted over and began to knead down the back of her neck.

"He must have been about forty then," Laidlaw said. "The girl was something like fifteen. I suppose her family wouldn't have it, even if she would have. They smuggled her off to one of those unwed-mother places and then after the baby they all moved up to Kentucky."

"And your father never told you anything about all that?"

"He kept me, though," Laidlaw said quickly, his hand working down the muscle of her shoulder, into the cramp he knew supporting the fiddle left her. "He always made me understand that I belonged here. I wouldn't doubt he meant to tell me sometime, but when do you pick to tell somebody that kind of tale about themselves? He never was that big of a talker anyhow, not about something like that."

"It's a hell of a story," Adrienne said. "So that's what's been on your mind all night."

"Well, no," Laidlaw said, hopping down from his seat on the fence rather abruptly. "As a matter of fact, it wasn't."

Nights that Adrienne stayed with him, Laidlaw could usually sleep all the way through. He wasn't sure if it was some kind of love or just the comfort of another presence, but he cherished a secret gratitude for it, whatever the cause. On the nights when he did wake restless, he'd still sometimes go out and run the ridge, but never for so long as when he'd been alone. Adrienne was a solid sleeper and most of the time it seemed she never missed him. Occasionally when he came back in she might be roused enough to mutter

"Where've you been?" and he'd say "Out for a walk," and then she'd be asleep again, and never seemed to remember it next morning.

Tonight he snapped awake as suddenly and rough as something breaking, and lay there staring up into the dark, hearing the rapid saw strokes of his breath. He still did not remember dreams, but this was more an apparition, coalescing out of the moonset night: Kate Sevier, with her calm handsome face of a backcountry madonna. The sweat he'd woken in began to cool and dry along his skin. He deliberately forced his breathing to slow down, and found that he could calm himself by remembering and rehearsing the first time he had met her, the only time they all had, that once in Japan.

Neither he nor Ratman nor Rodney had especially wanted to go along at all, and they all thought that Sevier was crazy and had told him so. Who but a crazy man would want three extra guys along to meet his wife for the first time in however long, a year? But Sevier had insisted on it and would hear no refusal, juggled the leave times and arranged the transport, till in the end there was no graceful way out, so they had gone. It came off much as they would have expected, awkwardly. Sevier kept them confused with the strangely stiff and formal country courtesy with which he treated Kate and all the rest of them equally, while Kate herself behaved with the detachment of someone in mild shock, as well she might have been, having come so far to such a powerfully strange place. Well, for a fact they had all liked her, and meeting in some other way they all might have got along more easily, but as it was, everyone's concern was to survive the few days without it turning out too badly, which it hadn't. It had only been perfectly pointless, and in that it was so unlike Sevier that Laidlaw began to wonder later if he had not had some knowledge of the future and so had wanted them all to meet her at least one time before it came.

Odd how even that thought seemed to quiet him now. Beside him, Adrienne slept steadily, borne along on the wave of her long, slow breathing. She lay on her side, facing out toward the room. Laidlaw turned parallel to her and closed his hand softly over her rib cage, amazed again at what a delicate thing it felt to be, light and fragile as matchwood. Her pulse came into him by his fingers, spread up his arm, and poured into the center of him, lulling him to let his head drop to the mat, and so he slept.

29

LAIDLAW WORKED his way toward the end of the second set against a building headache. Adrienne was fronting the group for the next to last number, playing the mandolin, singing out in her sharp clear voice "Shady Grove."

> My true love slighted me,
> Tore my heart in two . . .
> Because I was a pore little feller
> And I didn't know how to do . . .

Laidlaw muttered the chorus behind her, then swung the banjo around to the mike and drop-thumbed the high break on the open D-minor chord. As Adrienne picked up the second verse, he swung back. Every time he moved his head he felt a sort of thump that wasn't quite pain yet, just starting to head in that direction. He chunked the banjo softly, marking time while Martin started into his break, and scanned the front of the crowd. No stompers tonight, and he wouldn't complain of it. Goodbuddy was there, along with one of the overachieved young women whose company he favored, a pale blonde tonight, cased in such a hard shell of makeup and hair spray that she might have been dipped in shellac. At the next table to the right were some of the Giles group: Earl, Fowler, who now seemed to turn up almost everywhere Earl did, even Walter tonight, which was unusual, and a couple more Laidlaw couldn't quite put names to. Mr. Giles himself was not attending, Nashville being farther than he usually cared to drive at night. Laidlaw joined Adrienne in the next chorus, and turned back to study how Walter and Goodbuddy sat in nearly identical poses, leaning forward onto heavily folded arms, both faces blank and meaty. You might almost take it for a family resemblance, at least in this dim light . . .

He sang through the final chorus and chimed softly on the twelfth fret at the end of the song, then turned his back to the tables and began to retune to double C. Adrienne and Martin stepped toward chairs outside the lights, and Martin reached to the wall switch to turn off the two side spots, the last number of this set being Laidlaw's solo. Adrienne gave him a wink from the shadows, and he smiled faintly back, trying to concentrate on his tuning as his head gave him another dull thump. He had the feeling that something specifically unpleasant was just at his back, but maybe it was only Fowler. They'd had another of those queer disconnected meetings at the bar before the show, in which nothing had happened, nothing at all; whatever he might have in common with Fowler was nothing he wanted to discover. The tune he would play, just recently finished, had been partially inspired by that irrational revulsion . . . He hooked his toe around the leg of a metal stool and dragged it toward the front mike and sat down, hunched with his head low over the banjo, so that he saw only the drum and a patch of the floor between his knees. After he'd been a moment in this position the swell of conversation that had risen in the room rolled back and he opened his hands and began to play.

Nausea. The first part of the tune was meant to express a fully physical inward writhing, along with its companionate mental condition: unease climbing the scale toward terror. That part went on for a long time and as unendurably as he could make it come out. He kept his head dropped so low that the back of his neck began to ache, and after a minute he shut his eyes and saw blue, blue, purple, a bruise blackening as it rose. The music turned to a conjure spell and he used it to fasten a ring around the bruise and press it tighter and darker until when he switched over toward the less constrained melody it burst into a free flow of blood. As he played on, the melody gained speed and gradually sweetened its temper, relaxing as the first venom ran swiftly from it, becoming itself a bloodletting wound to dizzy, to intoxicate, and finally clear the head.

Laidlaw was weak but lucid when at last he'd finished it. He stood up a little shakily. The looming headache was completely gone. There was some applause but he could only take the vaguest notice of it. Down at the end of the front aisle between the tables, against the light of the doorway to the outer bar, there was a shadow of something terribly familiar, and an instinct let him know that this must be what the music had conjured up. Already now the shadow moved toward him as he stooped to prop the banjo against the stool and straightened up again. Somewhere out of sight Wilbur switched on the house fixtures and showered light all over the room, and

Laidlaw saw clearly what the shadow resolved to at the same time as he began to walk out toward it. Among the tables people had turned toward each other and begun to talk, but he seemed to hear nothing but a sort of high whine. As he went forward his arms lifted giddily from his sides and floated in the air, though he had sent them no instruction, and as soon as he was near enough his hands shot out and clamped on Rodney's upper arms.

"*Where did you come from?*" Laidlaw said, his voice breaking back to a whisper. Rodney had a grip on him too now, a tight clasp just behind his elbows, and his grin was wide enough to show the pink of his gums.

"From going to and fro in the earth," Rodney said. "And from walking up and down in it."

"No, man," Laidlaw said. His eyes felt hard and shiny. "You're not the devil . . ." His next words formed themselves with no forethought whatever. "You're the only one that knows me now."

"Man," Rodney said, with a slight shiver in his voice. "Don't you know that can be the devil too?"

Laidlaw shook his head and pitched himself forward to seize Rodney in a blinding hard hug that squeezed his own eyes shut. Rodney's knuckles were gouged into the muscles at the small of his back. His mouth had come slightly open against Rodney's neck and he could taste a faint sweaty sourness there. For a time he was aware of little else but the hiss and pound of his own interior as they rocked lightly together from the knee.

Then someone brushed Laidlaw and he raised his head and took a half step back. People had begun to get up from their tables and drift out of the room. He stood completely still, staring at Rodney. They were still holding on to each other by the elbows and leaning a little toward each other, as if for balance. Someone ran into Laidlaw fairly hard from behind, hard enough to nearly make him stumble. It might have been either Fowler or Walter, who were both shouldering by, but neither of them looked back and Laidlaw didn't think anything about it.

"Well," he said.

"Yeah," Rodney said.

"I've got one more set to do," Laidlaw said. "Come on and let's find you a seat. I'll get you on my drinks tab. You can stick around till later, right?"

"Oh yeah," Rodney said. "I'll be sticking tight."

*   *   *

"I thought I must've been dreaming there for a minute," Laidlaw said.

He drew on his cigarette and the head glowed back at him, reflected in the windshield of the truck. They'd parked at the back of a 7-Eleven where they'd bought a six-pack of beer that now sat in the damp bag between them on the seat. Laidlaw could have run free drinks at the Clawhammer but the bars were near closing by the time the last set was done, and besides, both of them still found it easier to be out in the dark, however odd it might have seemed to hold to that preference here.

"I had some doubts myself," Redmon said. "Saw that ad in the paper and just got a wild hair to come see if it might be you."

"Well, now," Laidlaw said. He couldn't quite make up his mind whether he should be thinking of him as Rodney or the old childhood name of Pepper. "What you been up to, all this while?"

"Nothing too special," Redmon said.

"Working?"

"Yeah." Redmon struck a match, looked at it a second or two, and blew it out. "I got a warehouse job just at the minute. Run a forklift and so on. Stack a whole mess of boxes."

A long low car pulled in off the road, its headlights sweeping across the truck as it turned to park around the corner at the front of the 7-Eleven building. Laidlaw heard the door bang, then a scrape of feet. Rodney's face looked stony in the harsh radiance of the burglar light behind the store.

"I had me an office job for a while there," Rodney said. "White collar. But it didn't work out quite the way I thought in the end."

"Well," Laidlaw said uncertainly. "Whatever it takes to keep you going, I guess."

"I suppose," Redmon said, dipping into the bag for a fresh beer. He flinched a little as his elbow grazed the seat back.

"That is one big momma bruise you got there," Laidlaw said. "How'd you come by that one?"

"Oh, you know," Rodney said. "Somebody just up and tried to club me dead, is all." His mouth pared back from his teeth for a flash. "But it appears he didn't quite succeed."

Laidlaw laughed a little uneasily. "Is that the truth?" he said.

"A righteous fact," Redmon said. "But hey, man, I'm ahead till yet."

"You ought to be getting some heat on that, I'd say."

"That's what everybody keeps telling me," Redmon said. "They must all think I don't know it."

"Well, shut my mouth," Laidlaw said.

"Ah, never mind," Redmon said. "Maybe I'm a little touchy. The sucker does hurt and that's the truth."

The car door banged once more and Laidlaw heard the motor crank. The headlight beam swung across them again as the car turned around and pointed into the road. Who was it, back there in the bar, who'd bumped him from behind? He blinked trying to picture the scene as others would have seen it. The car jounced out onto the road with a slight squeal of its tires. Laidlaw scraped his cigarette out on the outside of his door and let the dead butt drop down to the asphalt.

"What have you been doing yourself?" Redmon said. "Just what I seen you tonight, or you got a day job to go with it?"

"Pretty much what you saw, up to now."

"There a living in it?"

Laidlaw cracked another beer. "Almost, maybe. With some luck. This gig here pays real well, it's the best we've had by a long chalk. But it's about the first one we've had that paid anything at all to speak of, and I don't know how long it's likely to last. Still, I'm hoping something may come of it. We haven't been playing together that long anyhow, so I don't have any call to complain just yet."

"Well, sounds pretty good. If you like that kind of thing. You've got a lot better yourself than I remembered, got a fast hand on the banjo now."

"Thanks," Laidlaw said. "It's how I've been spending most of my time. I'd been kind of getting by on benefits and things, you know, but I'm about to the end of that now, so I need to make this music go or else I don't know what." He shrugged. "I grow a garden, a kind of one anyhow, and freeze what I can for the winter. I got some lambs to send to the packing house here before too long. But I doubt I'd really cut it as a farmer."

"You and me both," Redmon said. "Where are you living at, anyway?"

"In you all's old house," Laidlaw said. "Didn't you know?"

"How would I know?" Redmon said. "Are you really living in there?"

"Where else?" Laidlaw said.

"Well, damn if I ever thought about it," Redmon said. "I was out by there one day last winter, in fact. Saw smoke in the chimney but I never dreamed it was you."

"Who'd you think?"

"Some tenant," Redmon said. "I just never had a picture of you in there, somehow."

"I'd been in there plenty of times before," Laidlaw said. "Back when you all used to dandle me on your knee . . ." He lit another cigarette and passed the pack to Rodney. "I had tenants in there a while but they weren't any 'count, just let the place fall down, practically. So I propped it up a little and moved on in myself. Suits me fine, tell you the truth. I don't even use more than half of it, I just closed off the rest."

"Whole place belongs to you now, don't it?" Redmon said. "I guess you might sell it off if you got too hard up. Should keep you going quite a spell."

"Never," Laidlaw said. "I plan to stay. I could even live off of it if I had to for a while but it would be more than a full-time job."

"Don't I know it," Redmon said.

"Right," Laidlaw said. "This time last year, I could hire a little help. Now it's getting harder to find the money for it . . . I'd been hiring Mr. Giles and them, whenever I could pay them anything, that is."

Redmon turned and spat out the window.

"I know you don't much like him," Laidlaw said.

"I know he don't like niggers," Redmon said.

"Well," Laidlaw said. "I could do without the boys myself if it came down to it, though I'd sooner Earl than Walter. But Mr. Giles has got his good side, I'd say."

"It don't show where I can see it," Redmon said. "He ain't likely to be any good to me."

"Maybe you have a point," Laidlaw said. "Sorry I brought it up. The boys were in there tonight, I don't know if you saw them."

"Oh yeah," Redmon said. "They did come kind of jostling by. I wasn't paying all that close attention."

"Me neither," Laidlaw said. "But now I think of it, it's kind of funny they didn't come back in for the last set. They're usually pretty faithful."

"Can't say I missed them."

"Oh, and you know who else was there tonight?"

"Don't make me worry about it."

"Goodbuddy."

Redmon rolled his head on the back of the seat and laughed. "I missed him clean. You see much of him?"

"Not more than I can help it, really. He does drop in on the shows, though, and you know, beggars can't be choosers. Don't usually stay too long anyhow. He must've gone out at the break with the rest of them."

"Does he run with the Giles crowd now? I wouldn't really've thought it."

"You wouldn't say he *runs* with them. They act like they know each other, though. And you know Goodbuddy is just like a dog, he'll nose up to anybody for at least a little while."

"Ain't it the truth?" Redmon said. "Well, you all put on a pretty good show, anyway. That one you were playing right when I came in, where'd you get that from?"

"Made it up."

"Hey, that ain't bad at all. You make up all them other funny tunes?"

"Had a whole year to do it in."

Redmon opened his hands and examined his fingers, spread on the dash. "I guess you would have, at that," he said. "How did the end of your hitch turn out?"

"Boring, mostly," Laidlaw said. "I didn't do anything but sit around Nha Trang."

"Is that right? I kind of bet myself you'd get restless and cut back for the bush."

"*Hell*, no," Laidlaw said. "I had my ration of that and then some. I just kept on sleepwalking till the time ran out." He chuckled. "Matter of fact, I was so deep asleep one time I chopped my own toes off without knowing it."

"You fooling? How?"

"Just dropped a sharp-edged box on it and that was all it took. Sliced them clean off, all five . . ." Laidlaw pulled the necklace up from his collar. "Here's the proof if you don't believe me."

"God*damn*," Redmon said. "A box? You must've felt silly."

"I surely did," Laidlaw said. "Still do sometimes, in fact."

"A box. What was in it?"

Laidlaw laughed, tucking the necklace back into his shirt. "You know, I really can't remember," he said. "I think it might actually have been a big old case of beer. Something good and heavy, anyway. Screwed me up for a good while too, I didn't walk right for about six months."

"Yeah," Redmon said. "Toes are more important than you think."

"I do pretty well now, though," Laidlaw said. "I can walk fine, really. Can't run quite right but I'll pogo along if I have to. Just

retrained myself, see, like . . . like they say people can." He leaned
forward, hugging the steering wheel to him, and listened to Rodney's
breath sigh in and out. He'd said a little more than he'd intended, but
it looked like it would pass over. After a minute, when he saw that
Rodney didn't seem to care to follow up the subject, he sat back.

"That was a real nice tune, anyhow," Redmon said. "That first
one I heard you play."

"I appreciate it," Laidlaw said. "Coming from you. You still listen
to Mingus?"

"Would if I could. Just at the minute I ain't got any record player."

"I heard you whistling it still, though," Laidlaw said. "Back one
night last winter."

Redmon turned and stared at him. "Say what?"

"Time I told you, I guess . . ." Laidlaw said. "I was out in the
woods back of your daddy's house one night and you came walking
out whistling. I knew it was you right away by the tune. Thought
you might remember it, since you chased me up the hill a ways."

"That was *you?* Yeah, I do remember that now. I thought it was a
big old dog."

"Sure, but it was my dog I had with me." Laidlaw smiled. "I
could've reached out and touched you if I had a long enough stick."

"And you didn't say anything."

"I was scared to, if you want to know the truth. If it had been the
other way around I'd've been inclined to kill whatever it was and
shine a light on it later . . ."

"So you were there." Redmon shook his head. "Son of a *bitch.*"

"I figured you'd find the tracks next day," Laidlaw said. "Snow on
the ground, you could have trailed me all the way home."

"Maybe if I had stayed the night," Redmon said. "But I just went
on home and forgot about it. What were you doing back up in there,
anyway?"

"Nothing much," Laidlaw said. "Taking a walk."

"A walk. Seem like your back yard must stretch a good long way."

Laidlaw shrugged. "I wasn't sleeping too sound back then."

"Dreams?"

"Not really. I don't have dreams."

"Hey, man, everybody dreams."

"That's what I hear," Laidlaw said. "Must be I just don't remember
mine. Haven't had one I remembered ever since I got back."

"Must be nice," Redmon said. "I have a dream every once in a
while."

"Don't tell me about it, then."

"Don't worry," Redmon said. "I forget them quick as ever I can."

"I've been sleeping better lately anyhow," Laidlaw said. "For the most part. Got myself a girlfriend."

"I guess that might help you," Redmon said. "Who, that fiddle player?"

"Is it that easy to tell?"

"I was just guessing. Hey, she might be skinny but you know they say —"

"Not to me they don't," Laidlaw said.

"Didn't mean nothing," Redmon said after a pause. "What's her name?"

"Adrienne Wells," Laidlaw said. "I'll see you get a better chance to meet her before too long."

"Yeah," Redmon said. "Okay."

Laidlaw reached in the bag and rattled the empty cans. "Think we ought to spring for another one?" he said.

"I don't think we can." Redmon pointed. "Look there, the store's shut on us."

Laidlaw looked across the parking lot: the glow from the 7-Eleven's front window was gone. "So it did," he said. "Well, I might have something back out at the house."

"I don't think so," Redmon said. "I guess I'll just call it a night."

"Where are you living then, yourself?"

"In town," Redmon said. "Up there around Jefferson Street. A small place but my own, and so forth."

"Want me to ride you over there?"

"It's all right," Redmon said. "I got wheels parked over across the street." He got out of the cab and clapped the door shut and walked around to the driver's side to shake Laidlaw's hand.

"You know where to find me, then, at least," Laidlaw said. "Come on out whenever you feel like it. I mean it. I want to see you, man, okay?"

"Okay," Redmon said. "I can get there."

Laidlaw held the grip. "You know me," he said. *More than anyone yet alive.* But that second part he didn't say aloud.

Redmon drew his hand away and looked down on him, unsmiling. "I wonder if you know me too," he said.

His sneakers made no sound at all as he crossed the parking lot.

30

LAIDLAW SLEPT late, for him, and woke with the woozy feeling that might have come with a hangover, though in considering it as he came half alert, he didn't think he'd really had all that much to drink. He rolled onto his back and pulled the cover back up around him. The room was clammy and rather cold, and the light had a murky underwater tint. After a little while he made out the stuttering on the roof to be rain.

The dog was scratching at the back door. Laidlaw felt lazy, inclined to let her wait, but she wouldn't quit, and after a couple of minutes he turned over, pushed himself up into a crouch, and then stood. As he walked to the kitchen he could feel last night's interrupted hint of a headache settling back over him. The dog was twisted upon herself at the doorway, looking back at him over a shoulder. Laidlaw lifted the latch and turned her out. A white fog hung low over the back yard, with a drizzle seeping sluggishly down through it. The dog moved slowly out over the damp ground, her back humped up, and halfway across the yard the fog swallowed her.

He let the door fall to and reached a bottle of aspirin down from the shelf. He shook three tablets into his hand and swallowed them with a gulp of water from the faucet, went back into the front room, lowered himself back onto the pallet, and folded the blanket around him. His head thudded a time or two and then let up, and he felt himself gliding back toward sleep. Just as he'd begun to fade completely into a doze, the dog scratched again to be let in. His eyes came open, and he listened for a minute before he shoved himself up. The dog rubbed herself damply against him as she sidled in. Laidlaw walked back to his pallet and stood over it, debating; he still felt bleary but now it seemed more trouble than it was worth to lower himself back down. He stooped slightly to peer out of the window. Outside, the hillside was blanked by the fog. He straightened up and walked into the kitchen to start a pot of coffee.

The fog had rolled up to the kitchen windows, leaving them lifelessly pale. Laidlaw paced the room from end to end, an unlit cigarette stuck in his mouth. Dull rain coalesced on the window panes and ran slowly down. At one spot where the caulk had cracked, water was beginning to pool on the sill. Laidlaw tried the wet spot with a fingertip, then turned back toward the stove. The coffee had turned brown, bouncing in the pot's glass knob. He poured himself a cup and lit the cigarette.

In the front room it was dark and dank and he shivered a little when he stepped back in. The dog lay on her belly with her head stretched over her paws, staring gloomily out across the floor. Laidlaw moved to switch on a light, then changed his mind and went out the front door, taking a seat in the first chair he came to. The fog had settled itself snugly around the corners of the porch. The thump of the door closing made him look back that way, and when he saw Mr. Giles sitting silently at the far end of the porch he flinched, enough to slop hot coffee all down his forearm.

"*Damn* it," Laidlaw said.

He switched his cup to his other hand and began to wave his arm in the air to cool it, looking wide-eyed at Mr. Giles, who showed no sign of pleasure in catching him so completely out. When his arm had stopped stinging, Laidlaw got up and pulled his chair down to the corner where Mr. Giles was sitting.

"I never looked to see you there," he said. "We might have to fix you up with a bell or something if you keep on doing this way."

Mr. Giles said nothing. His eyes seemed to be fixed on a point just ahead of Laidlaw's shoes, and his face was as pale and glum as the day.

"What are you doing out spooking around, anyway?" Laidlaw said lightly. "Won't be Halloween for months and months yet."

Mr. Giles's face twitched. He took his hat off and raised his head to look at Laidlaw, who caught himself noticing particularly how his eyes were a razor's gray. It was no more than an instant before Mr. Giles dropped his eyes back to his lap, where the felt hat circled slowly through his heavy hands.

"Sorry weather we're having today," Laidlaw said. He knew for a certainty that something was the matter now, but he was not at all sure he wanted to know what.

Mr. Giles twisted partway around to contemplate the fog. "I expect it to burn off before too long," he said.

Laidlaw flicked his cigarette butt up over the rail and watched it vanish into the fog at the top of its arc. "You really think so?" he said. "I guessed it was going to just drip all day long."

"Ye'll see sunshine in an hour," Mr. Giles said with small enthusiasm. "Least that's my bet."

"You're the prophet," Laidlaw said, surprised to see Mr. Giles shift suddenly, as if he had been pricked. "I'd sooner you'd be right on this one anyway. I don't much care for this to keep up." He flapped a hand dismissively at the fog. "You want any coffee or anything?"

"No," Mr. Giles said. His hat completed another revolution through his hands. "I don't reckon I do."

"Well, you didn't come all this way just to catch me sleeping in, did you?" Laidlaw said. "I mean, seems like it's got to be too wet to work."

"Good thing we got your hay in at least," Mr. Giles said.

"You're right about that," Laidlaw said.

The dog scratched at the inside of the door and he got up to let her out. "Some watchdog," he said as she emerged. "Must've got used to you . . ."

Mr. Giles did not smile. The dog lumbered to the porch steps and stood there looking down them, unwilling to go farther into the wet. Laidlaw resumed his chair and as he did so Mr. Giles stood up.

"I best get on," he said. "Just meant to stop in and say hidy."

"Well, hidy hidy ho," Laidlaw said. "Sure you wouldn't rather sit back down and tell what's on your mind?"

Mr. Giles sat down with a thud and took his hat off again. He sent Laidlaw a glance as brief as a slash and then looked down at his knees. The denim of his overalls bagged around the prosthetic joint and he covered the knob with his hat and splayed his fingers across the crown. Laidlaw set his cup on the rail and idly drummed the wood beside it.

"Reckon ye'll be playen in town again tonight?"

"Sure will," Laidlaw said. "Any time you care to come I'll see you get in free."

"Well, I kindly doubt it," Mr. Giles said. "It's a right smart piece to be drivin by dark. I'll bet ye don't get home till late most nights."

"Well, I guess about one or two in the morning on average,"

Laidlaw said. "Gives me an excuse to sleep late, don't you know."

Mr. Giles fingered the tear at the peak of his hat. "I'll bet ye go later than that some nights." His eyes cut up quickly and then dropped again. "Some nights I'd bet ye stay gone till sunrise."

"If it rises at all," Laidlaw said. "Hang on here a minute." He tried a laugh but it caught in his craw. "What are you doing, planning a burglary? It wouldn't hardly be worth your while."

"Oh no." Mr. Giles bent low over his knees, speaking in a rapid strangled tone. "Just thought tonight might be a good night ye stayed out a while longer is all." He stood up quickly, quick enough to impress Laidlaw once again with how light on his feet he was for such a big man.

"Sit down, now," Laidlaw said. He lit himself another cigarette, though his mouth had gone suddenly dry. "I won't turn you loose before you tell me what's going on."

"Reckon I'm bound to," Mr. Giles said. He seemed more relaxed, though he kept on his feet. To be on a level with him, Laidlaw stood too.

"Don't ye know them boys get a little hard to handle at times," Mr. Giles said. "And been known to run with a low-down crowd too."

"What of it?" Laidlaw said, but he felt his skin draw tight and cold.

"I happened to hear some ugly kind of talk," Mr. Giles said. "They's a crowd of them thinken to come roust you, might be. Course it might not amount to anything at all."

"The hell you say," Laidlaw said. "It amounts to enough for me right now if they already picked out their *night*."

"Could be nothing to it," Mr. Giles said. "But ye might just be gone from here and be on the safe side. What I'd do."

"You would not," Laidlaw said. "You wouldn't budge a step off your own place for such a thing, not if I know you." He took a step backward, knocked over his chair, and let it lie. "But what I don't understand is where this notion came from in the first place . . ." He set the flat of his hand against a post and leaned, letting his eyes close. It was curious how calm he felt for someone being sucked down a bottomless descent. "I know what it is," he said, snapping his fingers as he opened his eyes back up. "Somebody just decided I'm a nigger-lover, that's what."

Mr. Giles turned and leaned on the porch rail, putting himself nose to nose to the fog.

"You can't tell me I'm wrong," Laidlaw said. "Now can you?"

"I wouldn't never mess in your business," Mr. Giles breathed out, so quiet Laidlaw could scarcely hear it.

"Now that suits me just fine," he said. He pushed himself away from the post, feeling himself sway to the edge of his balance, a little beyond. Mr. Giles still leaned weightily on the rail, his stare fixed on the fog that moiled over the yard. Laidlaw could not recall such a fog, he couldn't even see as far as the hackberry tree. He reached for the chair he'd overturned and swung it up, believing for an instant he would smash it against the post. But instead he set it back upright and dropped himself down into it, setting his fingers against the bridge of his nose and pressing sharp and hard. Mr. Giles moved around to face him and Laidlaw let his hands fall to his knees.

"No sir," he said. "I couldn't hardly ask any more than that, now could I? I just wish that the whole rest of the world would feel the same as you."

"If ye'd just be gone from here," Mr. Giles said slowly. "I know them boys, they ain't got all that much attention. They don't find ye here I expect it'd just blow on over."

Laidlaw glanced down at the cigarette in his left hand, which seemed to have sprouted a long ash since he'd noticed it last. The air had grown so oppressive that even the smoke seemed painfully slow to rise.

"Oh yeah," Laidlaw said. "It'll just blow over and fair up sure enough, the clouds are going to roll away and I don't doubt it, but I just *can't have anybody run me off my place*, now I know you understand that much." His hand shook slightly, bringing the cigarette to meet his mouth.

"I don't doubt I'd feel the same," Mr. Giles said, looking him full in the face this time.

"What are you doing out here then?" Laidlaw said. "If you don't mind the question."

"I hoped to reason with ye," Mr. Giles said.

Laidlaw snapped his cigarette out into the yard. "Hell with it. Reason with *them*."

"They get all doped up till they can't hear reason," Mr. Giles said, his eyes falling away again. "Don't you think I ain't tried it once in a while."

"The hell with it," Laidlaw said again. The dog came clicking across the porch to lay her head in his lap, and his hand settled unconsciously on a spot at the base of her skull. "The way I think of it, a thing like this is made just like a snake. Once you chop the head off, the body keeps on moving but it ain't really going nowhere."

"Don't hardly see how that helps ye," Mr. Giles said.

Laidlaw settled back in his chair, letting his legs uncurl before him. Now that the first vertigo had passed, he felt cool as if he were just talking to himself.

"What I'm wondering," he said, "is where's the head? I don't figure it would be Earl. His mind don't run in that direction. Not without help. That leaves us Walter. Now I'd say he's got the meanness for it, no harm intended. But I kind of doubt he's got the enterprise. Trouble enough if ever he moves but it'll take a mighty shove to get him going. Now, how am I doing?"

"Like a lawyer," Mr. Giles said. "I reckon it's a line of talk."

"So that leaves it down to somebody else. Somebody I don't know and you ain't even kin to. Just some loose son of a bitch . . . like Fowler."

Hearing himself speak, Laidlaw thought again of the shove from the night before, and felt a stony suspicion that indeed the whole thing might be down to Fowler. Odd where this thinking out loud might take you. But then again it could have been Walter who had jostled him.

"Him that's been running with Earl lately," he said. "You know who I mean?"

"I seen him a time or two," Mr. Giles said. "Here and about."

"And what did you think of him?"

"Can't say I care for him," Mr. Giles said. "He's got a piece missen, I'd say."

"I'm along with you there," Laidlaw said evenly, rubbing a circle around the dog's ears. "And that's what it comes to."

"Comes to what?"

"*Step on the head*," Laidlaw said. It might have been somebody else talking through him now. "*Get it before it gets you.*"

"I don't know if I altogether follow this head business," Mr. Giles said. "Way I see it they all just drink awhile, pop a pill, and just generally get each other all worked up."

"Well, you're closer to the source," Laidlaw said. "But what I'm guessing at is that Earl and Walter most likely wouldn't have *started* anything like this."

"Might be they didn't," Mr. Giles said. "But then where are we at?"

"Keep them out of it," Laidlaw said. "Keep them home if you can. Otherwise . . ."

Mr. Giles shook his head. "Be a whole lot easier if ye'd only stand clear."

"Well, I won't do it," Laidlaw said. "You know I can't."

"I figured it." Mr. Giles pushed himself up straight from the rail. "If that's how it stands, I reckon I'm gone."

Laidlaw stood up to see him go. He was still angry, but manners died hard. "What was the use of coming, then?" he said. "According to you, that is."

"I'll tell ye straight," Mr. Giles said. "So they don't take ye by surprise. I judged it'd fall out worse for everybody if they surprised ye." He took two steps across the yard from the porch and the fog reknit itself behind him.

Laidlaw walked into the house and smacked the screen door shut. He stalked in a wide circle around the edge of the front room, coming to a halt by the phone, staring at the smudgy section of the drywall where all the numbers had been scribbled. After a little while it came to him that he had better call Adrienne. His fingers felt slightly numb when he dialed the phone.

"So how's it going?" Adrienne said. Her good cheer irked him for no good reason. "Stay out late with your friend last night?"

"Oh, Rodney," Laidlaw said. He had not been thinking directly about him all morning. "Not too late. A little, I guess. I'll see you get a better chance to talk to him next time."

"Whenever," Adrienne said. "He seemed like a nice guy . . . You planning to pick me up tonight?"

Laidlaw tapped at the spot on the wall where her phone number was creased in blue ball-point. "That's just what I meant to tell you," he said dully. "I won't be able to make it at all tonight. I can't play, I mean."

"Can't *play?* Come on, whatever kind of hangover you have has got to clear off by dark, at least."

"I just can't make it," Laidlaw said. "It'll only be tonight. I'd like you to tell Martin for me if you would."

"Listen, you're not really sick or something, are you?" Adrienne said. "Because I want you to tell me if you are."

"I'm not sick," he said. "Why don't you call up Bob Reynolds and ask if he can fill in for me. I know he'd be glad to get the work."

"Maybe," Adrienne said. "Are you in some kind of trouble? You don't sound quite right to me."

"What kind of trouble could I get into?" Laidlaw said. "An easygoing feller like me . . .''

"You better be telling the truth," Adrienne said. "All right, I guess. Am I going to see you tomorrow?"

"Of course," Laidlaw said. "Come on out in the daytime. Or else I'll call you."

"Well, maybe I will," Adrienne said.

"Look, I'm sorry about tonight," Laidlaw said. "But you all have a good one."

"We'll hold your place," Adrienne said.

"I count on that," Laidlaw said. "See you."

He hung up and turned to face the door. Beyond the screen the dog stood, facing into the house to watch his movements. Out behind her it looked as if the day was getting brighter. Laidlaw took hold of his long table and dragged it a few feet out from the wall. For a long numb time he stood staring down at the floor, but he didn't want to open the hide-hole yet. When he turned away from it at last, he saw that two squares of real daylight had appeared on the floor below the east windows. Mr. Giles's prediction might prove out after all. He edged past the dog and went out on the porch. The fog was burning off faster than he'd have thought possible, lifting lightly away from the ground and dissolving as it rose. It was shaping into a fair transparent day, and yet he still felt cold all over. He crashed into a chair and started the long wait for dark.

31

DONE WITH his few evening chores, Laidlaw stopped at the corner of the barn to look back toward the house. Sunset stains were dragging down the hill like claws. To the east, behind him, the sky was its palest milky blue. He rested with his back against the weather-faded wall of the barn and watched until the sky's color deepened and the first few stars began to appear.

When the night had barely begun to turn black he went down to the house and warmed up a skillet of meal and drippings for the dog. He fed her on the porch and then went back inside. The table was still pulled askew from that morning and all he had to do was remove the length of quarter-round and flip the hinged floor section back. A damp dirt smell rose into the room from underneath the house, and Laidlaw hesitated for a moment before he hopped down.

After the last time he'd been in there he'd sealed the padlock against the wet with a plastic bag and tape, and it came open easily on the first twist of the key. Stooping into the brick-walled cavity, he unsnapped the lid of the trunk and felt rapidly over its contents, needing no light this time around. First he found the oily bundle of the shotgun and twisted up to shove it across the floor. Then he groped for a few of the heavy cubical boxes of shells and stacked them on the boards beside the gun. From his low angle, in between the table legs, he could see the dog snuffling anxiously at the screen. He shut the hide-hole and vaulted up into the room, closed the floor down, and went to let her in.

The dog was nervous; often she picked up his moods, and he wouldn't doubt she was sensitive to something troublesome in the air. She followed close on his heels as he went out to the smoke-house for a canful of salt. He left her standing on the porch, reentered the house, and unwound the twelve-gauge from the oily sheet. It was still good and clean, with no rust specks, and the pump worked as smoothly as he could ever remember it had. He pushed a swab through the barrel just to be sure of it, and then leaned over to prop the gun against the wall.

The shell boxes had gone soft at the corners, print fading, cardboard beginning to tatter, but he was sure enough the shells would be all right; they'd been kept dry. He dumped one of the boxes out on the table and began to pick open the puckered ends of the shells. The beads of loose shot made a brassy rattle when he dropped them into a coffee can at the end of the table. Laidlaw refilled each shell with the coarse salt from the smokehouse and then closed them all up again with a little tape across the ends.

Outside on the hill a ewe bleated three or four times, and Laidlaw paused to listen, but she had already stopped. He rolled the salt-loaded shells to one side and began to operate on another batch, using his kitchen knife to slice around the cardboard tubes just ahead of the brass ring, almost all the way through but not quite, turning each into a solid slug, or so he hoped. He hoped he wouldn't be firing anything like that either, but he wanted to be prepared for all eventualities. *Underkill and overkill.* He marked the brass butts of the slugs with scraps of tape so he could tell them from the others in the dark.

It was solid dark outside by this time, so that he began to feel uncomfortably pinpointed under the lights of the house. Through the open doorway, the rising insect chorus reached him. Adrienne and Martin would be pulling up to the Clawhammer about now, he'd guess, unloading the instruments, getting set up. He stood up and looked down at all the shells spread over the table. What he could have used was some kind of hunting jacket, but he didn't have one, so he went to a hook and got down the suit jacket he hadn't had on since the summer before. He filled the left pocket with salt shells, the right with the slugs, and split the unaltered ones between the two inside pockets, where they rode high on his ribs. The weight dragged the coat down, pulling at the shoulder seams; no doubt he looked ridiculous, but no one would see. He picked up the shotgun and put a shell from the left pocket into the breech and pumped it into place with a thunk: *salt.* One from the inside pocket, thunk: *shot.* The last from the right pocket, thunk: *slug.* With the last slap of the pump his stomach gripped up and his mouth twisted into a wry shape it would have been hard to take for a smile.

Salt, shot, slug. Try to remember that . . . The shotgun tilted on the pivot of his wrist, the barrel dipping toward the door. Laidlaw crossed the floor and flicked on the porch light, whistled up the dog, and shut her in the house. He could hear her raking her claws down the inside of the door as he walked up toward the track, the shells thudding against his hips as he moved. There was no moon, but the sky was clear and all the stars were there to see by. He got into the truck and, without turning on the lights, drove it down to the hay barn and parked it in the hall behind the tractor. By the time he passed the house again on his way back up the slope, the dog had given up and gone quiet.

A dozen yards from the fence and road, a gully ran almost the whole way up the hill to the tree line. At the track it dribbled off to nothing, but at the high end he knew it was deep as he was tall. He walked up it until it was just about waist-deep, climbed over a heap of stumps and brush he'd dumped in for a halfhearted try at slowing the washout, and knelt down. From here he could cover the whole approach from the gate to the house, and if he ran into trouble the deepening gully would give him cover almost all the way to the woods.

Bracing the gun on a spur of a stump, he sighted down the groove on the barrel to the bead, picking the corner post of the porch as his target. Of course he was desperate for a cigarette now that he'd decided to leave them in the house. He'd never smoked at all in the bush, and always missed it badly . . . A ewe and two stout lambs grazed their way toward him on his right, their fleeces an indefinite pale against the dark slope. As they came nearer he could hear the sound of their cropping more and more distinctly, a whisk of their teeth breaking grass. At a slightly greater distance the ram was grazing too, facing the same way. Laidlaw had not bothered to check the time, but Adrienne and Martin, maybe Bob Reynolds too, must have been into the first set already, and anyone interested would know by now he wasn't showing up. Unless anyone interested didn't show up himself until the later sets . . .

He heard an engine's whir rise and fall behind the hill, and half turned as the lights of the car angled up into the treetops and leveled back out, coming over the peak. The car's descent seemed dreadfully slow but it went on by the gate without stopping and sped off once it reached the flat. The drawn muscles in Laidlaw's belly and chest began to loosen. He was being strict with himself to make no noise, too strict probably, since it wasn't the jungle and the wait might be a lot longer than he thought.

No more than a habit, really. He could hear other cars now and again, swishing past on the paved road, but none turning in, and gradually, cord by cord, he settled himself down. Now he had no problem except a deepening of the cold he'd been feeling off and on all day and had nothing to do with the weather, which was mild to warm. No, he felt like he'd been quick-frozen, his skin was rubbery and numb, he'd have had to push a pin an inch or more into himself before it pricked live flesh, and of course it wasn't really cold at all, only a specialized form of fear. That first night in Nha Trang after his spell in the Mekong Delta, where he had not had a pleasant time, he was walking just a little after sunset, walking nowhere, just around, he was too numb even to get himself drunk, and Sevier put his head out of somewhere and said, *Hey there, home folks, over here.* Instantly familiar, the voice sucked Laidlaw into a dope-smelling dimness to meet Sevier and Ratman, just up from the Iron Triangle, and once they had all said their home counties Sevier began to pour out his stary dope-driven line of talk about how where you came from was what counted the most and home folks would always take good care of you when you took care of them, going on and on in the same flat gentle tone he used for everything he ever said. Sevier's eyes didn't match that calming voice at all, they'd already started to look like they belonged in somebody else's head, but it was better than half dark anyway, and Laidlaw was agreeing with everything he heard, taking his hits on the joint whenever it came around to him, nursing comfort from the familiar accent which had awakened the wish to trust he'd kept stunned for so long. Ratman wasn't saying much, he never did, just assenting, or dissenting, but Sevier was a one-man conversation whenever he took the mood. He'd had a duty change himself, it developed. He was starting a new recon team and he wanted Laidlaw on it, it would be the best and he would swear it, it would be so good, he had zeroed in on Laidlaw when he heard his voice in the lunch line earlier that day and had just been waiting for the chance to talk — and Laidlaw heard himself, felt himself going along with all that too. He barely knew what he'd agreed to when he got up to leave, but Sevier was so pleased he came out to walk partway with him, his talk still streaming out of him like rain. Lost far away behind Ratman's heavy dope, Laidlaw reacted poorly to the thick soggy darkness outside, but just as the terror was about to light up the rocket-propelled pinwheel of razors inside of him, Sevier brought him to halt with a hard arm across his shoulders.

You're afraid, aren't you? Sevier said in the same tone he'd have used for saying, that's right, keep on, and Laidlaw said, any sane man would be, and Sevier laughed and said, I can fix it, though, and Laidlaw said, I'd love to believe you, and Sevier gave him a little shake and said, it's obvious, you just become what you're afraid of. You become part of it. Laidlaw said, what? and Sevier said, like the dark. Carry a light and you're scared of the dark. So you put out the light and you're dark, it's dark, and your problem is gone. I know you've done that. Laidlaw said, yes, and Sevier said, it's the same, you become what you're afraid of, repeating it so evenly that it sounded perfectly rational, its weird logic burst into his brain with a stone-blind flash and fixed itself there so deeply that it remained true when he got straight the next day and then forever after, any time his mind felt for it. It was true that you couldn't get rid of the fear but you could learn to move around inside it, you could turn it into a chill or a blush or like now, transform it into the most subtle and thorough form of attention imaginable, that picked up anything and everything light-years before your mind.

What you were supposed to do with it back in the world was what Laidlaw would have liked to ask Sevier, who had so many answers, if only it were possible to ask, but he forgot all that instantaneously now, locking onto the rise and drop-off of another motor climbing the hill. When it hit the top he heard the motor cut and the lights went out a half second later as it started to coast. Laidlaw could see it anyway, a pickup with side rails, he could even see the silhouettes of a couple of men standing up in the back. The truck came very quietly, barely crunching the gravel, with a faint skidding sound every time the driver had to tap the brake. It came to a stop well short of the gate, just opposite the place in the gully where Laidlaw was crouched.

Heavy feet began coming off the tailgate; Laidlaw counted off three pairs of them. That made five men, or maybe six if they rode three in the cab. The truck had parked in a spot where the honeysuckle was so thick on the fence that he couldn't see it, but the men sounded less than a breath away. He listened hard for the cab doors closing, but he could only hear shoes whispering over the gravel. They were trying for silence, though they weren't all that good at it.

"I don't know —" a voice started, and another voice shushed it down in words Laidlaw couldn't hear. The first was Earl, plain enough, down to the whining slide his voice took on when he was very drunk, but he couldn't recognize the second. He was trying to make a guess if it might be Fowler, but really there was no telling; he'd hardly ever heard Fowler do more than grunt a word or two. And it didn't really matter anymore. A short conversation went on in whispers, from which Laidlaw could distinguish no clear word. For a second he glanced behind him and saw that the ram and ewe had raised their heads to listen too.

The fence gave a creak, and he switched back to see the shadow of a man coming across a low spot where it was clear of vine. Laidlaw swung the gun around and ducked lower down in the gully, his eyes fixed on the crumbling dirt of its wall. There was a sound like cloth giving and someone said "Goddamn" and was quickly hushed. Next he heard a familiar liquid clanking at the same moment he smelled gas. His hands tightened on the gun, but he held still. There was a rustle as the fence rose back and he heard lots of feet moving down over the grass. Behind, there was another patter as the sheep spooked and scattered farther across the hill field.

When the footsteps had gone definitely below him, he raised his eyes just over the rim of the gully. There were six of them down there, neatly outlined against the porch light now as they moved across the slope. Two with long hair, the fattest one was no doubt Walter, and that was all the detail he could make out. No rifle or shotgun visible among them, though pistols remained a possibility. And the middle two were definitely carrying gas cans. Though he had them where he'd meant to have them, clean back-lit targets one stinging blast could break up and confuse, the sight of the gas cans gave him a furious wish to do worse.

Laidlaw slid over the lip of the gully and slithered toward the low spot in the fence, using every bit of the stealth at his command, though he thought he was well out of pistol range, at least for drunks. Once over the wire he looked back for a second. The men had hesitated above the track, all of them facing down toward the house. Laidlaw went around the back of their truck at a crouch and squatted next to the rear wheel. There was a faint smell of dried manure rising from the bed. Laidlaw found the loose corner of his jacket lining and ripped out a foot-long strip and then another and tied their ends together with a bird's-eye knot. Quickly he unscrewed the gas cap and lowered the fabric all the way down the pipe, then pulled most of it back out. Breathing in the giddy petrol smell that fumed out from the cloth, he frisked himself for matches and found none. Naturally, they were down in the house, tucked under the wrapper of his cigarette pack. But the doors of the cab had been left ajar, that was why he hadn't heard them closing. A good chance that was Fowler's touch, if Fowler was in on it. He reached in and lucked on to a match book with his first grope along the dashboard.

Back by the gas pipe, he squatted and struck a match, cupping it back in his right hand till his left closed on the gun. It seemed to him that his hand had only half uncurled before flame closed the gap between the match and the cloth and then he was already jumping the fence and hitting the floor of the gully as the sudden blast and heat flared up behind him. He came to his knees and sighted the shotgun over the stump again.

There was a big yelling coming from the yard, and now he could see well enough what was wrong with the new strategy: he'd allowed them time to reach the house and left them nowhere else to go. Also it would be complicated to get out of the gully without being lit up by the burning truck. That was what you got for letting anger go to your head. He fired his first shell down into the yard, but the range was way too long for salt. A smell of burnt powder came as he pumped the gun and flipped the spent shell out. Someone answered his shot with a pistol, but Laidlaw was sure enough he didn't have a target.

He fired the birdshot shell and pumped the gun, watching a man with a gas can jump up to the corner of the porch. Too far away to tell who it was, though it didn't look like either of the Gileses. He clenched, unsure whether to fire the slug — he'd never counted on killing anybody or even coming close, but if he didn't do something he'd probably just swapped a blown-up truck for a burned-down house. That same pistol popped again from the yard. Laidlaw's finger twitched in the trigger guard, and he saw the right front window burst and the dog come hurtling out, striking the man chest-high and carrying him out over the porch rail to tumble in the yard. The gas can came apart from him and rolled jerkily toward the hackberry tree. The man was tucked up on his back, trying to kick, but the dog was all over him from every side at once.

The pistol popped and Laidlaw saw another man firing at the dog, moving in on her from the side opposite the house. He covered him briefly with the shotgun and then pulled it off and fired at the gas can. His dumb-lucky shot for the night: a shaft of flame blew ten feet straight up and the man with the pistol plunged off to one side. Laidlaw reloaded with desperate speed and sprang from the gully to run, stooping low, downhill along the fencerow, counting the pistol shots when they started again, *four*, then *five*. The confusion in the yard was such that no one saw him low-crawl over the track and dart for a clump of three trees by the fence. The pistol made a louder bang now he was closer. *Six*. The dog dropped low beside the gasoline fire and the man who'd been mauled rose to his knees. Laidlaw fired a barrel of salt at the nearest man to him, who screamed and ran off back of the house. The kneeling man also bounced to his feet to run.

Laidlaw fired another round of salt and heard something slap into the tree by his elbow. Someone he hadn't accounted for was shooting at him, moving in. He counted two powder flashes straight out of the barrel. Somebody had another gun and the wits to hold his fire, but it was still a desperation tactic, since he was out in the open and well set off against the house. Laidlaw made himself wait till the rushing form blocked the beam of the porch light and then fired to the center of the body. The man flipped over backward and didn't get up. Everyone else had already beat it out of the yard. Laidlaw's hands went slimy on the gun stock; if he'd mixed up the shells he'd killed somebody sure, even the birdshot would have killed at that short range.

Automatically he reloaded and when the pump slammed, the man on the ground got up and ran headlong into the creek. Only the wind knocked out of him, then. Laidlaw tagged him across the shoulders with a round of salt as he splashed out the other side, savoring the shriek which followed. He was still close enough for salt to tear up cloth and skin. He crossed the creek himself and stopped at the corner of the garden fence to fire the next two shells at the line of runners straggling over the low pasture.

From then on he knew he could have it all his way. The last two shots had driven the whole gang into the trees. Laidlaw veered into the woods himself and loped along a few dozen yards behind them, able to keep track of them all individually by the huge amounts of noise they made. When they hit the clearing by the orchard he opened up on them again with salt and drove them yelling through the blackberry brambles and up to the top of the ridge. Windmilling down the other side, they all got hung up at the fence by the roadbed, and he let them have two more flaying rounds while they struggled to get unsnarled. By then they seemed too beat even to howl when they were hit, so he left them to get themselves away down the road.

The shotgun barrel cooled in his hand as he walked slowly back toward the house, and by the time he reached the low field it was cold. The chill that had shrouded him all day was all gone now. The run had left him lightly warm, and the only other thing he could feel was relief. The truck fire had burned itself out without spreading, he saw when he let himself into the yard by the garden. The gas-can fire had burned down too, when it might have taken the hackberry tree, as he could see when he got closer to it. He was lucky; his losses were slight. Nobody killed and he hadn't been hurt. All he was out was one broken window, a nasty cleaning job on the shotgun, and a big hole scorched in the middle of the yard. It wasn't till he'd almost tripped on her body that he saw the dog was dead.

32

DAWN FOUND him lying on the frame of the derelict wagon back of the sheep barn, looking up at the fading stars and a thin trimming of the late-rising new moon. The sheep had grazed into a half circle close around him, mildly curious, since he'd been spread out there so long, so still. He paid them no attention, looking only straight up. As the sky brightened he could see a dim black dot hung high over the crown of the hill. When the light got stronger the dot sprouted wings and presently was joined by another. Now he could see that they were not stationary after all; both moved in long slack ellipses, paths which loosely interlocked.

Nearer him the smaller birds had already begun to sing, but Laidlaw noticed nothing but the slow and silent revolution of the buzzards around the sky. He'd carried the dog's body up the hill in the dark, and left it in the middle of a fairy ring of the old sheep bones. From the beginning he'd known she'd be heavy, but in the act her weight was staggering. The only way he could manage was to carry her slung across both shoulders. That way she'd bent him nearly double, and bled all down the back of his shirt. It amazed him that the carrion birds had come so quickly; it was inconceivable that they could have smelled her so soon. Still, they were supposed to have phenomenal eyesight too, and the body would make a sharp dark sign against the green knob of the pasture. He supposed the buzzards were not entirely sure of their reading, or else they would have landed by now. It would have been better to have buried the dog, he felt dully, but he was too discouraged to get up and do it.

For some time he'd been half aware of the noise of a big unmuffled engine coming close, and as it grew startlingly louder he sat up and saw an enormous blue tractor chewing its way down the road from the top of the hill. It tilted up at a crazy angle, one heavy-treaded wheel climbing the embankment, to squeeze around the burnt frame of the truck in the middle of the road. Once past, it bounced back down and stopped. The driver was a big man dressed in overalls, white T-shirt, broad-brimmed hat. When he got down from the seat and moved back toward the truck Laidlaw saw that it was Mr. Giles.

Laidlaw pushed himself all the way up from the wagon bed and walked down into the yard. The gas can he'd shot up the night before was shrapnel now, but the other was intact. Someone had let it drop in the creek and it had floated down and hung in the water gate below the line fence, where a culvert ran under the road. He waded in and fished it out and carried it up to the spot along the fence where the tractor had parked.

The cracking toes of Mr. Giles's old brogans stuck out from under the cab of the truck, with a long brown length of heavy chain swinging back and forth just above them. No other part of him was visible. Laidlaw set the gas can down and looked into the cab of the truck. The tank had blown forward through the seat, shattering the windshield. The side rails had caught fire and burned all the way down to the metal. The paint was bubbled and charred all over, but in places you still could tell it had originally been red.

"My God, they had your truck," Laidlaw said. Mr. Giles came sliding out from under the cab, hooking with his right leg to help propel himself. The left foot stuck out straight on the roadbed, digging a shallow furrow in the gravel. When he got up his eyes slipped over the place where Laidlaw stood as if there were nothing there at all.

"Well, I never had any idea it could have been yours . . ." Laidlaw let his arms flop limp across the top strand of the fence.

Mr. Giles turned his back and spat toward the far side of the road. "If ye had of just done what I told ye . . ." he said. "Here I meant to save us all some trouble and what happened but I did us all in. Got one boy practically skinned alive and t'other'n got dog bites clean through both his arms. Never mind about the *truck*, next to that there."

"Did you let them take it?" Laidlaw said.

Mr. Giles whipped his head around to stare a hole right through him. "Do ye really think I would?" he said. "They slipped off with it while I was feeden yesterday evenen."

"I believe you," Laidlaw said. "I wish it hadn't turned out this way."

"You and me both," Mr. Giles said. His mouth shut on a tight bloodless line as he turned to face off down the road.

"You know, it could have been a whole lot worse," Laidlaw said.

"Might be. Could have been a whole lot better too," Mr. Giles said. "They never intended to give ye any more than a shivaree."

Laidlaw picked up the gas can with both hands and pitched it over the fence into the roadbed. "Take a look if you recognize that," he said. "I don't know but what it belongs to you too."

Mr. Giles glanced briefly at the can, then raised his foot and set it on the sag of the tow chain. "Ain't none of ours," he said.

"Well, if I could find out whose it was I'd make him drink every drop," Laidlaw said. "Don't you know they meant to burn me out?"

"I don't believe it," Mr. Giles said. "At the most they might have burnt a patch of your field there."

"I don't care if they planned on burning a cross," Laidlaw said. "It don't make any difference to me. Don't you think I've had enough fires on this place without needing anybody to set me a fresh one?"

Mr. Giles didn't answer, only his shoulders hitched up a little. He moved around to the side of the cab, reached in, and chopped the gear stick into neutral.

"You'll have a high time towing that thing without anybody to steer it," Laidlaw said.

Mr. Giles turned his back sharply, walked over to the tractor, and mounted the seat. His hand lifted toward the ignition and then dropped away. He twisted back around and looked at Laidlaw through tight-screwed eyes. "Don't ye know," he said. "All my good help look like they're hard under the weather this morning, now what do ye say about that?"

"Well, what did they have to come here for?" Laidlaw said, but Mr. Giles had switched to face forward and the tractor noise drowned out the question.

"Why did they do it?" Laidlaw yelled, though he could hardly even hear himself now. The chain tightened as the tractor jerked ahead, then went slack as the truck began to slip after it. The front bumper smacked against the tractor's hitching bar, then Mr. Giles sped up to outdistance it, jolting on down the hill.

Laidlaw climbed over the fence to retrieve the gas can and then climbed back. The can had picked up a deep dent on its bottom edge from falling on the limestone spine of the road. Laidlaw set it down and straightened up. The buzzards were gone from the pale sky now; he guessed they'd found the resolution to come down. *Why did they do it?* Though he would have preferred to go to the woods, he knew the answer was not in nature. He kicked the gas can a little distance away from him and then started back toward the house.

The interior seemed dead or half aborted; nothing in it spoke to him of use. It was not more than some kind of intermediate zone, a waiting room where someone had camped for a time. He turned away from it and mounted the narrow stairs, stooping to pass under the lintel into the cramped upper passage. The door to the room overlooking the road had soaked up enough damp from somewhere to swell tight shut and it gave a tearing screech when he shoved it open.

The junk in the room was faintly lit by the small eave windows at either end. Laidlaw took hold of the door frame and swung forward to the end of his arms, hanging there to overlook the clutter. He felt a dizzy spin start up, maybe just because he was tired, but the contents of the room got little and began to whirl away underneath him, like the whole world must do below a buzzard's circling eye. He smiled at that thought and the room swung back upright and came still. From separate crannies, this, that, or the other thing seemed to signal him for attention. Legs of one table, top to another. Stack upon stack of moldy movie magazines and *TV Guide*s, old pill canisters and cough syrup bottles, all manner of empty containers, rags and tatters of worn-out cheap clothing. Doll furniture, most of it broken. On top of a heap below the east window a pair of tan pantyhose miscegenated with a man's stray sock. On the near side of it lay a pink baby doll with its eyes fallen shut and its limbs sprung halfway loose from their plastic sockets.

What the hell had he saved all this for? Laidlaw was dimly wondering. Oh, because it was less trouble to save it than throw it away. Something moved on the west window pane, drawing his eye toward it. An orange Volkswagen was jouncing down the road from the hilltop: Adrienne's car. Right, he'd invited her out this morning, sure enough. He stepped all the way into the room and leaned back against the door to close it. Dimly he heard the clink of the chain on the gate and then the VW pulled up behind his truck on the track. Adrienne got out and walked down toward the house, swinging her mandolin case at the end of one arm. Her head fell below the level of the window sill, out of his sight, and a moment later he heard a knock come on the downstairs door. A pause, followed by the whine of the spring expanding as the screen door was pulled open. She called his name a time or two and then the door whanged shut. Laidlaw switched his head toward the western window and saw her going across the field in the direction of the woods. Her hands were empty now; she must have dropped the mandolin inside the house. When she had gone out of sight behind the trees, he let his legs begin to fold. His back scraped slowly down the door until he was sitting on the floor with his knees pulled up underneath his chin.

To the side of his right hand was a pile of movie magazines, and he reached over to lift the one on top. It let out a musty stench when he pulled it open, and came soggily to pieces in his hands. Plain enough he'd missed a leak somewhere, or else a new one had sprung. He chucked the rotting magazine across the room and picked up the next, which was fairly dry, though there were brown water stains at the edges of the pages. The leaves of it ran by under his thumb; he scarcely saw the glossy polished faces. A loose photograph fell out onto his knee and he tossed the magazine aside and picked it up. A snapshot of a snaggle-toothed boy in a loose-fitting air force uniform, no one he'd ever laid eyes on before. On the back someone had written a date but the ink had bled and he couldn't read it. He flicked the photo with thumb and forefinger and watched it go fluttering a limp foot or so away from him. Next in the stack was a child's spelling workbook, only half filled in and most of the answers wrong, angrily gouged over with some teacher's red ballpoint. No help there. Laidlaw pushed the whole pile over and tipped his head back.

Farther into the room was a television tube with no case or works to it, sitting on top of a scatter of chipped 45 records, which were spread across a hump of colored rags. Between him and that lay a ruined umbrella, nothing left of it but the center rod and the hooked rubber handle. He took hold of it by the tip and began to rake the handle idly through the rest of the muck. It turned over a few items that didn't much interest him, and then he snagged the baby doll by its foot and hauled it over toward him. Its eyes were hung with little weights and when he lifted it they popped open with a clunk and stared at him, glassy blue with the glitter of mica.

Laidlaw gave the doll a shake, and the dead eyes rocked behind their long stiff lashes. It had no sign of any sex, and precious little personality. Still he remembered that Rodney's little sister, Deana, had once owned such a doll as this. Yes, and they'd both played with it too, one summer day in the powdery dust of track between the two houses, and he even remembered they'd got in trouble somehow, but for what? Dirt on their clothes, most likely. They'd have been no more than five or six; he recalled clearly how much bigger Rodney had looked back then, when the year or so between them made a gap as wide as the world. No chance it could really be the same doll, though, since the house had been cleaned down to the boards after Wat moved out of it. He knew that for sure from helping with the job. So this doll and all the rest of the plunder belonged to the last bunch of white tenants, and so it must possess the secret of how such people came to turn against each other.

He gave the doll another shake and the eyes winked back to let him know it wasn't such a mystery after all. The answer was heaped up all around the place he sat. If you were born into the middle of all this, there was little doubt what your life must be. Momma and Daddy could just about read and write their names and never needed to do more, never had to know a thing past farming. But now the land was too poor to keep you, and there were too many of you anyway, and you didn't own it and never would because all around you it was being sold off in half-acre scraps to the kind of people you were growing up watching on a half-broke TV that was your only peephole into a world you never knew was a dream until whatever day you finally learned it would never spit anything back your way but trash. Then whatever fury you could still feel would be bound to waste itself on the people handiest by. It wasn't such a wonder if you turned on the people going down in the same boat with you, not when they were the only ones you had any chance to reach.

Why sure, it was simple enough if you thought about it a little. He'd told that much of the truth to Mr. Giles that morning: it could have been a whole lot worse. All he'd left out was that no doubt it would be, soon enough. Before you know it . . . But he was tired of the whole business now. The doll's eyes clicked neatly shut when he tossed it onto the nearest pile of rags. A second later he slipped down to one side and passed out as his shoulder hit the floor.

Laidlaw was stuck in the middle of a dream, an awful dream and the only one he could remember having in years. The worst of it was he couldn't tell exactly what it was about. Only that Wat was down in the kitchen and there was something dreadful on the stairs. If he could just get down to Wat it might be all right, but there was no way he'd get down there, past whatever the thing was. Fear climbed up his throat, a strangling bile. Then his eyes dragged open and he found himself standing out on the porch with one hand locked to a post with a grip like death. He was partway back in the real world now, but it took him a second to understand that he must have been sleepwalking.

"Are you evil?" Redmon was standing at the foot of the porch steps, looking up at him with half a smile, hands hidden in the pockets of the light windbreaker he wore.

Laidlaw shook his head hard and felt his throat unlock. "No," he said. "Just tired."

Redmon's eyes narrowed slightly, like he was trying to read some secret message off his face.

"Come on up and grab a chair," Laidlaw said. "I'll be back out in just a second."

He walked a beeline through the house to the kitchen shelf where the bourbon bottle stood and took a hard pull right from the neck. The jolt of it straightened him up like a smack in the face might have. He stacked two jelly glasses into each other and took them and the bottle back to the porch.

"I must have dozed off there for a while," he said, pouring out a shot for Redmon. "I stayed up a little bit late last night."

"That right?" Redmon said, reaching for the glass. He took a drink and set the glass down, returning his hand to fondle something in his jacket pocket. "You came staggering out of that door like a blind man, that's for sure. I thought maybe somebody'd just been killing you a little bit, the amount of blood you got down your back."

"Oh, that," Laidlaw said. "My dog just died."

"Died hard, too, from the looks of it," Redmon said. "That big old thing I saw?"

"She was a better dog than I ever knew," Laidlaw said. "I don't think I appreciated her right."

"What did you do with her?"

"Hauled her up the hill to the boneyard."

"Shame." Redmon tapped a pack of Luckies and held it out to Laidlaw.

"Thanks," Laidlaw said, and took one.

"Is that your bug, too?" Redmon said.

"It's Adrienne's," Laidlaw said. "I guess she must be still in the woods." He took a look out across the field and saw the sun had switched to the western side; he'd slept the whole day through, it seemed. "You been here long?"

"Oh, I was poking around a little while," Redmon said. He pulled his hands out of his jacket pockets and scattered something rattling out over the floor. "And what did I find but twelve-gauge shells, and forty-five shells, and a few from a three-fifty-seven Mag, if I don't miss my guess." He pushed the dead casings across the boards with the side of his shoe.

Laidlaw shrugged. "That last batch of tenants must've had target practice, I guess."

Redmon laughed. "Get out of here, man, these things are practically still warm. Not to mention you're covered in blood and it looks like somebody blew a load of Eff You gas right out there under that hackberry. You been fighting the war over again, I can tell it. None of my business, maybe, but I was kind of curious who with."

Laidlaw sat down and poured himself a drink. "I had a band of loose fools come by," he said.

"What were they after?" Redmon said.

"Never did find that out for sure," Laidlaw said. "I got word they might be coming so I laid for them up in the gully." He pointed. "Let them have a couple of barrels' worth of salt when they came in and then they all beat feet."

"Uh-huh," Redmon said. "Meanwhile, they shot off a few clips at you and set a fire bomb in your front yard."

"Maybe it did get a little out of hand," Laidlaw said. "They were too drunk to hit the broad side of a barn anyway."

"Must have been pretty close friends of yours if you'd take such care not to damage them any worse. It'd been me, I'd been tempted to let them have something stronger than salt."

"Yeah, well," Laidlaw said. "Some of the Gileses were mixed in with them, but I don't think it was their idea."

"What idea?" Redmon said. "Now wasn't I just telling you that old man is poison?"

"He wasn't with them," Laidlaw said. "Matter of fact, he was the one to warn me they might be on the way."

"And put them up to it too, I'll bet."

"Never," Laidlaw said. "I don't blame you for thinking it but he's really not that kind. I can't say I share every opinion he has but he's a decent man at the bottom or he wouldn't have come out of his way to let me know to begin with."

Redmon shook his head. "I don't see you have that much call to stick up for him now."

"Well, you know what it means for somebody like him to make the least move against family, right or wrong," Laidlaw said. "It's more than a notion." He let out a sigh as he drained his glass. "I just wish I hadn't blown up his truck, is all."

"Say what?" Redmon said. "Man, why don't you quit wiggling and tell me what happened."

"Well, he told me they swiped it from him and I believe it's the truth," Laidlaw said. "He came by and towed it off this morning. Maybe he thinks he might collect insurance on it some way, there ain't much left on it to fix."

"Like, from the beginning," Redmon said, reaching for the bottle.

"I pretty well told you already," Laidlaw said. "I heard something might happen so I took a shotgun up the gully last night about dark. Pretty soon along comes a truck and parks just over the fence from me, that part was a fluke, I guess. Well, when the people in it came across the fence I saw they were carrying gas cans along."

"Out to burn you in your bed," Redmon said. "That's Ku Klux style."

"It's what I thought too at the time," Laidlaw said. "I'd been wondering since if they might've meant to just light some kind of fire out in the field or somewhere. You know, just to throw me a scare."

"Fat chance," Redmon said.

"I'll never know now," Laidlaw said. "Next thing was I lost my temper. I went over the fence and lit off the truck. Couldn't tell whose truck it might be in the dark and I wasn't really thinking much about it at the time. So while I was busy with that they got down to the house and I guess they would've burned it then, after I'd already burned the truck. But then the dog got out and tangled with them."

"Then they shot the dog," Redmon said.

"Yeah," Laidlaw said. "Then I shot one of the gas cans and it went off, they never lit it. While they were looking at that I shortened up the range and scattered them and ran them off through the woods." He shrugged. "I guess I peeled some skin off some of them and that's about all. They didn't hurt me or come anywhere near it. The blood's all from carrying the dog."

"But you're mad, aren't you?" Redmon said.

"I was last night," Laidlaw said. "Now I'm just miserable."

"Hell, what for?" Redmon said. "Sounds like you had yourself a big time." He stood up and put his glass down on the porch rail. "Meanwhile, I expect I've worn out my welcome."

"What are you talking about?" Laidlaw said. "I told you everything you asked for."

"All but what they came here for," Redmon said. "And you don't have to tell me that."

"Wait a minute." Laidlaw rose too, blocking the path to the steps.

Redmon's face turned hard and bright. "For what?" he said. "Come on, white folks, stand out of my way."

"Don't you call me that," Laidlaw said.

"Am I telling you a lie?" Redmon said. His face cracked. "All right, Laidlaw, I'll take it back. But just let me get by you."

"Hey, man," Laidlaw said, walking after him up toward the track. "You can come and go as you please, by me. I just don't follow this, is all. It wasn't *you* they raided."

Redmon tucked his chin in tight. "Oh no," he said. "I'd love to've seen what happened if they'd known where I lived at."

"To hell with them, they won't be back," Laidlaw said, spreading his arms out. They had reached the gate, and Redmon unlatched it. Laidlaw followed him through and let the gate fall open behind him. "It's just a stupid thing," he said. "That crowd don't mean a thing to me."

"*Now* you're lying," Redmon said. He swung his leg up over the saddle of the motorcycle.

"Nice bike," Laidlaw said wretchedly.

"Ain't it, though," Redmon said. "Goodbuddy loaned it to me a while back."

"You got to be kidding," Laidlaw said, and smiled a little in spite of his mood. "Now why don't you come on back to the house and tell me that one till I believe it."

"I don't think so," Redmon said. "Not today."

Laidlaw stooped down and picked up a rock and threw it wild, toward the garden. It bounced off the roof of his tool shed with a clang. He swung back around to face Redmon, sitting on the bike.

"Man, I don't believe this can be happening," Laidlaw said. "I want you to understand, I haven't been trying for all that much. I didn't ever ask for any friends, never asked for a girlfriend either, I didn't even go looking for the *dog*, for God's sake. All I wanted was to play a little music and live where the neighbors weren't too close and I could hear the birds. Now this. What did I do?"

"I'd say you practically kissed a nigger," Redmon said. "Out there in front of God and everybody. Think you needed to do any more?"

"You think I wouldn't do it again?"

"Just run it one time slowly through your mind, now," Redmon said. "We could have hunted each other up any time this last year, wonder why we didn't? It just wasn't that important."

"It is now," Laidlaw said.

Redmon shrugged. "We can't bring each other anything but trouble," he said. "Ain't no way it's going to work out any better."

"But I want it to," Laidlaw said.

"Is that a fact?" Redmon said. "Guess you're fixing to find out how it feels to not get what you want."

Before Laidlaw could answer, he had turned the key and kicked the starter. The bike roared, bucked up over the rim of the road, and a second later it was gone. Laidlaw sneezed from the dust it threw up, and scratched at his nose with his left hand. As the hand came away from his face he saw that it was shaking slightly, and he stared the tremor down until it stopped. It was a hangover from his nightmare, maybe; he still felt like he'd been turned inside out. He hadn't been more than half awake through the whole exchange with Redmon, and if it hadn't been for the plume of dust still spreading out across the fencerows he might have managed to believe he'd dreamed all that part too.

When he turned around to face the house and yard through the open gate, everything looked more or less the way it should. There was a charred ring under the hackberry tree, and above it the leaves on the lower branches had been withered by the sudden shock of heat, but with a slight effort that whole area could be overlooked. Anyway, it was beginning to get dark. The water maples along the creek were throwing long black shadows all the way to the house wall. Laidlaw saw that one of them was advancing faster than the others; it belonged to Adrienne, who was just coming in at the garden gate.

If she saw him standing up there by the road she didn't give any sign of it. He watched her come across the porch and go inside the house. A moment later the screen door creaked again and she came out with the mandolin slung to her shoulder, fingering out a swift jig in A major. Laidlaw felt himself beginning to go slack. It would be an unambiguous comfort, this one time, not to be alone.

Adrienne walked to the end of the porch and stood facing out toward the lowering stain of the sun. She began to linger on the tremolos and the tune slowed down and turned minor under her hand. The mandolin settled into a rich vibration and she took one step backward, as for balance, and began to sing.

> My Lord, He said unto me —
> Do you like this garden so fair?
> You may live in this garden
> If you will feed my lambs
> And I'll return in the cool of the day.

Fine hairs began to lift in a pattern that climbed the back of Laidlaw's neck; it was eerie to have someone else sing out what you had not even yet known you were thinking. He'd just reached out to shut the gate, but now he stopped with his hand barely resting on the chain. A slight chill had already begun to rise and enclose the evening in a cool grasp. It was the time of day when the light fell rapidly. At such an hour, on a day like this had been, you might welcome judgment almost as much as you were obliged to fear it. Adrienne paid out the melody achingly through both hands, to the moment where it overstepped itself and plunged down, and deeper down. When she began to sing again she'd found a lower note than he thought he'd ever heard her strike.

> Now is the cool of the day . . .
> Now is the cool of the day . . .
> Oh, this earth is a garden,
> The garden of my Lord
> And He walks in His garden . . .
> In the cool of the day.

IV

Last Go-Round

(1971—72)

33

IN THICKENING twilight Redmon pulled the motorcycle up to the side of Mosque 37 and Health Food Restaurant and got off. A mean wind sliced down on him as he pulled off his helmet, and he tucked his head down into the bomber jacket's fake fur collar. His hands had stiffened on the handlebars and he flexed his fingers wide to loosen them. The fitful cold of the first fall weeks was securing its grip.

He undid one of the luggage boxes and took out five cans of Spam. It was the custom at his new job to share out the contents of whatever damaged cases might come off the trucks, and from politeness Redmon always took what he was offered, though he couldn't abide Spam. Balancing the cans in a wavery stack, he walked around to the front door of the building. Inside it was very pleasantly warm. He went straight to the counter and put the cans down on it and sat on a revolving stool. Raschid was not in sight at the moment but he had trade: five or six people sitting in a half circle before the monstrous old black-and-white TV set he had erected on a card table in the front corner below the window. Right now its long rabbit ears were pricked to the local news.

Redmon waited, tapping an unlit cigarette on the counter. After a few minutes Raschid came out through the bead curtain that hung across the door to the back room. He had finished the turnip-shaped aperture over the doorway, and the mosque itself had been furnished with whatever he seemed to think it required. Though he still had attracted no more than a handful of halfhearted converts, he remained cheerful on the subject, under any form of teasing Redmon could devise. Also the restaurant side of the operation seemed to be prospering rather well.

"*Salaam aleikum*," Raschid said to Redmon as he slipped in behind the counter.

"Abracadabra," Redmon said.

Raschid snorted at him and turned to lift the lid of one of the big kettles on the stove behind him. A sweet curry smell steamed into the room as he stirred it up with a long steel spoon.

"Smells all right tonight," Redmon said.

Raschid turned and leaned forward on the counter. "Ought to taste good too," he said. "If I didn't miscalculate. You staying for supper tonight, you think?"

"Hadn't made up my mind yet," Redmon said. "I might just wait and see if somebody else tries it."

Raschid tapped the top can in the stack of Spam. "What's all this here?"

"Present for you if you'll have it," Redmon said.

Raschid started laughing. "Now what would I want with that monkey meat?" he said. "I wouldn't eat that even back when I used to eat things like it."

"Well, I'm not fixing to eat it either," Redmon said. "Maybe you could use it to stop cracks or something. Fact is, I thought you might know somebody somewhere that'd be hungry enough to give it a try."

"True," Raschid said. He swept the cans off the counter and stored them somewhere underneath.

"Pork and all?" Redmon said.

"I'll just tell them it was from you."

Redmon smiled. He laid the cigarette flat on the counter and began to roll it from one hand to the other across the Formica. "You know, they stock these little old flat cans of turkey and chicken meat too," he said. "Supposed to mash it up with a fork like it was tuna fish, so I been told. I keep waiting for a box of that to break one time, but it just don't seem to happen."

"Do you?" Raschid said. "Somehow the idea of that don't quite have me licking my chops, myself."

"It's nothing but curiosity," Redmon said. "I don't have all that much to think about, you know, standing around that place all day." He swiveled his stool and looked toward the TV. A big kissy mouth was rushing hard at the screen, accompanied by a zippy jingle:

> Ultra Brite —
> Gives your mouth —
> *Smack — zoom —*
> *Sex* appeal.

He snapped his fingers and turned back.

"Still thinking about making a change?" Raschid said.

"After while," Redmon said. "I had me a look at that UT night school. But I think I might wait till next fall and start even."

"They roll it all over after Christmas too, don't they?" Raschid said. "End of January, or something like that?"

"Well, they do," Redmon said. "But my parole'll be up if I wait till the fall."

"What's the difference?" Raschid said. "Think they'd stop you going to school?"

"Not hardly," Redmon said. "But I don't like them patting me on the head any better than anything else they do. Them breathing down my neck all the time, it spoils the taste of whatever it is."

"Well, could be," Raschid said. "Wait a minute now."

A young woman wearing an outsized man's pea coat over a white uniform had come in leading two children by either hand: a little boy and a smaller girl. Raschid went over and conferred with her, then came back and began to spoon rice and stew into three bowls. He put the bowls on the tray with two glasses of milk and a cup of tea, served the table, and returned.

"So," Redmon said. "What's the news?"

"No news." Raschid's glasses had fogged in the steam from the pots. He took them off and wiped them on the white sleeve of his robe and pushed them back up his nose, blinking. "How's your daddy getting on?" he said.

"Surviving, I suppose," Redmon said. "He fusses a lot about the shape he's in, but I don't know what it amounts to, really."

"You don't take him serious?"

"I tried to," Redmon said, batting the cigarette back and forth on the counter. "But when it gets down to going to see the doctor, then he don't want to go. But I figure he should be all right if that old buzzard he lives with hadn't picked his bones clean yet. Anyhow, I'm due to go find out the next day or so."

"Tell him I said hello," Raschid said.

"He knew what you were up to over here, I think he'd be mighty surprised," Redmon said.

"Why not give him a thrill?" Raschid said. "I'll serve him a free dinner any time he cares to come in."

Redmon picked up the unlit cigarette and began to twiddle it through his fingers.

"Smoke that thing," Raschid said. "You're about to drive me crazy with that fiddling."

Redmon dropped the cigarette into his shirt pocket next to the pack. "Ah, I doubt he'll ever claim it," he said. "He tells me it's more trouble than it's worth for him to come all this way into town."

"It's some distance," Raschid said. "I'll tell you who did make it in today, though."

"Who's that?"

"Your man Laidlaw."

"You're fooling," Redmon said. "He came in here?"

"Big as life."

"Hell on fire . . ." Redmon said. "You better mind out he don't have a lynch mob following him. What was he after, anyhow?"

"You," Raschid said. "He was looking for you."

"You're fooling with me," Redmon said. "What did he say to you?"

"Nothing much," Raschid said. "Asked for you by name, if I knew you, knew where you lived at and all. He'd been trying all down the street, I think. I saw him go into Brother Pig when he left here."

"What did you tell him?"

"Not a thing," Raschid said. "I don't know but what somebody else might have. He does know you live someplace around here, at least."

"Well, I might have told him that myself," Redmon said. "Did he know you?"

"How would he?" Raschid said. "I didn't know him till he said his name. He never laid eyes on me since he was a child, got no real call to remember."

"Well," Redmon said. "It's funny."

"You hadn't seen him at all since that business?"

Redmon shook his head. "Not a hair of him," he said. "It makes two, three months now, I guess, and I hadn't missed him much either. I do wonder what he's after, though."

"Easy enough for you to find out if you want to," Raschid said. "You remember where he lives at, don't you?"

"Are you recommending it? He should just be one more blue-eyed devil, according to you."

"No doubt about that."

"What are you trying to tell me, then?"

Raschid reached behind him to turn down the stove. "I wouldn't call it one way or the other," he said. "I'm just passing the word, that's all."

34

LAIDLAW STAYED up and up and up and up until he believed all
weight would leave him to go floating out above the bowl of the valley
altogether. In the deep of the night the cold began to grow raw, though
it was not yet quite a numbing cold. He went up to the hilltop above
the orchard and beyond it, as far as the second ridge that overlooked
the highway, before he turned back. The earliest trees to lose their
leaves had lost them and they crackled drily underfoot along with the
fallen seed pods and acorns and the drying stubble of the underbrush.
In whatever place a tree had gone bare there would be a latticed gap
in the cover through which he might see a section of the sky with a
few stars in it and the least hangnail of moon. Apart from that it was
very dark on the woods floor. He moved rather slowly, no quicker
than he needed to to keep himself reasonably warm.

Since the low field had last been cut not much had grown back but
some tall ironweed plants and a couple of thistles among them. The
short grass grew in uneven thick clumps that had begun to get dry
and papery with the cold. He stopped for a while in the middle of the
field to watch the spectral shadows of the ironweed moving in the
rhythm of the light westerly breeze. Though there was so little
moon the sky still seemed very light in the open, with the round
rollers of the tree-covered hills standing against it much more
darkly. But a shelf of cloud had appeared over the western hills, and
while he waited in the field it pushed itself all the way over to the
eastern ridge, closing down the valley like the lid of a box. The
breathless dark which succeeded stunned him enough that he felt he
might sleep, and he put his foot forward and began to walk toward
the fencerow, toward the garden and the house. But there was
something coming on the road, pushing a yellow column of light
ahead of it, up the gradual rise of the hill.

After he had watched it for a moment, he saw that its nagging peculiarity was that there was only one beam instead of two, and yet it was very quiet and went more slowly than any motorcycle he was used to seeing pass this way. Also it was very late for any kind of traffic, whatever it might be; there was not but an hour or so left before dawn. Still, he was somehow surprised when the motorcycle turned into his gateway and stopped there, just off the road. He went circling back around by the garden gate and the creek ford and so came to the lower corner of the porch, on the far side of the house from the gate to the road. The beam of the single headlight glared over the leaves still hanging to the snarl of honeysuckle vines and broke into slices of light falling through the slats of the gate.

After a little, the light died, and he moved quickly away from the house toward the fencerow, thinking that the rider's eyes could not adjust to the dark in the time it would take him to cross the yard. It was so pitch-black that he could hardly see anything himself. He went carefully up the hill, post by post along the fence toward the gate, straining his eyes at the tarry dark. He was near enough to hear the tick of the engine cooling before he could begin to pick out the outline of the bike and then the rider too, slouched over with one leg braced on the ground, and with a curious cannonball-shaped head. When he had just begun to discern it, the head revolved his way and spoke.

"Is that you?"

"Who else?" Laidlaw said.

He had come so near he needed to speak no louder than a whisper. Now he took a few more steps and came full in front of the gate. From there he could see the helmeted figure more clearly marked out against the faint chalk-white of the roadbed behind.

"What brings you out this time of night?"

"Couldn't sleep," Redmon said.

"I know," Laidlaw said. "I've had that problem at times myself."

The motorcycle tipped a little and Redmon shifted his bracing leg to bring it more upright. The gravel crunched, scraping under his boot. For some time more, he didn't speak. Laidlaw leaned his elbows on the unbroken part of the gate's top rail.

"Cold tonight," Redmon said at length.

"Come on back to the house," Laidlaw said. "There'll be a coal left in the stove yet if we have any luck."

The iron links of the chain chinked as he lifted it from the nail. The gate was sagging on its tilted post and it dragged over roots and hummocks of dirt as he hauled it open. Redmon hesitated a moment more, then swung out of his saddle and wheeled the bike quietly through the gateway, down the track toward where Laidlaw's truck was parked. Laidlaw shut the gate back behind him. He could no longer see Redmon once he had gone a few yards ahead, but he heard him knock the kickstand down and move away from the bike. Away up the hill a ewe bleated dolefully but she was too far gone in the night to be seen either.

Laidlaw turned from the gate and moved down the track with his right arm slightly crooked and held out before him. Near the truck's tailgate he discovered Redmon again by jamming his fingers into the back of his leather jacket.

"Dark as the cave," Redmon said.

"Sure is," Laidlaw said. "Let's go in."

They walked down to the porch steps, close enough to each other that their shoulders knocked together any time one of them made a misstep. Redmon went up the stairs first but paused and waited before the door.

"Ain't locked," Laidlaw said.

But Redmon still waited until Laidlaw had opened the door and entered, then followed him in close. *"Don't put the light on,"* he said.

Laidlaw stopped with his hand on the switch. They were both still speaking in forced whispers, he had no idea why. "All right," he said. "Shut the door, would you then?"

Redmon was still standing in the door frame. When he had stepped into the room and closed it, the darkness there grew denser still. Laidlaw went to open the drum of the stove. A chunk of bodock had held out during his absence and was smoldering smokily on the iron floor. He took up a long thin stick and poked it till a flame leapt up, then added a couple of pieces of dry hackberry.

"Well, drag up a chair," Laidlaw said.

The open stove door threw out firelight over the floor about as far as Redmon's feet. There was a squeak of wood on wood as Redmon brought one of the straight chairs nearer to the fire. He had taken off the helmet and put it somewhere and Laidlaw could see his face, brass-colored in the firelight, for a second before he shut the stove door.

"It's been changed," Redmon muttered. "Emptier."

"I had to clear it out," Laidlaw said. "Lot of people been through."

Redmon didn't answer. Laidlaw knew where he was by memory

but he made no sound at all and there was no light to see him by.

"It's the same old stove, at least," Laidlaw said, and took a couple of steps toward the kitchen.

"*Leave it dark,*" Redmon said.

Laidlaw nodded, as if the gesture could be seen, then went through the kitchen door and began to feel his way down the cabinets. It must not have been absolutely dark everywhere because there was a glimmer of reflection off the panes in the cupboard doors. He groped the left one open and felt for the whiskey bottle and a couple of jelly jars and found his way back to the other room, following the glow of the cracks in the stove.

"Take a drink?" he said, having arrived.

"Not but a mouthful."

Laidlaw poured a splash in a jar and held it out. Redmon's fingers came fumbling over the back of his hand before they got hold of the jar and took it away. Laidlaw sat down and had his own drink and then lit a cigarette. He heard the clink of Redmon's putting his glass down on the bare floor.

"Bottle's here whenever you need it," he said.

Redmon kept his silence. It seemed he scarcely breathed. Laidlaw had no definite notion what his mind might be traveling toward. "It'll be light soon," he said, as though it were a comfort.

"What do you do?" Redmon said.

"Do what?" Laidlaw said. Opposite him the other chair gave out a moan as Redmon's weight shifted.

"When you can't sleep."

"Well, I stay up," Laidlaw said, changing his own position, leaning to tip his ashes in the bucket near the stove. "I roam around in the woods, is what I mostly do."

"All night long?"

"Till about now."

"Ah," Redmon said. "I thought I never heard you come out the house."

Laidlaw moved to put more wood on the fire. In the light from the stove door he could see Redmon leaning far forward with his chin propped in his hands. His glass was on the floor by his feet and Laidlaw couldn't tell if he had touched it. Laidlaw dropped the end of his cigarette into the fire and shut the stove door back.

"Ever meet anybody out there?" Redmon said.

"Rarely."

"Living or dead?"

Laidlaw coughed out a sort of a laugh. "Living, always," he said. "Ain't no ghosts allowed in my woods."

"But don't you dream about them, though?"

"I don't dream anymore," Laidlaw said. "Didn't I once tell you that?"

"Yeah, but I do," Redmon said. "I'm telling you, I dream all the time."

"I don't sleep that much," Laidlaw said.

"I believe you must have said that too," Redmon said.

For an instant his face came alight again in the brief blaze of a match. He drew on the cigarette a time or two and then the spark lowered to rock slightly just off the floor, like it must be swinging at the full length of a slack arm. When Laidlaw offered the bottle again he drew no response, so he poured himself another drink and then, a while later, a third. The room was too dark for him to see the level of his glass and each time he dumped in more than he knew. The room was getting very warm, but still he stayed near the fire and kept it built up. The chinks in the stove glowed privately to themselves, throwing no light into the space of the room. A pair of screech owls had begun to hoot to each other in careful soft voices somewhere up the hill beyond the barns. The two windows on either side of the stovepipe were beginning to turn into pale gaps in the wall of darkness. By the time Laidlaw could see through them clear to the outside, he could also see that Redmon had slumped all the way down in his chair and was breathing hoarsely through his mouth in his sleep.

"Rodney," Laidlaw said. "Hey, Rod?"

Redmon's head jerked up and his eyes whitely widened. "What?"

"Easy," Laidlaw said. "Go on and lie down on the bed. Right there on the floor behind you. You'll get a kink in your back trying to sleep on that old hard chair."

"All right," Redmon said. "What about you?"

"Looks like I'm on the whiskey," Laidlaw said.

"All right, I will," Redmon said. He rose and swung himself around to sit down on the edge of the pallet.

"Take your shoes off, fool," Laidlaw said. "That's all I ask."

Redmon smiled and reached for his laces. A minute later he was on his back. By the time he had begun to snore the light in the room had grown quite clear. Laidlaw got up and put the bottle away, what was left of it. He drank the drink that Redmon had left and set both glasses in the sink, then went outside on the porch. Now he could see it had frosted hard during the night; a chillingly brilliant layer of ice spread all over the yard and across the pastures. It was crisp under his feet as he walked up to the sheep barn. He broke a bale of hay under his feet and scattered it out across the slope and waited there till the sheep came flocking down from the crown of the hill to eat it.

Afterward he climbed up past the pond and stood for a time by the three-strand fence at the edge of the woods, taking in the early morning quiet. Far off down the road a rooster could just barely be heard to crow, and apart from that the whole valley was as silent as if it had been closed away under a crystal bell. Below, the sheep were finishing the hay and beginning to scatter back out across the hillside. The peacock was still at his roost in his usual tree, neck retracted, head despondently tucked in, as though the cold and frost depressed him. Laidlaw had been a little drunk when he first came out but now the cold had sobered him considerably. He stayed where he was, watching the jeweled movement of the new light across the frost, until the sun had lifted itself entirely clear of the tree line behind him. The cloud cover of the previous night had swept on past, so that the sunlight came down unhindered from a deep untrammeled blue sky. There was no wind either; the smoke from his stovepipe was standing straight up. On his way back down he noticed that there was just the least wrinkle of ice on the surface of the pond.

Going back to the house he saw that Redmon was coming around from the side porch in his sock feet, carrying an armload of wood. He looked well at home there in the daylight; Laidlaw could imagine for an instant that he himself was the guest. He hurried up the steps to pull the door open. Redmon carried the wood in and dumped it by the stove.

"You're up early," Laidlaw said. "Sleep all right?"

"Like a baby," Redmon said. "I started the coffee, you don't mind?"

"Not if I get some," Laidlaw said, and went after him back toward the kitchen.

In the warmth of the house he felt a little tipsy once again and there was another giddy layer that came from his sleeplessness. Redmon handed him a cup. Whatever strangeness had haunted his gestures during the night now seemed to have passed on by.

"I been approaching the day in a backwards direction," Laidlaw said, motioning toward the bourbon bottle as he sipped on the coffee. "It might be an idea if I cooked us some breakfast."

"I could eat it if you did," Redmon said, and moved around to lean on the big white freezer Laidlaw had installed at the far end of the kitchen.

Laidlaw reached into the refrigerator for a sack of sausage and began to cut rounds from it, tossing each into the iron skillet after he peeled it loose from the cloth.

"Be damn if that don't look like home-grown hogmeat," Redmon said.

"I went in on a hog with the Gileses last year," Laidlaw said, and pinched his lip in his teeth as he heard just what he'd said. A silence was thickening behind him, he felt, but he didn't turn around to check. "You're in luck. This is mighty near the last of it. Don't look like we'll do it again this year, at least I hadn't heard from them."

"None of my business either way," Redmon said. "What say we just let it alone?"

"I'd just as soon." Laidlaw turned the heat on under the skillet and reached to the lip of the sink for his coffee cup. "See where you're still riding that bike you said Goodbuddy lent you. Weren't you planning to tell me that tale next time we ran across each other?"

"Oh," Redmon said. "Did I say that? Well, it was just . . . He sort of owes me a favor, you might say."

"What would you ever do to earn it?"

"Went to jail."

"No fooling?" Laidlaw said. "Man, that sounds like almost too large of a favor to be doing for old Goodbuddy."

"I never did it on purpose," Redmon said.

Laidlaw picked up a fork from the drainboard and pushed the sausage cakes around the floor of the skillet so they wouldn't start to stick. The iron was warm enough now that the meat was beginning to sweat out a little grease.

"Goodbuddy was what you might call uncommonly friendly right around when I got shut of the army," Redmon said. "Matter of fact, he asked me did I want to go in partners with him in the old real estate and development business there."

"Did he now?" Laidlaw said. "I wouldn't have thought —"

"Me neither," Redmon said. "I wouldn't have thought Clemsons'd have a boogie in the business, especially not the old man."

"You wouldn't say that either one would honestly be inclined that way," Laidlaw said. "But don't you remember some kind of a mess the old man was supposed to be in, between the Klan and the FBI and whatever? Back when you were little and I was littler. Don't I remember some people went to jail on that in the end?"

"But not old Clemson," Redmon said. "He snaked out of it. And still slithering around to this day. Anyhow, he was keeping kind of a low profile around our end of the trade. Goodbuddy had set him up his own little office there on the Hillsboro road and the old man didn't hardly come around there at all."

"I believe I've passed the place," Laidlaw said.

"You'd passed it this time two years ago, you'd have seen my name on the board out front."

"Man," Laidlaw said. "Partners with Goodbuddy."

"I know what you mean," Redmon said. "But it was about the only opportunity that knocked. If I look back I see I might ought to have gone into truck unloading right away and saved myself this mess of trouble, but I had bigger ideas at the time, don't you know? Also I never thought Goodbuddy could get very far around me with nothing but his black-market number and all those little tricks he picked up in the Quartermaster Corps. I didn't think he was smart enough. Still don't, if you come right down to it, but it does look like some other people was pulling his strings."

"And then what happened?" Laidlaw took up the fork again, turned the sausages over, and put a pot of water on to boil.

"Well, I had me a fine old time at the beginning," Redmon said. "Wore that white collar and tie in to work every day. I'd sit at my desk and talk on the phone, and I'd go out around the building sites, and I used to talk to all kinds of nice folks down at the bank. Then after about ten months we're all in court for about five different kinds of fraud and in the end it got decided that I had to be the one did it."

"Did what, exactly?" Laidlaw said. He cut into a sausage with the side of the fork but it was still showing a little pink.

"What I was told, more or less," Redmon said. "I expect you've seen that development there on the far side of this hill, down where Morgan's front pasture used to be. You know, the one that's fixing to fall down."

"Sure," Laidlaw said. "I understood that was a Clemson project. I only wish it had've failed before they spoiled that pretty place."

"I was all for it at the time, myself," Redmon said. "Hell, I was planning to live in one of the houses. But I'm not sure they ever really intended to finish it at all. We once started building on it and then some other gang the Clemsons was in with bid up the price on it and then they started to take out all kinds of bank loans. Then all of a sudden everybody was after us, and the next thing it appeared somebody had to go to jail."

"But you weren't in on it?" Laidlaw said.

"I didn't know I was," Redmon said. "But I signed a mess of papers, that was my problem in the end. They had me making all the trips to the banks. I was right pleased at the time, you know, getting all that responsibility so soon? Then at the trial it came out how it was the new partner let them down, practicing all this fraud and what have you."

The water on the stove had come to a boil. Laidlaw poured in some grits from a cardboard canister, then stirred the mix with a long steel spoon.

"And you couldn't bring it back to them in court?"

"Easier said than done," Redmon said. "Also I was sort of talked out of it. We all had the one lawyer, you know, who they picked. And first we were all going to get off together, and then it was going to be a suspended sentence, and then it was going to be nothing but a fine, and the next thing I knew I was getting that new suit of clothes with the numbers all over it."

"What was really in it for them, though?" Laidlaw pushed the sausage to the edge of the pan and began breaking eggs into the hot grease. "I mean, I don't see how they could get any money out, for one thing."

"But they could have," Redmon said. "It was all so confusing there at the end nobody could quite tell where the money had got to. I was the one supposed to know, remember, and I sure to God didn't. But I think they didn't mean for it to fall out just like it did. They had me stuck in there like a safety valve for in case something wrong, and looks like that's what happened. Also they could have been playing some politics along with it."

"For what?" Laidlaw said, flipping the eggs.

"Well, first they get their spade partner in there, the nigger in the window, don't you know?" Redmon said. "That gets them in real good with the liberals and the nigger-lovers. The ancient snakes out in Clemson country might not like it so well, unless maybe it was their idea in the first place. Then the spade partner gets busted and they get to pull a long face and go around saying, 'Well, try'n help one them boys'n see whar it gets ye.' And now nobody can say they didn't have their heart in the right place. Anyhow, that was what I started thinking when I was sitting around up there in Brushy Mountain."

"Hell, they never sent you there?" Laidlaw said. "For a little hitch on a charge like that?"

"I believe it was an accident. I just got on the wrong bus," Redmon said. "See, when they separated the sheep from the goats, everybody just naturally assumed I should go with the goats." He shrugged. "Wasn't quite as bad as they say, though I wouldn't care to go back. I sent off for a course or two. And I had me all kinds of time to think about things."

"I'd thought of killing off Goodbuddy if I'd been in your place," Laidlaw said. "Him and the whole sorry lot of them."

"I expect they'd send me back to the pokey if I was to try and do that," Redmon said. "Probably before I had time to get done."

"Sons of bitches," Laidlaw said.

"But they're cunning, you got to give them that," Redmon said. "They pulled a fast one on this old shine." He grinned across the room at Laidlaw, slitting his eyes up, then suddenly let his face go blank. "I did go see Goodbuddy the one time after I got out," he said. "Don't quite know what I was meaning to do. But the upshot was, I asked could I go for a ride on his bike and he never wanted it back till yet."

"Don't sound like Goodbuddy's usual style."

"No," Redmon said. "Well, he's a little scared of me, I think. He's been a little scared of the both of us, probably, especially after overseas. Or it might be he had his conscience hurting him. He promised he was going to send me cookies and things up there in the slammer, but you know I never got a one."

"That I believe," Laidlaw said, serving up plates. "Maybe I ought to ride over there one time and kill him myself."

"You don't have to on my account," Redmon said. "Why don't we quit talking about it, that breakfast looks too good to ruin."

They ate in the front room where there was a table, rapidly and without saying much, though Redmon passed a few complimentary remarks on the food. When they had done, Laidlaw put the dishes in the sink and then followed Redmon out in the back yard, where he'd gone to smoke a cigarette. It was a little warmer now, warm enough the frost had melted.

"Pretty day," Redmon said. "That hill looks handsome with the leaves turned on it."

"They're falling fast now," Laidlaw said. "We might take a walk if you got time."

"I'm not hard pressed," Redmon said. But neither of them moved from where he was standing.

"Spend a lot of time in the woods, do you?" Redmon said. "What were you talking about meeting people?"

"Nothing particular," Laidlaw said.

"Come on," Redmon said. "I told you my secrets."

"Well, I found out somebody was jacking deer by the woods pond," Laidlaw said. "So I went down there one night and jacked him."

Redmon whistled. "Serious? You get him?"

"I never intended to do all that much," Laidlaw said. There was an unpleasant twisting in his stomach, maybe just the coffee opening a quarrel with the whiskey. "I only meant to take his gun off him and scare him out of there well enough he'd stay gone. But when I once got there . . ."

"In the dark," Redmon said.

"You know it."

"How bad was it?"

"I know he couldn't have been hurt too bad because he got out of there some way, on his own hook," Laidlaw said. "I went back and made sure of that much. But past that I just can't tell you at all. Once it got started my mind got all jumbled up and . . . I don't think I knew right where I was at, exactly."

"You want to be careful about that kind of thing," Redmon said. "Sounds like you're pretty near living out one of my dreams."

"It could be I overreacted a little," Laidlaw said. "But he butchered a doe right there in my woods and left it there looking like you know what."

"Don't," Redmon said. "You know, I don't think I hardly stepped a foot in the woods the whole time I been back."

"You might like it better than you think," Laidlaw said.

"Sounds wonderful the way you tell about it," Redmon said.

"That was only one time in five hundred," Laidlaw said. "Besides, it's daylight now."

"Well, thank you for the offer," Redmon said. "I might try it next time." He started walking toward the house, and Laidlaw went after him.

"Wait a minute, are you leaving?" Laidlaw said.

"I got a couple of things to do," Redmon said, sliding in at the kitchen door. "Probably you could say the same. Where's the girlfriend, by the way, or did you quit on that?"

"Oh, she went off on a fiddling trip," Laidlaw said. "Got an out-of-town job for a couple of days, she won't be back till Tuesday. She'd be proud to know you anyway, man. Come back any time you want to."

"I might," Redmon said. He reached down and collected his helmet off the seat of a chair beside the front door.

"Or I'll come see you if you'll tell me where," Laidlaw said.

"I don't know," Redmon said. "It's not much of a place. I'm due to go by Daddy's house the next few days, though, maybe I'll pass by here coming or going." He paused. "You never tried there when you were looking for me?"

"No, I didn't," Laidlaw said.

"You hadn't been by there since you got out, have you? I know he'd have told me if you had."

"Well, I'll go," Laidlaw said, smiling crookedly. "Maybe I could go sometime with you."

"Maybe so," Redmon said, and pushed the front door open.

"I'll lay for you over there if you don't come back," Laidlaw said. "How did you find out I'd been looking for you, anyway?"

"Somebody told me," Redmon said. "You were getting pretty warm. What gave you the notion to hunt me up?"

Laidlaw shrugged. Redmon was standing with the light behind him, so bright Laidlaw couldn't make out his face. A sharp tongue of sunshine came in between his feet and made a hard-edged triangle on the planks of the floor.

"I wanted to see you," Laidlaw said. "I wanted it all to go back like it was."

"Well, it's not going to go back that way," Redmon said. "It's not the same place and too much already happened, you know the kind of things that can happen to people."

"I know." Laidlaw took a step closer but Redmon's face was still too deep in the shadow for him to read the expression of it. "But then we just have to make up something new."

"We'll see about it," Redmon said, moving all the way outside. "Sure, I suppose we could always try that."

35

REDMON PAUSED for a moment in front of Laidlaw's gate and
looked down at the powdering of snow along the ridgepole of the
house. It hardly seemed that much different from when they all had
lived there, not the house itself at least, not from the outside. In the
yard or on the track there would formerly have been a lot more odds
and ends of broken-down machinery that Daddy would be meaning
to fix someday. Laidlaw held on to nothing of that kind. Redmon
unchained the gate and pushed it open. Laidlaw's stovepipe was
smoking, and there was light at the windows. Behind and above the
roof's peak, the sky was darkening rapidly, stars already beginning to
come out. He rolled the bike through and knocked down the
kickstand and moved back to close the gate behind him. The coat of
snow on the ground was so fine that his footprints cut through it to
the dirt. He walked down the slope and up the steps to the porch to
knock on the door.

There was no answer, and after the second knock he stooped to
peer in at the near window, but he could see no one and in a moment
his breath had fogged the pane. If Laidlaw was not at home, that girl
Adrienne might be; he hadn't noticed her car anywhere, but sometimes they would switch. He straightened up away from the window
and reflexively looked down to the side of the door where Daddy
used to keep the key hid underneath a big white shell from the
ocean. But the shell was not there anymore, and the door was not
locked anyway. Redmon knew he was welcome to walk in, but
though he came out here quite often now, he never liked to enter
before he'd been asked. Instead, he walked to the high side of the
porch and looked out. It was pretty well dark already, but he could
see a shadow shaped like Laidlaw coming down the hill from the
barn.

"Hey, Rod," Laidlaw said as he came up the steps.

"Where you been?" Redmon said. "Out running the woods?"

"Just out to feed," Laidlaw said, touching him briefly on the shoulder. "Come on in the house. Cold, ain't it?"

"Bitter," Redmon said, following him in. His face, which had stiffened on the long ride out, could barely register the warmth of the room. Laidlaw opened the stove and threw in a couple of sticks and shut it back, then moved off toward the kitchen. Redmon sat down on the nearest chair and pulled the zipper of his jacket open. The room still surprised him whenever he first came into it; in his time it had been so choked with stuff that it had seemed about half the size it did now it was more bare. Laidlaw came back from the kitchen with two bottles of beer and passed one of them over to Redmon. His face was flushed a bright red from the cold. Redmon twisted the cap from his bottle and drank.

"Want a sip of whiskey to go along with that?" Laidlaw said.

"Nah," Redmon said. "Not yet awhile."

"Hungry?" Laidlaw said.

"I had something in town," Redmon said. "You go ahead and eat if you want to."

"I might make a sandwich or something," Laidlaw said. "Here in a minute. What's the news?"

"Nothing particular," Redmon said. "You looking for your girlfriend tonight?"

"No," Laidlaw said. "She's killing her own cats this evening. I was just on my lonesome till you showed up."

"Well, I was just on my way over to see Daddy," Redmon said. "Thought maybe you might like to go too."

Laidlaw's eyes slid away from Redmon and tracked some distance across the floor. "Now?" he said.

"Go on and have your sandwich. Ain't no big hurry."

Laidlaw stood up and took a long pull at his beer. "It'll keep," he said. "I was just going to eat because I'm supposed to, I ain't really all that hungry."

"Suit yourself," Redmon said. "Why don't you bring along your banjo?"

"You think?" Laidlaw said. He reached across to damp down the stove, then lifted the beer bottle and emptied it with another long gulp.

"He'd like to hear you," Redmon said. "I been telling him how good you got."

"Have you now?" Laidlaw said. "Well. All right."

"Also I been thinking," Redmon said. "We might could persuade him to get his fiddle out."

"All right, then," Laidlaw said, and stooped to take hold of the banjo case. "Guess we just as well both ride in the truck, won't have to get so cold that way."

Either side of the road the fields were sifted over with snow, and whenever Laidlaw glanced over he could see Redmon's profile sharply outlined against that flat white. Redmon held his beer bottle between his thighs, fingering the label. He had nothing to say the whole drive across to the highway and Laidlaw could not guess his mood. He was feeling mildly uneasy about the visit without knowing why, and Redmon's silence did not do much to reassure him.

Once they reached the paved road it was only a short haul up to the dog-run cabin. Laidlaw pulled the truck up behind another car and parked. Getting out, Redmon drained his beer bottle and slung it in the direction of an old washing machine that lay on its side at the edge of the yard, half overgrown with weeds and vines. Laidlaw turned his head toward the clang.

"What difference does it make?" Redmon muttered.

Not knowing, Laidlaw slid the banjo toward him off the seat of the truck, and closed the door after him. There was light showing at the window to the left of the dog run, but no one came when Redmon jangled the string of bells.

"Old buzzard must be gone somewhere," he said.

"I won't miss her if you won't," Laidlaw said.

The door opened just a crack when Redmon tried it, and then stopped. He unfolded a jackknife from his pocket and slid the blade up through the gap to turn back the latch. Laidlaw followed him into the dark passage.

"Mind your step," Redmon said.

Laidlaw went in gently, holding the banjo tight against his knee. A door to the left was outlined by cracks of light and Redmon pushed it open quietly and went through. When Laidlaw came to the threshold he could see where Wat was sleeping in a raggedy stuffed chair, turned over toward one arm, with his legs drawn up under him; he was small enough to almost fit himself completely into the chair seat, as a child might have done. In the yellowish light which shone on him from a lamp on a nearby shelf, he looked much younger than he possibly could have been, his coppery face smooth, unlined, handsome as Laidlaw remembered it from when he was a little boy. You could barely tell that he was breathing.

"Daddy," Redmon said, just in an ordinary speaking tone.

Wat came quickly upright, his sock feet hitting the floor with a soft thump. For an instant after his eyes had opened he looked as young and untroubled as he had asleep. But as his eyes came into focus his face collapsed into a maze of wrinkles; it seemed to Laidlaw that his age had dropped over him all at once, like a net, though he was smiling.

"*Pepper,*" Wat said. "Who that with you?"

"I brought him," Redmon said almost tonelessly. Laidlaw took a step farther into the room and set the banjo case down on the floor. Wat was looking a little confused, and he could feel his own smile beginning to stiffen on his face.

"Why . . . *Tommy.*" Wat's face broke forth in a light of comprehension. "Tommy," he said. "Ain't that *you.* Come on over here . . . and let me get a *good* . . . look at you."

Laidlaw walked over and put out his hand to shake. Wat's hand looked palsied as it came out to meet his, but his grip, once achieved, was strong as it ever had been. When the clasp was done, he kept holding on.

"*Tommy,*" he said. "How long you been back . . . *this*away?"

"A while, I reckon," Laidlaw said, a little disoriented by the offbeat emphasis of Wat's speech. It was something he had nearly forgotten, something which also seemed to have got a lot worse.

"I *hoped* . . ." Wat said, and momentarily seemed to lose the thread. "I hoped to *see* you . . . Tommy."

"I'm proud to see you," Laidlaw said. "You know I am. This last little while, I just been struggling to keep my head above water, back over there."

Wat's hold of his hand was like a caress, and still it unnerved him. He had been afraid of coming here for a long time and he could tell plainly that the thing he had feared was beginning to happen now, though he still didn't quite know what it was.

"Turn him loose now, Daddy," Redmon said, "if you want to hear him play."

Wat looked around, letting his hand come shakily undone from Laidlaw's. Gratefully Laidlaw backed away to sit on the edge of the bed, and leaned over to undo the fastenings of the banjo case. When he straightened up, drawing the instrument to him, Wat was still looking at him with the same bright-eyed fascination. Seemingly apart from his attention, Wat's hand worked through a pile of clothes and papers that came as high as the arm of his chair, until it came forth with a flat pint bottle. Softly Laidlaw tested the tuning, watching him drink.

"Do you reckon . . ." Wat said, lowering the bottle and clearing his throat.

"He's good grown now, Daddy," Redmon said, a slight edge of impatience in his voice. He had remained standing, so far. "He ain't hardly any younger than me."

Wat swiveled his head around his way. "Well, now I *believe* . . ." he said. "Pepper . . . best you step in the kitchen . . . and get a *glass* for Tommy . . ."

"The hell with that," Laidlaw said rapidly, and leaned across the gap to claim the bottle from Wat's hand. It was still uncapped, and he took a hard drink from it as quickly as he'd settled back in his seat. Had he been more in private he possibly would have screamed. As it was, he just breathed carefully through his nose, inspecting the bottle at arm's length with slightly runny eyes. The liquor looked a great deal like kerosene, except that when he gave it a shake, numerous small black specks rose from the bottom. He passed the bottle over to Redmon, who was looking down on him with a somewhat sour smile.

"Enjoy," Laidlaw said.

Redmon drank without comment, recapped the bottle, and set it down on the pile by Wat's chair. Wat's hand settled back over it, the fingers half-consciously stroking, as one might stroke a dog or a cat. Laidlaw, still with a scorching throat, struck up "The Arkansas Traveler," frailing softly, then beginning to drop-thumb. The banjo was brashly loud in the little room, though he wasn't using picks. He played through one break and then returned to the verse and quit when it was done.

"Aw now . . ." Wat said. "Ain't you done *good* . . ." His fingers slid around the walls of the bottle and lifted it again. "Who would have thought . . ." he said, and drank.

The whiskey seemed to have stunned his thought and he lowered his head and kept it down for a moment, hanging over the bottle's neck. After a little time Redmon reached down and took it from him and offered it to Laidlaw, who kissed the rim and gave it back. Wat's head came slowly up, and now his brown eyes were keen again.

"Ain't had sight of you in . . . a *long* time," he murmured. "A long *time,*" he repeated, shifting the beat. "I mean to *ask* you . . . Tommy . . . Do you recollect the time . . ." He stopped.

Laidlaw's mind scrabbled like a rat trying to get up the wall of a well, but Wat offered his memory no more definite clue, though the old man kept on searching his face as if he hoped for help.

"Yes," Laidlaw said finally. "Sure I do."

His right hand began to grope out another tune, sweet and reflective, "Omie Wise." Wat's mouth started to work and move, as if the music had released him. Laidlaw paused to hear what he would say.

"I mind your daddy, now . . . Tommy," Wat said. "I mind him . . ." He stopped and plucked the bottle where it hung loose from Redmon's hand, drank, and laid it down. "I wisht . . ." he said. "You know . . . how the times keep moven . . . they like to done passed us all by. You know, I wisht . . ."

His head hung. Laidlaw looked over at Redmon, who was still on his feet, not a shadow of any expression on his face.

"Come on and play with him," Redmon said. "Get that fiddle out now, let's hear you all play together."

"*Naw,*" Wat said. His smile lit up and widened, though at the same time it seemed like a stall.

"Let's try it," Laidlaw said.

"I can't *think* . . ." Wat said, frowning now. "I can't think *when* I last . . . had *hold* of that fiddle . . ."

"I remember that," Laidlaw said. "I remember how you used to play."

The creases on Wat's face smoothed out and for an instant he seemed as youthful as he had in sleep. With the help of both hands he pushed himself up from the chair and knelt by Laidlaw's feet to lift the skirt of the coverlet and peer up under the bed. Laidlaw put the banjo aside and got down on the floor to help if he could, but he couldn't see anything past Wat's shoulder. Wat began to haul one thing and another out from under the bed, pushing it all into the small clear space on the floor behind him. At last he came out holding an oval wooden fiddle case, splintered along the top where it curved the most. Laidlaw got up and put out a hand to help Wat rise, then put himself back behind the banjo.

Wat was in his chair again, opening the fiddle case across his lap. He first removed the bow and held it to the light as he tightened up the thinning hank of horsehair. Then he lifted the fiddle and held it vertically in front of him and stared at it for a couple of seconds before he nestled it carefully under his chin. Laidlaw sounded an A, and Wat twisted the keys until the fiddle came more or less in tune, sighting down the length of it as though it were a gun. The notes were wavery, not quite true. By the rear wall of the room, Redmon shifted from foot to foot.

Laidlaw commenced "The Arkansas Traveler" once again. After a bar or two, Wat came in behind, slightly sour. There was something the matter with their timing; Wat was not quite on the beat. After a little, Laidlaw changed tactics and began to try to follow the fiddle. But Wat was playing to no rational rhythm, and before long both of them were lost, so tangled up that finally Laidlaw just dropped out. It didn't seem to bother Wat, who kept on playing, his fingers falling one side or the other of most of the notes, a little sharp or flat. Laidlaw stole a look at Redmon, but he couldn't tell if he seemed disappointed or not.

Wat continued to play. He had slipped out of "The Arkansas Traveler" into something else, some withered tune that drifted from the instrument with a smoky fitfulness. Every stroke of the bow seemed fatally unsure but still the tune kept being patched together, and Laidlaw was not disappointed. He had had no definite expectations, which was partly why. In the middle of a phrase, Wat stopped playing suddenly to point the bow at him.

"I mind . . . *Tommy*," he said, and swallowed. "I mind this *hoss*hair . . . It came from your *daddy's* barn . . ."

"Well, I expect it did," Laidlaw said. "Do you recall what horse?"

Wat frowned. "I . . . I *gathered* it," he said. "*All* over, that's what I did . . . Don't you *know* . . . Tommy."

His eyes dulled a little, shortening range; he brought the bow back across the fiddle and the same drowned tune began slowly to rise. It was surely not disappointment that Laidlaw felt now, but an overwhelming sadness, almost sweet in its purity, the least complicated feeling he had had for some time. Though he hardly would have called it unpleasant, in a moment it had grown strong enough that he had to get up and leave the room, moving quickly and keeping his face turned away from the others. Stumbling a little in the close dark interior, he found his way through the kitchen and out the back door.

There was about half a moon, and though it was still low behind the trees on the brow of the hill it was already starting to make a lot of skylight. The snow in the back yard was whitely shining; it barely looked tracked, except on a path toward the outhouse and back. Laidlaw propped himself against the wall by the door and swallowed until he had got the sadness mostly down. Out here he could smell the wood smoke from Wat's stove; it must have been starting to go to the ground. Inside, the fiddle whined on for a while longer and then tapered down to a stop. He was half listening for speech, but could hear no voice.

A shiver ran over him and he folded his arms. He'd left his jacket inside, and it was getting colder. An outside light came on, just a weak bare bulb screwed in above the door frame. Automatically he moved farther away from it, down toward the corner of the house. In a minute the door creaked and Redmon came out to lean on the wall a few feet away from him, nearer to the light.

Laidlaw felt impelled to say something, although he didn't know what. "Well, I'd have to call that some mighty bad whiskey," he said, straightening up from the wall. "If they're making that themselves, I'd say they lost the touch." He paused. Redmon's face remained inflexible, and Laidlaw tried again to hit on something that might make him smile. "I'd known that was what we were going to drink, we could have drunk some oil or ate some lard before we came," he said. "You know, get that lining in your stomach before you —"

He almost snapped his head back in time, but not quite, and the punch got just enough of him to bring the taste of blood to the corner of his mouth. Redmon's second swing was already coming, and Laidlaw blocked it from the outside, openhand, and hit him back with a roundhouse slap kick, though not in a very useful place. He had used his bad foot to kick with and when he came down on it he fell. Above him, Redmon expelled an amount of breath with a grunting sound, bending slightly at the waist. Laidlaw rolled away from him and back onto his feet and took out running into the woods. He didn't really want to fight, particularly when he knew he couldn't win; Redmon had always been the better at this kind of hand-to-hand activity. Nor could he expect to outrun him, not anymore, but if he could make it into deep cover he might yet outmaneuver him. Behind, there was a sudden slam; Redmon had hung his foot on the fallen fence and gone headlong into the frozen ground, but he was up again quickly, and again beginning to gain. Laidlaw made a quarter turn and ran into the cedar grove. Once well into the dark he stopped dead, holding his breath. Redmon crashed on a little farther, not quite in the right direction, and came to a halt himself. He wasn't all that far away, near enough for Laidlaw to make out a hoarseness in his breathing.

"Hey, you still mad?" Laidlaw said, and got ready to run some more in case the answer was yes. He figured he could lose Redmon in the thicket and go back home across the ridge, supposing it turned out that bad. But Redmon didn't answer him, or even seem to move.

"Listen, I didn't mean anything," Laidlaw said. "I was just fooling around, that's all, just looking for something to say . . . I didn't have anything in mind. I'm sorry."

Redmon coughed.

"You all right?" Laidlaw said.

Redmon ducked under a low-hanging branch and came up standing beside him. "Yeah," he said. "Getting there, at least. I fell over something and knocked the wind out of myself, there when I was coming out the yard."

"Oh," Laidlaw said. "I was kind of wondering why you hadn't caught me."

"That's why," Redmon said, and cleared his throat. "I suppose I'm a little touchy."

"I'd say so."

"I don't like to see him get that way," Redmon said.

"No more than I do," Laidlaw said. "Don't hit me, but I wouldn't say being married to Martha had done him a whole hell of a lot of good."

"That's the truth sure enough." Redmon turned his head and spat into the snow. "He ain't been right since Momma died, that's when he really started in drinking."

"I know it," Laidlaw said.

Redmon was quiet. Laidlaw tasted the scrape on the inside of his lip with the tip of his tongue.

"I love the man, you know," Redmon said, his face lighting up as he raised a match to a cigarette. "He's my father — man, when I was little, I just about thought he had made the world."

"Right," Laidlaw said. "So did I."

"No you didn't either."

"All right, then," Laidlaw said. "I thought *my* father made the world, and Wat fixed it."

There was a long pause and finally Redmon laughed. His mouth was briefly illumined in the red glow of his cigarette.

"Got another one of them?" Laidlaw said with a slight shiver.

"That was the last." Redmon passed the cigarette. Laidlaw took two long drags and handed it back.

"He used to play a *lot* better than that," Redmon said. "Or am I crazy?"

"You're not any crazier than me," Laidlaw said. "He used to be good."

"He used to could build anything," Redmon said. "He could fix anything, no matter what. No matter if he never seen one before and didn't even know for sure what it was supposed to do. Man, I would like to know what *happened* to him."

"He's getting old," Laidlaw said. "I don't know if you want me to say it, but he's one of those people that just can't drink."

"It's the truth," Redmon said, passing the cigarette back. "He'd been a lot better off if they never invented whiskey."

Laidlaw smoked, warming his inside a little bit with it. A drink of Wat's liquor might have tasted better now. Where they stood in the thick of the cedars it was so dark even the snow did not reflect, but in several gaps not far from them the moonlight was coming brightly down. He passed the nub of the cigarette back.

"I see him now, it's like seeing a ghost," Redmon said. "I don't feel good about it at all."

"I know what you're talking about," Laidlaw said, and shivered again, harder. The scuffle and the run had warmed him some, but that was all gone. He had got some snow in his collar when he was rolling in the yard, and it was melting in an icy trickle down his back. "I used to always want to be near him. I'd follow him around, trail after him anywhere he went if he'd let me. And I believed whatever he'd say."

"Your mistake," Redmon said.

"I don't know," Laidlaw said. "He used to tell me he could bend horseshoes. That he could do it when he was younger, of course."

"That was nothing but a tale."

"Maybe," Laidlaw said. "I was dying to see him do it, you know. Kept after him about it for weeks, I guess."

"I bet you made him wish he never brought it up."

"Yeah, but finally," Laidlaw said, "finally I was pestering him about it, there in the hall of the barn, and he just got a shoe down from the wire. He took hold of it and just kind of *held* it for a while, it looked like to me, and then it broke."

Redmon turned around to face him. "He broke it, huh?" he said. "What, an old shoe?"

"Not all that old," Laidlaw said. "It had some rust on the outside but it wasn't worn down much at all and the inside was bright as new, along the break, you know. I remember that part especially, how shiny it was on the inside. He broke it right along the top."

"You must have been surprised by that."

"Nope," Laidlaw said. "When I think back on it now it surprises me some, but back then I just believed he could do whatever he claimed."

"And he did that for you," Redmon said. "Man, he —"

"What?" Laidlaw said.

"Never mind," Redmon said. "Hey, look at yourself, you're shaking all over. What you doing out here in shirt sleeves, fool?"

"I never meant to stay out this long," Laidlaw said.

"Right," Redmon said. "You're not hurt, are you?"

"Fat lip," Laidlaw said. "Not much of one. It'll go away. You?"

"I might end up with a sore rib," Redmon said. "Don't know if it was you or just when I fell."

"Why don't we quit doing that kind of thing?" Laidlaw said. "What do you think?"

"Good idea," Redmon said. His hand found Laidlaw's and squeezed. "Come on back down to the house and we'll get warm."

36

"Now you turn right," Laidlaw said.

Adrienne flipped her signal on and turned the Volkswagen onto Third Avenue. Laidlaw's left hand dropped and idly fiddled with the little stick between the seats that worked the heater.

"And then?" Adrienne said.

"Go on by that underpass," Laidlaw said, "and Jefferson Street should be coming right up. I believe you want to turn left."

Adrienne pulled a cigarette from her top pocket, and Laidlaw reached across to light it for her after she had made the second turn.

"Should be somewhere right along in here," Laidlaw said. "On the right, I think it is. Slow down some, this could be it."

Adrienne twisted her head around to peer past him. A low, square, green and white building was sliding past on the right.

"Don't see any sign," she said.

"Well," Laidlaw said. "It's in fairly small print. But that was the place. Mosque Thirty-seven and Health Food Restaurant."

"I didn't see any parking place, anyhow," Adrienne said.

"No," Laidlaw said. "Me neither. I guess you might as well just park on the street."

Adrienne pulled up behind a jacked-up rust-colored Impala and shut her motor off. The cold began to cut through the little car almost immediately. She drew on her cigarette and looked across the street. On the far side there was a junk stand, marked out for attention by a string of colored rags that hung limply from a wire above it, stirred by no breath of air. The junkman sat on a stool, still as if frozen, his face mostly hidden by the gray hood of the sweatshirt he wore under his bulky coat. A dark smudge of smoke rose from a tin can set between his feet.

"What are we waiting on?" Laidlaw said.

"I want to finish my cigarette," Adrienne said. "Health food restaurant, they might not let you smoke."

"I don't think you have to worry all that much about that," Laidlaw said. "Rodney smokes."

"Yeah," Adrienne said. "He smokes." She cracked her window to tip some ash out and then shut it back again.

"What's on your mind?" Laidlaw said.

"I just don't really thinks he likes me," she said. "That's all."

"Rod?" Laidlaw said. "What makes you think that?"

"Well, he never will look at me when he talks to me," Adrienne said, "for one thing. He always just looks right over my shoulder."

"Look," Laidlaw said. "He asked the both of us to supper. It's the first and only time he even asked *me* to come anywhere near around where he lives."

"I know," Adrienne said. "I understand that."

"So I don't get it," Laidlaw said. The window crank was missing on the passenger side, and he began to fidget with the worn brass stud where it used to fit on.

"I don't know," Adrienne said, and stubbed her cigarette out in the ashtray. In front of her face the windshield had begun to fog. "I can't really explain it."

"Well, I wish you could just get over it, then," Laidlaw said. "The man is my best friend, you know. He's just about my only friend, aside from you and Martin."

"I know that," Adrienne said. "I don't want to mess it up for you. But sometimes I think it would be better if I could just stay out of it."

"You can't stay out of it, though," Laidlaw said.

"Why can't I?"

"Because my people shall be your people," Laidlaw said. "I take you seriously too."

"Is that an order?" Adrienne said. "Because it sounds a little too much like one to me."

"It's a request," Laidlaw said, and reached to her. "A favor, that's all it is."

For a couple of seconds she held herself stiff, then relaxed and let herself come toward him.

"All right," Laidlaw said. "Better now? Now let's go on in there and try to have us a nice time." He let go of her and shoved the car door open.

"Better lock it, I guess," Adrienne said.

Laidlaw complied. They linked arms and walked down the block, heads tucked slightly against the cold. The weeds in the cracks of the sidewalk were still bushy, though dead. At the corner they paused to let an ancient dented Cadillac creep through the intersection, then crossed over to the front of the green and white building.

Inside, there were eight or ten people sitting at five or six tables, mostly arranged so they could see the big black-and-white TV. A couple looked up as they entered, and then quickly away, back toward the screen. Laidlaw glanced at the television himself. It seemed that a western was playing. There was gunfire and he could make out cowboy hats, though the picture was poor. Above the set, the plate glass of the front window was thickly steamed over.

"He must be late," Adrienne said.

Laidlaw swung his head back to the rear of the room. Redmon was not anywhere in sight. The owner of the place sat on a high stool behind the counter, head lowered over a book.

"Or else we're early," Laidlaw said. "I hadn't really paid that much attention to the time."

He walked across to the counter, his boot heels tapping lightly on the tiled floor. Behind the owner's stool, a good-smelling steam was rising from a pair of industrial-sized caldrons. Adrienne came up behind Laidlaw and settled herself on a stool. On the stove, a pot lid levitated, borne up by a cushion of foam, and the owner swirled quickly around to lower the temperature dial. When he turned back, his eyebrows raised at Laidlaw, though he did not speak.

"I'm looking for Rodney Redmon," Laidlaw said. "You notice if he's been in yet this evening?"

"Oh yes," Raschid said. "You were here before, back in the fall."

"Well, this time I have an appointment." Laidlaw smiled. Raschid's expression remained grave. Adrienne's stool squeaked as she swiveled around to face the front door.

"That's right," Raschid said. "Thomas Laidlaw."

"You know me," Laidlaw said, feeling his smile turn foolish on his face.

"I do," Raschid said. "But do you know me?"

Laidlaw stared, but he could search out no clue. There was some sort of nagging familiarity, but he could not make it more definite. A trace of a smile appeared on the other man's face, as if he were pleased that Laidlaw had failed.

"Prester," Raschid said. "I used to be Prester Ball."

Laidlaw's congealing smile relaxed and became more genuine. "Good Lord," he said. "Well. You used to come on the sheep-shearing truck."

"That's right," Raschid said.

"And I would bring you all out the cord to plug into."

"You remember that, do you?" Raschid said. "You were nothing but a little old boy, way back then."

"I might have known you if not for the clothes," Laidlaw said. "And the glasses, you didn't have glasses then." He put out his hand and Raschid looked down on it.

"Didn't have a gray hair yet back then either," Raschid said. After a moment more he took Laidlaw's hand and gave it a very brief squeeze.

Laidlaw turned around to Adrienne. "This is my good friend Adrienne Wells," he said. "And this is Prester —"

"I'm Raschid now," Raschid said, a smooth but speedy interruption.

"Pleased," Adrienne said. She put her hand across the counter, and after another hesitated beat Raschid took hold of it.

The front door banged and Redmon moved toward the group, a broad smile stretched across his face. "Well, well," he said, rubbing his hands together. "Looks like you're collaborating, brother man."

"Just being polite," Raschid said. "In honor of old times and everything like that."

"Them good old days gone by," Redmon said, turning toward the others. "I keep you waiting long?"

"No more than a couple of minutes," Adrienne said.

"Not too bad," Redmon said. "Why don't we get us a table?" He switched back to Raschid. "I reckon all three of us will have the special."

Redmon steered them to a square table in the middle of the room, where they sat down. Raschid had followed them with a tray, from which he dealt out cups and napkins and silverware. He nodded his head to them vaguely, and went away.

"What might the special be?" Adrienne said.

"Normally it's stew on rice," Redmon said. "Sometimes stew on noodles. Every once in a while he puts it on this kind of Arabian grits he makes. Not too often, though."

"What all else has he got?" Laidlaw said.

"Nothing," Redmon said. "Just a little packaged-up stuff. It's one man, one dish around here."

Raschid came back with his tray more heavily loaded, with three served plates and a metal teapot. He arranged the food on the table and straightened up.

"Thank you," Adrienne said.

Raschid went behind the counter without saying anything in reply.

Laidlaw inspected his plate: yellow rice with chickpeas and a good many other vegetables all mixed together, a sweetish spicy smell rising out of the whole. "Snappy service, at the least," he said.

"Right," Redmon said. "He's a pretty good cook too, unless he has a real off day. He knows how to make all sorts of things, but he likes to leave himself time to study his book."

"What is that book?" Adrienne said.

"The Koran," Redmon said. "Arabic, he's been learning it for years, or trying to."

"Oh," Adrienne said. "So he's serious. About being a Muslim."

"Very serious," Redmon said, lowering his fork. "He has to leave himself time to pray too. Five times a day he got to dash back behind that curtain and pound his head on the floor for a while."

"Is that right?" Laidlaw said. "I didn't know too much of that went on around here."

"It don't," Redmon said. "Though he does keep on trying to spread the word."

"Is he making any converts?" Adrienne said.

"Not hardly," Redmon said. "He's got a few churchgoing kind of ladies halfway interested some of the time, and that's about it. On the other hand, nobody lynched him yet either, which puts him way ahead on points if you ask me."

"Lynch for what?" Laidlaw said.

"How good of a reason does it take?" Redmon said. "I thought you were the man had the answer to that question."

"They're for killing off the white people, aren't they?" Adrienne said.

"In theory," Redmon said. "I don't think Raschid has killed off all that many till yet."

"Ah, I think it's coming back to me," Laidlaw said. "I hadn't had call to think about any of that for a good while." He winked at Redmon. "What say you and me change plates?"

Redmon smiled thinly back at him. "Too late anyway, I'd guess."

"Just fooling," Laidlaw said. From the TV there came another burst of gunfire. "Matter of fact, it seems like a real good meal to me."

"It *is* good," Adrienne said, nodding. "Mind if I ask how you know this man?"

Redmon glanced toward Laidlaw. "Well, he started out a plain old country nigger like me," he said. Adrienne dropped her eyes to her plate.

"He was a whole lot older than me," Redmon said. "But his daddy and mine were right good friends, so we used to see something of each other. Then he ran off to New York when he got about twenty-five, and didn't nobody hear from him anymore. But I happened to run across him a whole lot later on, when I was living up there myself."

"By accident?" Adrienne said. "New York's a big town for that." Laidlaw put his foot lightly on top of her foot, and she fell quiet.

"Summer camp," Redmon said with a smirk of sorts. "It so happened that we wound up going to the same summer camp."

"Right," Laidlaw said.

"After that, we kind of fell out of touch," Redmon said. "Everybody moving around and all. Then one day a year or so back I was just walking down this street and what did I see . . ."

"So he moved back down here," Adrienne said.

"To save our souls," Redmon said.

"And cook up a storm while he was at it," Laidlaw said, pushing back his empty plate. "This is one of the best things I've had to eat in a long time."

"It was good," Adrienne said. "Thanks for the invitation, Rodney."

"My pleasure," Redmon said. He poured tea all around and then got up and went to the counter. Laidlaw switched his chair around so he could look at the TV set, now playing the local weather report, and at the same time drop his hand onto Adrienne's knee. The big dark windows gave back an opaque version of the room, and he could see himself and her, vague and ghostly in reflection. Redmon came back to the table with a tin ashtray in his hand.

"Aha," Laidlaw said. "So you *can* smoke."

"Smoke till you choke," Redmon said.

Laidlaw reached for his pack and shook out three. Redmon's lighter went around the table, and then they all leaned back.

"What was on the forecast?" Redmon said. "I wasn't paying attention."

"About what you'd expect," Laidlaw said. "It's going to keep on being cold and snow if it feels like it. Or in other words, they don't know what it might do."

"Like usual." It was a new voice speaking, from a little above the table. Laidlaw glanced around to see a middle-aged man in a trim green uniform with no name tag.

"Well, Mr. Maddox," Redmon said. "Meet my man Laidlaw and his girlfriend, Adrienne."

Laidlaw stood up to shake hands. He saw the older man's eyes shift a little, taking his measure rapidly from head to toe.

"You known Rodney for some time?" he said.

"About since I was born," Laidlaw said. "We grew up more or less on the same place."

"That right?" Mr. Maddox said. "You mind if I sit down?"

Laidlaw glanced at Redmon, who frowned and nodded at the same time.

"Go right ahead," Laidlaw said.

Mr. Maddox lowered himself into a chair, keeping his back perfectly straight. He folded his hands on the table top and turned toward Adrienne. "Miss," he said. He bowed from the neck, and she returned the gesture. "Well, I'm proud to see you all come in here," Mr. Maddox said. He let his head drift a quarter turn toward the counter where Raschid was sitting. "Just don't let *him* get acrost you with all that devil business."

"Huh?" Laidlaw said.

"They say the white man is the devil," Adrienne said. "The Muslims do, I mean."

"Seems I need to brush up on this stuff." Laidlaw looked at Redmon. "You believing along those lines these days?"

"I believe the white man has got the upper hand," Redmon said.

"It's all foolishness," Mr. Maddox said, smiling underneath his mustache, making a backhand gesture in Raschid's direction. "Fact is, I suspect he don't really believe all that hisself."

"The hell he don't," Redmon said. "He lives it body and soul."

"Could be, could be," Mr. Maddox said, the smile wiped smoothly from his face. "Now, *this* man," he said, pointing at the television, "this man I like. He got something to say a body could believe."

Laidlaw and Adrienne turned, almost in unison, to look at the set.

The face of a man filled up the screen. Though his lips were moving, you couldn't hear what he was saying yet; instead there was an announcer's voice-over.

"You been following him?" Redmon said.

"Lately," Mr. Maddox said.

"Who is it?" Adrienne said.

"Brother Jacob," Mr. Maddox said.

"Oh yeah," Laidlaw said. "I heard talk of him. Heard him on the radio too, I think."

"Has he got any last name?" Adrienne said.

"Not that I know of," Mr. Maddox said. "Not that he ever uses in his work."

"I do remember him," Laidlaw said. "He's the one won't say if he's a black man or a white."

"Just somebody," Mr. Maddox said. "That's his claim."

"Some kind of a *red* nigger, more than likely," Redmon said, his mouth tightening down into a grim twist. "Wouldn't you say?"

"Can't tell one way or the other from the TV," Laidlaw said.

"Not from this one here, noway," Mr. Maddox said.

"I thought these kind of people hibernated in the winter," Laidlaw said. "You know, the revival circuit kind of shuts down. Where's he supposed to be at right now, you think?"

"Supposed to be preaching in some big hall," Mr. Maddox said. "Down there in Atlanta or someplace like that."

"Yeah, that's another thing about him," Redmon said. "He operates mostly in the Deep South. You wouldn't think he'd do too well down there, but seems like he does."

"Hush a minute," Mr. Maddox said. "I believe they might let us hear him speak."

The camera had drawn back quite some distance, far enough to show the heads of people in the first rows of the audience. The man behind the microphone had come to a pause in whatever he'd been saying, and stood with his right hand raised, palm-out, the first two fingers up and slightly crooked. The television let out a sound that might have been either static or a sigh.

"In the olden time," the speaker said, "there was a king had set his hand against a preacher. Though before, there'd been a time in their lives when they had been the best of friends. But after a while, they fell out with one another. Turned their hearts hard against each other. And would have come to violence and blood."

The camera tracked closer, framing the head and hand together. Laidlaw took in how the hand moved in moderating motions, something like a conductor's baton.

"In that olden time," the speaker said, "the people had a notion which was called the kiss of peace. Whatever man could give that kiss to another, then ever after they were bound to love one another. Whether they were friends or whether they were enemies, that didn't matter a bit. And so," he said, "and so the preacher set out to trap the king, *deceive* him into giving him that kiss of peace."

The speaker paused, and his hand shot up a little higher. Timing, Laidlaw thought, it's like a rest in music. The picture did one vertical roll and then came still again.

"Children of God," the speaker said. "This is what we *all* must do. We must learn to lay that trap for one another. Not to trap each other into ruin and murder, no, not that. No more, no matter if it's been our habit. But into Christian charity and loving-kindness — I say to you all, children of God, we must *trap* each other into the spirit of brotherly love."

His hand dropped sharply as a signal flag, and there was a sudden swelling of voices calling out. Then the picture switched back to the newsman, summing up and moving on to talk about a fire that had broken out on a Gulf oil rig earlier in the day.

"Think he's got the mojo?" Redmon said.

"I believe he's got something sure enough," Mr. Maddox said.

"It strikes me funny how quiet he talks," Redmon said. "It's about like you were listening to somebody think."

"I know what you mean," Laidlaw said. "I remember that from the radio, it sets him apart from all those other preachers. He's got everything timed down to the second too. He's a good performer, you got to at least give him that."

"That's all?" Redmon said.

"It's what I can see," Laidlaw said.

Adrienne rattled her fingers on the table top and stared across at Redmon, who shifted himself around to look back at her, hearing the noise. "So what if I give you that kiss?" she said.

"Why?" Redmon said. "You thinking about it?"

"Would you be bound to me forever?"

"I don't know," Redmon said. "You're only bound if you believe."

37

WHEN THE atmosphere in the house had become too oppressive, Adrienne put on Laidlaw's leather jacket and went to the door. Laidlaw had been hunched over the banjo for more than an hour, plucking a long chain of dissonant clusters, harsh as the calling of crows. As she went out, he raised his head and asked her where she was headed, and she told him she was going out to feed. It was already just about dark, but she knew he would leave it until Redmon made some move. Redmon, sitting with his feet on the stove's apron and his head hunched down between his shoulders, didn't look up when she left.

Her senses had all gone soggy inside the house, which was smoky and hot as an oven as well, they'd built up the fire so high, and she was grateful for the cold outdoors, which brought her back alert. It had stayed too cold for the snow on the ground to melt off, but it had been worn away in paths and patches the people and animals most commonly used. Earlier in the afternoon it had sleeted for a while, forming a brittle crust over the snow which her feet broke through step after step as she went up the hill to the barn. The catch to the feed room door had frozen into a little globe of ice. She found a butane lighter in Laidlaw's jacket pocket and held the flame of it under the metal while the sheep clustered urgently behind her, nosing at the back of her knees. When the latch gave, she pocketed the lighter, climbed up into the feed room, and filled a bucket with sweet feed. One of the half-grown lambs gathered itself and sprang into the room after her as she straightened up, and she shoved it back out with the edge of her foot, dropped down to the ground, and went around under the shed roof to dump the grain in the trough.

The sheep pressed frantically around the trough, struggling for optimal position. Adrienne went back and shut the feed room door and then got a bale of hay out of the room on the uphill side of the barn and scattered it farther up the slope. As she finished she saw the shadow of the little calico barn cat crossing a clean spot in the snow, and she called out to it.

"Here, kit, kit. Come on over here, kitty . . ."

The cat stopped and sat up, looking at her, but when she took a step toward it, it dropped back to all fours and darted through a gap in the boards into the rear of the barn. It was only a volunteer cat, as Laidlaw said, mostly wild, and neither one of them even knew its sex. Laidlaw would not have it fed, claiming both he and the cat would be better off if it was left to live on mice. Adrienne shrugged and walked down the low side of the barn, her hands balled in the slash pockets of the jacket for warmth. In the bare tree over the shed's overhang, the peacock had gone to roost, its tail hanging rattily down and its head tucked under a wing, so that it looked as if it had been decapitated altogether. Adrienne stopped to look off over the house and the icy white gleaming of the low field to the tree line and the curve of the hills which blocked off the horizon. The sun had already fallen out of sight and the fading colors of its passage lay above the hills in horizontal spectrum bands, purpling off toward a perfect black at the height of the sky's dome.

She worked her fingers in the pockets; they were beginning to stiffen, but she didn't feel at all like going back inside. The silences that grew between Redmon and Laidlaw always seemed morbid to her, though Laidlaw would insist that they were no such thing, if ever she tried to bring it up. True, it wasn't always like that. Half of Redmon's visits passed pleasantly and talkatively enough. The others soured into this stale inertia, where neither one of them seemed to have the heart to do much of anything but drink. Laidlaw never drank so much in other circumstances, and she guessed maybe Redmon didn't either. They were the kind that got each other doing it; she'd seen that a time or two before.

She stomped her feet and walked a little away from the barn, toward the iron skeleton of the rotted wagon. It was windless, utterly still; she felt she could have heard a footfall at the far end of the other field. Laidlaw had left a pack of cigarettes in one of his pockets, and she took one out and lit it quickly and put her hand back where it could keep warm. When things took this turn, her instinct was to keep out of the way, and she might just have gone on back to town if Laidlaw was not so stubborn about wanting her to stay. She would have thought that they might speak or otherwise get along more easily if she were not there, but there was no way of knowing that for sure, and what curiosity she had once had on the subject was dwindling away. All in all, things had not been going too well for the last couple of months. The winter clung obstinately to the country, harder and colder than it ought to have been. The band had had nothing but pick-up dates since the Clawhammer gig had run out, and Laidlaw was doing so little session work now that he was always short of money. Maybe that was wearing him down . . . There was no doubt but that he was strange. She doubted he had got any stranger, either; she was just beginning to pay more attention to it. She was starting to notice how wild he was at times, and not in any agreeably romantic manner, but simply feral, like the cat.

The cigarette had burnt short enough that smoke was leaking into her eyes, and she spat it onto the snow and trod out its red spark. The sheep were coming out of the barn and starting up toward where she had put out the hay. The yearling lamb that Laidlaw had bottle-raised stopped and turned in her direction, short ears pricked. It was a solid, chunky creature now, squared off by its winter coat of wool. Once in a while either she or Laidlaw would still feed it a bottle, just for fun. She stretched out her hand toward it and it came bouncing forward and began to suck her fingers avidly, with short thrusts of its thick neck. Already it had grown little curls of horn. She pulled her hand free and began to rub the lamb around the ears, reaching in to the animal warmth while it bumped at her shins with its muzzle.

The sound of a door closing made her look back down toward the house. It was dark enough now that she wasn't completely sure it was Redmon coming across the yard until he straddled the bike. He rode up to the gate and got off to open it, took the bike through, and dismounted again to close it behind him. She was pretty sure she had watched him put away half a fifth of whiskey at least in the course of the afternoon, but there was no sign of it in his movements, or none she could recognize at this distance, in this light. The headlamp of the bike came on, a little gravel spat from the rear wheel, and Redmon was gathering speed as he came up the hill. She thought he raised his hand to her as he went by, and she waved back just in case he had.

"Go on," she told the lamb, sidestepping it and moving away. "Go on, now, and get your hay."

The lamb followed her a short distance, but before she was halfway down the hill it gave up and trotted back to join the others. Adrienne went in at the yard gate and up into the house. Laidlaw was dumping an ashtray into the open door of the stove. She saw that he had tidied up the room a little and cleared the bottle and glasses away.

"You were gone awhile," Laidlaw said. "I would have done it."

"No point in letting it go till after dark," Adrienne said. "Anyway, I needed to get some air, it was getting stuffy in here."

"True," Laidlaw said. "Crack a window if you feel like it."

"I'm cold enough for right now," Adrienne said, and hung the jacket on a nail beside the door frame. When she turned back Laidlaw had gone into the kitchen and she followed him as far as the door. He was leaning on the sink, working his way through a stack of glasses and cups.

"I put some potatoes in the oven," he said. "We got a chicken, I thought we might bake it."

"Have we got any greens?" Adrienne said automatically.

"Check the freezer," Laidlaw said.

He put the last cup upside down on the drainboard and dried his hands on the seat of his pants. There was a certain heaviness to his gait as he came across the room toward her, though she might not have noticed if she hadn't been looking for it. Like Rodney he could carry a fearful amount of whiskey without much letting it show.

"I meant to tell you," he said. "Got a phone call this morning."

"Oh? Who from?"

"A man owns a roadhouse somewhere down around Bitter Springs," he told her. "Wanted to know if we wanted to play down there weekends for a while. Friday and Saturday nights. He was kind of vague about the money, but it would be a couple of hundred dollars, I guess."

"I don't think I ever heard of Bitter Springs."

"Me neither," Laidlaw said, shrugging past her on his way into the front room. "It even took me a while to find it on the map. It's an hour drive from here at least."

"Oh," Adrienne said. "That's not so hot, when you have to come back late and all. What's the name of the place?"

"The Buzzard. The Dead Cat . . ." He shrugged. "I forget exactly, but it's that kind of a place." He sat down in a chair and pushed his hair back from his face. "I hate to have to take it seriously, but it's been a real slow season."

"Well, I'm not saying I won't do it," Adrienne said. "I'm holding you to the window rule, though."

"I wouldn't try to break it anyhow," Laidlaw said. They had a basic agreement not to play in any bar with no windows, since those always drew the roughest trade.

"Good," Adrienne said. "Then we can see about it."

Laidlaw leaned back and locked his hands behind his head. Adrienne remained in the kitchen doorway, trying to think where she'd put her own cigarettes. The kitchen was beginning to smell a little bit like baked potato.

"I made a date to go down there and look at the joint next Saturday," Laidlaw said. "Week from today, will you be free?"

"Should be," she said. "I'll check my studio book whenever I go back to town."

"Looks all right, then," Laidlaw said, rocking his chair up onto its back legs. "Oh, Rodney might ride along too. I told him he could if he felt like it."

"Oh really," Adrienne said. "That's if he manages to make it home tonight, you mean."

Laidlaw dropped his chair legs back to the floor with a smack and frowned up at her. "Why wouldn't he?" he said. "He was walking straight when he left the house."

"You two make a bigger pair of fools than you know." Adrienne spotted her cigarettes in a mess of papers on Laidlaw's music table and stalked over to pick them up. "You get yourselves shot at two or three times and it makes you think you're just *immune* to getting killed in a wreck."

"Not quite," Laidlaw said, his voice almost inaudibly soft. "It just makes you not worry about it so much."

"Oh great," Adrienne said. "If that's how it is, I guess I'll just follow you two in my own car. Down to East Cow Flop, or wherever the hell it is."

"I don't drive drunk," Laidlaw said. "Not anymore, you know I don't. And I tried to get him to stay and eat and all, but he just wouldn't do it."

"Would you rather him around than me?" Adrienne said, regretting the words as they emerged; it looked like she was a lot angrier than she had suspected.

"You know better than that," Laidlaw said.

For a second it seemed that he would get up and come to her, but then she could practically see him changing his mind. Instead, he reached around to the wall behind where the banjo was propped and lifted it onto his lap.

"Pick up the fiddle," he said. "And let's have done with this foolishness." They solved fights more often this way than by making love.

"Not in the mood," Adrienne said.

Laidlaw shrugged, looking down at the banjo head. His fingers made a silent flex and then he struck an open D-minor chord and began to frail and sing to the music in a hoarse voice.

> My true love slighted me,
> Tore my heart in two . . .
> Because I was a pore little feller
> And I didn't know how to do . . .

"You won't get me with that one," Adrienne said. "I do it better than you."

Laidlaw nodded and smiled and changed the tuning, twisting up a couple of pegs. In a moment he'd begun a new song, a slower cadence.

> Once I courted a lady beauty bright . . .
> I courted her by day, I courted her by night . . .
> I courted her for love, and love I did obtain . . .
> Didn't have no reason nor right to complain . . .

She turned her back on him and went into the kitchen. On a sheet of waxed paper on the table, a whole chicken had mostly thawed. She balanced her cigarette on the edge of the sink, picked up a knife from the drainer, and hacked the bird apart in five or six furious motions. In the other room, Laidlaw had skipped ahead to the last verse of the tune.

> When I awoke to my senses again . . .
> I picked up a pen, wrote down the same . . .
> Come one and all, wherever you may be . . .
> Come pity my misfortune, my sad misery.

He ended it, and she heard his chair squeak as he changed position and retuned again. She got the iron skillet and arranged the chicken parts in it and sliced some onions and bell peppers over the top. When she straightened up from putting it in the oven, she recognized he was now playing "Wake Up, Little Maggie."

> I got drunk in the city
> And I stumbled and fell at her door
> She throwed her little arms all around me
> But she bid me come back no more . . .

The sad lingering phrases of the tune cut straight through her to the center, slowing even her heartbeat down by half. She brushed her cigarette into the sink to dispose of it and walked into the front room at the fluidly measured pace of a sleepwalker, to the table where she'd left her fiddle case. With her back to Laidlaw, she fingered out the basics of the slow bridge he was playing, and once she was sure of it she turned to face him. They played through the instrumental part a second time and when they had come back around to the verse again, she began to sing along.

> My head bows down like the willow
> And I'm lonesome like the dove
> Sometimes there's tears on my pillow
> When I think about my love . . .
>
> Oh, where is my little darling?
> That one I loved so dear
> She's gone away and left me
> And's a-courting some other one . . .

"Well now," she said, lowering the fiddle. "When did you pick that one up?"

"A while back," Laidlaw said. "I'd been saving it for an emergency."

Adrienne laid the fiddle back in the open case and drew a chair to sit facing him, her knees touching his. After a moment she reached up and settled her hands on his shoulders, holding him there at half an arm's length. Beside them the fire went on rumbling in the stove, and she could feel the heat warming the left side of her face to a flush.

"It's not that bad," she said. "I just don't understand what gets into you two sometimes. I know you're friends, but half the time you practically act like you hate each other. It gives me the willies when you get that way. I just don't know what keeps it going."

"Ah well," Laidlaw said. Letting the banjo slip back against his shoulder, he reached to lift the shock of hair from her forehead, and then let it fall back to the line of her brows.

"We have a lot of the same memories," he said. "Trouble is, not all of them are good."

"From the army?" she said.

"It goes back a lot further than that," he said, and twisted away to lean the banjo back against the wall. "His father, Wat, he . . . oh, I don't know. I just spent a whole lot of time with him when I was little. He was always willing to play with me and everything. My father wasn't what you would call the playful type."

"So where was Rodney during all this?"

Laidlaw dropped his head back and looked up at the ceiling.

"Over here, in this house, I guess," he said. "I didn't see him all that much when I was *real* small. Wat would be across the hill on our side, at the big house or the barn, most of every day, you know. But I stayed over here once in a while, if my father was gone off to Texas or doing the shows. I didn't get along with Rod so good then, really. He had a little sister nearer my age and I would play with her."

"Where is she now?"

"Dead." Laidlaw got up and began to walk around the room. "She got married to some bad guy from North Nashville when she was about sixteen, and a couple of years later he got high on some bad combination and stabbed her to death. With an ice pick, as I recall."

"Jesus Christ," Adrienne said.

"Right," Laidlaw said. "That's what I thought too. It was a real bad time for Wat. His first wife had just died then and it was around that time that Rodney went up north, and I didn't see him again myself till he turned up in the army." Laidlaw stopped in front of the mirror and shrugged at his reflection, as if to deny that he recognized it. "Anyhow, he never liked me all that much when we were little-bitty. Used to pick on me, push me down and stuff like that when he didn't think anybody was looking. Wat whipped him every time he caught him at it, but it never made him quit."

"Did you use to tell on him?"

"Never," Laidlaw said. "But when I got to be about nine or ten I picked up a stick and fought him back. And I gave him a real good telling off, and then we were pretty good friends after that. We would go fishing together and prowl in the woods and all. We hung around together all the time up until he got old enough to drive."

"How much older is he than you?"

"A couple of years," Laidlaw said, pacing in an S curve around the middle of the floor. "By the time I was sixteen myself, he was gone out of here."

"Slow down, will you?" Adrienne said. "You're making me dizzy."

"What?" Laidlaw said. "Oh." He sat down.

"And that reminds me," Adrienne said. "I never did think to ask you what you were tromping on my foot for, back there when we all went out to that restaurant."

"Oh, that?" Laidlaw said. "Well, he was in jail a little while up there in New York. Supposed to have been involved in some kind of an armed robbery thing, but I don't think he ever stood trial. I guess they weren't sure they had him cold, because all they really did was keep him locked up a few months or so and then offer him to go in the army. Which he jumped at, like anybody would have."

"You think he did it?" Adrienne said. "The robbery, I mean."

"Probably," Laidlaw said. "Not that we ever talked about it head-on. He'd already been over there a good while when we happened to meet up. And we were both just so glad to see somebody from home . . . So that's when we really got tight. And we made sure to take care of each other ever after that, but I don't know . . ." He hitched his shoulders and leaned forward on his knees, looking down at the floor. "It don't seem to work out the same back here, quite. I don't see why it shouldn't myself, but it seems like he's got some things eating on him."

"Seems like you got some things eating on you too," Adrienne said.

"What do you mean by that?" Laidlaw said, looking up at her sharply.

"I'm not real sure," Adrienne said. "But I've been starting to wonder where you go off to in the middle of the night."

Laidlaw jumped out of his chair and went into the kitchen. She heard the water running for a couple of minutes and then cutting off.

When he came back his face was dripping wet and his thick eyebrows were plastered up his forehead in strings.

"Didn't think you knew about that," he said.

"You must think I'm pretty stupid."

"No," he said. "I just thought you were asleep."

"But sometimes I wake up," Adrienne said. "Like when I get a feeling there's nobody there where you're supposed to be."

"Well, it's not anything, really. I just go out walking," Laidlaw said. "I just don't seem to need all that much sleep."

"Oh, no," Adrienne said. "You just get up every morning with rings around your eyes like a raccoon."

"All right," Laidlaw said. "I'll tell you the truth." He leaned forward and stared at her, his eyes wide. "It's because I don't dream."

"What!"

"Everybody is supposed to dream, right?" Laidlaw said. "But I don't ever have a dream, not a one. So when I'm supposed to be dreaming, well, I just get up and go walk around in the woods." He spread his hands palms-out and smiled.

"That simple is it?" Adrienne said, laughing a little in spite of herself. "If that's all there is to it, then I guess I give up. Let's go eat supper before it burns up."

38

THEY HAD decided, or Laidlaw had decided for them, to all go in the truck. Adrienne sat in the middle, with her feet up on the hump of the transmission, the place where Laidlaw usually rode his banjo. She felt crowded, though in truth she wasn't. Without the instruments, there was plenty of room for three, room enough for her to sit and even shift around a little without brushing shoulders with either one of the others.

It had got a little warmer, not all that much. Laidlaw and Redmon had both opened their windows to let out smoke, creating a chill little cross breeze. Over the dashboard, straight across from Adrienne, a small orb of steam had formed on the windshield; it would neither expand nor shrink.

Laidlaw had brought a cup of coffee along, and when he started up the ramp on I-65, she reached up to steady it. Once he had fit the truck into the traffic, she took a sip and wedged the cup back on the angle of the dashboard where it had been. The coffee was bitter and nearly stone-cold.

"Go on and finish it off if you want to," Laidlaw said.

"Thanks the same," Adrienne said. "But I really don't."

The conversation ended there. A green sign giving the distance to Birmingham flicked by on the right, pulling her eyes around in that direction. Redmon was slumped over against the right-hand door, staring moodily out the window, his head piled up into one of his hands. Smoke sputtered toward the vent from a cigarette he held there behind his head, seeming to come straight out of his close-cut hair. What fun, Adrienne thought crossly, turning to face the crown of the road again. Once more she had that irksome feeling that she had just interrupted something. It seemed so much as if she had blundered into this joyride by accident that she had to work to remember it had all been arranged.

Up ahead, the road's cut stretched on, broad, bland, and entirely uninteresting. Past the Franklin get-off, they lost most of the other traffic, and the road spun endlessly out ahead of them, vacant all the way to the sky. Laidlaw reached down and put on the radio: some crackly local station giving the farm report in row after dreary row of numbers. After about five minutes, Adrienne shut the radio off. Laidlaw cut his eyes toward her, but had nothing to say. The sky stood dully before them, climbing straight up from the horizon. You could not have called it either overcast or clear; it was simply flat, and colorless but for a faint metallic gleam. When they had accomplished thirty or forty miles down the road, it began to pulse at them at half-minute intervals, long strokes of heat lightning interrupting the daylight like some enormous photographer's flash.

"Looks like heavy weather up ahead," Redmon said.

"Yep," Laidlaw said. "We'll be running right into it, I'm afraid."

Although this was the first conversational opportunity that had occurred for some time, Adrienne could think of nothing to add to it. When the truck had rushed about ten more miles toward the rapidly darkening sky, she cleared her throat and spoke.

"If it's supposed to be around an hour to this place," she said, "then we must have passed it a little while back."

"I know, I know," Laidlaw said. "Sometimes it looks kind of shorter when you look at it on the map."

"Well," she said. "Are we going clear to Alabama, or what?"

She saw Laidlaw opening his mouth to speak but she never did hear what he said because at that instant the sky ahead of them was cloven in two by a bolt of lightning as wide as the whole road. It was unbearably bright and shockingly silent, and when it was gone it seemed suddenly dark as night everywhere around them. The smash and roll of the thunder following rocked her head back as the truck lunged forward into a wall of rain. The water was coming down practically solid; it was as if they had driven into a lake. Laidlaw was flipping on wipers and lights, but neither seemed to be a whole lot of help. Two spears of lightning came down at more or less the same time on either side of the highway, though it was harder to see them now, through all the rain. When the thunder had faded out again, Adrienne poked Laidlaw with the point of her elbow.

"Get off the road," she said to him. "No use trying to keep driving in this."

"Hell, I can't even tell where the road is to get off of it," Laidlaw said. But he lifted his foot from the gas and the truck veered to the right and coasted to a stop. There was a click as Redmon closed his vent. Laidlaw left the motor running, just set the parking brake.

"I do hope we don't get rear-ended by some other fool," he said.

"I believe we're on the shoulder all right," Redmon said, peering through the sheet of rain sliding over his window. "Near as I can tell."

"But will that help us enough?" Laidlaw said, turning around to face the other two, his grin eerily illumined by another flash of lightning. In the wake of this bolt, there came a crash on a different tone.

"There goes somebody's big old tree, or something," Redmon said. He was smiling too, she noticed.

"Yeah," Laidlaw said. "Or barn, even. Suppose we'll be next?"

"Supposed to be safe, sitting on rubber tires," Adrienne said.

"That's what they tell you," Redmon said. "I always did wonder if it was the truth."

"Here's where you stand to find out," Laidlaw said.

Adrienne was tensed for the next lightning strike, but none came. Instead there was some negligible change in the pace of the downpour, and it seemed to get a little lighter inside the cab. Still, you couldn't see an inch past the windshield, though the wipers lashed frantically back and forth.

"Praise the Lord," Redmon said with a short barking laugh. "I do believe spring is here."

He dipped into his jacket pocket and came out with a half-pint bottle of Bacardi 151 and held it out in the flat of his hand. Adrienne noticed how neatly the curve of the bottle fit within the borders of his palm, noticed too that the pink paper strip of the state seal was as yet unbroken. She shook her head at it and Redmon leaned across her to push the bottle near Laidlaw, who took it and wrenched off the cap. After he had drunk he leaned forward across the steering wheel and expelled his breath in a long wheeze.

"God*damn*, but that's hot," he said, passing the bottle back. "It's not even a liquid, it's a gas."

"You're getting there," Redmon said.

"Cork that good when you get through with it," Laidlaw said. "The smell alone must be drawing state troopers from miles around."

Redmon took a short drink, cleared his throat, and dropped the bottle back in his pocket. Laidlaw reached up above the sun visor, pulled down a map of the state, and unfolded it. After a minute he frowned and slapped the map shut.

"The turnoff ought to be somewhere right around here," Laidlaw said. "Hope I didn't go by it in this rain. Might even be able to see it from here, if we could see anything. Looks like we're apt to be late."

"Ain't no helping that," Redmon said.

Laidlaw slumped down in his seat and lit a cigarette. The smoke swirled around his head in a lazy spiral, clinging to him in the damp atmosphere. A thin rivulet of water was running in through his vent and dripping onto his knee, but he didn't seem to notice or mind it.

"These hard rains don't usually keep up all that long," Adrienne said.

Laidlaw rolled his eyes at her and slid farther down in his seat. But in another five minutes the rain had stopped as sharply as a tap shut off, and sunshine was cutting through the water-slicked windows of the cab.

"How do you like that?" Laidlaw said, taking off the brake.

Nobody bothered to answer him. He drove on down the interstate another couple of miles and got off onto a small secondary road that curved through a series of wide pastures. Adrienne turned her head to watch the fields slipping by. Before the rain there had been patches of snow still hanging on, but now they had all been washed clean away, and the gray of the fields was beginning to come up in green.

Laidlaw came to a T intersection, hesitated, then made a right turn. Woods came down to the edge of the road they were driving on. Every quarter mile or so there appeared a mailbox and a short drive leading up to a house trailer set on a block foundation or, more rarely, to a single-level prefab house. None of the dwellings looked particularly new, and yet they all seemed to have just been torn into the woods, a raw look to them Adrienne supposed they would never lose.

Laidlaw came to a crossroads and pulled to the side of the road before a reddish frame building with a good part of the paint peeling off. Opposite them was a square concrete filling station with the old-fashioned rounded-off pumps. On the far corner stood a barn-sized white clapboard structure with a square turret or steeple that suggested it might once have been a church, though its door and windows were boarded over now. Across from that was a sort of general store with two or three cars parked in front of it. The red building where they'd parked was marked with a big tin Coca-Cola sign over the door. There was a space on the sign for the name of the business, but it was mostly rusted out, and only the word CAFÉ was dimly discernible on it. The building was not otherwise distinguished except for a neon Budweiser sign which glowed in one of the small square windows.

"Are we lost, or just out of gas?" Adrienne said.

"No," Laidlaw said. "This should be the place."

"This?"

"I'm not promising," Laidlaw said. "The roads ain't marked any too good out here, if you notice. But if that café is the Redbird Café, then it's where I was supposed to meet the guy. About a half an hour ago, of course."

As Adrienne swung her head around to peer at the sign again, the door underneath it opened and a policeman came out and paused on the top step. At first glance she took him for a state trooper, because he wore that same kind of broad-brimmed hat, but his uniform was blue instead of tan, with a gold stripe running up the trouser seam. He wore his gun on a wide cartridge belt, each shell gleaming as if it had been freshly polished that morning.

"That's one hell of a police for a town this size," Redmon said.

"You suppose he's local or state?" Adrienne said.

"Got to be local," Laidlaw said. "That ain't a state car."

In fact, the car was a regular blue-and-white, a city-style police car looking very much out of place such a long way from any city. The policeman had come down the steps and walked over to the driver's side of the car, but instead of getting into it, he folded his arms along the roof and favored them with a long gaze. After a moment Adrienne grew tired of looking back at him, and found her eyes drawn to a long aerial set in the center of the trunk lid, or rather to its tip, where there fluttered a miniature American flag and beneath it a Confederate flag the same size.

"He sure is getting a mighty good look at us," Redmon said.

"I'd count on him knowing us again," Laidlaw said. "If he don't think he knows us from before. Keep that firewater out of sight. I'll be back in a second."

He got out, slapping the door shut behind him, and went over to the police car. For a moment he and the officer conferred, the policeman speaking out of the side of his mouth, never shifting his eyes from the cab of the truck. Then Laidlaw went up the steps and into the café. In a minute he had come back out in the company of a beer-bellied man who wore a green coverall and, incongruously, fancy cowboy boots and a new-looking Stetson hat. The stranger strolled over to join the policeman, turning to stare across at the truck himself. Laidlaw came over and rapped on Redmon's window, and Redmon rolled it down.

"This shouldn't take all that long," Laidlaw said. "Man's going to just ride me over to that place right quick. You all just stay in the truck and I'll be back in about a half an hour, at the outside."

"What in the hell are you talking about?" Adrienne said.

"They got a sundown thing," Laidlaw said, looking not at her but at Redmon, his hands tightening white on the top of the door. "Look, I didn't know —"

Redmon opened his mouth, but closed it without saying anything at all. His hand floated upward and then fell back onto the dashboard with the dead weight of a dropped brick.

"Just stay in the truck," Laidlaw repeated. "I'll be back right quick."

He turned sharply and went back toward the other two men. Half gaping, Adrienne watched him and the man in the coverall both climb into an old Chevrolet with fins. The car backed out, gasping, turned by the abandoned church, and disappeared. The policeman kept on staring at the truck throughout, but after another half minute he gave his head a long slow shake, got in the car, and sped off in the opposite direction, fast enough that the two flags on the aerial whipped wildly back and forth.

Adrienne turned to Redmon. "Do you understand this any better than I do?"

"Can't tell nothing about it, missy," Redmon said sourly. "Boss man says we spose to stay in the car, is the only thing *I* know."

"Don't give me that," Adrienne said.

Redmon turned away from her and wound his window up. He reached out to the dashboard and drummed his fingers on it for a few seconds and then stopped.

"What's got into everybody all of a sudden?" Adrienne said. "I'd really love to know what's going on."

Redmon shifted around in her direction again. His eyes passed across her and came to rest on something else. "Them as don't know, you just can't tell'm," he said in the same artificially slurred tone.

Adrienne sighed. "Everything's a riddle, right? So I give up, you can tell me the answer."

"Ain't no answer," Redmon said in his ordinary speaking voice.

Adrienne said nothing. She stretched herself out a little, moving into Laidlaw's seat behind the wheel, and looked out the driver's side window. The service doors of the garage opposite were open and two men were studying the underside of a mud-streaked white Ford which was raised on the lift. Otherwise there was no activity, not the least hint of movement anywhere around the crossroads.

"Bitter Springs," she said, shaking her head.

"Not too much of a place, is it?" Redmon said.

They let a period of silence pass, fifteen or twenty minutes' worth, perhaps. It was dank inside the cab, and getting colder by the minute. Adrienne crossed her arms over her chest and squeezed the edges of herself.

"Damn, it's cold."

"You had a key to this thing, we might turn on the motor and warm up that way," Redmon said.

"Wouldn't that be nice?" Adrienne said. "But he tore out of here so fast I never had a chance to get it from him."

"Boss man *always* knows what's best," Redmon said, reverting to the slur.

"Oh, for Christ's sake," Adrienne said. "Rodney, don't you think we could get along a little better than this? So long as we're going to be stuck together?"

"*You* ain't stuck *nowhere*," Redmon said, staring out through the windshield. "You can go where you feel like and do what you please. I mostly just do what I'm told, myself."

"Well, I wish I knew what was bothering you," Adrienne said. "If it was all up to me, I would just let you alone, stay out of your way, you know? I mean, if you don't want to bother with me, that's your business. I wouldn't even have to know the reason. But it does make a difference to *him*, you know, so what I want you to tell me is, what have I been doing wrong?"

"Nothing," Redmon said, the response pat and toneless. But he turned around to face her head-on, looking straight into her eyes for once, stroking the line of his jaw with one hand as he studied her.

"I never knew it was bothering you," he said. "I guess I hadn't give it all that much thought."

"Well, I've *had* to," Adrienne said.

"I see," Redmon said musingly. "Well, I guess I'm sorry. If I been making you feel funny, or what have you."

"I'm not after an apology," Adrienne said. "I'm just looking maybe for things to improve."

"All right," Redmon said. He dipped the rum bottle out of his pocket, uncapped it, and took a drink, then held the bottle out to her. "Have a drink on it," he said.

Adrienne sipped, just wetting her tongue. The liquor fumed into her whole head, radiant, white-hot.

"God," she said, giving him the bottle back.

"It's wicked, sure enough," Redmon said. "But it ought to warm you up a little."

"You wouldn't consider using something a little milder?"

"This here is the best value for the money," Redmon said, smiling a little as he pocketed the bottle. Adrienne laughed, the laugh blending into a shiver that ran fast and hard all through her.

"You are cold," Redmon said. His hand drifted out toward her shoulder and halted in the air a short distance away.

"You can touch me," Adrienne said irritably. "I'm not going to break or burn you or anything."

Redmon's hand came all the way down, like a helicopter landing. He squeezed the bone of her shoulder once quickly and drew his hand back away.

"There you go," Adrienne said. "I'm flesh and blood the same as you. No need for us to act like a couple of ghosts."

"If you say so," Redmon said. "You really are getting pretty cold, though."

"Don't you know it," Adrienne said. "Where's he got lost at, anyhow? He should have been back here ten minutes ago." It took some concentration now to keep her teeth from chattering. "This is stupid. What are we doing out here waiting to freeze? Come on, let's go inside, get a cup of coffee and warm up."

Redmon reached out again, as if he would restrain her, but she had already got out of the cab and banged the door shut. Hands jammed in her pockets, she went quickly up the steps and shouldered through the door of the café. It was only a small room, paneled with pine planks varnished to an orange shade, and it was very warm in there, almost steaming. There were just two square tables and a single booth fit into a cranny of the wall, and at the rear a high counter with a coffee pot on it, next to some big gallon jars full of things like red hots and pickled eggs. No one seemed to be attending it at the moment. At the table under the window with the beer sign four men were sitting, all of them fat in a greasy bloated way that puffed up their faces and slitted their eyes. They looked enough alike to have all been related, and were similarly dressed, in work pants and white T-shirts, none too clean. Three of them were involved in some murmured colloquy and the fourth stared dully at Adrienne, looking through her, it seemed, while his thumb idly riffled the edge of a deck of cards which sat on the table among coffee cups and a couple of beer bottles.

She turned her back to them and sat down in the booth, facing the door. Her hands had gotten painfully stiff out in the cold, and she spread them on the table top and began to flex the feeling back into them. It seemed that Redmon was not coming in, and that depressed her, just when she thought she had finally opened a crack in his reserve. But then the door opened and he appeared, hesitating on the threshold, then coming quickly over to sit down across from her.

"Look a here," Adrienne said. "I really would like it if we could be better friends."

"All right," Redmon said, his tone sure enough, though his eyes seemed somewhat uneasy. "I reckon I'd be willing to give it a shot."

"Shake on it?" Adrienne put out her hand. Again she sensed some odd restlessness to him; he seemed to be hovering a couple of inches out of his seat. Then his hand came out and grasped hers and quickly let it go. She watched it settle onto the table, a tan hand on yellow Formica. The index finger rose and tapped sharply three times, the sound of it strikingly loud, maybe because it seemed to have grown oddly still elsewhere in the room.

"I don't know," she said. "Maybe they don't wait on tables round here, we might be supposed to serve ourselves."

"Normally speaking, we don't serve niggers at all," a voice said conversationally from the table behind. Adrienne almost turned around, and then thought better of it. It was plain enough now what the trouble was, and it was making her feel fairly stupid. She locked her eyes onto Redmon's; his face was blank as stone. Behind, there was a noise of chair legs scraping on the floor.

"Course, we might be able to find *something* that would suit a special pair like you."

The speaker strolled around into her field of vision and propped himself up on the high back of Redmon's seat. A second man leaned down over the back of hers, near enough for her to catch a faint smell of stale sweat and tobacco.

The voice came just at the edge of her ear. "We just been kindly wondering . . ." it said. "If you all was related, or just good friends."

"Friends is what I bet," the man by Redmon said. "*Real* good friends, now ain't that right?" Adrienne looked up to meet the pair of flat eyes, pale green and oddly depthless.

"You know, we seen you swappen spit on that bottle out there," the one behind her said. "So we figured it had to be one or t'other."

A third voice spoke from the table in back of her, where she couldn't see which one it was. "Anybody would drink after a nigger would do most anythen else with one too, more'n likely. Ain't that what you would expect?"

Holding the eyes of the man in front of her as well as she could, Adrienne smiled, a bright hostess smile. She had been around such people a time or two before, and she knew that they could be shamed. There would be something she could say, a magic group of words that would shrink them down to their proper size, turn them back into children again. If she had been on home ground she would have known the phrasing right away, but in this unfamiliar place she was unsure of it. All she knew for certain was that she had to do something and do it quick. Redmon looked like he was about to do something himself, and if he did she thought they would kill him, at least, and maybe her too.

"Gentlemen."

She had not seen how Laidlaw got into the room, but he was there. The man who stood behind Redmon's seat straightened up and swung lazily around to include him in the group.

"Hey there, feller," he said. "These here people belong to you?"

"Yes sir, they do." Laidlaw's head was lowered, his eyes set somewhere around the other man's chest. "I hope they hadn't been causing you no trouble."

"Not beyond what we could handle if we had to."

"Yes sir," Laidlaw said. "I don't doubt that."

"Maybe you might like to see it," the man said reflectively. "You know, how we might handle this type of thing."

"No sir, I don't think we need to," Laidlaw said. "I expect we'll all probably just head on home."

"Is that what you expect?"

The man's hand rose and stroked outward as if he meant to thump

Laidlaw on the chest, but Laidlaw was no longer where he had been. Adrienne had not seen him move. It was if he had been invisibly translated from one spot to another one just out of reach, so that the other man's hand swept through a curve of empty space and slapped to rest against his thigh. She herself slid to the edge of the booth so the table would not be much in her way if she decided to move somewhere quickly.

"Yeah," the man said, frowning down at his empty hand. His tone had changed; the interest was dulling out of it. "That might be your best plan."

"Yes sir," Laidlaw said. "Well, we thank you." He turned toward Redmon and spoke more sharply. "Rodney, you go get in the truck."

Redmon stood up and walked stiff-legged to the door and through it. Laidlaw jerked his thumb at Adrienne, who got up from her seat. Guiding her with a hand set in the small of her back, he came out the door behind her.

"Nigger, don't let the sun go down on you in Bitter Springs," Redmon said. "Best not even let it shine on you there at all, matter of fact."

Laidlaw's hands were rigid on the wheel. His jaw muscles poked through his cheeks in knotty little twists. Overall, Adrienne thought, he looked about the way she felt.

"I wouldn't be driving so damn fast," Redmon said. "Unless you want to bring down that bad country fuzz on your head."

"Why didn't you just stay in the truck like I told you?" Laidlaw said through gritted teeth.

"Your girlfriend decided she just had to have a cup of coffee."

"*Go to hell,*" Adrienne said, not quite sure which one of them she meant. "Why didn't we just get the hell out of there when we saw what we were into?"

"Because it was too late by that time," Laidlaw shouted. "I had Mr. Policeman already telling me what I should do. Leave you all sit in the car and get my business fixed and get out after that. You think I *wanted* to hang around there?"

"Who knows?" Redmon said. "But I'm waiting on you to tell me what good-hearted people all them were, deep down inside."

"They were nothing but trash," Laidlaw said.

"You surely did pull the wool for them, though," Redmon said. "You did it real good. *Yassuh. Nawsuh.* Man, you got it *down.*"

"I can do it if I have to," Laidlaw said. "To keep from ending up somewhere nobody wouldn't ever find my body. I could also stay put somewhere if somebody told me to."

"But what I really want to know is, did you enjoy it?" Redmon said, pursuing his own train of thought.

"Not all that much," Laidlaw said.

"Well, but you looked like you just *loved* it." Redmon laughed. "Hell, you should have been a nigger yourself." He opened his bottle and took a long pull. "Come on, let's have us a drink on that thought."

Laidlaw accepted the bottle in his right hand, looked at it for a second, and smashed it over the edge of his door. It was the same easy movement he would use to break an egg on the rim of the skillet, and it looked so natural that Adrienne hardly absorbed the meaning of it until he took his left hand off the wheel too and shucked a shower of bloody glass from the palm of his right, scattering it out the open window. In an abstract disinterested fashion she saw that the truck was out of control, bouncing along the shoulder; then Laidlaw took the wheel again and wrenched it back into its lane. A slim trickle of blood was winding down the inside of his forearm.

"So what did you want me to do, kill them?" he said.

"Yes," Redmon said. "You should have killed them. People like that need to be killed."

Laidlaw turned and looked at him. To Adrienne, this look was completely indescribable, not because it had some special character, but because it had none at all. All the same, it was a kind of look she would have been pleased never to see again. He kept it up for a long time. Again the possibility of a wreck seemed lively, yet she still felt that it didn't really interest her all that much.

"I've sworn off killing people," Laidlaw said.

"Well, I call that a crying shame," Redmon said. "Because you were damn good at it."

Laidlaw turned his face back down the road, lifted his leg, and stamped on the accelerator as if he had in mind to crush it. The truck leaped forward so hard they were all thrown back in their seats. Adrienne let her head loll back, watching through narrowed eyes as the horizon screamed up toward them. So this is what it feels like, was all she could think now, not to care what happens to you.

39

IN DREAM *Wat was twelve again and climbing the buckeye tree. It was midsummer and the broad green leaves moved in a lively dance as the branches were fanned back by an uneasy breeze. Through a fork of the tree he could look over the road and down the hill across the back end of the Laidlaw place. But he wasn't much interested in the view, he was only after the buckeyes, reaching for more of the big pulpy pods and dropping them down through the branches to the ground where he would retrieve them later. One he ripped open while he was still in the tree, to find the rich brown nuts with their paler eyes, wrinkled into forms that smoothly fit his thumbs and fingers, so freshly shining they might have already been oiled. There were five or six in the single pod, enough to fill one of his pockets, five or six times the good luck that buckeyes were supposed to bring. But moving higher in the tree, he made a misstep and was falling, ten feet down to a place where the trunk had split and grown back in two parts against itself. He fell head down, too startled to cry out. His leg slapped into the place where the trunk was double, hard enough to part at the sections, which then snapped back on his leg like a vise.*

For a moment he hung upside down and swinging lightly, his arms in a helpless dangle and his head swollen with a rush of blood. Then the dream broke and he awakened to find he really did have a cramp in his leg which he couldn't stop. Dismayed, he watched the leg kick all the covers from the bed in vigorous, spasmodic jerks. He reached up to grip it with both hands but the cramp would not rub out immediately and the leg went on kicking of its own accord for a couple of minutes more. When it had finally stopped he lay on his back for a while and rested, looking up at a whorled water stain on the ceiling and wondering about his dream. It had been many a long cold year since he'd been fit to climb a tree.

Daylight reached in a long pointed triangle from the crack of the blind as far as the soles of his feet. At his right hand Martha's half of the mattress billowed yeastily up high enough to conceal the greater part of the room from his sight. Directly overhead in the corner, a square of the shelf paper he'd covered the ceiling with had come loose to dangle partway down; it had been like that for long enough for a spider to have knit a web between it and the wall. Some secret glimmer of light had made the web a silver spangle that drew Wat's eye. Not far from it a middle-sized honey bee hovered, droning; it might have been its small sound which had waked him. How a bee could have blundered into this perpetually darkened room was more than he could imagine, but here it was. Just as he noticed it, the bee flew a few inches forward and entangled itself in the web. The fat bulb-shaped spider had been hidden in a cranny above the paper and now it came running, throwing out its legs like little stilts, toward where the bee tumbled in its strands. It had come almost within a touch before it knew the bee for what it was, and Wat smiled to see it bolt back even more hastily the way it had come, back to its dark shelter behind the paper's curl. The bee struggled and thrashed itself free and went in a looping, limping flight across the room. Between the blind and the window glass it went on buzzing furiously, its wings whirring drily against the fabric of the shade.

Wat climbed over the rising of the mattress, stepped into his overalls, and went over to open the window so the bee could get out. The small current of air coming under the sash was warm enough that he left the window open after the bee had gone. Then he went back and balanced himself carefully on the edge of the bed for long enough to put on his shoes, smiling a little as he tightened the laces. Lately he had been in the habit of staying in bed till something happened that might qualify as a sign, and the bee's narrow escape struck him as a fairly good omen.

In this warming weather, his arthritis bothered him much less. He stood up, easily and fluidly for him, and walked quietly through the dog run to the kitchen. Martha was heaped in a chair behind the square table, her huge body monumentally still. She breathed through her parted lips with a slight rasp that was not quite a snore. He watched curiously as a fat housefly settled on her flesh just above her right eyebrow; her whole face responded with a great galvanic twitch to throw it off, yet she did not waken. It seemed possible that she had never come to bed at all the night before, for she was capable of passing an entire night more or less upright in that chair. Last evening they had quarreled over there being no whiskey in the house, which only meant that there was not enough for two. He had gone to bed thirsty and angry over it, but he felt better for it now.

Wat went softly around to the refrigerator, keeping a wary eye on his wife. Martha outweighed him by close to a hundred pounds and for some years had been much the stronger of the two. She was not above beating him when enraged and her rages often came without warning or provocation. Still fresh in his memory was a time she'd struck him with a skillet hard enough to crack three of his ribs. But this morning it seemed unlikely that anything would rouse her soon.

He took two slices of Bunny Bread from a plastic sack and stuck them together with a smear of margarine. It would have discouraged him to remain in the kitchen long enough to eat or even fix coffee, so he went back through the dog run and outside to sit on the cracked concrete block that served as his single front step. On the other side of the road a long slow line of cars moved along toward Nashville as far as he could see, as regularly spaced and paced as the linked cars of a train. He was up a good deal earlier than usual, feeling better too. In slow deliberate bites he ate the bread and margarine, his eye on the leisurely progress of the traffic, and afterward rolled a cigarette and lit it. This morning his hands were almost perfectly steady and it presented no real problem to construct the smoke. There were warm and cool currents running in the air by turns, like currents in a stream. By the time he had finished the cigarette, the traffic had thinned out to just an occasional car. He sat awhile longer on the step, watching two blue jays chase each other back and forth across the littered yard, and then got up and went back around the house to the garden.

The growth of weeds was not as bad as it might have been. He had been in already to pull the tallest and what was left he thought might just be turned under. For ten days or so he'd been meaning to plow, but he hadn't quite felt up to the job, not without a tractor, and nobody seemed to feel like lending him one, though he'd been asking around for the last few days. Over the fence from him there was a man named Peabody who had a mule and had told Wat he could borrow it any time he felt like he could catch it. But he hadn't quite felt like plowing with a mule before today.

He went stealthily back into the kitchen and got a limp bunch of celery out of the refrigerator and carried it outside again. Above his garden patch there was a gap in the fence that let onto a narrow trail through the trees, mostly overgrown now with the spring weeds. He went down it a quarter mile or so and came to Peabody's big pasture. Down by the far fence the white mule, Ghost by name, was grazing alongside of an old swaybacked chestnut mare. Wat crossed the field to Peabody's barn and found an old lead rope, softened with use, and tucked it all the way down into his bib pocket so the mule would not be warned off by the sight of it.

It was the mare who responded first to the celery when Wat got to that end of the field. He let her take a stick of it and then batted her away and walked slowly ahead toward Ghost with the wilted fronds stuck out at arm's length in front of him. The mule was bunched up, ready to run, but he stayed put until Wat reached him, and as he nibbled at the celery he seemed to settle down. When Wat circled his neck with the lead rope, Ghost gave one wild toss of his head, but quickly Wat came back around his nose with another loop of rope, and that seemed to quieten him. Holding the end of the lead, Wat began to walk him toward the barn. When he drifted off to the mule's right, Ghost all of a sudden set his hooves and began to fight the lead as hard as he could, nearly lifting Wat's feet clear of the ground. Wat shortened the lead and turned to face him. Ghost had always had big watery blue eyes, but now his right was fogged over with the white veins of a spreading cataract.

"Hoo, boy," Wat said softly, and switched himself to the mule's left side. At once Ghost fell calm, and Wat stayed still, stroking the soft gray nose to soothe him further.

"Near 'bout half blind, ain't you," he said, then took Ghost the rest of the way over to the barn.

The mare followed them at a little distance, whickering. In the hall of the barn Wat put Peabody's plow harness on the mule, looped up the traces, and led him back up the woods trail, careful to keep on the side he could see. When he reached his own yard he paused long enough to fasten the fence gap shut with two turns of the rusty wire, and then took the mule into the garden..

Nobody plowed much with mules anymore around here, and Wat had picked up an old plow blade for just about nothing, building a new frame and handles for it himself. Now he hitched it to the traces, pointed Ghost down the row, and gave him a cluck to get him going. Ghost was a good mule to plow, and well mannered generally too, his only defect a certain wariness of being caught, but Wat supposed he had not been worked in so long he'd grown incautious about that. The problem now was not the mule but his own strength. Spreading his arms to the handles of the plow brought some kind of dull weight deep into his chest, not so much a pain as a pressure, somewhere toward the left side. It wore at him, and made it hard for him to keep the furrows straight. A third of the way across the plot he had to stop awhile and blow.

"We old," he said to Ghost, leaning on the shafts of the plow. "We just getten too old, you and me both."

However, he was not in a bad mood. In spite of that nagging central numbness, he felt a lot better than usual. The weather was nice and the turned earth smelled good to him, and there was a mockingbird singing high in the locust tree that grew at the top edge of the yard. Nobody was rushing him to finish the plowing anyhow; he could do it in his own sweet time.

When he got done the sun was high, warm on the cross straps of his overalls. He led the mule back to Peabody's barn, unharnessed him, and turned him loose, speeding him back to join the mare with a light slap on the hindquarters. While plowing he had noticed that one of the harness straps was nearly dry-rotted through and now he found a sounder length of leather and replaced the bad one, prying the studs loose with the blade of his pocket knife and knocking them back into place with a stone, as there was no hammer handy. There was some neat's-foot oil in the tack room and he oiled the whole harness before hanging it back up. The little repair would serve as payment for the use of the mule, though chances were that Peabody was too old and too crazy to take much notice of either.

The work had brought a pleasant glow to his arms and legs, though the weight in his chest was as heavy as ever, and his breath was a little short. By the time he got back to his house, it was well past noon, but he wasn't a bit hungry. Martha slept on in that kitchen chair; she didn't seem to have moved a muscle. He stood in the doorway, looking over at her without much interest. Dawning in him was an appetite for whiskey, which more than anything else depressed him. It had been quite a while since he'd been far enough back from this feeling to get a good look at what it really was. Now it seemed to him that he wanted distraction more than a drink. Besides which, he knew that all the stash bottles he had hidden around the place were already tapped out. Beyond the kitchen window the balmy lights of the spring day flickered with the rising and falling of the breeze, and it came to him that this warm weather would bring rabbits and groundhogs out to laze in the sun, so that it might be a good day for hunting.

He went into the other room and knelt down to root under the bed. Back behind the fiddle case he found the shape of an old four-ten shotgun, wrapped in a towel so old all the nap was worn off it. It took most of his breath away to stand up straight again with the gun. Must be he was tireder than he thought, and his heartbeat now was a painful pulse. He waited until it had slowed and then went to a dresser drawer and got out a half box of shells and loaded the gun, snapping the breech shut with a satisfying thump. The rest of the shells he dumped in his bib pocket before he went back to the kitchen.

Martha's breathing had changed its pitch to something combining a gasp and a snore, and her mouth had slackened farther open. It was enough to make Wat wonder if she might not have something the matter with her. Without knowing he would do it he dropped one knee down on the seat of a straight chair and sighted the shotgun right on her temple, steadying the barrel on the top rail of the chair back. It stood within his power to change the conditions of his life in this way, if in no other. He drew back the hammer to see what that would feel like. It made a little clicking sound, and Martha's breathing stopped. In the ensuing silence he promised himself he'd kill her if she woke. As a matter of fact, he'd have to; if she opened her eyes on a sight like this, it would be him or her. Wat had only been in jail once and then not long, just five or six hours on a drunk-driving arrest, until Mr. Laidlaw had come down to get him out. He didn't suppose he'd survive much jail, not at his age and the shape he was in, so it would be the end of him either way if she happened to come to. She didn't breathe for such a while that he wondered if she might not have died of her own accord. From outside, he could still faintly hear that same mockingbird calling. Then Martha snorted and began to snore again on a different rhythm, drowning out the birdsong. Wat eased the shotgun's hammer back down, pushed back from the chair, and swiftly left the kitchen.

He went up the hill back of the house a certain distance and then cut to the left and went on, following the hill's curve around, one of his legs lower than the other on account of the grade. It seemed harder to walk that way, and yet the sense of laboring felt distant from him, as if his own self stood somewhere above it. There was not anything you could have called a trail; he only picked his way where it seemed easiest. After half a mile or so he found that he was passing above the graveyard. Through a screen of trees he could see the headstones flashing a sun-washed white as though they were moving instead of him, but he didn't pause for a closer look. Instead he veered away and went farther uphill, struggling all the way to the top of the ridge.

Along the ridgetop it was clearer, easier going, trees set farther apart and not so much brush among them. He went back south slowly; he could feel his heart flopping like a fish inside of him from the effort of the climb. The treetops around him were busy with squirrels but somehow he didn't think of taking a pop at one. It was like he was on his way to some particular place, though truth to tell he didn't even know just where he was. He came to a fallen fence, and once he had stepped across it he couldn't have said for certain whose land he was on. Most likely that fence marked some property line, high up there on the ridge like it was. He stopped and considered, resting the gun butt on the ground. The angle of the sun was tightening so that the light came in slanting lower from the west, though it was still strong enough to warm the whole right side of his body. It must have taken him longer than he'd realized to climb up all this way.

It crossed his mind that if he didn't turn back now, he might end up having to find part of his way home in the dark. But he didn't feel ready to go back, and anyway, it would be downhill when he started home, so he'd cover the distance faster. He shrugged to himself and shouldered the gun and went on. After a ways longer the ridge line began to make a smooth turn to the east. He could have told it from the fading of the drone of the cars on the highway even if he hadn't had the sun to go by.

Just up ahead of him there was a copperhead stretched out on a big flat rock. A warm slash of sunlight came in low between the trunks of two trees and fell just on it, holding it there in a bath of warmth and light. Wat stopped and covered its head with the shotgun barrel. The snake lay in slack coils, not knowing anyone was near. In the stillness while he thought about killing it, he felt he could practically hear his heart fluttering, which puzzled him, since he'd been walking easy a good while now, up here on the flat. The thought came to him that the old snake was a long way from where anybody was apt to surprise it and get himself bit. Also there was a chance it wasn't really a copperhead at all, but one of those water snakes that looked just about the same. You could only tell the difference by the shape of the eye and a couple of other delicate signs that needed you to be closer to the snake than you really wanted to get.

He lowered the gun and kept on going, making a good-sized loop around the snake to give it all the room it might need. Still, it seemed too thoroughly drugged by the sun to take any notice at all of his passage. About a hundred yards farther on, the trees thinned out down the slope to his right, the sun came through them more fully, and he saw he had reached the edge of a cleared hillside. It was not fenced, though there was such a thick patch of buckbushes just past the trees that it almost looked like they'd been trained into a hedge. He walked up to where the buckbushes started and looked out to try to see where he was. The pasture went all the way down to a fence with a dirt road running alongside it, but there was no house or barn or any kind of clue at all to whose place it might be. He noticed he couldn't hear the highway any longer. The oranging sun was sitting right on top of the line of the western hills.

Wat lowered his eyes to get them out of the glare. The pasture had been terraced to keep it from washing out, and in the flat furrow of the terrace nearest him one of the biggest groundhogs he had ever seen was eating on the new spring grass. The groundhog grazed about like a cow would, just eating and eating and every now and then taking a step that carried it forward on a straight line. In the sunset light its fur had a reddish sheen. It was almost like they were supposed to meet there by appointment, only he, Wat, had been just a little bit late. He made a quick calculation as to what the groundhog would probably weigh dressed out and then threw down on it with the gun. But with the stock to his shoulder, it struck him that perhaps the range was yet a little too long.

Some bigger animal had cut a narrow trail going back and forth from the field toward the buckbushes, and Wat eased quietly along on that, holding the shotgun at his hip. When he got clear of the buckbushes he kept on going, laying his feet slowly and carefully down and getting nearer and nearer. The groundhog looked too fat and happy to have any idea it might be in trouble. Wat had come practically within clubbing distance before he decided to stop. The groundhog moved forward a little more. It looked like it was eating the clover out from under the longer grass. Wat brought the gun up to his shoulder again to cover its blunt head. Then, to his own surprise, he lowered the gun and rested its stock on the toe of his shoe.

Funny as it seemed, he just didn't much feel like killing anything today. Not that snake that was probably poison, and not this groundhog either, though he could have used the meat and had come a long way to get it too. He was still thinking about why that might be when the gun went off all by itself. Or at least, he felt the big slam of it kicking into his shoulder, though there was no answering boom and he didn't think he had lifted it back up. Then again, it was the wrong shoulder, the left instead of the right. Either way, the kick was enough to knock him down.

His face was turned in the grass so he could see the groundhog making its way off with a fat waddle that made its whole hind end wag. *What kind of fool way is that to run!* he thought at it. *I could have caught you with my two hands.* He did not feel especially uncomfortable, though his left leg had folded up under him and there was something hard and sharp poking into his side. There was a big pain stretching down his left arm as far as the elbow and it was strange how little that bothered him, considering how bad it was. The only thing he lacked was a cigarette, and with his right hand he dug in his bib pocket till he found the cloth tobacco sack among the shotgun shells and could pull it out. However, it seemed like too much trouble to try to roll a cigarette one-handed, and he didn't seem to be able to move his whole left arm at all.

He kept on lying there a while, just resting. The tobacco sack lay on his belly, going up and down with his breath. He could see where the shotgun had slithered a little ways downhill from him in the damp grass and he thought he had better pick it up just as soon as he got himself pulled together, before the rust got started on it. The sunset was almost blindly bright on his face; it made his eyes squint up of themselves. Behind him it seemed like it was getting dark too quickly, but he couldn't get his head around to see what was throwing that long cool shadow. The sun was coming up toward him fast like a ball rolling up the hill, till he saw all it really was was somebody walking up toward him, a black shadow outlined against all that light. He felt pretty sure it was his son, sure enough to think of calling out his name, but then he saw that really it was Deana. She was wearing the white dress she'd been married in and buried in and her left arm was crooked around behind her to hold hands with others of his kinfolk who were coming along after her all linked together in a chain. Her right hand was reaching down to him, and he was thinking that that should have scared him, since it was a ghostly kind of a happening, but all it did was make him feel like singing. And he would have sung something, sure enough, if he could just have got his mouth to move.

V
Soldier's Joy
(1972)

40

LAIDLAW AWOKE with a sort of snap and sat up full of a feeling that something had happened or was fixing to happen that needed his attention right away. He switched his feet around to the floor and rubbed his eyes till they came clear. By the dim shade of the light at the windows he thought it was probably between six and seven, but it was already quite warm in the room. Adrienne rolled over toward him on the mat; her hand drifted slackly across his back.

"Where you going?" she mumbled, her eyes still shut.

"Just something I wanted to check on," Laidlaw said.

He got up, put on a shirt and pants, and walked barefoot out onto the porch. There had been a heavy dew and the overgrown grass of the yard was shining with it. The last layer of the morning mist was slowly peeling away up the hillside past the barns. In the space on the road side of his front gate an army-green pickup truck was parked, and Laidlaw thought he might have heard it stopping through his sleep; it could have been that sound which woke him. Mr. Giles was standing just past the front end of the truck, resting his elbows on the top rail of the gate, letting his arms dangle over. Laidlaw stared. After a little time he perceived that Mr. Giles was not planning to come through the gate just yet and so he walked up through the yard to greet him, the wet grass swishing between his bare toes.

"Long time," Laidlaw said, coming up to the gate with a smile.

Mr. Giles nodded his head, the movement as much a duck as a nod, and then raised it again. It looked as though he might have lost a little weight, or at least his face seemed less fleshy than before, the bones more plainly apparent, eyes a little deeper set.

"Reckon so," Mr. Giles said.

There was a stalk of grass set in the corner of his mouth and it jogged up and down when he spoke. To Laidlaw this seemed an alien mannerism. In fact, he did not quite seem to be able to make sense of Mr. Giles's whole aspect. His eyes looked watchful, guarded really, but the rest of his face had no particular expression.

"New truck," Laidlaw said, glancing at it and then back.

"Ay," Mr. Giles said. "Had it near about a year now."

"Well," Laidlaw said. "Then I don't suppose this is a test drive."

"Not hardly," Mr. Giles said. He rolled his forearms apart from each other across the gate rail, so that his hands turned palm-up. "Thought ye might be getten ready to set out the garden."

Laidlaw grinned. "I'm a step ahead of you this one time," he said. "There's not but a couple of rows of beans left to plant."

"I'll not trouble ye then," Mr. Giles said. He withdrew his arms from the gate and stood up straight.

"It always goes quicker with two, though," Laidlaw said.

"All right then," Mr. Giles said.

When he saw that Mr. Giles would not open the gate for himself, Laidlaw reached down to unlatch it and drew it open far enough for him to be admitted.

Mr. Giles did not seem to want to come inside the house, so Laidlaw left him on the porch and went quickly back to the kitchen, where he found that Adrienne had been up long enough to make coffee. He poured himself a cup and then went back into the other room to hunt for his socks and shoes.

"What's going on?" Adrienne said, coming to stand in the kitchen doorway. "What's got you all stirred up so early?"

Laidlaw tied his shoelaces, stood up, and came toward her. "Mr. Giles is back," he said in a low tone. "We're fixing to go and work the garden a little bit."

"Oh," Adrienne said. "I thought we'd got that about through with yesterday."

"There's still the beans yet," Laidlaw said. "Besides, I think he mainly came to make peace and I don't want to lose the opportunity. He's not one for making strictly social calls, you know."

"I'll go out and tell him good morning, then," Adrienne said, tucking in her shirt. "Then I might just stay in here and practice, as long as you all don't need any extra help."

"Fine," Laidlaw said. "Like you say, there's not a whole lot left to do."

The spring whined as she went out though the screen door and he heard her say something to Mr. Giles, just what he couldn't make out. He gulped some coffee fast as he could without burning himself and then turned to the kitchen sink to wash his face. When he was done with that she had come back in the house. Laidlaw kissed her on the cheek.

"If you have to go to town," he said, "come say goodbye before you do."

"I doubt I would need to go before noon."

"Oh, we ought to be done before then," Laidlaw said.

In fact, there were only two rows of beans to plant and it took them under an hour to do it. Mr. Giles worked in virtual silence, as had always been his habit. When they had done, it seemed to Laidlaw as if nothing more was going to be said. Maybe there was nothing that needed to be, after all.

"Got a little lumber there in the back of the truck," Mr. Giles told him as they came out of the garden gate. "Long's I'm here I might just as well mend ye your front gate."

"It's been needing it," Laidlaw said.

They walked side by side up to the road, and Laidlaw helped Mr. Giles lift the gate down from its hinges. Mr. Giles stepped across the gateway and stooped into the bed of the truck for a plank and a saw and a hammer and nails. A couple of sheep, attracted by the unfamiliar activity, began to wander toward them across the hillside. From inside the house there came the faint trill of the mandolin.

"How's the family?" Laidlaw said, figuring now if ever might be the time to bring it up.

Mr. Giles stroked a pencil stub along the width of the new one-by-four and began to saw along the line. "Pretty fair, I reckon," he said when the butt end of the wood had fallen. "I hadn't heard a whole lot of them lately."

"What, are they not living with you anymore?" Laidlaw said.

"Not this last little while," Mr. Giles said. "Truth to tell I got a mite tired of haven them underfoot all the time, big old grown boys like they are. Anyhow they gone into town to try doen some factory work for a spell."

"What factory?" Laidlaw said.

"That Goo Goo plant."

"You're fooling," Laidlaw said.

"I just about wish I was." Mr. Giles pulled the last nail free of the broken plank on the top of the gate, straightened up, and turned to face him. "Can you just picture it? Standen there all the day long, not doen but one thing? Some little fiddlen thing too, you know." He made some ambiguous fidgeting motions with his hands.

"I can, but I don't know if I want to," Laidlaw said with a crooked smile. The thought of Walter, in particular, at the Goo Goo plant inspired him with mixed feelings. "What is it exactly that they do?"

"They just wrap up them candies," Mr. Giles said. "Stand there and roll'm up in that silver paper, don't ye know. They have to do so many a minute or the belt gets ahead of them. I'd as soon work on the *county* farm, myself."

"But it pays pretty well, don't it?" Laidlaw said.

"So I been told," Mr. Giles said. "Doubt they'll last too long at it, either one. Earl now, he figures to work along till he can quit and draw money from the government like they do."

"Oh," Laidlaw said.

"Ay," Mr. Giles said. "We kindly fell out over that little notion."

The ram and two black-faced ewes had come up a little too close to the open gateway. Laidlaw picked up a green stick and swished it through the air a time or two to drive them back. Mr. Giles knelt down and fit the new plank into the gap on the gate where the old one had been, then reached behind him for the can of nails.

"Don't believe ye knew my first wife," Mr. Giles said.

"I don't think so," said Laidlaw, who hadn't known the second wife either. Mr. Giles hammered in a nail with three good licks and Laidlaw bent down to hand him another.

"She came from down around New Orleans," Mr. Giles said, and set the second nail and drove it. "Mixed blood, she was, a lot of them are, down around that way. You wouldn't know it to look at her."

Laidlaw picked up the whole can of nails and held it in reach of Mr. Giles's hand.

"I been thinken on her a good deal lately, don't rightly know why," Mr. Giles said. "But I believe she was about the best wife I've had. She never did have no children though."

He sank several more nails in quick succession, drawing his arm far back and striking the heads dead center with each swing. Then he got up and motioned for Laidlaw to come and help him hang the gate back on the hinges. When they were done they had ended up on opposite sides of the gate again.

"That nigra boy you like to run with," Mr. Giles said. "I see where his father done died."

"I didn't know you were keeping up," Laidlaw said. "Didn't know you had any traffic with him."

"Only knew him to say hello to maybe," Mr. Giles said. "But you know he was a right good carpenter when he was a young man. He raised barns just about all over this county."

"I know it," Laidlaw said. "He built a couple on this place."

"Yep," Mr. Giles said. "He knew how to do it right too."

"He could do a number of things," Laidlaw said.

"And they ain't so many left as can," Mr. Giles said, and slapped the new board on the gate with the heel of his hand. "Well now," he said. "I reckon I'm gone."

"Don't you want to wait till I get you some money for this job?"

"Oh, most likely I'll get by tomorrow and put ye some paint on this plank," Mr. Giles said, walking around the front end of the cab. "It'll keep that long, I expect."

Laidlaw stayed by the gate until the dust the truck had raised began to settle. Then he wandered back down toward the house. The sound of the mandolin had stopped and when he went in he found Adrienne in the kitchen eating a fried egg sandwich.

"Hungry?" she said.

"Not too," Laidlaw said. "I was thinking I might go walk in the woods a while."

"Oh," she said. "Want company?"

"I don't know," Laidlaw said shiftily. "I might want to go kind of fast today."

"Ah," Adrienne said, and turned her head away from him to look out the window. "Well then, I might be gone by the time you get back. I've got a thing or two to take care of in town."

"Will I catch up with you this evening?" Laidlaw said.

"If you're lucky," Adrienne said, her smile slightly brittle.

Laidlaw blew her a kiss from where he was standing and quickly went out. By the garden he paused for a minute to survey the new-laid rows, resting an arm on the top of a locust post. The palms of his hands were a little sore, more from the work yesterday than the little he'd done today. He turned away from the garden and went across the field toward the fence and the trees. Once he was well into the woods he began to run. But today he could not quite get his mind to empty.

He had about made up his mind last night not to do this at all. Then this morning he had felt less sure about what he had decided. When Mr. Giles had appeared he had made one of those stupid bets with himself: if they got done in time he would go and if not, not. Now he was stuck with going when nothing would be gained by it, and he had probably hurt Adrienne's feelings into the bargain, for no better reason. Nothing to do but keep on running until the stitch in his side became so painful he could hardly think about anything else.

By that time he was just short of the top of the ridge and he stopped and bent near double, panting, holding himself up with an elbow crooked through the fork of a maple sapling he'd nearly blundered into. Once he'd got the breath to straighten up, the sweat he'd raised had already cooled on him. At dawn it had seemed to be shaping into a hot day, but there had been some turn in the weather and now it felt as much like spring as summer.

Stretching out his back, Laidlaw bowed the sapling away from the arch of his body. Here under the well-leaved trees he could not find the sun certainly enough to know the time of day, but he thought it was probably just off noon in one direction or the other. The light came streaming brightly down in nearly vertical lines through the branches, and he saw for the first time how the woods here were full of spiders. All around him there were great webs spun from tree to tree and each with a huge spider sitting quietly at its center. Of some species unfamiliar to him, they came in a spectrum of vivid colors and had a curious sort of pyramidal shape. It occurred to him that he had probably knocked down a good many of these webs when he was running blindly up the hillside.

His breath back at last, he went on at a walk, picking a way between the webs. There were so many that he had to go in a wild zigzag all the way down the other side of the ridge, but once he was across the dirt road there were less of them, and he speeded up, going almost fast enough to reawaken the cramp in his side, not quite. Out of some gathering reluctance he went much more slowly over the moss that lined the ground all through the cedar grove. When he was almost in sight of the clearing that ringed round the graveyard, he heard a shovel blade striking stone and he stopped altogether.

But the sound was not repeated, and after a little space of silence had gone by, he stalked up carefully to where he could see. Someone had been doing a little tending, especially around the newer graves lower in the plot, and the weeds had been cut back nearly to the trees, mowed or more likely just whacked short with a swingblade. In the sharp noon light even the oldest stones shone a wonderful white. There was no marker yet by the new grave, only a big hump of earth with two long-handled shovels sunk into it. And there was no one anywhere around, so he must have imagined that sound he'd thought he'd heard. Two grackles settled onto the mound and began to squabble over something they'd detected in the dirt. Laidlaw took note of its orangish color; they had gone deep enough to cut into the clay, and it would have been hard digging too, since it was fairly dry.

He began to move around toward the path at the bottom of the graveyard, keeping far enough back that no light from the clearing could fall on him. If his own father had been yet alive, he was thinking, he would already have bought and paid for a stone to be set at the head of that fresh slash in the ground. Why had he not done something about that himself? It might take Rodney months of saving to get it done: he'd have no help from Martha, that was sure. Death on the installment plan . . . Clearing his throat, Laidlaw thought he tasted bile. Keeping comfortably in the cover of the trees, he walked parallel to the cleared path until he had come in sight of the white frame rectangle of the church.

If his father had been yet alive they would both have been inside there at this minute. From his distance the swell and retreat of the prayer and song was no more distinct than the movements of some ocean far away, yet had he so chosen he might have been inside there to hear every word spoken plain as death itself. As his father would have done, he might have sat in the front pew, half strangled in the formal clothes he almost never wore, waiting to be called upon to testify. The black folks might scream and shout and tear their hair if that was what they felt like doing, but being white folks, he would have been expected to remain stiff and slightly distant, perhaps even allowing himself to seem somewhat uncomfortable, until the moment came for him to rise and face them all and speak the longest, most important words he knew in honor of the dead.

Laidlaw, who had been holding very still, began to weave his head back and forth in such a way that the church came in and out of sight on either side of a scaly-bark hickory tree right in front of him. Without much planning to, he struck the trunk of the tree with his right fist, chipping off a piece of bark which went whirling off somewhere behind him. Rather pleased with the sensation of the impact, he went on hammering at the tree for several minutes, switching his feet back and forth to bring one foot or the other forward, until he slipped over something round and fell. For a time he lay winded, on his back, looking up at the smooth bare patch he'd cleared on the bole of the tree, and then he sat up again. The knuckles of his right hand had split, and bringing it to his mouth he licked and nursed the little cut as though it were the very taste of life.

The truth was he might have gone in even now, dirty and bleeding as he was, like he had come from some brawl or other. There would have been some, at least, who would have known him and made him welcome too, and he would have known their faces if not all their names, and some such too-little-too-late appearance might in fact have been better than nothing at all. The catch was that Rodney had not asked him, and without the invitation he could not get himself to cross the threshold. Although perhaps it was too easy to tell himself he wished to God he had been asked.

There was a sound and he got up with one of the easy catlike movements he had memorized and backed a little farther from the trail. Four men, one of them Rodney (looking strange in a borrowed black coat too long at the sleeves for him), carried a plain wooden box out of the door of the church and loaded it onto a tiny and ancient gray truck. The other three men were old, white-headed, and the handful of men and women who filed out of the church after them looked like they were getting on too. The truck started with a cough and a roar and began to go draggingly up the rough trail, which was just barely wide enough to accommodate it. A straggle of mourners came along behind it, most looking like they found the going difficult. Laidlaw kept retreating softly away, but he could not seem to turn his back. Rodney had climbed into the bed of the truck and stood now with his arms folded over the roof of the cab, looking out ahead of him with a rigidly fixed stare. Weeds and branches stroked at the sides of the truck as it proceeded, and Laidlaw saw how narrowly it fit into the trail, as tightly as the coffin would fit its shaft of entrance to the ground. This was the time to say a prayer, but he could not remember one, and once he thought he was out of earshot he turned and ran like hell for home.

41

HE HAD GROWN unused to sleeping alone and that might have
been why the pallet felt cold to him when he woke up shortly before
dawn. Outside it was shivery cool still and a thick roll of fog lay
along the hollow path of the creek, blotting out the trunks of the
maples and mock orange trees. He went over and waded barefoot
across the creek and stood against the fence of the big field,
watching the last stars fade out with the slow gain of daylight. In the
bluing darkness he smoked a cigarette slowly and deliciously, half
hypnotized by the rising and falling arcs of the red spark in his hand.
After he had put it out he remained for a long time without moving
at all while the light rose higher all around him.

When the fog had begun to lift out of the creek bed and dissolve
itself into the warming air, he heard something coming toward him
from the water gate by the road. He cut his eyes around to look at it:
something the rough size and shape of a groundhog, lumbering along
on all fours. It noticed him when he turned his head, and sat back on
its haunches. Then he saw its long-fingered front paws and robber's
mask and the ringed tail stretched straight out behind it across the
damp clumps of grass. The raccoon looked at him with canny eyes and
then dropped back on all fours, squeezed under a gap in the field fence,
and moved over to disappear in some secret place in the hedgerow
along the road. No doubt it was the same coon that prowled so craftily
around the house sometimes. He'd seen the tracks often enough
before, but never the animal itself, and now he felt happy that they
had exchanged this glance, as though it meant good luck.

Smiling slightly to himself, he crossed over the creek and went
back up into the house. He was alert enough by this time that there
seemed to be no point in making coffee, and he came out of the
house again, still barefoot, carrying the banjo on its strap. At the

western corner of the porch he stood rocking lightly from foot to foot, picking soft and idle patterns with his naked fingers. His left hand felt slightly tacky, sliding up and down the neck, and his fingertips were a little sore, though not really enough to bother him, up underneath the layered calluses. The moist dawn air closed in the music; each note went a little way out from him and seemed to stop.

The sun had risen fast enough behind the hill that a band of bright clear light had appeared at the western edge of the field and was broadening nearer and nearer to him. When it had come about halfway across the field, he heard the sound of some machine passing through the acoustic cushion on the far side of the hill, its sound reemerging as it came over the top. Laidlaw turned around to see what it was: Rodney on the motorcycle, his head in the helmet a perfect black sphere. The bike made no more than a low drone, an extraordinarily polite sound for a motorcycle, Laidlaw thought. When Redmon dismounted in the gateway one of his legs appeared to give way beneath him, and he sagged into the lower gatepost, where he remained for some little time, resting. Then he pushed himself up, opened the gate, wheeled the bike through, and walked a reeling snake line down to the house. Halfway there he stopped and yanked his helmet off and let it drop on the long grass of the yard. It rolled a short crooked distance and came to a stop against a hidden stone. Laidlaw's hands went jerky on the banjo, the music coming out like a tic, a spasm.

When Redmon had come up the porch steps Laidlaw stopped playing and muted the strings with the heel of his hand. "Morning," he said with a nod of his head. "You look like you might be a little shaky today."

"It's possible," Redmon said, leaning heavily on the porch rail. The words came out sluggishly, as though his mouth and tongue had thickened too much for them to pass freely.

"What'll you have?" Laidlaw said. "We got whiskey if you want to keep on with it."

Redmon rolled his eyes, doubled himself over the rail, and vomited quietly into the yard. Laidlaw was struck by how he somehow managed to do this in almost complete silence. It was over quickly and in a moment Redmon straightened back up and gave a low cough.

"Don't think it would really help me," he said. "Not right now."

"I guess not," Laidlaw said.

Redmon backed up a step and lowered himself into a chair.

"Sorry," he said, making some studied motions to balance his weight. "I didn't think I was going to do that."

"It don't matter," Laidlaw said.

He went in the house and came back with a quart jar full of water. Redmon took a sip and bent over to spit it out from the edge of the porch. He swallowed the second gulp, then poured some water into his palm and slapped it onto either side of his face. With a long sigh he sat back in the chair.

"What's up?" Laidlaw said.

"Oh, I got the misery," Redmon said, his voice coming more distinctly.

"You get any sleep at all?" Laidlaw said.

"I must have dropped off a couple of hours ago. But then I had me a dream that blew me straight through the roof."

"Worth telling about?"

"Not on a bet." Redmon laughed, or maybe he croaked. "I just forget them as fast as I can. You've got it lucky, you know, not dreaming."

"To each his own poison," Laidlaw said lightly. "You want to go in and lie down awhile?"

"Ah?" Redmon said. "No, that's all right. I'll just rest up in this chair a little bit."

"Sit tight, then," Laidlaw said. He unslung the banjo and set it against the clapboard wall. "I better go get the sheep fed before they wander off."

"I'll be here," Redmon said, flipping a hand over in an ambiguous gesture.

Laidlaw climbed to the barn and did the feeding. Hanging above the cap of trees on the peak of the hill was a wisp of daylight moon, insubstantial as a feather. He had still not put his shoes on and his feet picked up dust from the bare patches around the barn, but the damp grass of the hill pasture wiped them clean again. As he came back up the porch steps he saw Redmon make some careless movement that almost overbalanced him, so that he had to slap his hand to the wall to stop his chair from falling over to the side. When he had it back on all four legs again he shot a glance at Laidlaw's feet from under the sinking lids of his eyes.

"You'll end up with hookworm, won't you, going barefoot to the barn?"

"Will I really," Laidlaw said. "If it's time for advice giving already, I might say you probably ought not to be riding around on a motorcycle any time you have this much trouble sitting up in a chair."

"Is that a red-eyed fact?" Redmon said. "Well, but I'm here."

"More or less." Laidlaw sat down next to him and picked up the banjo again. For a couple of minutes his hands jittered nervously over the strings.

"Put that damn thing down, why don't you," Redmon said. "Plonkety-plonk all the day long, sometimes I think you never stop."

"Whatever pleases you," Laidlaw said. He put his banjo aside and lit a cigarette, but smoking alone didn't seem to give him enough to do with his hands, so he got up and went into the house and came back with a bottle of beer.

"Starting this early?" Redmon said.

"Just trying to catch up."

Redmon smiled. "At that rate you won't gain on me much," he said.

"You want one yourself?"

Redmon leaned over and groped on the floor for the water jar. "This'll do me for right now."

"All right," Laidlaw said.

He put out his cigarette and began to pick at the label on the beer bottle with the hand he'd freed. The air was steadily clearing but it was still very quiet during the gaps between the episodes of breeze which stroked through the leaves of the trees in the yard. A sharp line of sunshine was walking up the porch steps, and between the shadows of the tree trunks the yard was streaked with bars of light. Not far from the fencerow, the wren hopped in figure eights, getting a little nearer to the feeder stone with every circuit. Laidlaw balled up a damp scrap of paper and flicked it over the porch rail. His hand was glittering with tiny flecks of foil from the label. He turned it over and squinted at the cut between his knuckles, which had scabbed over rough and black.

"You been fighting?" Redmon said.

"I only hit a tree."

"Did you whip it?"

Laidlaw smiled. "Call it a draw."

"You must have been mad about something, then," Redmon said.

"Not exactly," Laidlaw said. "Somebody died."

There was a silence followed by the sound of the wind running through the trees again, like a long expiration of breath. It was cool yet and Laidlaw felt it raise the short hairs along the back of his neck. He watched a gray squirrel walk down the trunk of the hackberry tree and stop three feet off the ground, screwing its head one way and another.

"I was there in the woods when you all came out of the church," he said. "I wondered at the time you didn't see me."

"Had my mind on other things," Redmon said. "You could have come in and heard the service."

"I don't recall that anybody asked me."

"It was in the paper big as life."

"Yeah," Laidlaw said. "That's how I knew when it was going to be."

"You could have come along to it, then."

"Don't you pull this on me now," Laidlaw said. "You know I couldn't come in there without you asked me. If you set this up to make me feel bad, then you ought to be ashamed."

"You should have been there," Redmon said.

Laidlaw sprang out of his chair and stood vibrating.

"Goddamn it, don't you think I know it?" he yelled. "All he used to do for me and I never paid him back a lick. Ever since the day I was born, you know that. Used to change my britches for me, used to warm up that baby bottle and feed me just like a woman would —"

"You don't remember any of that," Redmon said.

"But I been told it. Don't you think I know all he did? Why, it was like was my —"

"*Don't you say it*," Redmon said. His face was shattered in a thousand tiny lines, starred like a fractured pane of glass. "Don't you never. He was *my* father. *Mine*."

"All right," Laidlaw said, his voice slackening. "All right, I know that well enough."

Redmon leaned forward, clenching his own knees. "Sure he did it all for you. Everything, he did it for *you*. Broke that horseshoe for you, man . . ." Redmon's face squinched up a notch tighter. "Because he liked you better than me. And do you know why *that* was?"

Laidlaw fell back into his chair, limply as if his strings had been cut from above. "No," he said. "I don't know why because it ain't so."

"I'll tell you, then. It's because you *white*."

"Don't," Laidlaw said.

"Come home every day *talking* about you, telling every little thing you did, all about how *smart* you were —"

"Don't do it."

"By God, you were the one he spent his care on —"

"Stop it, now," Laidlaw said. "You can't think that. It's not the truth. Don't ever think it."

Redmon sank back into his chair. His whole face suddenly began to sag, as if at that moment he'd just gone to sleep, although his eyes were wide. "No," he said. "It's not the truth. Not the whole truth, anyway."

"Not any part of it," Laidlaw said.

The squirrel was sitting up on the feeder stone, nibbling at something it held in its front paws. Laidlaw leaned forward and got a pebble from a coffee can full of them he kept by for such occasions and snapped it hard in the squirrel's direction.

"What's that?" Redmon said, starting.

"Just an old squirrel scaring off my birds," Laidlaw said, pointing to where the squirrel had run halfway back up the hackberry tree.

"Oh," Redmon said. "Let me get a taste of that beer."

Laidlaw picked up the bottle and passed it to him. "All that hollering does tend to dry out your throat," he said.

"Right," Redmon said, nursing the green bottle, gazing out toward the road. "I don't know what made me say all that."

"Forget it," Laidlaw said. "You had your father to bury and you had too much to drink."

"I suppose." Redmon pulled the bottle away from his mouth and looked down through the circle of its neck. "I just hadn't got anybody to talk to no more."

"Did you used to talk to him a lot?"

"Nope," Redmon said, sipping again. "Not hardly at all, as a matter of fact."

Laidlaw lit a cigarette and passed him the pack.

"I don't belong to anybody now, I guess," Redmon said, and blew a chain of smoke rings.

"No more do I," Laidlaw said. "I don't belong to anything but this land."

"And it's not even yours," Redmon said. "He was here a long time before you all came."

"What, now?" Laidlaw said.

"Daddy was." Redmon's voice was quiet, unstrained this time. "You all didn't do anything but buy it. And then you put him off it in the end."

"All right," Laidlaw said. "All right, then I'll give it back to you."

Redmon shifted in his chair to face him. "What in the hell are you talking about?" he said, pointing his cigarette straight up into the air.

"I'll split it with you, I mean," Laidlaw said. "Down the middle. You can have from the top of the hill all the way over to the road on the other side."

"That's the best piece of it," Redmon said. "That's the show place."

"Damn right," Laidlaw said.

"You wouldn't give that away to nobody."

"It's no good to me," Laidlaw said. "If I as much as set foot on that side of the hill I just about go to pieces."

"Sell it then, why don't you?"

"That's what I won't do, right there," Laidlaw said. "But I could let you have it free."

"No, man, I must be dreaming," Redmon said with a puzzling smile. "Nobody just gives away land like that."

"Always a first time, so I'm told."

"You're just pulling my leg."

"Then call me on it," Laidlaw said. "Courthouse ought to be open in another hour, I could deed it over to you today even, probably get it done by noon."

Redmon switched his head away to look through his smoke out over the yard. "Maybe you would do it, at that."

"We'd be neighbors that way," Laidlaw said. "I'd help you build some kind of house over there . . . If you were once living there, I'd feel different about crossing that line."

"And what did you have figured we'd live on?"

Laidlaw shrugged. "We could grow some kind of cash crop, maybe, or run some stock. It's all just been sitting there waiting for somebody to think of something to do with it."

"No," Redmon said, beginning to shake his head slowly from side to side. "No, I couldn't take it."

"Why not?" Laidlaw said.

"You'd only do it because you're crazy," Redmon said. "It wouldn't mean anything but that."

"That's where you're wrong," Laidlaw said. "I'd do it for justice."

Redmon stretched his neck and spat over the porch rail. "There is no justice," he said flatly. "You've seen enough of the world to know that."

Laidlaw sat silently for a space of time; he couldn't think of a word to say. He began to suspect that in the future he would not be able to know for certain how seriously he had meant this offer, though at this moment he would surely have followed through on it. Redmon was also very still.

After a little while the army-green truck came over the top of the hill and crept down to park in front of the road gate. Mr. Giles got out and stood by the open door of the cab, looking down toward them, but he didn't wave or call out. Presently, he slapped the door shut and walked around to take a can of paint and a paint brush from the rear of the truck. Laidlaw felt his insides start to shrink.

"Is that who I think it is?" Redmon said.

"More than likely," Laidlaw said.

"So you're hooked up with them again," Redmon said.

"He happened by yesterday and fixed that gate," Laidlaw said. "First I'd seen of him in a good long while."

Redmon did not reply. Laidlaw watched Mr. Giles paint the bare top slat of the gate, moving the brush in a long lateral stroke. It took him no more than a couple of minutes to get finished. With his usual measured and deliberate movements he put the paint can and brush back in the truck bed, and then came through the gate and began to walk down toward the house.

"What, he didn't come but to paint that one board?" Redmon said. "Don't hardly seem worth the trip."

"I wouldn't wonder if he had some other jobs out this way, you know how they do," Laidlaw said. "Also I owe him some money from yesterday."

He should have been going to look for his wallet, but he felt too numb to get himself moving. There didn't seem to be much in the next few minutes for him to really look forward to. Mr. Giles's inexorable approach had taken on the curious slow-motion quality that accidents can have sometimes when they're happening to you. When he had come up the porch steps, Redmon got up with extraordinary care and stood supporting himself with a hand on the chair back.

Mr. Giles nodded in Laidlaw's direction and then removed his hat. "Saw lately where your father died," he said to Redmon.

"That's right. We buried him yesterday, as a matter of fact."

"It's what I'd heard," Mr. Giles said. "I'd been wondering how it came to happen."

"Heart attack," Redmon said.

"He had heart trouble."

"He used to complain about it some," Redmon said. "Nobody put a whole lot of stock in it, though. Any time you got down to seeing a doctor he never did want to go. I figure now he was probably scared to."

"Don't care for doctors much myself," Mr. Giles said. "I wouldn't care to die in no hospital neither one."

"He managed to miss that part of it," Redmon said. "He was out hunting when it happened. Gone about ten miles from home too. They figure he was probably lost."

"I doubt that," Mr. Giles said. "He knew all this country pretty well is what I understand." His fingers worked on the edges of his hat, but he kept on looking straight at Redmon. "I never did know him any too well but I know he was a good man in his time and I hoped to tell ye I'm sorry he's gone. I wish now I had've known him a little better maybe. Ain't too many like him left and I don't see no more comen along."

"No," Redmon said, "I know what you mean."

"If I think on it I expect him and me was more like than ever we knew," Mr. Giles said. "Well. I had it in mind to tell ye I was sorry." He put out his hand and Redmon took it without missing a beat. Then Mr. Giles had his hat back on and was walking back up to the road. Redmon sat back down in his chair, spread his hand in front of his face, and looked at it.

"I forgot to get him his money," Laidlaw said, watching the truck go on down the hill.

"He forgot to ask you for it," Redmon said.

"You know it cost him something to tell you all that," Laidlaw said.

"Could be," Redmon said. "It cost me something to stand there and listen to it too."

His face began to crumble an instant before he could get it covered in his hands. He leaned forward, elbows on his knees, his fingertips dug into his head above the eyebrows. Long shudders ran across his back like a series of electric shocks.

"See how hard on you it is to hate people?" Laidlaw said. "It's just the most exhausting thing."

Redmon sat back in his chair and lowered his hands from his face. His eyes were dry, though meshed with red. "You know, I been thinking a lot about that preacher."

"Which one is that?" Laidlaw said.

"That brotherly love one, Brother Jacob. You know, we saw him on TV one time."

"The quiet one," Laidlaw said. "I remember who you mean."

"What do you think of him?"

Laidlaw turned his hands palm-up on his knees. "Not a whole lot either way," he said. "Least you could say is, he's got a good act."

"No," Redmon said. "No, but I get the feeling he's real."

"He always could be," Laidlaw said. "I hadn't really thought a lot about it."

"He's going to be in Nashville," Redmon said.

"I've been hearing about that," Laidlaw said. "About the middle of next month."

"I really would like to get to see him," Redmon said. "Up close, you know, not just in a big crowd."

"How bad would you?"

"Pretty bad," Redmon said.

"Well," Laidlaw said. "I might could fix it."

Redmon turned around and almost glared at him.

"How?" he said. "How could you do that?"

"Be real simple if it worked," Laidlaw said. "His front men have been asking around for bands to play when they have that big rally. I'm told they try to use some local bands just about everywhere they go. They want to have one bluegrass group but there hasn't been anybody wanted to get mixed up in it so far."

"You really think you can get in on that?"

"Probably," Laidlaw said. "If I can talk the other two into doing it. Lord knows a little exposure wouldn't hurt us any right now."

"I'd like it," Redmon said. "I'd like it if I had the chance to say hello."

"I'll see about it," Laidlaw said.

"I'd appreciate it," Redmon said.

"I owe you," Laidlaw said.

Redmon didn't say anything more after that, and they both sat quietly listening to the wind combing again and again through the branches and to the flittering calls of all the birds. Redmon's breathing grew slow and regular, his hands loosened and slipped to his knees, but when Laidlaw checked he saw his eyes were still open, though there was no telling just what he was looking at.

42

BROTHER JACOB'S organizers were scattered all over the place, in hotels and motels in a couple of cases, but more often in spare nooks and crannies of other people's houses. There were even one or two, Laidlaw understood, who had put up at the Union Mission. Also they tended to keep moving around, fast. Laidlaw tried chasing them by telephone all morning long before he gave up and decided it would be just as well to go into town and try to run them down in person. There was a man named Peter Hatch, who he could make most of the arrangements with, and Hatch turned out not to be all that hard to find. But to get it totally nailed down he also had to talk to somebody named Bill Shannon, who was the one it was a real challenge to catch up with. Shannon stayed about one jump ahead of him all through the afternoon, and it was four-thirty or so before Laidlaw finally found him drinking coffee and taking calls on the pay phone of a tiny three-table restaurant out on Charlotte Avenue. By the time they had shaken hands on the business it was after five, and when Laidlaw went back outside he saw the road was completely choked with cars.

He stared, cursed, then climbed into the truck and bashed the door shut after him. It had been very hot all day and the cab was scorching, so that it hurt his hands to hold the wheel. He had to wait around five minutes before somebody paused to let him turn into the slow-motion crunching of the traffic. No question of going fast enough to raise a breeze; in fact, any movement in his lane was just about imperceptible. He sat slumped behind the wheel, sweating heavily, his skin adhering to the black plastic seat cover through a damp patch on his shirt. Whenever he had to shift, the gearbox gave out menacing clanks. At least he was headed east, away from the setting sun, but the chrome on the cars ahead of him caught flaring reflections of it and threw them back into the corners of his eyes. Laidlaw squinted; he was starting to get a headache. It would take him at least an hour to get back to the country at this rate. The jam he was in right now had probably been started by cars backed off the I-40 ramp, still half a mile up ahead. That was when it occurred to him that Rodney would probably be getting off work about this time. He turned off Charlotte the first chance he got, onto the short dead-ending side streets to the north, where there was not all that much traffic. He zigzagged his way over to Twelfth Avenue and then drove up to Jefferson Street.

After he'd found a space by the side of Mosque 37 and Health Food Restaurant, he kept on sitting in the truck for a while, despite the painful heat. There was plenty of traffic on Jefferson Street, though it hadn't come to a dead halt the way it had on Charlotte. Laidlaw stayed plastered to the hot vinyl for long enough to smoke a cigarette. He had been back here a time or two with Rodney, but never yet alone. Every time he looked at Raschid he saw something like a shadow of the former Prester Ball, and he wouldn't doubt he made Raschid a little edgy too, in ways he was uncertain of.

The traffic would stay unbeatable for about another hour, that was the sure thing. He got out, dropping his cigarette on the pavement and grinding it out with the toe of his shoe. Then with an odd twinge of shame he bent over to retrieve the butt, but as he stooped, he saw there were a hundred others flattened there; he couldn't even make out which one might be his own. Shrugging, he turned the corner of the building and went in through the screen door of Mosque 37 without allowing himself time to hesitate. Inside it was dim and conspicuously cooler, with a stiff breeze coming down from a big fan on a pole in a rear corner of the room. It was also surprisingly crowded, and it looked like Raschid had hired some help; two teenage girls were going back and forth from the counter with trays of food and drinks. But the most startling thing was that a good many of the people scattered around the tables were white, so that Laidlaw didn't really stick out the way he expected to, and usually did. He blinked and walked over to the counter and sat down on a stool. Raschid was loading heavy white plates from three of his big stew pots. When he had filled a tray he passed it to one of the new waitresses and then moved along the counter in Laidlaw's direction.

"You're doing a land office business, looks like," Laidlaw said. "I see where you got people working for you now."

"The Lee sisters," Raschid said. "Yes. We been pretty busy these last couple of weeks. What will you have?"

"You got ice tea?"

Raschid nodded soberly and moved away. Laidlaw revolved on his stool to look over the room. He'd never seen it half so full before; almost all the seats were occupied, but he didn't see Rodney anywhere, as he'd hoped he might. A brown man sitting against the far wall raised a hand to greet him: Peter Hatch. Mildly surprised, Laidlaw waved back. He thought the man in green that Hatch was talking to might be Rodney's friend Mr. Maddox, but he wasn't dead sure. There was a clink on the counter behind and he turned back to pick up his glass of tea. Apparently there had been a lull in the orders, for Raschid had settled on his own stool behind the counter.

"Hot one today," Laidlaw said, sipping the cold tea. It was not sweet, but had a faint flavor of mint to it. "Here's what I need."

"It's supposed to keep on hot all next week," Raschid said, gesturing toward the television.

Laidlaw glanced over his shoulder. On the TV a man stood in front of a weather map, reciting the local forecast. Above the set, he saw that part of the plate-glass window had been cracked. Somebody had fixed a flattened cardboard carton to a section of the pane, with silver duct tape along its edges. He turned back to face Raschid.

"Looks like you're drawing a different crowd," he said.

"You mean all these white folks?" Raschid said.

"Well," Laidlaw said, "it does make a change."

"And all from out of town," Raschid said. "Just about every one of them but you."

"Is that right?" Laidlaw said.

"They all follow that Brother Jacob," Raschid said. "Or go ahead of him, I guess I should say."

"What are they, some kind of freedom riders?" Laidlaw said.

Raschid snorted. "Do they look like it to you?"

Laidlaw turned back toward the center of the room, flicking his eyes from one table to the next. Everything he saw seemed to answer *no*, whether it was the clothes or the shoes or the teeth or just that it was essentially a different kind of face. "I don't suppose," he said.

"They're none of them college kids," Raschid said. "Or Yankees either. All country people, they come up from south of here, Georgia and Alabama and Louisiana, even."

"Ah," Laidlaw said. "I wouldn't have thought people like that would stray so far off their land."

Raschid stroked a thumb along his lower lip. "These mostly don't own any, I don't think," he said. "They're tenant farmers, you know, they're used to moving around a little. There's some that tried mill work, or factory work, got laid off and hit the road that way. A lot of these here have been picking up odd jobs here around town."

"I wouldn't have thought —"

"— there'd be so many," Raschid said. "Yes. It does tend to take you a little by surprise."

"So it's black and white all traveling together like that?"

"All jumbled up," Raschid said. "That's what it's like."

"I wouldn't guess that would be your dish," Laidlaw said.

Raschid moved his broad hands over the Formica, as if he meant to smooth it down. Laidlaw felt an involuntary pulse of memory: a picture of the young Prester Ball laying hands on a sheep and swinging it up onto the shearing truck with a great sweeping motion.

"It makes me curious, is the least I'll say," Raschid said. "Of course, it's apt to raise some trouble too."

Laidlaw peered back at the cardboard patch on the window. "Have you had any of that yourself?"

"Only a speck," Raschid said. "Every now and then we get a carload of white trash come tearing through here. Drunk and hollering and throwing stuff, you know."

"Nasty," Laidlaw said.

"Not too serious yet, though," Raschid said. "This is not somewhere it would pay them to get out of their cars. But a bunch did put that crack in my window, driving by."

"Just general meanness?" Laidlaw said. "Or because you been serving these people?"

Raschid took off his glasses and polished them on his loose white sleeve. "Could be either, it's hard to tell," he said. "I also got a few of them sleeping there in the back."

Laidlaw cut his eyes toward the turnip-topped door. "You letting white people sleep back there?"

Raschid settled his glasses back on his nose. "It wasn't getting that much other use," he said.

Laidlaw winked at him. "Would you let me?"

Raschid grinned, but only on one side of his face. "You got your own place to sleep," he said.

"You're surprising me," Laidlaw said. "I wouldn't have expected you to get behind this kind of a thing."

"I'm curious, like I told you." Raschid went back to smoothing down the counter, looking at the space between his hands. "This is a different sort of a thing than I've really known of before, and I'm wondering where it might be going to go. Not everybody is going to be that pleased with it, I don't think, black or white either one." He raised one hand and waved it toward the room. "These people here are a peace-loving crowd but they stand to bring out a good few that aren't. You know, they're stirring up the soup."

"Think so?" Laidlaw said.

"Where you been lately?"

"Out in the country," Laidlaw said. "I can't really think when I was last in town. I got no TV and I don't read the papers all that much."

The two Lee sisters stood at the far end of the counter. One rapped her tray sharply with the back of her knuckles. Raschid swung around on his stool and called out to them.

"Serve it out yourselves a little while, why don't you?" he said. "Don't you see I'm talking to the man?" He leaned back toward Laidlaw. "Hadn't been anything yet but some ugly talk. No killing or burning yet, nothing but threats. But things are getting wound up kind of tight and that rally's still a good little while away."

"I never heard of this bunch having any bad trouble before."

"You never heard of them getting this far from home, either. They used to sort of just inch along in their own area. Now they're getting bigger and moving faster and that's a risky business, if you ask me."

"You expect there'll be some trouble at that rally?" Laidlaw said.

"I'd say the chances were good for it," Raschid said. "Why, you planning to go?"

"With the band," Laidlaw said. "We're set to be part of the live entertainment."

"You're surprising me," Raschid said.

"'I wouldn't wonder," Laidlaw said. "I surprise myself sometimes."

"Better start watching your back," Raschid said.

"Oh?" Laidlaw said. "Tell me some more about these threats. You been getting any personal ones?"

"Not more than a note under my door every once in a while."

"Saying what, exactly?"

Raschid pressed his palms together. "Different ways I could be done in, and so on. Different ways somebody could be, that is. They don't have my name on them. You know, these people don't really have a whole lot of imagination."

"What people are you talking about?"

"Did you think they would be signed? They just say KKK on the bottom of the page, things like that."

Laidlaw picked up his tea glass and gave it a shake, but the ice had melted and it made no sound, only the liquid moved in a silent swirl. He set the glass down again without tasting it and lit a cigarette. Raschid was staring at him, his eyes slightly magnified by the lenses of his glasses.

"What's the matter?" he said. "You a member?"

"What in the hell do you take me for?" Laidlaw said, his voice shaking slightly.

"No telling," Raschid said, smiling in a way that exposed the points of his teeth. "They don't normally show their face. Just like they say a man can be a nigger and it not show. All it takes is a drop of that black blood to do it."

"I don't hold any of them opinions," Laidlaw said.

"Maybe not," Raschid said. "But you're still white."

"If you say so," Laidlaw said. "But if you really thought I was that kind, I doubt we'd be having this little talk."

"Why, I never knew you were such a logic picker." Raschid's smile loosened and much of the tension went out of his voice. "All right, then," he said. "I take it all back."

"Whatever." Laidlaw drank off what was left in his glass. He felt a little easier now but he was still more than ready to leave. "I was kind of looking for Rodney, by the way. You expect he'll pass by here this evening?"

"Been and gone," Raschid said. "I expect you'll find him at home."

"And where's that?" Laidlaw said.

"You don't know?" Raschid said. He frowned, picked at a fingernail, and told him.

In the twilight, Laidlaw stood before the low building marked with the pale enormous numeral 2. Raschid had not known just which was Rodney's room and there were no names anywhere around the outer door. Laidlaw turned the knob and the door groaned inward.

Inside it was almost completely dark. Down at the far end of the hall a small bulb in the ceiling leaked a radiance too weak even to reach the floor beneath it. Laidlaw had not known wattage as low as that existed. There was a gigantic black man, dressed only in a grayish union suit, lurching down the hall toward him, blocking out most of the faint light. Funny thing to be wearing in this heat, Laidlaw thought, but maybe he was crazy. He moved in an unstrung way that suggested he was drunk or drugged or mentally ill or some combination of all three.

"You another one of them puke-face Jesus-lovers?" the man inquired. His delivery was so indistinct that Laidlaw had to think it over for a minute to understand what he'd said, and in the meantime the man tripped over his own feet and fell with a smash against the wall.

"I'm looking for Rodney Redmon?" Laidlaw said stupidly. "You know which one is his?"

The man didn't answer, and when Laidlaw took a step closer he saw that his eyes were half shut and showing only white. Farther down the hall a door opened, spilling a pale wash of the fading daylight over the floor, and from inside a voice called.

"*Shut up* out there, for Christ's sake."

Laidlaw went toward the sound, but when he arrived the doorway was empty. Cautiously he peeped in and saw a room more bare than not, with stained green walls and the huge gray motorcycle incongruously leaning against one of them. Redmon sat on the unmade bed with his knees drawn up, a couple of pillows smashed between his back and the wall, looking up at the ceiling. On an upended peach crate by the bed a small radio hummed and buzzed. Beside it there stood a pint of rum, uncapped but mostly full.

"What are you doing here," Redmon said tonelessly.

Laidlaw came all the way into the room and pushed the door shut behind him with his heel. "We're on with Brother Jacob," he said. "I just came by to give you the word."

"That's good," Redmon said in the same empty voice.

"I guess you'll have to learn to play the harmonica right quick," Laidlaw said. "You know, so you can come out there on the stage with us and look useful."

Redmon went on staring up at the ceiling, without so much as a ghost of a smile on his face. Laidlaw looked up himself to check what might be there to see, but he could make no sense of the pattern of cracks. He paced across the room to the windows. On another peach crate in the corner a small electric fan was revolving; whenever it tracked all the way to the left it made a strangled squeaking sound. Its breeze made no dent on the heat in the room. Laidlaw propped his haunch on the window sill.

"Hell," he said, "I thought you'd be happy."

"Oh, I am," Redmon said. He pushed himself a little farther upright and reached to turn off the radio, then picked up a pack of cigarettes that lay beside it on the crate. "You caught me at a bad time, is all."

"Didn't mean to barge in," Laidlaw said. "I was just in a hurry to let you know about it."

"It's all right," Redmon said, blowing a single smoke ring upward. "You hitting the bottle?"

"I barely tapped it," Redmon said. "You want a taste?"

"Nah," Laidlaw said. "It's too hot for raw liquor."

He could not seem to pull his eyes away from the motorcycle. Against the water-marked wall it looked so glossy and clean and new that it seemed to draw all the light of the room into itself and reorganize it into a silvery glow. The column of stale air the fan thrust out cut back and forth across his knees. That squeak could get on your nerves, he thought, if you had to listen to it for long.

"I can't quit thinking about my daddy," Redmon said.

"That makes good enough sense to me," Laidlaw said. "Considering he just now died."

"That's not it," Redmon said, "what I'm thinking about. I mean, he was a talented man. All those different things he could do, you know? And he dies himself a five-year death in that damn shack there by the side of the road, now why did it have to be that way? I just can't get it off of my mind."

Laidlaw stood up to look out the window. There was a squirrel moving sluggishly across the patchy, drought-damaged grass outside. "You need to shift yourself out of this place," he said.

"Hah," Redmon said. "Is that what you think? This is my own little corner I'm stuck in here."

Laidlaw turned around to face him. "Is that my fault?"

"What kind of a stupid question is that?" Redmon said. "I couldn't tell you whose fault it is. Ain't nobody's fault. All I know is, I been backed in this corner one way or another and it just keeps on getting tighter and tighter and littler and littler . . ."

Laidlaw came across the room and sat down on the edge of the bed, about six inches from Redmon's bare foot. "The offer stands," he said.

"What if I took it?"

"Then you'd have it."

Redmon blew some more smoke toward the ceiling. "Could I sell it, then?"

Laidlaw didn't reply.

"You know, could I call up Goodbuddy and sell it off to him to put a mess of those little square houses on and take that money and slap it in the bank?"

"No," Laidlaw said. "You know that wasn't what I had in mind."

"Then I wouldn't really own it, would I?" Redmon said.

"All right," Laidlaw said. "If that's the way you want to be."

"What did you have in mind to do about it?" Redmon said.

"Be your friend," Laidlaw said. "Come see me again when you get in the notion."

He went out the door without looking back and pulled it shut quietly after him.

At the top of the hill above his house, he cut the lights and motor, clipped the gear stick into neutral, and let the truck roll. By the first bend it was moving so fast already that he could barely keep it out of the ditches, but he was as loath to touch the brake as if he'd bet money that he wouldn't. He slewed in and out of his own gateway without even trying to stop, cutting up a big fishtail of gravel and shooting on down over the limestone washboard, every pock in it threatening to jar the wheel clean out of his hands. Across the neighboring pasture he could see headlights coming toward the crossroads and he knew that if the other car turned in they were set for a head-on collision. The only thing he wasn't sure of was if he was going fast enough for the wreck to kill him, or if it only felt that way. The car went on by without turning and the truck lost its momentum quickly on the flat section of the road, coasting to a stop a few dozen yards short of the corner where the mailboxes were.

It was still warm out, too warm, and the atmosphere was thick. Laidlaw sat still behind the wheel, taking shallow breaths of the dense air, and then got out and walked the rest of the way to the corner. Down in the left-hand pasture, tendrils of fog spread out from the trees along the creek like fingers of a spectral hand. The dome of the sky itself was clear and starlit, and there was a bright sliver of moon. On either side the snarls of honeysuckle vine in the fencerows were coated with fine dust from the cars going up and down the road. In the starlight the dust had a silvery glow and the roadbed itself had turned bone-white.

Laidlaw went around the corner and pulled open the bent tin door of the mailbox on the left. When he touched what was inside it his hand snapped back as if something had bitten it. It was nothing, just a slice of the rough construction paper like what children use in school, but his hand had recognized the texture and recoiled. Shaking his head, he reached in again and took it out and tilted it to catch the thin light. It looked like all the others had, folded over twice and closed with a square of cellophane tape which glittered with a dim reflection from the sky. He carried it back to the truck and tossed it unopened on top of all the others in the glove compartment. His breath still seemed to be coming a little short, and he rested for a little longer before he turned the truck around and pointed it back up the hill.

43

WHEN THE motorcycle pulled up the next morning Laidlaw was inside the barn dipping sweet feed for the sheep, which was probably why he hadn't heard it coming. He hopped down out of the feed room to see that Redmon had already come to the gate and was standing between where he'd propped the bike on its kickstand and the spot where Laidlaw's truck was parked. Redmon was looking down at the dry ridged ruts of the track. Watching him from the corner of his eye, Laidlaw went around the front of the barn and dumped the feed into the trough under the roof's overhang, then kneed his way back through the crowding backs of the sheep. The brief movements of their narrow hooves stirred up small puffs of dust that rose a few inches from the ground and then settled slowly back. Laidlaw saw that Redmon had moved off the track and hunkered over the grass as if he hoped it was going to tell him something. He closed the feed room and walked back down the hill in that direction.

"Dry around here," Redmon said, raising his head as Laidlaw came up.

What he had been looking at were the deep cracks that cut into the earth between the hummocks of grass that were beginning to turn a silver shade, as though it were fall already instead of midsummer. The larger cracks were wide enough for Redmon to slip his index finger into.

"You just now noticed?" Laidlaw said. "Ain't rained in nearly a month."

Redmon stood up. "Don't make that much difference to me, living in town," he said. "I guess you must be right, though."

"It gets muggy all the time but it just won't rain," Laidlaw said. "I keep thinking it's bound to break pretty soon."

"It hurting you?" Redmon said.

Laidlaw shrugged. "Not a whole lot yet," he said. "Don't have enough stock to need all this much pasture anyway. I been watering the garden. The only thing that really worries me is fire."

Redmon nodded and turned downhill, walking back toward the truck, his hands in his hip pockets. When he reached the tailgate he turned around and leaned against it. Laidlaw came along after him, blinking in the brightening morning light. The night before, he had only got to sleep toward dawn, and now his eyes were puffy, his vision slightly blurred.

"I been riding you kind of hard lately, I suppose," Redmon said, not quite looking him in the eye.

"You might say so." Laidlaw walked past him and propped himself on the side of the cab. With one hand he reached up and began to finger the knurled edge of the gas cap behind the passenger door.

"I've had a number of things on my mind," Redmon said, "but no call to drag you into any of it."

Laidlaw picked at a peeling callus on his left ring fingertip. "Why not?" he said. "Do you think I would mind it?"

Redmon was looking away from him, back in the direction of the road. Laidlaw saw his shoulder lift and fall.

"You're white, that's all," Redmon said. "It comes down to it, you're bound to stick with your own kind."

"Come off it," Laidlaw said. "When did that make any difference between you and me?"

"That you ever noticed," Redmon said.

"I'm not thinking any kind of thing like that and you know it."

"You don't have to think it," Redmon said. "You've got the choice."

"Hell," Laidlaw said. He reached for cigarettes and found he had none.

"You mean well, that's your problem," Redmon said. "You just want to be some comfortable spot in between everything, but there ain't no such place."

"What got you so interested in Brother Jacob, then, if that's the way you feel?"

Redmon's shoulder rose and sagged again. "Couldn't really tell you," he said. "I'm not making perfect sense to myself, that's part of what *my* problem is."

"Look here," Laidlaw said. "I don't know if it would make any difference to you, but there's some that say I'm an honorary nigger myself."

Redmon's head screwed around to stare at him; his eyes were hard as little stones. "What do you think you're talking about?" he said.

"Easy now," Laidlaw said. "Wait until I show you."

He reached in through the open window of the cab and pushed the button of the glove compartment. Redmon came up behind him to peer over his shoulder as he shuffled through all the double-folded sheets of construction paper. Some fluttered from his grasp, scattering across the seat and the floor. At length he found the one he wanted and straightened up out the window.

"Here you go," he said, unfolding the stiff sheet.

Redmon gripped the free edge of it and they held the message between their two heads.

ANYBODY THAT WOULD LIVE IN A NIGGERS HOUSE
IS NOT ANY DIFRENT FROM ONE

TOUCH NOT PITCH LEST YE BE DEFILED

The three lines were typed all in capitals, and all of the *N*'s were out of formation, cocked up above the line and turned a little crooked. Toward the bottom of the sheet, below the second fold, was a black-inked outline of a rearing horse with a robed and hooded rider. Beneath the horse's hind hooves some rather ornate lettering spelled out WHITE KNIGHTS OF THE KU KLUX KLAN. The whole image seemed to have been put there with a rubber stamp, and its outline was slightly smeared, as though somebody's hand had slipped in affixing it.

"I'd shut my mouth if I were you," Laidlaw said with half a smile. "Don't, something's liable to fly in there and build a nest."

Redmon's gape closed sharply, his teeth meeting with an audible click. He elbowed Laidlaw out of the way, opened the truck door, and reached in to scoop up the rest of the scattered pages.

"They use a different color just about every time," Laidlaw said, the same crooked grin pasted to his face. "I always appreciate that part."

Not answering, Redmon began to spread the colored pages on the hood of the truck to read them, laying them down one on top of another, color by color: red, blue, green, yellow, orange . . . Phrasing differed from page to page but the sentiments expressed were much the same and the rubber-stamped silhouette of the Klan rider appeared on each. The line TOUCH NOT PITCH LEST YE BE DEFILED was frequently but not invariably repeated. Redmon pinned the stack of papers under the weight of his hand and lifted his head to Laidlaw.

"How long you been getting these things?"

"Over the last three weeks or so," Laidlaw said. "Once or twice a week I'll find one stuck in my mailbox down yonder." He pointed off toward the end of the road, as if Redmon didn't know where the mailboxes were.

"And you hadn't done anything about it?"

"Do what?" Laidlaw said. "I may not look that busy to you but I still don't have time to lay a week-long ambush on my mailbox."

Redmon tilted his head back over the pages. A weak dry breeze caught the corners of them and fanned the layers of color back.

"Kind of monotonous, aren't they?" Redmon said.

"Yep," Laidlaw said. "That's what your man Raschid said about his, matter of fact."

"What, has he been getting these too?"

"He didn't tell you?"

"Not a word about it."

"Well, I was asking about all these new people around his end of town when I was by there yesterday," Laidlaw said. "I guess I kind of got him on the subject. I mean, I hadn't felt all that much like talking about these here myself."

"And you say he's been getting these same things?"

"He didn't show me," Laidlaw said, "but I gather from what he said it's something similar. Though I don't suppose they would be calling him a nigger-lover, for instance."

"That wouldn't hardly make sense, would it," Redmon said.

"These ones here have kind of a personal touch," Laidlaw said. "That's one of the things I least like about them."

Redmon refolded the top sheet along its creases and looked at it front and back. "Don't have your name on it anywhere," he said.

"No," Laidlaw said, "but they appear to know some things, you see what I mean, like who all used to live in this house before I did, and so on."

"Like how you like to spend your time with me," Redmon said.

"Ah, well," Laidlaw said. He tapped his forefinger on the smudgily stamped figure of the Klansman. "It's all kind of a disappointment, you know? I really had thought these bastards were out of business now."

"You have a talent for fooling yourself," Redmon said. "Forgotten that visit you had last year?"

"That was a prank," Laidlaw said.

Redmon snorted and looked away from him. Again he shuffled through the pages, and this time an unopened one slipped out of the pack and fluttered off the hood to the ground. "Hey, what about this one?" Redmon said, stooping to pick it up.

"Must be the one that came last night."

"You didn't look at it yet?"

"It was dark when I picked it up," Laidlaw said. "I won't carry those things inside my house."

Redmon slid his thumbnail under the square of tape and paused.

"Be my guest," Laidlaw said.

Redmon peeled back the tape and unfolded the paper. "Damn, take a look at this one," he said.

Laidlaw craned his neck to see.

DONT STAND NEAR THE NIGER PREACHER IF
YOU DONT WANT TO GO THE SAME WAY AS HIM

TOUCH NOT PITCH LEST YE BE DEFILED

"Their spelling is poor," Laidlaw said.

"They got the Bible part down all right."

"I expect they copied that."

"Forget about their spelling," Redmon said. "Their information is *good.*"

"Too good," Laidlaw said. "I only set the thing up yesterday, the son of a bitches beat me home."

Staring Laidlaw straight in the face, Redmon began to whistle "Goodbye, Pork-Pie Hat." At the end of the second bar he stopped, leaving the last note quavering, suspended.

"Hadn't heard that one in a while," Laidlaw said.

"I only do it when I'm in this particular mood."

"Ah," Laidlaw said. "What say we go up and sit by the pond a while? I wouldn't mind getting off my legs for a minute."

As they came over the rise of the pond's lower lip, two big snapping turtles that had been sunning on the bank scooted out into the water with a sort of skimming movement. Because the pond's surface was mostly covered with thick mats of algae, their descent didn't make much in the way of ripples. All around the edges of the pond were smaller splashes of frogs flinging themselves into the water.

"Goddamn," Redmon said. "Did you get a good look at that

second one? He wouldn't hardly have fit in a foot tub. Make you one fine turtle stew if you knew how to catch him."

"I never did figure out how to make it not taste like mud," Laidlaw said.

"Pepper helps," Redmon said. "Red pepper pods."

They walked around to the high side of the pond and sat on the slope above the drooping willows. In the drought the pond had shrunk upon itself and it was ringed by a yard-wide mud flat, spotted by the cloven hoofprints of the sheep. At the outer edges the mud had dried hard and begun to crack.

"You suppose there's any fish still in there?" Redmon said.

"I doubt it," Laidlaw said. "It's mostly silted in by this time, not very deep anymore. If there was any left, I expect the turtles got them."

Redmon lit a cigarette and passed the pack to Laidlaw.

"Careful where you throw that match," Laidlaw said, drawing in smoke.

Redmon leaned forward and flicked the matchstick out onto the slick surface of the mud. "It's dry, sure enough."

"You know it," Laidlaw said. "Like I told you, fire's the thing that worries me."

"You fixing to have more trouble than that."

"Yep," Laidlaw said. "I know that too."

"Won't you back out of it?"

"No."

"Why not?"

"Because I'm stubborn," Laidlaw said. "It's in my blood. My daddy died of it, after all."

Redmon whistled another bar of his tune and stopped. "And what would you say my daddy died of?" he said.

"I'd say they both died of being themselves, in a way," Laidlaw said. "And you know, I can think of a lot worse ways to go."

"You don't want to be joking now," Redmon said. "This has got the earmarks of a pretty bad thing. It's not likely to stop at note passing, you know."

Laidlaw worked a rock loose from the hardened earth beside where he sat, held it in his palm and looked at it. It was a flat triangular cake of limestone, embedded with fossilized fronds of seaweed, slightly larger than his palm. He tossed it up a couple of inches and it slapped back against the heel of his hand.

"Don't suppose it's likely to, at that," he said.

"I don't think you better try coasting through this one," Redmon said. "You need to be thinking what you're going to do."

"Right, right," Laidlaw said. "I will in just a minute. That last note was the only one that sounded like doing something. All the rest just looked like aggravation."

"Ain't no small-time thing anymore either," Redmon said. "There's a long distance to cover between you and Raschid."

"He might draw that kind of attention all on his own, don't you think?" Laidlaw said. "It could just be a coincidence."

"Get out of here," Redmon said. He rubbed his cigarette out on a dry patch of dirt and rolled the butt between thumb and forefinger until it began to shred. "Sometimes I think I ought to just invest in a white robe and a funny hat and get over there behind Raschid myself. Cut loose from white folks forevermore . . ."

"Me included?" Laidlaw said.

"Have to be."

On the far side of the pond the head and shoulders of a black-faced ewe appeared, grazing her way halfheartedly up the slope. Behind her, Laidlaw could just see the curled horns of the ram.

"Then what would you do for family?" he said.

Redmon laughed aloud. "Now's the time you're going to claim kin?" he said.

"I'll claim we've known each other a good deal longer than anybody else yet alive."

"Well," Redmon said. "That could be one way to look at it. But how much difference does it make? Maybe a man just ought to go on."

"And end up where?" Laidlaw said. "No, I'd rather hang on to what part of my history I can."

"Even if you get in a fix like this one?" Redmon shook his head. "I wouldn't have thought you'd interest yourself in this amount of trouble."

"I wouldn't go out of my way looking for it, no," Laidlaw said. "But hell, Rod, sometimes you act like you think I don't know right from wrong."

"Sometimes *you* act like you don't."

"Well," Laidlaw said. "The difference ain't always that obvious."

"And what about now?"

"Oh, this one's plain enough for me," Laidlaw said. "This one's a fairly easy call."

Redmon whistled a few more bars and then cut himself off with that same abruptness. He plucked a long straw from a clump beside him, set it between his lips, and breathed through it with a faint hissing sound. "What if I could tell you who's sending those notes?" he said, the straw weaving as he spoke.

"Well," Laidlaw said. "I'd say that might produce a tactical advantage."

"Goodbuddy," Redmon said.

"And you just now called me a safe player?" Laidlaw said. "I wouldn't figure him into anything like this, ain't no money in it."

"But you know how he'll swing with the strongest wind," Redmon said. "I don't say he thought it up but I know he's got a hand in it."

"How do you?"

"Give me a chance and I'll show you," Redmon said. "We might slide around his office tomorrow and see can we catch him alone. Sometimes he'll work by himself on a Sunday."

"You sure about this?"

"Dead sure."

Laidlaw got to his feet, the limestone chunk still cramped in his hand. "In that case, I can probably get him to come here straight-away."

"Didn't know you two kept company," Redmon said.

"We don't," Laidlaw said. "But I know the magic words: 'I'm thinking of selling.' That should have him over here like a shot."

"I believe that," Redmon said with a short spitting laugh.

Laidlaw said nothing. He looked past the pair of sheep, down the hillside. All those colored sheets of paper had blown off the hood of the truck and the breeze was carrying them along the track and among the patches of dry grass. He hefted the rock in his hand again, then threw it up in a looping arc and watched it come down to punch a hole in the algae in the center of the pond. The muffled sound it made was just enough to spook the sheep, who went stiff-legged for an instant and bolted down the slope.

44

GOODBUDDY SAT on one of the porch chairs with a clipboard wedged between his plump knees, talking rapidly, now and then waving an arm, mentioning various numbers. He wore a blue and white jacket that somewhat resembled seersucker and was already marked with widening sweat patches under the arms. In fact, his whole face seemed hot and damp, even in the shade of the porch, and his blond forelock was plastered wetly to his head. It appeared to Laidlaw that excitement or some sort of strain must be making him sweat so much, since it was not all that hot yet, and it was dry. In the pauses of his speech, his tongue licked up to moisten the pink swell of his upper lip and retracted; each time it looked as if he found that the taste of himself was good.

Laidlaw answered him readily whenever an answer seemed called for, keeping his tone bright. Every couple of minutes Goodbuddy motioned him to come look at some figure he had jotted on the clipboard, but Laidlaw stayed where he was, on his feet beside the corner post. On a slow pulsing beat he pushed himself away from the post and then let himself drop back against it, catching his weight on the flat of his hand. A metronomic slapping sound was produced by the regularity of this movement. Goodbuddy spoke with sustained animation for about a half hour and afterward appeared to be winding down. Since he had not raised the subject of tearing down the barns, Laidlaw brought it up himself, and found that this part too went over easily enough. In a moment they were walking down the porch steps side by side, still chatting, and turning in the direction of the hay barn.

Goodbuddy was walking fast and a little jerkily, since he wasn't paying much attention to where he put his feet. Laidlaw let him get a little ahead. His pale hair had darkened from his sweat and was stuck in a whorled shape around the thin spot at the peak of his skull. The peacock went across the path a few yards ahead of him and Goodbuddy stopped to contemplate it. Laidlaw came up beside him.

"Well, there's my old peacock," Goodbuddy said. His thumb stroked the edge of his lower lip. "So, he's still hanging around?"

"Still hanging on," Laidlaw said softly.

The peacock's sinuous neck made a forward stroke and it picked at something in the dry grass. After a moment it lifted its head and walked on, slow and splayfooted, in the direction of the creek.

"Shy bird," Goodbuddy said, dropping his hand to his side.

"Not too," Laidlaw said. His mouth had gone a little dry. "I'll see about getting him put up for you pretty soon."

"That might be handy," Goodbuddy said, striding out ahead once more. "Seeing that you're planning a move . . ."

"I'll see —" Laidlaw's tongue had suddenly swollen up, so that it felt too thick to use for speech. Leaving the phrase unfinished, he cleared his throat. Goodbuddy had come to a halt at the creek bed.

"Ever get crawdaddies out of here?" he said.

"Not in a while," Laidlaw said. "Not when it's this dry."

Goodbuddy planted one oxblood shoe in the pale dusty gravel and took an exaggeratedly long step across the slim trickle of water that still ran. Here at the crossing place, the creek had practically no banks, and Goodbuddy had only to take a half step up to be back on the trail that ran on toward the barn. Laidlaw knelt down beside the thin rill of water and dipped the ends of his fingers into it. It felt tepid, but beneath it the rounded stones were polished, gleaming. He grasped one to lift it out, then changed his mind and let it go. A little way down the creek the banks were higher, the bed narrower, and enough water had accumulated to form some little pools.

"Catch one there?" Goodbuddy said.

Laidlaw glanced up and saw him outlined against the blank gray wall of the barn. "No," he said. "I was just —"

Since Goodbuddy was not paying much attention, it didn't seem to matter if the sentence got finished or not. Laidlaw felt just slightly giddy when he stood up, but the feeling passed from him in a moment. Goodbuddy had gone on to the barn, saying something over his shoulder about board feet. There was the track of a single wheel pressed in the dust along the path, but Laidlaw didn't suppose Goodbuddy would notice it, or make much of it if he did. He lit himself a cigarette and walked up.

Goodbuddy came up to the double barn doors, reached out to stroke one of the vertical planks, and took a step back. He pursed his lips, paced off the front end of the barn, and made a note on his clipboard. Laidlaw stood a little distance away, smoking and tapping his ash into the wide apron of dust in front of the barn. Goodbuddy tucked his clipboard back under his elbow and began to walk off the long dimension. Halfway down, the long gray wall threw a cold shadow over him. Above the place where he had paused, the trap door to the hayloft had swung open, disclosing a hollow black gap. Its hinge squeaked as a breeze moved it slightly, and something about the sound made Laidlaw feel clammy for a second. He looked away from the trap door, down at the ground, and stirred his ashes into the dust with the toe of his right sneaker. Goodbuddy nodded to himself, did a quick calculation on his pad, and came back.

"Yessiree," he said, tapping the clipboard with the eraser of his pencil. "This is about premium for barn siding, I would say. Course, I could tell that from the road . . . Now you got this and you got roughly the same amount, I'd guess, out of those two little barns up on the hill."

"Then there's the horse barn," Laidlaw said. "Back over there on the other side."

"Well, but that's painted, right?" Goodbuddy said. "See, what really goes these days is this natural color, this gray." He felt behind himself to touch one of the boards again.

"Oh," Laidlaw said. "I hadn't been keeping up with it."

"Course, you might want to save out some to keep for yourself now, too," Goodbuddy said. "I got my den at home paneled in it myself. Looks real nice, I'll tell you."

"I bet so," Laidlaw said. "I'll think about that. No rush, I suppose?" He dropped his cigarette and stepped on it, shifting his weight.

"Oh no," Goodbuddy said. "You got all the time you want for that."

"Want to look at the inside?"

Goodbuddy frowned slightly. "No need to that I can see," he said. "I can pretty well tell what there is from out here. Just an estimate, you know."

"There's some interior walls," Laidlaw said. "Stalls, and so on." He paused. "Mostly *brown* wood, I believe."

"Sure," Goodbuddy said, shrugging. "Can't hurt anything, can it?"

Laidlaw came forward and dragged open one of the big double doors. Because it had sagged from its hinges, the ragged corner of its end plank scraped a toothed pattern on the ground as he hauled at it. The hall of the barn was quite dark and the daylight Laidlaw had admitted did not seem to penetrate very far into it. The ceiling was low and the hall was narrowly hemmed in by closed stalls. Three quarters of the way to the rear wall the loft floor ended, and a fair amount of grayish light leaked in from the open trap door on the higher level, illuminating a well-like space from the ridgepole down to the dirt floor. Laidlaw could see Goodbuddy's squatty silhouette against this light, groping his way forward, pausing to peer at the side walls along the way. In the daylit area there was a length of rope hanging down from a high rafter; the rope was white nylon and had a soft sheen. Below the rope, the big motorcycle leaned into the wall where Laidlaw and Redmon had put it to be out of Goodbuddy's sight when he first arrived. As Laidlaw's eyes adjusted to the dim, he began to make out the pattern on the back of Goodbuddy's jacket. When Goodbuddy saw the motorcycle, Laidlaw thought he froze.

Then Redmon stepped out from behind the corner stall and stood in the area of light. The queer angle of the light's entry gilded the top of his head silver and left his eyes hidden in deep sockets of shadow. Goodbuddy screwed his head around to peep inquiringly at Laidlaw, and then looked back at Redmon. His arms rose a little out from his body and settled back to his sides.

"Hey there," he said.

"*Hey,*" Redmon said. "Goodbuddy."

Goodbuddy half turned toward Laidlaw again, then shifted back in Redmon's direction. "Well, now," he said. "This sure is a surprise."

"To you it is," Redmon said. He shifted his feet a little farther apart and smiled, his teeth bright and clean looking in the shadow of his face.

"You all are up to something," Goodbuddy said. He turned sideways and set his back to the wall so he could see both of them at once. He raised a hand and pointed at Laidlaw. "You never did mean to sell this place?"

"Not hardly," Laidlaw said. "I thought I let you know that a good while back."

"Why, sure, but I thought you changed your mind," Goodbuddy said. "I've seen the stubbornest holdouts do it, once they get a good idea what kind of money they're sitting on."

Laidlaw shook his head. Goodbuddy lifted his other arm and spread his palms flat against the empty air. The clipboard slipped loose from under his elbow and raised a splash of dust from the ground, but he didn't appear to notice it.

"Hey, no need for any misunderstandings," he said. "After all, we all of us go a *long* way back. All of us growing up right here in the county, and all in the service together too . . . I used to think about you two all the time, out in Nha Trang and all those crazy places . . ."

"Oh yeah," Redmon said. "We thought about you a good deal too. Every time a shipment turned up short."

Goodbuddy's hands made some more stop signals, and his eyes flicked back toward Laidlaw. "You know, I never had anything against old Rod. Some might say I did but it's just not the truth. I always did everything I could think of to do for him. Give him a good job when he come out of the army, now it's not *my* fault if that didn't work out." He gestured toward the motorcycle. "Look how I just let him have my bike there. Why, the fact is, he practically stole it from me, and I never did a thing about it. I could have had him arrested any old time. Why, he'd've been a dead man riding that thing around town, if I had've just opened my mouth —"

"Is that a fact?" Laidlaw said.

"What say you tell us a little more about how that would have worked?" Redmon said.

"Uh," Goodbuddy said.

Redmon pulled the sheaf of colored construction paper from his hip pocket and fanned it out in front of him like a hand of cards. "While you're at it," he said, "we'd also kind of like to know just exactly where these came from."

"Hey now," Goodbuddy said. "I didn't have *one damn thing* to do with that there."

"Of course not." Redmon tossed the papers up over his shoulder; Laidlaw watched them drift to the floor in the weak grayish light. Then the light shifted, dimming a little as a breeze brought the trap door partly closed. "But for somebody had nothing to do with it," Redmon said, "you sure can recognize it at a good long range."

"You can't prove anything off of that," Goodbuddy said.

"But we ain't in court," Redmon said.

"You all tricked me," Goodbuddy said.

"How does it feel?" Redmon said. He shook his head. "You ought not to been too cheap to get that typewriter fixed, Goodbuddy. Every time you wrote *nigger* it put that cockeyed *N* up there above the line, the same way it did when I used to type on it."

"I never wrote any of that myself," Goodbuddy said.

"I didn't much think so, as a matter of fact," Redmon said. "All I want is you tell me who did."

"I can't *do* that," Goodbuddy said.

"Oh yes you can," Redmon said. "Whether it takes you a long time or a short time, that part is all up to you."

Goodbuddy's arms fell back against his sides. He straightened up away from the wall, but it didn't much look like he would go anywhere.

Redmon broke out of his stiff straddle stance and took a step toward him. "What do you bet I know what you're thinking?" he said. "If you had've done one little thing different. Say, if you fixed that typewriter, for instance, then you wouldn't be here now."

He paused. Laidlaw turned himself slowly around and began to walk toward the light at the front door of the barn.

Redmon started speaking again, softly, but he could still hear it. "Or it could be just some real small thing," he was saying. "If you brushed your teeth or not this morning. Picked out one tie or another one to wear to the office. Walked to your car in ten steps instead of eleven. Any little thing like that would be enough to change your whole future, till you would have ended up somewhere else and not here." Redmon laughed and cut himself off sharply. "But that's the catch, Goodbuddy. You can't go back, can't change that one little thing. And every least thing that you did, why, all it did was bring you right up to this."

"So?" Goodbuddy whispered.

"So here you are."

Laidlaw was through the doorway then, blinking in the harsh daylight. He turned and shoved the barn door shut and leaned his weight against it. As he did so he heard a couple of heavy thumps with a hiss of breath sandwiched in between them. It seemed that he felt shocks of impact coming to his hands through the wood, but he thought he must be imagining that part. He pushed himself away from the doors, gagged unexpectedly, and bent over double, but he had not eaten anything all day and the spasm passed without producing anything. When he straightened up he felt a sort of feverish ache behind his eyes. The dry wind blew and the trap door cried out on its rusty hinge and he thought of that pale streak of daylight going on and off inside the barn. From behind him, inside the building, there was a creak and a groan as if the whole structure had taken on a new weight.

The wind died down and the hinge shrieked again as the trap door settled back into the position where gravity took it. Laidlaw walked a little way from the barn and looked out past the house at the hill above it. The white backs of the sheep were spotted across the slope below the barn. Three deer were coming cautiously down from the tree line toward the pond, their hides almost matching the sere brown pasture that they crossed. Mechanically Laidlaw reminded himself that the drought brought them nearer the house in daylight now because they were getting desperate for water. He turned back around. The barn was a gray hulk against the parched dun expanse of the field behind it. Above, the sky seemed bleached of its color; the sun was a hot invisible whirl. Laidlaw was listening for a scream, but it would not come. He had bitten through his lip, and blood was pooling in the space in front of his bottom teeth. The hot taste of it seemed to revive and strengthen him, dispelling the shaky feeling he had had before.

Never mind the blood was his own. Laidlaw swallowed, coughing slightly, and shifted back in the other direction. The deer had reached the upper bank of the pond and stood, alert, between the willows. A ewe bleated below the barn, but the deer did not retreat. The sound carried sharply in the hot dry air, and still, still, there was no scream. It was a thing that was just in people, Laidlaw reminded himself, swallowing again with some difficulty. That was what you learned in time: it was in people to vivisect each other right back to the core. It was in the others and it was in you just the same and the only real difference was who had the upper hand. Tired of swallowing, he bent and spat a shower of blood into the dust. A few stray droplets flecked onto the canvas of his shoes. Although he would have liked to smoke, it looked like it would be too messy to get involved in it.

He walked down to the creek and sat with his back against one of the squat mock orange trees and blew a narrow stream of air across his lower lip, trying to dry out the cut. From the corner of his eye he could see the peacock taking a dust bath between the roots of the next tree down the line. When the cut had formed a lumpy scab, he lit a cigarette and smoked it with his eyes shut. Some time after he had put it out, he heard dragging footsteps going past on the path, but he didn't open his eyes to see what was happening until he heard the motor of a car start up.

What he saw, with a small tick of surprise, was the green Volvo making its slow way down the hill. Everything about it seemed perfectly ordinary. He stayed seated against the tree until the car had gone around the corner, and then looked back at the hillside above the barns. The deer had either bolted or gone down so low within the ring of the pond that he could no longer see them. Probably the noise of the car starting had been enough to frighten them away. He got up and turned around. Redmon was standing in the open doorway of the barn and Laidlaw walked up to join him there.

"He left under his own steam, did he?" Laidlaw said.

"Why not?" Redmon said. "Where were you?"

Laidlaw peered over Redmon's shoulder. At the end of the hall of the barn the nylon rope hung in the same slack dangle as it had before, only now there was some curious knotting of its lower end.

"You know," he said. "I try to avoid the occasion."

Redmon frowned. "You cut your lip."

Laidlaw tried the bitten place with his tongue. The cut had formed a thick rough scab, which prevented him from closing his mouth comfortably. If he rolled his eye down he could just see a blackened corner of the scab.

"You lost your taste for it," Redmon said.

"Not exactly," Laidlaw said, feeling how his speech was slurred and softened by the changed shape of his mouth. "I told you about that deer hunter?"

"What of it?" Redmon said.

Laidlaw blinked and shook his head. "Never mind," he said. "I thought you'd hung him. When I heard that rafter give down."

Redmon snorted. "What would have been the good of that?" he said. "Would you feel like gravedigging in this dry ground?"

"It was so quiet, though," Laidlaw said.

"I thought there better not be too much noise," Redmon said. "Well, but you missed it." He joined his hands behind his back and pushed the double fist upward, the movement forcing him to stoop.

"I just tied him like so and then hoisted him over that beam, see?" he said. "Puts a devilish strain on the shoulders. And him overweight like he is." Redmon relaxed and straightened up, clapping his hands together.

"Good God, yes," Laidlaw said. "Where did you come up with that idea?"

"I read about it while I was in the pen," Redmon said. "It's something they used to do to witches."

"What was the object of it?"

"Make them say they were witches, of course."

"Of course," Laidlaw said. "Well? Did he say he was one?"

"Not quite," Redmon said. "He admitted to being acquainted with some."

"And what are they all up to these days?"

"Different things," Redmon said. "Nothing much to do with us, directly. But they're planning to shoot Brother Jacob at that rally."

"Oh yes," Laidlaw said.

"Surprised?"

"No," Laidlaw said. "Not really." He tapped the hard shell of the scab with his forefinger and felt a faint and distant pain.

"What do you plan on doing about it?"

"Wouldn't I just love to keep clear of it, though?"

Redmon shrugged. "Up to you, I suppose."

"I bit his ear off," Laidlaw said. "At least, when I try to remember what happened, that's what I *think* I did."

Redmon peered curiously into his face. "If I'm supposed to know what you're talking about," he said, "I have to tell you that I don't."

"Ain't no stopping, once you start," Laidlaw said. "Oh well, forget it, I guess."

"Look," Redmon said. "You're not being asked to save the whole world, you know. Just remove a grain from the great store."

"Right, and what difference does it make?" Laidlaw said. "Everything just keeps on being like it was."

"What if it does?" Redmon said. "The difference is you. You've said where you stand, that's all."

Laidlaw sighed, puffing out his breath like smoke. "All right," he said. "You know, we're going to need some wherewithal."

"That's the spirit," Redmon said, slapping a hand on his shoulder. "What have you got?"

"One pump shotgun and a Kabar knife," Laidlaw said. "How about you?"

"I got a can opener," Redmon said. "I hope you weren't expecting better."

"That's not going to cut it," Laidlaw said. "Hell, now we got to do a robbery just to get started."

Redmon stroked his jaw, considering. "Maybe not," he said. "We might could get some stuff from Ratman."

Laidlaw stared at him. "Have you lost your mind?" he said. "Ratman is in a locked ward in Walter Reed or somewhere. I doubt he could even get his hands on a metal spoon."

"That's where you're wrong, my friend," Redmon said. "Ratman is living in a trip-wire camp up there at Fort Negley."

Laidlaw squeezed his lips tight shut, feeling the same slight prick of pain. He wasn't sure if he believed the news or not, but it was interesting either way.

45

THE NIGHT before they went to Fort Negley it finally did rain, a long slow soaking rain that stopped just barely before dawn. It was not enough to heal the cracked earth all the way, but it made the leaves on things uncurl and look a little brighter. The roads were still wet when Laidlaw picked up Redmon and drove back around to the empty switching yard behind the city cemetery. There was a short twist of graveled road that went up the hill a distance from the tracks to dead-end on a flat rectangle that might once have been intended for a parking lot. Laidlaw stopped the truck on the rain-darkened gravel and got out.

"Careful how you bang that door," he said.

Redmon made a face at him, then stared balefully up the hill. It did not look particularly steep, but the whole hump of it was a verdurous wet snarl.

"Man, you know what a mess this is going to be?" Redmon said. "I still say we might just as well go up the road."

Laidlaw folded his arms over the roof of the cab and looked out across it. To the east, past the railroad tracks, he could see the fairgrounds, mostly still and empty now. The rides were set up in the small amusement park that operated there all summer long, but it was too early in the morning for them to be turning. A man in a brown coverall, doll-sized at this distance, went from one machine to another, checking the works and leaning over to make adjustments. Above, the sky still lowered with dull-bottomed clouds, but in one place the sun was cutting a white column through them.

"You're sure he's up there?" Laidlaw said. "It wouldn't be just a rumor."

"Ninety percent," Redmon said. "Ain't no *sure* thing left on earth.

I'm telling you I saw him dead-on down at the VA that time I went to try for the sleeping pills."

"And it was really him."

"I was as close to him as I am to you now."

"Why didn't he know you, then?"

"Doubt he saw me," Redmon said. "I was half in another room. But I followed him on out of there. I'd've known him from behind, just by that walk." He took a few paces across the lot, miming Ratman's scuttling step.

Laidlaw stared, then turned his back. He went to the edge where the gravel met the tall weeds and scuffed at a small pile of beer cans with the toe of his shoe. Somebody had been using the place as a go-parking spot.

"And you followed him all the way back here?" Laidlaw said, rehearsing the story. He felt like it might encourage him up the hill if he was to hear it all over again.

"Pretty near," Redmon said.

Laidlaw turned back around. "How near?" he said, and waved an arm at the bushes. "I mean, could you mark the spot?"

"Close enough, I'm telling you," Redmon said. "There used to be a wino camp up there, only somebody run all of them out a while back. Some wild man loose from the army, that's the talk. And that's the way I put it together."

"Right," Laidlaw said.

The clouds parted farther from the sun and a pool of warmer light spread toward them up the hill. The wind rose for a moment and brought a shrieking sound from the loose sheets of tin on the abandoned Block Brothers factory around the curve of the hill to the north. Laidlaw looked in the direction of the noise and blinked. A man was sitting on the roof between the tin towers. He had a metal chair to sit on and he was eating a lump of something white and feeding scraps of it to a big black crow in a wire cage.

"Hey, look at that," Laidlaw said. "Somebody living over there now?"

"Don't know," Redmon said. "Like I told you, there's all kind of squatters and things around here."

"I thought I saw him myself, you know, one night down on Lower Broad," Laidlaw said. "Somebody looked just like Ratman, but you know, the mind plays tricks."

"You saw him, all right," Redmon said.

"Yeah," Laidlaw said. "Still don't mean he really was there."

He walked back around the tailgate of the truck and cocked his head to look up the hill. No trace of the old fort could be seen through the trees and the heavy brush.

"Well, ain't getting no earlier," Redmon said.

"If he *ain't* up there, no point in us going," Laidlaw said. "If he *is* up there, we better not go by the road."

"Mister Smart," Redmon said. "All right then, you're on point."

Laidlaw smiled thinly at him and stepped off the patch of gravel. He walked through a few yards' worth of weeds and then came under the shadow of the taller trees. Redmon was following at a distance of about a dozen yards, and making too much noise, Laidlaw thought, coming through the soggy bushes. He turned back and pushed the heel of his hand downward as a gesture for silence. Redmon frowned at him, but quietened his movements. Laidlaw went ahead, circling around toward the north side of the hill as he climbed.

Up beneath the trees it was a lot steeper than it had looked from a distance. The long drought had eaten into the ground cover like mange, and now the bare patches had turned into slick mud under the rain. Laidlaw had to take special care not to slip and fall. Every ten or fifteen yards he stopped and searched the terrain ahead of him, high and low. No doubt that tramps and drunks had been using the area, since the woods floor was strewn with trash. But there was nobody to be seen, and whenever he stopped to listen he could hear nothing but the chatter of the birds.

The sun came out completely from behind the clouds, lighting up the scattered clearings in the woods through which they moved. It was getting hotter, and was still muggy from the rain. He was beginning to sweat a little, no matter how slowly he was moving. He stopped, holding on to a maple sapling to keep from sliding back down in the mud, and looked back the way he'd come. He was high enough on the hill now to be level with the Block Brothers' third-floor windows, which he could see across the way, flat black holes in the brown rusting walls of tin. By some illusion, the wall seemed almost near enough for him to touch. The man had left the space of roof between the towers but his chair was still where it had been and next to it the crow hopped from foot to foot on its perch, turning in a slow circle inside the cage. Just down the slope, Redmon was catching up to Laidlaw, walking with exaggerated cat-foot steps.

"What's the holdup?" Redmon said, his voice just barely below a normal speaking tone.

Laidlaw poked a finger in his ribs as he came within reach. He opened his mouth and let a word escape so softly it was more like it had been imagined than said: "*Quiet.*"

"You're making too much of this," Redmon said, but now he too was barely breathing the words. They held their heads close together to be able to hear each other's speech.

Laidlaw pointed higher up the hill. "We're almost to the road here," he said. "We're going to have to cross it."

"So?" Redmon breathed.

Laidlaw shook his head. Redmon stepped around him and walked up to the level of the road. Although his motion looked impatient, it was inaudible even from as near as Laidlaw stood. After a moment he followed and stopped behind Redmon, just below the level of the roadbed. The brown grass that had grown all across it was damp and matted by the rain, and the old ruts could be seen as parallel depressions in the growth.

"Ain't nobody been along here in a *long* time," Redmon whispered.

Laidlaw nodded. "Not driving, anyhow."

He watched Redmon's eyes flick along the matted grass in the roadway. Redmon took a long silent step to the middle of the road and with one more stride was on the other side of it. After a second of hesitation Laidlaw went after him. During the instant he was out in the open he felt his skin shrinking tight to the bones of his face, but nothing happened to him before he was back into cover.

"Easy does it," Redmon said, peering into his face.

Laidlaw bobbed his head again. "All right."

Redmon climbed farther up the hill, moving with the same deliberation Laidlaw had used when he was in the lead. They had not gone very far before there was a clanking and squealing down below them on the tracks, and they both stopped. It looked to be a long way down the hill to the spot where Laidlaw saw, through a gap in the trees, the engine nosing behind the wall of the old factory. The train was long and moving slowly and it took ten minutes to go past. When the last car had disappeared behind the wall, Laidlaw kept on looking. On the far side of the tracks he could see the rich corpse-fed grass and the pale tombstones tilting in the old cemetery under the shade of its trees. The passage of the train had left an odd silence behind it, which it took a few minutes for the birdsong to refill.

"Come on," Redmon breathed, and pointed the way. A clear grassy passage ran between the bushes all the way to the place at the crest of the hill where the sky had become visible between laced branches of the trees.

Laidlaw shook his head at it. "Too easy," he said. "We're too close now."

Redmon used both hands to shape a gesture of disgust, but he let Laidlaw go past him into a tight tunnel through the brush. The little round leaves of the bushes Laidlaw was creeping through were still heavy with rain and they dampened him as he found his way on. They had come far enough around to the west now that he could hear the traffic on Eighth Avenue. The next time he looked over his shoulder he had a view out above the factory roof to where the Life and Casualty building broke the downtown horizon. Up ahead there was a path which seemed to run all the way to the top of the hill.

"Here's where the winos been using," Redmon said as he caught up.

"Yeah," Laidlaw said. "Not lately, though."

The path was marked all along with trash but the bottles were half sunk into the mud and the cans were rusted through and there were no tracks, or none since the rain.

"Look there." Redmon pointed.

Laidlaw sighted down his finger until the overgrown bank above them changed before his eyes and became one of the pointed buttresses of the old star fort. "Getting warm, sure enough," he said.

A fresh ray of sunshine cut down through the trees and, just where the path turned by the wall, Laidlaw saw it fleetingly gleam on a length of fish line stretched a couple of inches off the ground. The line was too fine for his eye to follow — in fact, he was barely sure he'd seen it at all — but in the brush at the side of the path from it he could make out a sapling bowed back to the dirt. There was a cardboard cylinder lying casually across its leafy end, hardly distinguishable from the rest of the trash, but it gave Laidlaw an idea. When Redmon made to move ahead, Laidlaw caught him by the elbow.

"What now?" Redmon whispered.

"Watch."

Laidlaw rooted a bottle out of the ground at his feet and flipped it end over end a couple of yards up the trail. When it hit the fish line, the bent sapling snapped up, throwing off a bright shower of rain water, and flung a three-foot snake writhing and striking into the middle of the path.

"Sweet Jesus on a stick," Redmon hissed.

"Our mascot," Laidlaw said.

In the circle of sunlight where the trip wire had been, the copperhead twisted its thick reddish body in and out of elaborate knots. Laidlaw could tell it was still leashed to the fish line because the cardboard tube it had been hidden in was jerking in time to the snake's every movement.

"You see what I have against using the roads and the trails and all," Laidlaw said.

"Oh yes," Redmon said. "Say no more about it. I have to tell you, whatever I was looking for wasn't this."

The snake, wound in a tight coil, was for the moment still.

"It's not really our department, no," Laidlaw said. "That's basically a tunnel trap. Very popular around Cu Chi, you know, where Ratman did his first tour and all."

"Where Ratman became Ratman," Redmon said. "Do you suppose he comes down here and feeds that thing, or what?"

"No idea," Laidlaw said.

"Think we ought to kill it, maybe?"

"Let's leave it," Laidlaw said. "It's not ours to be killing, after all."

He worked his way around the far side of the sapling to a place just past the point of the wall. The broad base of the stone triangle was sunk into a dirt embankment, and he began to inch his way up it. Once he had lifted his eyes above the wall he saw that he was indeed upon the first line of defense. There was a broad bare space some twenty yards wide between him and the second inner star-shaped wall. The lines of the inner fortification were blurred by the brush and the short scrubby trees, but he could make out the general contours well enough. The scrub along the inner walls was thick enough to give good cover to anyone inside, but if anyone had Laidlaw under observation he wasn't doing much about it.

Redmon scrambled up beside him. "This is it, hey?" he said, his lips brushing Laidlaw's ear. "This goes clear around, I guess."

Redmon flicked his hand toward the bare swath between them and the inside wall. The whole area was a field of Queen Anne's lace, grown hip-high and flowering a ghostly white. Inspired by a low breeze, the flat-headed blooms moved in regular strokes like waves. Their billowing made Laidlaw feel that everything else might begin to float.

"Going up?" Laidlaw said.

"Why? Are you?"

"Can't say I care for the exposure."

"Maybe there's a better way," Redmon said. "Might as well keep on going around."

He scooted down below the level of the first wall and began to walk counterclockwise, reversing the partial circle they'd made during the climb. Laidlaw went after him. When they had come back around to the east side of the hilltop, he saw that the ferris wheel had begun a slow revolution in the fairground below, while beside it a flying jenny swooped and whirled.

Redmon had come to a halt before a sort of stone-walled pit. "There's your wino nest," he said.

Laidlaw looked down. The stone hole was half roofed over with heavy timbers roughly the dimension of railroad ties, over which was spread a moldy green tarpaulin. About half the covered space seemed to have kept dry through the recent rain but the shelter showed no sign of recent habitation. There were the same old silted-over cans and bottles, a supply of decaying rags and newspapers, and a padded jacket with one sleeve ripped away. Damp grayish matter leaked from the torn seam. The whole shelter had a loamy disused smell.

"Nobody home," Redmon said.

"Nor has been," Laidlaw said.

There was a crash to the left and both of them crouched reflexively. An enormous white cat had jumped down out of a hickory tree and was now strolling by on the far side of the shelter. The tip of its tail was black and its eyes were a spooky brilliant blue and if it knew that the two men were there it didn't seem to care anything about it. Laidlaw watched it walk up beside another of the star-point walls and disappear among the stalks of Queen Anne's lace. On impulse he moved up closer to see if he could tell where it would go. The cat had vanished under the flowers, but after a minute it reappeared, climbing the inner wall and slipping through a pile of cut brush at the top of it.

Funny to think of anybody bothering to cut brush all the way up here. Then Laidlaw saw that one of the sticks was pointed a different way from most of the others; straight at him, in fact. He shifted to the left to test it and saw that it did track him.

"Hey, man," he called. "It's nobody but us."

The gun barrel did a little woggle and then cocked up toward the sky, as if a support had been removed from its opposite end. Laidlaw pushed himself up to the top of the wall, out into the open, and stood with his hands spread away from his body, ostentatiously empty. Behind and below him he heard Redmon sucking in his breath. Blood thumped heavily in the sides of his head, and he had time to think he had made the distinctly wrong decision, before Ratman appeared on the inner wall beside the pile of brush.

"*Hot* damn," Redmon said, and climbed up to stand beside Laidlaw.

Ratman hopped down from the wall and came toward them across the twenty-yard clearing. He had on holey blue jeans and a field jacket and no shirt, and his hair hung lankly down the sides of his face. The Queen Anne's lace came high enough on him it appeared as if he were wading a stream. It looked like he was opening a wake behind him, through the tossing bone-white blooms. When he had covered about half of the distance his face twisted up and he began to cry.

Redmon got to him first and Laidlaw, a half step behind, saw Ratman's hands lock hard across his back. Ratman's screwed-up face was pressed tight against Redmon's neck. The long scar that ran from his ear to his chin like an off-balance sideburn was turning purple as his face turned red. He cried in very loud strangling barks and Laidlaw, acting from a memory, gave him the meaty edge of his hand to bite down on. Feeling the clamp of Ratman's teeth brought back the way Sevier's hand had felt and tasted in his mouth, one night a good long time before, the first time he had ever killed another human being. But of course it was all different here and now; all three of them might howl as loud as they pleased, and it wouldn't make any difference at all who heard it.

46

"ALL RIGHT," Redmon kept on saying. "All right, now, all right."

His hands worked up and down the space between Ratman's sharp shoulder blades. Ratman choked and spat Laidlaw's hand back to him. He wasn't crying anymore. Laidlaw flipped his hand over to inspect the bluing teeth marks on the fleshy edge of his palm. Ratman came out of Redmon's clasp, took a step backward, and stood looking down at the ground. After a moment he sniffed and wiped his nose on the back of his hand. There was a red rubber band around his wrist and he shucked it off and used it to pull his hair back and fasten it to the base of his skull. Then he raised his head and looked at them out of his pinkish eyes. The scar, the shape of a small three-fingered hand stroking down his jaw, was fading back to its usual dull color.

"You got yourself all worked up," Redmon said.

"Yeah," Ratman said. "What brought you all? I hadn't been looking for anybody."

"A little recon," Redmon said. He pulled out his cigarettes and offered the pack to Ratman. "Heard there was somebody up here sounded like it could be you, so we thought we'd come on over and check it out."

Ratman plucked loose a cigarette and screwed it into the side of his mouth.

"Didn't mean to take you by surprise this way," Laidlaw said.

"I seen you coming," Ratman said.

"We sprung your trap back there," Redmon said.

"I seen you do it," Ratman said. The unlit cigarette wagged up and down as he spoke. Redmon and Laidlaw exchanged a quick and slightly nervous glance.

"You knew it was us the whole time, did you?" Laidlaw said.

"Sure I did."

"Then could I ask you what you were doing still sitting up behind that thing?" Redmon pointed at the brush pile.

"Couldn't get my mind made up," Ratman said, "how bad I wanted to see you all or not. I been some mad at you all, don't you know. Off and on for quite a spell."

"Jesus," Redmon said. "You feel like you're getting over all that now?"

"It's all right, I guess," Ratman said. "You can come on up."

He turned sharply around and walked through the rippling bands of flowers toward the inner wall. Redmon lit his cigarette and went after him; Laidlaw brought up the rear. A flight of stone steps came through a narrow gap in the wall and the three of them climbed up in single file. The innermost ring of the fort was a long elliptical area bare of anything much but patchy grass and a few weeds. Some scrabbly young locust trees grew around the perimeter. The big white cat was sitting by the brush pile, licking a forepaw, but as Ratman came nearer it dropped to all fours and sidled away. The brush had been laid in a rough V formation and at its apex a Browning Automatic Rifle stood on its stubby tripod. Behind it was a big slab of granite the approximate dimensions of a coffin, and Ratman sat down on a corner of it. Redmon passed his cigarette down to him, and Ratman drew a light off its coal.

"Antique you got there," Redmon said, squinting at the BAR.

"Works, though," Ratman said. His smoke stayed gone for a long time; finally a faint wisp of it reappeared.

"I wouldn't doubt it," Redmon said. "I expect you got this neighborhood pretty near outgunned."

Laidlaw coughed and cleared his throat. "What was it you said you were mad at us about?" he said.

Ratman glared up at him. "You know damn well," he said. "Having to go do it. All by myself that way."

"That was nothing but luck," Redmon said. "You pulled the short straw, is all."

"Might be," Ratman said. "But I ended up mad about it just the same. I had the feeling we all should have went in the end."

"That's not what we decided."

"No, it ain't," Ratman said. "But still."

"So," Laidlaw said. "Did you go?"

"Hell yes I went."

"How'd it go?"

"You're a son of a bitch to ask me that, Laidlaw," Ratman said, his voice cracking as it rose. "You might try it for yourself if you're hot to find out what it's like."

"I'm sorry," Laidlaw muttered. "I didn't mean anything, nothing at all. All I wanted to know was, did she blame you?"

"You know it." Ratman's head sank between his shoulders; his hands crossed and dangled over his knees. "She blames the lot of us, as far as that goes."

"Well, but if you get right down to it," Redmon said, "he never would have made it back nohow, not and been the same as he was. You know, he was a long way gone."

"I'd like to seen you try telling *her* that," Ratman said. "Besides which, we all of us was a long way gone."

"Ain't it the truth?" Redmon said.

As if for confirmation, he looked at Laidlaw over Ratman's stooped back, but Laidlaw turned away without responding and strolled a few yards down the inner curve of the wall. From this eminence he could again see as far out as the fairgrounds. The amusement park looked busier now, the tiny rides dipping and spinning, and he could just barely hear carousel music mingled with the cries of children, each sound miniaturized by distance. When he blinked he was surprised to see that the scene remained, since for a moment he had believed that it was only one of those brilliant flashes of image that would appear out of nowhere inside your eyeballs when you'd gone too long without sleep in the bush and started to make up for it with those sharp and sudden waking dreams. *A long way gone.* Another blink, its instant of darkness, was enough to make him wonder if the whole history of his return was just another of those hallucinatory explosions, if he was really still in the bush, after all. "Eyelid movies," Sevier, who had had some term for everything on earth, had called them. It appeared that he had anticipated everything too, except for the problem of assigning that visit somebody had to make to Kate. Of course, you had to presume he hadn't counted on getting killed the way he had either, although it had seemed to all the other three that he was expecting it all along and wasn't the least bit surprised when it happened.

People all around them were constantly getting themselves killed in the most stupid ways imaginable, and one of Sevier's axioms had been that all that sort of thing was avoidable and therefore shameful if it happened to you; if you had to get it you owed it to yourself to get shot or have your throat slit, something neat and inevitable like that. But what happened to him in the end was hardly anything but a fluke. They were coming back from something that hadn't worked out the way it was supposed to and which in fact had lost them their two indigenous personnel. Another one of Sevier's proverbs was that indigs were dispensable, but these ones had been in charge of knowing the way in and out, so maybe it was the loss of them that had caused the trouble, or maybe it was the decision to try to move so far at night, though otherwise, Laidlaw supposed, all four of them might just as well have bought it.

Sevier figured he could dope out the directions, so he was walking point in the wet inky dark. Laidlaw was slack man when it happened. The jungle was black as death and you couldn't see an arm's length ahead of you. So every few yards Sevier would halt and let Laidlaw come up to him, and then Laidlaw would wait for Ratman before he himself went on. Then Rodney came up as the drag, and that was how they kept in contact. It was all pretty much SOP, except that they were moving a bit faster than usual because of everything going wrong and what they hoped they had left maybe not all that far behind them. Laidlaw had not seen or heard or suspicioned anything wrong until he heard Sevier hissing at him, the voice seeming to come straight out of the ground under his feet.

"Watch your step," Sevier said, and Laidlaw crouched down on all fours and felt his way over a big slime-covered stone. It didn't seem to be more than about a three-foot drop into the stony ditch on the other side of it where Sevier was lying on his back.

"What's the matter?" Laidlaw whispered.

"Broke my leg," Sevier said back.

"You can't have," Laidlaw said. "Falling off that?"

"Reckon I must've landed wrong," Sevier said. "I might have broke it in more than one place. You better let me have some morphine."

By the time Laidlaw had fed him the tablets by touch in the dark, Ratman had caught up with them, and Laidlaw had to stand up to stop him from slipping down over the slick face of the rock himself. While they waited for Redmon to get there, Laidlaw hunkered down again. He was tempted to strike a light to see the situation better, but Sevier read his mind and told him not to do it. There must have been a spring somewhere behind the rock. On his knees in the mud and gravel of the ditch, he could hear the trickle of the water, could dip his finger in the rivulet where it ran out from under Sevier's thigh, and he could hardly believe that it was really too dark to see any glint of it, even though it was so close. When he ran his finger down Sevier's hurt leg he felt how it twisted to cross the thin stream in two different places that weren't at the knee; it felt less like a human limb than some kind of a big rubber corkscrew.

"How bad?" Sevier said, already sounding a little goofy from the pills.

"The limit," Laidlaw said.

"Ain't that a caution?" Sevier said. "Well, listen up, here's what we do."

Redmon had got to the stone by that time, and all three of them did their best to argue, but nothing they said could do any good. For a long time afterward Laidlaw had had to wonder if Sevier had really had the right of it or if it was just that they were all so deep in the habit of doing whatever he said, but at the time he'd seemed to have a fairly invincible case. He couldn't walk and the idea of carrying him the necessary distance was not even worth thinking about. They were still miles away from the extract point and miles the wrong side of the line as well. So there was no way of getting a chopper in, even if, as Sevier underlined, they'd known their exact position. Staying put, for any or all of them, would under the present circumstances have amounted to group suicide. So by process of elimination, Sevier told them, you arrived at the obvious answer. It was also his idea that the three of them should all pull their triggers at once, so that none of them would be tempted to think later on that they hadn't fairly shared the blame.

Laidlaw remembered that Sevier had said, *You have to do it*, though without saying what, and then over and over, *Do it, do it*, not with any special urgency but with the level incantatory tone of a hypnotist, while they all knelt over him in a frozen silence, not doing anything at all. Finally Sevier had turned himself over, using his arms and the one sound leg, to give them the back of his head as a target. Laidlaw remembered that Sevier seemed to have passed out from the pain at that point, and he *knew* that they had carried out Sevier's suggestion before he had time to wake up again, but he didn't actually recall anything about that moment, no grip on the trigger, no crack or muzzle flash. His next true memory might have been minutes or hours later on, when they were moving again in the thick hot night, keeping closer together than they had been before, and he saw the flare of a match from the point position. Redmon had lit a cigarette.

"Put that out before you get us all killed," Ratman said.

"What difference does it make?" Redmon said.

And Laidlaw felt as if sacrilege had been committed: you never smoked in the bush at all and you especially didn't do it at night, and that was dogma. Nevertheless they were soon all smoking and standing in a bunch (thus breaking another cardinal rule) and nothing further happened to them. And not one of them said a word to another before they had put out their cigarette stubs and pocketed them.

"It'll be light soon," Redmon had said.

Then they had all gone on.

"He's right," Laidlaw said aloud.

Without being fully aware of where his steps were tending, he had drifted back to the rectangular slab where Redmon and Ratman were now sitting side by side.

"Who's right?" Redmon said. "What about?"

Laidlaw pulled a tick off the inner curve of his wrist and flicked it out into the grass. "Ratman's right," he said. "We probably all ought to have gone. I'd bet you that's why he made us all go meet her in Japan that time. It's what he would have expected."

"I guess that just makes one thing we didn't do his way," Redmon said.

Ratman stood up and thumped a fist into his palm. "Don't hardly make no difference," he said, and then unexpectedly he smiled.

Laidlaw was not quite prepared for it. Ratman's teeth were set slightly apart and the black gaps between them made them look pointed, though really they were not. All of a sudden he seemed almost blithe. He had fallen into these sudden shifts of mood during the last month or so before he'd rotated out, but Laidlaw was no longer accustomed to them.

"Hey Ratman," Redmon said, rolling his eyes at the empty spread of grass, "what I wonder is, what do you do when it rains?"

"How long you been up here, anyway?" Laidlaw said.

"Since the spring." Ratman's smile blanked out. "I like the quiet, nobody near you." His face screwed up, then cleared again.

"Right," Redmon said. "How many of those little trail traps you got laid?"

"All I need," Ratman said. "Come on and I'll show you something."

He turned with his customary ducking motion and crossed over to the western side. Over there a section of the wall had tumbled out, down to the lower level, and Ratman skipped nimbly down over the uncobbled stones and then turned to the left. Beside the fallen stretch of wall a massive doorway was set back into the central mound of earth. Ratman slipped into it like a lizard going into a crack and was swallowed by the dark beyond. Laidlaw hesitated on the sill. The stone posts of the door were almost as wide as the gap between them, which was black as tar. From within there was a hiss and then a brilliant blaze of light. Ratman had lit a Coleman lantern. Laidlaw stooped under the lintel and went inside, with Redmon following him.

"Well, I'll be —" Redmon said. "Snug as a bug in a rug."

Laidlaw passed his hands over the rough-cut faces of the huge stones of the wall. "Bone dry," he said. "Whoever built this thing knew what they were doing."

"They built it for a powder safe," Ratman said. "That's my supposition."

Laidlaw stepped into the center of the area. The ceiling was low; he could stand straight, but his head came just short of grazing it. The available space was not very large and a fair amount of it was taken up by rows of packing cases stacked along the walls. Laidlaw flattened his palm on the ceiling and then took it back away.

"You could last out the winter in here," he said. "Figure out a way to heat it and you could."

"I been studying about that."

Ratman was sitting on a wooden crate beside his lamp and a Coleman stove and a sleeping bag, rolling a joint out of a Baggie he'd dug out of somewhere. Redmon stood at the rear of the vault, in the shadow thrown by Ratman's hunched back.

Redmon reached into one of the top packing cases and took out a can of Spam. "Hey, I can get you a deal on some more of this," he said. "If it's what you fancy." He thumbed up the lid of the next box. "What do you need with all this Pet milk?"

"The snakes like it," Ratman said. He pulled the joint through his pursed lips to dampen it and then struck a match.

"I see," Redmon said. "Mind if I ask how you got all this stuff up here?"

"Humped it," Ratman said, offering the joint to Laidlaw, who shook his head. "A bit at a time."

"*Jackpot*," Redmon said.

He bent over a long narrow crate on the floor and lifted out two M-16s and an M-14 and propped them against the wall. Laidlaw's eyes fastened onto the rifles. All three were taped to break their outlines. Redmon straightened up and turned around, holding up a bouquet of banana clips.

"And Claymores too," he said. "I won't even ask you where you got the Claymores."

"Around," Ratman said. "What's it to you?"

"Since you bring it up," Laidlaw said. "We were kind of, ah, hoping to borrow a thing or two."

"And maybe you along with it, now I think," Redmon said. "This project's a little undermanned."

Redmon bent to put the clips back into the case, then straightened and flung one of the M-16s at Laidlaw, who caught it reflexively by the narrow part of the stock and held it at arm's length from him.

Ratman screwed around in Redmon's direction. "What's it about?"

Redmon plucked the joint from between his fingers and took a long hit. "You know that Brother Jacob that's coming to town?"

"Not to pay any attention to," Ratman said. "I know who you mean."

Redmon passed him back the joint. "We heard some bad crackers were planning to kill him at that rally," he said. "Klansmen, in fact."

"I don't traffic with none of them," Ratman said. He peered back up at Laidlaw.

"We had in mind to stop it," Laidlaw said.

"How did you?"

"We hadn't gotten all that far with it yet," Laidlaw said. "We were just kind of scouting for munitions first."

"You need to have a plan, I'd think," Ratman said.

"Are you in?" Redmon said. He came and squatted by Ratman and took the joint from him again.

"Don't know yet," Ratman said. "What's the plan?"

"We'll get it figured out," Redmon said. "We'll fix you up as nice of a plan as you want."

Laidlaw knelt down facing them, and leaned to put the rifle

against the near wall. Somehow he still couldn't seem to peel his eyes off of it.

"Are you falling in love with that thing or what?" Redmon said. "Your eyes are starting to go googly there."

"I had pretty well counted on not ever picking up one of them again," Laidlaw said. "It's kind of a funny feeling."

"Surprise," Redmon said.

Laidlaw frowned down at the flagstones under him, then tapped them with his knuckles. "This is old stuff here," he said. "This goes back to the War Between the States."

"It's history," Redmon said.

Ratman looked up. "*Yeah*," he said. "Will they put us in it?"

It seemed like another one of his shifts out of nowhere, but Laidlaw was getting used to them again now.

"They'll get it wrong," Redmon said. "That's what you can count on."

47

"EVERY TIME this thing stops moving," Redmon said, "it heats up just like it was a stove."

Laidlaw nodded his head absently, twirling the wheel to reverse the truck on the slab in front of Martin's shop and backing it up to the door.

"You ought to get some air conditioning put in," Redmon said.

"Are you planning on paying for it?" Laidlaw said. "Quit complaining and let's start shifting the business."

When he stepped down out of the cab he almost thought he could feel the concrete burning up through the soles of his shoes. It was a little past three in the afternoon, peak heat, and Redmon was right enough, it was broiling everywhere.

Redmon came out of the cab on the other side, and Ratman, who'd been riding silent in between them, ducked out after him. Laidlaw unlatched the tailgate and let it down, flinching a little as his fingers grasped the hot metal. The huge bass case lay on its back, the curved lid giving it something of the look of a beached whale. It did not seem to have shifted any during the ride. Ratman vaulted up into the truck bed and stooped to shove the case slowly across the rusting runnels of the floor to the tailgate. Laidlaw and Redmon each gathered an end of it into their arms and lowered it delicately to rest on its side on the slab. As the case twisted sideways, it let out a series of muffled clanks.

"Damn but that's heavy," Laidlaw said, setting both hands to the small of his back as he straightened up. "Feels like it gained weight on the trip."

"Don't you know it," Redmon said, and turned toward Ratman. "If you hadn't made us pack all those Claymores in there, this thing would be a whole lot easier to deal with. You know we ain't going to need them things, so what's the use in humping them?"

Ratman, who was standing in the truck bed with his arms crossed on the cab roof and his eyes lost somewhere out on the busy street, let a few seconds go by before he faced the others. "Don't *know* what you need before you need it," he said.

"Hell, it ain't going to be a war," Redmon said. "All it is, is a —" He shut up.

Adrienne was standing foursquare in the shop doorway, her angular fists cocked on her hips. "Hey, Rod," she said grimly.

Redmon dipped his head to her.

Laidlaw walked over to the doorway and leaned against the frame. "Hey there," he said. "I don't believe you met my old friend Ratman."

"Not yet," Adrienne said. "My pleasure."

"Yes'm," Ratman said, and retracted his head into his collar, like a turtle.

Adrienne reached for Laidlaw's shoulder and pulled his head down toward her. "Where the hell you been?" she hissed. "Don't you know we need to practice? The damn rally starts tomorrow, if you didn't forget."

"Well, I got hung up, kind of," Laidlaw said. "One thing and another . . . Anyway, there's time left in the day."

"Not for me there's not," she said. "I got a session starts at four. Which you already knew about."

"Well, but there's always after it, right?"

"I'm going to *sleep*," Adrienne said. "Not everybody keeps your hours."

Laidlaw spread his hands and flapped them. "Take it easy," he said. "Don't mind me. I can always fake it."

"Well, you're not checked out on the new tunes, hot dog," Adrienne said. "Besides, don't you know there's a place we have to back that gospel choir? Boy, I'll die laughing watching you try to fake that."

"Martin hadn't got no session, does he?" Laidlaw said. "I'll just have him run me through the new moves."

"I think you better," Adrienne said. Her eyes cut to the bass case. "Now what is that?"

Laidlaw shrugged. "A bass," he said. "A stand-up bass, don't you know? *Bomp* bomp, *bomp* bomp . . ."

"No kidding," Adrienne said. "What did you have in mind to do with it?"

"Well, I thought Rod could just play along with us," Laidlaw said, smiling. "Tomorrow's Sunday, you know, he don't have to work."

"You did, did you? Is that what you thought?" Adrienne stalked over to the bass case and tugged at the handle. The frame of it creaked in a couple of places, but it didn't raise as much as an inch from the ground.

"What's it made of, brick and mortar?"

Redmon groaned and turned away toward the road.

"Right," Adrienne said. "You know, I watched you all pulling that thing off the truck. What kind of bass takes three grown men to lift it?"

"All right," Laidlaw said, speaking in the general direction of Ratman and Redmon, "I'm going to tell them about it."

Redmon spun back around toward the shop door. "What's that you say you're going to do?"

"Can't you see we have to?" Laidlaw said.

"No," Redmon said. "Sure can't. But I reckon it's your funeral."

"Come on and tell me," Adrienne said. "I can hardly wait for this one."

"Let's go inside, then," Laidlaw said. "I need to tell it to Martin too."

In the close interior it was dark, but scarcely any cooler. There seemed to be no lights turned on, even in the back. Laidlaw groped his way toward the sound of Martin flat-picking "Black Mountain Rag." At either corner of the rear wall a pole fan flailed at the dead air, the pair of them running heavily as twin beaters mixing batter. Between them in the faint seepage of light from the row of grimy windows, Martin hunched over his small guitar. He finished out the lead break on the tune and hit a high chime on the E string before he looked up.

"Mighty fine," Laidlaw said. From his rear he heard a snort as Adrienne lit a cigarette and expelled the first blast of smoke.

Martin was blinking up at him. "Ah," he said. "We looked for you a little sooner."

"Playing in the dark, are you?" Laidlaw said.

"Too hot to burn the lights on a day like this."

"I know what you mean," Laidlaw said. "It's might near too hot to think."

Back toward the front of the shop, there came a couple of crashing sounds and Laidlaw heard Redmon's voice, cursing from the tone of it, though he couldn't make out the words.

"What's that there?" Martin said, craning his neck toward the noise.

"The world's heaviest bass case," Adrienne said, and stuck a finger into Laidlaw's side. "Our boy's just fixing to tell us what's really in the thing."

"Guns," Laidlaw said. He backed up to one of the folding chairs and dropped himself into it.

"What, now?" Martin's forehead crinkled up. He set the guitar against the wall beside him and began to massage the bridge of his nose.

"I hope you're joking," Adrienne said.

"Well, I ain't." Laidlaw lowered his head toward his knees. The smothering heat of the interior had brought a new layer of sweat out on him, stinging where it ran into his eyes.

Martin cleared his throat and leaned back in his chair. "Can't say I follow you too well yet."

Laidlaw looked up. Redmon had come quietly along to stand in the shadows just behind where Adrienne stood. He didn't see Ratman anywhere, but guessed he might be exploring the shop, never mind the lack of light, for Ratman had the eyes of an owl.

"There's supposed to be some trouble," Laidlaw said. "Tomorrow, at the rally."

"Ay, could be," Martin said. His hair stuck up, stiff with sweat, where he had run his fingers through it. "But bringing guns to trouble don't usually make it no better."

"Spoken like a sane man," Adrienne said. She stared down at Laidlaw. "I believe this heat must have melted down your brains."

"Supposed to be a killing, what it is," Redmon said.

"Kill who?" Martin said.

"The main man," Redmon said. "Brother Jacob."

"Who says so?" Adrienne said.

"We got word of it," Laidlaw said.

"The kind we couldn't help but believe," Redmon said.

Adrienne folded her arms across her chest. "Take it to the police, then," she said. "It's not your business to take care of."

Redmon let out a partially choked laugh.

"You got to understand," Laidlaw said. "This is somebody gets threats like some people get flowers."

"Besides which," Redmon said, "the police ain't apt to miss him all that much noway."

"So what's your idea?" Adrienne said. "What have you all got in that case, anyhow? Heavy artillery is what it feels like. You going to walk into a crowd of a thousand-odd people and just open fire?"

"We considered that problem," Redmon said.

"And how did you solve it?" Adrienne said.

"Not too well," Laidlaw said.

Martin pulled a blue bandanna from his shirt pocket and wiped at his face and sneezed. "You all stirred up the dust," he said. "If he gets all that many threats like you say, what makes you think there's anything to this one? Might be nothing'll happen at all."

"We got a feeling," Redmon said.

"It might be nothing will," Laidlaw said. "I sure to God hope that's how it'll turn out. But if something does happen, then I don't want to be caught standing around with my thumb in my mouth. I want to be set up to do something."

"Good God," Adrienne said. "Is that the extent of your planning?"

"Pretty near," Redmon said.

"I don't like one thing about all this," Adrienne said.

"Didn't much figure you would," Laidlaw said. "That's why I'm telling you . . . To give you an out, you and Martin both."

"What, not play, you mean?" Adrienne said. "Break the date?"

Laidlaw nodded.

"It's funny times, you know," Martin said. "I can't hardly make sense of all that goes on." His eyes traveled uneasily across Redmon's torso. "But I couldn't abide that kind of a killing."

"Best keep away from guns, then, is what I think," Adrienne said.

"Ay." Martin looked at Laidlaw. "I'll go on and play with you. Like usual. I don't mean to handle no guns, though. Wouldn't know what to do with one anyhow. I was too young for Korea."

"You'll be taking a risk," Laidlaw said.

Martin pursed his lips and nodded. "I know it," he said. "If it does come to anything, you'll give me what warning you can."

"All right," Laidlaw said. He looked up at Adrienne, who flipped her wrist over and inspected her watch.

"I'll be late for my session," she said.

With a neat pivotal movement, she stepped around Redmon and moved off toward the front of the shop. Laidlaw got up and went after her. The brightness of the doorway hurt his eyes as he watched her silhouette dart across it. He could hear Ratman prospecting in the dark somewhere to his right, but he could not see him, and he followed Adrienne on out the door, blinking in the sudden sharp daylight. The afternoon sun was beginning to tilt and lower, bringing violent flashes off the chrome on the cars passing up and down the street. Laidlaw squinted around until he saw Adrienne standing by her Volkswagen, tapping her fingers on its rounded roof but making no move to get into it yet. When he moved toward her, she turned and slouched down, propping her elbow on the door latch.

"Well, now what?" she said.

Laidlaw swiped a hand across his upper lip and shook away the film of sweat. "I wonder," he said. "Am I going to see you tonight?"

"What the hell kind of a question is that?" Adrienne said. "What are you worried about it for, anyhow? You figure you might be dead by *tomorrow* night?"

"I doubt it," Laidlaw said. "I hope not." He tried to smile. "All right, then, where should I start?"

"Do you want to just tell me what you're trying to do?"

"Well," Laidlaw said. "You might say I'm trying to do what's right."

"Why can't you just do what'll keep you living?"

"Don't think I wouldn't rather," Laidlaw said. "I kind of got backed into this one."

"You look a lot like you're running to meet it, to me."

Laidlaw paced a step in either direction, then turned around to stare at the shop. A sharp line of shadow bisected the cinderblock wall; in the sunshiny part there was a spigot with a short green coil of hose hung on it.

"I just do what I have to," he said.

"You've always been a little strange," Adrienne said. "I've not minded any of that. Have I ever? But I never thought you were bone crazy before."

"I'm not," Laidlaw said. "At least, I don't think I am."

"No, you're just stubborn," Adrienne said. "And reckless along with it."

Laidlaw walked in a semicircle, his heels making dead thumps on the concrete, and halted facing her again. "You'd think it was all right to just stand by and see somebody killed that way?"

"No," Adrienne said. "I didn't say that. But you all don't even have a plain idea of what could happen, much less how to stop it."

"It's still better than nothing," Laidlaw said. "To my mind."

"And would you really have gone ahead and not told me anything about it? Me or Martin either one?"

"No, I wouldn't have," Laidlaw said. "It was just that they probably'll be checking everything pretty close tomorrow. Easier for that case to get by if it goes in with the whole band. But I never would have done it without letting you know."

"You were thinking about it, though," Adrienne said. "And Rodney would have just run it right by us, I'll bet."

"I know you two don't get along the best in the world."

"I get along just as far as he'll let me," Adrienne said. "After that, I just let him alone."

"Well, I wasn't picking on you about it," Laidlaw said. "Didn't mean to be."

"What about that other one you're carrying along? Him with his eyes spinning around in opposite directors? He looks like he just ran off from some madhouse somewhere."

"Ah well," Laidlaw said. "I'm afraid you're not far wrong on that one."

"So you plan on turning *him* loose with some guns."

"Well, they're his guns," Laidlaw said. "'As it happens . . .'" He took a step nearer her and stopped, letting his hands fall back to his waistband. "I don't blame you. Feeling like you do. You better go on or you'll be in trouble with that session."

Her head tucked in, she went past Laidlaw to the wall of the shop, where she crouched down and turned the faucet on. The hose jerked and belched stale air and then some warmish water splatted out onto the slab. Adrienne swiveled away from the splash, then pushed both of her palms up under the flow and left them there. After a moment she cupped some of the water and slapped it into the sides of her face.

"It's running cold now," she said as she stood up.

Laidlaw came over, unwound a length of the hose, and set his thumb over the brass ring to spray himself, drenching his face and hair and shirt. The surprising cold of the water delivered him a fairly solid shock. Adrienne laughed and backed up as he lowered the hose and shook himself all over like a dog.

"Well, I better go on," she said. "See you tomorrow at the show."

"You will?" Laidlaw said. "I thought —"

"Oh, I plan on being there," Adrienne said. "I'll find you out there at the park."

Laidlaw reached to take her head between his hands. He lined up his fingertips along the muscles of her neck and rubbed his wet thumbs over the bone below her eyebrows.

"That's good," Adrienne said. "Feels cool."

"What do you want from me?" Laidlaw said, and watched her eyes roll shut.

"I just want you alive," Adrienne said. "And me too, for that matter."

"Oh, I know that much," Laidlaw said. "Ain't that what everybody wants?"

48

BY THE TIME he left the farm it was just beginning to get light, and all the way into town it was foggy. Long cottony rolls of mist stretched across the road, interspersed with patches of grayish daylight. Laidlaw picked Redmon up on Jefferson Street and then swung back around to the Fourth Avenue underpass, where Ratman had come down to meet the truck, as he'd agreed to. No one had a word to say during the drive to Martin's shop. Laidlaw recognized a tingle in the atmosphere, though the only outward sign of it was Ratman systematically biting each of his fingernails down past the quick. Laidlaw had borrowed a key to let himself into the empty shop. They reloaded the bass case quickly, with one of them muttering a short instruction now and then, but little other talk.

"Might as well not bothered loading it on and off," Redmon said tonelessly when they had all remounted in the cab.

"It could have rained," Laidlaw mumbled.

No one responded. Halfway across town, he pulled into a 7-Eleven and bought three carry-out coffees. They rode on west, sipping, the cups steaming gently through bite-sized holes in the plastic lids. Ratman's bloody cuticles stood out sharply red against the Styrofoam. Redmon lit a cigarette and smoked it with nervous haste, as if he thought somebody might take it from him if he didn't get done with it quickly.

Laidlaw kept his eyes fixed on the road. The town streets were quiet and almost empty, the few cars they passed bound for early church. By the time they had reached the gates of Percy Warner Park, the fog had mostly lifted and it was already starting to get hot. Inside the gates, the road was marked one-way, a narrow black ribbon climbing a tight curve through the wooded hills.

"How big is this place, anyhow?" Redmon said, dropping his dead cigarette stub through the vent.

"Right sizable," Laidlaw said. "I couldn't give you a number, though."

"Do you know where you're going?"

"Can't tell that either," Laidlaw said. "No, wait a minute. There it is."

Around the bend they had just turned was a large clearing along the slope. On the high side of the hill there were some rusting ranks of bleachers, and below, a light wooden platform had recently been raised. Ten or twelve people were milling around on the stage, and some of the out-of-state pilgrims were already waiting quietly in the bleachers or sitting on blankets spread on the grass nearby. A couple of dozen cars and trucks were parked on a pull-off from the road some fifty yards downhill from the platform, and Laidlaw came to a stop at the end of one of the rows.

"No cops out yet," he said.

"Nope," Redmon said. "Looks like we got in under the wire. Before much longer, I bet they'll be stopping people at the gate." He got out and slapped his door shut after him. Ratman slipped out behind Laidlaw, sliding underneath the wheel.

"Hey, you all are bright and early." Peter Hatch was hailing them, striding rapidly down from the platform. Ratman went furtively around the back of the truck, to avoid an introduction, Laidlaw guessed.

"You look all frazzled out already," Laidlaw said.

"We been right busy." Hatch drew his sleeve across his damp face. "I'm worrying about the weather too. You don't reckon it'll rain?"

Laidlaw looked up. It was overcast still, the sky a flat blank shade, but there was a patch too bright to look at directly, where the sun was trying to burn through.

"Well, the ground could use it," he said. "It ought to clear on up for you, though, or that'd be my guess."

"Hadn't you got any tent to put up?" Redmon said.

Hatch laughed. "We outgrew tents a good while back," he said. "This ought to be a real *big* crowd too. If the Lord's willing . . . You all want to come and meet Brother Jacob?"

"Sure would, if he's already here," Laidlaw said.

Hatch motioned and started back toward the platform, Laidlaw and Redmon following a few paces back.

"Hey," Laidlaw said, giving Redmon a nudge. "Don't that look like Raschid up there?" He pointed toward a spot below the left-hand corner of the platform, where a white-robed figure stood in conversation with a slighter man in a black suit.

"Well, I do believe it is," Redmon said. "And it looks like that one there might be the man himself he's talking to."

Raschid turned toward them as they came nearer.

"Look at you," Redmon said. "What brought you out to this?"

"Call it curiosity," Raschid said, taking a few steps away from the other man.

"That's what killed the cat," Redmon said.

Raschid smiled faintly from the corners of his mouth. "Satisfaction brought it back," he said.

"Here's Laidlaw," Hatch was saying to the man in the black suit. "And his friend . . ."

"Rodney Redmon," Laidlaw said.

"Laidlaw," Brother Jacob said musingly. His voice was tenor, with a humming quality, a sort of overtone. He shifted from one foot to the other, his upper body moving a little stiffly, as if he were made of metal underneath his coat.

"The banjo player," Hatch prompted him, "with that bluegrass band."

"Well, good," Brother Jacob said. He put out his hand and Laidlaw took it briefly.

Brother Jacob smiled and moved over to shake hands with Redmon. Laidlaw studied him from the toes up. His shoes looked expensive, and so did the suit. His shirt was a rich cream color and had the look of silk, a little fancy for a tent preacher, perhaps. A thin black tie was snugged up to his throat. Above the collar, his face was nondescript; colorless was the word that came to mind. It was not a face to notice or remember if you didn't have any special reason to.

"Well?" Brother Jacob said. "Do I look all right to you?"

"I . . . I'm sorry," Laidlaw said. "I never meant to stare at you that way."

Brother Jacob took a step backward, sweeping an arm toward Laidlaw at the same time, as if to underline his presence for the others in the area. "Where you been using, banjo man?" The preacher's voice, though soft, had a throb in it. "You got a funny look in your eye."

Laidlaw's glance roved round the others. He thought he could make out a glimmer of amusement behind Raschid's small glasses, but Hatch's and Redmon's faces were blank. Still, Laidlaw did not enjoy the publicity that the preacher's gesture had given him. He felt that he was about to be drawn into some parable, and he was not enjoying the feeling.

"You've been in some strange places, I'll surmise," Brother Jacob said. "You've had a look at some curious things."

"I used to walk by the light of the moon," Laidlaw said without knowing why he'd started with the truth.

"Did you, now?" the preacher said. "What did you see?"

"All right," Laidlaw said. "I saw my shadow." Now he could feel the rhythm; it was one he knew, and he was less reluctant than he had been at the beginning to be drawn down into the pace of the litany.

"Oh yes," Brother Jacob said. "Don't we all see that?"

"Well, but I didn't know it," Laidlaw said. "I took it for somebody after me."

"Have you got somebody hunting you, friend?" The preacher's right hand shaped waves in the air; he was keeping a beat. Grave-faced, the others leaned in closer.

"It feels like I do, from time to time," Laidlaw said.

"I wouldn't doubt but everybody's had that feeling," Brother Jacob said. "Well, then what did you do?"

"I hailed him. Asked him, what did he want with me?"

"How did he answer?"

"Said he would follow me clear into eternity."

"And then?"

"Then I moved, and he moved, and I knew he was mine."

Brother Jacob smiled and let his hand drop. His fingers tugged absently at the cloth of his trousers. "All right," he said. "So now you know."

"Know what?" Laidlaw said.

Brother Jacob frowned, though his tone stayed light, and almost teasing. "What you been looking for, banjo man? What is it you want out of this world?"

"Nothing particular." Laidlaw looked down at the tops of his shoes and saw that one of his laces had come undone. "Maybe just to be left alone."

"Well, but God won't *let* you alone, friend. He's a stalker. He'll dog your tracks."

Laidlaw jerked his head back toward the truck, where Ratman was still circling around in the area of the tailgate. "I've heard it told there ain't no God," he said.

"No doubt you have," Brother Jacob said. "That's what the fool said in his heart."

Laidlaw looked him back in the eye. "Do you yourself truly believe?"

"Well you may ask." The preacher's voice went suddenly low. "Maybe He's left us. Maybe He's just gone off, like some claim it. Don't make no difference anyway."

"What's that you say?" It was Raschid's voice asking the question, but the preacher, though he hadn't moved any nearer, now seemed to be talking only into Laidlaw's ear. And Laidlaw had the perplexing suspicion that no matter what use he'd planned to make of it the preacher had meant what he was saying all along.

"The point is, what did He do when He was with us? He loved people, that's what He did. Only not with a fool's blind love, the way some misremember it now. He loved out of the full understanding. He'd see down through every darkest turn of your soul, know you better than you knew yourself, and love you still in spite of it all. Saint Paul called that charity. And charity is God among us, even to this day. And that's what I believe."

"I see," Laidlaw said. "Yes sir, I think I might follow you that far." He bowed from the neck, turned, and began walking away, without saying anything more. He walked stiff-legged, awkward as someone fresh out of deep sleep. Halfway across the space between the platform and the truck, he halted and knelt to retie his flapping shoelace. The flattened clumps of grass around him were still pale from the drought. He plucked one of the whitened blades and set it in his mouth to chew, then got up and walked on. The other men were still standing quietly near the preacher, watching his receding back.

It was Redmon who broke their little silence. "What call did you have to go and tell *him* all that for?" he said.

Still looking after Laidlaw, Brother Jacob groped toward Redmon with his other hand, and took hold of his shoulder. His face had the vacant clarity of some transparent empty vessel.

"It's his time," he said, and turned his face full onto Redmon, his cat-colored eyes coming back into sharp focus. "It's not your time, my friend, and I'm starting to doubt if it's mine either. It's just his time."

*   *   *

Ratman wandered away from the truck and started off toward the nearest grove of trees as Laidlaw came closer, but Laidlaw paid no attention to him. Earlier he had wedged the banjo in behind the bass case, to make room for the others to ride in front, and now he reached in and lifted it down. He opened the passenger door and slid the case lengthwise along the seat and unclasped the lid and raised it. A brush of his thumb across the strings showed him it had kept in tune during the trip. He pulled the banjo in to him and fastened the strap across his shoulder as he twisted back up out of the cab. His mind had slipped into one of its blank spaces and his hands were moving so smoothly over the neck and drum and strings that he did not even feel their touch, while the music itself seemed to be smoking up from somewhere deep inside his head. Gradually the dry wisp of grass between his lips became sweet to him.

He paced up and down before the front end of the truck, playing, scarcely aware of his own movements or of anything he saw. Though the light was getting a little brighter, the clouds had not parted and everything was still tinged with gray. Now and again another car pulled in, discharging groups of passengers who climbed the hill to join the others on the bleachers, though there were hours left before the rally was due to begin. An electronic grumble began on the bustling platform, where somebody had apparently started a sound check. Hatch, Brother Jacob, and Raschid still stood in a tight cluster below the platform and twenty, twenty-five yards to the left of it, but Redmon had detached himself and was coming down toward Laidlaw.

"Well, you're full of surprises," Redmon said. "I never knew you could talk in riddles that way."

"Mmhm," Laidlaw said, and kept on playing. He was calm but he felt there was little conversation left in him. "Live and learn." The grass stalk still rode on his lower lip.

"Yep," Redmon said, propping his hip on the hood of the truck. "This place'll be full up by the time it starts, they keep on coming in like they are."

"Mmhm," Laidlaw said, playing and pacing side to side.

His eyes inattentively began to track a line of five or six cars that had cruised slowly past the area where everybody else was parking to pull off, all in a row, on the road's shoulder farther up the hill, parallel to the stage area but a good hundred yards from it. The cars were mostly old Fords or Chevys, so the newish green Volvo, second from the rear, looked distinctly out of place. Indifferent, Laidlaw shut his eyes to hear the music better.

"Yonder comes your band, after all," Redmon said.

Laidlaw blinked his eyes back open and rotated around. Martin's car had just pulled into the growing rank, and he and Adrienne were getting out, unloading instrument cases. Adrienne waved, and Laidlaw nodded, still unwilling to lift his hand from the banjo head.

"You all came in one car?" he said as they came within earshot.

"Easier to get away later," Adrienne said, settling her fiddle case on the floor of the truck. "There's apt to be a traffic jam, I think."

"Now what is that gang up to?" Redmon said, looking back over his shoulder at the small caravan of cars parked up the slope. "They must have packed one hell of a picnic."

Laidlaw reversed his direction and looked where Redmon was staring. The men in the cars were getting out leisurely and beginning to gather around their open trunks. It wasn't so strange that all of them were white, but it was a little odd that they were all men, since the other carloads had held more women and children than not. Still, he didn't catch on to what was the matter until he felt Redmon stiffen beside him.

"Wait a minute," Redmon said in a splutter.

He lunged toward the rear of the truck, laid a hand on the wall, and vaulted up into the bed. The springs rang under him as he landed. Laidlaw stared at the cars on the hill, still abstractedly playing on. Of its own accord his pick hand had sailed up the neck to pick up the deeper, throaty notes. Vaguely he took in that the last weapons were being handed out from the trunks of the several cars, and the men, some twenty in number, were moving across the slope in a long straggling line. The span of a football field or so still separated them from the stage. Sliding his hand back and forth toward the drum to bring out the shimmering sound, Laidlaw squinted at the sloppy column. There were some deer rifles, a couple of shotguns, and a surprisingly large number of stubby little submachine guns, several different makes. The men were not moving with any particular urgency, and no one seemed to have taken in the meaning of their presence any more definitely than he had himself. The sound check continued on the platform: *testing, one two,* between whines of feedback. On the bleachers, the pilgrims perched quietly as crows on a telephone wire.

"Laidlaw!" Redmon's voice was a scream with the highs flattened out of it. *"Get cracking and help me open this thing."*

Laidlaw moved as if through soup. Slowly, with terrific care, he unslung the banjo and leaned in the cab to replace it in its case. When he had shut it up and straightened again, he saw Ratman running back toward the truck from the woods. He was running full tilt with his hair fanned out behind him, and there was a look in his face that let Laidlaw know that something serious was happening back toward the stage area.

"Oh no," Redmon said, and stood bolt upright in the truck bed with his arms hanging down at his sides.

The armed men had reached the group below the platform. Someone had clubbed Hatch to the ground with a gun stock and two other men were helping kick him down the hill. He rolled over and over with his elbows tucked up; tight around his head, as though he'd had practice at it somewhere before. Laidlaw could not make out where Brother Jacob was, but Raschid's white robe stood out plainly in the mill. He heard two weighty thumps of a shotgun go, as if from under water, and Raschid's back flared out in red. His body toppled over backward, the stained cloth of his garments floating down around him gently as a parachute settling into a field.

"There's your warning," Redmon groaned. "'Everybody hit the deck.''

He himself was full in the open, and nothing was coming their way as yet, but Laidlaw kept himself mostly covered by the cab of the truck. Adrienne and Martin were both hunched by the front wheel, their backs to the action, Martin hugging his guitar case vertically between his knees. Ratman reached over the wall of the truck bed and passed Laidlaw an M-16 and two clips fastened end to end with duct tape.

"Good man," Laidlaw said.

He slapped in a clip and went up to the nose of the truck, holding the rifle at his hip. From the platform came the light popping of one or more small-caliber handguns. Laidlaw saw several men drop running from the stage, led, he thought, by Bill Shannon, who was brandishing a pistol and firing wild. Somebody among the Klansmen perforated him with a submachine gun, and he ran on a few steps more before he pitched forward into the withered grass. If there had been another pistol, it too was silenced now. The couple of men who had turned back were picked off before they could cover the twenty yards back to the stage.

"The son of a bitch, he lied to us," Redmon said. "This ain't a hit. It's a snatch."

Laidlaw scrambled back toward the rear of the truck, trying to move quickly, though he still felt weirdly sluggish. Ratman had assembled the BAR and was ducked behind it, training it up the hill, but there was no good target, since all the gunmen were clumped tight around Brother Jacob and beginning to hustle him back toward their cars. Laidlaw thought a couple of them looked just slightly familiar to him.

"Would you look at that puke-faced bastard?" Redmon had been holding another M-16 slack against his thigh, and now he raised it like a pointer. Laidlaw saw Goodbuddy for the first time, standing in the open door on the far side of his Volvo. His face was crumpled, practically green; he looked like an outsized ten-year-old getting ready to cry. Redmon snugged the gun stock into his shoulder.

"Hang on," Laidlaw said, spitting out his grass stalk. He'd spoken too late, but when he heard the four-shot burst his torpor finally left him. Redmon sank down on one knee. "Goddamn mouse gun," he said. "Go on, you, fall over. I know I hit you." There was a beat, then Goodbuddy's face went slack and obligingly he fell over out of sight behind the car.

"You ought not to done that," Laidlaw said. "That's the kind of thing'll get us all in trouble."

"It's an eye for an eye," Redmon said. "Besides, that's what you get for trying to play the middle, Laidlaw."

As he finished the sentence he abruptly flattened himself on the floor of the truck bed. Some rounds were passing high overhead; whoever was returning fire had never learned to shoot downhill. Ratman replied with a hoarse burst from the BAR. Laidlaw watched a shell casing chip a wedge of black paint from the corner of the truck and go spinning off at a cockeyed angle.

"Careful, damn it," Redmon said. "Don't, you'll hit the preacher."

"It's a problem," Ratman confessed. Automatic-weapons fire was continuing to clatter down in their direction, though with no great accuracy.

Laidlaw reached up and unfastened the tailgate. "Come on down," he said. "Their aim gets any better, they'll hit you through the rust holes."

He ran stooping toward the end of the line of cars. Behind him he could hear Ratman clashing the BAR down off the tailgate. The last car on the rank was a white Ford Fairlane, and when he reached it Laidlaw raised up over the hood for long enough to squeeze off a couple of rounds. The Klansmen bunched up and froze in a way that reminded him of his sheep. He was gratified to see that a good twenty-five or thirty yards still separated them from the cars they'd come in.

"What's the drill?" Ratman whispered in his ear.

Laidlaw half turned, enough to see that Redmon had taken up a position at the trunk of the white car. "I'd say you're welcome to anybody that breaks out of the pack," Laidlaw said, loud enough for both the others to hear. "But the main thing is keep them cut off from their cars."

He ducked and weaseled under the front end of the Fairlane, leaving Ratman the firing position by the hood. By the time he had a clear view out the other side, a man had strayed over toward the roadway. Laidlaw opened up on him from the partial cover of the wheel well and watched him twitch and tumble down. Redmon had fired at the same time, and there was no telling who had the kill. The return fire was coming in closer now; Laidlaw could hear glass splintering in the window frames of the car. The range had shortened up considerably. Then the BAR took up a jackhammer pounding, and the return fire stopped. Laidlaw watched Ratman's heavy rounds lashing up low ripples of dust from the parched ground. The Klansmen had changed their direction and were starting up the clear defile beyond the bleachers toward the trees.

"Well, what the hell," Redmon said. "Now they're going in the woods."

"That's right," Laidlaw said. "Now they're going where we want them."

49

A MINUTE or two after the last of the Klansmen had passed through the tree line, Ratman and Redmon went scurrying after each other back toward the truck, each bending low. Laidlaw came out from under the car and walked after them, erect and exposed and moving quite slowly, but no one tried a shot at him from up on the hill. The M-16 rocked up and down like a seesaw, dangling at the full length of his arm. He came to a stop beside the open tailgate. Redmon and Ratman were kneeling in the truck bed, hastily raking various materiel into a couple of green knapsacks. Martin sat where he had been sitting, drawn up on himself beside the front wheel. Adrienne, however, had raised herself up enough to peer out across the hood toward the platform and the bleachers.

The area near the platform was scattered with the dead, five, six bodies, all unmoving. The single Klansman they had brought down lay on his face at some few dozen yards' distance from the rest. On the stage itself nothing now moved, and all the people in the bleachers seemed frozen; only in the concussive silence that had succeeded all the shooting, a single woman's voice screamed and screamed. Laidlaw saw Hatch rise up from the field like a corpse coming from the grave and move uphill in the direction of the shrieking. By one of the still bodies he paused and bent down, as if he'd suspected some sign of life, but he must have been disappointed, for he did not linger any length of time. He went on, painfully it appeared, his arms holding himself in tightly around the ribs. Soon after he had reached the bleachers the screaming abruptly ceased. The quiet which came after seemed a solid thing, its texture interrupted only by the rare tremulous inquiry of some startled bird.

Holding the rifle at a 45-degree angle across his body, Laidlaw experimented with blinking the whole scene away, shuttering his eyes till they saw nothing, wrapping his hands tighter on the gun as if they might mold it into something else altogether. But when he allowed himself to look again, it was all as it had been before, and the rifle was still just what it was. Its shape and balance felt wrong and awkward to him now, much as the banjo had done that first summer of his return, yet what was now before him was far more real than any other thing.

"Pull yourself together," Redmon said to him sharply, tightening the cord on his knapsack. "We got business yet to take care of."

"Ah yes," Laidlaw said dreamily. "So we do."

Redmon hopped down off the tailgate. "Ideas?" he said.

"Obviously," Laidlaw said, "we track."

Adrienne pushed herself up off the hood and moved a step nearer to them. Laidlaw caught her by the elbow and drew her a little away from the others.

"If you want to be useful," he said in a low voice, "then you and Martin get the cars out of here. Get shet of that bass case, dump it in the woods or something, and go wait over on Highway a Hundred . . . There by the golf course, you know where I mean?"

"I know," Adrienne said. "What about the case, is there anything left in it?"

Laidlaw leaned into the truck bed and dragged the case toward him. The M-14 was still loose in the bottom and he took it down and briefly demonstrated its operation to her and to Martin, who had now also stood up.

"What's all that tape doing on it?" Martin said.

"Breaks the line of the thing," Laidlaw said. "It's camouflage, but you won't need to worry about it." He looked over his shoulder at Ratman. "You got ammo for this?"

Ratman rummaged and produced a couple of clips, which Laidlaw passed over to Adrienne.

"Better stick it all up under the seat while you're driving," he said. "There'll be police coming along pretty soon, I expect."

"That's right," Adrienne said. "The police'll *have* to be coming now. Why don't you all just wait . . ."

"I doubt they'll be bringing the army," Redmon said.

"Enjoying yourself?" Adrienne said. Her voice had a hint of a break.

Laidlaw reached into his pocket and took out the truck key.

"Ain't that much police could do," he said. "Not that I'd leave to them, anyhow. You go on. We'll be all right."

"You don't know that," Adrienne said. But now she seemed calm. "You better be telling the truth, though." She smiled rather thinly and touched his sleeve and climbed up into the cab.

Laidlaw turned around to Ratman, who was slipping his arms through the straps of the second knapsack. "I'll take that," Laidlaw said, reaching. "You've got the BAR to lug."

Ratman surrendered the pack and Laidlaw shrugged into it. The truck's motor coughed into action, making the loose tailgate shudder. The three of them scattered to let Adrienne back out. Martin made a stiff nod in their direction, and carried his guitar case off toward his own car.

"We better move," Redmon said.

"But not straight after them," Ratman said, hefting the BAR.

"No," Laidlaw said, and turned his head to follow the road up past the place where the Klansmen had parked their cars. The tree line ran raggedly from the curve at the road's highest point back across the ridge, some forty yards above and behind the bleachers. It would be just as well to stay out of range of that. Lower down, laterally across the road from the place where the three of them now stood, he saw that the woods were thick enough to cover a circling movement up the hill. He cinched the knapsack higher on his back. "We can go up the other side of the road there and cross back once we get to the bend."

In single file they went across the roadway and into the woods on the other side. Once they were a few yards into the cover of the trees they turned and began to go uphill. Martin's car was winding down the road in the opposite direction, following the truck. When the motors had passed out of earshot, the same spooked silence resumed; it seemed only to be underlined by the loud low-frequency hum that all along had been coming from a bad ground somewhere in the sound system on the stage. When they came abreast of the Klansmen's cars, Redmon, who'd been leading, paused. Goodbuddy lay on his back on the sticky black asphalt. His open mouth suggested a snore; one arm was flung out like a careless sleeper's. There were some beer cars and a pint whiskey bottle scattered downhill from him; it was like he might have been passed out drunk.

"Well, you got him, sure enough," Laidlaw said in a neutral tone.

"Free kill," Redmon said. "He owed us anyway."

"We ought to do something about this here transport," Ratman said.

"Right you are," Redmon said.

He and Laidlaw shouldered their rifles and began firing single rounds in an uneven pattern. One by one the cars began to heel over on deflating tires. When the echo of the shots had faded, they spread out and moved on up the hill, to cross the road at its next U-turn. A short distance into the trees on the other side, Laidlaw stopped and looked back over at the people on the bleachers, maybe thirty-five or forty of them all told, and all almost rigidly still. Most were facing the vacant stage, as though mesmerized by the electric drone that still drove through the speakers.

"They ain't doing a whole lot, are they?" Ratman said.

"What would you do?" Redmon said. "That crowd laid down their guns before they started on this road."

"They're civilians," Laidlaw said, thinking he recognized that same mute torpor from another time and place.

Redmon faced up the wooded hill. "Well, look at that," he said.

Snagged on a low bush a few yards from them was a blue nylon cap with a Budweiser patch sewn on it. Laidlaw glanced at it and then looked on up the hill. At the top of the rise, light came in flat wedges through the sparsely set trees.

"Up and at'm," Redmon said.

"Go slow," Ratman said.

"Why bother?" Redmon said. "These people ain't any more than a bunch of drunks. Didn't you see that mess of bottles down there by those cars?"

"They got machine guns," Ratman said.

"Kit machine guns." Redmon tilted his head and spat on the ground. "They send off for those little kits and then file down the flange . . ."

"They still got'm," Ratman said. "Don't make me no difference where they got'm at."

Sevier would not have let such an argument go on quite so long Laidlaw was idly thinking. Any of the others might pick at each other a little while, but it didn't much matter what they said, since soon enough they all knew that Sevier would squash the whole debate and let them know what they had to do. Only not this time . . . Redmon was taking out a cigarette.

"Don't smoke," Laidlaw said.

"What?"

"Listen," Laidlaw said. "I'm pretty sure I recognized at least one of them people. It's an old Special Forces guy name of Fowler."

"Never heard of him," Redmon said.

"I barely did," Laidlaw said. "I only met him in a bar a time or two. But if that's who it is, then he might know some things. Now some of this gang is drunk and a lot of the rest are probably fools but they got a lot of fire power and they got a prisoner and they outnumber us pretty bad. And they already know we're here."

"We got to take it seriously," Ratman said, "you mean."

Redmon shrugged and put the cigarette back in his pocket. "Ever what you say," he said. "All right, what would you be doing if you were them?"

"I wish you wouldn't ask me that," Laidlaw said, "because they ain't making a whole lot of sense to me so far. I don't quite see what's in it for them, doing a kidnap like they are."

Ratman snapped the back of a fingernail on the breech of the BAR. "It don't have to be what they first had in mind," he said. "Probably we already fouled up whatever plan they started with. They'll just be trying to go with the flow."

"That figures," Redmon said. "They're shook up and they're running. Got a hostage they might hope they can do a deal with if they get themselves cornered somewhere along the way."

"They'll be wrong about that part," Laidlaw said.

"That's what we hope," Redmon said. "So where you think they're going to go?"

Laidlaw held up his parted thumb and forefinger as a makeshift map. "The park's a triangle," he said. "'We're up here toward the little end right now." He wiggled his index finger. "They go west, they'll hit Highway a Hundred pretty quick. But down south it widens out; they might get almost to the county line without once coming out of the woods. Which might be what I'd try if I was them . . ."

"Not me," Ratman said. "I was them I'd be trying to double back around and get back to my cars."

"I don't know why I asked that question," Redmon said. "Only way to find out is follow the trail." He pointed to the hat again.

"Fine with me," Laidlaw said. "Just be careful how fast you run up on them, though."

Redmon smirked and trotted up the grade. Laidlaw left him a twenty-yard lead and then followed. Ratman trailed at a similar distance, carrying the BAR somewhat awkwardly clamped under his right elbow, his left hand supporting the muzzle and tripod. A little before the top of the hill, Redmon plastered himself onto the ground and squirmed slowly ahead until Laidlaw could see only the soles of his shoes hanging over the rim. He waited for him to stand again before he himself walked on to the peak.

Redmon was already a good way down the far side of the hill, moving slowly, sweeping his whole upper body on a 180-degree band in front of him and aiming the rifle wherever he looked. However, there was no movement anywhere in this next hollow, and even the birds were singing again, their earlier disturbance forgotten. The trees were thin enough that you could see for a good long way, and Laidlaw was struck by how easy it was to move on this terrain, where the ground cover was not dense enough to hinder. You could have gone miles and miles in one day. But with the drought it needed fanatical care to move without rattling what dry brush there was. Laidlaw's body was limber, at an artificial ease, but he could feel the back of his neck beginning to stiffen with the strain of his concentration. The heat was climbing steadily as the sun and he was beginning to break out in big blots of sweat, heaviest where the knapsack rode his back. Somewhere well back behind them he could hear the cry of several sirens converging on each other.

Halfway down the hill they cut across a narrow footpath and continued with no pause. At the very bottom there was a shallow stream bed, dry for so long it was full of white dust. They stepped over it and spent ten or twelve minutes climbing the next steep grade. Again when he neared the crest Redmon dropped to the ground and low-crawled the last few yards, holding his rifle pricked out before him. This time when he had come to the head of the rise he froze and raised a cautionary finger. Laidlaw inched his way up near him.

"Listen here," Redmon breathed in his ear. "There go the elephants . . ."

Laidlaw cocked his head. Down the far side of the hill he heard the tramp of many feet and cracking brush and once in a while a muted voice. Ratman had caught up and was now lying prone just in back of them.

"Noisy, ain't they?" Redmon whispered.

Laidlaw nodded.

"Think this Fowler would use a drag man?" Redmon said.

"Somebody might go see," Laidlaw said.

Leaving no time for further discussion, Ratman laid down the BAR and slithered into a patch of dry buckbushes and over the hilltop. Redmon shot Laidlaw a sober glance and moved off a fair way to the left. Downhill from them, the sounds of general movement gradually grew fainter. Laidlaw repositioned himself behind the BAR, leaving his rifle on the ground where he could reach it handily. After some ten minutes Ratman reappeared at a point about halfway between them and they closed in.

"Do they have one?" Redmon said.

"Not now they don't." Ratman stabbed his knife in the ground to clean it and settled it back inside his waistband.

"Showboat," Redmon said.

"What are they doing?" Laidlaw said.

"They're going in more or less of a circle," Ratman said. "Don't know if they mean to be or not."

"Are they using one of those cleared trails?" Redmon said.

"Yeah," Ratman said. "An old one, looks like."

"Can we get ahead of them?"

"We could catch them coming out on the top of the next hill if we make good enough time."

"All deliberate speed," Laidlaw said.

This time Ratman took the point. They were moving faster now and with imperfect silence, but Laidlaw thought the other group was making so much racket of their own that they were probably safe enough. And in under five minutes Ratman had brought them 45 degrees around the gentle curve of the ridge; when they stopped to listen Laidlaw could tell they had worked their way a useful distance in front of the Klansmen. Just where they had halted, the old footpath, partly overgrown but still hard-packed under the brush, slipped over the spine of the ridge and ran on the gentlest upward grade for some way along its back.

"Beautiful," Redmon said under his breath.

Ratman stepped behind Laidlaw and began rooting into the knapsack on his back. "What do you think about Claymores now?" he said.

"I'm going down on my knees to you, man," Redmon said. "But how long do you think we got?"

"Hush," Laidlaw said. He waited. "I think they stopped."

"They must have missed their drag man," Ratman said, loosening a roll of wire. "They'll be coming a deal faster once they find him, I bet."

"What if they go off the trail?" Redmon said.

"Then we're screwed," Ratman said. "But there ain't much anywhere else to go before they get up here. It's good and steep on the other side."

"Where's the preacher?" Laidlaw was already helping Ratman lay the Claymores, as if he knew the answer to the question.

"About halfway back," Ratman said. "I figure a number one should just about do it."

"I'm going in for him," Redmon said.

"There ought to be two, at least, doing that," Laidlaw said.

"Oh good," Redmon said. "I guess you better run get your girlfriend."

"He's right, we ain't got no choice." Ratman was backing up on his hands and knees, unrolling wire from the mines he'd set to cover the first kill zone. " 'Cause you and me got to be where we got to be. Now let me have that knapsack."

"I'll help set up the other end," Laidlaw said.

"Just gimme it," Ratman said. "And take your other clips."

"Which way are we leaving?" Laidlaw said.

"Back," Ratman said. "You better try to cover it too. I'll support you soon as I can."

"Terrific," Laidlaw said. "So you'll drop the flag."

"No, that's got to be the snatch element," Redmon said. "*Right* when you hear me bust one, bring it on down."

"I hear you," Ratman said. "See you all to home." He took the pack and the BAR and trotted, puffing slightly, toward the head of the trail.

"You look worried." Redmon frowned.

"What about?" Laidlaw said.

"Can't tell that by looking," Redmon said. "You all right?"

"You're the one with call to worry," Laidlaw said. "Better quit talking about it."

"*They're moving*," Redmon said. "Positions, good people."

Then he was gone. Laidlaw fell on his belly and burrowed backward into a snarl of tall weeds and vines. Redmon was out of sight but Laidlaw felt sure he was already set for the snatch.

Anyway, they had all done it before, and done it right more often than not, but it worried Laidlaw how short-handed they were now. The wires to the mines were gathered under his left hand, and he squared off his extra clips beside them. His hands were steady but slightly numb, and they felt a long way from his lightening head. When he noticed the amount of poison ivy he'd crawled in among, he had to squelch the urge to laugh out loud. Then he heard them coming up the trail and his heart started tolling like a midnight bell.

Walter Giles was the first man into Laidlaw's kill zone, and from the way he was moving Laidlaw guessed something had thrown a fairly good scare into him, though he couldn't have told it from his face. Walter had never known more than a single expression. Laidlaw would not have said he was surprised to see him there, not really. Ratman was going to kill him for sure, but he had no time to decide what he thought about that, besides which, there was no helping it. They were coming fast, as Ratman had predicted, and the next three men through were nobody he'd ever set eyes on before. Fowler was the fourth man, stalking along with his eyes hard as little nails, twisting the nose of a heavy pump shotgun from one side of the trail to the other. Laidlaw's hand pulsed in his trigger guard; he wanted Fowler dead in the worst possible way, not out of vindictiveness but simply as a pragmatic concern. If Ratman had had time to set up right he might get more than the first four before anybody could find cover, but it was just a shame he didn't know Fowler on sight.

While he was worrying about that, eight more men passed through the kill zone, and then Brother Jacob appeared, moving fast and stumbling a lot. Laidlaw was relieved to see that he didn't seem to be either chained or tied. He was holding his hands on the top of his head, and whenever they slipped down, the man behind him poked him in the small of the back with a rifle barrel to make him put them up again. Now they were going at almost a jog, and as they passed, Laidlaw's breaths began to come shorter and the numbers started ticking in his head. At *six*, he heard Redmon shoot and instantly he blew the Claymores and was firing himself, bringing down the first man in his zone and reversing the taped clips in time to get the second man too. Jittery, he burned through most of the second clip with no real target, but stopped himself when he felt the barrel warming up in his left hand.

Nobody was standing or firing in his area anymore, and he took the chance to change to the second pair of taped clips. His hands

were just a little slippery, but he could still use them all right.
Ratman had done a nice job setting the mines; the woods were full
of the kind of noises people made when they had just had their legs
taken off at the knee. At the head of the trail the BAR sustained a
monomaniacal pounding and Laidlaw guessed that Ratman had
managed to take the front end of the column in enfilade; the big gun
had a happy, productive tone. Then he saw Redmon come crashing
down by him, holding the preacher by the elbow and almost
dragging him along. They passed and ran on down the hill, and
Laidlaw made a hair's shift in the direction they'd come from. By the
trunk of a slender sycamore tree, a red-headed gap-toothed man was
kneeling and sighting a rifle along the path of Redmon and the
preacher's retreat, with the noon sun pouring down all over him,
softened and tinted by the green of the leaves. It was Earl Giles, sure
enough, a perfect target, and Laidlaw felt that it was not his own life
but Earl's that whirred backward through his brain like a drill, while
Earl remained immobile as the relief on a marksman's medal and
still not firing a shot, and nothing seemed to happen at all for a long
declining time. Laidlaw heard one of his internal phantom voices
crying, *Shoot him shoot him shoot the bastard now*, but he thought
he knew he would not do it until he heard his own gun chatter and
Earl was gone. Gone. A deep black rim of something began to rise up
and blot the sunlight stripes between the trees; against it golden
sparks were dancing. Laidlaw's ears were ringing and his head
pained him at the temples. Ratman had turned up, hardly a hand's
span from him, and was moving backward down the hill, still with
the BAR covering the area of the bushwhacking.

"Fall back," Ratman said.

"No, you," Laidlaw said, and waved him down.

After Ratman had departed he held his position and kept on
holding it for a good long while after it was time for him to
withdraw, out of a feeling, a conviction really, that something more
was going to happen. But nothing did. He guessed from the cries he
kept on hearing that the Klansmen must have abandoned their
wounded, but after all, he tried to assure himself, there'd been
nobody hurt but the enemy.

50

ADRIENNE SAT in the broiling truck cab, lighting her next cigarette off the butt of her last one, keeping it up until her mouth had acquired the taste and texture of burnt newspaper. The air was so dense the smoke didn't want to move out of the truck, even though she had the windows rolled all the way down on either side. Through the windshield, a hundred yards up the highway toward town, the humidity hung in a particulate curtain, shimmering slightly in the hot, dull light. Whenever she glanced up in the rearview mirror she saw Martin's car nosed up on the shoulder behind the dangling tailgate of the truck. Martin himself could not hold still. He was perpetually in and out of his car, walking nervous circles around it, or coming up to her window as if with some pressing message, then not saying anything at all. Finally after an hour or so had leaked away, he asked her for a cigarette. Adrienne looked up at him with some surprise.

"You don't smoke," she said.

"Well, but I used to," Martin said. "Give it up, oh, fifteen years ago, I expect."

His wide moon face was damp, clammy; he'd sweated clear through his light cotton shirt and it stuck to him in flesh-colored patches. Adrienne turned up the denim flap of her top pocket and offered him a Marlboro. Martin held it up to his eye as though it were a specimen of something unheard of, shook his head slowly, and passed it back.

"What's the matter with it?" Adrienne said crossly.

"I figure I best not, that's all," Martin said. "Best not take it up again." He paced several steps away.

"A day like this you might count yourself lucky if you lived long enough to catch cancer," Adrienne said.

Martin froze for an instant with his back to her, then paced on to the end of the tailgate before he turned back. "I ask myself, why did we take this here job in the first place?" he said.

"There was those that said we needed the work," Adrienne said.

"Beyond that," Martin said. "Beyond that. Putting our foot right spang in all this mess of trouble."

"I know what you're talking about," Adrienne said. "Best I can figure is, *this* batch of trouble came looking for us."

A black Corvette materialized out of nowhere and roared past them toward town, going so fast it was almost hydroplaning on the stagnant air. Martin sidestepped in front of the truck to get farther out of its way, then followed its passage with his head.

"Would you just look at that rascal fly?" He shook his head and came back around toward the driver's door, eyes aimed at the ground. Adrienne watched her cigarette fizzle out at the edge of the filter, and pinched her pack again, but it was getting skinny.

"I keep looking for cop cars and not seeing any," she said. "Wonder where in the hell they are?"

"We're a good step out of their way over here," Martin said. "Whatever's coming'd be coming from town."

"Well, I guess I know that," Adrienne said. "What I'm really wondering is what *we're* doing here, I suppose."

"Thought that was what I was asking you," Martin said. "No ma'am, I never cottoned on to this preacher all that much in the first place. Never give him a whole lot of thought one way or another."

"Does that make you in favor of seeing him killed?"

"No," Martin said. "No, I'm against that."

"That makes you and me both."

Adrienne popped her door open, got out, and reached under her seat to drag out the M-14. After a quick glance up and down the road to see that nothing was coming, she threw it up to her shoulder and cracked one off at the nearest speed limit sign. The muzzle bucked up on her: a clean miss.

"What the —" Martin's face squinched up. "You quit that, now."

"I hate to wait," Adrienne said, and shot again. The top corner of the tin sign folded back with a loud clang, and she felt her face creasing into a weird smile.

Martin clamped a hand on her elbow. "Hush a minute," he said. "Can't you hear that?"

Adrienne looked to where he was pointing, across the deserted golf course toward the trees. Nobody was doing any golfing today, and she could understand well enough why. Everything was so dry the grass was approaching the same color as the sand traps, and never mind the heat. At first there was nothing but the echo of the M-14 in her ears, but then she could make out a distant rattle of shots somewhere off in the woods.

"You hear it?" Martin said just as the noise stopped. Adrienne nodded.

When the firing started up again she could tell it was coming nearer, fast.

Laidlaw was coming at a slow aimless walk back down the hill from the ambush site. His head was still humming and his sense of direction was all out of whack, so he didn't know for sure right where he was or what might be up ahead. Odd how he didn't seem to recognize much of anything about the way they'd come. His hands and feet felt heavy and alien to him and he was staggering slightly as he walked. But soon after he had got across the second hilltop he saw Redmon coming toward him at a brisk trot.

"The hell you been?" Redmon said. Laidlaw gazed upon him, speechless, then waved one arm ambiguously behind him.

"We thought something had got you sure," Redmon said. "Yawing around in the woods like this? Come on now and let's look lively."

He reversed himself and went back down the hill in a rapid skidding zigzag, his rifle counterbalancing him at arm's length like some lethal outrigger. Laidlaw started after him. They had not gone much farther before he was able to make out where Ratman and the preacher sat on the ground just short of the clearing where the bleachers were.

Ratman swiveled around on his haunches as Laidlaw came up. "Hey, you all right?"

Laidlaw's tongue was still thick and numb, but he flexed it a time or two and thought it would work. "More or less," he said. He raked his nails down the inside of his forearm. "Think I caught a real bad case of poison ivy, though."

A wave of nervous laughter ran around all three of them. Only the preacher sat silent, looking down at his hands. When the laughter had stopped, Laidlaw lowered himself to his knees and laid his rifle flat beside him. Of a sudden Ratman took up laughing again, but no one joined him this time. It sounded peculiar, him doing it all by himself that way, and after a little bit he stopped. Laidlaw covered his face with his hands. There was a silence that might have gone on and on except that in the middle of it one more siren started yowling up the road.

"What's the matter, friend?"

It was Brother Jacob with his soft voice, speaking into the blank where the siren had died. Laidlaw dropped his hands, feeling the backs of them brush over the dry stubble on the ground. He stared at the preacher through shrunken dry eyes.

"Did you ever kill anybody?"

"No, I never," Brother Jacob said.

"I doubt if you can help me, then."

"You don't know I haven't done worse," the preacher said. "I will tell you one thing, though."

"What?" Laidlaw said through a sourness in his mouth.

"Ain't nowhere you can't come back from. *Nowhere*. I'm telling you true. Do you remember what I said to you before?"

Laidlaw nodded.

"I want you to think on it, then," Brother Jacob said. "Soon as you get time."

"I'll try to," Laidlaw said.

Ratman jumped up without any warning and started peering up through the covering branches overhead. Above them there was a loud flogging of helicopter blades.

"Where'd that come from?" Redmon said, starting up himself. Through a tattered space in the treetops Laidlaw saw the small helicopter loop over them and then eddy away back down over the clearing. It had no markings he could read, neither police nor military.

"They borrowed a traffic chopper," Ratman said, "what I'll bet."

"I think we better not hang around." Redmon took a few steps toward the edge of the clearing.

The pilgrims had come unglued from the bleachers at last and were wandering alone or in unfocused groups all over the open hillside. Half a dozen police cars, dome lights revolving, were pulled in catty-cornered all around the stage, along with a couple of camera trucks.

"I can't go down there," Redmon said musingly.

"Oh?" Laidlaw said.

"Don't you know I'm still on parole?" Redmon said. "I'm not

supposed to get caught with a pellet gun on me, much less all this here."

"Well, that's so," Laidlaw said. "As far as that goes, I wonder if any of us would make out that much better."

"You know I'll speak for you," Brother Jacob said from behind them. "So will all my people."

"It would make it awful complicated," Redmon said. "I expect you better just go on down there by yourself."

"Think they might take a shot at him, though?" Ratman said. "If he surprises them coming out of these trees?"

"I doubt a Metro cop could hit much of anything at this kind of range," Redmon said.

"Oh, I feel lucky," Brother Jacob said. He stood up and straightened his lapels. "I thank the lot of you for that."

"Well," Redmon said, turning his face away.

The preacher smiled and raised his hands palm-out. "Hope to see you," he said. "Somewhere down the line . . ."

He let his hands drop as he might on stage when making a point, and with two long strides walked out into the clearing and started down the slope, not once looking back. In all the commotion no one noticed him at all before he came level with the bleachers. Then the pilgrims began to approach, one by one and forming a bigger cluster. It was like watching iron filings drawn along after a magnet. Laidlaw tipped forward, not quite falling, and pressed his forehead against the rough bark of a hackberry tree.

"Hey, what's the matter?" Redmon said.

"Nothing," Laidlaw muttered. "Nothing, I just got the weirds. Ah hell, I'll tell you, I just shot Earl Giles."

"Did you?" Redmon set his hand softly between Laidlaw's shoulder blades. "That's what's eating on you, is it?"

"You know it." Laidlaw hugged the tree. "Right when you and the preacher came by, you know, he popped up just like a duck on the shooting arcade."

"Take it easy," Redmon said. "Don't you know he ought not to been there?"

"Right," Laidlaw said. "But whoever said *I* was supposed to be roaming around with a gun in my hands? That's what I need to know." The tree was small enough he could lock one hand over his other wrist, which seemed to help contain his trembling.

"Hey, you got it that bad, do you?" Redmon said. "But if he was where you say he was, he must have been throwing down on me. Now if that was all the choice you had, are you really thinking you did the wrong thing?''

Laidlaw shook his head, the left side of his face batting into the bark. "I'd do it over again too, most likely," he said. "But now what? You got a life-sized picture of how I'm going to go meet the old man? Tell him, well, we killed your boy, both of them as a matter of fact, because it seemed like the best thing to do at the time?"

For a moment Redmon said nothing. He dragged a hand along his jaw line, over and over, while he considered. When he looked over at Ratman, Ratman only shrugged. Laidlaw's back was shuddering but his face retained a metallic immobility.

"Turn aloose, now," Redmon said. "Right now."

He reached around Laidlaw's back and neatly broke his hold on the tree. Grasping him by the shoulders, he pulled him upright, and once he had him balanced straight, let go. Laidlaw stayed standing on his own, his shoulders slumped and his head down, but he looked a much more promising spectacle than he had when wrapped around the hackberry.

"You never did but what you had to," Redmon told him. "Don't think about it any other way. You had to do it and that's all."

"I know that," Laidlaw said. "Ain't nothing says I have to be happy about it, though."

Redmon inspected the ground for a time, then raised his head and once more met Laidlaw's eyes. "Well then, maybe you can think about what the preacher told you."

"Sure I will," Laidlaw said. "Soon as I get the time." He bent down and got his rifle and wiped it with the tail of his shirt, though dry as it was there wasn't anything much to wipe. "We better get a move on," he said.

"Good," Ratman said. "Where to?"

"Straight west, that way." Laidlaw pointed. "I had Adrienne go wait for us over there on Highway a Hundred."

"What if she didn't make it?" Redmon said. "What if she didn't stay?"

"Then it'll be your turn to think up something," Laidlaw said. "Troublemaker. We might just as well go find out one way or the other."

Ratman hefted the BAR, and Laidlaw reached across and flicked him on the shoulder.

"You think you took care of Fowler?" he said. "I was kind of wondering. He was up there toward the head of the line."

"I got me a mess of them, is what I can tell you," Ratman said. "I never did stop to ask them their names."

"Thought you might say that." Laidlaw slapped his gun barrel once into the flat of his left hand. "Oh well."

"Let's shake a leg," Redmon said.

Ratman nodded and began to walk west. Laidlaw watched his back till it got small and then picked up the slack position. As before, what most immediately struck him was how easy and rapid the going was. It didn't seem like any more than a walk in the woods, and these were tamer woods than his own. Moving ahead, he maintained an attentive watch: treetops, ground cover, left, right, center. After he had covered some hundred yards, he looked back once to verify that Redmon was in place. Redmon raised his hand to him. Laidlaw was still near enough to see the white in his smile, and he was somewhat cheered by that as he went on.

Though he didn't know exactly how far it was to the highway, he thought it was certainly under a mile, and they should be passing well north of the ambush site. With the sun hanging directly overhead, direction was less than perfectly sure, but they were in the narrow tip of the park and all they had to do was go reasonably straight and they were bound to come out near enough the right place. In this area of the woods it was all calm, just as it should have been, with the birds singing loud and happy and the squirrels busy high up in the trees. A walk in the woods, one more of many. Though he was still alive to the least flicker of movement or whisper of sound, he wasn't thinking anything; his mind was clear. It was a kind of happiness, that clarity. Up ahead, he saw Ratman start a small brown rabbit, and he smiled as it thumped off into the brush.

The racket of the helicopter came spiraling overhead and then receded once again. Laidlaw could hear how it moved in loosening concentric circles. Nobody could have seen anything below the trees, that much he was sure of, but he was still relieved when the rotor noise faded away entirely.

They had to be getting pretty close now. Downhill to his left were three picnic tables grouped just beyond a mushroom-headed dead end off the park road. Beside the nearest table, a small white dog sat panting. Laidlaw passed on. Now he could plainly hear the occasional car droning up the highway. When he saw a sand trap in the clearing off to his right, he knew that Ratman had piloted them straight to the golf course. Beyond it, an empty span of roadbed threw off the steely sheen of stilled river water. The first intimation he had that anything had gone wrong was when Ratman stumbled forward and then broke into a run.

It was the classic bad-news connection, and Laidlaw could hear firing at both three and nine o'clock, which made him think it was probably an *X*. He rushed at the vertex, firing full auto, which was the only thing to do, if not especially hopeful. Just try to get out of the kill zone, fast. As he closed the distance between himself and Ratman he saw a wedge of the back of Ratman's head fly off, a long black hank of hair flagging from it, like a scalp. It was very obviously one of those things you would go right from observing to trying arduously to forget, with the least intermediate period of contemplation possible. Laidlaw hadn't even heard the BAR before he heard it stop. Evidently Ratman had missed Fowler, after all. As he ran past the body someone's head bobbed up not more than five feet from where he'd been expecting it might, and he fired into it three times and ran on.

If he wasn't down or ·dead so far, he thought he might have actually made it clear through. Behind him he heard the BAR start up again; with luck that meant that Redmon had managed to recover it. He was running down the edge of the golf course now, barely inside the woods, with just one line of trees strobing by across the pale broad sweep of green, and now he saw the black truck careening toward him, swerving to narrowly miss a sand trap. His stomach rolled into a frozen ball. He wanted to wave the truck away, but if he moved into the open he stood to get shot before he could deliver a signal of any kind. He was automatically changing clips and still running when he heard the stutter of a submachine gun quite near him match up to a thudding blur across his chest, and his body exchanged the solid ground for air.

His return was a slow buoyant transit along the wavery corkscrew path of a feather or a seed pod. What he saw were the white *X*'s that crossed the doors of his father's horse barn, for he'd been translated back to a time when he was very small, when he'd been kicked square in the stomach by his own ornery little pony and dumped on his back with the wind knocked out of him. His father's face appeared hovering over him: *Get up, boy, get up right now,* he said.

There was the bristling face, its weather-worn hide, but now for the first time Laidlaw could recognize the shock in his eyes. Why, he was scared, he heard himself thinking. *I never knew anything scared him.* Opening one eye, he saw a short distance across the close-cropped grass of a desiccated putting green. Where his rifle might have landed he had no idea.

"Get up, Laidlaw, get moving, fool!"

All along it had been Redmon's voice screaming over the whine of an angry gear. Laidlaw raised himself on one elbow. As he moved a great warm weight shifted away from his center, but he didn't feel any pain. For an instant he saw Adrienne hauling on the wheel of the truck to slam it into a bootleg turn. Redmon let go of the BAR, which he seemed to have been firing across the roof of the cab, and scrambled back toward the tailgate, stretching his arms out. Laidlaw got up and ran a few staggering steps, enough to lock his hands on Redmon's before his legs noodled out from under him. Another vicious transmission noise, the truck shot forward, and he felt his feet dragging back over the dry grass and then through a patch of sand, he thought, before Redmon had somehow gathered him in and rolled him up into the truck bed on his back.

Straight up, bare tree branches clawed out toward each other; Laidlaw couldn't fathom what acceleration of time had caused them so suddenly to lose all their leaves. The branches locked in a bewildering spin, and beyond them the sky was a deep blue whirlpool with a tiny white dot of a cloud just covering the point where it all sucked off into nothing at all. The truck jolted some farther distance over rough ground and then he felt it fit itself into the smoother hum of the highway's surface and begin to gather speed. Redmon's face cut in between him and the vanishing sky, and all of a sudden Laidlaw thought that he could read the future there.

"Don't lie to me," he said. "Have I had it?"

"Nah, man, what you talking?" Redmon said. "We'll see you patched up good as new."

Laidlaw meant to shake his head, but once it rolled over it just wouldn't come back up. Through a rust hole in the wall right beside him, he saw the road's shoulder pouring past, brown and blurred as floodwater.

Redmon pinched his chin and pulled his head back straight. "Don't you quit on me now," he said.

"Ah," Laidlaw mumbled dimly at him, giggling through a sticky thickness down his throat. "I never saw a black man look so pale."

"You think you're funny?" Redmon said. "Hey, we still got a house to build. Are you taking back all you said?"

"Get out of here," Laidlaw said. "Don't count on me to be around for it." Half of his voice was coming out his mouth the way it was supposed to; the rest was issuing from some new aperture elsewhere.

"I know you wouldn't go back on a promise," Redmon said.

"Not on purpose," Laidlaw said. For no good reason he wanted to laugh, but he thought it would hurt too much if he tried it. There was pain waiting for him somewhere nearby, and he didn't want to give it an opening. Besides, it was serious business here: he ought to be keeping his promises. He saw Rodney's face as through a pinhole, worried and expectant too. Laidlaw made his stiff lips move. "What do you want, my blessing?"

"That don't matter one way or the other." Redmon's voice turned confident as he sat back on his heels. "I won't let you go either way."

There's girls in Boston dancing tonight
The redcoat soldiers are holding them tight
When we get there, we'll show them how
But that ain't doing us no good now . . .

— "Soldier's Joy," traditional